W9-CMP-751

Consent of the Governed

Consent of the Governed

A Political Novel of
High Intrigue and Conflict
by

Gerald P. Balcar

OLIN FREDERICK, INC.
DUNKIRK, NEW YORK

Library of Congress Cataloging-in-Publication Data
Balcar, Gerald P.
    Consent of the governed / by Gerald P. Balcar

Printed in Canada

ISBN 0-9672357-0-7

**For
Sherry,
Peter
and
Joanne**

**In Memory
of Sidney Edlund**

"Some people live in
the past; some live in
the present. I live in
the future; it is a pleasant
and exciting place."

**"... Let us love our country
and walk in the light of the truth"**

The Reverend Canon
Ivan Harewood,
Chaplain, House of
Assembly of Barbados.

CHARACTERS

(in order of appearance)

Tony Destito - Corporate Vice President for Development, PENMET
Ian MacAuliffe - Chairman & CEO, PENMET
Ward Cowell - Chairman & CEO, ACP (American Carbon Products)
Erla Younge - Senior Vice President Farthergill & Slawson (Public
  Relations Firm); Director of Doctrine & Intelligence Group, POLACO
Marsha Fox - Political Consultant, POLACO
Ruth Farrencolt - Marsha Fox's Assistant
Erwin Festener - Vice President for Government Relations, ACP; Capital
  Action Group, POLACO
Helene Courtney - Vice President for Public Affairs ACP; Staff Director,
  POLACO
Alex Peterson - CEO of Wainwright & Jordan (Investment Banking Firm)
Madeline Cowell - Ward's second wife
Warren Hatch - President, MacPhail Foundation; Consultant, POLACO
Rollin Tinton - Associate Professor Trinity College; Consultant, POLACO;
  Director of Recruiting, Training, and Election Group, POLACO
Louis Fischer - Ph.D. from the Allendale Foundation; Director of
  Intelligence, POLACO
Harold Smalley - Ph.D. from the Allendale Foundation; Assistant to Erla
  Younge
Edgar Slaughter - Chief of Security, POLACO
Ansell Monroe - Captain of "Norma;" Tony & Jean Destito's friend in
  Spanish Wells
Betsy Monroe - Ansell Monroe's wife
Jean Destito - Tony Destito's wife; Member, Pennsylvania Democratic State
  Committee
Denise Williams - Public Affairs Consultant, PENMET
David Gibson - Attorney with Bergman, Harris, Gibson, Lindau, &
  Seaberg; Special Consultant to PENMET & Ian MacAulliffe
Terry Leelan - Professor of Political Science, Cornell University; Adrian
  Daggett Campaign Director
Stephanie Comstock - Corporate Vice President of Finance, PENMET
Alvin Carter - Director of Security and Asset Protection, PENMET
Susan MacAuliffe - Ian MacAulliffe's second wife; Chief Executive Officer,
  Pennsylvania Liberty Foundation
Nancy Letersky - Vice President Public Affairs, PENMET; Director of
  Communication, Daggett Campaign
Adrian Elliot Daggett - Illinois governor; Democratic presidential candidate
Pamela Petrusik Daggett - Adrian Daggett's wife
Francisco Rodriguez - Ian MacAulliffe's valet
Lucinda Rodriguez - Ian MacAulliffe's maid
Dianne Daggett - Daughter of Adrian & Pamela Daggett
Anne Russell - Senior Vice President, Evans and Copeland (Public Relations

Firm); Director of Publicity, Daggett Campaign

Alan Jacobs - Account Leader, Jeremy Reubin & Associates (Campaign Consultants); Political Director, Daggett Campaign

Carrie Watkins - Helene Courtney's Administrative assistant; Director of Human Resources, POLACO

Michelle Proust - Intelligence Analyst, POLACO

Bill Haber - Intelligence Analyst, POLACO; Michelle Proust's beau

Paul Melius - Specialist, Industrial Security & Investigations; President, Melius Associates, Inc.

Elizabeth "Liz" Daley - Melius Operative a.k.a. Cynthia Reese

Janos Krypska - Melius Operative a.k.a. Joe Frozzi

Karen Crezna - Regional Coordinator in Iowa, Daggett Campaign

Merrick Reynolds - Staff, Jeremy Reubin & Associates; Director of Daggett Campaign in Iowa

Ryan Keeley - President & CEO, Mississippi Valley Chemical and Pharmaceutical Company; Member, POLACO Executive Board

Mendos Sadovan - President, Utilities International; Member, POLACO Executive Board

Radion Gallosey - Member, POLACO Executive Board

Bernt Umrich - President, Eurochem; Member, POLACO Executive Board

Mitchell Fiddler - Director of Finance, Daggett Campaign

Dominick Kluczinski - Mitchell Fiddler's Deputy Chairman; Director of Administration, Daggett Campaign

Roger Bennett - Director of Issues Staff, Daggett Campaign

Steve Zimmer - Campaign Director for Willis Porter

Steven Hatford - Republican Presidential Candidate

Richard Sandellot - African-American Democratic Candidate for Presidency - Ohio

Cybill Chubb - Edgar Slaughter's Chief of Detectives

Pat Stabler - Assistant Producer, POLACO Television

Parker Lothan - Senior Vice President, Rossberg & Janowski (Polling Firm)

Earl Hanley - Executive, Gateway, Inc.; Member, Sioux City Council; Karen Crezna's beau

Louise Sczyniac - Anne Russell's Chief Press Aide

Amy Camisona - President, Lady Garment Workers

Jack Wood - New York staff, Daggett Campaign

Louellen Parsons - New York staff, Daggett Campaign

Veronica Torblad - Involved with accusation of sexual harassment against Adrian Daggett

Daphne Poltrac - Writer; PENMET mole on Harbour Island

Sharon Gilling - Editor; PENMET mole on Harbour Island

Annabelle Linden Mayberry - Adrian Daggett's Accuser of sexual harassment

Broderick Rose - Private Investigator, Rose Associates, Inc.

Marylou Michaels - Operative, Rose Associates, Inc.

Quentin Locksley - Attorney, Adrian Daggett's personal law firm

Sandy Gordon - Branch Manager, Clayton Missouri Trust Company

Hugh Daggett - Adrian Daggett's father

Eleanor Daggett - Adrian Dagget's mother

George King - Former Sandellot Campaign Staff working for Daggett

Campaign
Lucile Cush - Former Sandellot Campaign Staff working for Daggett Campaign
Randall Dustin - Campaign manager, Hatford Campaign
Ross Chamberlain - Political consultant, Hatford Campaign
Carolyn Masiac - Administrative Assistant, Senator Steven Hatford
Laurie Pinta - Computer Specialist, POLACO
Carlos Himenez - President, Agricultural Workers Union
Jorge Carraballes - Staff Director National Labor Council
Olaf Jenson - Chairman National Labor Council; President, Paper & Lumber Workers Union
Orrin Egglinton - President, Center for the Resistance of Expansion of the Atomic Power (CREAP)
Maxine Marshal - President, Women's Movement to Stop Nuclear Pollution
Josh Smitton - Vice President, Nuclear Powers Issues, Center for Environmental Recovery
Mark Klippstein - President, Nuclear Power Association
Wilma Westcott - Chairwoman, Department of Environmental Sciences at Rutgers University
Julia Manilla - Chairwoman, Association for Minority Economic Development
Miles Ruskin - Colonel, Special Recovery Force
Sam Black - Captain, Special Recovery Force
Corinne Clayton - Lieutenant, Special Recovery Force

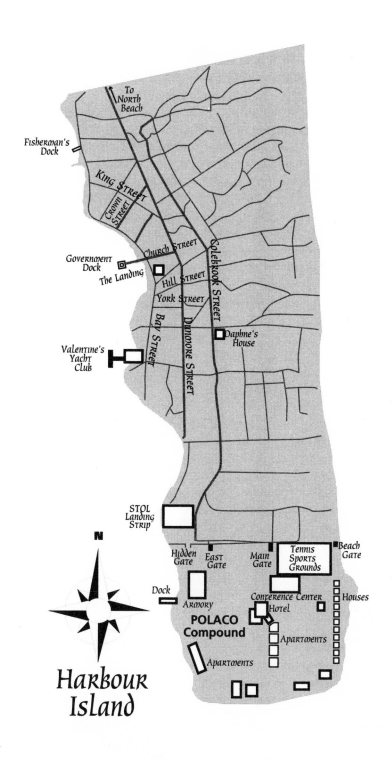

Harbour Island

☆ PROLOGUE ☆

THE "WHOMP-WHOMP" of the helicopter blades echoed off the water as the Royal Bahamas Police Force pilot skimmed low across the surface of Eleuthera Sound on a sunny morning. The passenger, Chief Inspector Charles Whitfield, sipped coffee as they left Nassau behind and watched the passing islands, reefs, and shallows of his maritime homeland. He saw sailing yachts and powerboats knifing through the blue water trailed by foaming white wakes. He wondered if any carried illicit drugs and whether drugs were involved in the murder he was about to investigate on Harbour Island.

This onetime bastion of British tropical culture lay to the east of Eleuthera Island, separated by a two-mile bay that offered partially protected anchorage to the town of Dunmore. The town clustered around two docks, one built by the government and a private dock owned by Valentines Yacht Club, which the self-proclaimed the best bar and restaurant in town. Churches, stores, restaurants, pubs, the lesser hotels, and the only bank were an Bay Street along the shore or on its intersecting lanes. Outside the center were houses of permanent residents and then the winter homes of the seasonal residents. The best hotels and homes were found along the eastern shore, hovering on a bluff above the celebrated pink sand beaches facing the rollers of the Atlantic.

Development on Harbour Island had slowed after The Commonwealth of the Bahamas gained independence from Great Britain in 1973. Interest began to perk when some artists and writers discovered the island's charm. A reputed American research institute then purchased the entire southern quarter of the island for construction of a very large facility.

Whitfield thought about the quiet island and its history. There was never much trouble, that the three resident constables who also covered North Eleuthera and Spanish Wells with their auxiliaries, couldn't handle. Now they had an apparent rape/murder of an American woman who was the assistant to the head of the new institute.

The helicopter zoomed over Eleuthera which stretched to the horizon and the lush green of Harbour Island appeared. It took two minutes to cross the bay where Whitfield spotted the bright uniforms of his colleagues and sand colored jeeps that would carry them to the crime scene.

The resident police sergeant saluted as Whitfield ducked toward him under the blades. He casually returned the gesture and shook hands.

"Good morning, sir."

"Good morning, sergeant."

"I think you should see the body first. We should be there for the identification. Someone is on the way from the institute."

"You're certain?"

"Yes, her card was in her wallet."

"Not good."

"No, sir."

They drove down the main road of the island going north and through the backside of Dunmore. On the other side of the town they climbed a hill passing an old quarry where they veered to the left toward the isolated north beach. The road became a dirt track before they came to a police van where two auxiliaries were on guard. Whitfield walked toward them and saw a naked white woman with straw blonde hair lying face down on the edge of the beach where it interfaced with the bushes and grass. He saw that she was youthful and in good physical condition.

"Who found her?" Whitfield asked.

"A couple who had come to swim. They called us from the phone booth at the north end at 2:20 this morning."

"No one has touched anything?"

"We had a guard here immediately. Her wallet was in the glove compartment of her jeep around those trees." He pointed southward. "Sheila Thompkins, executive assistant to the chairman of the institute."

"What was she doing here?"

"Apparently swimming. There are clothes in the jeep."

"Theory?" asked Whitfield.

"It was a hot night. She came down to swim, skinny-dipping. She was alone and didn't see a boat drawn up on the beach or anchored nearby. She was a beautiful woman splashing nude in the water. Some men crept ashore and got her."

"Why would they kill her?"

"From depravity or to prevent identification."

Bending down, Whitfield could see bruises on her neck. "She was strangled."

"Looks that way."

"Other marks?"

"Bruises on her wrists and ankles where they held her."

Whitfield thought these might be significant. Staying on the grass, he walked around to the jeep. He saw her clothes on the backseat; expensive looking shorts with a matching shirt beside court shoes. There were footprints and other marks in the sand between the jeep and the water. A heavy rain the previous afternoon had cleaned the sand so that only the recent marks were visible. He avoided making tracks when he returned.

"Who's coming to identify the body?"

"The security supervisor. His name is Mike Anzarra."

"We need to establish her whereabouts last night, and the same for loose, unattached males."

"We'll make the inquiries. The institute people usually hang out at Valentine's or The Landing."

"See if there is a log-off time on her computer."

"Yes, sir."

Ten minutes later, with the help of Mike Anzarra, they had their identification. Sheila Thompkins was indeed the executive assistant to Ward Cowell, chairman of the institute.

"How long has she been working here?" Whitfield asked Anzarra, who had a military demeanor and appearance.

"About nine months."

"What did she do in her job?"

"She was the operating boss for Mr. Cowell," Anzarra said, poker-faced. "She did the contracts and the budgets and enforced them. She did all of the planning, the hiring, and she looked after all of the corporate, legal, and financial stuff."

"How many employees?"

"Seventeen, I think."

"Did Sheila have any friends or connections outside the organization?"

"She was divorced and her children are in boarding school. A man came to see her two or three times a month. I've seen him. He stays at the Coral Sands or the Romora Bay Club."

"Did she stay with him or did he come to your compound?"

"Mostly at the hotel."

"No local connections?" asked Whitfield looking Anzarra in the eye.

"None that I know of."

"Then we need to know where this boyfriend is and where he was last night. I see she looks athletic."

"She ran or swam every morning and played tennis most evenings."

Whitfield asked to see her apartment and her personnel records. On the way there, the sergeant told him that Cowell's secretary had died two weeks earlier with her husband and two teenage children in a gas explosion in their home. Whitfield remembered the news of a shaken community. There was only a brief police investigation.

In the apartment he saw evidence of a search; pillows were awry and two drawers were slightly ajar. He found letters from Tyler Lenhardt, the man Sheila had been apparently seeing. He was president of a regional waste management and environmental remediation company. From her resume he gathered they were both from Chardon, Ohio. She went to Georgetown and was captain of the women's track team and president of her sorority. With an MBA from Columbia, she started work on Wall Street. She soon left to join a growing chemical company in New Jersey and to marry. When it was time to start a family she suspended work for four years. She then returned to the company, which had been acquired by American Carbon Products, a giant multinational of which Ward Cowell was president. When her marriage ended she came to Harbor Island.

Whitfield wondered why an MBA from Georgetown and Columbia, who was obviously capable, worked as an executive assistant. Then he saw her salary was $180,000 a year, plus travel to and from her home, plus living accommodations in the compound.

"Nothing makes much sense," said Whitfield to the sergeant. "Local men don't become rapists and murderers just because they see a naked woman swimming."

"Maybe they're not local."

"Tourists don't do it either. Also, there are no signs of a struggle."

"Maybe they were criminals who happened by, chief inspector."

"Then why didn't she just run to her jeep and drive down the beach to the compound? The key was in the jeep. She could have run away on foot in the dark."

"Maybe she tried to put on her clothes."

"Doesn't look that way. Be sure to photograph them. Take the camera up in the chopper and shoot the nearby area. Maybe we'll see something we can't see on the ground."

"Yes, sir," said the sergeant.

Whitfield had seen no blood or tissue under Sheila's nails, just the bruises. Who was it who was armed with cords for a garrote? Some of the answers could come from knowing her movements on her last evening.

He called Tyler Lenhardt at his office. His secretary cheerily volunteered, when Whitfield asked, that Lenhardt had been in the office until the early evening the previous day and then had gone to address a dinner of stock analysts. When Whitfield spoke with Lenhardt he told him the bad news. After he got control of himself Lenhardt said he would be at Harbour Island that evening if possible.

THE NEXT DAY, after considering the sergeant's report, the coroner's report, and the aerial photographs, Whitfield reached a surprising conclusion. Sheila logged off at 8:12, had dinner at The Landing about 9:00, and had left just after 10:30. She was not seen thereafter and had not returned to the institute. The aerial photo showed various footprints going to the water from the jeep and also from the body. Other photos showed only three vehicle tracks leading to the beach: Sheila's jeep, the golf cart of the couple who found her, and the first police van. The coroner and the autopsy reported bruises on her face and upper body, and concluded that the ones on her wrists and ankles were from her being tied. The lab reported semen samples from three different men.

It seemed likely that the perpetrators waited for her at the restaurant, kidnapped her and drove her to the beach in her jeep. That would explain why no other vehicle tracks were found in the sand. Then she was taken to a boat offshore where she was probably questioned relating to the search of her apartment. Then she was raped and murdered. It was made to appear she had taken a moonlit swim. It was a professional job. Someone had taken out a contract to have Sheila Thompkins murdered and was also interested in obtaining information from her.

The sergeant and his men visited all of the hotels on the island in search of clues. The few unattached male guests were in their rooms before eleven. They questioned each one of them at their little head-quarters in the town building. They asked at the docks about boat arrivals. The water taxis brought no one unknown or unaccounted for. There was no record of any visitors at the institute. Whitfield assumed the perpetrators used a launch from their yacht to sneak ashore to Sheila's apartment.

The principle clue was not, in itself, evidence. Whitfield did not believe that Sheila put her fashionable clothes in the jeep. She would have put them near the water where she swam. Also, if she intended to go swimming, where was the towel?

When he told his boss, The commissioner of police, about this, they both realized a professional killing of Sheila Thompkins might mean that Ward Cowell's secretary and her family may have also been murdered in some connection to the institute.

A FEW DAYS later, a report of an explosion in the Exuma Cays was flashed to the Bahamas Air Sea Rescue Association. A rescue hel-icopter found wreckage. The police marine unit sped to the scene with orders to pick up bodies and as much debris as they could find. The diving team found the wreck in a trench almost 150 feet down and photographed it. The registry computers showed the vessel was owned by Mikla Almast, the director of information systems at the institute on Harbour Island.

Whitfield went out to the site by helicopter and made several dives himself. He found the explosion site and ordered samples to be cut from it. There were no signs of bodies or body parts. They brought all the clothes and papers to the surface. There were no wallets or watches and only a little inexpensive jewelry.

"No bodies, no wallets?" Whitfield said to the lieutenant com-manding the police vessel.

"They wouldn't last long if there was blood in the water," the lieu-tenant replied. "Anything they were carrying or wearing would be dragged away to wherever the sharks took them."

"But, no passports?"

"They were blown away by the explosion, or someone could have boarded the yacht and taken the people and whatever they wanted."

"Why? You don't run drugs into Florida with a sailboat if you blow it up?"

"Someone who was an enemy?"

Whitfield telephoned for Almasy's resumé and talked with Mike Anzarra. The fax he received showed the director to be an exceptional computer professional and had been an Assistant Professor at Case Western Reserve. Anzarra said the director was sailing with his girlfriend from Cleveland. The Cleveland police reported she was on a trip to Harbour Island. The forensic laboratory found evidence of explosive materials with the signature of plastique. This was another professional job.

"WE NOW HAVE three probable murders connected to the institute," Whitfield said ending a report to his commissioner and the minister of national security, who oversaw police matters among other responsibilities. "One has to suspect a connection, or more specifically, that someone at the institute ordered the killings. How could it be coincidental?"

"It is unbelievable that there is a connection," said the minister. "This is a research organization."

"What sort of research?" asked Whitfield.

"They say they're in political science and economics," the commissioner responded.

"If they say that," the minister emphasized, "that's what we must believe. You know what they've done so far for us."

"What do you mean?"

"Investments, Whitfield. Large deposits in our banks, large purchases of bonds, participation in venture capital funds. They have also signed a tax payment agreement which will provide much more revenue from Harbour Island."

"Then it's sensitive?"

"Quite."

"Maybe they wonder why three of their people died in a month. We can explain part of it. It may help them to understand."

"Unless, as you have suggested, they already know," said the minister.

"In which case they would be concerned that we knew," said the commissioner.

The minister paused. "I don't think we'll take the chance. They don't know we have a first-class investigative capability. They probably assume we don't."

"If my theory is correct, the perpetrators are related in some way to the institute, and are not a threat to Bahamian citizens or visitors," Whitfield told them.

"True, they aren't," the minister said as he stood to end the meeting. "At least we can be sure of that. Excellent work."

"Thank you, minister."

Two accidents and one rape/murder by persons unknown were recorded. The investigations were suspended.

Whitfield still thought about the apparent crimes. It made no sense that enemies of the institute would have killed these people. Why, however, would someone in the institute or associated with it order these murders of apparently competent people? The only explanation was that they knew something they shouldn't. So if information associated with the institute warranted murder to protect its secrecy, then there was something about the institute that was probably not legal. He wondered who Ward Cowell really was and what this institute was really doing.

The minister of national security was troubled and told the prime minister about the investigations and the conclusions. After hearing the story the prime minister was similarly troubled, but he agreed with the decision to proceed no further.

☆ Chapter 1 ☆

WITH THE SUNDAY *New York Times* business pages folded on his lap, Tony Destito looked out the left side window of the luxury Gulfstream jet flying to the Bahamas from National Airport in Washington. The plane had winged south behind a line of thunderstorms and turned toward the ocean over the coast of South Carolina. He could see the chain of the Sea Islands hugging the mainland and identified the Kiawah Resort below by relating it to the buildings of Charleston.

While it reminded him of the heinous crime of slavery, Charleston had the charm of its original antebellum buildings and ambiance. As a technical marketer for Pennsylvania Metallurgical Industries, PEN-MET, he had worked with engineers at the Charleston Naval Shipyard to help design new destroyers. He remembered bringing his wife, Jean, there. They had a memorable romantic night at the Planters Inn where she played at lovemaking as a southern belle after walking around the South-of-Broad section visiting homes from which secession banners could have hung. She had become infected, she said, with the spirit of the Old South where "women were brought up to please men."

Her present view differed. She was a militant feminist with a seat on the Pennsylvania State Democratic Committee and would have been an uncompromising abolitionist. He visualized her slim figure maintained by exercise and an active life. It made him miss her and the Sunday afternoon and evening he had left behind. They would have played tennis with friends. He would have had dinner with his children, Barbara and Martin. College was getting Martin's attention in his junior year at prep school. Barbara, just a freshman, was interested in science and boys. Tony and his daughter discussed her projects and her curiosities as often as they could.

Of all the Sunday missions, this one was something different. For two months, Ward Cowell, Chairman, CEO, and scion of the founding family of a Fortune 10 firm, American Carbon Products, ACP, had badgered Ian MacAulliffe, Chairman and CEO of PENMET to come to a meeting at the ACP corporate retreat on Harbour Island in the Bahamas. Ian, to whom Tony reported as corporate vice president for development, resisted. Finally, he made Cowell agree that Tony could represent him. For Tony this was further evidence of the trust of one of the nation's greatest business leaders.

At age 46, Tony and his staff oversaw and worked on development activities in divisions and subsidiaries in ten states and a dozen countries. The corporate culture allowed any idea to be heard and risks were risks, which everyone took. Employees of PENMET were empowered to contribute and be productive long before the word appeared in business books. There were corporate politics to be sure, but Ian did everything he could to eschew it. Ian was Tony's hero and mentor.

In the visit to Ward Cowell, Tony assumed PENMET was a target for some kind of involvement. The company had a reputation that was sought after. Its corporate vice president for public affairs, Nancy Letersky, and all the PENMET divisions received dozens of requests for various involvements every week. In this case Ian and Tony had to sign complex confidentiality agreements after review by outside attorneys. Whatever was to be revealed was considered a secret.

Tony glanced at the woman seated opposite him who had flown from New York on the USAir shuttle. She had an Ivy League look with a slightly thickening figure. Tony saw hardness in her eyes and cynicism in her smile when he met her. She was Erla Younge. Her card told him she was a senior vice president of Farthergill & Slawson, a premier international public relations firm serving a creamy list of clients charging creamy fees. Two ACP staff people who had flown from Cleveland and two academic-looking men from Washington started a bridge game, and tapped the corporate liquor. Two women, also from Washington, were working from their briefcases. Ruth Farrencolt, a lanky, dark-haired girl in her twenties seemed to Tony to be on her first ride on a company plane. The other was Marsha Fox, medium height and slender with dark hair falling around her face. He speculated her jacket and slacks cost three weeks wages of the average office worker in a PENMET plant.

Flying over water, Tony, a sailor and yachtsman, liked to see the landfalls. They passed over Grand Bahama and then began a descent turning toward the small airport on the north end of the island of Eleuthera. In front of the pastel yellow and white wooden terminal, a welcoming party waited with cars and a van. The stewardess signaled that Tony should go forward to be first off. As he stepped down, Erwin Festener, the ACP Vice President for Government Relations based in Washington, came forward to greet him. With balding, sandy hair and a paunch, Erwin had enjoyed too many good lunches and dinners in Washington without enough exercise.

"Hello, Tony. Welcome to North Eleuthera," he said.

"Erwin," Tony smiled, "Good to see you."

"Good to see you too, but we're sorry that Ian isn't here with you."

"You know how he is about traveling and seemingly clandestine meetings."

"Clandestine?"

"That agreement we had to sign makes it feel clandestine."

"It's a process. You'll see what we have for you soon enough."

They climbed into a Mercedes 530. Another car was there for Erla Younge, Marsha Fox and a tall, good-looking woman meeting them who introduced herself as Helene Courtney. He saw the others pile into a van with the luggage appropriately distributed. As they drove eastward toward the dock on the bay opposite Harbour Island, Erwin redirected the conversation, "Have you been here before, Tony?"

"Two years ago Jean and I chartered a yacht with some friends from Spanish Wells."

"How'd you get to be a sailor coming from landlocked Pittsburgh?"

"I was like Ted Turner, not good enough in college to play football or baseball so I sailed."

"You play tennis well."

"I rarely beat Jean and now I lose to Martin."

"My son can beat me. It's a stage we go through. We want you to enjoy your stay. The weather will be warm enough to swim in the ocean and we have both hard courts and clay courts."

"No grass?" Tony smiled.

"Don't suggest it. The grounds keepers would start a project. Tennis grass won't grow very well down here."

"You could import the soil from Wimbledon."

Erwin chuckled. "There are still some nice resorts, but Harbour Island stalled after the British gave independence. The economy is winter tourists and people with winter homes. There are a few artists and writers. Most of the land south of the town was undeveloped. We bought all of it including some houses and a tennis club. When good adjacent property comes up for sale we usually buy it."

Tony wondered about the size of whatever it was. A quarter of the island was over half a square mile. "Why not a warmer winter climate?"

"The cooler winter helps us convince the IRS this is a business necessity for conferences and retreats. It's lovely in the spring and fall; not too hot in the summer. If you tire of the food, the best fish restaurant in the world is in Spanish Wells. It's handy because of the harbor. When hurricanes threaten we send our boats there. Charming little town."

"It is. We have friends there."

"You do?"

"When we picked up the yacht, we stayed at the hotel where the locals come to party. We were invited to a barbecue at one of the Captain's homes. Last year they came to visit. They're special people."

At the dock Tony saw a fishing yacht and a fast cruiser. The cars drew up to the cruiser, and the van to the yacht. He and Erwin, Erla, Marsha, and Helene Courtney climbed into the stern. The drivers and one of the crew handed the luggage on board, and they went powering across the water toward the island two miles away. Helene was Ward Cowell's Vice President for Public Affairs. Tony thought she looked more relaxed than Erla, and he saw she was trim and moved like an athlete. He sensed something of the guardedness of the public relations profession.

New electric cars, in which ACP had invested, were at ACP's private dock. The British-Colonial hotel into which they were ushered was gleaming and spotless. Men and women liveried in the peach and gray of the ACP logo helped with the luggage. Tony had been tempted to ask what the plan was, but he waited. As they were unloading, Erwin said, "Ward would like to see you when you've freshened up. Then if you would like a game of doubles..."

"With you, Erwin?"

"We'll play mixed doubles. I think you will enjoy it."

After Tony had hung his clothes in what was obviously the VIP suite, they met in the lobby. Erwin led him to a large and elegant conference room paneled in light oak with open casement windows overlooking the celebrated pink sand beach. The smell of the sea was in the air. Ward Cowell stood at the head of an antique table where there were bottles of mineral water at each place. Helene and Erla sat in leather chairs. Standing with him to greet Tony was Alex Peterson, CEO of Wainwright & Jordan, a huge investment banking firm. Alex was tall and a little heavy, but with a handsome face under blond-gray hair often seen in business magazines. Equally well publicized, Ward was slender with brown hair properly colored showing some gray. Tony was then introduced to Deidrich Kirchener, executive vice president of Nordstall GmbH, a German steel combine and Takesheki Emoto, chief development officer of Shinwa Meiwa, the largest metals company in Japan, both similar to PENMET. He exchanged bows with the Japanese executive.

After the introductions, Ward asked, "What can we order for you Tony?"

A steward appeared.

"Were you well fed on the plane?"

"With two stewardesses on a Gulfstream, I was well fed," Tony said. "Mineral water is fine."

"How is Ian?"

"He's very well, Ward."

"Well, we are very sorry he couldn't join us."

"Ian is Ian. He is a good delegator. He lets us do the worrying."

"What does PENMET have to worry about, the star stock of the Dow Jones average?" Helene asked, with a raise of her brow.

"We worry about staying that way," Tony said and then asked, "Have I come to a meeting of the Tri-Lateral Commission?"

"Nothing that public, Tony," Ward said. Despite his tremendous authority, he was fidgeting. He cupped his hand over his mouth for a moment. "Thank you for sending the Confidentiality Agreements. We have your word that you and Ian will maintain confidences regardless of your decision on what we ask you to do?"

Tony wondered why he would ask such a question.

"You have our signatures and our word."

"Very well then," Ward said, "let's get down to why you're here."

Tony got out his portfolio.

"I'm a note taker," he said. "I hope you don't mind."

"Just remember your agreements, and be careful with the notes," Ward replied. "You do have shredding machines in your offices?"

"To protect us from industrial espionage from Germany and Japan."

There was some laughter, but he made a point. Why was he here with these two competitors?

"As you well know, Tony," Ward began, "great changes have occurred in corporate America and in Europe and Japan in recent years as multinationalism has evolved. I refer to the size and scope of the manufacturing, service, and financial industries. The world is becoming increasingly complex from every point of view beyond anything that science fiction writers could have ever imagined. We have divided and subdivided and even further subdivided our companies into individual technologies, which require specialization in resources, and increasingly risky investments, which may lead to big gains or big losses. Similarly, our organizations have expanded. As you know, there is a Japanese company that advertises it has 20,000 products. How many products does PENMET have?"

"About 7,000 that we can identify by specification."

"Multiple products, multiple industries, multiple factories, all focused on world-scale corporate development and financial objectives," Ward said. "The concern that many of us have, Tony, is the fact that the political development is not likely to parallel our pace of corporate development and overall economic development. In fact, the political development is going in reverse. We are increasingly beset with incompetence in political leadership. Our 'leaders' make their decisions based on public opinion polls rather than leading that opinion, and the reason they don't lead opinion is they don't really understand the issues and therefore can't.

"American Democracy has become hopelessly mired in bungled political struggles. The situation is not so bad in most other industrialized countries, but what happens in Washington is paramount. We are still the driving market of the world, and we are the superpower.

"In the past, corporations have pleaded their case with the various lobbying devices and more recently utilized the media to stop a national health insurance program. Am I insulting you Tony, by telling you things you already know?"

There followed a moment of silence. Ward seemed to be giving him the opportunity to say he wasn't interested.

Tony was shocked at the direction this was taking. He wanted to say that PENMET didn't deal in politics and leave, but his instinct was to get the details.

"No, Ward," he said. "Tell the story the way you want to."

Ward smiled meaningfully.

"Thank you, Tony," he said. "Right now, we consider the political structure of the United States to be increasingly unstable. As a result of the politicized and incompetent leadership, issues are propagated by the media, single interest groups and advocacy groups who distort meaning and use premises which are false or manipulated. We have been in a running battle with these groups for years. Meanwhile, the politicians ride false issues toward personal objectives.

"As the interest and advocacy groups wail their woes and fear monger, they capture media attention and threaten individual politicians. Rabid fringe environmentalists have stopped nuclear power in the United States. With environmental regulation, we were at the point where it cost more money to build a new factory on a brown site than on a green site, totally at odds with rational environmental objectives.

"Reducing military power in the United States is also at odds with rational foreign and industrial policy objectives, regardless of how much social spending we might see necessary. We all know that defense spending stimulates new technologies, which almost all of us can use. How much does the general public understand about those technologies? How far can the general public see into the future? In fact, how much time does the general public even spend studying these issues that we all live with? On top of all of this, we have the plaintiff lawyers hounding us with lawsuits!"

Tony felt tension in his stomach. He had heard this in variations from businessmen all over the world. But there was a big difference. Here, they were organized and intended to do something.

"There are three key threats to our global businesses," Ward said. "The first is the possibility of political action motivated by advocacy groups that would irrationally try to regulate corporate expansion worldwide, limit the markets, or limit our ability to use our assets and borrowing power as we see fit.

"Second, there is the threat of the ignorance of the general public that mostly doesn't exercise the vote. They are vulnerable to the appeals of the false prophets.

"And the third threat is a huge risk of mistakes by the people in positions of power. Our military policy is an example. Here we are, the most powerful nation on earth. In the Gulf War we proved that no one can fight the United States. But our politicians harp that we cannot use our soldiers and risk lives. They were afraid to send our soldiers into a place like Haiti which couldn't have fought effectively in The Spanish-American War.

"With leaders afraid to use our force, we are vulnerable to awful results. Sometimes men and women have to die for their country, and protecting the global economy is essential if they want any quality of life at all. Politicians who can only follow public opinion have led nations to disaster in the past. What is needed are politicians who will tell the people the options and lead public opinion."

"Politicians," Tony said.

"What this meeting is about, Tony, and what this place is about, is that those of us who can afford it intend to take greater political control of events. One of the results of populist politics is giving us the opportunity. The era of the ironbound incumbent is going to partially disappear if term limitations spread. The opportunity is for us to back candidates in an increased number of Congressional elections with whom we have understandings on certain issues. This is a long-term effort. Candidates have to be recruited, established in local elections, and then those who prove themselves will move forward into Congressional and state elections to influence the national scene. We will move our people into the state capitols, into Congress, and eventually into the White House. The founding fathers, brilliant as they were, never foresaw aviation, space travel, electronic communication, computer data processing, and wire transfers of funds. They never foresaw overpopulation, either. The Constitution is getting old, Tony. We need to get to a form of government that can get things done a lot faster. We need some structural changes, changes that give corporate Americans more voice. Changes that bring an intellectual government into power instead of bickering men and women of no more than modest ability. Changes must be made that might limit the scope of the voting public, but not the rights of individuals, except to stop the founding and perpetuation of illegitimate single-interest constituencies and advocate groups.

"The broad goal is to take greater political control. The purpose is to preserve the context in which our companies can best function in terms of fiscal, monetary, and other aspects of public policy. Our main thrust will be to get people into office who understand the world and agree with us. Do I shock you, Tony?"

"No, not 'shock,'" Tony lied. "But, it's a huge new concept."

This was another point where he could have politely left. He knew he needed to report this fully to Ian.

"Good, Tony. It is time that you, Erwin, and these two ladies play some tennis. My other friends and I will play a quick nine holes. Unfortunately, they cannot stay for dinner. We'll talk more then."

In his suite to change for tennis, Tony wished he could hear the conversation on the golf course. Three important people had come a long way to support the pitch he had just heard.

THREE SETS OF tennis ensued pitting Erwin and Erla, who were both well taught and had played together, against Tony and Helene. They lost the first set. Tony was wrapped up in what Ward Cowell had said. Helene kept it competitive, however. She moved across the court easily and could swing two-handed both ways. She was powerful and magnificent to look at, with firm arms and legs, high breasts and a classic face that was flushed with determination. Tony got into playing and they took the next two sets.

He found a maid waiting at the suite to press his slacks and sport shirt for dinner. In the shower he wondered about the scope of Ward's plan. Ward Cowell and his friends could well do what Ward started to describe. There was a whole day of presentation planned for tomorrow. Tony could have politely excused himself, but his intuition told him to find out all he could. This was no dreamy concept. Something had germinated, and was being fertilized with large amounts of cash.

If major players of corporate America took this course, what would happen if it leaked? They would have detailed plans for spinning various excuses. It would be cheaper and much more effective to put their own candidates into congressional office than to try to reeducate new ones every eight years in the House and every twelve in the Senate. Money would still be a problem for candidates, a problem which Ward Cowell and his group would solve for their chosen ones.

They gathered for hors d'oeuvres on the terrace overlooking the ocean. Helene, Erla, and Erwin were there with Madeline, a madonna looking blond, Ward's second wife, who had met Ward when she was a lawyer with the company's principal law firm in Cleveland. They were on the side of the island facing away from the sunset. The light showed the clear azure blue of the Atlantic and the lush planting through which there were glimpses of the pink sand.

Over dinner there was talk of politics and events at PENMET. Then Ward refocused the conversation. "Tony, you've had some time to think about what I said this afternoon. What's your major concern?"

"I think you are tinkering with fundamental rights and liberties in the Constitution, if that is the breeze on which you are tacking."

"Good metaphor, Tony. Maybe it is the outcome in the end, but I believe most Americans don't understand their liberties anymore. I also wonder if they even care. Hardly half of them vote in critical elections; less than half vote in state and local elections. In primaries, it is hard to get anyone to vote at all.

"Then when they do vote, what are they voting for? Party platforms used to mean something. There were newspapers to read that discussed platforms and philosophies. Sure there was hucksterism. There were slogans and songs. But there was debate and political dialogue by people everywhere: general stores, workingmen's clubs, country clubs, university pubs, and at home. Today, we have sound bites and a population which spends six hours a day gawking at their television sets and rarely talking to each other. The democratic process has become too shallow for the modern world, and it has to be changed. People don't care as long as they have their paycheck and their rule of law. What else do they want? With our plan we will move into an exciting future."

"Government by the elite?" Tony questioned.

"The elite have always governed. Democracy needs educated people and today only educated people can really participate."

"Don't you think politicization goes in cycles? I mean at some point we throw the rascals out."

They continued the discussion. After the dishes were cleared, Ward and Madeline apologized that they had to telephone some family on the West Coast. Erla and Erwin also made excuses. Tony found himself alone with Helene on the verandah. The sea air was velvet. Helene asked the steward for tea, Tony joined her.

When they were alone she asked, "Is there anything more I can tell you?"

"I need more time," he said, being careful. He guessed he was purposely left alone with her, for another opportunity to leave graciously.

He looked out over the broad night sky, black and full of stars away from the lights of America.

He looked at Helene.

"Take an 'e' off the name, and yours could be the face that sent a thousand ships to Troy," he said.

"You're flattering me," she replied.

He realized it was the wrong thing to say.

"Maybe whoever said it had nearly as much to drink as I have."

"If I had a racquet I'd swipe it across your butt," Helene joked.

"Please don't. You're too strong."

"You deserve a bruise."

Tony saw a glint of curiosity in her eye. They talked of clarifications and the compound and then getting some sleep.

Back in his suite, Tony called home and then spent almost an hour typing notes on his laptop. Normally he would have dictated, but he was convinced the rooms were bugged. He activated his computer password to protect his privacy. He was sure Ian would want to oppose this if he could.

IN THE MORNING Tony thought it would look best if he went running on the beach. He called for breakfast to be sent up and hoped to avoid any contact before the morning briefing. On the famous pink sand, however, he found Helene running toward him from the north end. They exchanged greetings, breathing hard, and left in opposite directions. He carried away a mental image of her face flushed under her tan and her smile at meeting him.

In the shower, he concluded he would generally support the plan until he could see Ian. That would give them the most information.

An electric cart driven by a smiling local man took him through a manicured garden of trees and flowers, past newly built houses and utility buildings to the other main building, the conference and business center. It was pastel plaster in tropical style and had an arched verandah at a circular drive.

Tony was ushered to a white-walled conference room where soft-seated chairs had been arranged around a massive light oak table matching the woodwork. Extra seating for an audience faced the podium, screen, and white board. The ceiling was high enough to accommodate a full brace of audio-visual equipment. Ward was at the table with Helene, Erla, Erwin, and several others.

Ward explained that this would be a briefing on the details of the concept, to be followed by a tour of the facilities. Helene took over and introduced the key personnel starting with the well-known conservative ideologue Warren Hatch, president of the MacPhail Foundation. He was a stocky man with a brushcut and a singularly uptight demeanor. From his foundation he dispensed largess to conservative researchers, educators, and television producers, and spewed out articles prepared by his capable staff.

Marsha Fox, who was on the plane, was introduced as an independent political consultant based in Washington. Ruth Farrencolt was her assistant. Helene recounted that Marsha had worked on the Reagan and Bush campaigns, and reeled off three successful senatorial campaigns.

An intelligent-looking and elegant African-American man wearing a brown sports coat with matching shirt and slacks, was Rollin Tinton, a Rhodes scholar with military service as an infantry officer in Vietnam, a Ph.D. in economics, and a full Professorship at Trinity College.

Finally, there were two Ph.D.'s from the Allendale Foundation, Louis Fischer and Harold Smalley. Tony knew that Washington foundations provided salaries for mid-range government managers when their party was out of office or when patrons retired.

Tony got up to shake hands with everyone.

Helene yielded to Warren Hatch. "I'm sure Ward has outlined what we are about Tony," Warren began. "He views it as a solution to certain problems. My view is a little different. It is a fundamental change in the way things are done in democracies...tantamount to the Glorious Revolution of 1688 in England without bloodshed or mayhem.

"We will create a new political organization of greater power and discipline than has ever been seen before. The purpose is to maintain and improve the worldwide context for the development of large multinational companies. The goal is to establish substantial political influence in the United States government to control relevant events. We will get to our specific objectives later. More important is the means we have developed."

Warren went on to explain there would be four main groups. The video screen flashed on with an arty organization chart. The Recruiting, Training, and Election Group under Rollin Tinton was to have all of the functional resources needed to scout and recruit candidates, train them, finance them, and win elections.

The Capital Action Group, headed by Erwin, was an effort to refocus corporate lobbying in Washington to strengthen and unify it.

Warren portrayed the Doctrine and Intelligence Group, where Erla was in charge, as the source of doctrine and philosophy with appeals to the majority of the American people. This was also described as the strategic group where the deep thinking would be done. He said intelligence reported to Erla and she would be responsible for interpretation.

The Communication Group, Warren continued, would be the gurus and practitioners of main line public affairs, advertising, other communications, and fundraising. They would produce profuse amounts of television, radio, and print advertising, press copy, and literature to appeal to voters on all levels. A leader was to be recruited.

When Warren turned the podium over to Rollin Tinton, the display changed to an organizational chart of his Recruiting, Training, and Election Group. Rollin presented the concept to literally scout candidates as they run in local or state elections, much the same as a major league team would scout athletes. He showed the training plan which would be largely one-on-one with consultants working with candidates. The training was to be comprehensive, including organizing support, writing speeches, media relations, and fundraising. He described a "campaign support unit" which would draw on Communication Group assets to help with campaigns and tackle special problems in the field. The training was to be highly automated with video, but still personalized. The last unit he described was Political Analysis. This, he said, would do analyses of congressional districts, state legislative districts, or even county districts to help with planning. They would receive information and data from the campaigns, planning groups, the intelligence group, and other sources and would work with campaign staffs to plan individual campaigns with local issues treated properly.

When it was time for questions, Tony tried to get information as to the size of the group. Rollin didn't bite. Warren turned the meeting over to Erwin to stop the discussion.

The audiovisual flashed to a structure of political Washington, on which Erwin commented, and then to the Capital Action Group, which he explained. He showed how there would be joint planning and the use of both the Doctrine and Intelligence and the Communication Group resources. There would be much more intense analysis of particular issues to develop the best possible communication support. Erwin indicated that when constituent support was needed, this group would marshal it. He projected they would organize task forces on specific issues and, if needed, mass attacks on Capitol Hill.

When questions were invited, Tony tried again to get at how many people would be involved. Erwin refused to answer.

Warren jumped in again to stop the questions and brought Erla to the rostrum in her elegant sports outfit of blue and beige. With her head cocked looking down at him, she described how they intended to crystallize the development of philosophy and doctrine.

"One reason," she said, "for the confusion of the American political scene now and over the last few decades has been a lack of real doctrine. During the Clinton administration, the Republicans opposed everything and wound up not knowing who they were even after they took over Congress. The conventional wisdom is that definitions must be simple for the public to comprehend them. But if they are too simple, they fail to guide the thinking of candidates and office holders and are probably not meaningful to most people.

"Once every four years a group of not necessarily competent people get together from each party and in the course of five or six days, they draft a 'platform.' Substantially, more competence and many months are needed. You know how many issues there are in politics, Tony. The national candidates have to transcend issues to the local level since 'all politics are local.' Our purpose is to form doctrines which help in the transcending. It's no small task."

Tony wanted to ask if the intelligence function included dirty tricks. At that point Warren suspended the meeting so that Helene could show Tony around the facility. They would get back together at lunch.

Tony looked sideways at his watch. It was barely past 10:30 a.m. He wondered what it was they would show him that would take until lunch.

ON THE MAIN floor with Helene, Tony walked past conference rooms and classroom facilities. Corridors led to wings of sleeping rooms. In the rear of the lobby, Helene gestured to an elevator. She smiled at him when they stepped inside, and he noticed how perfect the color of her off-white outfit was for her tanned complexion and brown hair. She unlocked the control panel to reveal four buttons and slipped a key into one of them. It lighted and the elevator which Tony assumed would move upward, suddenly dropped for some distance.

When the doors opened, they entered a small reception area with several doors. He heard the hum of ventilators. Helene opened one of the doors and they stepped into a corridor.

"Before Ward purchased this property," she said, "we heard of the legend of caverns used by pirates during the days of the Spanish Main. With aerial photographs, the company geologists found them. The enticing legend for the tourists turned out to be true. We own the land and buildings above them. We built the hotel, the conference center, some of the houses, and other buildings. In these caverns we found pieces of eight, Spanish dollars, gold and bronze jewelry, and bronze chains. The pirates may have captured slaves and made them work a plantation for provisions or they may have imprisoned captives. Under the guise of repairing the damage from a hurricane, Ward reconstructed the caves and ventilated them at his private expense. This is still going on. It's like a bomb shelter."

She pushed a button, and a door opened with a hiss of compressed air. They entered a large high-ceilinged room with 15 or so computer workstations facing a huge conformal map of the world projected on a smooth curved wall. In front of them was a large oblong conference table, and at the rear was a projection room with a dozen lens apertures.

"This is the intelligence center, Tony. It hasn't been fully wired yet, but this is where all of our information will be collected. A few stations have been connected."

"All you need is a satellite track," Tony joked.

Helene laughed. "It's not quite that complicated. The map shows the time zones and windows close-ups of any area we might be interested in. Most people here will be working on regular assignments or projects. The A-V can bring any local situation from our computers. It also brings up data analysis. It is supposed to have any data we would ever need stored. This is Louis' thing. We all hope our Allendale Ph.D. knows how it works."

The room was square; the ceiling two stories high. The offices were around the perimeter on a mezzanine. It all looked very intense. Tony wondered how Bahamas Telecom could ever handle this. He assumed they were being paid to do it, or being paid to allow Ward and his organization to infringe on their monopoly.

They walked down the hall and Helene made another turn, opened another door, and stepped into a high-ceilinged gallery with seemingly natural lighting. Workstations lined the center on the ground floor amid a semicircle of offices on the mezzanine. A large photographic mural of a Harbour Island scene was projected at the far end of the room on the entire wall.

"We want people in the intelligence section to feel they are in a control room environment where they have to be precise in their analysis and careful in their language," Helene said. "This is for the Doctrine and Intelligence Group from whom we want creative thinking."

In front of the offices was an open area of conference tables, where people could wander out of the offices to meet and talk. There were conference rooms at the end of each row with windows facing the atrium. Each office had blinds that could be lowered for privacy. On the mezzanine level he heard a phone ring. Erla's office was probably up there.

Tony saw the mural was a live picture.

"That mural can be switched by moving or changing the cameras," Helene said. "The idea is to show the outside to make this feel like it is on the surface. When they first installed it, I was down here and took a few minutes at lunch to get some sun. I didn't know there was a television camera that could see me, much less zoom in on me."

She smiled. He sensed her warmth and vulnerability. He also counted the workstations in this underground world.

Across the hall there was another atrium about half the size with another live mural. In this, there were six workstations and offices around the floor with open spaces and conference tables.

"This is for our support staff for Erwin Festener. He hasn't given us a complete concept of it yet."

They continued down the corridor, chatting about the changeable murals, and whether people in the atriums might become disoriented. Rounding a corner, they nearly bumped into a tall man with khaki pants and a matching shirt that seemed almost like a uniform. Helene introduced Edgar Slaughter, the chief of security. He was lean and hard with thinning sandy hair, a light mustache, and an overly familiar look in his eyes.

"I heard you were visiting us," he said. "Has he signed all the agreements?"

"Yes," Helene said.

"How do you like our evolving headquarters?" Edgar asked.

"I think this place is fascinating."

They moved down the corridor, passing a flight of stairs going downward.

"Where is the security department?" Tony asked.

"You can't see it until you officially join us," Edgar said behind them.

"Edgar enforces procedure," Helene said, with a touch of pique, as he ducked into the stairwell.

"I see," Tony said.

An elevator whisked them up to another, warehouse-type building on the surface. Outside, they walked down the main street through the garden area and back toward the conference center. Tony realized it was nearly a half a mile and calculated that the underground system was nearly 700 yards long. He wondered how much of it she hadn't shown him.

"Why all of this Helene?" he asked. "Why here on Harbour Island?"

"Access is controlled. We are outside the United States, but still very close. If we have trespassers, we have a friendly government to expel them or throw them in jail, whichever we ask."

"Is it that important to be out of reach of American law?"

"We want to be beyond the reach of American snooping."

"What about electronic surveillance?"

"You heard what Edgar said, Tony. We don't take anyone down to the security department until they join."

"How many people do you have now?"

"We have 14 professionals and a total of 33 on the payroll. Just the beginning."

They passed the tennis courts.

"When you come back we'll have our gym done, complete with a running track and we'll be able to play basketball and volleyball, rain or shine."

"You like volleyball?"

"Almost as much as I like tennis. It's a real team game."

A luncheon was served in the executive dining area, designed like a German cellar restaurant. They joined Erla and Warren Hatch.

"What do you think of our project, Tony?" Hatch asked after the pleasantries.

"How could I be anything but impressed?"

"You see we are very serious about this."

"There must be some code name for all this," said Tony.

"POLACO."

"Political Action Commission?"

"Political Action Coalition. It's part of our public relations strategy to avoid sounding threatening or sinister," replied Warren.

"You mean you will be able to explain all of this if *60 Minutes* or a flying squad of *Newsweek* reporters overruns your fortress?"

"I think we can, Tony. We are exercising our right to know, to understand, and to be heard."

"But aren't you interfering in American politics from an offshore location. Isn't there something illegal about that?"

"Not if we are Americans."

"Why do you have intelligence reporting to Erla instead of being a separate function?" Tony asked.

"The most important use of intelligence is to understand the facts about the people to be able to create doctrines and philosophy with broad appeal. If intelligence were a separate department, Rollin's group or Erwin's would monopolize it with their questions. Reporting to Erla as part of the Doctrine and Intelligence Group gives Erla first dibs. The operating people always want more than they really need."

After some more discussion, Warren adjourned the lunch to

resume in the conference room in a half-hour. He also announced a tennis tournament after the meeting to see if anyone could beat Helene and Tony.

In his suite, Tony rushed to type as much as he could.

WHEN THEY REASSEMBLED in the conference room, Warren went to the lectern and snapped on some new charts.

"Now that you have seen the concept and the assets, and you know the purpose and the goals, let's get into the objectives," he said. "You already know, of course, that we want to maintain a strong military establishment with continued development of technology as a paramount program. We already know the U.S. military is the best protection for our assets abroad.

"Second, we want to influence the federal regulators to mitigate their paranoia about the securities markets and brokers. The securities laws need to be refined. The banking laws are burdensome. We have a lot of items on the infrastructure agenda. We want money spent on the railroads and highways. We can lose significant basis points of our gross national product by having trucks standing in traffic jams.

"We need to stop all of the legal wrangling that goes on. It is so simple. If a plaintiff loses a case in Germany, he pays the defendant's legal fees and is normally assessed a penalty by the judge. We have to insist that plaintiffs take that risk in the United States."

Warren continued, "We understand that the entitlements of Social Security and Medicare are sacred ground. However, we'll fight any attempts at national health insurance because of the huge costs that businesses could incur. We'll struggle against further entitlements.

"On the matter of welfare, there is a big question mark. We believe there has to be some form of population control among people who cannot be educated to participate in even lower middle class jobs. Not an easy thing to sell."

"Who knows what might happen with an appeal to the greed of the middle class?" said Tony.

"That's probably the strategy. Do you want to comment, Erla?" asked Warren.

"In something like that, Tony, you can only generalize. It is expensive to support people who cannot support themselves because of the expectations. We've had many conversations about alternatives: back to the CCC, federal workfare programs and so forth, and population reduction makes the most sense."

Warren steered to the next subject. "On the matter of crime, and on workforce development for that matter, we all know our main problem is drugs, and our objective is to bring about the imposition of the death penalty for drug traders using the Singapore model. We've been screaming at the Latin Americans to cut off production. The Latin Americans have been screaming at us to stop consumption. Neither one is possible. What Singapore has discovered is that you can stop the marketing."

"Do you intend to also treat the addicts on the Singapore model?" asked Tony.

"Yes. I think we will support that."

"On the matter of international terrorism, we like the idea of an international tribunal which tries those caught. We'd have an internationally sponsored and monitored exile place where these people would spend their lives or long sentences at hard labor. I don't think the liberals will object.

"The final issue is the environment. We all know that regulations are wildly out of control. We've created a school of environmental advocates who are as intense as any political effort. This may be the most difficult area of all, Tony, but it is going to have to be rationalized. We did get the trading of emissions credits halfway done. We have to get the responsibilities of cleanups off the backs of companies that have nothing to do with the polluting, and we have to promote the use of brown sites rather than green sites. We have to fight the lunatic fringes who have too much influence. They have been allowed to stop nuclear power and harbor dredging because our politicians are afraid to confront them. Questions?"

"I don't see balancing the budget, Warren," Tony said.

"Large corporations and their owners don't necessarily want the budget balanced. We deficit funded the expansion in the Reagan years."

"I thought it was an accident."

"We shifted the focus of federal expenditure away from social welfare to sophisticated military hardware to maximize the pressure on the Russians and the benefits to business. Supply side economics was probably foolish, but if it worked it would have been great for us. It still led to benefits. As far as the deficit is concerned, as long as it does not exceed a certain percent of gross national product, who cares? We invest our money in good government bonds and let the taxpayers pay the interest. The IRS is a reliable collection agency."

Marsha Fox looked at Tony. "You can tell the liberals it is the redistribution of income. You take from the laboring class and give it to the capitalists and managers."

Tony hadn't thought of that.

"What about internationalism?"

"A long-term objective. We have to be sure we are not restrained by some right wing, anti-foreign populism," replied Warren.

"Civil rights?" Tony glanced at Rollin.

"We are for equality of opportunity and using the human assets of all races. We hope the African-American community will merge with the white. Good race relations are good business," said Warren.

"Would you strengthen EEOC laws?"

"No, no interference. We'll promote the idea in our companies. That's the way to build race relations too. When it's done with laws it's too emotional. We can make it real on our own."

"Occupational Safety and Health?" asked Tony.

"Blow it up. Our position is that it was, like the labor union movement, once necessary and is no longer needed. All we get are meddling bureaucrats creating unnecessary regulations."

The discussion continued. Tony probed as much as he thought he should. Helene, Erla, Marsha, Louis, Rollin, and the others answered. He tried to relax and focus to get everything in mind.

After an hour and a half they broke up to change for tennis, while several went off for golf. Tony pounded more notes into his computer. He wondered who else was in. Was PENMET a key to something for POLACO? Would Nordstall and Shinwa join if Ian did?

At the tennis courts a tournament was organized. Tony and Helene easily won it. Then Helene challenged Tony to a game of singles. She broke his second and fourth service games to take the set. She was fast in the backcourt and a terror with passing shots. He tried to come to the net; she top spinned over him. He was delighted just to watch her play.

At the net he said, "Are you the resident tennis coach or is there somebody better than you?"

"We play a lot here," she laughed.

☆ **Chapter 2** ☆

THEY WERE TO have dinner that night with Warren, Marsha, and Harold. Warren had an emergency. When Tony and Helene got back to the club, Marsha and Harold had started drinking with Louis Fischer and two new arrivals. Helene suggested she and Tony have dinner alone and recommended Spanish Wells.

With executive ease she commandeered one of the cruisers. Twenty minutes later they were seated together in the stern slicing up the bay channel to round the north headland of Eleuthera just before sunset. A while after they turned westward, the little town glided toward them with its quaint houses of pastel pink and white. Winding through the narrow harbor channel, their skipper showed off his maneuvering and fast reverse to kiss his gunnel against the quay at the Echo Marina. Tony jumped out with a line and then offered Helene his hand. He had the sensation it was the first time he had touched her.

They walked the quarter mile to the Sands Hotel and found a lively crowd of tanned men and blonde women in the bar. Tony glanced about for his friends, but didn't see them. The maitre d' greeted Helene and they were quickly seated at a side table. Vodka and tonic quickly arrived British style with lemon and Schwepps. They talked as they dallied through conch chowder, a tasty fresh salad, and succulent lobsters. Helene measured Tony. Some of the corporate executives who had visited were, in her judgment, essentially phony men who had plied their way by buttering their boss' bread or undermining those who were more competent. One reason she liked ACP was there were few phonies. The culture was "be tough minded and know your stuff." Problems were expected to be solved, not excused. If managers couldn't cope and staff couldn't produce, they left.

From reading his bio she knew Tony had a rich background. She knew Ward had been skeptical of contacting PENMET about POLA-CO. The culture at PENMET, she had read, was very productive and indicative of good leadership. She suspected Tony Destito was part of that good leadership. It wasn't all MacAulliffe or his division chiefs. It had to come from a dedicated and highly competent central staff. She heard stories of executives who couldn't make the grade being pushed aside.

Tony had a handsome face with nice smile lines, and intense dark eyes. He was over six feet tall, husky and muscular with dark, wavy hair. There was a sense of truth in him. She started to feel a little aroused. He was no ordinary man.

"What brought you out here Helene?" he asked.

"I was divorced and had to get a job, so I went to work for Ward. What else does a single girl accustomed to a certain lifestyle do in Cleveland?"

"You weren't working during your marriage?"

"Part time, with my old firm. I did the volunteer stuff, too. You get sick of that."

"What's it like being out here?"

"It's lonely, but when I feel bad I think about the salary."

"Is the job exciting enough?"

"I wish it weren't on Harbour Island, but it's exciting, Ward is exciting. His people are exciting; the companies that have come into POLACO are exciting. In my wildest fantasizing, I never was doing anything like this."

"Not too many people ever have an opportunity like yours. Why so many women in top jobs?"

"I'm sure you've noticed no one is married. When this enterprise gets going we're going to be one busy group. I'm here all of the time. Erla will be here most of the time. Marsha will be here most of the time. They're both ready to move in. We'll finish their apartments next week. They are older single women. We can't come out here with husbands. Men can't come here with wives. Powerful men need women a lot more than powerful women need men. And powerful women have trouble getting men because most of the ones they meet get scared of them."

Tony thought he would have to try that on Jean.

"Do you think Ward is exploiting you?"

"Hardly by the salaries he is paying."

"Is it a harem arrangement?" he asked tentatively, but it was part of the reasoning he had to do.

"Heavens no, Madeline would have us all mutilated."

"There has to be some pairing."

"I'm not sure I like this line of questioning, but yes, there is. I guess we encourage it between the analysts and secretaries. We have to limit the people who know about POLACO, so if an analyst marries an analyst, or a secretary marries an accountant, or computer specialists marry each other, or if they just go to bed, that's fine."

"Do you believe in this enough to be sacrificing your happiness?"

"Somebody has to do something about the United States. Somebody has to do something about democracy all around the world. Some countries in Europe may work because of their homogeneity. Maybe Japan does. In the United States, we wonder if we know who we are. I don't have a lot of time to consider meanings. It's a huge task, Tony, and Ward relies on me. Sometimes I think I'm an overpaid professor of political science. Sometimes I think very big." He suspected there was a soul in this woman.

"You have been in public affairs. What school?"

"I went to PITT, Tony. My parents weren't wealthy."

He had expected Smith or Stanford. "Did you study political science?"

"Oh, yes."

"Your father and mother?"

"My dad is still working. He is a tool maker for a glass fabricator in Toledo."

"That's home?"

"Yes, my mom worked part time, but when my brother and I came home from school she was there. I can't imagine what it is like for kids who don't come home from school to a mom. She now works at Wal-Mart. She likes it and they're flexible so she can fly to see my kids in Westport."

"They are with your ex?"

"There is nothing else I can do. The divorce was reasonably friendly."

"He resented you?"

"He couldn't handle that I made more money than he did. It was crazy, but it also made him look weak to me."

"Does he work in New York?"

"Now he does. He's bureau chief for *The Economist*; smart, but stiff. He has the whole United States to look after, but he spends most of his time in New York and Washington."

"I assume you know all about me, Helene."

"Yes, your bio was very detailed." She also knew that he called his wife last night and told her he loved her and that he spent an hour with his computer. Security had gone in to see if they could copy the notes, but found he had locked them out with a password.

She wanted to ask him if he were making notes or doing some other work, but for the moment, her feelings pushed against her job. She thought he might be sizing her up as a lonely female, but she wanted to believe that Tony was above that.

Tony felt a looming presence near him, and turned to look up into the smiling face of Captain Ansell Munroe holding the hand of his blonde wife, Betsy.

"You're right, Betsy, it's him by God, but the wrong girl."

Tony laughed and stood up to embrace his Spanish Wells friend. Betsy hugged him and held up her cheek for a kiss.

"I've some explaining to do," Tony laughed. He introduced Helene and briefly told of the connection.

"I saw that fancy cruiser you came on. It's still waiting for you, very fancy; very expensive."

"I didn't see 'Norma' when we came up the channel."

"Aye, I was up sun from you. Right behind you. I saw you with this pretty lady in my glasses."

"I am awfully glad to see you," said Tony. Please join us. Have you had dinner?"

"Aye, and it's first night back." Tony knew this had special meaning. On the first night home after a trip the crew gathered with their wives and girlfriends and the captain paid for the drinks. There was a party, but it usually ended early as the couples became anxious to get home.

"How was the trip?"

"Profitable, and invigorating except to be away from Betsy here. Lance Wallens, remember him? He was bitten by a barracuda."

"Is he all right?"

"He's fine, but I still had him helicoptered off to Nassau. He'll fly back tomorrow. He couldn't get on the flights today, too many of your people, Miss."

Helene sensed she had better not get into questioning about the island because this captain would probably be interested. "I thought barracuda were only scavenger fish?" she said.

"Barracuda, pretty lady, are like people. Out of every 500 or so that you meet, there is going to be one mean bastard." Everyone laughed.

"It's time for partying, Tony."

"That's what I am afraid of."

"You've finished your dinner. Let's go to the bar and I'll spend some of my new dollars and we'll talk about the news."

There was no denying Ansell. He was the owner and captain of the "Norma," the largest fishing boat in Spanish Wells with a crew of more than twenty and a reputation for always coming back with the best catch. The fishing was done by deep diving, and sometimes by trapping lobsters.

Ansell was the fifth or sixth generation of his family who moved from South Carolina after The Revolutionary War. They still spoke the English dialect of the 18th Century. He was handsome, clear minded, and could have his pick of the girls. He picked a beauty. He and Betsy had three school-age children. Tony and Jean were arranging for the eldest, a son now twelve, to come to Pennsylvania for prep school. The boy had a good mind and Ansell wasn't going to let him waste it in Spanish Wells.

With Ansell just back, Betsy could hardly stop touching him. In fourteen years of marriage she had probably spent no more than four with him. He was a common councilman in Spanish Wells and a man of the sea. In this culture, there was always concern when the men left. Even with radar and satellite navigation, the sea still claimed victims. And, there was the legend of the Bermuda Triangle that the Spanish Wells people had to laugh off. They were inside it.

They joined the men from the "Norma" with their women at the bar. Several men cast admiring glances at Helene followed by knowing smiles at Tony. Two of them flirted with her and pinched her. Tony warned her about sexual harassment in 18th Century English society. She laughed, and said she could handle it.

They talked about local news and gossip. The subject of "the sheltered people," the product of too much intermarriage in the town came up. Ansell said they might cure it by inviting some well-qualified males to add some new genes. He asked Tony if he would be interested, but then said that he wouldn't qualify because of his dark eyes. Whenever Helene and Tony emptied their glasses, Ansell was there with two more drinks.

As the group broke up, Ansell and Betsy invited them to come for a sandwich at their house. Helene suggested maybe there was something else Betsy would like to do that evening. Betsy said that she would have to feed Ansell first anyhow. They snacked. Betsy asked Tony all about Jean and his family. They talked about the school the young Munroe would attend. Then Ansell turned the conversation to the subject of rumors.

"Start a good rumor on Spanish Wells and it will reach the other end of the island before you get there," Ansell said. "There's plenty of rumors flying around about Harbour Island. Is it true you're going to build an amusement park there? Like Disneyland?"

Helene giggled.

"No, not quite," she said. "It is a corporate retreat, for business, and I don't think we'll be building anything else."

"What about the accidents?"

"What accidents?"

Ansell smiled.

"Just rumors," he said.

Soon after that they said their good nights, and just before Tony stepped into the taxi, Ansell wrapped him up in a bear hug.

"Be careful," Ansell said. "There are rumors."

HELENE LEANED AGAINST him in the stern of the cruiser as it rumbled over calm, moonlit water. Her face was more beautiful than ever. At the POLACO dock Tony scrambled up and held out his hand for her. A security man with a golf cart took them to the hotel. As they started up the stairs to the hotel door, she took his arm.

"I have to hold on to you," she said. "I lost count of my drinks. How do those people do it?"

"In the 18th Century life was hard; you did a fair amount of drinking."

"She kept holding his arm in the elevator. When they were outside her apartment, she turned and kissed him. He put his arms around her.

"I wish there were men like you on this island," she said.

She held her face up to his to be kissed again. He could feel the smooth shape of her back and her hips and her breasts pressing against him.

She might become the most powerful woman in America, he thought. But what was he doing? He had his wonderful Jean. Helene separated from him, smiled as she opened the door and said, "Good night."

For the first time, he felt an intense attraction to another woman. He was completely aware of this woman in a way he had been only once before, when he had fallen in love with Jean so many years ago.

Then he thought about Jean. He knew what had happened would be a big problem with her, but at the moment, he couldn't understand why. It was like he had entered another life on Harbour Island. A life separate from home.

Lying in bed trying to turn his brain off he couldn't help comparing the two women.

THE FINAL PLANNED event of the visit was a meeting with both Helene and Ward Cowell. Ward looked at Tony with curiosity. No doubt he had had a full report on the night before.

"Tony, you've seen it, you know what it's about, and you're still here," he said.

"Yes, Ward, I'm still here."

"Does that mean you're interested?"

"It's hard for me to not be interested," he said.

Ward was obviously relieved to hear that, so much so that Tony thought what he suspected might be true, that Ward had a deal with Nordstall GmbH and Shinwa Meiwa to come in if PENMET came in.

"Then you need to know what we expect of our members."

"That would seem appropriate."

"We've asked everyone who is coming into this to invest $1/10$th of 1% of last year's revenue as a deposit on which you will receive interest and then to provide an annual fee of $1/20$th of 1% of your operating profit."

Tony tried not to look surprised. "Ward, that's $45 million."

"And with your large gross profits, your annual fee will be about $10 million."

"Ward, we hardly spend $10 million on all of our trade associations."

"This is not a trade association, Tony. You know what it is. I think you and Ian have to decide whether you are going to be a part of it."

"How do we take this to our board?"

"We have all of the documents and representations on the investment that you will need. It's a use of surplus cash. Ian can manage that."

"But the annual fee, Ward?"

"Add it to your operating budget."

"Ward!"

"Tony, we can't have too many participants in this, so it is expensive."

Tony realized that was true. Too many companies would increase the risk of disclosure.

They had to have common interests. If Helene was going to become one of the most powerful women in America, Ward was going to become one of the most powerful men. He had already built a headquarters big enough to accommodate the ambitious adventure. Maybe that was the motive: tens of millions of dollars, or hundreds of millions to make Ward Cowell the kingmaker of the United States. No, it had to be serious. The others would ask the same question. Apparently they were satisfied it was real.

Helene rode with Tony on the cruiser back to North Eleuthera and to the airport.

They stood alone by the plane.

"I hope I'll see you again," she said.

"I would like that very much."

She slowly moved to kiss him. As their lips met, she closed her eyes.

THE ACP GULFSTREAM jet took Tony directly to Harrisburg. As he descended the steps, Jean drove her BMW onto the tarmac. The copilot and stewardess brought his luggage. Inside the car he kissed her.

"Looks like ACP recruits stewardesses from a modeling agency."

"They don't compare to you, no brains," he said.

"How was the trip?"

"I'll tell you about it." He leaned and kissed her again.

She wondered, "Something wrong?"

"Are you home tonight?"

"Yes."

"Good, I need you to be home tonight."

They talked of family things on the way to the large house that Jean persuaded him they needed after he became a vice president. It was an imposing colonial on five acres in a rural suburb beyond the West Shore Country Club. In the back there was a hard surface tennis court and a swimming pool.

Jean Somerville Bartlett was a skinny, sexy blonde he met at a fraternity-sorority exchange. The first time he saw her, a bell clanged in his brain and he never was interested in another girl. She was bright with serious blue eyes. Her hair shook when she moved.

He was a senior when he met her, she was a sophomore in Government and English. At Cornell, the engineering program was five years so they were married as students and he crammed in an MBA. His family liked Jean the moment they met her. But, when Jean took him to her home in Cambridge, it was the crowning event in the disaster of her leaving Massachusetts to seek an education. Alfred Emory Bartlett, her father, head of the family investment banking firm, had negotiated with her regarding the schools to which she would apply. History was to be her major with a literature minor. A husband was his objective and who would she meet at Cornell? He complained the school was one-third Jewish, and one-third immigrants. She said that was just fine. He sputtered; her mother cried.

Jean was his prize. He loved the slim, muscled girl who could out-shoot all the boys with a basketball, and fake them with a hockey stick. Cornell beckoned to her to play basketball and softball, and she went to the Ivy League school furthest from Boston. Then she brought home a handsome, highly intelligent man who was Italian. Her mother was dismayed, the grandchildren wouldn't have blue eyes! The official announcement of the engagement was entirely handled by the Bartlett family PR firm.

Antonio Guiseppe Salvatore Destito was third generation American in a family that remembered its heritage. Tony's great grandfather, Paulo, and his young bride came to America in 1878 in the midst of the great immigration. They went to Pittsburgh where he was a structures engineer for the Pennsylvania Railroad. Their son, Salvatore, saw Italy for the first time in 1919 as an American infantry captain who survived the final paroxysms of the Great War.

When he returned to Pittsburgh, he started importing, and established a retail business in fine Italian silk fashions. He married Isabella Pochielli of Sienna, and his first child, born in 1920, was Guisseppe or "Joey," Tony's father. The import business faded with the Smoot-Hawley Act and the Depression. On the retail side, the Destitos parleyed their savings and expanded when retail property was cheap. With good products, good services, good prices, and good people, the risk paid off.

Guisseppe had two brothers. The youngest, a marine lieutenant, was killed in his first action on the beach at Iwo Jima. Ruggero went from college to sea as a deck officer on a destroyer. Guisseppe went to Carnegie Tech as a star student in engineering. All of the Destitos, got good grades to avoid the wrath of Salvatore. After army O.C.S.,

Guisseppe was assigned to the staff of a new secret project. For months there were only occasional phone calls, and censored letters.

He was invited to stay in the army and did so until 1950 when, as his mother nearly despaired, Major Destito fell in love. She was Antonia Lucci from Sonoma, California, an assistant professor at PITT. California was then, impossibly far away, but the Destitos traveled west for the wedding and embraced their new in-laws.

Joe Destito found a good job with a steel company, and rose in the ranks to become a superintendent. Tony was named for his mother. The retail stores prospered and Tony's brother, Paulo, trained to take them over from his uncle. His sister, Janell, became an internist. Salvatore and Isabella lived to see her graduate from medical school. Guisseppe and Antonia expected even bigger things from their eldest. He did not disappoint them.

Tony and Jean were married in Ithaca on neutral ground. Jean hoped her family would respond to the love that radiated from the crowd of Destitos that came. They didn't. The reception was at Tony's fraternity house where the toast to the bride and groom was on a terrace overlooking Cayuga Lake. They flew to Nassau, stayed at the Sheraton British Colonial, and made passionate love in every possible setting. Jean took loving droughts of life every day, and jumped out of her clothes whenever Tony winked.

When Tony picked PENMET, they moved to Chicago where he worked in plant engineering demonstrating his technical brilliance and leadership ability. This was tested when he was assigned to head a faltering facility in Detroit. He moved the weak people to other jobs, or let them go, and replaced them with competent men and women who were motivated to achievement. He formed teams and preached that teamwork was mainly unselfishness. With the union cooperating he empowered the workers. Everyone greeted him when they saw him. Tony hired women and minorities into management and professional jobs. More than a few of the girls had crushes on their tall, darkly handsome, pleasant-faced boss.

Corporate Human Resources suggested that Tony have some time in marketing. He was assigned to Washington and took over relations with the U. S. Navy. He showed he could establish relationships outside the company and deal with political people. He brought in contracts and as a Product Manager used his imagination in communications as well as technical development. He caught Ian's attention by now, and was brought to Harrisburg to the Central Research Department and showed his team building again. He gave people credit for their accomplishments and avoided politics. He was selected to head the new technical advisory section of the corporate staff from there.

In each city Jean connected quickly; an advertising agency, marketing for a publisher and in political campaigning. Martin was born in Detroit and Barbara in Washington. In Harrisburg, Jean freelanced as a consultant and then went into politics. She was welcomed, and put her energy and rich ability to work. Jean rose quickly.

CARRYING HIS BRIEFCASE and suit bag, Tony pushed through the front door. He was assaulted by their Springer spaniel; their Abyssinian cat appeared, who never had feline aloofness, and rubbed against his leg. Jean came in from the garage lugging the tennis bag. She reached in for the used shorts and shirts, and shoved them in the laundry chute.

"What's so mysterious?" she said when she came back.

"Come upstairs, I have to practice telling you, so I can tell the story to Ian."

They sat in her study with his lap top open so they could read the screen while he talked.

"An underground office complex? It's Ian Fleming or Tom Clancy. Why?"

"They want to control access and to keep a very low profile. They probably have agreements for protection from the Bahamas government. Helene Courtney said trespassers would be thrown off the island or jailed."

"What's she like?" Tony became concerned. Did Jean sense something?

"Smart, powerful, like you."

"Warren Hatch, I've met him. Isn't he a 'kook?'"

"Could be, but a smart one."

"Whose idea is it?"

"I'm not sure; could be a Washington Business Roundtable meeting that adjourned to the bar."

"What are you going to do?"

"That's Ian's call."

"What do you think?" He felt her probing him.

"I think it is very dangerous and we should try to stop it."

"So do I. How?"

"I'm not sure. We're cramped by a Philadelphia lawyer's confidentiality agreement. We can't just expose this. Who would believe it?"

"There's a lot they could hide behind. If it became public it would scare off supporters, but it sounds like the support is already there. We may have been the last catch they went after. Big deal to have the ultimate tip-of-the-hat from PENMET. If you go in, they have more reasons to give if they get caught."

What a smart wife, he thought.

"If they've got all the money, what would stop them?" she continued.

"I don't know, we'll start looking at it tomorrow."

"Do you think Ian would agree with this?"

"I'll bet dollars against Belgian Francs he'll be as scared as I am."

"You hungry? I'll make something to eat."

"I was stuffed down there." He thought of the dinner with Helene and felt a guilt pang. He decided not to tell her he saw Ansell. She would want to know the details.

He took her hand, and said, "Come and hug me a little, I missed you." She punched the stereo to the classical music station. He stretched on the couch in their sitting room. She got on top of him and kissed him. He pulled her shirttails out of her slacks so he could feel her skin. A few minutes later she got up and locked the door, and turned to him unbuttoning. He saw once more that her breasts were as firm and her belly as flat as he ever remembered.

That night he held her close to him, feeling her familiar body. He was wakeful as he tried to estimate the changes the trip to Harbour Island and Spanish Wells might make in his life, and hers.

☆ **Chapter 3** ☆

IAN MACAULLIFFE'S FAMILY had fled Scotland in the depressed 1920s to Pennsylvania. His father Andrew, a brilliant metallurgist, found a job in the burgeoning aluminum industry and rose rapidly in its ranks. After a corporate crisis to expand plant capacity speedily enough to provide the basic material for the aircraft industry prior to World War II, Andrew convinced some investors to stake him and built a company that made them all many millions.

With his father's brilliance, his mother Wilima's warm character, and a Presbyterian upbringing, Ian took over at a young age and led the company to heights far beyond any of which his father ever dreamed. Utilizing a substantial cash flow, a high share value and awesome technology, Ian spread the company into steel, brass, copper, and new high performance metals. He then moved into plastics, chemicals, and ceramics worldwide. In every market, PENMET was the low-cost, high-quality producer. In addition to endless ideas and know-how, it also had effective control of many prices.

As was his custom, Ian MacAulliffe rose from his desk as Tony crossed the office to greet him. He was well muscled, 5'10", shorter than Tony, with gray hair still tinted its original blond-red. His high-cheekboned face was pleasant, curious, and tough, mirroring the essence of his character.

"You wanted a private meeting, Tony?"

"I think it has to be, sir, because we have signed Ward's confidentiality agreement."

"Aye, sounds ominous. Let's use the small conference room."

Ian's private conference room was decorated as his office was, with tasteful art mainly from Scotland and with cultured masculinity. Blue leather chairs surrounded a mahogany wood table. Cream white carpeting lightened the room.

Sarah Anderson, Ian's tall raw-boned secretary of many years, followed them with a coffee tray delivered from the executive kitchen. As always, there were muffins and bagels.

Tony relaxed in the familiar surroundings.

He told the story chronologically so Ian could picture the events in sequence. Smart people at PENMET knew that his mind worked that way. Tony left out the end of the evening with Helene Courtney. Ian interrupted a couple of times for questions, and Tony could see him taking it in through his extraordinary brain. He made notes on a pad in a leather folder.

When Tony finished, Ian responded. "This is very heavy, Tony. The heaviest thing anybody has ever brought back to me. Ward Cowell is many times over rich. He wants to be the kingmaker, and he has a persuasive argument. He'll get support. Too many of us are frustrated with government and by the democratic processes themselves. My father always feared this kind of thing because of what happened to Britain in the '20s. We have to take this very seriously."

There was silence while Ian thought, and Tony knew it was best not to speak.

"Do you know who else is involved, other than Nordstall, Shinwa Meiwa, and Wainwright?"

"They don't give that information until you join."

"I can understand that."

"I think the reason Kirchener and Emoto were there and said virtually nothing was Ward was showing them he could deliver us. I think if we come in, they will."

"Some endowment-raising technique this college has."

Tony laughed.

"I think consumer products companies won't take the risk. Surely not airlines or the auto companies, where the principals are so clearly known," he said. "The public reaction could be bad."

"This is the financial group. They are very powerful, Tony. It's also the chemical group, who feel threatened by environmental and energy conservation. Paper companies are probably in it, and the pharmaceuticals and medical equipment. They all fear government. They fear they can't influence government decisions. The way some of them lobby they should be afraid. They can't define their own issues and arguments."

Ian leaned back and folded his arms.

"What worries me is their thinking," he continued. "Ward Cowell says people don't understand the issues, then he frames them in terms of 'us and them,' 'for and against,' 'friends and enemies.' The advocacy groups are not the enemy. Ignorance is the enemy because it allows the special interest groups to manipulate. The 'either-or' logic Ward is using is not any different from the techniques of the groups he is complaining about. It doesn't reflect reality and leads to bad decision-making. And the more powerful the group that uses it, the more dangerous it is for the rest of us."

Ian paused and then said, "Write it up Tony. Do it on your computer. Let me have the report tonight. We'll talk tomorrow, first thing."

"Yes, sir."

"Good job, Tony."

"Thank you, sir."

Tony pleaded a minor tropical illness so he could take everything home and print out his report in privacy. He finished by mid-afternoon, and called for a messenger to take it to Ian. He then got on the phone about his regular projects.

Later, he found Jean in her study about to make a call. He put his hand over the phone, leaned down to kiss her and said, "Is it too late for a matinee?"

"Why, you were positively energized by this Bahamian climate."

"Only by missing you. You'll be scuttling off again to one of your meetings."

"You're the one who is away all the time!" she protested.

TONY WAS AT the office at eight the next morning. The PENMET headquarters was a stainless steel, aluminum and glass structure built on the west shore of the Susquehanna River, an exquisite seven stories high with an office penthouse on top. There were courtyards where employees could leave their offices in warm weather, and on the outside there were galleries where they could look down at the long bridges over the rapids at the fall line.

On a separate pylon, there was a large gleaming stainless steel sign, "PENMET," which was brightly lit at night. Alongside were two tall flagstaffs. A great flag of Pennsylvania flapped beside the Stars and Stripes, both clearly visible from Front Street on the city side of the water. When foreign visitors came, their flag replaced the state flag.

On the birthday of Andrew MacAulliffe, they flew the traditional flag of Scotland, the blue and white Cross of St. Andrew, the patron saint for whom the founder was named. On the national holidays of nations where they had installations they flew their flags and reported it in the local newsletters.

Tony's secretary, Joan, was at her workstation when he arrived. She told him that Ian had called. He grabbed the file from his brief-case and walked to Ian's reception room shortcutting through the boardroom. A long mahogany table with white leather chairs was the central piece. On the walls were photographs of every factory, and key employees. Cabinets held product samples and the exhibits were changed for every meeting. Ian presided over his empire with great good humor and insight. Board members were constantly reminded of employees, factories, and products.

Ian was on the phone and waved Tony toward the private confer-ence room. The coffee service was already set and Tony was pouring himself a cup when Ian came in. Without speaking, he helped himself, and they sat down in their respective chairs.

"We cannot judge this, Tony. We both have ideas of what it means, but we have to make a very precise judgment. It's my guess these people are ready to attack the Constitution and destroy American democracy or at least twist it beyond recognition. That has far-reaching implica-tions. Nobody has come up with a better means of government yet. Democracy has flaws, but the others are far worse.

"We have to figure out what these guys are really planning. It will require breaking our confidentiality agreement and calling in our advisors. I want you to form a team. We can trust Denise Williams on public affairs, but what political scientist can we trust with this piece of lighted dynamite?"

Tony thought for a moment. Denise Williams had the finest brain in public affairs Tony ever came across. David Gibson, Esq. was the long-standing outside attorney with the Madison Avenue firm of Bergman, Harris, Gibson, Lindau, and Seaberg. "We should ask Dave Gibson to look at this and be protected by attorney-client privilege."

"Aye, ask David, Tony, if he can recommend someone. Tell him we need an adviser we can trust with a secret more important than any we have ever had. Ask Denise. We must limit the number who even know there is a secret."

"Yes, sir," he said.

Tony felt uneasy as he went back to his suite of offices.

THE NEXT AFTERNOON, he flew to Ithaca to meet Dr. Terry Leelan, the preeminent political scientist at Cornell, whom Denise Williams had known well in graduate school. A private dinner had been scheduled at the Statler Hotel, which was operated mainly by hotel management students.

A limousine took Tony through the familiar campus where he and Jean had come to homecomings and where they had walked together as students. In the waning light he heard the carillon clanging the evening song. It always made him sentimental.

At the hotel desk, he asked for Professor Leelan and from behind him, a short light-haired man in a tweed sport jacket jumped up and came forward.

They had a free-ranging conversation. Tony already knew that Leelan was loved by his students and acclaimed for his lectures. He was a prolific writer and researcher, one of those rare professors who combine great academic skill with great teaching. He was also the right person, Tony decided, to explain the intricacies of political action to Ian, and whomever else might have to hear about it. Tony offered to pay him $2,500 a day for the consultation, plus expenses.

"Why so much?" the professor asked.

Tony told him he would find out.

The following Monday, a plane went to Ithaca to fetch Dr. Leelan to PENMET, where he interviewed with Ian. Another plane brought Denise Williams and David Gibson from Teterboro, the historic business airport in New Jersey that served Manhattan.

Denise was a gray-haired lady of 62. She became a consultant when she stepped out of agency life to raise her family, and she was so successful she never went back. Her retainer with PENMET was an annual salary to most of her profession, and Tony knew there were three main clients plus others whom she helped. She had a good deal of feminine handsomeness, featuring bright blue eyes. David Gibson was in his early seventies and liked to play tennis. He was tall and straight with only a little gray and looked like he could beat Jimmy Connors. He usually wore the latest style suits.

An aura of suspense surrounded the meeting. Tony told both David and Denise this was the most confidential matter to come before a company executive group since the Manhattan Project.

In the private conference room, Ian introduced Professor Leelan. Everyone had received Leelan's curriculum vitae by Federal Express. Ian was obviously pleased with him. He joked about bringing so potent an academic onto capitalist turf.

An hour and a half later, Tony had finished telling the basic story. Ian set the ground rules. There were to be questions of clarification only. David Gibson was the first to break the silence.

"Who are these people?"

Denise said, "Opportunists. They've seen something in the system, and they want to take advantage."

"I can see why you're keeping it so secret," said Professor Leelan.

Ian broke in. "I have a few questions to ask the professor, then we'll have lunch and continue. If we need more time we'll have dinner here tonight. We may need to think about this overnight, and meet again in the morning."

There were murmurs of approval.

Ian turned to Leelan.

"Terry, is this rational? Does it make sense that this kind of thing can be accomplished in the United States under the present system of laws and under the Constitution?"

There was a pause.

"I am afraid it makes all too much sense," Leelan said crisply. "A group of very powerful corporations have joined together to change laws. Can it be carried out? Well, if it is done with the expertness of the people Tony has described as involved, it can. It is rational, Ian."

"Aye, I thought you'd say that," Ian replied. "I wondered if it was something halfway thought through, that Ward's ego carried the rest of the way. You don't think so?"

"I have to think about this quite a bit, Ian, but I do believe it is rational and that he has probably consulted others in organizing it. Warren Hatch for example."

"Okay, you've heard the names of the key people: Hatch, Erla Younge, Marsha Fox, Harold Smalley, and Louis Fischer. What is your assessment of those people?"

"You forgot to mention Helene Courtney," Leelan said. "Helene was a published scholar of political science at a young age when she was doing her graduate teaching at NYU. She took on lobbies, a much less researched area, because it is very hard to get inside and difficult to document. She went into public affairs before she married.

"Fischer, I know by reputation and, of course, everyone knows Warren Hatch. Fischer is competent, but I have always wondered about him. He left teaching at the University of Iowa, went into government, and is now at the Allendale Foundation – or was. I certainly wouldn't give him less than a 'B.' Hatch and Fischer are the kind of people you would have to involve in something like this, because most professors wouldn't deal with it. If the organizers were smart they wouldn't even ask them."

Denise added, "I can tell you more about Erla Younge and Marsha Fox. Erla was an extremely bright student who has demonstrated good work in everything she has done. She had been with Farthergill for some time. I met her and have dealt with her; she's plenty competent. Marsha Fox has spent most of her time in political campaigns. She was at Farthergill as well. In her early thirties she was running the Washington office and was effective. She and Erla are both good writers and have television experience."

"Rollin Tinton?" Ian asked.

"He's an academic," said Leelan, "well published. I've heard he does a lot of consulting. Is he at Trinity?"

"Yes," said Tony.

"We need to find out a lot more about these people," Ian said. "My next question: is there anything in this that is illegal? What are the legal boundaries, David?"

"It will be a research job to cover all of the points. However, there is a chance they could keep it legal, probably by setting up foundations or political action groups. Terry knows more about this than I do."

"I agree with David," Leelan said. "There are a lot of laws drawn in various directions. In general, if they don't conspire to overthrow the government by force, they're not going to get into a lot of trouble; nothing they couldn't talk their way out of."

"That may be the key issue here," said Ian. "How do they explain what they are doing if they get caught?"

"That may depend on how they get caught," Denise said, "and what they are doing. They should be backfilling. If they are caught, it is questionable if any of the existing interest groups would attack them. The Republicans wouldn't. It would be up to the media."

She mused for a few moments.

"I don't see what they are doing is going to be particularly dangerous to them," she said, "in view of what they think they'll gain."

Tony judged the ad hoc advisory group was working very well.

"Having asked what would happen if the information leaked, how secret do you think it can be kept?" Ian asked.

David answered first. "I think this is a CEO-only arrangement or at least very senior officers like Tony. They keep secrets," he said. "The amount of money they ask as an investment and the annual fee is hideable by these large companies. One reason they are dealing only with the largest is that with very few members, the secret is safer."

"I think hiding these amounts is straining the accounting rules, David," said Ian.

"You have accounting experts of all kinds working for this company, Ian," David said. "You had better let Stephanie Comstock in on it. You'll have to let her in anyway when the time comes to present a $45 million investment to the board, if we are going to get into this."

Tony winced at involving Stephanie. She was a tough sell on most new projects.

Terry Leelan shot back, "Are you intending to help finance this thing, Ian?"

"This is the reason for having this meeting. We'll invest in it only as part of a means of stopping it. By joining we would maintain access to intelligence."

"You would spend the money for that?" asked Leelan.

"This group will decide, if I agree with the conclusion," Ian joked. They laughed.

"Back to the security issue. What about employees, secretaries, industrial espionage if our conclusion is to fight this group?"

"Maybe you need to have your security director in on this, too," David said.

"We can't have too many people know about it. We've technically violated a confidentiality agreement by talking to you," Ian responded.

"We can trust Stephie Comstock and Alvin Carter, Ian," said Tony.

"We'll stop for lunch. Tony, give Alvin and Stephie a copy of the write-up, and make sure they show it to no one. Print it off your computer yourself, and see if they can come in around two. Have them clear their schedules for tomorrow at least until lunch."

"Yes sir," Tony said.

Tony arranged a quick closed-door meeting with Stephanie Comstock, corporate vice president of finance, and Alvin Carter, director of security and asset protection.

Stephanie was a tall woman just turning 60 who challenged just about everything that anyone proposed. She was a genius at finance who had come to work for Andrew as an early woman Harvard MBA. After she had proven herself in lower-level jobs, Andrew, and later Ian, had seen that she took the fast track. Ian had suffered the innuendoes in board meetings that finance was a man's game and that he had pushed her through her election as chief financial officer when she was 40.

In her relations with Wall Street, Stephanie won special respect, and PENMET stood out in the early days because of her personal prowess. She underwrote much of the growth through the banks and the sale of bonds and gained prominence carrying out a series of domestic, Eurobond, and foreign currency financings. She understood the institutions, molded concepts they could accept, and won respect in the financial markets worldwide.

Politically, Stephie would probably agree with what Ward Cowell was doing, being that she was so conservative, Tony thought. David Gibson was right, however. She would have to know, because of the presentation to the board. She could also provide her extraordinary financial insight into POLACO.

Alvin Carter, in his fifth year with the company, was from a leadership family in the Cleveland's African-American community. His father had been a police captain. After completing the criminal justice program at Ohio State, Alvin joined the Cleveland Department, where he rose to be chief of detectives. He had taken early retirement to join PENMET.

Tony explained the meeting with the three consultants and asked Stephanie and Alvin to read the document he had given them first, then join them when they thought they were ready.

Then he went back to Ian's offices. The food had been kept warm on the buffet table. It was oatmeal-coated perch, a specialty of Scotland, which Ian particularly liked.

After lunch, they resumed with Stephanie and Alvin present. Alvin took his place at the table looking a little dazzled by what he had seen.

Stephanie was aggressive as usual in speaking her mind. "I think I get it, but we should all have a clear view of the underpinnings," she said.

"Good point," said Ian.

"If they have asked us for $45 million as an investment, I see a large amount of money being accumulated from a small number of companies who can afford it," she said. "They probably have well over $700 million. They will be careful with the investment and they will want some liquidity.

"To carry this out, Cowell started with his own money," she speculated. "Probably put up a fair amount which was paid back when the investments closed. There's plenty there. They're using some of the capital to build the facility, but they will have the security of having a lot left if they need it. The question is the spread between what the capital earns wherever they have invested it and the interest they have promised to pay to make it a good-yielding product. It's probably favorable, but they could use the annual fee to cover a negative spread. This could be good for the Bahamas if they are lending it in Nassau. It would be a way to multiple quids pro quo."

"That's what I pay you so much for, Stephie," Ian said, "Good analysis."

Ian refocused. "Another question for you, Terry. Where will this thing be if it is outstandingly successful in ten years?"

For a moment everyone thought about the question.

"It might take more than ten years, Ian, for this organization to be positioned to initiate matters of their critical interests or block any legislation before the Congress," Leelan said. "I may misjudge the ultimate intent, but I believe they would attempt to elect a President and a Congress that would stack legislation their way. It takes a lot of thought to see how this will evolve."

"My concern, Professor, is what Tony said about tinkering with the Constitution," Ian replied.

"That is a danger. I gather, Tony, that they were baiting you to see if you responded."

"That's how I saw it," said Tony.

"It's more than that, Ian," said Denise. "They wouldn't have talked about changing the Constitution unless they have some goals in mind."

"Tony mentioned," Leelan responded, "the possibility of a corporate state."

"They mentioned liking Japan," said Tony.

"Japan might be at least a partial model," said Leelan. "Japan is a country where large corporations have great influence. They establish the social contract. They diluted anti-trust, banking, and securities regulation. They have maintained the non-tariff barriers to imports."

"Let's keep to the point," said Ian. "Tinkering with the Constitution."

"It appears they are thinking of a series of Constitutional amendments," said Leelan.

"What would they be?" asked Ian.

"Oh," Leelan gestured, "ascribing greater powers to the executive branch and specifying them; withdrawing powers from the states and investing them in the Congress to centralize things. They could move the Federal Reserve under political control. Give me some time and I'll list a few more."

"I think it's more than that," said Denise. "Ward Cowell could well be aiming at a state in which suffrage is limited. The population control thing is a direct infringement on certain liberties. There is more to this. The reforms they cited to Tony are potential popular issues. They could stir issues enough to get their people elected or frustrate people sufficiently so they would agree to give up democratic institutions. They probably intend to do both."

"Germany and Italy in the 1920s and 1930s," said Leelan.

Ian listened to the discussion for a while. "What do you see as real threats to big business, Terry?"

"Business is a natural target for political maneuvering. Militant young assistant secretaries in a liberal Department of Justice could look for an issue to ride. They could find something related to antitrust, then try to break up large companies. A liberal Congress conceivably would support them. Even capitalists argue that the unfriendly takeovers that result in selling off divisions to get cash are healthy, because units remain smaller and more efficient. The sheer size of companies today is frightening to some. It will probably become an issue and the POLACO people foresee that.

"An economic downturn might raise questions of forcing investment into the United States. From Ross Perot to Jesse Jackson there has been talk of protecting American jobs. Populism seizes a democratic country from time to time. One motive for POLACO could be that the companies intend to export American jobs and they are afraid of the government for that reason alone. Those who seek power for power's sake will use any issue or motive they think will benefit them. The value of free markets has been recognized, but the trend can reverse. A successful demagogue could appear.

"Then there is the huge question of the competence of those who govern. They aren't that good. The party system has broken down to entrepreneurial candidacies at all levels. POLACO could be a grouping of unprecedented resources to undertake such candidacies.

"It gets back to your first question, Ian. Is what Ward doing rational? Yes, it is rational, in the sense that big business has issues to be concerned about. These big companies are trying to reduce the political risk."

"It's complicated," groused Ian.

"They used to call economics the 'dismal science'," Leelan said. "Political science, history, and economics are difficult because the laws are vague and change with human experience.

"To get at what you are looking for, Ian, it is not a process, but it's people. We are in the era of entrepreneurial candidacies, particularly for the Presidency. Groups form to support particular candidates. I have always wondered if there might have been a group in Southern

California who thought they needed to find a President who 'could play the role' and decided to make Ronald Reagan Governor of California and then President. That was a corporate-oriented government that would have been highly successful except for the deficit funding and a few overzealous policies. The POLACO people know that and they are entering the game. The more I think of this the more I think that is the main motive in substantial control of events."

"But," interrupted Ian, "where does that lead?"

Leelan closed his eyes, then opened them.

"If any one group controls access to elections and controls the individuals that are elected, forces will be let loose," he said. "Power corrupts. I have to think about it.

There are many scenarios."

"It's not all to be solved by public relations," interjected Denise. "There would be a gradual development of protest like the Vietnam War in the streets."

"And," said Leelan, "it would not end by ending the war. It would advance to a political crisis."

"What about the companies involved if they are identified?" asked Ian, "What happens then?"

"They could use a variety of excuses. Everyone could say everyone else was doing it so they wanted to be on the inside."

"For $45 million?" exclaimed David.

"Why don't we leak it?" said Ian.

"Because we would be tied up in lawsuits by those confidentiality agreements forever," said Tony.

"Damn the lawsuits. That's what we have a legal department for," said Ian.

"We would risk the management of the company, Ian," said Tony, "and, we are personally liable."

"I saw the agreements and I agree with him, Ian," said David. "We shouldn't have signed them."

"The more important question is: who would believe the leak? They would fog that in so fast. The releases are probably already written," said Denise.

"We should focus now on what our purpose, goals, and objectives should be," Ian declared. "If we can come up with these, then you lasses and lads can become a joint task force to determine the options and respond to Cowell."

There was another pause.

"I'm think this is a great threat to the country and to basic freedom," stated Leelan.

"I agree with Terry," said Stephie. "There are other things we can use the $45 million for."

"Don't think about the money," said Ian.

"I hope you all see the danger in this to fundamental American institutions," said Leelan.

"That is my first concern," said Ian. "It's not as though what they are aiming to do is wrong. In many cases the action they propose is needed; it's the way they are going about it."

"Does that give us a real purpose here?" asked Leelan. "We want to stop it?"

"If we think this is a threat to the Constitution of the United States we have to do something," said Ian.

"Why are we always it?" asked Stephanie. "Can't we just not join and forget about it?"

"How could we know about the threat and not do something about it?" asked Denise.

"How could you do anything that would risk the corporation?" asked Stephanie.

"It's when good people do nothing, Stephie," said Ian.

Tony realized this was the conclusion Ian had reached. He looked at Alvin Carter who was sitting, listening, and thinking. In the style of a junior person he didn't pipe in at meetings, but Tony could sense Carter was putting it all together.

"Am I correct, professor, to think this could turn very mean and could get fascist and become the end in itself?" Alvin asked. "It could maybe become racist?"

"It's reasonable to say it could happen, Alvin. If one group has all of the power and they become confused, or if another movement starts that threatens them, things can get out of hand quickly," Ian responded.

Tony looked at Ian and he knew the decision was made.

"All right," Ian interrupted. "I really appreciate this dialogue. You're a great group. Let me give you the parameters now. First, I would like to have some kind of forecast as to what might happen, and where this could lead the country. Second, assume we want to resist this thing. What can we do to stop it? Third, and at the same time, we must protect the company. Keep in mind whoever belongs could stop buying our products if they found out we were working against them. There are risks, but I consider us fortunate to be informed, and fortunate to have the personal ability and the wealth, and I mean mine, to resist. So I want to know the options to resist and how do we respond to Cowell? To join or not to join? I don't think we can string him along."

"You're talking big risks," said David. "Let them pass to someone else."

"Who, David?" asked Ian. "We can't go around recruiting opposition. Suppose these people 10 or 15 years from now, have changed the Constitution. How does that affect our corporate stewardship? How does it affect us as citizens?"

Ian stood up. "Take them to your area, Tony," he said. "Keep the doors closed and let me know when you're ready. Why don't you stay here for dinner? You're the chairman, Tony."

AT HARBOUR ISLAND Helene, Erla and Edgar met with Ward on the PENMET membership. Helene had mixed feelings. She was attracted to Tony Destito and she knew he was attracted to her. If PENMET joined she would see him.

"Who has anything to report of fact?" Ward asked. "Edgar?"

"Two telephone calls to his wife and one to his secretary. He asked for a meeting with Ian MacAulliffe when he returned."

"Anything else? What about the questions he asked?"

"He was curious," Erla answered. "I thought he was trying to get dimensions. He probed us about the intelligence activities."

Helene knew Ward was edgy about Tony. He had never been happy about the pitch to PENMET. They didn't fit the group. Several superbly managed companies were in POLACO, but some were led by greedy executives focused on short-term results. PENMET was famous for its substantial creative thrusts of new products and technologies. There was no preliminary contact with PENMET. Others wanted to see them in.

"Any insights at your dinner with Tony, Helene?"

Why was she nervous? "He does have a friend in Spanish Wells. I met him. Erwin told me about him. He's very smart. He understands what we are. I think he'll recommend they join." Afterward she could not determine a reason why she said that.

Later Ward telephoned Alex Peterson about his uneasiness. Alex tried to calm him and said that PENMET would follow their economic interest.

"I trust MacAulliffe but then I don't trust him," stressed Ward. "I can't picture how he would react to this. For one thing he didn't come himself."

"He never does if he can manage it."

"I sense danger."

"All right, take some action. If you are suspicious and really sense danger use your assets."

"I think we should stop our solicitations at this point unless you've got some indications of real interest."

"There may be one or two, but I agree. We have a fair percentage of the gross domestic product represented in this organization."

Ward's uneasy feeling increased; he'd had it many times. He thought it was good to doubt once in a while and check judgements and avoid overconfidence.

WHILE TONY'S ADHOC group deliberated, Ian returned to business. His days were full, but not harassing. He didn't scurry from appointment to appointment. He delegated as much as he could. He gave his people responsibility and expected them to come to him only when they needed decisions or help. He wielded the power of the world's most profitable multi-national corporation. He was proud of his people and proud of their achievements.

His counterparts ran about the world, visiting people and doing deals. Ian let his division people do that. His major divisions were large companies in their own right. He let people come to see him. No one could fail to be impressed by PENMET's headquarters; they had all of the materials they needed to persuade people to enter the arrangements they wanted, and to sell their products.

Sarah stepped in to say that Ward Cowell was on one of his private lines.

He had thought about this possibility. He picked up the phone.

"Well, Ward, you've got us thinking," Ian said. "It's quite a story Tony told. How are you and Madeline?"

"Everyone's fine. Are you and Susan all right?"

"Just fine."

"Do you have any questions?"

"There are a lot of things to consider about this, Ward. Tony has given me a full report. He was impressed, particularly with your staff as well as the concept."

"Can I report to my colleagues you're on the positive side or on the negative side?"

"I think you can say we're shading on the positive. There's a lot to think over as I am sure you've had others tell you."

"Yes, of course, Ian, I understand."

"We're anxious to know who else is involved. Do I understand the terms of this agreement are that we have to come to a positive decision, then you will tell us who is involved and if we choose to withdraw we can?"

"After you've made your initial deposit of which 10% would not be refunded."

"I understand, and I don't think that's unfair."

"Keep in mind the confidentiality agreement."

"You don't need those agreements dealing with us," said Ian.

"I know that, Ian, but I have to follow the form as you know."

Ian changed the subject, "How is the new program going down in Venezuela?"

"It's bugging us to death, Ian. Now I know why you only have two plants in Latin America."

"We're building two more, Ward. Get good local people."

"What do you think about China?"

"I'd like some clearer banking information and clearer political channels. I will be there soon; the staff has a lot for me to look at. I don't care for the human rights situation, but we decided the best thing to do was invest and hope it changes. We'll go in by acquisition."

"The classic PENMET technique. Buy it cheap and turn it into a jewel. How many times have you done that, Ian?"

"A few."

"Probably two dozen, Ian. I am jealous of your ever-growing technology and expertise. When do you think you will have a decision for us?"

"I can't say precisely, but I will call two weeks from today, or Tony will."

"That's fine, I appreciate your input, Ian."

As he put the phone down Ian felt there was tension in Ward's voice. After the long harangue of who would visit Harbour Island, Ward had not mentioned anything about his sending Tony instead of going himself. He wondered what it meant. He concluded Ward either needed PENMET for some financial reason or was concerned about what he might do.

He would see what Tony's group came up with, but he had an idea of what he was going to do, and if Ward was concerned, it was justifiable.

☆ **Chapter 4** ☆

THAT EVENING, IAN and Susan were at their townhouse on Front Street where they stayed during the week in the winter, or when they were entertaining in town. Ian left Tony in charge, lest Ian impose too much of his power on the deliberation. Their main home was the MacAulliffe estate southeast of Gettysburg, where Andrew MacAulliffe had bought a thousand acres of exquisite Pennsylvania countryside. There he built the MacAulliffe mansion of gray stone in the Scottish style. There were barns for horses, two tennis courts, a spa with an indoor swimming pool, an outdoor swimming pool, and a nine-hole championship golf course.

Ian and his father started a Scottish hamlet as housing for some of their employees and as the setting for a Scottish pub and restaurant. They imported the food and chef and the two places became popular in central Pennsylvania. Stores were added and a quaint shopping village emerged, all Scottish true to form in light gray stone. The MacAulliffe's made money on the things they did because they did them well.

The restaurants and the village were Susan's, Ian's elegant second wife. His first wife was the tragedy in his life. His father pushed him to Oxford for economics and business after chemistry at Princeton where, as a graduate student, he met Evelyn Wallace, a spirited Scottish girl with raven black hair and blue eyes, tall and stately, with a great love for life. She could sing and dance and could have become an entertainer. She majored in history and literature and began a career in writing. Her talent was quickly recognized. Ian fell for her and pursued her among considerable competition and won her as a deep love developed between them.

Her father was Earl of Auchencairn. They were married at the family church on the north shore of the Solway Firth. He and Evelyn made their way back several times each year for ceremonial events and to visit her family. Ian enjoyed the town in Galloway surrounded by the rolling hills of the lowlands.

Despite their differences and the demands of his work, they had a sharing relationship in which Ian found refuge and great happiness. His wife was popular in the company and visited the offices often. They had three children, Robert, Mary, and James. The youngest was just four years old, when on an early April afternoon, Evelyn had been at a luncheon meeting. Driving back through a spring snow shower, a runaway truck crashed through an intersection and crushed her Buick convertible. Ian was on the phone when his secretary dashed in and stammered, "Mr. MacAulliffe...Evelyn...an accident...on line one." He ended his conversation and pushed the lighted button. An urgent masculine voice said, "Mr. MacAulliffe, I'm Lieutenant Babcock at the Third Precinct. Your wife's been in an accident and she is being taken to the hospital. You have to come immediately. I am sending a police car. It will be at your entrance in two minutes."

With sirens screaming, he was sped through the wet streets to the emergency room where he was led to her bloody, broken body. He spoke her name. She opened her eyes. He had to hold his ear close to hear her say, "I love you, God be with you, take good care of the children." He knew she had fought to stay alive so she could give him this message. The memory of that moment always made his eyes moisten and his throat clench.

The family and his friends rallied. Andrew and his mother were in Europe. They met the Earl and Lady Wallace at Heathrow Airport in London and made the sad flight together. The wake, funeral, and reception were jammed with employees, officers, and managers sharing their young leader's terrible loss. Customers and vendors were there to show their respect. Civic leaders and politicians did the same.

Ian stayed home with the children for a week and then gave them over to their grandparents and disappeared. Andrew knew he was on the Greek Island of Santorini at the vacation house of an Italian friend who phoned from Milan to offer it. He took one book, *The New International Bible*, and spent most of his days reading it and making notes. He had food sent in. He cooked. He walked on the beach and climbed the hills. When the peak of his grief washed out two weeks later and he finished the reading, he phoned one morning from Paris and went back to work in the European headquarters office on the Rue d'Anjou. In four days he was home and life began again.

After many months, his friends started to introduce him to women. He set a schedule for spending most of his spare time with the children, but he got away for a day here and there and one weekend a month. He took the children on vacations. He went on trips with his current liaisons. When he had just turned 43, he met Susan at a theater party in New York at the elegant old Chemist's Club on 41st Street. He saw her first coming down the stairs; tall, sharp nosed, elegant with a warm easy smile and reddish brown hair. She had been widowed by cancer and left with two children at age thirty-two. The courting was across the distance between Harrisburg and Darien on the Connecticut coast.

Their feelings developed into a deep love. They took vacations together as a couple and then with their families. They were married at her church. Their parents and their children were present along with their close friends. The officers who reported directly to Ian, selected long-time employees and their wives were ferried by chartered DC 9 to LaGuardia Airport and bussed across the Whitestone Bridge to Connecticut.

Their honeymoon started at the Carlton Hotel in Cannes. They wandered down to Montpelier and walked along the shore of Palovas. Neither had seen the restored medieval city of Carcasonne so they drove there. They drove into Spain and then to Pau and Lourdes where they prayed at the great shrine. Susan said if the Blessed Virgin Mary did appear it surely would have been here with the incredible beauty of the Pyrenees forming the background. They then flew back and moved Susan's household to Harrisburg for their life together.

Susan was a product manager in fashion fabrics. After she married Ian, she stayed active in the family interests. She was his companion, his hostess, his confidant, his lover, his best friend, and his private business analyst. When he first told her about POLACO she was stunned.

TONY ORGANIZED THE group he guessed would continue as a task force, and they worked through the definitions of the critical issues. He commandeered the guest offices to which David and Denise were accustomed, but where Terry Leelan felt flattered with a plethora of computers, a private fax, and full access to the Internet.

It was 8:00 p.m. before they gathered for dinner. They resumed at 9:00 the next morning.

At 3:30 p.m. the next afternoon, they assembled in Ian's large conference room. Sarah brought the usual refreshments and Ian took his place at the head of the table. Tony started, "Ian, we have worked over the questions and the issues. Terry will lead this presentation. It's mostly political and he's the political scientist."

Ian chuckled with the others and nodded toward Terry.

"I would like to review your question, 'What is the likely outcome of this POLACO if it were to proceed forward?' We can assume if this group continues to be effective and is not restrained, that within 25 years or sooner, after electing its candidates to successive congresses and a couple of presidencies they would have appointed a majority of the Supreme Court. Challenged and overtly illegal initiatives they put through Capitol Hill could be approved by the Supreme Court. They could take over the United States seemingly legally. This is probably their real goal. They would rely on their new dialectics and the related propaganda to create a justification. The result of that Ian, would probably be civil conflict. It would be a matter of the development of leadership. The POLACO government will control communication and may survive. But, it's likely an underlying minority will oppose them. Eventually, competent leaders will emerge and there will be conflict initiated by those who believe their liberty has been compromised. There is no greater cause for action in history."

Ian felt his skin get clammy. The faces around the table were uncomfortable and grim.

"It is conceivable that with great wisdom in its leadership, POLACO could be limited and rational. But, they are spending a huge amount of money. Control is the probable objective. POLACO is not a single person or single power focus. Rather, it is a group and groups get in trouble because of their decision-making processes. If they are well structured and decisions are made in an orderly way, success is possible. If they are not well structured, which is usually the case, decisions are disorderly without adequate process. Political groups get political within themselves and start to make mistakes."

"Business is benevolently authoritarian for that reason, Terry," said David.

"Businesses with orderly means by which they make decisions are successful. If the decision-making process is disorderly, my guess is that the companies are less successful or fail."

"A good observation," Ian said. "That's why we Scots are stingy;

it's to stay orderly." Everyone laughed. He broke the tension.

"There is an inevitable conclusion," Terry continued, "which does not require speculation. Regardless of purpose, the attempt by any single group to monopolize political access should be resisted. The POLACO method is wrong.

"You've asked for the options to resist or stop POLACO and whether PENMET should join. Our conclusion is that PENMET should join unless we decide not to take action against them. By joining we establish access to information and communication with the operating council. We might even have an option of calling for and urging dissolution. This is not a high probability again because of the money that has been spent. But, Tony has projected marketing 'Hotel Underground' with all kinds of exotic happenings. He's volunteered to organize it." More chuckles further relaxed the seriousness of the occasion.

"It is possible to expose the whole thing," Terry postulated, "on a gradual basis by third parties without overtly violating the confidentiality agreements or at least without exposing you, Tony, or the corporation to legal action. The result from the exposure is questionable as Denise has argued. Would anybody really care? If the real objectives were clear, most Americans would react. But, these will not be clear. Rather, they will be obfuscated. They can hire the best of the best to create an intense public relations campaign.

"The eventual disclosure is almost certain. The architects have probably calculated that they can avoid disclosure long enough, then if they are exposed, the majority of the American people might well accept what they have done. That's probably the main reason they have this doctrinal development going on. It adds the greatest possible substance to their program. If they are positioned to argue that they have acted in the best interests of the people, perhaps there will be no social upheaval. If there is no protest, they will have taken over substantial control of affairs. We've tried to find an option that might entail some risk, but could produce decisive results and stop what is happening."

Ian's face wrinkled. He liked bold thinking.

"We think that you and others who are like-minded," Terry measured his words, "could make another intervention into the political process, but one that is wholesome and honest. This is to undertake a successful, entrepreneurial presidential campaign that would bring to power a truly-competent and well-meaning President. It should be someone fully capable of organizing an administration and governing the country to reverse the political deterioration on which Cowell and his group would feed.

"This is an expensive proposition and one to which there are serious regulatory and legislative restrictions and limitations. But, if it could be done for the next election – no easy task – it is possible that by creating solutions to the fundamental problems and reversing the national political erosion and popular mistrust of government, we could stop POLACO by seizing their legitimate issues. A competent administration in office would take away POLACO's reason to exist.

"This would have to be followed by a campaign to reestablish the party system and to create means and structures within the parties to bring forward competent men and women of goodwill to run for political office. This is another complex task, but without it, entrepreneurial candidates would reappear and the danger to the democracy would gradually resume."

Ian saw the idea. "I agree. We have watched growing evil in many situations in this country and the world without taking action. Now, unless we somehow engineer a counter force, Ward Cowell will let loose a monster that could swallow the Constitution. We'll take this on. I'd like some time to think about it. Would you all stay one more night?"

The dialogue continued. Denise reviewed the public relations options to explain involvement by PENMET first and then the other corporations should POLACO be exposed. She posited that the companies had joined in an informal trade association of multinational corporations to develop analyses of the political processes in various countries. "The coalition undertook a study of complex political issues to rationalize them for their executive staffs, board members, and shareholders," she said mimicking a POLACO spokesperson. "Lobbying is the right of any corporation or corporate group to present a case to a government. On the matter of assistance to candidates, everyone has the right to help candidates who represent opinions they favor and to support them to the limit of the law. With regard to recruiting candidates, what is wrong with urging competent people to serve, and help them to do so?"

The discussion went on until 6:30 p.m. when Ian left, and Tony realized they hadn't ordered dinner. He called Jean with a request to serve dinner for five guests who couldn't go to a restaurant and continue their talk. Jean apologized that she would be out for the evening, but she agreed to call the caterer. Barbara would study in her room. Martin was to be at junior play rehearsal and had a ride home.

He had intruded on Jean's schedule; she was getting ready for a meeting of her own.

At the bar in Tony's family room, cheese, shrimp, and crackers with fruit were waiting. People from the restaurant that Jean used for these occasions were preparing a Pennsylvania meal of pot roast, mashed potatoes, string beans, salad, and corn bread. The special task force was still there, making notes and discussing the issues when Jean came home at 10:30.

SUSAN WAITED FOR Ian in the Front Street den where they watched the *PBS News Hour*. He made a scotch and soda, poured sherry for her, and clinked glasses with her. A maid served broiled cod and vegetables with Scottish bread.

"I received the recommendations from the consulting group on the matter of POLACO. They agree we have to resist this."

"I should hope so, but how can you possibly stop them?"

"Dr. Leelan has suggested we run someone for President, a top-grade candidate from outside Washington, who will turn things around in American politics and government. If we reverse the trend we take away POLACO's reason to exist."

"Run somebody for President?"

"That's what he suggested. If a force is being developed which will gain control of access to candidates for elections and possibly take over the country, then there has to be a counter force. Leelan is very good. We would have deliberated for months before we came up with that."

"I'd like to meet him."

"I was going to bring the group here tonight, but I need time to think. This discussion is more important. I'll have to do what Ross Perot did; use our personal fortune to start a movement."

"Why don't you run?"

"That's not for me. It has to be someone with political experience."

"You have had plenty."

"I don't want to look the self-serving fool like Perot and Steve Forbes. We have to find the right person."

"You want to start a political movement, a new party?"

"I think we have to form a group to support a particular candidate. We are allowed legally to seed that group with substantial funds, but I am going to have to raise the money to put this candidate across. It might cost us as much as $50 million."

"50!"

"That's to move a candidate to the stage where funds can be solicited and to make public funding available."

"Why so much?"

"Maybe it will be less; I have to pay my own expenses. We can't charge it to the company. I'll have to pay other peoples' expenses. We have to find someone who is the very best for the job. I'm not sure whom they are going to recommend yet. I'm not even sure anybody exists that can pull this off. I wanted to talk with you about it beforehand."

"It's your money," said Susan.

"It's Terry Leelan's idea to move quickly and take POLACO by surprise."

"How would you organize it?"

"Leelan is very imaginative, but also careful and I think he can give strategic direction. Denise Williams is the best there is. David Gibson would be the lawyer. I think Terry Leelan could be put in. Stephanie and Alvin Carter are involved. And, Nancy Letersky could be, she would be a significant weapon."

"Isn't that too close to the company?"

"Gibson has to tell us."

"You've just spent $2 million on your consultants."

"There will have to be others. I want you to be one of them. We will establish a foundation. I want you to be in charge of the main entity."

She was flattered, and also flattered to be married to one of the greatest business leaders in the history of the United States, who also happened to be a warm-hearted, well-intentioned man. She smiled, "I'll help you spend your $50 million, except I thought you'd make me First Lady."

"We could run you for President."

"I could probably do the job, but there are better women than me. How about a woman vice president?"

"I'll have to refer it to my advisors," he replied.

"How are you going to get this done and leave for China?" she asked.

"I'll delegate it to Tony Destito. He's got a good consultant as a wife too."

"I should charge you."

"You could negotiate your salary with Gibson."

"It wouldn't look good if I took a salary. We'll manage without the $50 million."

She knew that 50 million dollars was hardly 2% of their $2.5 billion liquid wealth. The book value of their stock in PENMET was over three times that. If they added everything together: the farm, the real estate, the mortgages, the stocks and bonds and calculated the value of PENMET shares at market, it was over twenty billion. They never added it up. The rest of the family was worth another ten billion or so on the same basis. Ian voted their stock.

Ian put his wealth to good uses. She knew that when he retired much of it would be given away anyway. Their prenuptial agreement arranged that neither she nor her children would ever have a financial worry.

"Well, $50 million was not all that happened today," said Susan changing the subject.

He looked at her with a trace of alarm in her eyes. "Something bad?"

"Cindy was arrested in New Orleans."

He was stunned. She saw his feeling for her and her daughter whom he loved, but who never really accepted him. "More drugs?" he asked.

"Yes."

"This is the third time?"

He stepped toward her and took her in his arms. She held her arms together against his chest.

"Did you call David?"

"No, I called the lawyers we used last time and wired $25,000."

"Bail?"

"She's accused of selling."

"I don't believe that."

"Possibly a self-serving prosecutor," she said.

"Everything must be done quickly. Does the firm understand that? Before they size up the situation. A trial of Ian MacAulliffe's daughter could be sensationalized to gain notoriety. Don't give them time to think or to drum up phony evidence or circumstances." They sat together on the couch in their bedroom suite sitting room.

"I'll call them tomorrow. What do we do with her? She's had the best treatment available."

"She will not allow us to love her," Ian said. "There are two possibilities, mental illness treatment or the discipline of the military."

"She won't do either."

"Tough love. Maybe she has to go down to the bottom," he said.

"Too dangerous. Evil people would find out who she is."

Ian pondered the dilemma. He was resourceful, but nothing was harder. A stay in jail might help, but she would be on the phone screaming at her mother if they didn't pay the bail. She had little respect for the law. There was, however, a glimmer of hope in her talents and charm.

An idea came to him. "I can send Stephie down to see her. She had the problem, I think with a son. She is a woman at the center of the wealth and power of the company whom Cindy knows and who won't take any nonsense. Maybe she can appeal to options that Cindy could take that would get her into deeper treatment. We have to get a diagnosis, if there is a pathology, or we don't know what we're dealing with."

"We can't impose on Stephie. She's busy and she has a life," Susan said turning toward him.

"Stephie will take it like an assignment and plan to win. She'll do it. She can take some time in New Orleans."

Susan leaned to kiss him and couldn't hold back the tears. He held her and patted her hair. His heart cried with her. A minute later she said, "I'm sorry," She stood up, "I need a shower."

Wearing only undershorts he lay on top of the bedspread reading when Susan returned. Her hair was still damp when she sat opposite him in a terry robe. "There's always a way with you. You never give up." He smiled. She slipped the robe off her shoulders and pushed herself naked beside him. He admired her form, only a little puffiness in the stomach. Her breasts were soft and her nipples erected. Her arms and legs were trim from her high-energy life with just a little extra flesh and softness. "I'm going to make love to you."

The next morning the group reorganized along the parameters of Ian's conversation with Susan. The Pennsylvania Liberty Foundation would be formed of which Susan would be Chief Executive Officer. It would dispense funds and hire consultants. David, Denise, and Terry would send their bills for services to Susan. Tony would remain on PENMET's payroll. Leelan would continue at Cornell, with a leave-of-absence to work on the campaign. He would receive $7,500 a week.

WHEN IAN AUTHORIZED forming the team to develop the program Leelan had suggested, he also proposed they include Nancy

Letersky whose judgment he greatly respected. It was also hard to have Denise Williams working on something that Nancy didn't know about.

In her early 40's with a buxom figure and a warm dimpled smile framed by dark brown hair, Nancy had been the vice president of public affairs for a small producer of specialty alloys. When some sudden reversals caught the small producer with excessive debt, PEN-MET acquired the company. Ian would normally meet individually with the key people; a shrewd judge of whether executives could do their job, he was right about three quarters of the time and very wrong on only one in ten. He was right about Nancy.

A graduate of Douglass College at Rutgers in journalism with a master's in television arts, Nancy was one of a new generation of well-trained young people in communication. From a traditional Polish family, she grew up second to the last of six children. Her father was a metalworker who, during World War II, built aircraft engines at the Curtiss Wright factory in Woodridge, New Jersey. An achiever, he became an engineering technician with the Metal Improvement Company which opened the new technology of shot peening of metals to hugely increase fatigue resistance for the aerospace industry.

He made sure that each of his children was thoroughly schooled in Polish Catholicism, in patriotic Americanism, and in a desire to rise above the working class. One of Nancy's brothers who went to St. John was already a millionaire. Another worked his way through Stevens as a commuter student and was a corporate officer. Nancy received a scholarship to Douglass for leadership and academic achievement at Woodridge High School. At Rutgers, she met a mechanical engineering student from Newton, New Jersey in Sussex County. After they graduated, her brothers gave her a wild Polish wedding and they went to live in Hazelton, Pennsylvania where her husband was an engineer for a company producing metal powder products. She worked for the local television station in Allentown, who was happy to get her, and she rose quickly.

Pressure developed in the marriage because of the odd hours she spent as a news producer. In ten years, she won every award that was given. There were two children, and while raises had come every year for her husband, her salary had rocketed upward. She had the opportunity to go to a station in Philadelphia and the fissures appeared in their relationship. She gave it all up and started writing while the kids were in school so that she could be home when they returned. She did articles and columns for regional newspapers and became a stringer for the *New York Times*. An assignment to write and produce a television series for a public interest group came her way. Her work attracted the attention of the chief executive of a growing metal alloy producer who needed a strong person to handle the communication program. She joined the company; then she met Ian MacAulliffe. When she knew the marriage could not be healed, she left it and took back her maiden name. She moved to Harrisburg with the children, while their father sank into alcoholism.

THE THREE CONSULTANTS and four PENMET employees decided to meet in Manhattan. They determined they would not meet at the same office or hotel more than once. They started at one of the Blumberg Harris conference rooms on Madison Avenue. On the first day, David Gibson reviewed the legal issues. The second day, they went over the critical issues to determine how their candidate would propose to yank on the control stick of government to pull the country out of its political tailspin.

Their theme would be to accuse the political establishment of dealing in foggy perceptions of issues rather than the reality that confronted the nation and the free world. Reality would be their focus. Their candidate would define the reality and would deal with the real issues ranked on a scale of importance. They would distinguish between perceptions and reality and would not accept that perception was reality.

Taking on the tough issues would also mean taking on the tough lobbies like the lawyers, the health care industry, the government employees union, the educational unions, possibly the banks and the financial community, and the multitude of advocate groups. However, in each issue there would also be support and they would try to coalesce that into the national interest.

In Harry Truman style, they would tell what they believed, regardless of the polls. They would cite the mistakes and motives of previous administrations. They would call for debate to seek the truth. They would look to history and try to bring forward a sense of it. In all aspects of the major issues their administration would lead thinking and not follow it.

Their general strategy with the candidate yet to be chosen would be to raise political competition to a new level. Once the candidate was established the plan was to get endorsements from Democratic leaders. They would concentrate on winning the Iowa caucuses and the New Hampshire primary, but would organize fully in all the critical states. They would move quickly to achieve local political endorsements.

The organizations established in each of the key primary states would be with paid staff. As quickly as possible, volunteers would be recruited and trained. The money would be funneled through every means possible to keep everything legitimate. New fundraising would be undertaken with a well-structured and well-trained group.

To handle this strategy and to elect their candidate they would gather the best possible staff of professionals who would share the purpose. To access data quickly for analyses, they would retain FIND SVP for rapid on-line services and for their survey work. PENMET had been a FIND client for almost 30 years. They determined to retain Jeremy Reubin Associates as a political consulting firm anticipating that they would contribute the most to the plan. Denise was Reubin's champion, believing that Reubin was one of the few genuine companies in the business. For public relations and communication they needed a firm with offices throughout the country and personal relationships with the media. Once again, it was a question of time. They had to get attention quickly. They chose Evans & Copeland. Denise championed them, reporting on their professionalism and good work with a strong client list at fair fees.

By then it was Friday. Each of them felt surrealistic. Could all of this really be done? Occasionally one of them would ask, "What is the reality?" and get a laugh. But it was no easy concept to grasp. Stephanie called a plane to Teterboro for the Harrisburg contingent which also carried Terry to Ithaca.

On Monday, in a meeting at the Hyatt Regency on 42nd Street, they reviewed the strategic and organizational matters and set themselves to the question of the candidate. There was some wrangling about how to do it.

They went around the table when Tony called for nominations and each put in a name except Terry's candidate was also Denise's. Deliberation began to choose someone who could carry out the strategy if anyone could. Tony got a private dining room at the Cornell Club where they talked until after ten. FIND SVP delivered dossiers of the people they had nominated.

Terry Leelan followed the proceedings carefully and made only limited input. He was already concentrating on how to persuade his candidate to run, knowing he was going to be the inevitable choice.

By Tuesday afternoon they worked their way to where there was only one name left and decided they should still consider others. There was a new round of nominations. Deliberations began again. By midday Thursday it was clear that Terry's first nomination, Adrian Elliot Daggett of Illinois was the overwhelming best choice. Over a period of two weeks they had fashioned a potential campaign that would win the presidency and selected a man to lead it.

JEAN WAS OUT when Tony got home exhausted on Friday evening after a final day of working over details. He treated himself to some good vodka while he wondered if Daggett would accept. The son of a skilled factory worker, Daggett had graduated from the University of Illinois at Champagne-Urbana as an industrial engineer and went to business school on a scholarship at Stanford. He became an expert in finance and then set about learning marketing. He joined a mid-size company in specialty metals as a plant engineer, but he quickly broke out of that to financial planning, to field sales support, and the job of business manager for one of their major lines.

Moving up to the management group, he went back to finance. He built and maintained strong relationships on the manufacturing side and always looked for greater competitiveness and productivity. The company was acquired in a stock transaction in a friendly take over. The President and CEO moved over to the acquirer and eventually became their chief executive officer. Adrian was tapped by the board to step into his seat as CEO, jumping over a dozen senior contestants.

He landed there at age 42 with his agenda prepared. Four years later the profits had doubled and volume was up 60%. New projects were jammed into research and development. The bureaucrat middle managers who had been in the company for years saying "no" to new ideas had relocated. Action and procedures were streamlined.

Then, the Board of a very large company in a related industry beckoned to him to perform what was a rescue. Peeling away layers of management, he took down an entrenched bureaucracy and put the right people in charge of marketing, research and development, manufacturing and finance. He reinvigorated the culture of the company to focus on the customer instead of the process and the technology. He was perceived as a miracle worker.

After seven years, the Illinois Democratic State Committee came to him in need of a miracle in Springfield. They knew of his ability, but they also knew of his brilliant speeches made so by a low-key and very effective charisma. At first he resisted them, but then became attracted by the idea of testing his ability in government and his communicating in a political campaign. His business success had made him many times over a millionaire. He could do what he wanted. So he quit and started to work for virtually nothing. He found it to be much harder, but he also discovered that he was a natural candidate.

During his career, he had learned to speak without many notes. He focused on the audience and used his understanding of state and regional issues and of policies and people. His worldview was that of an enlightened business executive. Financially and socially, he was more conservative than most Democrats. Not born to wealth, he was a Democrat by birth. His family had been on the lower rungs of the social ladder. He was glad he could give his father and mother a prosperous old age. They tended to resist it and kept their home in Ohio. He bought two condominiums at Fort Myers and during the winter they lived in one of them.

He had a number of love affairs, but each time stepped back from marriage. Then, while visiting a laboratory doing tests for one of his major customers he saw an unusually attractive young woman, a Ph.D., working at one of the scanning electron microscopes. She had light, almost blonde hair draped over her shoulders. She appeared feminine and somewhat shy, but when she stood to shake his hand her hazel eyes looked into his and he felt she was peering at the inside of the back of his skull. He asked her for dinner the next weekend and soon found himself deeply in love with a complex and powerful woman. He found she had the same beliefs and gave him a few to consider. They shared golf, tennis, and the classics. Their dates were for concerts, opera, and ballet. He often took her to church. The love became mutual and they became intimate.

She was Pamela Ann Petrusik from Kenosha, Wisconsin. Her father and mother both worked in the auto plant there. She lettered in sports, was always on the honor role, and was a leader. She went to the University of Wisconsin and did her advanced degrees at Northwestern. When they married Pamela was 26 and Adrian 40. Their relationship grew to be one of wholly sharing their lives. She continued her career in physical chemistry. Adrian had just turned 43 when their first child was born. Part of the mystique of his Governorship was his youngish wife and teen and preteen children whom he so obviously loved. Pamela was a warm, cultured, and charming first lady of the state. The other condominium in Fort Myers was for her parents who had urged her and her sister to seek the greatest possible achievements.

While their son and two daughters were born and grew up to school age Pamela stayed home. The Daggett's settled in the Fox River Valley west of Chicago. Pamela found a farm where they could have the horses she had always wanted and built a house. Seemingly going broke on real estate, they also had a small apartment on Lake Shore Drive in Chicago so they could enjoy the culture of that great city.

In politics, Daggett was a great persuader. His natural leadership skills brought him the admiration of people who were genuinely trying to accomplish something for the State of Illinois. It brought him the enmity of those who were trying to preserve their position, or wheel upwards politically. As a public speaker he became terrific. He scoffed at politicians who read their statements on C-Span. He once leveled at a political dinner, "Don't vote for someone who has to read his statement. Vote for the person who wrote it." Awards poured on him from management groups and trade associations. The Chairman of the State Committee told him he could be governor forever. He stayed only two terms.

Mulling it over, Tony thought there was a strong chance Daggett could be persuaded. Ian said that he personally wanted to see whomever they had chosen. Tony agreed, because the full force of Ian's presence would be needed.

When Jean came home, he told her of the decision and she was pleased. "Power is best given to those who don't want it. Daggett never pursued the Presidency when he was urged to. He and Pamela would be ideal."

"Why didn't he accept a run for the Presidency?"

"Because of the issues. He was in favor of National Health Insurance. He was militant about the lawyers, and in favor of a strong American presence in the world, accepting the role of the world's policeman. It didn't play well with the national committee. He was a free trader and a fiscal conservative that was questioned, too."

Then she asked, "What role are you going to play in this?"

"Ian hasn't been real specific about what I will do."

"You need more women on your committee."

"Who do you have in mind? Susan stayed out because she felt she might overwhelm it. You could compromise your position on the state committee."

"What makes you think I will cooperate with you?"

"When you see our positions on the issues, I think you will."

"What's your position on EEOC?"

"We are for it."

"How much? I'll bet it's not a primary issue."

"We haven't gone through all of the issues yet."

"Well, make sure you put that on your list."

"We can't go through the issues in detail until we know who the candidate is. He might not agree with us. We're not going to dictate to him."

"Not a bad idea. I have to draft a statement to use at the labor luncheon tomorrow."

"I was hoping for some hugging time."

"I'll be up soon," she promised, but by the time she came he had fallen asleep.

Four hours later Tony woke up and felt Jean beside him. His mind churned over the bizarre situation. He recognized the syndrome; he was not going back to sleep, and moved toward Jean who responded a little. Sometimes she would roll over and hug him sleepily, and once in a while they would make love in the middle of the night.

This time she didn't move. He rolled out of bed trying not to disturb her and groped his way toward the bathroom. Finding his robe, he slipped it on and headed for the library where there would be books, and a drink if he wanted. He wondered if Ian was awake, too.

ON MONDAY MORNING the company planes gathered the attendees for a meeting at Ian's house so Susan could attend without attracting attention. Jean fixed some poached eggs for breakfast and Tony was eating his bran cereal when she sat down opposite him.

"You really think you can create a candidate in less than two years, and get him elected President?"

"We're going on the advice of Denise and Terry Leelan."

"I don't think it's doable. You want to run somebody to win the Democratic nomination and the general election and he doesn't even know about it yet!" Jean remarked.

"It's the best chance to stop POLACO."

"It's going to cost big, big money. Can you afford it?"

"It's Ian's money."

"But he can't spend all of that legally."

"That's one of our problems. We have to research the campaign finance laws. In the primaries, they're not so restrictive."

"Tony, I don't think you should try to do it."

"Jean, we have to do something."

"Just expose them."

"We can't. We have signed a confidentiality agreement. Besides, who would take any action? Denise says she is not sure anyone would do the story. She questions the believability. Just think now if you didn't know the details and you read about this in a newspaper or saw a *60 Minutes* item on it; would you be motivated to do anything about it?"

"Well you know me, I would."

"Okay, what's your anticipation of what Mr. and Mrs. Middle Class would do?"

"I think they would be concerned."

"But, would they take any action is the real question."

"I see your point. That's what Cowell's banking on."

"One of his basic premises is that the people of the United States don't care enough about these issues to deal with them."

"How are you going to get them to care?"

"Our attack is on the political establishment which doesn't tackle critical issues anyway."

"If Mr. and Mrs. Middle Class don't care about this new special interest enough to try to stop it, why would they care about the tough issues?"

"Are you testing the idea, or are you against it?" he asked.

"I am in favor of stopping them, but I don't think this is the way. Can't you go to a federal prosecutor and get an investigation going? I don't like to see you trying to do the impossible, Tony, you're too bold sometimes."

"I need your help on this."

"I'll help you, Tony, but I think it is going to disrupt our lives."

ON HIS WAY to the MacAulliffe mansion, Tony decided he would have to go over the whole program point by point with Jean to see where her objections were. If he couldn't win her over, their lives, indeed, would be disrupted.

The task group gathered to give their report in the spacious library at the MacAulliffe mansion. From floor to ceiling there were books. The impressive collection begun by Andrew was expanded by Ian, Evelyn, and Susan. Ian's valet, Francisco, had jury-rigged a table civil-service style with Ian's writing desk at the head. A coffee service was on a buffet from which the maid, Lucinda, served them. A fire crackled in a hearth opposite the desk.

Terry reviewed the issues they had discussed. Their main conclusion was the vitality to offer the truth as they best understood it in facts, logic, and background on the tough issues which people would understand because they are interested in their country. He outlined the plan.

At one point Ian observed, "If the consultants and the campaign staffs themselves don't know any more than the sound bites about issues, are we in danger of a politics of crude reasoning? We may stop transcending to the issues themselves which have become so much more complex. It is perilous if we don't use modern communication to address them properly."

Terry Leelan fully understood Ian's nature when he heard this. He knew Ian was more than a good executive, but had not seen his depth. "We're mostly already in the state of 'crude politics,'" he said.

David Gibson knew about Ian's depth, but he felt Ian was set upon a perilous course.

Denise Williams was focused on the goals and the difficulties in reaching them, and on the dangers to the country that Ward Cowell seemed destined to let loose. She wondered if Cowell himself had ever considered them.

Tony had the same thoughts. Was Cowell aware? Was Helene aware? He thought about her and of what might happen to her.

At the end, Ian said, "You have all done an excellent job. There isn't a group in this country that could have done better. You are all at the top of your professions. I agree, Terry, some significant structural reform might be needed. The system frustrates us because it fails to consistently deliver competent candidates for national office."

"I am also impressed," said Susan. "I didn't think it was possible to organize a movement that could act fast enough to preempt POLACO. I see how you've started to engineer it. You are not in any way de-emphasizing the need for grass roots action and state organizations. All of this cannot be done by Madison and Park Avenue. Sorry, Denise."

"Politics is essentially local,'" Denise quoted.

"All right," said Ian. "We have the plan before us but there is a key element to implementing it."

"Yes," said Terry, "the candidate."

Terry described how they arrived at the recommendation of Adrian Daggett. Ian listened carefully forming a picture of Daggett in his mind, "This is a good selection and you used a good process. Is there any problem of health or past scandal that has kept him from seeking high office? Are you sure about him?"

"None that we have seen in the exhaustive information we have received from FIND SVP and other sources," said Tony.

"Then the next question is, how do we persuade this man to give his life for his country. Why hasn't he tried before?"

Denise answered. "Running for President is a huge task, Ian. The process is horrendous and risky. Money is the central problem. What you have to do to get it is a worse problem. The process of selection is totally entrepreneurial. The parties have little input except to provide the format of the competition."

Stephanie asked, "What is it that makes people get into the groups? Pardon me if this is a silly question."

"It's not silly," Terry replied. "Some groups gather around legislative candidates because they feel they are supporting the best person for a particular job, but most seek access. They want to be sure they will be heard. There is little patronage.

"Individuals in the presidential and gubernatorial campaign groups want something for themselves. They have ambitions. The President and the Governors make appointments. There is substantial patronage anywhere. In the big states it is huge and in Washington there are 7000 positions. The big players expect cabinet or sub-cabinet jobs, ambassadorships, White House positions, or jobs as administrators. Supporters in the state organizations will get deputy assistant or deputy administrator posts or appointments to commissions. For patronage you spend time and money for the appointment and for the spoils you get after surviving in the administration if the campaign wins.

"It's money, fame, and power. Power serves big egos. Henry Kissinger, when he was with the White House, said 'power is the ultimate aphrodisiac.' Remember, he was a bachelor for awhile."

"Nixon probably told him he had to marry after he said that," Ian quipped. "At least we relieve the circumstances with regard to money. POLACO does the same."

"In this entrepreneurial system," said Denise, "we don't necessarily get good appointees because the people that help and expect to be rewarded are not necessarily qualified."

"This is the main reason for the frustration of the companies in POLACO. It's the incompetence and distorted values of the people in government, not only politicians, but also the appointees. Hopefully we will bring in people who can come up with solutions to the problems," Ian added.

"No easy task," responded Terry.

"Now," said Ian, "let's turn to the question of how to persuade Adrian Daggett to accept and gather a competent group of men and women who will also change their lives for the same purpose."

"We all think you have to make the presentation to him, Ian. We need to show him what we propose and the extent to which we are willing to help," suggested Tony.

"The funds at the moment are yours," said Terry.

"I agree. He needs to know I will support him with my personal funds. We need to prepare a proposal to him. I also believe that we have to tell him why we are doing this."

"We have already started drafting," said Tony. "Nancy is doing a document which makes the case."

"I look forward to seeing it," said Ian, looking at Nancy.

She smiled at the compliment. "We'll keep it low-keyed, not flashy, but impressive enough to show that we are dead serious. I hope you can help me with this Susan."

"We have complete desktop publishing computers in the village," Susan said.

"Keep us all updated," said Ian. "Let me think about how this is best done, Terry. You will have to be with me."

"How are we going to arrange the meeting?" asked Terry.

"I know him," said Ian, "and he knows me. I'll phone him. Alvin, you've had naught to say."

"Aye," said Alvin, and got a laugh. "There aren't too many security matters except secrecy, Ian. The real time security starts with the announcement of the candidacy."

"God willing, we'll soon be preparing for that."

They talked until lunchtime. Lucinda served a delicious crab soup with a salad. After they broke up, Ian went to the office. At four o'clock Adrian Daggett returned his call and they made an appointment for the following Thursday, enough time Ian thought, for Susan and Nancy.

☆ **Chapter 5** ☆

IAN MADE THE appointment with both Adrian and Pamela Daggett. He wanted them to hear the story from him. He thought about including the immediate Daggett family, but he was concerned the teenage children were too young to keep the secret. He decided to take Terry. Nancy and Denise, bright and powerful women, would relate to Pamela and add their towering expertise in answering questions. David would come since there would be legal questions and Tony would pick up any points which Ian might miss, and he could tell the POLACO story first-hand. Susan was in New Orleans with her daughter, Cindy, trying to work through a drug rehabilitation program for the third time. That lively girl had all the qualities of her mother, but had switched off life's main line to a bad sidetrack. Ian knew it hurt Susan, but he knew she was strong enough to deal with it.

Denise and David met in the Atlantic Aviation lounge at Teterboro Airport two days before the meeting with Adrian Daggett. In thirty minutes they touched down at Harrisburg. Everyone was together in the afternoon to review Nancy and Denise's presentation. Nancy tried out a title, which digested the thinking so far: "New Reality in American Politics." Underneath her title was the Presidential seal. Inside was a spread on each of the policy points with support data in graphic form.

They worked on it as a group to gather everyone's ideas. The following day they reviewed and rehearsed how they would approach Daggett, with continued work on the presentation for Ian's final review. There was back and forth e-mail with Terry Leelan.

On a clear wintry morning, PENMET's Falcon jet swished them to

Ithaca to pick up Terry and then thundered off west to the DuPage County Airport near St. Charles. High above the world they had coffee and talked in temporary isolation. No one used the phones or fax. They all concentrated on the forthcoming meeting.

Two limousines fetched them to the office building downtown where Adrian Daggett oversaw his interests. He did some venture capital investing, very limited consulting, and worked on the information he needed for the boards on which he served. He also prepared his lectures and did his writing. He had a staff director, an administrative assistant, two researchers, and two secretaries. A local CPA firm handled the money.

They were ushered into Daggett's conference room. It had large glass windows, which looked down at the frozen Fox River. It was furnished traditionally and decorated with paintings of Illinois scenes. It seemed to represent a modern man who held traditional values. A tray of coffee, low-fat pastries, and fruit was on a side table.

Pamela and Adrian came in and everyone was introduced. Adrian was over 6-feet tall and was half gray. He had a ruggedly handsome face; Nancy thought she saw a slight paunch. Pamela, not tall for a woman, was blond and stunning. She glowed with exercise and good health.

"Now you have to break the suspense, Ian," said Daggett gesturing to the seats at the table. "Pamela and I are very curious about why you want to see us."

"We haven't been able to speculate," Pamela said smiling.

"I don't think I have to do anything more than reflect on the confused and frustrating state of political affairs in our country," said Ian.

"We talk about the incompetence and misdirection at least three times a day when we hear the news," said Adrian. "We write letters; we get nice responses. They often suggest we should make some additional contributions."

"Several weeks ago," Ian began slowly, "I commissioned a study headed by Tony which included Nancy, Denise, Terry, David, and two others from our company to examine the state of the American polity, to tell me what they thought needed to be done. They have given their report, defining what they considered to be the key issues. It gave substantial substance to the thinking we all have. 'Sound bite' politics has created 'sound bite' thinking by the electorate and has turned off many good people to the political process. Tough issues are almost ignored because most of the politicians in office don't know what to do about them. Or, the concern is that such issues would result in controversy which the political establishment might not know how to manage. The lawyers, health care, overseas involvement, weapons proliferation, the debt, trade issues, employment, are all very complex. Very few politicians are equipped to deal with them and, there are powerful lobbies and advocates with which they have to contend."

"You forgot civil rights, abortion, monetary policy, and the environment," said Daggett with a smile.

"I'm a stingy Scot in giving examples," said Ian smiling back. The group around the table laughed and relaxed a little.

Ian paused and looked Adrian in the eye. "Of the various solutions which were proposed, the paramount one was to seek a Presidential candidate from outside Washington who understood the processes and the problems of getting things done; one who could manage the issues and achieve valid objectives, and at the same time explain to the people, the Congress, and the rest of the government the real meaning of the issues. This would hopefully set a new course for political thinking. Dialog is needed in which the issues are to be constructively defined, as opposed to hammering on each other with the 'Gottcha!' rhetoric the press adores."

"You mean," Daggett grinned, "you really can't tell the people all they need to know in nineteen words?"

"That's what I mean. One of the beliefs that we have put into a tentative manifesto is that the American people are not all stupid and should be treated as if they could understand. The average reading level may be eighth grade, but there are a great many people in the United States who are achievers and who are concerned about the political process and the future of the nation. They recognize they can change the future. Right now we need someone with charisma to run for President who is smart enough to understand the issues, articulate enough to communicate to the people, and has the skills to manage them by delegating tasks and recruiting effective people to carry them out."

"Running the United States is a lot different than running a corporation, Ian," interrupted Daggett. "Democracy lets a flood of opinions and interests loose."

"I am aware of that. Washington, Lincoln, the Roosevelts, and Truman were reasonably successful. We have also been studying the reasons why people don't run for President. Terry can wax eloquent about that. This group of staff and consultants, Adrian, has considered the issue of who the person might be to lead the nation. In intensive consideration they compiled a list and your name is at the head of it. In order to undertake important changes in the political system and in policies, the country needs somebody like you because the people now in Washington obviously can't do it. We think you are the best choice. My purpose in coming here today is to show you the type of support that we are willing to give to you. We want you to make the race. I know what I am asking."

There was a long pause.

"If any other CEO of a Fortune 50 company had come here and said what you just said, I would immediately suspect his motives. You're acting in the national interest?"

"That is correct. 'When good men do nothing...'"

"I understand. You're asking me if I am willing to make the sacrifices necessary. Are you willing to make sacrifices too?"

"Susan and I have talked about it. I'm sorry she couldn't be here. We have a daughter in trouble."

"We're sorry, Ian," Pamela said. "We saw a news clip."

"Susan and I have agreed to use fifty million dollars of our personal funds in this pursuit. We intend that it will all be used legally to begin the campaign. We'll make ourselves fully available to seek other necessary funds. I will come up with whatever support you need so it won't be necessary for you to do more than the normal fundraising. I will personally seek the endorsements you will need. A program is being drawn."

"Ian, I have huge admiration for you and your company, but do you think you can pull this off?"

"If I didn't think there was a strong chance of success, Adrian, you know I wouldn't suggest it."

"You want to start a separate political movement with me at its head, to win the nomination of the Democratic party?" There was another pause, and he continued. "How can we possibly do this in two years? It's just over a year to the New Hampshire primary. There aren't ten people there who know my name. People in Iowa and Indiana might know who I am along with the Illinois immigrants in the retirement states. I have never held national office."

"You were one hell of a governor of Illinois, Adrian. You could have been governor of Illinois forever."

"I know and I got tired of the political bickering, constant nights out, constant travel, and the petty attacks by opponents and the media. We wanted our private lives back. There are the children to think about. It's not easy to be the son or the daughter of the governor. They are all still in school. Donald is at Yale, Linda is at Columbia, and Dianne is at Blair Academy. We sent them all out of the state for a reason."

"Professor Leelan, does this make sense?" Pamela asked.

"I can tell you, Mrs. Daggett, in my experience, there isn't any substitute in this country for a warm-hearted, good person in the White House who is competent to lead. This is a very serious issue to me. The process of election, however, is something that is unattractive. We will take away some of the unattractive features of the election process that chase warm-hearted, good people away."

Ian wondered if that was quite the right way to put that point. There was another pause.

"I have no illusions about what you are asking me to do. I have thought about it and I believe I can do the job, I just don't know whether I want it. I know enough about economics and foreign affairs and the legalities of Washington processes, but I have always shrunk from it. I don't even have an organization in Illinois. The Democrats pleaded with me to run and saw that I got elected. They were the organization. A good one."

"You made some very good speeches," said Leelan. "I have quoted them in some writing and in classes. In fact I have differentiated you from certain other governors. In this group of people who were mulling over this issue it was I who put forward your name."

Daggett responded, smiling, "I appreciate your compliment, Terry. Denise, I've met you a couple of times. What are we getting into? Is it possible?"

"Everything is possible if there is a plan and a strategy. And, we have taken the liberty of developing something to show you. Nancy has that."

Adrian turned to Nancy. She handed bound copies of the presentation to everyone and began the explanation. "We've put together the essence of a primary campaign for your approval, which would extend into the general election with some modifications. We have recommendations for you on how we would present you."

Nancy gave her presentation in 10 minutes. Ian watched Adrian and Pamela, and saw they were taking it all in with interest. When Nancy finished, she said, "These are principles, Governor Daggett, which we think are key to success in the present political structure. We're anticipating you from the things that you have said in the past."

"This is an excellent presentation; what I would expect from PEN-MET. You put a lot into it. Ian, I still don't see the reason. Why are you doing this? Fifty million of your own money!"

"I've given you the apparent reason and I suppose I have to give you another reason."

"Another reason?"

"I am sure you will keep this confidential as it must be. In telling you, I am violating an agreement, which I have signed. Being present here, Tony is an accessory before the fact because he has also signed the agreement and he has also given his personal word that he would not divulge the existence of another movement. I have to tell you, Adrian, that we are not the first. There is another movement."

A serious look came over Adrian Daggett's face as though he were anticipating what Ian was about to tell him. Pamela looked intensely at him.

"There is a group of corporations, which put in $1/10$th of 1% of their annual revenue as a deposit and then pledged $1/20$th of 1% of their operating profit as their annual fee. The apparent leader is Ward Cowell and Alex Peterson is much involved."

"Cowell? Peterson? What are they up to?" asked Daggett with a tinge of anxiety.

Ian gestured to Tony. "Tony has been there to see them. That is how we have learned of this."

Tony said, "They're on Harbour Island in the Bahamas, based in a large office complex, all built underground. It's called the Political Action Coalition, or 'POLACO.' Warren Hatch is the chief professional."

"Hatch?" exclaimed Daggett. "Him?"

"Yes."

"He has no scruples, no morals."

"I think you know him better than we do," said Ian.

"How are they funded?"

"$1/10$th of 1% as a deposit."

"For us it would be $45 million."

"That means a huge amount of money has been gathered, if they have 20 companies like you. And, what is their self-proclaimed mandate?"

"They say," said Tony, "their purpose is to provide a continued beneficial environment for multinational corporate operations and development. Their goal is to assume greater control of national events. They intend to do that by centralizing lobbying; by developing a centralized doctrinal and intelligence group; by providing expert communication services; and by establishing a program of recruiting candidates, training them, and establishing fundraising to get them elected."

"Ward Cowell, Alex Peterson, Warren Hatch. Who else?"

"There were representatives there from Nordstall and Shinwa Meiwa apparently to hear the pitch that Ward made to me. We think that there may be a deal that if PENMET joins, these other two companies will also join." Tony then summarized a description of the underground offices and the staff.

"So they've already organized. Are they going to start with Congress or are they going to attack state legislatures?" Daggett asked.

"Both. Part of the candidate development program is to take people out of the state houses and move them to Washington."

"So they're out there in the Bahamas with a highly integrated, capable political staff with the most modern equipment, an intelligence capability that is probably better than the CIA's all aimed at intervening in American government."

"That seems to be the case, sir," said Tony.

"And you, Ian MacAulliffe, have found out about it and are single handedly organizing the counter force. And you want me to be the candidate of the counter force to make the tumultuous changes in government that must be done to preempt them?"

"To take away their reason to exist and to blunt the well-crafted appeals they will make," said Ian.

"This is full of risks, Ian," Adrian said.

"Aye. Susan and I have talked about them. Terry can tell you the analysis we have come to, which is the reason we are here."

"Focusing power in too few hands, Terry?" asked Adrian.

"Yes, sir, that is the essential question. We couldn't see in this case, except for a miracle, that this would not be a threat to the Constitution."

"Anything like this that is even half-way subversive is in fact subversive. I imagine they say they will stay legal."

"That's what they tell us."

"I don't think for long," said Daggett. "A scheme like that doesn't stay legal. And, God knows who else is involved."

"Essentially they are frustrated with the democratic processes," said Terry. "They are trying to make what they consider reasonable changes, which on the face of it, may even be reasonable, but which will not stay that way."

"Why not disclose what you know and call for an investigation?"

"They have all kinds of excuses and ploys already packaged. They are a study group; they are a think tank; they are trying to make good changes," said Denise. "They could appeal to the need for change and that they are trying to offer alternatives. Disclosure could be an opening for them to criticize. It's a good chance that they would just continue. The perception of good intentions could be created."

"The other question," added David, "is who would investigate them. They could befuddle the bureaucrats. They are offshore. It's likely they would control whatever the Bahamian Government would say or do."

"Keep in mind," Nancy interjected, "that these companies are also big advertisers, particularly in the national media, and in some cases may even own or control newspaper chains, television, and radio stations."

You're right," said Daggett. "Once that much money and effort is in motion, it's hard to stop."

Ian was pleased at how Adrian was responding, and how informed and smart he was. His group indeed did come up with the right candidate.

"You'll have to give us some time," said Daggett. "Pamela and I have to talk about this."

"I quite understand. But, you recognize there is some urgency to put the machinery in motion."

"I'm going to have this reviewed by my own legal group, but I will confine that to one attorney, the name partner in the Chicago firm. That will be covered by attorney-client privilege. Who should he talk with?"

"David knows all of the details. Pamela, are there any questions that we should answer for you?"

"Probably two dozen," said Pamela. "Let me have some time with this. I might like to come and talk with Susan."

"Susan will be back as soon as she can. I can ask her to fly directly up here."

"That would be nice, Ian. She can call me. I would like to see her."

After the amenities they left. They didn't talk about it until they got to the plane. Seated around the table in the lounge Ian said, "That was a good job. I think you've sold him. When he saw Nancy's work he knew how serious we are."

"I think you sold him," said Nancy.

"No. You all did a good job and I am grateful for it. We'll see what happens."

ON SATURDAY MORNING Pamela met Susan in a small conference room at the United Airlines Red Carpet Club at O'Hare. From
the windows they could see planes taxi by and baggage and service
carts scurry around them.

Pamela knew what Adrian was getting her into. She visualized a
gubernatorial campaign 30 times over. Adrian had determined with
her that they would not seek the highest office. She expected they
would retire early with partial activity, and enjoy their family, each
other, and as much travel as they wanted.

Halfway through the second term as governor, Adrian wanted to
get back to private life. She didn't mind the public eye as much as he
did, but then he was the focus. She sensed now that he was restless.
A sincere, truly competent man, who had been in leadership roles so
much, he was too young to step entirely down. The writing absorbed
him, but was not fully satisfying. Now, the ultimate challenge was
laid before him. She knew after the PENMET delegation left that his
mind was made up except for her, the children, and due diligence.

The first part of her conversation with Susan was due diligence.
Was Susan as committed to the race as Ian was? Was there any hid-
den agenda? Would Ian really spend $50 million to start a movement
to correct problems with which the great democracy was now beset?
Any wavering on Susan's part would be a signal to warn off Adrian.
There was no such sign; there was every assurance.

The next subjects were family, security, and the risk. She and Adrian
had not yet completed raising their children. How would they be protected? What thoughts did Susan have about how to involve them?
What did Susan think of the natural danger to a candidate from
kooks or crazies? Susan suggested that the children should be brought
to a family meeting, and offered to have PENMET planes pick up the
three and fly them to St. Charles. She did not think they should be
told about POLACO. Susan told Pamela about Alvin Carter, and
assured that there would be no skimping on expenses that would
insure everyone's safety.

Pamela's final concern was rating the chance of success. She wanted to know what Susan really thought. She was not going to disrupt
the lives of three children and agree to all the other risks on a ten to
one betting line. Susan's response was that if they did it right, Adrian
would win the nomination. Her reasoning was that the others were

not ready to compete at the level the new campaign and Adrian would set. The essential strategy was to raise the level of competition.

The Daggett's regular travel agent arranged for the immediate family to gather at a conference room at the Continental Airlines' Presidents Club at Newark Airport the next day, and for a private dinner at the Airport Marriott. She and Adrian would take an early Continental flight while limousines brought the children. She could imagine her tall, beautiful Dianne getting into the limo at Blair. She would dig it. Linda would think it pretentious and might take the subway PATH to Penn Station in Newark and a cab to the airport.

There was growing suspense at the Club as four of them gathered around the table drinking coffee and waiting for Dianne. When she swung into the room with her long gait, shoulder bag swinging, she reached for her father to hug him and asked, "What's the big deal, Dad? Someone ask you to run for President?"

He kissed her cheek. "I guess you could say that's what this is about."

AT 10 A.M. the following Tuesday, Ian placed a conference call to Denise Williams, Dave Gibson, and Terry Leelan. He invited the others to come into his office, then announced that Daggett had accepted, subject to a review of the details of the plan. Within an hour, Terry Leelan requested a leave-of-absence from the university. Denise Williams organized meetings with Evans & Copeland concerning their public affairs and with Jeremy Reubin & Associates concerning campaign consulting. The following morning Tony and Nancy were in a Learjet back to St. Charles.

Adrian and Pamela Daggett wanted to be absolutely sure they understood the parameters of Ian MacAulliffe's backing. There was to be as much "soft money" as David Gibson would allow to be invested in the campaign support organization. Ian would pay for his own consultants who would work with the campaign planners and otherwise participate with Gibson's limitations. Loans would be made to the campaign, and guaranteed by Ian. There were to be no strings of any kind attached anywhere. Daggett would not run unless he was his own man, and Ian would have it no other way.

Nancy and Tony went through all of the arrangements with Daggett and his staff and noted down all of their questions. They left to accumulate the answers.

In New York, David Gibson researched what agreements could be made, and was in touch with Daggett's attorneys who were embarked on a parallel task. It was more Adrian Daggett wanting to be certain of the legality of everything, rather than in anyway mistrusting Ian's word. The laws were so complex that a technical violation could be made without anyone's knowing about it and later could become a campaign issue.

"We can't start a multi-million dollar campaign and lose it because our attorneys had overlooked something," Daggett philosophized.

In their suites at the Pheasant Run Resort, Tony and Nancy worked to put the deal together. Tony talked for an hour with one of Gibson's top people. They thought there should be a general agreement between Ian and Daggett, but then realized that this was difficult.

Denise Williams scrambled with David Gibson between the new Pennsylvania Liberty Foundation, Evans & Copeland, and Jeremy Reubin & Associates working out retainer agreements. The lawyers raised all kinds of questions. Large amounts of money would flow from a very wealthy man and his wife into political action and there were rigorous constraints.

Coopers & Lybrand, long the established accounting firm of PEN-MET, also served Ian's other interests. They suggested retaining a second firm to avoid any possible conflict-of-interest. They settled on a local Harrisburg firm Jean Destito suggested, which had campaign experience and whose character was unquestioned. The partners were flattered by a retainer from the MacAulliffes and terrorized by the thought of being found to be responsible for information getting loose.

By 8:30 p.m. Tony and Nancy had everything on their computers ready to printout. Nancy had crafted a time-flow chart, and brought it to him. Tony asked, "Some dinner?"

"Is there still time for a swim?"

A few minutes later they were doing laps in a heated indoor-outdoor pool. Tony jumped out in the freezing cold, did a passable jackknife and dared Nancy, who couldn't refuse. She pushed up out of the water to the board and paused to make her jackknife perfect. Tony saw her sturdy, full-bosomed figure.

The weekday evening had thinned out the dark oak-paneled Baker's Wife dining room. Under lithographs of 18th Century country scenes they ordered vodka and tonic and clinked glasses. Nancy toasted, "To adventure," with a smile into Tony's eyes.

"Did you ever think you would be doing something like this?"

Tony asked.

"I fantasized it. Entrepreneuring a business and running for public office are the two greatest challenges. I've always thought I might be involved in one or maybe both as 'the PR Lady.'"

"How would you feel about working full time on the campaign?"

"I'd like to, but I am not sure how we would arrange that."

"How do you think it would affect your career?"

"I hadn't considered it. Are you concerned?"

"There are so many ways this thing could bomb. I would be considered responsible for it."

"So it bombs. It is Ian's responsibility if you want to play that game. Isn't that the way everything is supposed to be at PENMET anyway? We all agree, we all take the risk?"

"Nancy, you, Ian, Stephie, Alvin, and I are the only people in the company that even know about this."

"So far."

"It isn't the track that I thought I would be taking."

"You asked me about my career. Well, if this is successful and I am part of the public relations operation I would expect to be at least White House press secretary. If not, I want to be an assistant secretary of something."

"Why not secretary?"

"I'm sure I can do some of the cabinet jobs down there. But, if it were to really happen, I'd want to be close in."

"Being deputy Secretary of State these days means you are out of the loop."

"It seems that way. What job would you want?"

"I'd like to stay at PENMET."

"Come on, Tony."

"Okay, I would like to be under secretary of defense for advanced development."

"You're selling yourself short. You are much better than most of the people down there. I have been around them enough and so have you."

"I'm not sure how good I really am in a public forum."

"You'll do fine, I'll coach you."

"We're both talking fantasies?"

"I don't think so, Tony. We have put together a plan that can elect Adrian Daggett President of the United States. I doubt very much that anybody else in the race so far has as good a plan or the caliber of people we have to carry it out."

"Nor the money."

"By all means, but I've known campaigns that have had oodles of money, poor management, and incompetent people and they have all failed. I can also cite a bunch of poor candidates who got elected because they were well managed. Anyway, it is fun in a sense. I know it is going to be very hard. This is the first of our late nights."

"You're looking at the challenge, and the opportunity."

"That's right, Tony, maybe I am. Where do I have to go at PEN-MET? I love the company. I love talking about it. I love writing about it. Ian is fantastic. The executive staff is probably the best in the country if not in the world. Ian's senior division people are all good, not a phony among them. But I don't aspire to be president and CEO of PENMET or even a division CEO."

"Learn enough about finance and engineering and you could do it, Nancy."

"Tony, I am a PR person, so maybe being White House press secretary is what I have to aspire to. After that, I could open my own firm and make oodles and oodles of money. When you become CEO, I will charge you what I am worth."

"You better not bank on that."

"You are the short betting line, Tony. Ian was 35 or 36 when he took effective control. You are the youngest and most capable of the corporate VPs. You have the leadership skills and you could write technical manuals for all our divisions. You know the plants, the products, and the markets. I was waiting for Ian to come in and tell me to prepare the releases. He can't, now. He has to stay in control. If Ward Cowell gets wind of what we are doing, he will attack us in many ways."

Tony was surprised, "You've been thinking about that?"

"Denise and I have had a session on it."

"Our company absorbs us."

"What else does a single girl over 40 have to do?" Nancy said.

"You don't look it."

"Nice of you to say that, Tony. I would like to be press secretary while I still look good."

"If you become the most glamorous press secretary ever, you could surely write a very good book. It would be a best seller."

"What do you think is the most important thing to accomplish to put Daggett across in the primaries?" asked Nancy.

"I think it is to differentiate his using reality. If Adrian Daggett can put across reality and the complexities and show his personality and innate capability, that will define his campaign and everyone else's. We can make them play our game. We can also differentiate his philosophy because he has one. Not many candidates do."

"Bring that up tomorrow," Tony suggested.

THE NEXT MORNING they went over all of the structural issues. Nancy went over Daggett's speaking engagements. It was in her mind to fire the first shots at major speaking engagements to draw the press in. It was necessary to build up some anticipation and press background. Something else was germinating in Nancy's brain related to her belief that there was no longer sufficient debate of national issues. She wondered why television didn't present good debate. And then, there was Tony: interesting to work with, attractive, a warm guy, very competent, and very married. She had fantasized about him before. Maybe in the course of the campaign she might meet someone old enough and mature enough to take her on. She was daydreaming when Daggett interrupted saying they could spend some time on issue positions.

For the next few hours, Daggett reviewed his positions on foreign policy. Concerned, knowledgeable, articulate, Adrian Daggett grew into a giant in her eyes, and the Daggett for President campaign began in earnest.

SUSAN MACAULLIFFE CAME to New York with Nancy to join Denise in a meeting with Evans & Copeland concerning their retainer agreement. After it was initialed, Anne Russell, Senior Vice President, who would be in charge of the campaign account for the agency, spoke of an initial strategy which paralleled Nancy's thinking. Tall, blonde, and glamorous, Anne was the best account person the agency had. Some thought she was the best in the country.

"After seeing the positions Adrian Daggett wants to take," Anne said, "he should appear before trade groups interested in his issues where we can invite the media to experience him. We need to form an issues staff of experts. We need to be better at the issues than any campaign has ever been. There should be groups who consider only a few; maybe only one. My thought is that the foundation can retain them."

"It's rare that anyone of Adrian's stature talks about transportation," she continued, "it is, however, a critical issue which concerns many people. Politicians don't deal with it on a national scale because they get hit by 'anti advocates' and transportation is expensive. I think the American Road and Transportation Builders would be delighted to have him. Their convention is in February. We'll check other major events for open dates. The question is, how fast we can get the papers prepared and some damn good speeches written for whom I gather is a very good speaker?"

"You'll like the way he uses your materials, Anne, but make no mistake, he'll want complete control over the content," said Denise.

"When it's the right time," Anne continued, "after we have some attention, we'll rumor a possible run with probes into New Hampshire and Iowa. If you're not a Presidential candidate in those states there isn't a lot of interest. We'll need endorsements from the key primary states and some big-time Democrats. There should be a group that asks him to run."

"So now that we've appointed our public relations operatives and our political consultants, and we have FIND on board, we need an issues staff," Nancy said.

"It's an important step," said Anne. "It's a step that a lot of candidates don't take. It's expensive, but we have to come up with fresh ideas and lots of detail if we are going to tackle the tough issues and deal in reality which is complex."

"Your idea to have panels on different issues is important," said Susan. "Much more intense than the typical issues advisors."

"Issue people usually find out what people want to hear and tell the candidate and the speech writers," Anne said. "One of the points of your plan is to present these issues properly and fully regardless of what the people want to hear and to force your opponents to play at a higher level of campaigning. For that we need a new model issues staff. We have to have good people, properly focused. We have to analyze the other candidates' positions," Anne said.

"FIND SVP is working on the history of all of them – on all of the issues. It's becoming a complex matrix which demonstrates frequent changes of view," Nancy told her.

"Amazing," said Anne.

WARD COWELL'S PHONE rang. It was Helene. "Tony Destito just phoned. They're coming in."

"No bargaining?"

"Not a sign of it."

"No questions?"

"None."

Ward paused. That wasn't quite right. Maybe they would bargain and question on the way to the closing. "Okay, make up the prospectus and get it to them. Did he say when?"

"They have a board meeting in six weeks. He said they could do it if we got the documents ready, otherwise he would poll the board."

"I'd like to have it done at the meeting. Can you do it?"

"It's already underway. Aren't you pleased?" She was, for reasons of her own. She would see Tony again. She wanted to see him.

"Of course, I'm pleased," he tried to say convincingly.

"You don't sound pleased."

He didn't know whether he was or wasn't. The more he thought about Tony Destito and Ian MacAulliffe, the more he wondered if it was a mistake to invite them in. He thought a little more, and then dialed Edgar Slaughter and invited him to a private lunch.

Slaughter came in carrying his signature black leather portfolio.

Ward motioned him to the table that had been rolled in.

"Are things coming together, Edgar?"

"I think so, sir. The clearance procedures and assets are in place. I have the best investigators ready and the best cooperation I can get from the FBI and credit agencies. I've started enlarging the security force."

"You're sure that the people you are cooperating with are trustworthy?"

"They don't know POLACO exists. It all looks like a secret business project; not uncommon these days."

"This secret mustn't leak, Edgar. Particularly before we accomplish something."

"Understood, sir."

"What guarantees can you give?"

"It depends on how we enforce the security and how we operate."

"Tell me what we need to do that we're not doing."

"Leaks occur when someone intentionally lets out information. We can mitigate that by our recruiting practices with thorough checks and detailed files. The other means is to monitor all conversations and activities so that we find out if someone is planning to spill us."

"You mean listen in on all the calls and bug every room?"

"Correct. Without doing that, I cannot give you a guarantee that everything is being done to stop a leak."

"That is invasion of privacy."

"Yes, sir. You do it now to your guests; why not employees?"

Ward winced. He had been persuaded to bug the guestrooms to make sure whom he was dealing with, and for an early indication of their reaction to the initial briefing.

"How important is it?"

"You want the maximum security."

"You want to bug people like Helene, Erla, and Warren?"

"For maximum security we should."

"They're not going to talk!"

"Are you sure?"

"Of course, I'm sure! I recruited them." What was this man thinking?

"Part of security is monitoring changes in people who have access to sensitive information. Here, everyone knows the existence of the underground offices. From there, ascending with responsibility, people have access to more and more sensitive information. This is like a weapons project where all personnel know something is happening, but a lesser number know the details. It's unlike a weapons project in that it is more sensitive to breaches and almost everyone can breach because they know enough to cause us harm."

"You're scaring me."

"The Manhattan project was a great security success. A large number of people were involved and there were no leaks."

"There was a leak, to the Russians!"

"That could have been prevented by what I propose."

"You want to record what goes on in Helene Courtney's apartment, and in Erla Younge's, and in Warren Hatch's?"

"It is necessary for maximum security, sir."

"What if they're making love or having intimate moments?"

"We'll know who it's with."

"Let me think about it. Is there anything else?"

"Yes. The most likely low-level leak will be the local employees from Dunmore, Spanish Wells, or Eleuthera. The most likely intentional leak will be from middle-level employees who will steal documents or take photos. That is usually related to personal feelings, but sometimes can be doctrinally influenced. Senior employees are usually emotionally mature and don't get upset. A conflict of doctrines can cause them to take action. That was the case in Manhattan."

"Your clearances and good recruiting are supposed to take care of that."

"As I said, people change. You have to recognize, sir, that you're engaged in politically sensitive activity that is subject to misunderstanding. Some people will come to believe you are threatening the Constitution."

"We're trying to preserve it," he positioned.

"I'm only describing the risk, sir. There is a concern with the locals. We have to know if someone is talking outside the compound. Say they get drunk at a bar or at a party."

"How are you going to find out about that?"

"The same way police do. By informants that are paid to listen."

"Can we do that?"

"We can."

"What difference does it make? Everyone in the town knows that something is going on here. The Spanish Wells people know."

"Our rules strictly forbid talking about the operation to anyone. We have to enforce the rules if you want them to be respected. Once a breach is allowed, further breaches occur cumulatively. A little information here and there and an investigative reporter comes to town."

"Okay, we have to know if someone is talking. I agree, any leak is a leak. Can you do this with your budget?"

"Yes."

"Then get it started. We'll have more and more locals coming in. Our mainland employees will also be coming in."

"We'll pick up anything on them in the upscale places. We'll cover them."

Ward didn't want to know any more details. He found himself involved in decisions that he hadn't anticipated. But, there had to be security.

"Then, sir, there is a question of punishment."

"How do you mean?"

"What we do to people who violate the rules."

"We fire them."

"That may just make the matter worse. Then they will really start talking."

"We'll have agreements with them. We'll sue them and harass them. Everything has to be legal, Edgar. Also, it has to be explainable to the public."

"We must have other means to keep the secrets. If a person breaks the rules they have to be reprimanded or punished. If we are limited to reprimand we take a risk of exposure. We need a means of punishment, sir."

"How?"

"It would have to be incarceration or corporal. Corporal is better because it carries with it the threat of being repeated even after discharge."

"What do you mean by that? "Ward felt himself being swept into something he didn't like.

"We ask the police to pick someone up and bring them to us. Or, we get them."

"You want to be the justice? It sounds awful!"

"You have to have security. To have security we have to be able to punish breaches."

"What do you propose?" Ward began to sweat.

"Corporal except that we use electric probes instead of bamboo or leather straps. The probes don't leave marks. The man or woman found guilty by administrative procedure is taken to a room where they strip and the pain is inflicted."

"We can't do anything like that. If that leaked we'd be dead!"

"It can be done so that nothing is provable. We can deny everything. Remember, the only recourse anyone has is to a friendly government."

Ward, at one time had thought about this. He planned to shift Edgar's reporting line to Helene to let her handle the problem. She would do better than he would. And, there had been events in the early days of the founding of POLACO which he would like to forget. "Let's get to that another time. Take no action at the moment."

They concentrated on their food. Ward sat back from the table. "When I first spoke with you, I asked about industrial intelligence and how much it would cost to put a mole in a corporation. What did you tell me?"

"It depends on what you want to find out."

"I want to know if anything is going on that we should know about."

"If it's that generalized, we could try bugging. That's detectable to anyone with the right equipment, but it usually yields something beforehand. I would put someone on the job and take the usual steps: gathering the executive garbage, getting profiles on the players to see who might be bent, hanging out where the office people hang out, listening and asking questions at unguarded moments."

"What does that cost?"

"For a good and safe job, 15 to 20 thousand dollars a month without a mole. With a mole another 10 to 15. It's not sensible to rely on a mole alone. The other work can bring out corroborating or conflicting evidence."

"This has to be very confidential between us. No one else will know except who I may tell. I want your plan to crack the PENMET headquarters in Harrisburg. Can you do that?"

"PENMET? Aren't they members?"

"Didn't you recommend that we bug our own employees?"

"You think they're a mole?"

"Never mind what I think. Let me have your plan. Contact no one. We won't ask for quotes. Tell me who you consider to be the best and we'll worry about the cost later."

"Can you give me two or three weeks?"

"Yes."

Ward knew he was starting something on a hunch, but his hunches had almost always paid off. He came to the decision to watch PENMET because he could see little risk in it. Perhaps the information would quell his anxiety about them. Or, if it didn't, then he would be sure. There was a benefit in both results.

☆ **Chapter 6** ☆

WITH HER PROFESSIONAL smile, the Continental flight attendant handed Tony his first-class lunch on his way to Miami and
Harbour Island for the closing of the PENMET "investment" in
POLACO. In his briefcase were the warrants and representations,
and the authorization procedures by which he would transfer $45
million to the designated investment company on receiving the signed
note. Ian had slipped the investment past the PENMET Board.
Helene had arranged the POLACO side. It had taken weeks for them
to assemble the papers.

All that had happened since they first traveled to Harbour Island
seemed unreal. At Ian's direction, he was now engaged in a major
political effort to elect a President of the United States to thwart
POLACO.

Anne Russell's people were in contact with major trade and industry groups where Daggett would give benchmark speeches. Alan
Jacobs, the account leader at Jeremy Reubin & Associates, the campaign consultants, was making contacts and starting organizations in
Iowa, New Hampshire, and the other primary states. Panels of
experts on the critical issues were formed into an unprecedented
issues staff to upgrade the campaign's thinking and its presentation
ability. Ian's $50 million commitment looked smaller as the tasks
grew. Anne Russell had, however, pressed for the issues work. She
was focused on raising the level of competition as the means to win.
Tony knew that in most competition this worked. Whether it would
work in this political race remained to be seen.

Daggett and his group melded smoothly to the operation. Daggett was in charge, and Terry, on a leave of absence from Cornell, was the campaign director. Tony and Nancy had continued to accomplish substantial work on the campaign with Susan MacAulliffe, but for the most part it looked like the two vice presidents were doing their jobs as usual. Pains were taken so there would be no clues of the involvement of Ian or PENMET.

The charter operator's limousine picked Tony up at the baggage claim and took him to the general aviation depot on the Miami Springs side of the airport. The plane was a Beach turbo prop. When they were off the ground, he used his cellular to call Helene to give her the ETA. It was a bright clear day as they passed over the Gulf Stream. He could see Bimini on the right and the Berry Islands ahead. New Providence and Nassau were just visible to the south and soon the long sweeping shape of the Eleuthera loomed on the horizon.

Helene was beside the Mercedes on the tarmac. She wore a causal dress that looked like it had been designed to show off her figure. As the left engine prop stopped rotating and the door opened she came toward him smiling. She kissed his cheek and grabbed his computer while he took his briefcase and tennis bag. The co-pilot struggled out of his seat and came down the steps to open the luggage compartment and carry over his garment bag.

They chatted as she drove to the ferry dock where he saw she had brought the fast cruiser. Soon she was in the stern close to him while they pounded across the bay. She told him that more people had been hired for the 12-weeks-on, one-week-off routine. The intelligence center was now partially operating and Erwin had started the lobbying function.

"I'm glad you came back," she said.

In an office in the conference center, they spread the files of papers for the closing. Tony had to do PENMET's part himself. Because of the confidentiality, no lawyers were allowed.

The transaction was between PENMET and a Bahamian Investment Company issuing bonds for development in the Bahamas, the Caribbean, and Central America. He and Helene went through the agenda item by item with various certificates, warrants and representations, exclusions, the loan contract, and the note. As the final step, she gave him the signed original note and he telephoned the main PENMET bank where someone was waiting to wire transfer the funds. A few minutes later, Ward's secretary brought in a confirming fax that the funds had arrived.

"An old-fashioned closing," he said, referring to the modern style on the telephone after Federal Express or UPS had delivered the documents. Helene handed him a list of the POLACO members. He looked it over and smiled.

"No objections," he said.

A celebration dinner followed at Valentine's restaurant in Dunmore. Helene drove him up in one of the electric carts. It was a cool evening and small fireplaces were glowing throughout the restaurant. In a room of cream colored wallpaper hung with watercolors of London in matching frames, they joined Ward, Madeline, Erla Younge, and Warren Hatch.

They sat down on light blue stuffed chairs to a dinner that befitted the closing of a $45 million transaction. The hors d' oeuvres were caviar on toast points with Russian Vodka, an admirable combination. Champagne followed and then smoked salmon and Brie on home-baked crackers.

The conversation was light when Madeline whispered to Ward that he should invite some toasts. Ward eyed Tony before he raised his glass. He was pleased that the recruitment of PENMET had finally been accomplished. This would end the risk of soliciting members with the two which agreed to follow PENMET. But now that he had seen Tony again, his suspicions were aroused once more. He guessed Helene's apparent interest in Tony, and it made him more defensive.

"To our newest member, the distinguished Pennsylvania Metals & Materials Industries, the most profitable of the Dow Jones Average and of the Fortune 50," he said. "Welcome Tony. We anticipate your contributions both financially and intellectually."

"Hear-hears" rang out from around the table.

"To Ward Cowell and those others who started this enterprise," Tony responded. "To the human intellectual resources you have gathered. May this all bring forward the reforms we seek in a manner which will revitalize American democracy."

There were more "hear-hears."

Tony immediately regretted what he said, however. He was too honest to be a spy.

"Now that we set the character of this occasion," Ward said wryly, "I want you to hear about the progress we have made. Helene has done an extraordinary job bringing people in and getting things organized. Warren has the intellectual directions increasingly charted. Erla, who has the critical task of coming up with the defining elements of this enterprise, has her group more and more focused. Helene tells me that Erwin is finally getting his atrium organized. I can see how much that is going to contribute. Rollin would be with us tonight, but he is off testing the concepts of his group in Michigan."

Tony wondered if POLACO was also focusing on the mid-western states. Were things happening faster than they were scheduled?

"But let's hear from the other members of our party, and then you can tell what you think," Ward said. "Helene, Would you give further overview?"

Helene batted her eyes.

"When you were here before, Tony, we had about 30 people on the payroll," she said. "We're now up to 72. We'll look at Louis' intelligence center tomorrow. You'll be able to see where he is getting us with his computer systems. Tomorrow afternoon we'll join a meeting of the doctrine development group. That staff is about half complete.

"The medical department is set up. People here require health care. This is on the south edge of Dunmore in one of our buildings. It'll be available for anyone on the island at a very low cost as one of our contributions to the community.

"Our security department has expanded. We are, as you know, focused on maintaining secrecy. Tomorrow, Edgar Slaughter, whom you've met, will show you the measures we are taking. Oh, and the gymnasium is almost ready. Now, if it rains we can play volleyball."

"We're going to name it after Helene," Ward interjected.

"This is going to be a comprehensive facility," Helene said, smiling. "We are going to get a masseur for Madeline who hurt her back water skiing last week."

"That scared the hell out of me, Tony," Ward said. "We were towing double behind the cruiser. She went off to the right and hit what looked like a shark in the water. We were out too far. She laid perfectly still, floating, until we spun back to her. Warren was playing captain and he guessed what it was."

"It was probably just a Hammer Head," said Hatch. "He was more scared than any of us."

"Sorry to hear you were hurt, Madeline," Tony said, "but I'm glad you all get to play while you're down here."

"We sure do," said Erla.

"Keeps everybody sharp," said Ward.

"And," Helene said with an exaggerated scowl, "if you interrupt me one more time..."

The group muttered to silence.

"We're trying to develop a culture in the organization," Helene continued. "We are on an important mission. Security is necessary so we can work without interference. We work hard and we play hard. We're serious and are loyal to the organization and the mission. We have the best possible team with the very best equipment. And, there is much more to do."

She stopped and smiled at Ward.

"We still argue about the scenes that appear on the atrium screens," she added. "I think they cost a lot of money. Some senior guy was persuaded to try them by a very good salesman."

Tony saw she could joke with Ward and visualized an informal culture despite the controlling structure. She could direct any of the operating groups. Very important if there were any sudden changes of heart by key people. Recruiting senior people would be more than difficult because of the location. That was why Ward was using Farthergill & Slawson and Marsha Fox. They were professionals doing a job for a fee. Helene was his person whom he knew and trusted.

"Erla, you have to speak next before Warren or he'll cover everything you want to cover," Ward said.

Erla smiled with a hint of introverted embarrassment.

"I view our activity as the key new concept at POLACO," she said. "There are a lot of new concepts, but it is the idea of a doctrine that gives us the greatest chance for success. Political concepts and ideas need to be defined and related to a doctrine. This has to be much more than 'we have to get government off the backs of the people,' or 'government is the problem,' or even 'that government that is best which governs least.'

"The American middle class is fully aware that the world is more complicated than it once was, but we are denying complexity in American political life. Newt Gingrich and his 'revolution' was too simple. We're providing a philosophy which has to offer solutions to the basic questions before Americans. This will bring about the renewing of American democracy that Warren always talks about. Obviously, we have interests, but they are not unlike the interests we lobby on Capitol Hill, at the White House or at the agencies now. I hope I didn't take up anything that Warren wanted to say."

There was laughter.

"Now you can talk, Warren," said Ward.

"What more is there to say?" quipped Hatch to more laughter. "You've heard Helene's overall view of our progress and Erla's further definition in what we are attempting in her group. This new force of American politics will come about only in a long-term perspective. Recruiting and training men and women running for office is not the only training we have to do. We have to recruit and train people to operate POLACO. We are an instrument of that new age. We come from the groups in the society that have the resources and know-how to bring the polity into that new age. We're going to do it in the interest of economic development. It is development that is going to fulfill mankind, and we are not very far along with it. The real hope for the world is multinationalism in business, which bestows the fruits of investment in every nation. We're marshaling political support in the United States to that purpose."

"You all do recall that we have sponsors who have interests?" asked Ward.

"I thought we all had the same interests," said Helene. They all laughed.

Tony saw this was some kind of inside joke related to the banter that would have to go on in a place so loaded with talent.

"Now, I must yield to the former attorney practicing corporate law at Mathias, Lind, Stephens and Lane, the celebrated law firm of the great city of Cleveland," said Ward.

"I thank the chairman for his generous introduction," Madeline said.

Everyone laughed. Madeline stood with her hand on Ward's shoulder.

"I see here the evolution and development of an organization which has great potential," she said. "I do the lawyering here, Tony. We have to have an inside attorney because even with the attorney-client privilege we would take some risks. Erwin told me that you thought the confidentiality agreements were comprehensive. Thank you, I appreciate the compliment."

"He didn't say 'comprehensive,' he said 'burdensome,'" Helene quipped to laughter.

"He signed them; that proves they were well drawn," Madeline said. "It's nice to be part of this growing nugget of competence on the world scene. I'm very proud of all the people we have, of my husband, and all of his colleagues. I am proud to be a part of this. I keep it legal. So far, there has been no overreaching proposals that I have had to trim."

Ward led the applause.

"Now, we shall hear from our guest," said Ward, nodding to Tony.

Tony had been thinking on and off of what to say. He had an outline in mind.

"When I first came here, I wasn't sure what I would find," he said. "Because it was Ward who invited us, we knew it was important. I never suspected how important the trip would be relating to the future of America and the future of world business. I am impressed by the human resources that have been gathered, by the excellent quality of the thinking, the concepts, the organization, the facilities, the legal management, the food, the setting, and the tennis."

"You have to try the scuba diving and the water skiing," said Madeline.

"I'll stick to snow skiing if there are sharks in the water," said Tony. "Well, you made me forget what I was going to say. Let me do this." He picked up his glass. "Here's to success and may your accomplishments be satisfying and fulfilling."

There was a loud chorus of "Hear-hears" to that.

The evening ended jovially. The others went to their electric car and Tony and Helene walked to the cart. The air was now cold. Tony took off his jacket and draped it around Helene's shoulders. She pulled it around her and felt his warmth in it.

"I can take you on a tour of the town, except you'll freeze," she said.

"Maybe the cold will help me digest all of that food," he replied.

"Ward gave me a bottle of his famous Armagnac. I'll warm you up with that."

Tony smiled. "Where does this Armagnac come from? I've seen it in France. If I remember, it was expensive."

"It's good Armagnac. Ward told the development director of the department in France where a big ACP plant was built that he liked Armagnac. When he got back to Cleveland there was a case of it waiting. They send him a case every Christmas. He keeps three bottles for himself and gives the rest away. I'm cold, are you?"

"Yes."

"To the Armagnac."

IN HER APARTMENT, Helene asked him if he would like to hear some Mozart. He saw the sofa in a living room attached to a small dining area, admiring her choice of paintings, especially the brilliant blue seascape on the wall opposite him. She brought the Armagnac on a tray with two snifters.

With a grin in her eye she said, "To not being so drunk this time."

Then she held up her face to his and he kissed her.

"Ward seemed in good form tonight," he said.

"He's usually serious and finds it hard to relax," she said. "He's always pursuing something. That was Ward at his best. He can be fun."

"So, I take it you've gotten busier?"

"Much busier," she said. "I think I would rather have Erla's job than be in charge of everything. She gets to concentrate entirely on ideas. I like to put ideas to work, but I also like to think them up."

"Putting them to work is just as important. Without that, they aren't worth much."

"A view from a man of action as well as ideas."

"You're complimenting me too much."

"I don't know, look where you are at your young age."

Tony grinned.

"Why don't we sit down?" said Helene. They had been standing talking as though they were at a cocktail party, sipping the Armagnac. It was the smoothest brandy he had tasted.

She sat on the love seat and he on the couch listening to the mellow Mozart.

"So, nothing has changed around here except the amount of work?" he asked.

"The balance in my bank account keeps building up," she said. I hardly have time to get it invested. I try to talk to my children every night."

"I'm surprised the local studs aren't lining up to meet somebody like you," he said.

"What am I going to talk to a Spanish Wells fisherman or to a resort type in Dunmore about?" she asked.

"What about men here?"

"I'm their boss."

She asked if he would like another drink, and he handed her his glass. She came back from the kitchen with the glasses full and sat down beside him on the couch looking at him. Her very Hellenic face, high cheekbones, and expressive eyes fascinated him. Her hair was perfectly cut. She was wearing an informal cocktail dress with a wide neckline that showed off her tan and the curve of her strong shoulders.

"You know," she said, "Ward gives the kind of dinner party we had tonight only when he knows his guests are real people. It's a compliment to you. He knew you could handle it. He won't do it with people he thinks are phony."

"I appreciate that," said Tony.

He liked this woman who was seducing him. He found her attractive in many ways. There was going to be a struggle between PENMET and POLACO. But what did this have to do with it?

She put down her glass and took his hand and put it on her hair. He let his hand drop down to her shoulders and guided her to him. She reached to kiss him and then turned so she fell into his arms.

"You're wonderful," he said.

"Let's listen to the music."

After a minute, he kissed her; the third time their tongues touched. He touched the small of her back and then her hips and her legs.

"It's good to be back," he said.

She left him for a few minutes and came back wearing a flowered silk Japanese robe. She sat beside him and then turned herself across his lap facing him and kissed him. This time she pulled her robe open to show her perfectly shaped breasts with large excited nipples. He pushed the robe away to see her tan stomach. As he held her he felt her back muscles under her soft skin. He opened it further to see her strong legs.

When she stood by him to unbutton his shirt, he saw she was one of those rare women, like Jean, who looked better naked than dressed. She smiled at him as he looked.

THE NEXT MORNING, Helene drove Tony to the Conference Center. She put her hand in his while she drove. They had parted company at around 2 a.m., and now they were happy to be reunited.

They trotted through the Conference Center lobby, stepped into the elevator and went down into the underground complex. The first stop was the intelligence atrium where the computerized map presentation system was now working.

Tony met two computer people, Julie and Jeffrey, who both looked like body builders. They demonstrated how the software could project maps of anywhere in the world in detail on windows created in the large world map. They asked him the address of his boyhood home, and in about eight seconds a map of his street in McMurray, Pennsylvania appeared.

They then asked him a place he would like to see.

"Shinagawa," he responded.

They asked him to spell it, and up came that southeastern portion of Tokyo with the Shinkansen Line railroad station marked. He could see the Pacific Hotel, his preferred place to stay in Tokyo.

They then demonstrated outlining a county in Ohio, windowing up the names of the county legislators, the county executive, the mayors of key population centers and their department heads. The bio of the chairman of the county legislature came up in another window.

Tony turned to Helene and asked, "How did you get all of this programmed?"

"We were able to purchase some of it," she said. "The maps are almost off-the-shelf. As information comes in, operators input it. It will be available to all of our computers in the master net."

In the Doctrine and Intelligence Group atrium, all of the workstations were in place, two secretaries were busy, and several offices were occupied. Erla was on the mezzanine.

Helene took him to her office suite in the executive atrium and introduced him to Carrie, her administrative assistant, and Rose, her secretary. Tony noticed that Carrie, a bright-eyed African-American woman in her mid thirties, was eyeing them with interest and that she and Rose, a pleasant-faced older woman, exchanged glances. He realized some how they must have signaled to the women that there was romance on the scene.

The next stop was the security facility. Helene explained this was one level below with a private elevator to one of the houses for quick access to the surface where the vehicles were parked. She said the security force often practiced scrambling to surround the ferry dock, to patrol the beach, or to close off streets leading to the compound.

"Edgar Slaughter was in counterintelligence in the DIA," Helene said. "If we had batons I'm sure he would want to use one – you know a swagger stick. He has made a few far-reaching suggestions that Ward wants me to handle. He has been reporting directly to Ward, but that is going to change. Soon he will have to report to me."

It took a key to operate the elevator downward and another key to open a powered door to a small antechamber. From behind a thick glass window, an uniformed woman looked up, smiled at Helene and buzzed open the door into the reception office. Helene signed the register where her name was already printed and Tony did the same. A computer stamped out visitors' badges, blue for Helene and white for Tony.

The receptionist led them past a half dozen small offices to a larger office decorated with the pictures of military scenes and the regalia of a former officer. It had a large wooden desk with two telephones and something that looked like a control panel.

They were making themselves comfortable in the leather chairs in front of the desk when they heard the sound of the security chief's footsteps striding down the hall. Slaughter was dressed in the same khaki pants and shirt he wore when Tony first met him, and he looked as lean and hard as ever.

"You were supposed to be here 15 minutes ago," was his greeting.

"We're sorry, Edgar," said Helene, but the look in her eyes was anything but sorry.

Something like a smile flickered over his face.

"We're glad to hear you are now officially a member, Mr. Destito," he said. "You're from Harrisburg? I was once stationed at Carlyle."

"I know the town well. You were at Letterkinney?"

"No, at the War College," Slaughter said. "Did you play golf?" he asked.

"Not often," Tony said.

"I liked your West Shore Country Club when I could get on."

"You have a good course at the War College, I have played that," Tony said concluding the usual military greeting.

"Now, let me tell you what our mission is here. First, we have to maintain the integrity of the area so that no unauthorized persons ever get into the hotel, the conference center or any of the houses, and of course, into the underground facility. We now have more than 70 people employed in the complex. We will establish entrance and exit points where a system will react to magnetic cards that we will all carry. Everyone will show a card to a sensor to enter every area. This will record the time and date as is commonly done in plants with high security.

"Our second mission is to prevent theft, particularly of documents, by anyone. We will have inspections of briefcases, portfolios or packages at each entrance and exit point with facilities for searching people if we get tips or if a document or anything else is reported missing. We will have computer access to the copy machines so that none will work unless a card is shown by a person authorized to use them. The machines will have computer memories not only to record the number of copies made but also what was copied. We also have a means of determining when disks or CDs are copied and by whom."

"Edgar takes his responsibilities very seriously," Helene said. "He has developed this document control system with a software company in Atlanta. It's his idea. As you know, Ward is paranoid about anyone finding out about POLACO, much less being able to prove it."

"What happens if someone steals an access card?" asked Tony.

"The loss of an access card must be immediately reported," Slaughter said. "We will advise our employees to have them with them at all times. This will include a photographic ID and also the thumb print. We will match the print by computer. All of the employees will be fully fingerprinted.

"We will establish security levels on a need-to-know basis. With regard to trespassing, we assume there are people who will want to get inside POLACO to access information, documents, or simply to photograph the underground facility. If we do find some unauthorized person here, we will interrogate him and then turn him over to the local constables. If the person is a citizen of the Bahamas, we'll have to file charges. If he is from outside the Bahamas, we can either file charges or ask for him to be sent home."

"How many people will you have?"

"I need 30 people to forcibly guard the perimeter. There are six on duty at the locations that we have to watch, with six on in other jobs who are on ready reserve, which gives me basically an infantry squad on duty. We have no police support at all here except for three constables and a half dozen auxiliaries."

"The document system sounds almost impossible," observed Tony, wondering if he could get some more insight.

"It's difficult, but we won't find out if it works unless we try it."

"I wish we could just trust people," said Helene.

"So do I," said Slaughter with an imperious look.

"Our third mission is to control loose talk," he said. "Obviously we have employees who are janitorial and secretarial; we have accountants and analysts, chefs, cooks, and waitresses. Eventually there will be more than 200 people in the underground complex. There will be another 20 or 30 employees who work on the surface at the hotel and center. There are also my own people. We have three plainclothes people who are local plants. They spend their time listening in various places to hear what people are saying about us and report back."

"Interesting thinking. You've gone through the process," said Tony, trying to win him. "What do you intend to do if you find out someone is in fact talking outside the facility giving away information or carrying out information? Let's say for example, a secretary," questioned Tony.

"We're still discussing that question," Slaughter said. "We expect we would be able to detect that fairly quickly. The existence of the document control system will not be known and people will think they can copy one or two documents and take them out.

"Let's say for example that Helene's administrative assistant, Carrie, was bribed or needed money in such a way that she was willing to sell POLACO documents. If we saw that she was copying or printing off a particular document that we consider sensitive we would then ask Helene if she had instructed Carrie to do this. If not, then that day we would search Carrie on her way out. And, I mean strip search. I am going to equip the search facility with a x-ray to determine if anything has been swallowed. We're thinking about whether to randomly search people."

"We may be thinking about it, but we're not going to do it," Helene said. "We have to be very careful with all of this. We have highly motivated people here and we have to maintain that motivation. Security can't be onerous, Edgar."

"But it also has to be effective, Helene. My orders are to make it effective."

"I will refuse to allow my people to be randomly strip searched, or searched at all unless you have clear cause."

"I have to agree with Edgar, Helene," said Tony. "The security is paramount and people have to be conditioned to it because they are the ones that make it work."

Helene gave him a look that told him they would discuss this later.

"It's the group itself that can let us know if they think anyone is violating security," Slaughter stated.

"We're not going to have people tattle on each other." Helene seemed about to raise her voice.

"I don't mean tattling, Helene, I mean telling us if they think there is a violation."

"We'll talk about this another time, Edgar."

"It's part of the game, Helene. Any of us that have been in the service know that you have to report security violations, otherwise you yourself are at fault," Tony said, feeling another strong look from Helene. "What do you intend to do about people who violate security?"

"That's still a matter of discussion," Slaughter said. "We have detailed employment contracts with everyone that specifies their obligation to keep everything about POLACO confidential. So far, prosecuting under the employment agreement is all that we are able to do, although I think there should be other means. There certainly should be vigorous interrogation of anyone we catch either from the outside or inside."

"It's a critical question, Edgar," Tony said. "You are in a unique situation with a highly secure facility and no police structure around it."

He felt another glance from Helene without looking at her eyes.

"Do I assume that you have a fourth mission to maintain control of the streets?"

"This has not been specified, but we can control the island," Slaughter said. "If the police were to lose control, or were threatened, we could mobilize three squads of well-armed and highly-trained men and women with some extra ex-military volunteers. That's a full platoon. We have riot control equipment coming to us. We'll have the right response for any development."

A landing on the island by U.S. Marines crossed Tony's mind.

"We would assume that any apparent civil disobedience would be aimed at penetrating us," Slaughter said. "Now let me show some more of the facility. Our time is almost up."

He rose and held the door.

"Just turn left and walk down this corridor," he said.

Across the way was the squad room where the shift briefings were held. It had a large detailed map of the facility.

They walked through that room to the electronic control center. There were television monitors of all of the entrance points. The sergeant of the shift sat at a desk in front of the screens with a computer that could call up any camera position and look in any atrium or other area. Tony noticed a bank of CD ROMs which he assumed were for recording the day's transactions at each gate. He saw that there was a closet for the storage of disks, and he wondered if this was also the bugging system.

They went further down the hall into what Slaughter described as the interrogation room, equipped with a table and chairs, one of which had straps on it for restraining a person. Helene asked about the straps, and Slaughter said sometimes people become hysterical.

Further down the hall, they were shown two steel cells, typical police lockups.

"We have to have someplace to put people," Slaughter said.

Tony complimented the planning.

Slaughter then walked them to the elevator and put in his key.

"Glad you have joined us," he said, as the doors opened.

"Thank you," Tony said. "I look forward to working with you."

When the doors closed, Helene spun around and glared at him.

"Do you really mean what you said about all of this?"

"Let's discuss it tonight."

"I'll remember to ask you."

ON THE MAIN floor of the atriums, they walked back to the conference center elevator and took it up to Ward Cowell's office. In his private conference room a small buffet was laid out with salad, breads, fruit, and smoked fish.

Ward came in to greet them.

"I hope you didn't have a headache like I had, Tony," he said. "Good morning Helene. That champagne tasted good last night."

"It was a lovely dinner, Ward. Thank you so much," Tony said.

"We'll get something to eat and talk for a few minutes," Ward said. "I'm sorry that Warren and I have to leave this afternoon. I want you to talk with Erla. She would like your input on the doctrinal side. Unfortunately, Erwin is not here. He had to schedule meetings in Washington. January is, as you know, start-up time. I want your input Tony. We know how good you are."

"Thank you for thinking that Ward."

Helene interjected, "Are there any questions that you want to raise with Ward, Tony?"

"I was interested in the security system, Ward. I think Edgar has done a good job."

"I wonder if he isn't overzealous," Ward said, "but so far there are no leaks and no trespassers."

"I think his document system is an useful innovation."

"Helene actually pointed out the need for something like that, and there it is."

"You know what I think of some of these methods, Ward," Helene said. "I don't like intimidation."

"You know we can't take any chances," Ward said. "I don't like it either. Edgar is trained to deal with kinds of people we don't know how to deal with. Whenever the security thing bothers me I think about what would happen if *60 Minutes* or *The New York Times* got a hold of this prematurely. They would happily let us swing in the wind. Anyway, you are taking over Edgar."

"That will be a challenge," said Helene.

"We want communication, Tony, but nothing on paper outside of here," Ward said. "To contact us use e-mail. We also think it best that you don't contact any of the others. One thing that I am pleased with is that you will be down here trying to keep Helene's tennis ego in check. Nobody can beat her."

"That task is beyond me," Tony said.

Tony concluded that Ward wanted to see if there were any specific things that he wanted to say. There weren't. The luncheon ended quickly.

With Erla, he could tell she was getting into her job of developing the doctrine as he saw her with her staff. Erla had the scope of intellectual interest that helped her understand the appeals that might be made. They chatted about the importance of issues in campaigns.

Tony watched to see if there was any mention of issues experts or issues groups. It looked like the focus on doctrine development was aimed at justifying POLACO's self interest.

Helene came to fetch him at 4:00.

"Ready for tennis?" she asked.

"I've been looking forward to it for weeks," Tony smiled.

Helene looked magnificent in her white shorts and top in the bright sun. They dispatched their doubles opponents in two sets. Then Tony tried again to beat her in singles. Some parts were a struggle. At one point he led, but Helene rallied to win.

With singular grace, she came to the net to congratulate him on his effort, her eyes shining.

IT WAS MUCH cooler when they met again outside the lobby entrance. The sun was almost down. Helene wore jeans and a loose fitting sweater. Tony also wore a sweater. They rode a cart to the west beach and a Caribbean restaurant not nearly so posh as the night before.

A hostess who showed pride in knowing Helene led them to the best table. The special was flying fish, fresh caught. They decided on the fish with a salad, conch chowder, and sweet potatoes grown on the island. She mentioned to Tony that English bitter was available, Courage, to be specific.

When the drinks came, they clinked glasses and Helene said with a smile, "Now you have to tell me what you really think of Edgar Slaughter and the security operation."

Jean would have come at him, guns in hand, if he had voiced an opinion of which she disapproved. Helene addressed their disagreement with a smile, a clink of glasses, and a quizzical look in her eyes. Was it emotional maturity or that he wasn't married to her?

"Look at it from his point of view," Tony said. What's his responsibility? How does he look at the world? What's his background?"

"I know, Tony, I have read his bio three times, but jail cells, chairs with restraints? What else do you suppose is down there? He's willing to use third degree methods, I know."

"I don't think that he would do anything that you or Ward had told him not to," Tony replied. "But he is going to argue a lot, and if something goes wrong, you'll wind up being responsible for it."

"Your analysis?"

"Ward has told him the missions: to keep trespassers out, to keep documents in, to find out who is violating the rules, and to assure the safety of the compound in the event of something like societal unrest," Tony said. "He's thought it through."

"There has never been anything like that here, not even in Nassau," she interrupted.

"When you've got an investment like this and no adequate police to protect it, you've got to protect it yourself," Tony said. "It's like Barbados. They didn't have an army, so some adventurers decided to take it over and loot it. Fortunately the police held them off long enough for French marines to arrive from Martinique. Now they have a disciplined force of 300 trained troops. Mostly they take part in the parades and worry about their rifle slope, but everyone knows they're there."

"But, Tony, I think he is taking it too seriously."

Tony shook his head.

"He has very little police support," he said. "He has to be the force of the island. The duty of the police is to secure the streets. He's got to have the force to do it, and he's seen that he does. He needs his uniforms in order to establish this group as the force."

"I don't like this military and police stuff," she said. "How do I handle him?"

"Like anything else, you'll have to find out about it," he said. "You have to spend the time to experience it. Go on their practices and training. Shoot the guns. You can do anything you want to do. You have all the brains and body you need. Let the people in the department see that. Show them their mission is important."

He wondered if he should tell her to make sure the troops were loyal to her and the organization and not just to Edgar.

"I just wish they weren't necessary," Helene confessed.

"Don't let them know that."

"I won't," she said. "I hope you really don't think you had to tell me that."

They talked about other things: the history of the island and the Bahamas and how third world countries would progress. For some reason, they did not talk about themselves.

They went back to her apartment, and she put on the music. This time Beethoven.

They stood in the middle of the room and kissed. One kiss was long, deep, and passionate, not to be forgotten.

She took his hand and led him to the bedroom, they undressed hurriedly but he slowed the pace of foreplay so that when he went inside her, she cried out.

Afterwards, as they held each other, thoughts about his alliances back home surfaced in Tony's mind. He looked at Helene holding him with her eyes closed. He could fall in love with her. Tony remembered his reality: he was married to Jean and was working as a double agent against POLACO. He continued to watch her and wondered what she was thinking.

☆ **Chapter 7** ☆

PAMELA DAGGETT WAS youthful enough to wear low-cut gowns when going with Adrian to black-tie affairs. He admired her new blue dress that matched her eyes as she adjusted his tie. They were about to descend from their suite at the Hyatt Regency in Atlanta to a private reception with the officers of the Aerospace Industries Association and their dignitary guests prior to the annual convention banquet. Anne Russell's people had arranged for him to substitute for a senator who, under reelection pressure, decided to accept an invitation in his state after having agreed to appear. They promised a much better speech than the senator would have given.

Anne was resplendent in a French designer gown of white and gold which showed off her carefully coifed auburn hair. Adrian thought Pamela looked just as young as Anne, even though she was five years older. Any man would be proud to be with either of them. They were the stars of the little performance of association leaders, congressmen, senators, and industry heavyweights in a mirrored room where shrimp, oysters, and little sandwiches were served by girls in space costumes.

At the head table, Pamela was seated next to the president of the Association's wife so they could chat while Adrian made the final review of his notes. The audience was at tables of eight in tuxedos, full-dress uniforms, and formal dresses from the far left to the far right of the podium. It was a tasty meal, but he only nibbled enough to avoid hunger pangs. The president introduced him as a former governor and business leader, expounding on his resumé from a text that Anne's people prepared for the AIA speechwriters.

From what Adrian could see, the audience was dutifully present and applauded dutifully as he rose to the platform.

"It is an honor to be with the leadership of the American Aerospace Industry, which has accomplished so much for so many people of every country," Adrian said. "One would have to be culturally isolated not to have experienced some benefit from the work of this industry. In every respect your accomplishments amaze the thoughtful observer. But, there are those in the political establishment in Washington who seem to not fully recognize this and for them I have a few bullet points.

"A few years ago some fun research was done to illustrate the importance of communication to commerce. In 1820, a commercial transaction between New York and San Francisco took nearly a year. A merchant ordering from New York sent a letter with a bank draft by packet around Cape Horn, taking four to five months in the pre-clipper days. It took another four to five months for the merchandise to come back, plus the days or weeks for the process by his agent.

"When the railroads connected the coasts, it still took a minimum of seven days for the order to be delivered and a month to get the merchandise. Today, the fax or e-mail order is sent by satellite link; the related bank clearances are by similar computer transactions. The order can be on an air freighter and arrive the same day it was placed.

"The economic pace that spreads the benefits of growth would be impossible without the communication and transportation which your industry has created. Now manufacturers in South East Asia can deliver light goods to San Francisco almost as quickly as their competitors in Oakland. You can imagine the benefits to people in remote locations who are now tied into modern society.

"Everyone who values peace and economic development owes thanks to the great institutions of this industry and to those smaller companies, sometimes very small, who support them with all types of technological achievements."

He was interrupted by applause.

"This industry has been a focus of American technology during most of the 20th Century," he said. "It was born in this country. Many companies in this industry have become legends, as have many individuals. There are people within the industry who are perhaps not known widely, but who are nonetheless important beyond description."

There was more applause.

"The benefits which this industry has wrought for this country go far beyond the best missiles, the best aircraft, and the best space vehicles," he said. "I wonder how many people wandering the Internet recognize that virtually all of the developments of computer technology arose from the needs of this industry. I wonder how many people who dial a number in France and have it ring in five seconds remember that the satellite link originated with this industry. How many people driving a new car know that its instrumentation and control came from the development of aircraft and missile on-board monitoring systems? How many patients in hospitals, as they are hooked up to one or another of the modern diagnostic devices, recognize their origin in Project Mercury and its sequels? How many patients undergoing advanced surgery recognize that most of the materials being used are products of research aimed at advancing the capabilities of this industry? Such materials are used in applications from cardiac surgery to earth moving. This industry is a national asset of the greatest magnitude. Bullet point one for the political establishment of Washington is to understand and respect your vast achievements."

Adrian paused for sustained applause as the audience rose.

"In the course of doing miracles of metallurgy and electronics," he said, "this industry handed the weapons to young American men and women and to our allies that made them triumphant in World War II, allowed them to prevail in Korea, and showed in the Persian Gulf that you can't fight the United States in a positional war. You have accomplished the incredible task of providing weapons that fit every reasonable means of response that American foreign policy might require. The second bullet point to the present Washington establishment is to keep clearly in mind that this industry is essential to our defense and to our world position."

There was more sustained applause.

"No other country has an industry like ours," he said. "Indeed other nations covet it. Our European allies recognize the need for aerospace capability because of the great issue of maintaining the peace. You are the key instrument of the world for maintaining peace. For 40 years of Cold War, this industry accomplished that. I've heard that the Cold War is over, and we no longer need to invest so heavily in aerospace technology. I am not so sure that we should stack our shields and bullet point three for the political establishment is to recognize the reality of history. Nothing is fixed in Eastern Europe and Russia. That democracy can flourish there is by no means certain. There is still the chance that a venomous hand could be put back on the nuclear trigger. And, there is still a nuclear trigger."

There was a burst of applause, but this time it was short-lived. The audience wanted to hear what he would say next.

"Keeping the peace also means dealing with outlaw nations who obtain nuclear devices or chemical or biological weapons and may in fact bring one into the United States or an ally country," he said. "The rulers of those nations must be absolutely certain that the assets of their country will be hostage to the pinpoint strikes of a modern strategic force serving the cause of peace."

There was long applause. Adrian smiled and bowed his head while waiting for it to die down.

"The world brings surprises," he said. "What a surprise we had at the nuclear establishment that Sadam Hussein had developed and his attempt at chemical and biological weapons. Now we face the reality that outlaw nations could acquire nuclear and other weapons through the evident trade of such weapons in illicit circles. The difference between the United States and such an outlaw in terms of power is that we can deliver any weapon, at any time to any place and keep delivering them. No one should ever doubt that the United States will do that if it is threatened or if any of our allies are threatened. Bullet point four for the political establishment is to keep that in mind. This industry has given our armed forces the capability to respond to nuclear blackmail, to respond as may be necessary to outlaws, and to enforce nonproliferation."

This time cheers were added to the applause.

"Democracies have an underlying propensity, when danger passes, to de-emphasize armament to save money or to increase social welfare," he said. "Armaments are expensive.

Soldiers are expensive. But, it is also expensive to lose wars or to be at the mercy of evil states or evil individuals. It is expensive to live in an environment of lawlessness. It is expensive to pay tribute to avoid harassment. The United States, as a new country, sent a disciplined force to the Mediterranean 200 years ago to deal with the outlaw states of Tripoli, which other nations with greater power were willing to pay off. Now the issues are many times more complex than in those simpler days. The members of the political establishment must keep in mind the image of the cruise missile coming into an opponent's bedroom window. This industry made that possible. The military doctrine of limited and appropriate response is vital to our leadership position. You established this and that is bullet point five."

Cheers and applause interrupted.

"The United States now leads the advance of human civilization into space," he said. "This is a huge vehicle to peace among the industrial nations. It is also the means to achieving the advanced technologies of the future that will keynote international competitiveness and further advances of knowledge. Bullet point six is that the political establishment must recognize that the benefits of advances of technology are substantially related to economic advancement.

"Everyone has detractors. Your detractors may well be the grandchildren of those who shouted that Britain and France should not resist the early expansion of the Nazis in the 1930s and that the United States should isolate itself from the troubles of Europe. Their action assured World War II would happen. Pacifism is comfortable and cheap. Peace has a price.

Maintaining freedom has a price. This industry deserves the lasting support of the American people and their elected representatives. There are many more reasons than national pride or power that we should advance into space. Aerospace must continue to be the central focus of American industry and it must continue to be 'The American Industry.' I urge you to assert yourselves armed by the understanding of the true meaning of what you do and what you perpetuate. Thank you."

There were many cheers and a long-standing ovation. After Adrian was formally thanked and the program ended, people flowed from the tables to the rostrum to meet this man. Pamela looked at him with emotion. She knew the country needed him. Anne Russell looked at him with glistening eyes and a glow of accomplishment, daydreaming about where this new adventure, the most important of her life, might lead her.

Typically, the audience at AIA meetings included staff members from congressional committees on science and technology, communication and transportation, and the armed services, usually with wives. Erwin Festener with his feminine and pleasant-faced wife Cecelia was seated at a front table with John and Roslyn Poole and two other couples. John was the staff director of the Armed Services Committee. They were chatting with warm feelings about the speech when Congressman Wallace Bennett, a Republican from San Diego and the third ranking member of the Armed Services Committee came over from the head table to interrupt them.

"What was this all about?" he asked, as though John had erred in not telling him who Adrian was beforehand.

Poole knew the Congressman was connected to a probable run for the White House by Senator Steven Hatford. He said, "I'm not sure, but I thought it was a good speech."

"It was too good a speech. Have somebody find out why he was here," said Bennett. "Who invited him? You know what I mean."

"Yes sir."

The Congressman looked at Erwin Festener

"Do you know anything about this, Erwin?"

"No, Congressman," Erwin said. "I thought it was a good speech, too."

"I was just curious why we get the former Governor of Illinois."

"Maybe they wanted a good speech," Erwin said.

Anne Russell's group was successful with the wire services. They got two column spreads on the business pages in Los Angeles, Seattle, Wichita, Houston, Oklahoma City, Tulsa, and Atlanta. Almost 40 newspapers in Illinois used it, including the Chicago papers. 52 television stations picked up the TV tape release. 30 of those were in Illinois. The others were mainly in Aerospace distressed communities: San Antonio, Wichita, and Oklahoma City. The industry papers and magazines gave him headlines and one cover. Anne was pleased with the results.

AS A POLITICAL professional herself, with years of image-making and issue-shaping experience, Jean Destito liked what she heard. But, her experience in political public relations had made her cynical. As a member of the Pennsylvania Democratic Committee, she had seen a number of good, honest candidates suffer defeat.

"You'll never get Adrian Daggett elected with this kind of talk, Tony," she said, after reading through the campaign's position papers. "People don't want to hear about reality; they don't want to hear about plans, and they don't want to hear about fighting wars overseas. You may call what they want 'pap,' but it's what they want."

"I think that's what is wrong with the system, there is too much 'pap' and not enough thinking," Tony replied.

"The people don't want to think," she said. "They want attractive candidates who speak nicely and who tell them what they want to hear. They want perceptions, which become their reality. Sometimes they get tired of the old lies, so they elect someone who will tell them new ones."

"The system has to be remodeled, Jean, in order to make it work," he said. "If people are not going to face reality, we are going to wind up with a dictator who will do it for them. Maybe that's the mechanism that's going to come and swallow us. If people are not going to face reality in their decisions and in choosing their candidates, if they reject reality, then eventually there will be fascism."

Jean clicked her tongue in dismay. She thought he was more sophisticated.

"Tony, it doesn't work that way," she said. "The way it works is a group of people put forward a candidate or a political party puts up a candidate and that candidate does what he must to get elected. The issues are defined in a way that brings about election and after the election all the promises are off. Then if they are competent they manage the government well enough so they keep getting elected, until the time comes to 'throw the rascals out.' That's the way it is now and that's the way it always has been."

"The country has changed, the world has changed, technology has changed," said Tony. "Everything is infinitely more complicated. The time has come for a leader to change the system. It's like Harry Truman and George Marshall. The Marshall Plan was essentially responsible for the peace in the second half of the 20th Century."

"Truman brought people around who could manage the government, including Marshall, and they did something right. But telling people what you are going to do about problems and issues is not going to get you elected," Jean insisted.

"And that's what brings incompetent people into government in positions of authority who don't know what to do and have to pretend they do while they scramble around for advice."

"That's always been the system," she said. "People in government reach out for advice. There are a huge number of issues. Nobody can be an expert about every one of them. Nobody can have an opinion about every one of them. The people recognize that. By taking so many issue positions, you're going to expose yourself and Daggett to someone attacking each one."

"Don't you think the people will care more about these issues if they are properly explained and if the problems are defined?" he asked. "Why can't a candidate for the presidency talk to the American people like he would talk to stockholders, explain the problems, and tell them what he is going to do about them?"

"The American people don't care about the problems, Tony. They only want answers. They don't want them to be anything hurtful. Politicians play on these strings. If they think they can get a particular response to an issue they will spin it into a perception and then try to get people interested in it, but you're trying to get people interested in everything."

"Maybe we could afford that at one time," he said, "but we can't anymore."

"Tony, you don't get elected with unpopular positions," she said. "Look at Fritz Mondale. He told people he was going to raise taxes and got blown away."

"Fritz got blown away because of his lousy staff," he said. "They took a colorful warm guy and made him into vanilla pudding. I can hear the meeting now, Fritz, you can't do this, Fritz, you can't do that, Fritz, you have to do it this way. We're going to let Daggett do what he wants to do and be natural."

"Tony, I don't want you to lose this," she said. "Try this definition. You and Ian have to elect someone who is not beholden to POLACO. To do this you have to come up with a formula of positions that will appeal to the electorate and let you get elected. Don't change too much, don't make big waves, don't promise too much."

"I understand that, but I also understand that the system is not working," he said. "Too many issues are being dodged and we are not getting good candidates running for office."

"Well maybe POLACO's system is a good one to get good candidates," she said. "And I'll tell you something, they know how to get them elected. I'm not sure that you do. And they're going to have the benefit of choice and training."

"We shall see," he said.

She made him angry. Here was a new concept of political campaigning that he had worked hard to develop and she had ridiculed it. She felt that Tony and his cohorts were blundering into attempting something that was impossible. He also felt destabilized because he had such high regard for her judgment and her ability. She was a professional political person in every sense of the word. Was it possible that she was looking at the wrong side of things and not at the opportunity to uplift? Or was the whole idea wrong?

Leadership in Tony's view was always uplifting. Why couldn't the American people be brought to a higher level of understanding and political dialogue? Her arguments concerning what had always worked might be true, but wasn't there one essential difference? There was now a hugely greater communication capability. Also, what about the general good sense of the American people? Was he that out of touch?

THE WINDOWS OF Ward's office were closed for an ocean storm. Harbour Island was getting its annual watering by the North Atlantic winter weather, which tracked from the south along the Gulf Stream. Edgar Slaughter arrived to review his plan for the penetration of PENMET. He took a mug of black coffee and asked, "Can you be more specific as to what you're looking for, Ward?"

"Something is not right about the PENMET membership. I feel a threat from Ian MacAulliffe. I don't know whether he agrees with what we're doing or not. He sends Destito down here, he won't even come himself."

"He sent $45 million. Doesn't that convince you?"

"That man is so rich he doesn't care. Besides, it's not his. All of this is structured to use corporate funds."

"If he had a motive to oppose us, wouldn't he have to cover it personally? He couldn't oppose us with company money."

"True, but something isn't right, Edgar. Everyone else tried to bargain. Ian just sends his man with the closing papers."

"Maybe that's his style."

"I want you to find out if anything is going on regarding MacAulliffe and Destito that would be detrimental to our program. How will you look and how much will it cost?"

"I will employ a very reliable operator in New York, Paul Melius & Associates," Edgar said. "We'll do the peripheral stuff like getting at the executive waste paper and computer printouts. But, we must send operatives with good cover to meet PENMET employees at their hangouts to ask questions and listen to the shoptalk. Important moves by a corporation usually leak that way. The idea is to ask questions at unguarded moments."

"How much?"

"It will cost $35,000 a month for the operatives and the periphery activity."

"If it doesn't work, how much to get in a mole?"

"Assuming only one, about $20,000."

"No one is to know of this except Madeline," Ward said. "She'll arrange payment through our New York law firm. Why don't we do the mole first?"

"That takes time. Sending two operatives will be much faster than one."

"Do it the way you think is best."

AT HER COMPUTER in the POLACO intelligence center, a woman named Michelle Proust considered the former governor of Illinois who had just completed his third speech picked up by the national wire services. This one had been to the American Road and Transportation Builders Association, where action had focused on what new highways and railroads contribute to American competitiveness. Her job was to notice events like the ones he was creating and to investigate them.

It looked like Daggett had good public relations support. She wandered through Internet files and found out a lot about him. She e-mailed a summary to her colleague Bill Haber and asked him if he knew anything about Daggett.

A half-hour later he stopped by her station. Considering the press coverage at this early stage he agreed there was deep backing on Daggett. Michelle sent a memo to Louis Fischer to enter Daggett's name on the list of prospective Democratic candidates. Bill invited her to dinner the next evening after a volleyball game.

Two days later with a printout of Michelle's first report on Daggett in hand, Louis stepped up on the mezzanine of the Doctrine and Intelligence Group atrium. Erla saw him and they sat down at the conference table outside her office.

"It's nice to breathe some fresh air."

"The air down here isn't fresh. It only looks that way from the mural."

"It's fresher than the air in my office – something's wrong with the ventilator. I called about Daggett. It's reasonable to conclude that he has decided to make a run, or is seriously testing the waters."

"Is that coming from nowhere?"

"No. He has a strong base in Illinois, a two-term governor. When he retired from the governorship, there were people who wanted him to go further, but he said he was leaving politics."

"Somebody has to be backing him. Are there endorsements?"

"So far we haven't got anything in the data bank."

"Send it to Erwin."

ALAN JACOBS WRANGLED an invitation for Adrian to try the heart of the reality story with the New Hampshire Democratic Committee. The occasion was a fundraising dinner at the Mill Inn Restaurant in Manchester.

Adrian was to introduce the reality campaign and its policies regarding debt. In New Hampshire this was a test and a risk. It was one of two states which had no income or sales tax. The government lived off real estate taxes, partly paid by out-of-state summer residents and by tourists, and a liquor monopoly serving more Massachusetts citizens than their own. There was also a lottery. But, it was the location of the critical first primary. A fast start from the gate in New Hampshire would mean credibility and momentum for the whole primary season. He was going to call for increased taxes to pay the debt. The speech would prove the viability of the whole reality premise.

The main meeting room was lined in dark stained heavy timber. White plaster walls were decorated with framed posters of mountains, woodlands, and New Hampshire life. Other than Nancy, Tony and Alvin Carter were the only two PENMET representatives who stayed in the serving area. Four detectives hired for the occasion knew Alvin was in charge of security. It was time for the campaign to start and Alvin needed the experience of handling one of these dinners.

Manchester was the commercial center between the Concord, the capital, and Nashua; the headquarters of The Nashua Corporation, the largest manufacturer in the state. Anne drew people from that company and other businesses. The idea of a reality campaign attracted Republicans who were willing to contribute to the Democrat's expense fund to hear about it. Anne and Alan hoped the presence of business people would balance the audience in favor of practical economics.

Introduced after the preliminaries with rousing prose by Anne's writers, Adrian began with a compliment to the state's motto "Live Free or Die." He spoke of the frailties of democracy and the ultimate requirement for good leaders who would, among other things, see to the involvement of the people. He spoke of the possibility of losing democracy by mismanaging it.

He questioned the use of polling as a means to establish policy and warned that political leaders must tell the people the truth and not what they want to hear. Without the truth, he said, the people have no basis for judgment. He pointed out that in fiscal matters the political leaders of the United States had been bereft of their duty. The subject of a potential fiscal disruption because of the buildup of the national debt was rarely, if ever, mentioned. He said without sound finance, corporations cannot do well and neither can nations.

Adrian accused the Reagan presidency and said the debt which must be repaid was their terrible legacy of the lack of proper budgeting, untimely tax cuts, and the acceptance of impossible assumptions. He said the Reagan era showed that history's greatest nation could succumb to financial foolishness. He cited the facts that the average American household was obliged to pay $4000 per year in interest alone and that their share of the debt was nearly $60,000. This was equal to $1.39 of debt for each dollar of income.

He referred to the seeming triumph of balancing the budget, but pointed out that this was partially an accounting maneuver. He said the budget needed to be balanced in real terms and that the further reality was that it would be necessary to pay down the debt until the USA was a creditor nation again. The time had come to take the medicine for the illness the Reagan administration mistakes had wrought upon the country.

He described the rueful events of inflation, recession, and austerity to which nations succumbed if their currency fell drastically on the international markets. The mechanism, he explained, was caused by raising interest rates to defend the currency. This would, in turn, choke off investment and start recession even though exports increased with inflation injured by higher priced imports. He said the United States was not immune if its debt was too great. The alternative was currency collapse, which would wipe out wealth.

"If I choose to run and am elected, then you will know that, by God, I will reverse this trend of keeping the people ignorant and I will awaken the people to the fiscal dangers," he said. "I will not allow the United States to fail because all its politicians could do no more than promise tax cuts. I will tell the people the whole truth and I will make this unpleasant issue an example of how other politicians have failed the trust of the people. I will not fail that trust."

Adrian spoke sincerely and almost sternly. The audience listened intently; there was hardly even a cough. When he finished, there was a moment of stunned silence and then the room erupted into cheers and whistles and a standing ovation. People crowded forward around the rostrum to shake his hand.

The leaders turned around and directed the crowd in a cheer of "Run, Run, Run!" Pamela grasped his arm, leaning up to kiss his cheek. The talk around the rostrum lasted for nearly an hour. When Alan called it to an end, his people had the names of volunteers and supporters from the cream of the state's Democrats and many substantial Republicans willing to work for Adrian.

The press coverage ignited. The New Hampshire, Chicago, and Illinois papers carried the full story. In Sunday political review articles, Daggett was mentioned in the New York Times and the Washington Post. Television stations used the tapes in Illinois. The New Hampshire stations picked it up.

The next day, on the European money markets, the dollar rose strongly in heavy trading.

☆ **Chapter 8** ☆

IAN ARRANGED THREE meetings with US senators on the same day. The junior senator from Pennsylvania hosted him at lunch in the Senate dining room and listened intently to the proposition. He was flattered that the distinguished CEO came to see him. When he found out why, he became excited. He agreed on the spot to join the deputation to ask Adrian Daggett to run with their endorsement, conditional on Ian recruiting other people. Because there were no anticipated candidates from Pennsylvania, he would bring this to the attention of the Pennsylvania State Committee. The senator didn't bring up the connection between Jean Destito and PENMET. Ian didn't see a reason to bring it up either.

The senior senator from Illinois kept him waiting for 15 minutes, but he used the time to look at the pictures crowded on the reception room wall and to reread the briefing on the senator prepared by Alan Jacobs' people.

Once Ian was ushered into his office, the senator came from behind a large, flag draped, carved desk to shake his hand warmly and gesture to a green leather couch and chairs.

"I hope you haven't come to tell me you are going to close your factory in Gary," he said.

"No, I'm glad to say I'm not."

"You'd be surprised at how many CEOs come in to tell me they are closing or opening factories. It's to remind me of corporate power."

"I'm here on a personal mission."

The senator cocked his head. "Well then, what can I do for you?"

"This meeting is about Adrian Daggett," Ian said. "I have become extremely interested in his possible candidacy for the presidency. Many people in business and our institutions feel the need for much more professional leadership in the White House and are willing to back someone who has business as well as government experience. I've met with Daggett and his family and have pledged support. We're putting together the strongest possible group and an ample contribution from my personal funds. My purpose in coming to see you is to ask you to gather senior Democrats to ask Daggett to make the race. Our public relations firm, Evans & Copeland, and our political consultant, Jeremy Reubin & Associates think that's a good place to start serious talks."

"I've seen clippings about his speeches."

"Part of the prelude that we have started to play."

"He sounds like a Republican."

"He will," Ian said, "but he also is in favor of solid support of the United Nations, NATO, or any defense treaty to preserve peace, and he's for national health insurance."

"Thank God. I hope he'll not change his position when the clamor starts."

"He won't."

"What are his other positions?"

"He'll be strong on keeping a budget surplus and paying down the debt in the near term with revenue increases and a big downsizing of government. He'll blame the Republicans for tax cuts, and more debt. He'll focus on the amount of interest people are paying from their own pockets to fund the debt."

"Mondale went down on that one."

"We think there is a way of explaining which will make a big difference. Who can be against reducing indebtedness?"

"Good point. The sooner we do it the better. We have been mired in inaction because the leadership is afraid of the issue. They seem to think it will go away. It's hard to talk to people about international markets and bank liquidity."

"I have a group that is going to try," Ian said. "They will keep testing the reception. There is another issue of a restriction on speculating in currencies by American corporations. If we could tone down currency speculation, it might reduce the pressure on weaker currencies. It could be a vehicle to bring the international markets into the campaign. We could question why we have so much trading."

"Could be a good idea. What else is in your bag of tricks?"

"We'll probably come out with a National Health Insurance

program. A solution has to be found. If it can be private, fine, but if not, it has it be a government solution."

"You're really taking it on, aren't you? Who is putting this all together?"

"I have my best man on it, Tony Destito. He's coordinating a group of experts I've hired to help, headed by Professor Terry Leelan of Cornell."

"Leelan is excellent. He's down here quite a bit with Cornell's Washington program. His disciples visit. I see them when I can. Where's Daggett on abortion?"

"He's going to try to keep government from getting between a woman and her God, but he is also going to claim it as an issue with little real importance compared to nuclear or bio-weapons proliferation."

"That's a good idea too."

After some further discussion the senator asked for a confidential memorandum outlining all of the positions Daggett intended take. He said he would telephone as soon as he read it. He reminded Ian that there wasn't a lot of time.

The senator liked the issues summary. His staff wrote it into a confidential letter which was circulated to certain members of the Illinois delegation, and others he knew would be interested. Alan Jacobs' staff followed up and suggested holding a meeting of those interested in the Daggett candidacy to air all of the questions that they might have.

Anne and Alan met personally about the meeting at the Press Club and decided it should be held in Washington without the press. Working with the senator's staff, they sent confidential messages to everyone on Capitol Hill who had received the senator's letter and asked if they would like a meeting. They said they would.

THEY CHOSE THE Hyatt Regency ballroom close to the Capitol for the meeting. Invitations were sent by messengers who returned for the responses. Donald, Linda, and Dianne Daggett flew to Washington to be on hand.

Anne Russell, looking beautiful, and Alan Jacobs were the greeters with the tall, silver-haired senior senator and his wife. They decided Adrian and his family would not be in the reception line. This would build up some suspense and avoid preliminary discussions or confrontations.

The senator called the meeting to order and introduced Adrian and Pamela and their offspring, who appeared to polite applause. While the appetizers were served, they went to each table and greeted everyone. The handsome family made a good first impression.

When the appetizers were cleared, the senator rose and gave the microphone to Adrian. He thanked the Senator for arranging the meeting and referred to the position summary and papers which everyone had received and asked for the first question. A number of hands went up and he pointed toward one table. A portly gentleman rose.

"Hamilton Frasier, 23rd district of California (that's Pasadena) come to the Rose Bowl Parade," he smiled.

"We all want to do that," Adrian retorted, returning his smile while the audience clapped.

"Your positions on the defense industry and your speech to the AIA interest me. How much spending do you think is appropriate for technology development?"

Adrian recognized a test of how specific he could be.

"If I'm elected, I will appoint a commission to work with the Pentagon on technology development that will relate to the Aerospace industry and spin-offs to other industries. I know there are many commissions in Washington, but this is one step we have to take. Call it refocusing government and redefining its mission."

Hamilton remained standing. "You also have a position on health care which sounds daring."

"I certainly do. Health care in the United States is supposed to be the best in the world. The reality is otherwise because of access. It is utterly incomprehensible that millions of individuals cannot get it and wind up seriously ill in emergency rooms. Virtually every other country in the industrialized world has a health care system that is universal, some form of national health insurance. We can do that privately if we think it is going to cost less. Perhaps the Tennessee plan is possible in other states or on a broader scale. The key point is everyone must be covered and there must be limits on the escalation of cost. Covering everyone means that we will not turn mentally ill patients out of hospitals to wind up living on the streets. Are we the kind of society that does that?"

Another hand raised. A lean man with white hair rose.

"Senator Willis Cartwright. You say you want to raise a question of reality concerning the national debt and speak to the point of paying higher taxes to tranquilize the international currency and securities markets. I hasten to advise you to remember the political adage: 'never vote for anything that takes more than two minutes to explain.' Would you comment on that, please."

"Senator, we have to transcend that wisdom so that we can use more than two minutes to explain an issue. The tough issues are complicated. But, maybe we can make this one simpler by saying our purpose is to assure the international markets will never have a reason to speculate against the dollar because of its strength and the skill by which it is managed. We must further specify that any revenues raised for that purpose must surely be used for that purpose which is to assure the fiscal stability of the nation."

After two more exchanges, the Senator from Illinois suspended discussions so the entree could be served. When the plates were cleared, the Senator stepped back to the rostrum with Adrian, called things to order, and said, "Congresswoman Spense asked for the first question of this session."

An attractive brunette rose and smiled at Adrian.

"Governor, for years I have tried to get our party and national figures to deal with the realities of our transportation infrastructure and the planning that needs to be done long term. This issue never gets into the news because politicians rarely talk about it."

"This is an area in which the absence of good planning is potentially dangerous," Adrian responded. "There are some states which want to do away with the federal program and keep the highway trust fund taxes. It's some form of madness. Montana and Pennsylvania have about the same number of Federal highway miles. Pennsylvania has a huge tax base to maintain the roads. Montana is very thin on people and traffic to tax. Yet freight from the coasts and the industrial Midwest expect to use the interstates in Montana.

"Also in the United States, we are not maintaining the universal quality of our roadways. We are not using new technologies because they are expensive. The question is, what is cost effective? If higher capital means lower annual costs, that's the way to do it."

"Governor, I will support you for the office you seek."

"I will support your Committee on Transportation and Infrastructure," Adrian replied.

He pointed toward a handsome African-American in a dark blue blazer and tan slacks.

"Congressman Andrew Harper. Are you going to add a balanced budget amendment or propose one, and if you do, what kind of amendment would you foresee?"

"I know you are a fellow businessman, Congressman," Adrian said. "The laws of economics prevent corporate management from overspending without paying severe penalties. But there is no similar restraint on governments. My belief is that a balanced budget amendment is absolutely necessary to restrain government and I will propose it, but with a different structure from the one that failed under President Clinton."

The senator said, "Please recognize Senator Reston."

A scholarly-looking man in his 50s stood up.

"I want to shift to foreign policy, Mr. Daggett," he said. "I understand your vision and I support it, but aren't we going to be vulnerable to arguments that we are trying to be the world's policeman?"

"The world has to have police," Adrian said. "My judgment is that it has to be done through the United Nations, NATO, or existing treaties. These treaty groups or the United Nations have to be certain of the American support for any reasonable enterprise. We can't go through the Bosnia argument, the Kosovo fumbling, or the Gulf War argument each time something important happens. In the case of Kuwait, if we had failed to push back the Iraqi invasion, a nuclear war could have occurred between Israel and Iraq. In the case of Bosnia, Europe and the United States failed to take action against an openly racist government which was promoting ethnic cleansing and look what happened. How many other racist politicians did we encourage?

"During the debate on Bosnia we were challenged to remember the words of the memorials for the holocaust for World War II: 'never again' but we let it happen. It was Thomas Jefferson who propounded a foreign policy based on morality. I know it costs soldiers lives and wounds, but that's what evil men assume democracies will not accept. The resolve of the United States has to be expected by anyone who would do us harm or do harm to our allies. Back to John F. Kennedy, 'we have to bear any burden to support a friend or to support freedom.' We have got to get this country back to where it was when it was reaching for the moon. The world has to be certain of our resolve."

"I thank you sir," Senator Reston said. "I agree."

The questions continued. The meeting ended with warm applause. The next day Alan Jacobs started collecting support spreading his agents around Capitol Hill and downtown.

IN THEIR SUITE on the top floor, Pamela and Adrian gathered with their offspring.

"You were great, Dad," said Linda, hugging him.

"Smooth, best I've seen you do," Donald added.

"You swung 'em, Pop," Dianne told him. "You're going to be a great President."

"All of my professors are for you. One, I think, wants a job," said Donald.

"Mine, too," said Linda.

"You can have a rally anytime at Blair," Dianne claimed.

"We should have rallies at all three campuses," declared Adrian.

"I don't know about that," said Linda.

"There's going to be security with you from now on. They'll work with the campus police and the local police," Pamela told her brood.

"What does that mean?" asked Linda.

"Bodyguards." said Pamela. "Alvin Carter is an associate of ours and will provide this until the Secret Service takes over."

"Why, does that scare you?" Donald asked his sister.

"We're not at the point of no return yet, but we will be soon," Adrian said. "I can still back out."

"How could you do that after tonight?" Donald wondered.

"By cooking up some inside-the-beltway spin about family responsibilities. The job's too awesome, and so on."

"The job is too awesome for anyone but you, Dad," said Dianne. "You have to do it. We can't have anymore Washington bullshit."

"Dianne!" Pamela cautioned her youngest daughter.

"Politicians down here are playing with government. They're not governing. There is nothing in front of them but the next election and their retirements," Dianne stated with her chin up.

"I agree, Dad," said Donald. "That has to change. You have to make it happen."

"Your father is saying that he will still back out if you want him to, if it affects the family adversely," Pamela summarized with a warm feeling.

The five of them went into what they called a family hug, standing with their arms around each other. Pamela kissed Adrian's cheek.

Downstairs at the motor entrance where a limousine was waiting, flashes went off as they emerged. The meeting had been leaked.

The next morning, the picture was in the Post with the caption, "Is this the next first family?" Adrian wondered if Anne or Nancy had done it.

WITH THE ASSIGNMENT from Ward Cowell, Edgar Slaughter flew to New York to visit Paul Melius, a specialist in undercover industrial work. He had been part of the intelligence community of Washington to which Edgar had belonged. In the CIA, Melius had jobs in analysis and running agents. He was very good at putting a total story together.

Melius' office was in the Lincoln building. The space was not luxurious, but it made the right impression. The best of the plethora of law firms headquartered in Manhattan were within walking distance. In five years, Melius had developed a reputation for not failing.

Before seeing him, Edgar drove to Harrisburg to look over the ground Melius would be working on. He checked into the large tourist/conference center in Hershey with an assumed name and began forays to Harrisburg. He drove into the parking lot at PEN-MET headquarters and through the neighborhoods around the facility. He located the nearest TGIF and Houghlihan's where Melius' agents might meet with PENMET employees. He made notes in his laptop after each trip and collected copies of the Harrisburg telephone books and local directories. He subscribed to the local paper to be sent to his lawyers.

"This will not be quick or easy," Melius said after Slaughter had laid out the problem.

"Are listeners the right choice?"

"Usually works best. I have two regulars. We'll pay them through the lawyers."

"We would like to get a mole inside," Slaughter said.

"That's expensive and you have to wait for the right opportunity."

Edgar elaborated on Ward's concerns.

Two days later, Elizabeth Daley, who would be known as "Cynthia Reese" and Janos Krypska who would be "Joe Frozzi," left for Harrisburg. Liz was from San Fernando Valley and went on athletic scholarships to Stanford where she argued incessantly with her parents about her goal to be in the CIA. She persisted and won a job as a field agent. After some inside years and two successful field assignments, she got caught up in the internal politics. She quit in disgust. Several friends referred her to Paul.

Janos, from Omaha, was trained in the military where he earned a university degree and all the stripes an arm could hold. He was referred to Melius and mustered out to join him even though he was offered a commission.

Midwesterner Janos put money into a home in Pound Ridge in

rural Westchester. In his basement he built a workout room where he and Liz could practice hand-to-hand and otherwise keep fit. They were lovers, but Liz kept an apartment in White Plains.

Both were young enough to spark on the singles scene. Liz was attractive in any hair color. She was tall at 5'9". Janos only an inch taller was rugged and good-looking. He never had a problem approaching women.

They each took month-to-month furnished apartments. Liz's cover was an assignment from an international bank which could be confirmed. Janos was with a Greek engineering firm in bridge building. Thus equipped, they joined the Harrisburg yuppie scene.

After three weeks of socializing, they had sheets of notes in looseleaf binders about PENMET employees and about the company, but absolutely no indication of any political action. It seemed to be a dream place to work. Employees were not ready to betray confidences.

They knew that eventually they would come upon disgruntled people, part of any company. But there was a big question whether they would have access to sensitive information. It was evident that disgruntled people didn't get promoted at PENMET which was as nonpolitical as a company could get.

They did find one significant piece of information. The Corporate Public Affairs department was expanding, and was looking for additional professionals. Liz had good writing skills. She had been published in some trade journals, and was working on a novel. She had taken literature, journalism, and writing courses for a minor in communication at Stanford. They put together an unsolicited application letter and a resume that couldn't be turned down and sent it to Nancy Letersky.

A few days later Liz's fax rang inviting "Cynthia" to phone for an appointment. PENMET would, of course, pay all expenses. She went through the interviewing process and wound up in front of Nancy, who thought she was plucky and capable of a variety of assignments, even working on the campaign. "Cynthia Reese" was hired as a "Professional Associate."

In her first weeks, "Cynthia" started slowly as every good employee does and made few recommendations. She then began to contribute and establish herself. She was indeed being well compensated. The $6,000 plus a month from PENMET and $10,000 from Melius made it certain she would bank nearly $90,000 in cash under her true identity. She joined in employee groups for sports and recreation and scouted for particular men to seduce if necessary, always the best way to information. Her problem was finding out who had the information she was after.

Ward Cowell was pleased. He was much more comfortable knowing there was someone inside PENMET's executive suite. Further comfort came from the negative reports indicating no involvement in activity that would affect POLACO's interests.

After a few weeks, Liz Daley, who swore she would never work for a large company, started to like her job and the people. However, her weekly reports to Melius kept her in touch with her reality. They were worth $2500 each in cash plus expenses which were another thousand dollars a month for her evenings out and weekend trips with people from the company. She wrote off a membership in the best health club to keep in shape and started beating everybody in racket ball. She became involved in the meetings and the PENMET annual report. She met Ian MacAulliffe and Tony Destito and liked them. Nancy and Tony, she noticed, had frequent conversations and that they traveled together with apparent regularity. She noticed Nancy was away a great deal, but that was not uncommon. There seemed to be something confidential that Nancy was working on with perhaps, one or two other people, but that was also not uncommon. She would check on it when she had a chance.

With no results on his side, Janos moved back to Westchester without his favorite bed partner.

THE NEXT TEST for the Daggett campaign was the environmental issue. Anne, Nancy, and Alan judged that a clear statement was needed to mitigate the impact of the concept of needing to sell federal assets in order to pay the debt. Anne Russell and her people earned their fee by arranging for Adrian to speak at the National Convention of the Sierra Club in St. Louis at the Adams Mark. Because this would be controversial, she and her staff saw that the press coverage would be thorough. They no longer had to persuade the wire services to attend. CNN, CNBC, and C-SPAN off the campaign feed, scheduled it.

The hotel faced the Mississippi by the great arch commemorating the role of the city in the opening of the West. It was warm enough and Adrian, Pamela, and two of Alvin's detectives went jogging on the levee and through the park. Evans & Copeland saw that cameras were there.

Adrian was the luncheon speaker in the ballroom. He watched

Pamela, slender and elegant, go among the people she was meeting for the first time with poise and warmth. He saw that Anne stood back from her to allow her room. Tables were still being set up to handle the overflow crowd when the president of Sierra Club began his introduction. Adrian stepped up to the podium to rousing applause.

He started with illustrations in history of decisive action in government which was accomplished by the dedication of individuals. Women's rights, he said, took its course, as did the abolition of slavery, the civil rights movement, and the American Revolution itself. The environmental movement, he said, was a late example and deserved huge credit for sensitizing the nation to the impact of the industrial revolution on the environment.

To dramatize the significance of the accomplishment, he cited a report from Germany where 10,000 polluted sites were located of which 5,000 required remediation. Many of these resulted from unregulated pre-industrial revolution activities. He asked the audience to imagine what would have happened if industrial expansion had occurred without new regulation. He said the world owed a debt to those who recognized the threat and worked so hard to bring action. The audience interrupted with applause.

More applause came a few moments later after he told them continued vigilance was necessary and that the job would continue to ask governments to take longer-term action.

There was less applause when he called for absolving the liability of companies which occupied polluted sites, but who had not caused the pollution. He pointed out that brown sites must be used instead of green sites and that the public had to protect companies in international competition from excessive remediation costs if they were not responsible for the cause of the remediation.

When he proposed there be no further construction of fossil fuel power plants except for cogeneration, and that the French model of nuclear power be adopted worldwide the audience became uneasy. The feeling increased when he suggested that the pollution from the fossil fuel plants was infinitely greater than from the nuclear plants and that the safety of the nuclear plants could be properly managed. Activity at the press tables noticeably increased as reporters were typing furiously.

He related the need for worldwide action to deal with the specter of general air pollution and global warming. Citing the reality that the atmosphere was finite he recommended that the environmental lobby focus on this as a key objective for the future, insisting on global agreements. He said new power for ground transport would be required and this would have to be electricity, hydrogen, or a synthetic, clean burning gas. Electricity from a non-polluting source, he said, was the best choice and further burning of fuels must be reserved for industry and for air travel. He asked that the movement guard against over-reaction or irrationality and keep its work science based.

He paused briefly to see if there would be a reaction and he could feel the silence. The press tables were still busy.

He concluded by saying the movement was still vital to defend what had been achieved and to deal with the threat of global warming. He reemphasized the need for rationality in order not to discredit the movement and render it ineffective.

There was sustained applause.

As it started, the Sierra Club president turned to him and said, "Would you take questions?" Adrian said he would.

Anne Russell, at one of the press tables was excited by the obvious interest and sensed that something was going to happen.

The questions came rapidly.

"I am against the sale of any federal lands or the development of any federal lands for the payment of the national debt," one man said. "I have never heard of such a thing before and cannot understand how anyone can come forward with that proposition. This is totally opposed to the environmental cause. How can you justify that?"

"If the economy of the United States is damaged by failing to pay down the national debt, there would be no money available to do anything for the environment," Adrian said. "Environmental issues are tied in directly, as are all other interests, to maintaining the integrity of the American government. If we lose that, we will have to rebuild everything and we will rebuild it with an environment that has suffered much depravation."

"You cannot possibly be in favor of the environmental cause if you promote the development of atomic power," another man said. "Atomic power is a danger to the environment and to human life. I am unalterably opposed to building another nuclear plant anywhere. I agree that alternate sources of power generation should be found, but these are the wind and the sun. In the meantime, there is less danger from fossil fuel plants in my judgment than from nuclear plants."

"I know about Three Mile Island and I know about Chernobyl," Adrian answered. "Tell me about all of the other incidents of the question of nuclear power plant safety."

"There have been dozens of instances where radioactivity has nearly been released or has been released into the atmosphere," the man replied. "The atmosphere will not tolerate a great deal of this."

"I want to know about the instances," Adrian insisted.

"Well I don't have them with me," the man said. "I have read about them in various newsletters and various magazines. You can't expect me to cite them point by point at this time without any preparation."

"My belief is that there are very few, if any, other instances."

"Well isn't Chernobyl enough?"

"Chernobyl was an inadequately designed nuclear facility being operated by drunken engineers and doesn't serve as an example," Adrian said. "The example is the kind of plants that have been built in France where each has improved on the preceding. The French have seized leadership in design safety and waste handling. The Chernobyl plant could never have been permitted in France or anywhere else. The air in France is clean. It is not consistent with the character of the environmental movement to descend to fear mongering about radiation. If we cannot be science-based, we cannot take action. If power use grows 4% a year, air pollution will grow with it if we use coal and oil.

"Nothing in technology is 100% and no one can give a certain pledge that a nuclear accident will not occur. We can all, however, be absolutely certain that fossil fuel combustion is atrophying the atmosphere of the earth, possibly damaging the ozone layer and surely is a cause of global warming."

"I think the danger of the nuclear plant is the amount of waste that they create," a woman said. "We stopped building fast-breeder reactors because they produced weapons-grade fissionable material. Other reactors produce potentially harmful virulent waste and society should not have to deal with this."

"I'll again go back to the analogy of France," Adrian answered. "They have a technology to deal with the waste. For 20 years they have also been reclaiming fuel rods and putting the high level radioactive wastes in glass inside stainless steel cylinders and burying them deep in granite on the Cotentin peninsula near Cherbourg. Why can't the United States do that? The waste is far less dangerous because it is controlled."

Hands were raised throughout the room.

"You really think the government should institute tighter regulations on industry or on individuals. Industry is straining with the regulations, now."

"Do you believe in the ozone hole?"

"Of course."

"Well, so do I."

There was more applause as the meeting ended. As people rose, some started to filter down toward the rostrum to talk further. At the press table there was a rush to pull out cellular phones. Conflict had appeared. Adrian took some positions and defied "right thinking" and now he was news. Anne smiled to herself, seeing the power in the man and what she could do with him.

Watching the tape the next day, Alan Jacobs was not so comfortable. He questioned the unorthodox strategy. Yet in the back of his considerable mind, he realized that orthodoxy was always evolving and always changing. He saw the reaction here of a special quality of candidate who meant what he said and could think for himself. So much of politics was presenting a candidate of modest ability and trying to make something out of him or her. Not easy, he reflected. Yet what would happen to Daggett?

There were opponents in the primaries. The senior senator from Michigan was in the race and was gathering forces. A western governor was also in. The two were well known and politically astute. They were gathering staffs that were experienced in the major primary states. Each had a solid financial base and could be expected to raise adequate funds. At the next meeting of the campaign group, Daggett's people would have to focus on the competitors. The Iowa caucuses and the New Hampshire primary were growing closer day by day.

He wondered if they could do it in time.

The wire services carried a solid story of the environment speech and it was picked up broadly. The television stations in Chicago and throughout Illinois used it. The three cable networks taped it for stories on the national evening news. Inquires came from investigative reporters, journalists, and television producers doing environmental pieces. Anne was delighted. Jean Destito was not.

"You're leading with your chin, Tony," Jean almost shouted at him, "You've got to test things first."

"We will say what we believe."

"Read your polls. You can't go against public opinion."

"Responding to the polls is a despicable practice. It denies leadership."

"It may be despicable, but it works."

"Does it really, or does it make people more cynical about what professional politicians do?"

"That's not true," she said.

"Politics should be a noble profession and we are trying to ennoble it. We need another Jefferson, we need another Lincoln."

"Is Daggett your Lincoln?" she asked.

"I hope so."

"If Lincoln ran today he would have to run his campaign the way I am telling you."

Tony was saddened to witness the hardening of Jean's once winsome personality. "You may be right," he mused, "but we have to prove that we can elect a Lincoln today or our democracy is not worth much at all."

NANCY HAD SEEN to the preparation of careful material on Adrian and his family. It showed the promise of nobleness. Packages of information about Daggett were going out to all the media, and to political journalists. Copies of his speeches were going out to all Democratic leaders. The background material was building up. The senior Senator from Illinois called a press conference and gathered all who would initially endorse Adrian to co-host the formal announcement.

Alan Jacobs' target was to have 100 prominent Democrats publicly back Daggett. The Senator was able to get half of them from Congress. Alan went to see those who stalled and brought them in along with some others he knew well. From the past they brought in four former committee chairmen.

State leaders signed on and were brought to Washington to participate. The New Hampshire leadership was enthusiastic, and provided a big push to others. With members of the Democratic National Committee and state chairmen, the goal was reached. Democratic CEO's of Fortune 500 companies agreed to come. Some Republican CEO's who also wanted to endorse Daggett asked to come.

Of the total of endorsers, 103 prominent Democrats and 34 business leaders were scheduled to appear with Adrian at the Hyatt Regency. A stage was constructed in the draped, chandeliered ballroom. It would be crowded with the supporters seated around Adrian, Pamela, and the children. The rest of the floor was jammed with reporters and cameras in front of an invited audience of staff and party members. Alvin Carter was in the background with a new campaign security chief. Anne and her staff led people in the right directions. The reporters received press kits with photos and tapes.

There was a strong sense of media support for this new person on the national scene. Anne and Nancy knew some of it was genuine. Other reporters were interested only in conflict and an ongoing story about it.

At exactly noon, the senior Senator from Illinois, his silver hair gleaming in the lights, rose to the microphone and called for order. He spoke briefly of the need for facing the truth in government and facing the truth of the tough issues of the new century. He summarized the issues about which Adrian had already spoken. He said the endorsers had urged Adrian to run, stretching the truth a little, and that Adrian had been persuaded.

"Ladies and gentlemen, it is a great honor to present a man from the reality of business and government who will bring reality to Washington, where it has been absent for many years. In 1860 we sent a man from Illinois to face the crisis of our very existence as a nation. May God grant this man the same success, The next President of the United States, Adrian Daggett of Illinois!"

Adrian took the microphone amid a standing ovation replete with loud whistles and cheers. After the room quieted, he said, "It had not been my desire to seek higher office after considering the impact on my personal life and on my family. But it has become increasingly evident that the political establishment in Washington is not able to bring to the American people the reality of the American situation in this forthcoming campaign. Most Americans feel the need for it, but it is the duty of political leaders to define it and to do it. In recent years, the leadership of the United States has not.

"Many Americans are concerned about paying their bills. They know that to participate fully in the future, their children must attend college. Many are concerned how to pay for that. The standard of living of many Americans has declined. Many worry that their children will face a reduced quality of life. There is abiding concern for our international position and the viability of our economy in the international economy. Many are concerned about the cost of health care and access to it. Many are concerned about intrusive government regulation of industry and commerce.

"Many are concerned about the permissiveness of our society and the decline of moral standards. Many are concerned about the lack of basic honesty of the society along with ever growing litigiousness. Many are concerned for their personal safety and about crime. Many are concerned about the deterioration of the infrastructure and declining energy supplies. Many are concerned about the reappearance of racism in the nation. All must be concerned about preserving world peace in this nuclear age.

"Something is wrong. The political leadership has not tackled the tough issues or even attempted to bring them into the public forum. These are issues that are hard to understand, and which cannot be explained in two minutes, much less in 20 seconds. It is incredible that after so many years after the Reagan deficits we still accumulated debt without any idea of how much we can stand. Many of you are aware that American families pay an average of $4,000 interest on that debt every year. Many are aware that the United States is a debtor nation.

"There are many Americans who are not sure they can provide health care to their families and to themselves. We have the finest health care in the world, but many Americans cannot access it. Many Americans are concerned about the legal system and the use of it for corrupt gains. Faith in the law has eroded. Faith in moral standards has eroded. Trust has eroded.

"Many Americans are concerned with other countries and whether we're protecting ourselves and others from outlaw nations and terrorists. We are concerned with the spread of nuclear weapons and the possession by some nations of chemical and biological weapons. We're concerned about the environment and the obvious effects of industrial civilization regarding global warming, ozone attrition, and acidification of the water supply and aggregate pollution of the air and water.

"These are all tough issues, and tough issues require tough action: money to be spent; taxes to be paid; budgets to be cut; laws to be changed; and armed service personnel to be put in harm's way.

"The campaign that I will mount will tell you about the tough issues and what I will do about them if elected. The theme is reality. What is real, what is true, what is happening, and what we need to do about it. I am not coming to ask: are you better off now than you were four years ago? I'm going to ask if the country is better off. I'm not going to say we are going to cut taxes. I'm going to say that taxes may need to be increased. I'm not going to say blandly: 'we'll keep the budget balanced.' We are going to pay down the debt.

"But I'm also going to tell you that we will not abandon a social safety net nor will we abandon the environment. We will be conscious of the critical role of education. We will define the reality that is besetting our people with uncertainty, and we will show how the energy of the American people can be reinvigorated to move this country forward to its greater destiny. I will be portrayed by my political opponents as a 'tax and spend' Democrat and will be vilified by conservatives. But with faith in God, in the American Constitution, and America as a nation, we will carry the message of reality.

"We will offer a choice: do you want meaningless sound bites and empty generalized promises and perceptions, or an understanding of what is really going on? We will call on the American people to deal with the tough issues. We will relate them to our history and to the history of others and decide what should be done. There will be discussion and debate, let the truth be found and the best action and policy be the result. This is my promise for the campaign. I have faith in the ultimate judgment of the American people when a majority of them know the truth. This campaign will win. Thank you."

There was strong applause and hands shot up. Adrian didn't know the press corps. The first question was representative. "What is your position on abortion?"

"I think on a scale of importance of one to ten, the issue of abortion is about a minus three. I am not going to discuss it or debate it. I'm going to simply say, as I have already have said, whether or not to have an abortion is an issue between a woman, her family, and her God. Government should not get between people and God on this matter or any other and I'm certainly not going to." He pointed to the most intelligent face he could see.

"What do you mean by paying down the debt?"

"I mean that we will start paying off the obligations of the United States."

"How are you going to do it?"

"Watch me. I'm a businessman and I know how to reduce costs. I also know how to raise revenues and I can read a balance sheet. My administration will redefine the mission of every department of government and staff those departments according to their mission. We will determine goals by undertaking a process little known in government, but which guides the very essence of successful business. It's called planning. This is not the place to get into the details. There will be a speech about planning." He pointed to a well-dressed woman.

"You have said in a speech in New Hampshire that you believe the United States is the world's policeman."

"Tell me, who is the world's policeman if it's not the United States? Do you want to live in a world that doesn't have one? Most politicians say by knee-jerk that the United States should not be the world's policeman. Ladies and gentlemen, if we are not the world's policeman there isn't going to be one. Somebody with the power to take responsibility has to take it. Peace is achieved by someone exerting power to prevent lawlessness. That is reality. The United Nations should be the focus of this action. That institution should be reformed and equipped for the task.

"In Bosnia we allowed a repeat of ethnic cleansing, the chief atrocity of Nazi Germany. We allowed it to happen because we delayed supporting the European nations with our power. Intervention was called for at an early stage when Slabodan Milosovec's intentions were clearly recognized. We should have stopped the hate mongering before the process got started and let the world know that civilization would not tolerate it. We didn't learn from history. The first time the lesson was wrought upon Europe by a gang of thugs who were the essence of evil. 'When good men do nothing, evil has its day,' and that is the reality." He pointed.

"Does that mean the United States is going to intervene in every possible conflict?"

"It means that the United States has to demonstrate that it has the resolve to do so wherever and whenever necessary and render full support to the United Nations and NATO and any other commitments. If outlaw leaders like those in Serbia think we do not have the resolve, they will seek their own evil ends. If we do not have the resolve, how can we expect European countries to be involved? As the major economic and military power, we are critical to enforcement and support of the United Nations." He pointed to a reporter he thought he recognized.

"You have remarked that you feel additional regulation of the financial markets is needed."

"Sales of stocks and bonds to the public are regulated by securities laws which require complete exposure of all aspects of the business of the company whose securities or obligations are being sold. There are now other instruments of investment which are more like gambling games. In certain segments of the commodities and foreign markets manipulation may be going on and speculative ebbs and flows may not be of benefit broadly. An investigation and possibly regulations or legislative proposals will be forthcoming from my administration."

A chill came over Anne Russell as she watched the news being made. Within the next 24 hours everyone in the United States who read a newspaper or watched television news or listened to the radio, would have heard his name, know some of his positions, and associate him with the reality theme. Would the term 'reality' inspire or frighten them?

The hard grind of campaigning began the morning after the announcement, at the factory gate of the Borg Warner plant near Chicago.

"Good going, Governor."

"We need another President from Illinois."

"We need a man from the Midwest."

They touched his shoulder. One clapped him on the back and shouted, "Run those bums off."

The first results of Alan Jacob's polls came in 56% favorable, 32% unfavorable, and only 12% undecided.

Lunch was at the St. Charles Rotary Club. There were cheers and applause when he came into the room with Pamela. The scheduled speaker had gracefully yielded. He was introduced again as the next President from Illinois to do what Abraham Lincoln had done, preserve the Union. Daggett had scared some, angered some, and won many. The media and cameras followed him. In the afternoon, he toured a small metal recycling company in North Chicago greeting people and discussing their technology.

In the evening he was at a Torch Club meeting where he made a brief statement and took questions. The next morning, he and Pamela were in Cedar Rapids at the gate of the Collins Radio Company division of North American Rockwell. They toured Quaker Oats and Adrian spoke at a Lions Club luncheon. In Des Moines in the afternoon they toured the hospital and then worked a mall. He took questions at a Kiwanis dinner.

The next morning they were at the Nashua Corporation in New Hampshire. Everyone felt the momentum. In Washington, Alan Jacobs answered inquiries from more potential endorsers. They made their separate announcements to show the building of Daggett's "bandwagon" which was beginning to roll.

☆ **Chapter 9** ☆

DAGGETT HAD NOT only lifted off his campaign with the American people, but he also sparked the attention of the POLACO staff.

Michelle Proust's weekly reports on Daggett became daily and they were more than bulletins. They included discussion of Daggett's stands on the issues, which were much more readily available than the other candidates' positions, thanks to his extraordinary forthrightness and Anne Russell's media impact. Helene and Erla conferred in an informal meeting on his announcement in the conference room of Erla's doctrine and intelligence group.

"Daggett is off to a fast start," Louis Fischer reported. "He worked Chicago the day before yesterday, Iowa yesterday, and is in New Hampshire today. He's scheduled to be back in Chicago tomorrow. There will be a big fundraiser there next week."

"Where is the money coming from?" asked Helene. "Is he capable of doing this himself?"

"I doubt it, but it looks well organized and very well financed," said Erla.

"He has called in some chits," Helene speculated.

"Could be," Erla said. "Louis, what's your assessment?"

"It looks like a well-organized campaign and something of an unusual one," Louis said. "He is taking on the political establishment with some unusual issues positions. He is telling people what he thinks and not necessarily what they want to hear."

"What do you think Daggett is?" Helene asked Marsha.

"Sounds like a Boy Scout."

"Michelle?"

"Seems to be a well-managed campaign. I printed out a summary of the positions so far." She handed everybody a five-paged stapled spread.

"Do you know him, Marsha?" Helene asked.

"I met him several times when he was governor of Illinois and once when he was down in Washington testifying. He's a strong powerful guy, but a Boy Scout. How could anyone expect to get elected when he's telling everyone not only there will be no tax cuts, but they may have to pay more?"

"Has he said that?" Helene asked.

"Up in New Hampshire, he spoke of the bitter medicine we all had to take."

"What was the response?"

"They liked it all right, but that stuff doesn't stick to the ribs. Eventually it causes nausea."

"What will we do to get a volunteer into a campaign in Chicago?" Helene asked. Louis' operation included half-dozen bright, experienced women on his payroll who lived in the Washington area. Their job was to volunteer for political campaigns and then report on what they could learn.

"We could send a professional. They'll be hiring as fast as they can. This could be a higher level if we sent a good one."

"Everyone we have is good, Edgar," Helene said. But, she knew what he meant and she thought of Michelle. The girl was smart and more than good looking with brown curly hair, a classic face, and a sexy figure. She would tend to be accepted if the hiring authority was made.

Michelle had been dating and seemed serious with Bill Haber, another analyst. Both came with good references from member companies. "Let's give that some thought," she said.

The next morning Helene called Slaughter and asked if she could come and see him. Ward had finally told Slaughter that he would be reporting to her. His face had been absolutely blank when he heard it. Where their relationship would go from here was up to her. Seated, relaxed in his office with coffee she said, "Ward really felt he couldn't give you the time you deserved. Few in our position like to deal with security, but the issues are very important. And all of the ones you have raised have to be addressed."

Edgar nodded, poker-faced and focused. His military culture would always call it a demotion.

"First," she said, "I want to ask if you really believe that you have enough people with only two effective infantry squads with a third in reserve? Do we need to recruit one more squad of men and women who would like to go through the military training and serve as a second in reserve? That way you'd have two for guard duty and two that you could fully deploy if there was a real disturbance."

"I think a second reserve squad might be desirable," he answered quietly. "You never know what exactly is going to happen."

"I know, and I respect your ability to deal with it," she said. "Why don't we both make up a list of people who might be able to be part of that second reserve squad. Put my name down first."

"You?"

"Yes, Edgar, I want to go through the training. I want to learn how to shoot a gun and do hand-to-hand combat. I think I can do well at it, and it is something that a good many people here should know. It's also good exercise."

At that he cracked a smile. "That it will be," he said, "Shall we put down Michelle Proust's name for the training? That was the person you were thinking of to be a mole in Daggett's campaign, wasn't it?"

"I hope I wasn't that obvious."

Slaughter looked at her. "You strike me as the kind of person who is obvious when she wants to be," he said. "And I am sure Michelle got the message too."

"Do you think she'll do?"

"We'll find out in the training," replied Edgar.

"I know that you are going to do some outside intelligence activity and that the first assignment was to insert a mole in PENMET," Helene said. "Keep me informed about requests for the outside work. I'd like to know and have some input, particularly if you are questioning anything."

"The external stuff is risky."

"The 'volunteers' you or Louis have to insert into campaigns are fine with me because everyone does it. I think you are going to do it better than everyone else. No need to talk with me about that unless there is a question of funds. On the bugs, I know that you have permission from Ward to listen in on conversations in the complex.

"My concern about that is to keep everyone's confidence. Once someone hears a rumor that could have resulted only from a bug, we are going to blow the whole system. The difficulty will be recruiting people who can keep confidences," said Helene.

"I think I can do that. They will be professionals from the mainland."

"I know, but we would have to have too many of them, and that in itself would spark concern. The senior people know that the guestrooms are bugged. I don't want them thinking they are also being subjected to eavesdropping. There's a morale issue here."

"But there is also a security issue. We have to know when someone is wavering and I'm not sure that it's not going to happen," said Edgar.

"Neither am I. Here's what I propose. I'll determine if any people might be disenchanted in any way. I will tell the senior people to report to me and also to you, anyone in their organizations who they think might be considering betraying us. I will have to make the decision about senior people, but you're authorized to proceed with any others. I would like you to share that with me and we should discuss any people if you have doubts or questions. How does that sound?"

"Like a reasonable compromise. You're right that any knowledge of the bugging, should it become known, could be counterproductive," Edgar agreed.

"I have notes about your discussion with Ward about punishment and interrogation. I know he got upset," Helene said. "However, I understand the problem. Organize what you think we need, then we'll review it. You are right that you have to be able to keep someone quiet on the island who has a loose tongue. You're also right that this could be done without taking a great risk. We'll assess the risk in each circumstance. Also, I want you to put me through the interrogation process so I can best understand it."

"You mean you would subject yourself to this?"

"Have you gone through it?"

"Yes," he answered.

"I don't see any other way that I could make the judgment. I know that is not going to be fun. I think a good policy might be that only people who have been through the maximum punishment and interrogation can order it."

"But it means you would..."

"It means that I would have to take off my clothes?" Helene interrupted. "Yes, I know that would be necessary."

Slaughter blinked at her. "There's more to it than that," he said. Helene kept her gaze steady and nodded.

Soon they had 14 volunteers for the reserve company, including six hotel, kitchen, and janitorial people to whom they offered extra pay. Marsha's assistant Ruth Farrencolt was among the other staffers who joined. Helene wondered if she wanted some time away from Marsha.

THE NEXT WEEK with the Broncos Edgar kept at the airport on the main island and all of the other vehicles available for rent, they convoyed down the outer shore. After they set up their bivouac, they did some conditioning exercise including a mile run in the sand. In the afternoon they were given their weapons. Edgar believed in the Army's standard sniper riffle for target practice, and had the latest Berrettas as a regular weapon.

Helene had not handled a gun before and followed the instructions Edgar and one of his detectives gave in loading and holding for fire. There were a series of targets set up in front of a large sand dune. On signal, they blasted away, then checked their score. This went on; standing, kneeling, and prone, until Helene's shoulder felt like it couldn't take another recoil. After that they practiced with shields and batons which were to be their riot weapons with the Berrettas in reserve. They also had water canons. Keying off Helene's idea, Edgar had them all line up and he fired it at them. They experienced the force and the wet clothes. As the sun went down they ate their combat rations, and collapsed into delightful sleep.

The next day Edgar put them through the obstacle course and was surprised how well Helene handled it. She scrambled over the barriers and did the ladder walk as fast as the young men. She could strip, clean, and reassemble her rifle while the others were still fumbling. At target practice that day, he told her to watch Michelle's eyes when she fired the gun. He said if she closed them not to send her on the mission to Chicago. She didn't. Helene also kept her eyes open and started to hit the bulls-eye with both weapons.

In midafternoon they started the hand-to-hand combat with riot weapons. After dark, they bathed in the ocean. Helene luxuriated in the sense of the water on her skin after the sweaty exercise. She went to sleep under the stars, thinking of how she would tell Tony about this adventure. The next day they did the obstacle course again and started karate and jujitsu training. First, Edgar paired the women with each other, and then with men. Helene's partner was an African-American detective, who did some of the listening in Dunmore. He was afraid to touch her until she decked him and put her hands on his throat. After that they had fun trying to throw each other around.

WHEN HELENE CAME in for her weekly briefing with Ward he greeted her with "So you were out on bivouac?"

"Military training is nothing unusual. All the Israeli girls do it."

"Well, I think it's smart to take the time. You need to know about it and you are winning him over. What did you do about the punishments and the interrogations?"

"We have a plan of how to handle that. It will take a little while."

"What's your plan?"

She told him.

"What. You mean you would do it?"

"Yes that's what I mean. I have to understand it to understand him. Once I've done it, he will accept my decision."

"Well, I leave that to you. You're becoming a really good manager, Helene."

"I'm not sure I like managing."

"It's hard to imagine anyone doing it better. I sense this organization is very productive."

"I'm reasonably pleased. Our recruiting has been good. It's recruiting, recruiting, recruiting."

"In business it's managing, managing, managing."

"Time for your questions," she said.

"What's happening on the Republican side?"

"Senator Hatford is the obvious front runner, the rest are about even."

"Stephen Hatford is able to take positions on every issue that will satisfy everyone?"

"Not really. It just sounds that way when you hear him. When you read his stuff, he's running against Washington. He is able to do that since he was reelected last year."

"The Democrats?"

"Daggett has jumped ahead. Senator Porter is second. Governor Perona is third. Daggett seems to be very well organized and very well financed. He's running against everything. He seems to be pro-business in many respects, but has more than hinted at market regulation where markets aren't needed for investment."

"Derivatives?"

"He wasn't specific, but promised a speech on the subject. We'll see. Jeremy Reubin is the political consultant. Evans & Copeland are doing the publicity."

"He must be well financed," Ward said as it occurred to him that Ian MacAulliffe could afford to back Daggett.

"How is Rollin doing?" he asked.

"The testing didn't go well. Most of the candidates running for office are not the quality we're looking for.

"What is Rollin doing about it?"

"We're looking deeper and I'll get an exact count of how many people he considers potentials from this test."

"Too bad we didn't find Daggett. Okay, we'll test out the intelligence unit with him. See how much we can find out by next Tuesday. What about campaign moles?"

"We're going ahead with Hatford, Price, and Nable on the Republican side and Porter and Perona. They are all in Washington. Daggett's campaign headquarters is going to be in Chicago. We've submitted Michelle Proust's resume, the tall, pretty, dark-haired girl."

"Are you sure about her?"

"We suggested the military training to her. She keeps her eyes open when she fires a rifle."

"Who told you about that?"

"Slaughter."

"It used to be a man's world. Now you're learning all the tricks. The PENMET mole?"

"Nothing significant to help with your paranoia."

"I hope that is what it is. You want to tell me about your relationship with Tony Destito?"

"We've started an affair. I know of no rules against it."

"I don't make rules against nature. If we're successful we will get rid of the sexual harassment legislation or at least mitigate it."

"I prefer mitigating."

"Then I assume this relationship is a conduit of information from Tony?"

"I'd rather it not be. Remember we haven't proved the paranoia."

"I have to be able to rely on you, Helene."

"You can."

LIZ DALEY A.K.A. "Cynthia Reese," had done her PENMET assignments for the past ten weeks, earning her double salary, but she had little to report. She was on her way to meet Melius at the Strasburg Inn near the main railhead of the Strasburg Railroad. She knew Melius respected her judgment, but there was still not much to go on. It began to look like the answer was negative. She knew his questions would help her to recall material events and set new perspectives for things to look for. She also knew that she had to be reinforced; PENMET was drawing her in. She liked working there and she particularly liked working for Nancy. She needed to be reminded that she was on a second mission.

Melius had taken a suite. When she arrived, he led her into the pine-paneled sitting room. Grilled salmon for dinner was warming in the chaffing oven under the table on which small Caesar salads and a loaf of fresh bread were spread, with a bottle of Chardonnay.

"I gather you like your job."

"I'm glad I do. It's challenging, but it's fun."

"Do you report directly to Nancy?"

"The organization is very informal and assignments can come from anywhere. Administratively I report to Reeves Fullka, Director of Publications. He's very good.

"Who do you normally associate with," he asked, "like going to lunch?"

"We don't go to lunch. We can order from the staff kitchen so we don't have to go out. A lot of times we meet at lunch in our conference room. It's part of the culture. The company is profitable and generous, probably profitable because it is generous. But, it's not generous with staffing. We all have a lot to do and the assignments keep piling up. There's always something to think about."

"Is there any conversation of any kind about PENMET's joining POLACO?"

"Not a whisper."

"Tony Destito is probably handling POLACO," he said. "Have you met him?"

"The first couple of days. He and Nancy see each other at least once a day."

"Destito went to Harbour Island. He is involved in POLACO on behalf of PENMET. He might be a lead person to watch. Why would Destito be seeing Nancy? Is this a flirtation or is it business?"

"He seems to like her; I think she likes him," she said. "He's in charge of corporate development. There are rumors of a big new product coming out. I think Nancy's department would be invovled in a big introduction.

"So it could be related to the prospective introduction of something new."

"I believe it's something big," she said. "So far just rumors, but its often enough I believe there has to be some validity."

"Who would know about POLACO? Obviously MacAulliffe and Destito. They certainly would have brought Nancy into it, would they not?"

"They respect her judgment. I met Ian MacAulliffe when he came to see Nancy."

"What's he like?"

"He's a very people-oriented type of guy and he thinks way ahead. They tell me that when you have a meeting with him, there is always food offered."

"That doesn't sound Scottish."

"I understand he's very generous."

"People who have been as successful as he usually are."

Liz sipped her wine and gazed at him.

"What are you looking for?" she asked.

"As I told you, we need to find any kind of resistance or some kind of counter-measure in the direction of POLACO that MacAulliffe might be undertaking," Melius said. "Ward doesn't trust him and doesn't feel he's committed to POLACO."

"Forty-five million is an investment that any company considers carefully."

"True, and we assume that it has been considered carefully by these people. Of those who know about POLACO there are three residents at the headquarters, MacAulliffe, Destito, and Letersky. They are the only leads we have, so we have to watch them. Let's get back to Letersky and Destito, you think there is an affair?"

"Could be. I wouldn't rule it out. She's single. He's married to a beautiful woman who's on the Pennsylvania State Democratic Committee. She's from a Boston Brahmin family. The people in the office who know her don't give me a lot of positive vibrations about her. She's very powerful; maybe nothing more than jealousy."

"Back to the patterns. I think you have to keep a record on how often Tony visits, and how often they travel together or have lunch together and so forth; everything that Tony and Nancy do together. Then we have to examine Nancy. I think you have to keep a record of her travel."

"I've been doing that. I have some notes that can tell me when she's been traveling with Tony," she said opening her portfolio. "I think they have been away together three times since I've been there."

"Now the question is: what would they be doing?"

"I thought I was just supposed to listen and not detect."

"I think we are going to have to do some detecting."

☆ **Chapter 10** ☆

IN THE LOG on Nancy and Tony Destito, Liz Daley, A.K.A. "Cynthia Reese," found a pattern and she admonished herself for not recognizing it earlier. Several days per week, Nancy seemed to leave at lunch and come back as late as 6 p.m.. Considering the focus on the department from the whole company, it was strange that Nancy was gone so many times when she was not traveling. Melius spotted it.

Melius speculated it might be important to know where Nancy was going, and suggested that Liz find out if she was at her apartment complex. During several days when Nancy was away, Liz went to the condominiums and couldn't find her car anywhere. There were garages. She called Nancy's telephone number and got only her private voice mail. Senior people do not often answer the phone. She wouldn't herself if she were having an affair. Within the pattern, sometimes there were three straight days when she was away after lunch. Melius wondered, if it were an affair, how hungry she was. Liz pointed out Nancy was single. She knew what that meant since she was aching for sex herself.

She often thought about the $6000 a month in cash going into her accounts. If this were the dry hole she thought it was, soon she would be headed back. She might decide to stay at PENMET provided she could disassociate from Melius. Her real objective was to become a writer. She had a lot to write about. Right now, she needed capital. Not bad at investing; she bought $2,000 worth of airline stock in 1993, and sold it for a $30,000 profit. That money started her investment account which had appreciated almost 50% since.

Money was independence.

Another pattern emerged. Tony and Nancy took a trip together every two weeks, on Wednesday, returning after work on Friday. On one Friday after such a trip, Nancy came back from an absence and after dropping her briefcase, left in the direction of Tony's office. Getting up to go to the ladies room, Liz looked in Nancy's office and saw that three briefcases were there and the door was unlocked. She went to the ladies room, then to the water fountain and walked toward Tony's office where she heard voices including Ian's and Nancy's. She went back to her office and wrote a hand written question for Tony and moved to drop it on Joan's desk so she could hear the conversations. She couldn't make out the specific words, but she sensed they were intense.

She had an opportunity to take a quick look at the brief cases. She wrote a note to Nancy to attach to some materials she might be interested in to give her a reason to be in her office. In the briefcase that Nancy took on the day missions she found files of notes and drafts of literature, ads, speeches and releases relating to the Daggett campaign along with memos on which Nancy was copied. Her whole time in Nancy's office was about 20 seconds. She went back to her own office with her heart pounding to make notes. She was still there when Nancy came back into the area and waved to her. She saw Nancy leave with the Daggett briefcase.

At her apartment, she dialed a number in New York, let it ring three times, then hung up. A few minutes later the phone rang. She told Melius what she had found. Melius knew that Nancy was a Democrat and active in volunteer work. He also knew that they had no proof of anything. He called Edgar Slaughter who reported the finding to Helene and Ward. The answer came back that they should look further.

Melius sent two operatives to tail Nancy. On the very first try, they tracked her to the Scottish Village where she parked by the village offices. The next day they observed the same. Two days later, Melius, with a false identity, rented a car at the Harrisburg airport and drove to the Holiday Inn in Lancaster. In operations, it was important not to stay at the same place twice. Melius usually worked his way down from the Ritz Carlton if one was available.

The following day he walked around the village and had lunch at the Scottish Pub. In the shops he purchased a plaid sweater and a Scottish cap plus a sweater for his girlfriend. The offices were in the building where Nancy's car was parked; he took some casual pictures and then returned that evening for dinner at the restaurant. He brought an *USA Today* to read, and watched what was going on in the restaurant and along the street. He looked for signs for security. There wasn't a uniform or plain clothes in sight at anytime. At night there were no boulevard lights as there would be none in Scotland. The night lighting was quaintly 19th Century electric.

The next day he returned and strolled some more, particularly around the office building looking at the locks. A few more casual pictures were taken in the role of a tourist. He telephoned Liz and told her he'd be back and drove his rental car to New York, planning how to find out what was in that office. He phoned Janos who had an established cover as a construction and road equipment salesman in the Northeast.

ON THURSDAY, ACCOMPANIED by a freelance operative, sometimes-actress, Doris Hill, Janos claimed a reservation at the Inn in the afternoon. Janos and Doris were posing as a couple taking a long weekend wandering around Pennsylvania. They strolled and shopped, had dinner at the restaurant; went to the pub and returned to their room where they slept on opposite sides of a king-size bed wearing pajamas. The next day Janos strolled into the Scottish Village office and asked to see the general manager. The reception room was on the ground floor. A wide staircase led up to the main rooms.

"Mrs. MacAulliffe doesn't see visitors without an appointment. Do you have an appointment with her?"

"I'm sorry I don't. My wife and I were visiting the village. We're taking a long weekend. I wanted to see if we might do business. I sell all types of road and off-road equipment, snow plows, spreaders, cranes, tractors, and also warehouse equipment like forklifts."

"I hope you've enjoyed your stay," said the receptionist enthusiastically. "Let me see if there is someone who can speak with you."

"I'd appreciate it. I'd be happy to wait."

She got on the phone and spoke with Mrs. MacAulliffe's secretary. He stepped around the perimeter of the room to look at paintings of the village pretending not to listen. The receptionist was pleading his case. "Someone will be down in a minute."

"Thank you very much. Are you very busy here?"

"Oh yes, there are lots of people coming and going. I have to make sure no one goes upstairs unescorted."

"Well I can understand that. Are all of the offices here?"

"No, the transportation offices are in the garage. I expect you'll go there."

That was not good news. "Who has offices here?"

"Mrs. MacAulliffe, the sales and catering people, the accountants and there is a project going on, people from the company are working on it."

"What do you mean – from the company?"

"The MacAulliffe's own PENMET, or at least a lot of it."

"They do?"

"That's how they could afford to build the village. Isn't it super? I love working here."

"It's a really great place. How'd they do it?"

"Mr. MacAulliffe is a Scot. He loves Scotland, but doesn't have the time to go there as much as he likes so he built this. He brought in chefs and imported Scottish food. He wanted to share it and promote Scotland. It's been very successful."

"What's the project?" Janos asked trying to keep up the good mood.

"We're not supposed to talk about it."

The same closed door that Liz had found. Footsteps on the stairs made him turn. Approaching him, was a slender auburn-haired woman, elegant in gray-brown jeans and a paisley Gucci blouse.

"I'm Susan MacAulliffe," she said extending her hand. "I'm sorry, I have some guests, but I appreciate your stopping by. You need to see Gus Carlsen, but he's not here right now. Can we call you when he returns? His office is at the garage. Would you like to wait here for him? I don't want to trouble you."

"It's very nice of you. I'll wait. I'm fascinated by your village."

"Thank you, I wish we could talk, but I'm going to be tied up for the day."

"It was nice of you to come out of your meeting. I didn't have an appointment."

"Perhaps the next time you come," she suggested.

The MacAulliffes were good enough hotelkeepers to return the compliment to customers wanting a hearing. Janos selected a chair by the window. He could see no wiring for an intrusion alarm. There was no visible camera and he couldn't see any sensors. There was nothing like bar code or magnetic card restrictions. When the receptionist left for a bathroom break, he used a pocket camera to photograph the lock. Reading a magazine, he chatted occasionally with the receptionist to see if he could learn something by just sitting. He also thought about seeing Liz.

Through the window he saw a Chrysler convertible draw up. A minute later a woman carrying a briefcase came in and went to the stairs, "Hi, Nancy, early today?" said the receptionist.

"Hi, Chris. Yes, much to do. I'm here for lunch. Are the artists here?"

"There's a bunch of them up there," Chris commented as Nancy disappeared up the stairs.

"That's one of the company people. She's a vice president."

"Your company has good-looking officers."

"Don't be sexist," Chris responded, smiling.

He was getting a small relationship going.

"I wonder if Susan called Gus on his mobile?" said Chris as she dialed the phone. "I guess he's off-line."

The next visitors were a young Mexican couple, a slender, olive-skinned girl and a burly darker man. "Buenos Dias, Senorita," the man said as he entered.

"Good morning," the girl said pushing her hand against his face and smiling.

"Buenos Dias," smiled Chris. "You didn't come last night?"

"We helped with a party." They went to the stairs. "We're setting up the lunch. We'll clean after that."

"They work for the MacAulliffes. He's the valet and she's the maid. They're here from Mexico, to learn English. The MacAulliffes have a home in Mexico. They clean the offices and they serve meals here when there are guests."

When Janos could, he took a paper from his jacket and wrote notes in Hungarian, to be sure he didn't miss a detail.

When Gus Carlsen showed up, Janos was directed to the garage and got a look at the equipment. There were two fire trucks with ladders to reach the highest building, two snowplows, a big snow blower, and two large trucks, which did the regular plowing, and the sanding and salting. Surprisingly, he saw two fully-equipped police cars. In the course of his 'sales pitch,' he asked about burglar alarms and learned that they were satisfied with what they had. Going out the door of the office, he couldn't see any wiring, and he assumed there weren't any alarms. He couldn't find any cameras either.

Eager to see Liz, Janos sent Doris back to New York by train so he could stay for the weekend. He cautioned himself because of the risk he had taken sitting in the village office. Chris and Gus Carlsen could now identify him, as well as Susan MacAulliffe. Risks were part of industrial espionage, but were harmless, as crimes were not usually involved. The stress in his groin won out. He dialed PEN-MET from a pay phone.

"You shouldn't call here," Liz whispered.

"Let's have a nice weekend."

"Where? You can't come to my place."

"Name a resort with a good dining room, suites, an indoor pool, and a workout room."

"Paul stayed at The Strasbourg Inn. It looked all right. I think it's got everything." She envisioned being naked with Janos and making passionate love in the paneled rooms.

"If you don't hear from me again, I'll be there. When can you get there?"

"By 6:30. What name?"

"Frozzi. See you, lover." After he hung up, he realized that could be another mistake.

The best suite was $350 for two nights with breakfasts. Paying in cash, he picked up a bottle of Stolichnaya and some orange juice for Liz's favorite cocktail. She called on the house phone ten minutes early. When he opened the door he was wearing the hotel robe. She stepped in, dropped her suitcase and kissed him as she pulled off his robe. She led him to the bedroom where she threw off her clothes and stood before him. He stepped to her and ran his hands over her skin. She grabbed him and swung him onto the bed. Two hours later room service brought salad, lamb chops, and a bottle of Beaujolais. They spent the weekend in bed except for room service in the mornings, long swims before lunch at the pool, and a Saturday evening pot roast at the Plain & Fancy restaurant nearby.

MONDAY IN NEW York, Janos waited while Melius reported to Edgar through an attorney's office. Now they knew that something was going on in the village offices and that Nancy Letersky was definitely involved. Whether it had anything to do with the Daggett campaign was conjecture and what that meant to POLACO was indecipherable. Melius told Edgar that getting anything further would require the risk of breaking into the offices, unless they could wait for a mole to be inserted. Twenty minutes later, Edgar authorized the risks. This wouldn't be boring, but Melius didn't like it because he was the one taking the big risk. At this point, his fees tripled.

They went over their notes thoroughly. There was no sign of alarms. The two police cars had to be considered. There were no cameras or any visible surveillance. Janos and Melius both checked that. They had maps and photos of the buildings and the lock they would have to pick. They would make keys. With luck there would be no sign of forced entry, and they would use cameras on the documents. Early Thursday morning was chosen as the date. Melius wanted to move quickly once he knew the target because it could disappear.

Janos would be the leader of the entry team with Doris. Another freelancer, Amos Bryce would drive a rented van. They recruited a locksmith. Melius had the personal communication gear used by the secret service. Each would be able to talk with the others. Their weapons would be nightsticks, brass knuckles, knives, and 38's. They would be masked for the entry. Amos and Doris would be paid $5,000 in cash doubled for success and the locksmith, $2,500.

On Wednesday at noon, they left New York. Doris had the van and Janos a rented Bonneville. The locksmith with his truck went via I-78. The others took the New Jersey Turnpike to the Pennsylvania Turnpike and rendezvoused near the village. Amos took the car and went to the village as a tourist. He parked near the office so that he would have to pass the door to get to the car from the restaurant and pub. Walking and shopping until the stores closed, he went to the pub for supper, taking a newspaper to read. A pleasant smiling waitress served him a salad and Scotch pie. He kept looking for security and had in mind to ask someone. Janos had not done that and in his experience a place like this could not be without something. Maybe the MacAulliffes were so rich they didn't care, but their insurance company would. Maybe the location lulled their security people to inattention.

In gathering darkness, he strolled to the car looking around for anyone watching him. At the door of the office, in a 10 or 12 second pause, he fitted three blanks in the lock. He looked again. There was no one.

While Amos enjoyed a good supper, the others located suitable hiding places as a staging area should something go wrong. They left the Bonneville in one of them. Sandwiches, fruit, and snack food carried from a deli in New York was their dinner.

The prospective keys, as carefully done as possible, were ready in an hour and the locksmith sped away for home in New Jersey. While they waited for the pub to close they went over the plan and the signals. There would be someone at the Inn desk all night. They assumed that person to be the only security who would call the police if anything happened. The activity would die down when the last guests returned from their evening.

Amos took one spin in the car to look things over at 11:30. Two cars were still at the pub. At 12:30 they were gone. At 1:15 the van rolled into the village lot. They tucked it around a corner from the office entrance. They waited a full ten minutes. Janos and Doris now in black pants and sweaters with black sneakers, jumped out the back of the van, and ran low along the wall and around the corner to the door. The first key didn't work after a minute of trying. They went to the second; another minute. They were calm. The third would theoretically open the door. They turned the lock when one of the village police cars skidded around the other corner shining lights right at them. The loud speaker blared the command "Hold it right there!"

Janos breathed the emergency signal into the microphone and drew his gun. He yelled, "The right front!" He and Doris stood in place, and fired at the police car tire and then lunged to the side and pumped shots across the top of the windshield. Amos careened the van around the opposite corner and screeched to a stop as Janos and Doris leaped into it. By the time the security people had their doors open and their guns out of their holsters, the van was red lights turning onto the road.

Making sure they weren't followed, they headed for the Bonneville in a copse of trees near an Amish farm. Janos and Doris stripped off their black clothes as they went. They threw the weapons, cameras, and radio gear into the car. Making sure there were no fingerprints they left everything else in the van. After listening for traffic they wheeled out onto the highway and scooted a mile to their second hideaway. They took the guns and after wiping them thoroughly, threw them into a swamp they had located on the way. They ate more of the snacks and sandwiches, then they slept.

The next morning they were a car-sharing group in the rush-hour traffic across the Susquehanna and through the southern part of Harrisburg. On the radio, they heard the report of the attempted break-in and the shooting at the village police car. Village security personnel, a man and woman in the car, were cut by spalling glass.

On the bridge over the historic river, they looked back at the

PENMET headquarters building.

TONY COULDN'T BELIEVE the telephone call from Alvin just after 2:30 in the morning. Jean answered it sleepily and handed the phone across the bed. 30 minutes later, at the hospital, Alvin told him what had happened.

"How are our people?"

"They are both still in surgery. The girl took a bullet in the left shoulder when she was trying to draw her gun. They were both cut by spalling glass and lost a lot of blood. I am told they are in no danger."

"I'm glad of that. Were these people trying to shoot them?"

"I don't think so. They first shot out the right front tire and then fired across the top of the windshield. They could have intentionally hit Roxanne if they saw her gun, but they were not shooting to kill."

Tony considered this briefly.

"Can we catch them?"

"There was a third perpetrator in the van which picked them up. Roxanne scrambled the state and local police. Lance was blinded from his facial cuts. In the time it took the police to react they could have gone several miles in any direction."

"What were they doing?"

"Apparently they had keys to the village office and were getting ready to go in."

Tony's eyes narrowed.

"That's where Nancy and Susan are working."

"I know," said Alvin. "It's the only reason I can think of for a professional job on the village office in March."

"What do you mean 'a professional job?'"

"The police tell me they obviously cased and photographed the lock and used blanks on the lock from which a locksmith made keys. Same as if you locked your keys in your car."

"POLACO?"

"Could be."

"Why would they try it?"

"If it is POLACO, they think we are involved in the Daggett campaign and they are looking for proof."

"How would they find out?"

"Through a mole."

"In the campaign?"

"It could be the campaign, it could be Cleveland," Alvin said, "or it could be here in Harrisburg."

"Couldn't it just be a leak?"

"That's possible if somebody is going through the garbage in Chicago."

"Could you tighten that up?"

"I certainly will," Alvin responded.

"We'll have to be careful. We cannot reveal the significance of this. Does this have to get in the newspapers?"

"I don't think we can hold this back, Tony. There are people here in the hospital that know about it. If these people are who we think they are, the police will find the van with their clothes in it and other paraphernalia. Right now they are in another car somewhere waiting for the morning rush hour and then they'll leave by blending into the crowd."

"Can't we stop them?"

"We'll try, but there are thousands of cars, Tony."

"Will they try this again?"

"I don't think so. Industrial operators don't like their people to trespass. Much less fire their guns."

BY 7 A.M. Ian and Susan were at the hospital. They visited Roxanne who was able to smile and shake hands. Lance's face was bandaged. His wife was awed by the MacAulliffe's. She didn't know of Ian's deep concern for all of his employees. When any worker was seriously injured or killed on the job anywhere, a corporate officer showed up. In the United States Ian and Susan would attend a wake and a funeral with as many as the Falcon would carry. Just after Alvin and Tony had breakfast together at the hospital, they received a message that the van had been found.

When he and Tony arrived, the police were already cataloging its contents. It was registered to a rental firm in New York City. The credit card used was in an established false name; the person didn't exist, but the bill still got paid. They found the black coveralls, hats, masks, and sneakers which reiterated that the perpetrators were professionals.

Tony and Stephanie were to meet that morning with Ian. He hurried home to change. Behind closed doors and with only the three present, they reviewed their relationship with POLACO. Ian wanted to be sure that they got all possible information, but also kept up the pretenses of interest. Since Stephanie knew of the POLACO relationship, Ian assigned her to make a visit to Harbour Island and assume some of the liaison duties, particularly those related to finance. Perhaps her visit would steer away any suspicions and keep up their good relations with POLACO.

SPRING AT HARBOUR Island brought all of the colors of subtropical flowers to the gardens in the POLACO compound. Fresh green leaves appeared on the deciduous trees; the palms took on new life sprouting branches and buds where the coconuts would grow. The pink sand, shiny after the winter rains, gleamed against the azure of the ocean. It was difficult to think of politics, economics, and government on the hotel verandah overlooking the Harbour Island beach in the warming sun.

A meeting at the conference center was underway to review the first phase of doctrine development. Since this was mainly discussion, they had the blinds up and the windows open, letting in bird song and ocean breeze for the inhabitants of the offices-in-the-caverns who appreciated it despite their imaginative muralized environment. For them, it was delicious to look out real windows and smell the freshness of the morning.

Marsha, Harold Smalley, and Louis were seated with Erla at the massive oak table facing Helene, Ward, Alex Petersen, Rollin, and Erwin on the other side of the table. Behind them was the staff. Edgar Slaughter was in the front row near Helene.

Erla Younge was discussing in a casual and confident manner. "Our work on doctrine development has focused on defining the new ideas of a political movement. Our angle is to mold concepts and beliefs that everyone can reasonably accept that will allow people to differ on individual issues, but still support our candidates. Doctrine gets confused with issues because of single-issue groups. To them their issue is doctrine. Doctrine is also confused with the generalizations politicians use to avoid issues. Adrian Daggett is taking on all of the issues under one doctrine of 'reality.'

"Doctrine is philosophy that can hold people together or tear them apart. It has to be defined. 'Family values' sounded well, but what were they? What is 'reality?' Doctrine is not developed by speechwriters. It requires the collective wisdom of people at all levels if it is to be successful."

Ward smiled pleasantly. Erla neatly explained the definition without appearing to do so. Alex either didn't get it or wanted to rattle her, "This sounds like a graduate seminar, Erla, not what I came to hear. What have you accomplished with all the money we have spent?"

It was a mistake to think he could unnerve Erla. "The problem with almost every losing political campaign, Alex, is the lack of a common justification for their generalizations."

"We have a practical mission here, not an academic one," said Alex.

"And, I'm trying to say that if we don't use our full capabilities to carry out our mission we will fail," rejoined Erla. "The greatest wisdom we have to offer is to develop a doctrine to support POLACO's goals."

"These are the overriding doctrinal points. The distinctions with issues can be vague. But these are some truths to support positions on issues. She passed out a paper summarizing the POLACO doctrine.

1. Economic development is required for all societal improvements including: education, environmental conservation, health care, and welfare. The expansion of these programs is not possible without economic growth. The cost of social programs cannot be higher than economic growth permits. Therefore, political policies must promote growth.

2. The most important element of growth is non-interference. Almost any type of interference is counterproductive. Taxes and other policies that reduce the propensity to invest or for entrepreneurs to take risks must be avoided.

3. Economic free enterprise is the most productive means to progress. Individuals and corporations must be free to use their money as they see fit and to raise funds for new enterprise.

4. Free enterprise is also the best means to progress in specific activities, particularly health care and education. Continued leadership in these areas depends on maintaining a strongly competitive environment. In higher education, the US leads the world because our colleges and universities are competitive.

5. Markets must be free. Markets are self-regulating. When a product is obsolete, the markets will reject it. The markets discipline the management of corporations. They determine if products are competitive and if management is viable. They also discipline

governance. If a nation is mismanaged, the market for that nation's securities and currency will speak.

6. The essential business of government is to assure freedom, to protect the social peace, assure the rule-of-law, protect the owner-ship of property and commerce, to provide the required infrastructure, and to conserve resources.

7. Enforcement of laws and the peace must be international in scope and promote the international cooperation of responsible governments. Resources must be conserved on an international scale.

8. American volunteerism is the best means of helping disadvantaged people or others in need. Government funds for welfare and education are best utilized at the local level with a minimum of bureaucracy.

"This still needs work, which is the reason for this meeting," Erla said, and discussion ensued. The discussions were interrupted by a secretary who informed Helene and Edgar that they were needed in the security offices to receive a phone call from a Mr. Melius.

At the security office, Edgar waved for her to close the door. "Paul, Helene Courtney is with me," he said. "I'll put you on the speaker."

"Good morning, Mr. Melius."

"Good morning, except we don't have good news."

Melius related the details of the failed mission.

Helene quickly overcame her initial shock.

"Good heavens, Edgar. Why did they shoot?"

"The security car had ordered them to stop. They used their guns as a surprise to get time to escape."

"Can this be traced, Paul?"

"No."

"What's the report on the injuries?"

"Treated and released."

"How'd your people miss the cameras?" Helene asked, avoiding any tone of accusation.

"I was there myself. There were no cameras in sight. They must have been in the trees around the periphery, probably guarding the mansion as well as the village. Infra red.'"

"They waited while your people waited," Edgar interjected.

"To make the grab in the act," Melius added.

"Bad luck, Paul. What else do we have to go on?"

"We know the Mexicans who work for the MacAulliffes also

clean the office. The only chance now is to buy in."

"Do you mean bribing?" asked Helene.

"Yes, it's more risky yet."

"Ward can make that decision."

They returned to the ideological meeting. When the discussion was over and the room emptied, Helene told Ward what had happened. He squinted at Edgar.

"Why didn't we accomplish this mission?" he asked. "We are supposed to have the best of everything, including people."

"It looks like a new, low-profile technology," said Helene. "They didn't spot the surveillance system."

"I thought this guy was the best," Ward snapped.

"He is, Ward. This is half-way a mistake. Half-way understandable."

"We finally get some information that makes us suspicious that MacAulliffe may be doing something," Ward said, "and we blow the climax."

"Neither you, Edgar, Melius, nor myself were on the scene," Helene said.

"What are the options?"

"The one I like," said Helene "is to forget about it and rely on the mole. We have a chance to get one into the campaign. We've associated Nancy and her office with Daggett. We'll get something eventually."

"Suppose we can't wait."

"Anything else involves more risks," cautioned Edgar.

"You reported the Daggett materials in Nancy's possession and the activities at this village office," Ward said. "We need to know what it means. Why would Nancy be involved with Daggett so intensely? And Daggett, coming out of the wilderness preaching the new word. Who brought him? Why does he change his mind to run after only two years? If someone wanted to preempt us, the one thing they could do would be to bring out someone like Daggett and try to elect him. Is MacAulliffe backing Daggett to preempt us?"

"If Daggett is competent, doesn't that meet one of our objectives?"

"We have very complex objectives, Helene, and it's doubtful that a Democratic President would meet very many of them," Ward said. "It already seems that Daggett favors market regulation."

Helene gazed up at the ceiling as she thought about Ward's last comment.

"We still need proof. I have to have proof before I can consider action," Ward continued.

"What's the next step?"

Edgar told Ward about the Mexican couple. "We can try to bribe them to let one of our agents substitute for the girl. If they don't agree then we can give them an alternative they can't refuse."

"I don't like it."

"It's you who wants the information, Ward," Helene said.

"There's another way you might get it, Helene."

"There is no hope for documents. I can try for what Tony will tell me, but that is a low chance. I'm planning on seeing him anyway."

"All right, try both ways – but be sure one works," Ward said. "There is something going on, I know it."

Helene frowned. She didn't like the assignment. She didn't like what her relationship with Tony was about to become.

Melius was also less than pleased with the turn his assignments had taken. He didn't like the idea of bribing or strong-arming. He thought of declining the assignment, but he felt he had already accepted it. Had he seen the cameras and detectors in the trees, there would have been no incident.

TWO WEEKS AFTER the shooting, dressed in black with a mask ready, Melius was crouched in the underbrush along the road between the mansion and the village, peeking through his own infra-red binoculars. He waited until he saw Francisco and Lucinda get into their car, and signaled.

The road in its mile route curved at one point downward over a bridge and then upward. At the low point the sight distance was out of range of the security cameras. Melius had them fully evaluated this time. When the car was committed, he signaled again on his radio. One of his men, driving a rented Mercedes, came from the opposite direction to the bridge. As the Rodriguez vehicle traversed the bridge, the Mercedes swerved to block them. Two others who had hidden under the bridge dragged the couple out, urging them in Spanish to make no sound. They gagged and tied them in a practiced way and pulled them into the Mercedes and then rolled toward the mansion to a turn-around. Melius drove the Rodriguez car out of the village.

The village police at their monitors in the transportation building saw only the Rodriguez car leaving and heading toward the town. The Mercedes excited no suspicion.

At a nearby rest area, a large trailer truck was parked, the driver apparently sleeping. The two cars drew behind it. Melius and his men pushed their captives into the trailer, and when the door closed, lights came on and the blindfolds came off. Francisco saw they were inside a long metal box with battery-powered lights, rusty metal folding chairs and a card table. Along the sides were several picnic coolers and boxes for food and drinks. There was a smell of kerosene from a heater. Francisco and Lucinda were shoved onto two of the chairs and held there. They saw five masked men and two women. One of the men asked if he could rely on Francisco to keep quiet. He nodded and the gag was pulled down.

One of the men spoke slowly, "Mr. Rodriguez, we apologize for the way you were brought here, but we want to make you an offer you cannot refuse. There is certain business we wish to do in the office of the village. We will remove nothing and nothing will be missing. There will be no investigation and no one will ever know anything about it. We only want access. For it, we will pay you $10,000 in cash. Let me show you the money. Have you ever seen $10,000 before? How much is that in new pesos? How would you like to send half as many pesos to your relatives in Mexico? We've arranged that. Let me show you four Bancomer money orders. We only need to write in the name and address."

Francisco looked at the money and the bank drafts, but was too frightened to answer. Melius and his operatives knew that they had him.

"Okay, Mr. Rodriguez, you don't have to answer. We'll tell you what you have to do. This lady," he said, indicating Doris whose hair had been dyed black, "will accompany you in Lucinda's clothes on your night's duties. You'll tell her what to do. She'll help you. You'll drive her to the office and then back here. She will make sure you do."

Doris lifted her sweater showing some skin and a 9mm automatic in her belt. She didn't show the camera.

"To be absolutely sure, we're going to keep Lucinda here. If you don't return, when and if you see her again, she will have a lot to tell you or maybe she won't be able to at all. Will you help us, Mr. Rodriguez, and your relatives?"

Francisco weakly nodded, now sweating. There was no other

choice. Lucinda was terrified.

"All right, now we need your wife's clothes." Lucinda was jerked upright. The man holding her pulled off her jacket and gestured at the buttons of her blouse. She bent as she unbuttoned it. He pulled it off and then gestured at her belt. She slipped out of her jeans and stood in bra and panties covering her midriff with her hands. "You have a very attractive wife, Mr. Rodriguez," he said. He jerked her hands behind her, snapped on handcuffs, and pushed her back into the chair. Doris slipped off her jacket and put it around Lucinda's quivering shoulders. Lucinda looked into her eyes, hoping to see an ally. Doris took the clothes to the end of the box, and came back wearing them.

The monitors at the village security center saw the familiar couple going to work. The audio monitor heard only a man and woman speaking Spanish. The cameras did not detect Melius' ninjas watching with infrared glasses. Nor did they observe the two support cars parked just outside the surveillance perimeter. Doris took a minute at a time to go through the files and desks in the area where she found the Daggett material, not breaking the rhythm of the cleaning. She checked the controller's desk. In Susan MacAulliffe's office, she found financial records.

When she was finished, Doris brought Francisco back at gunpoint to the truck. The surveillance men had returned. She nodded at them as she stepped to the darkness to change.

"Sit down, Mr. Rodriguez, you did very well. We made a deal, and you shall have your money and the money to send back to Mexico. But, first, I need to tell you that you must not ever tell anyone ever that we have been here. If you do we will find out about it and then come to punish you and your wife. Nothing like that will ever be necessary if you don't tell anyone. No one will ever know we have been here. You saw at the office nothing was taken. All you have to do now is to enjoy the money and send it to your family. That is a joy. And you should enjoy your pretty wife. We've only looked at her. If we have to come again we'll have a taste of her. You understand, Mr. Rodriguez?"

Francisco managed a nod.

"Good."

Doris gave the jeans and blouse back to Lucinda. The man behind her jerked her to her feet and swiped the jacket off her shoulders. Lucinda blushed and put her arms in the blouse and buttoned it. She pulled on the jeans and zippered her jacket.

"Very well, Mr. Rodriguez, let's go to your car. You are to go directly to the mansion. We will follow you to be sure."

The truck was soon on the road back to New York, its driver thinking only of how to enjoy the extra two thousand dollars for this unusual trip.

IN HARRISBURG, TONY'S phone hummed. Joan announced Helene Courtney on line one. Momentarily fearful that someone would guess the relationship, he intellectualized his way out of that quick thought. "Hi, how are you?"

"I'm talking to you on my cellular phone."

"Are you sure Edgar Slaughter doesn't have a frequency scanner."

"Whatever that is, it doesn't matter, he works for me now."

"Well, that must be fun."

"I'll tell you about it. Is it too late for some good skiing?"

"A friend of mine once told me that the best time to ski in Vermont was the last week in March. He used to tabulate the total snowfall and that was the time with the deepest base. The surface is another question."

"Let's try it. Can you get away?"

"Oddly I can. Jean is on her annual visit with her mother."

"I'll be on a direct flight from Orlando to Albany that arrives at 4:30. I'll get the car and the hotel. Nobody will ever know you were there."

At the main square of the colonial village of Manchester they enjoyed the quaint scene of its white-sided buildings as snow fell. On one corner the Congregational Church marked the site of worship with a tall steeple. Across the street, a block of fashionable stores displayed upscale fashions. Opposite was the great Equinox Hotel where an elegant suite awaited. Its block-long, white-columned porch and front roof of two widows-walk peaks dominated the street as light from great coach lamps and from full length windows gleamed on freshly fallen snow.

The low-ceilinged lobby was warm and inviting with a blazing fire in a giant hearth. Smells of cooking wafted down the hall from the main dining room and kitchen. The room was white with oak furniture and red leather, with floral-patterned pillows scattered around and oversized paintings of scenes from early New England.

They changed into ski sweaters, headed for the bar, and at a table before the fire, they ordered vodka and tonic with lemon.

"Tell me about the latest exploits of the women's tennis champion of the Bahamas."

"I'm losing my game. We don't play as much. Edgar is ahead 4-3 in our series. He's 55 years old and sometimes, when he thinks he has a good serve, he comes to the net."

"And you top-spin lob over his head."

"Not off those serves."

"How are the rest of the mural people?"

"We are doing well. The computers are working. We're very interested in the Daggett campaign. We get daily reports. It's good practice to follow him. People are training themselves in their jobs. Erla is really shining with her work. We've all bet Warren that Daggett will be the nominee."

"So you think Daggett is going to make some progress?"

"His polls are good and he is raising money like crazy. He seems to be organized and was well financed from the beginning. Do you know who's doing it?" Helene tested.

"Is it the Chicago crowd?" Tony asked feeling deceptive.

Helene noted he answered the question with a question.

They were the last in the dining room so they were served quickly, sharing a spinach salad followed by a succulent fresh trout done in wine with capers. They started a bottle of Chardonnay and then took it to the suite. There he led her to the bedroom where he lit the fire. By the firelight, he undressed her, kissing her thoroughly as each garment fell away.

Helene, a quick shopper, coolly spent $1,500 the next morning in the Alpine Village at Stratton. She was dressed in her new purple, green, yellow, and black outfit with insulated longies. Over her felt peaked hat were Bolle goggles. She carried her new Olin 180's with the latest and best Salomon bindings and the latest Salomon boots. They took their first run down the lower half of the mountain on a green dot easy trail. Tony saw she was an accomplished skier. Then they rode the gondola to the top and schussed down the broad Upper Meadow trail, marveling in the delicious clear air and shining snow.

Because it had been some time since they had both skied challenging terrain, they arranged a private lesson at the ski school for lunchtime. After that, Helene took to the diamond trails diving down them like a racer to wait at the bottom for Tony. He was able to get down the trails and had fun doing it, but he couldn't match her speed. In the gondola on one trip up to the peak she snuggled and kissed him. At the end of the day, they agreed on one long, slow run on the Meadow trail. She kissed him again in the gondola.

They took turns soaking in the tub. He called his office, watching her as she dried off and smoothed lotion on her body. Nothing required him to interrupt his short holiday. At the store across the street from the hotel, Helene bought another ski jacket and pants. They walked to The Country Inn, a quarter mile north. The lobby and living room had been on the cover of country magazines. The high-ceilinged room with a balcony was exquisitely decorated in 19th Century Vermont with antique furniture, lamps, china and silver accessories, and paintings and photos of past eras. At a table in the bar they drank hot buttered rum and ordered rack of lamb with rosemary mint sauce and Mateus Rosé for dinner. When the hostess took them to their table, the salads were served with hot bread and rolls.

"Is there anything you don't do well?" he asked her.

"You mean in athletics? I don't know dink about sailing. You're good at that."

He remembered she had read his bio.

"How did you, from Ohio, learn to ski like that?"

"It was how we made the winters bearable. When I was at Columbia we were on the way to Vermont or the Catskills by mid-afternoon on Friday. We'd stay four to a room. From Cleveland we went to Lake Placid or Vermont. One of our close friends had a share of a 'ski house.' When the kids were old enough, we took them. That was more like local motels and pizza."

"Did you make mad passionate love when you were alone?"

"Not like you and I are learning to do," she said. "That's another thing you're good at."

"It takes two to be good," said Tony.

"But, one can spoil it. I haven't told you about Edgar."

"You're sure it's not secret."

"There are some things I won't tell you, but I was dreaming about you under the stars on the beach at his training facility." She related the story of the bivouac.

"Are you working, or having an adventure?" he asked.

"The best advice I've heard was from one of my professors at PITT. 'Seek adventure.' I've always done it. So have you, I can tell."

"Adventure. You're an adventure for me. And, danger."

Helene's face grew serious.

"I don't want to be, but I like you. As you may guess, I don't wait to be chosen. I choose."

"Like Maggie in 'House of Cards.' She was murdered."

"Better to take the risk."

"Goodness, a male feminist." The waitress smiled when she heard that as she cleared the salad plates.

"Ian is one. He likes women and no one can threaten him."

"Is he happy in his marriage?"

"Very much, I think. He lost his first wife." He told her the story.

"Is there any reason Ward should be afraid of Ian?" Helene asked.

"I can't imagine Ward being afraid of any one."

"Ward has got a thing about Ian," Helene said in a soft voice. "He doesn't trust him."

"Just about everyone trusts Ian to do the right thing," Tony said thoughtfully, not sure he said the right thing.

"What is Ian's real feeling about POLACO?"

"He would prefer that it wasn't necessary. He doesn't know whether it is, so we joined."

That was a lie, but not too grievous. "What do you think of POLACO?" he asked.

This was a crucial question now. The question their whole relationship might depend on. At first, Tony himself was seduced by POLACO, but Ian had raised him to a new level of understanding and Daggett had shown him hope, so important to doing the right thing. He wanted to tell her that, but he knew he couldn't. Indeed, it almost seemed like she suspected him.

"I wonder sometimes if there is a hidden motive," she said. "On the surface it meets a serious need. Someone has to put something real together. The think tanks don't work."

"It is un-American to criticize think tanks."

"When some philanthropist realizes in his soul that something is wrong with the country he forms a group and creates a foundation to think it through and make recommendations," she said. "What comes out are academic papers written by people who could never carry out the recommendations. What Ward has developed is to merge the new thinking with action. We develop our ideas and then know reasonably well that we or somebody we influence can implement them. This is not to say that the other way doesn't contribute, but it can't ensure the necessary action."

"I thought 'the pen was mightier than the sword.'"

"It's ideas that are mightier, but they have to be put to work. The work has to be organized and financed to be effective. You know the story."

"What do you think that the hidden motive might be?" he asked. "Could it possibly diminish freedom?"

Helene smiled.

"These are businessmen, not communists."

"Do you believe in freedom?"

"Very much."

"Good, then we'll have to keep in touch."

They took a bottle of the Mateus back to the Equinox. She undressed in front of him by the fire in their suite. He stood up and kissed her and started to undress; she helped him. Then she got cushions from the sofa and pillows from the bed and arranged them in front of the fire. "You'll have to let me stay on top."

He got comfortable on the floor and then lifted her onto him. They both felt the warmth of the fire. She held back between flights of intensity of foreplay. He waited for her. Twice they paused while he added wood to the hearth. Her orgasm, when it came, was long and sustained. He kissed her tenderly while she cried out. His orgasm was intense as she kissed him and touched him. After he held her for a long while, he found some more wood. They sat naked on the cushions enjoying the warmth of the fire and drank a glass of the cold wine.

TONY WAS SORE the next morning and wasn't sure he could chase Helene around the slopes again. They ordered one Vermont breakfast of bran cereal, fruit, and coffee from room service and split it. Helene decided to put on shorts and a halter under her long underwear and ski at Bromley, which faced south. Tony warned her she would be cold at her age.

By afternoon, when warm from the exercise and bright sunshine, she peeled off the ski suit, handed him her cell phone, and took a run in shorts. He followed her down the slope which was steep and narrow. As she did a quick turn, she spun out of control and hit her back on a tree. She caught the edge of her ski on a slab of ice, breaking it off and twisting her leg.

Tony rushed to her. She tried to get up.

"Stay down!" he said as he stepped out of his bindings. It looked like her back could be broken and maybe her leg. He could see she was in pain. She reached out to hold his hand as he knelt beside her.

He put his jacket around her.

"Don't worry," he said. "No matter how bad it is, I'll take care of you."

She squeezed his hand while he reached in his pocket for her cell phone.

Before the ski patrol arrived, he stood all four skies up in the snow to warn off other skiers.

"Maybe I am too old for this," she said shivering. He didn't say a word.

Helene's back was badly bruised, but nothing was fractured and her knee was sprained. It wasn't as bad as it had looked, but a stay in the hospital and bed rest was obligatory. Tony sat with her through the night, holding her hand and talking to her. They talked about their children and about their lives.

Whenever the cell phone rang the next day, she described her accident but told everyone to stay away. To both of them, PEN-MET and POLACO seemed like they were a distant past.

Tony delayed his departure as long as he could. But after two days and three nights, he knew he had to leave.

"Don't worry," he smiled to her. "You'll be back leading POLA-CO in no time."

"Tony," she asked, "do you love me?"

"Yes," he said.

"And, I love you."

The next visitors to Helene's hospital room were Ward and Edgar. Their condolences regarding the accident were short and then Ward did the talking. Slaughter stood behind him, scrutinizing her. He handed Ward a stack of photographs from his briefcase.

With a red face, Ward laid the photos before her one by one. Doris had been profuse in her coverage of the Scottish Village office. In addition to the photos, they had a drawing of the layout showing where each of the documents had been seen.

The documents in the photos told the story very clearly. Susan MacAulliffe and Nancy Letersky were involved in the high-level planning of the Daggett campaign. Professor Terry Leelan was the campaign manager. There was frequent involvement of Tony Destito.

"Well," said Ward, "what do you think?"

Helene closed her eyes and shook her head slowly.

"Looks like they're trying to fix the government. Why?"

"It's not for our benefit," said Ward. "I knew we shouldn't have tried to recruit PENMET."

Helene shifted uneasily in her bed. This was a blow, but not unexpected in her view.

"What do we tell the executive committee?" Ward asked.

"Tell them," she said, "we know our enemy."

After they left, Helene remembered Tony's saying almost cavalierly, "You'll be back running POLACO in no time." Was he secretly glad she had been laid up by this accident? No. Regarding PENMET and POLACO, he had answered her questions with questions, but his concern for her had been genuine.

Later that evening, Tony called her.

"How are you feeling?" he asked.

"Much better. I'll be flown back to Harbour Island tomorrow."

"I thought you were going to your parents. You are in no shape to work. I'll call Ward."

"Please don't," she said. "They'll take good care of me." There was a pause on the phone and then he said, "I don't know when I can get back down there to see you. It's very busy here for awhile."

"Well," she said, "you might not see me, but you will be hearing from me."

☆ Chapter 11 ☆

THE MEMBERS OF the executive committee, in a sense the board of POLACO, along with Alex Peterson and Ward, were chosen by the membership. Despite his red hair and a flushed and puffy face, which gave him the look of an alcoholic salesman, Ryan Keeley had become President and CEO of the Mississippi Valley Chemical and Pharmaceutical Company. He was the professional executive of the group with a chemical engineering degree from Stanford and an MBA from Wharton. He'd been in the industry for his entire career and with MVC for 25 years rising through the ranks from project engineer.

Radion Gallosey was the immigrant success story of the last half of the 20th Century. He founded a marine insurance company and built it into a huge conglomerate with holdings in transportation, manufacturing, auto parts, and trucking and shipping lines. His reputation for ruthlessness evoked fear among the management of any company that he targeted. Nine out of ten of his acquisitions were successful. He picked on poorly managed companies where he replaced the management and on overstuffed companies where he pruned layers of excess bureaucracy. Cartoonists took to associating him with a pruning hook. His wiry build and aspect of a malicious guardsman lent to that characterization.

Mendos Sadovan, president of Utilities International, also founded the company he now ruled with absolute authority. Stocky and barrel-chested, he was an imposing personality whose large head was adorned with closely-cropped gray hair.

Sadovan was considered tough. He put together a relentless series of takeovers, some friendly, some not. Sadovan always replaced the CEO of any acquired company. He had contempt for the world's executive establishment and considered an MBA to be useless in the real business world. After an acquisition, he sent in his cost cutters, raised the profits, and then decided whether to keep it or sell it. His schooling was in Europe.

Bernt Umrich, president of Eurochem, a German-based chemical producer with broad interests in the United States, represented the foreign members of POLACO. He graduated from the University of Hamburg. He was tall and impeccably dressed. A full head of straight blond hair complemented his pleasant, regular facial features, giving him a somewhat deceptive look of benevolence. The seventh member was Helene, representing the professional staff.

Each of the American members flew on his private jet to Opa-Locka, the business airport of Miami, to which Ward Cowell sent his Gulf Stream. Bernt came by Lufthansa first class the day before, and spent the night at an apartment he kept at Fishers Island. He sent his mistress in advance and would enjoy a few days with her in the sun, secure on the island where access was completely controlled, and away from the gray German winter.

Helene flew across to greet the visitors. Ward was at the airport on North Eleuthera. They both apologized for the suddenness of the meeting and dodged what it was about. They met in the conference center in the room with the large oak table where windows were opened to the breeze and a coffee buffet was at one side with pastries and finger sandwiches.

Radion Gallosey did not wait for Ward's preliminary explanations. "Okay, Ward, what is all of this about? I assume something has leaked."

"No it hasn't. It seems we have developed an enemy inside the gates."

"What gibberish are you talking?" asked Gallosey.

"I wish it were," said Ward. "But, one of our members has turned against us and is attempting to establish a means of countering us."

"MacAulliffe?" Ryan Keeley asked.

"Good guess," said Alex.

There was a long pause.

"Damn it, Ward. What the hell have you allowed to happen?" asked Sadovan, his deep voice booming. "You brought us into this with all of the assurance that this would stay strictly confidential."

"It's still confidential," Ward assured them.

"What the hell is he doing?" asked Keeley.

"He's behind the Adrian Daggett candidacy."

"He's behind that? I sent that guy a contribution," said Keeley.

"We have evidence that MacAulliffe selected Daggett and is supporting his candidacy in order to preempt our organization."

"What do you mean, 'preempt?'" Gallosey growled.

"By electing Daggett, he thinks he can reverse the political deterioration we would otherwise exploit. The objective is to stop us, and we have to assume electing Daggett is only the first step."

"Daggett's the one who is talking about regulating the markets?" asked Sadovan.

"That's right," said Alex. "We don't want a gooney like that in the White House."

"How did you find out about this, Ward?" asked Sadovan.

"We have a mole in PENMET's P.R. Department, who observed some strange behavior by the P.R. director going to the Scottish Village offices three or four times a week. Our security group arranged for those offices to be penetrated and we have photographic copies of papers."

"You what?" said Keeley, as if he had not heard correctly.

"I said, we penetrated these offices."

"With a mole?"

"I told Ward to use his resources," said Alex. "We had to make a decision to find out what was going on."

"That was the Destito guy who came down here?"

"That's right, his name is Tony Destito," Ward said. "Helene was with him last week skiing."

Sadovan turned to Helene. "You're having a fucking affair with this guy whose company's turned against us?"

"There is some good fucking in the affair, Mr. Sadovan, but we don't use that language around here," she said, "I tried to use the opportunity to find something out and couldn't. However, in the meantime, Edgar Slaughter planted the mole."

"I don't like this, Ward. Using your security people on a member," said Keeley.

"What's wrong with it, Ryan, if it protects us?" asked Gallosey. "At least we know what's happening. What made you suspect him?"

"I'm not sure, Radion. I wasn't comfortable."

"Are you investigating any other members?" asked Sadovan slowly.

"No."

"It's hard for me to imagine spying on PENMET," said Umrich.

"Something like this would never be done in Europe."

"I wouldn't have gotten where I am if I didn't take action when I felt it was necessary," Ward said."I didn't like the idea of recruiting PENMET and I was right."

The others blinked at him.

"So MacAulliffe is backing Daggett?" asked Keeley. "He has always been a Democrat. Maybe that is why you mistrusted him, Ward. Daggett is a good candidate, maybe the best in terms of his ability and essential character."

"We know the purpose, Ryan," Ward said. "It's to preempt us."

"Why is he doing that?"

"He knows our long-term objectives and doesn't like them."

"What is he, a member of the flower people?" sneered Gallosey. "Is he a Harvard man with dimples on his knees?"

"He went to Princeton and Oxford," said Alex. "I wouldn't underestimate his ability."

"So he took over his daddy's company," said Gallosey.

"And multiplied it by ten in real terms," said Alex.

"Let's let Helene give a report on the intelligence to show you what we know so far," said Ward.

"I printed this out with the essential data. Don't lose it please, Gentlemen." She took them through the document explaining the sources of information.

Ryan started the discussion. "So we have a campaign organization MacAulliffe seemingly put together. We have MacAulliffe active in supporting Daggett. He thinks he's countering POLACO. So what?"

"Daggett seems like a damn regulator to me," said Sadovan. "He wants to regulate the markets. That's the wrong direction."

"I agree," said Gallosey. "That's one point and the other point is control. We want to get into a position where we have more than a little say about what happens politically. We have a huge investment in this, Ward."

"That's why I called this meeting."

"Look at those positions," fumed Gallosey. "National health insurance, market regulation, paying down debt, raising taxes. If these things happen on your watch, Ward, it's not going to look very good."

"Okay, we understand the problem," said Sadovan. "What are the options?"

"Why do we have to do anything?" asked Keeley. "We can just stick to our program. You always said it was long term, Ward."

"One of the reasons that we thought we could be successful with

POLACO was the inherent weakness of the current leadership and lack of public confidence in it. If Daggett becomes a competent leader, that position will change. It will be more difficult to manipulate public opinion if he is guiding it and feeding it realistic stuff. Our long-term success would be jeopardized."

"And further," said Alex, "if he is elected with a sympathetic Congress we could find ourselves faced with national health insurance, market regulation, investigations, anti-trust pressure, and who knows what. He knows who we are. We have to assume MacAulliffe has told him about us."

"Options," said Keeley again.

"We could, as Ryan has suggested, not do anything specific," said Ward. "Then we can weigh the events to see if our long-term goals are indeed being endangered."

"Damn it, we've already gone over that. MacAulliffe's purpose is to defeat our long-term goals. You mean to say we should sit here and watch it?" rumbled Sadovan.

"The first option is out," Ward said. "The second option is to use our resources to develop some fundamental communication and a groundswell of support against Daggett. This is to be sure that he comes across as a tax-and-spend liberal and focus on his pocketbook issue of no tax cuts with a balanced budget."

"That ought to be a good way of killing him off," said Gallosey. "Define him as the multitude of his predecessors."

"The problem is, he's already defined himself. The issues are going to be discussed one by one, with reality brought into them. He is going to apply what they call a 'reality test' on other candidates and their views. He is going to focus on reality," said Ward.

"Then we have to fight his reality with a heavy dose of perception," said Radion. "We have to keep somebody like that from being elected."

"The third option is to become directly involved with the Hatford campaign," Ward continued, "assuming that Hatford wins the Republican nomination, we can offer soft-cost services at the most affordable prices. We can also establish opposition through various advocate groups, other advertising and publicity, and general agitation. You are right, Mendos, the focal point has to be on the pocket book issue, which in the short term means taxes. We'll offer a pay-down-the-debt with a big tax-cut perception. This has been done before and has worked for the candidate, if not for the budget."

"We mustn't do anything illegal, Ward," said Keeley.

"We will stay within the letter of the law."

"What about the moles?"

"I think we should leave them right where they are."

"We can always take them out if we have to. But let's keep listening. There is more valuable information to be had," said Gallosey. "Let's make sure there are no mistakes. You've got us all potentially exposed."

"Should we consult the other members?" asked Ward.

"We'll call them," said Gallosey. "Now, I would like to meet privately with the other three outside members."

"Is that appropriate? I am chairman," said Ward. "You can discuss anything you want in front of me."

"We can meet here or we can meet at the Romora Bay Club," said Gallosey.

"We will, of course, respect your wishes," Alex interjected.

Shuffling papers, he, Ward, and Helene got up and left the room. Ward was burning. "Who the hell does he think he is?"

"That's what happens when a board is considering removing the chairman and CEO," said Alex.

"What do you mean?"

"They want to talk about us, Ward. We've scared them."

"You mean MacAulliffe?"

"That, and the way we found out about it."

"We're in that kind of game," said Ward. "They'll understand."

They sat on a couch and chairs around a cocktail table. Helene ordered coffee and mineral water to be brought up. They talked about the means of contending with Daggett and some other business.

An hour later, Ward knocked on the door and asked about lunch. Keeley came out and told him to order it for everyone. Another 30 minutes went by. The luncheon buffet was rolled out of the elevator by two waitresses. Helene's assistant, Carrie, acted as hostess. Ward gestured that she should knock.

Sadovan appeared at the door. "We're finished. We'll talk while we eat."

They went in. Gallosey and Umrich were still huddled. Ryan came to Ward. "Sorry, but there are some things we need to do without you."

Places were set at the table and the buffet laid out.

"This business of a mole at PENMET," said Sadovan, obviously the leader, "how many others are there?"

"None," said Ward.

"Good. There should be no more without the approval of this committee except in the campaigns if you want to put them there. You do agree?"

"We have to be able to defend ourselves," Ward said. "I have to have the authority to protect our interests. No, I don't agree."

"We don't mean that. We mean no moles in any member companies. If it ever got out that there was another you'd lose this organization."

"I thought that our security group proved itself very well."

"It was a dumb thing to do, Ward, even though it was successful," said Sadovan. "No more! Did you know about this, Helene?"

"Not until it was done."

"I thought not."

"The ground rule is you have to get our permission for any future forays like this."

"Just a minute," Ward protested.

"No, Ward. That's the way we want it," said Keeley. "You're not going to do it again. If you do, we'll replace you."

"Next," said Sadovan, "each off us will talk with certain of the others. We'll spin it as an accomplishment of your excellent sixth sense. We're going to tell them of the mole, but we'll say that you had our approval. Personally, I'm glad you smoked this out. Your security group is first class; the same as your staff. Congratulate them for us, Helene."

"I certainly will."

"We're going to tell the others that you're going to use that staff, Ward, to defeat Daggett. We'll explain the danger he poses. You have to do everything you can do to stop him. We agree with your view that the deteriorating political core of the country is key to our interests. We want it to keep deteriorating. Do you think you can stop him?"

"It should be easy when a candidate says taxes will be raised."

"This is no ordinary candidate, Ward. This is not an ordinary politician who was elected by making empty promises. This man was hand-chosen to be governor of Illinois by the Democratic party professionals. Now he is hand picked to be the candidate of a new machine. This machine is very well run, with some of the top people in the country supporting him and with some substantial backing to get started."

"We'll prepare a formal assessment of the situation and what we will do about it."

"Good."

Helene tended to become calm in critical situations. Now she was very calm. She saw that Ward was on the defensive and needed time to counter Sadovan's attack. "When shall we have that for you?" she asked to interrupt the questioning of Ward.

"When it's ready, but we want you to get going on it. There needs to be a crisis team organized, Ward. We are that in one sense, but we need to be ready if anything leaks."

"We have all kinds of plans," said Ward.

"We know, and it's well done, but there has to be an organization reporting to Helene and Erla to carry it out."

"We brought our clubs as you requested, Ward, as a cover. Are you going to invite us to play?" asked Ryan.

"How many will we have?" asked Ward.

"I'm for some tennis. Do you play?" Sadovan asked, looking at Helene. "I hear you're pretty good."

"You want to find out?" Helene challenged.

"For a hundred dollars a game in singles."

Helene let Sadovan win his first service then took six straight games. She had apparently recovered quite well from her skiing accident. She and Erla then won two doubles games against Sadovan and Harold Smalley. She played well as she contemplated what she was learning from Gallosey and Sadovan about the use of power.

He wrote her a check for $1,000 and she smiled as she placed it in her bra.

DAGGETT PROVED EARLY that his message would raise money. A critical decision came up whether or not to take federal funds. If they did, there would be spending limitations that might reflect back on the soft costs Ian was supplying. If they didn't and the flow of contributions suddenly dried up they might be at a disadvantage vis á vis the candidates using taxpayers' money. Mitchell Fiddler, a long-time friend of Daggett, and an experienced and well-connected financier, joined the campaign as finance chairman. His deputy chairman was Dominick Kluczinski of Chicago who had really delivered. In the campaign treasury they had $17 million based on a fundraiser in Chicago and one in Springfield. The Illinois elite were anxious to elect their man. Contributions arrived from every state as the Daggett campaign gained momentum with its unique candidate and "get real" message.

Arrangements were in place for fundraisers around the country. Volunteers came forward from a groundswell of support from all classes that wanted someone competent to take charge. An organization of Republicans for Daggett started fundraising and came up with 900 contributions and $700,000 in a few days and promised much more. Alan Jacobs was enthusiastic about their early breakaway nine months before the primary season, which indicated some sophisticated Republicans considered Daggett better than any of their prospective candidates.

Dominick Kluczinski was also a hero for the building he rented just outside the loop. The owner was delighted to lease it temporarily, hoping that the Democratic machine would make use of it after the election.

It was a large eight story 1930's brick with new windows. On the first floor there was a substantial reception room where young campaign volunteers served as receptionists and guides. The second floor held administrative offices for the personnel, recruiting, and accounting functions. The state liaison offices were on the third floor. On the fourth floor there was a training unit with classrooms. The polling offices and the intelligence unit were on the fifth floor. Part of the campaign media group under Nancy which prepared special literature, position papers, press releases and newsletters for the state staffs shared the floor. The rest of the group was on the sixth floor along with computer hookups which sent material for printing around the country. The seventh floor was the media center; Anne Russell's domain. From there, dozens of campaign people and Evans & Copeland employees worked with media throughout all the states, either directly or through the state campaign offices. On the eighth floor were Terry, Anne, Alan, and their rest of their staffs; guest offices for Tony, Nancy, and Susan; and an office for the candidate who was there whenever possible for training sessions. There was also the boardroom.

Kluczinski, who was soon appointed director of administration, had furnished the whole building with passable used rentals. He turned up computers, copiers, fax machines, offset presses, a full telephone system, storage racks for immense quantities of papers, and floppy disks, book shelves, files, and shredding machines; and he even included TV production equipment from a production studio that had been upgraded. Kluczinski reminded Tony of an executive grade Master Sergeant scavenger supplying the needs of his regiment.

In the boardroom, Terry called the senior staff to order in its first meeting at the new facility. Anne, Nancy, Tony, Adrian, Terry, Mitchell, and Dominick, gathered with a new member, Roger Bennett, Terry's choice to head the "soft money staff." While better called "the issues staff," they were to generate detailed proposals and ideas for the reality campaign and the reality government. This was located in offices in an industrial park near the airport in Cleveland. The thinkers suggested New York or Washington would be best, but Daggett wanted them located in a city where they could find reality. This was also Bennett's home. He was a leader of Cleveland's African-American community, a distinguished law professor who had private practice experience and had served as a deputy Attorney General in Washington, as well as in the governor's cabinet.

The meeting started with informal progress reports from each area of the campaign. Its main mission was to consider a report on the primary opposition:

Opposition Profile
Report to the Senior Campaign Committee
Terry Leelan, Alan Jacobs, and Staff

Candidate: Willis Porter – Michigan
Status: The most significant competition, a former governor and now a senator. Early front runner.
Profile: Porter is a reasonably intelligent guy and is a courageous campaigner. Rarely picks an issue of any substance. Not a spectacular governor, but served two terms in Michigan. He is attractive, has pleasant mannerisms, and gives a good speech, but deals only on perception.
Issues: He'll speak about what needs to be done about the environment, education, lawyers, regulating the economy, and insuring job security, but will never make a real proposal. He is pro-choice.
Trust Rating: Average
Constituency: A mix of minorities, labor and middle class who feel the need of protection or assistance. He has the backing of some wealthy liberals who want access to him.
Organization/Staff: Fairly good. They'll come up with a good campaign. Steve Zimmer is the campaign director.
Fundraising: He's on the Environment and Public Works Committee, the Armed Services Committee, and the Banking Committee, as well as Appropriations and he will call in the chits.
Summary: He's up for re-election in two years. He has gone nega-

tive in his campaigns. It's reasonable to say that his campaign staff will do anything they think will help them win.

Candidate: Marilyn Findlayson – California
Status: Only political experience is four years as a state legislator.
Profile: Glamorous heiress to the Magnuson Electronics Corporation fortune. First female candidate for President running with her own money.
Issues: Reducing taxes and simplifying the tax code, but taxing the rich more than the poor. Big on law enforcement and protection of minority rights.
Trust Rating: She hasn't really developed a story yet. Tends to ignore the advice of her staff.
Constituency: Trying for traditional liberal support groups.
Organization/Staff: They're putting state organizations together but are mostly political neophytes using this campaign to gain experience. P.R. and political firms are OK.
Fundraising: Paying for her own campaign out of a net personal worth of over $500 million.
Summary: She'll concentrate on Iowa and New Hampshire to see how well she can do. She's filed everywhere. Options are open, chances for success are indistinct.

Candidate: Richard Sandellot – Ohio
Status: Former congressman, University president, Secretary of the Interior, and entrepreneur.
Profile: A very able son of a clergyman from High Point, North Carolina. Graduated from the University at Chapel Hill, did a masters and Ph.D. in economics at Harvard and MIT. His undergraduate degree is in chemistry. Cum Laude in all. He founded a company, went to Congress, and became president of Bowling Green – An African-American to boot.
Issues: Same reality and truth as ours. Focused on secondary education, electoral reform, reducing the influence of lawyers, keeping the budget in surplus, restructuring taxes, and getting the debt paid off. He has also suggested selling national assets. Favors universal military training or universal national service.
Trust Rating: High.
Organization/Staff: Amateur. There are only a few on salary. The rest are volunteers, fellow academics, and business friends.
Fundraising: He's underfunded and doesn't have the organization

to change this.

Summary: A very worthy candidate – the only other on real issues in a realistic manner. Should be courted as a possible member of a Daggett administration.

Candidate: Robert Ramsdell – Minnesota

Status: Former speechwriter for left-wing ideologues. Political hanger-on in various places. Former Congressional candidate and employee of the Democratic party. Spent some time at Brookings.

Profile: The reincarnation of Pat Buchanan as a Democrat. A graduate of Clemson in political science and history. He did a master's at the University of South Carolina, then joined a publishing company in Richmond. He has supported himself by writing and politics.

Issues: He is against free trade, NAFTA, WTO, and favors high tariffs.

Trust Rating: Poor

Constituency: The disenchanted who feel that the system is stacked against them. The little guy against the privileged.

Organization/Staff: His staff consists of mainly friends who are helping him. Outside the early primaries, he's got some organization in New York, Michigan, Illinois.

Fundraising: Surprisingly strong. Somebody is investing in the campaign, could be foreign – possibly the Iranians or another enemy.

Summary: Will focus on Iowa and New Hampshire and then Georgia, Florida, and South Carolina. Objective seems to be no more specific. He dreams of starting a national movement of some kind.

"Alan, Terry, thank you, well done," said Adrian as he finished the report. "Are there any material changes required in our program to deal with these candidates?" asked Adrian.

"Except for Sandellot," Terry said, "they're all vulnerable to our basic strategy of dealing in reality and attacking the political establishment which will not respond to it. Now, with the reality we will create some perceptions." That drew laughter. "The perception has to be that we mean what we say."

"I'm not so sure people will understand all of this," said Mitchell.

"We should talk about Nancy's idea," Alan said. "I think she should present it. It is a means of elevating the issues to our benefit which I respect very much."

"Let me hear you talk about it," said Nancy.

"It's Nancy's concept to establish a series of televised debates. The show would be a debating society with regular members and guest experts. It could focus on specific technical or legal aspects of any one of our positions. Take for example, our education programs, bringing back school prayer and teaching about religion in the public schools. This is going to develop a lot of debate. Who will do the teaching? What laws prevent the teaching of religious history or philosophy? And so on. Now you take over, Nancy. You're a television person."

"I would like to organize a kind of loose society of fairly regular people who appear in the parliamentary format which is open firing questions at each other rather than the formal collegiate format. It's called 'Westminster-style debate.'"

"The show 'Great Confrontations at the Oxford Union' was not very successful, Nancy," said Terry.

"I know, because it wasn't done with an eye toward good television. It may have been good debate, but good television requires that the show sparkle with characters who become familiar and who can draw a response from the audience and the press."

"I like the idea, Nancy," said Adrian.

"So do I," said Alan. "If we're going to be so brash as to attack the issues squarely and objectively, this will help. It will smoke out the special interest and advocate groups with big perceptions."

"How does everybody else feel about it?" asked Adrian.

"I think it is great and will be cost effective," said Tony.

"Great opportunity for some spin-off," said Anne.

"Good. Get to it, Nancy," said Terry.

And so they deliberated about the reality and how they would define it. The difficulty was that reality was sometimes bitter medicine and rarely included sugar to help it go down.

ANOTHER SENIOR COMMITTEE was formed and met almost simultaneously with a similar mission in a different jurisdiction. Erla, Warren, Harold, Louis, Marsha, Rollin, and Edgar were organized by Helene into a special campaign management group to gather support for the election of anyone but Daggett. Ward had decided after consulting with Alex, that Helene would lead this group because he wasn't sure of Warren Hatch in real combat. Ward told Hatch his main focus was to continue building POLACO's intellectual resources and assist in the action against Daggett, which would be conducted with Helene in charge. Hatch readily agreed, demonstrating a distinct distaste for accountability. POLACO had evolved to Helene being in full charge with Warren Hatch as the nominal ideological director. More and more, Erla was in the ideological role as matters grew complex in real application.

Rollin Tinton was to continue recruiting candidates and building for future elections with all possible speed, following the original strategy for which the supporters with their substantial funding had originally joined. The field forces would, however, assist as necessary in specific states or constituencies in defeating Daggett. They considered it unlikely that Daggett could win against Hatford, if they used their resources effectively.

To legitimize support for Daggett's opponents, two foundations were established which would make appeals to conservative donors and be generously supported by POLACO and its members. This meant recruiting people to run those.

Helene and her group left no time in developing strategies aimed directly at the Daggett threat. They drafted a series of countering papers attacking the Daggett positions as a start with "Harry and Louise" type television commercials. They staged speeches for prominent conservatives and made ads out of them. Those two techniques provided lively, TV-friendly attack videos against Daggett and were refreshing changes from the drab format of many political commercials. The staging of speeches had the added benefit of providing other grain for the public relations mill and developing relationships with regional and local organizations. The ads would be out early. The pressure against Daggett would build as soon as production was finished and would continue.

Another main strategy was to provide superior production and creative services to friendly candidates. By doing production work on the island, they could cut costs and keep control. The Communication Group Atrium was to be refitted for TV production with a crew and writers brought in.

The "foundation founding," as it was dubbed by the staff, saw the creation of the Southern Conservative Coalition based in Jacksonville, and the William Foulton Organization in Leesburg, Virginia near Washington. A third was the Fund for Liberalism established in Pittsburgh to feed materials to the candidates opposing Daggett in the Democratic primaries. Gifts of $100,000 each came from the 24 members of POLACO.

One further strategy was to expose chinks in the seemingly white

armor of Knight Daggett. Since he had run in only one political campaign for governor of Illinois against a disorganized and incompetent
opposition, not much research had been done. He married late so the
chances were good there were affairs prior to the marriage. Perhaps
women who felt wronged by him could be located. Better, they might
find incidents which could be construed or misrepresented as sexual
harassment. They would check all of his college loans and his
finances for defaults and irregularities. Every detail of Daggett's life
would be the subject of the inimicable scrutiny. Paul Melius sent two
operatives to each city in which Daggett had resided.

As the time approached to report status to the executive committee, Helene kept Ward continually briefed so he could think with her
about how to handle it. He, in-turn, updated Alex.

This time Radion Gallosey picked up Ryan Keeley and Bernt
Umrich in Miami at Opa-Locka to show off his new DeHaviland
while Sadovan came directly to North Eleuthera in his own
Gulfstream.

The meeting started with a tightly worded presentation by Helene,
spiced with their copy and storyboards for the commercials, and a list
of the conservative speakers and the organizations they would solicit.

Gallosey made the first comment, "I hope you realize that the key
theme is taxes. This guy wants to increase taxes instead of cutting
them. I'm not sure you have that clearly in mind. He's going to have
all the reasons to do this and lots of justifications. You have to have
counter justifications. People will love you for your reasons to vote
for lower taxes. Americans have probably intuitively realized for
years that taxes need to be increased to pay off the debt, but every
successful politician has let them avoid it."

"You'll see that in our materials – the ads and the statements,"
Helene answered.

"You're going to have a lot of academic chatter in those statements. What you need is the visceral stuff. Make the people dislike
Daggett for the tax issue and you got him. Show them he's putting the
government's hand deeper into their pockets." Gallosey spoke with the
convictions that his own pockets were at risk.

"We are going to mark him as a 'tax and spend' Democrat," said
Ward.

"That's not going to do it," scowled Mendos Sadovan. "I agree
with Radion. This has to be visceral. You need to get someone
tougher than Farthergill to deal with this. You have to hit those people
in a way they can't defend themselves. You have to pin them so they

can't back away from the perception they are going to raise taxes."

"We can be visceral about that, but that is not going to carry the debates. We have to think through the whole campaign, not just one issue," said Helene.

"Political campaigns are not an academic exercise in this country. There is no debate, only a media circus. You have to make the circus perform as you want," said Sadovan.

"There are signs that this campaign will be different," said Alex. "That may be the most dangerous part of it."

"Why should this be any different than the last bunch of nonsense? The media ran the whole thing fumbling as they were. After New Hampshire they said Dole couldn't win. Then he swamped them all. I had my people telling me that Lamar Alexander would be the nominee," said Gallosey.

"Each campaign has its own tone," said Ward, "set by the candidate. This is going to be different. We have a candidate proposing to run on reality. We have to be ready for him. This could be a truly issues-oriented campaign."

"Issues bullshit," said Gallosey. "There is one issue – taxes. The one who convinces everyone that he will cut taxes wins. That's what I mean by visceral. Working people vote for bigger net pay. They don't give a shit about anything else."

"How would you answer the position that the debt transfers income from the middle class to the rich?" asked Helene. "Shall we just ignore it?"

"Who's going to listen to that crap?"

"Anyone who is thinking about his net pay check. People don't think taxes are the only problem. They know something else is wrong," said Helene.

"Helene has a point," said Keeley. "These are complex communications and these are complex issues. Any candidate who puts forward the old ideas without any support is going to be butchered in the debates."

"What debate? I told you there is no debate in American politics," Gallosey raised his voice.

"There will be this time. Do you think the primary candidates or Hatford can handle Daggett without any preparation? Daggett would chew them up. He's got the best staff ever in a campaign," Helene asserted.

"Yes, and you know it intimately," Gallosey taunted.

"That's better than you know it," Helene fired back.

"Academic twinkies," chided Sadovan.

"Far from it, Mendos," said Alex, "we have our hands full. Look at what they have accomplished so far."

"I expect – and I think all of us expect – that you are going to defeat them," said Gallosey. "You have more resources at your command than anyone in politics has ever had."

"Are you sufficiently 'negative,' as you say over here?" asked Bernt. "You have to find something to question Daggett's character, or he might win on trust. I don't think the others command much trust."

"We're doing the research," said Helene.

"There has to be something," Sadovan predicted.

"He has always had enough money to pay his taxes and to support his family. He is an honest man. He goes to church."

"So do the Mafiosos. I mean to accuse him of poor judgment or of misunderstanding the issues. Say that he is not up-to-date," said Bernt.

"That may be hard to do if we're not as up-to-date as he is," said Alex.

"Then yell that he is going to increase taxes," Gallosey almost shouted.

"That may not be so easy because he has other things he wants to do with the money," said Ward calmly.

"Focus on taxes and find the weak spots in his character," Sadovan said in a low voice. "I don't care what else you do provided it doesn't make us lose."

"Negative campaigning backfires," warned Keeley.

"What resources do we have for dirty tricks? Maybe it will take that," said Gallosey.

"We're not considering any. They also backfire," said Ward.

"That is when they are not properly used. I'm going to send you a consultant in dirty tricks," said Gallosey. "I'll expect you to use his advice."

"We'll consider it, Radion, but if we don't think we should use it, we won't." said Ward.

"Then when that decision is made, I want you to call another meeting of this group."

"There is no magic in dirty tricks," said Helene. "Don't expect that they will win the election. It's going to be won by the staffs who plan and execute the best strategies."

"I have confidence that you will do it, Helene," said Keeley amiably. "Call on me for whatever support you need."

"Don't be afraid to call them names," said Bernt.

"Enough of this," Sadovan said raising his hands. "Now, I have been having dreams of playing tennis with Helene again."

"Were they sexual, Mendos? You like to be beaten by women?"

He laughed with the others to show he could take a joke at his own expense. On the court she saw that he had practiced his serve. She let his first two look-alike aces whiz by her and then turned it on and beat him 6-1 twice.

☆ **Chapter 12** ☆

ADRIAN'S NEW HAMPSHIRE team, which reported directly to Alan, chose Manchester, New Hampshire for headquarters in a building close to the lair of the archconservative newspaper, the Manchester Union Leader. They figured if the editors had to pass their signs each day they would get more negative press from the newspaper. This, Anne Russell said, was positive for New England Democrats.

The schedule evolved with travel concentrated on Iowa and New Hampshire and the "Super Tuesday" states. Big events and big time fundraisers were included. In Seattle, they set a record for gifts from the Boeing crowd and their vendors. Adrian believed what he had told the Aerospace Industries Association in every sense. Alan and Terry thought if they could keep that theme, playing it would assure them of all three West Coast states and Texas in the primaries and in the general election.

Pamela traveled with Adrian except when the children were home. Then they began to invite Donald, Linda, and Dianne to join them. Dianne's blonde, all-American teenager good looks and natural, outgoing personality proved to be a major asset. Once, when they were working a mall and she was in front of them shaking hands, Pamela and Adrian stopped to watch. When Dianne realized she was working the crowd alone she walked up to her father with a big grin pretending to kick him in the shin and then hugged him. TV cameras caught the incident and it became a staple replayed whenever news was short that day.

On foreign policy, they decided to introduce a controversial position concerning foreign involvement and "the world's policeman" question. Analysis showed New Hampshire would be receptive to this stand. Adrian was personally moved by the motto of the state "Live Free or Die." He keyed off that at a regional Chamber of Commerce dinner in Nashua with full Evans & Copeland inspired coverage by the wire services and television. In the speech he recalled the defeatist slogan, "Better Red than dead" of the late 50's early 60's when Russia seemed to be gaining in the cold war. He extolled "Live Free or Die" as New Hampshire's defiant response to the cowards who would surrender the country that had the overwhelming weapons superiority of the Nuclear Triad of submarines, missiles, and manned aircraft. He compared the courage of New Hampshire people with fear-mongers. The reality was that courage was essential to the success of nations.

He said it was necessary for the United States to maintain peace and to prevent nuclear proliferation. The world had to have a policeman and the United States was the only nation with the power to do it, through the United Nations, NATO, and other international bodies. He also said it was necessary to maintain a strong military presence in Europe and Asia, recognizing that danger still existed from the former Soviet Union. He said that the lives of American soldiers and sailors may have to be risked to protect the interests of the country and the free world and to make possible a peaceful future. He said the US would have to urge the reform of the United Nations and support it with American resolve to promote and preserve peace. He said the safety of everyone depended on peace.

The result was a standing ovation. The press, looking for conflict and controversy, carried it broadly. The next day, every American who read a newspaper or watched TV news was aware of the Daggett campaign. Editorials and commentary around the country were split. Adrian made news while the other candidates made mostly talk.

Daggett was so good on his feet, so interested in people, and so well supported by Pamela that the staff decided in some appearances he would not give a "speech." "The speech" was made famous in the Nixon campaigns when Nixon would say the same thing in a different way attempting to hammer home the themes. Instead, Daggett would use the entire time of his appearances to take questions. They tried it at a Lions Club meeting in Waterloo, Iowa and it worked well. It gave people a feeling of connection. Adrian's intelligence and personality began capturing the attention of the informed and engaged citizens of the country.

EVEN KAREN CREZNA, the youngest and least experienced of the Daggett field coordinators in Iowa, knew it would take more than the candidate's intelligence and experience to win a national campaign. She was assigned to the Northwestern quadrant to set up local organizations because that was the least populated quadrant with only one city and a few towns. She was successful in Sioux City and met Earl Hanley. There were now volunteer coordinators in each county reporting to her. She got together with them to help recruit more volunteers and to plan activities. The program was print and radio based with television to follow. The focus was preparing for Adrian Daggett's visits with tight scheduling and effective advancing for which she would be responsible.

Despite the uncertain prospects, Karen and Earl Hanley developed a relationship. After the Sioux City meeting, he drove to Des Moines the next Saturday to take her to dinner and stayed and took her to church and dinner on Sunday. They never lacked something to talk about; his work, her work, their roots in Iowa, their feelings about the country, their parents, and about religion.

She arranged to be in Sioux City at the end of the next week. After that, they talked on the phone every day. A day seemed incomplete if he didn't call and speak to her.

When she was traveling, the evenings were full. She tried to get enough sleep. Before breakfast she did a two-mile run. The campaign encouraged her to invite Democrats to meals to have enough time to talk through the Daggett program. She used meals to interview prospective salaried people and to check their table manners as Merrick advised. She often thought about being 23 years old and having an expense account of thousands of dollars a month. Her father probably filled one out five times in his life.

The politics of endorsements were thrust on her. Some county chairmen were willing to step forward and endorse Daggett, potentially the strongest candidate. Others held back saying they wanted to wait until he visited the county. Others indicated patronage would be necessary. Careful records were kept. A strong candidate like Daggett gave his representatives a strong negotiating position. She learned how to use it and to handle herself with people who averaged twice her age. She didn't let the patronage issue dampen her enthusiasm. It was part of the adventure she was living.

Earl helped. He had some insight into politics. She really liked him. He was intelligent; a reader like her; and he liked classical music. He had grown up in Davenport, one of four children of an agricultural equipment dealer who suffered heavily as government programs changed and farm equipment sales fell disastrously, aggravated by consolidations and voluntary liquidations. What had been a comfortable and cultured household, became strapped for money. His father sought to save the business while his mother returned to work, first as a high school teacher and then as an assistant principal. Earl won both academic and athletic scholarships at Coe College in Cedar Rapids. He was the star wide receiver on the football team and a pitcher with a sharp breaking curve ball, a burning slider, and professional baseball prospects. During his senior year, against Cornell College, the traditional football rival, he jumped high to catch the winning touchdown pass in the end zone with no time on the clock. He held on after a hit to strip the ball, but coming down his legs were entangled with two defenders and his right knee dislocated. He writhed in pain while the crowd went wild. His professional athletic career ended before the first tryout. He told Karen ideas were more important than fast balls.

After a week in the field ending in Sioux City to visit Earl, Karen was headed to her office in Des Moines for a staff meeting. On the way back she deliberated about becoming intimate with him and how wonderful he was not to push her. His kisses were sweet and churned her insides. She thought about what would happen after the Iowa Caucuses. If she was doing well she would stay with the campaign. If Daggett won, she hoped for a position in Washington. Separation from Earl was impending unless she wound up in Iowa City to study law.

The meeting scheduled was to review progress and put together a final plan. Karen was pleased to the point of embarrassment with what she had accomplished compared to the other field coordinators. As an illustration for her report she had enlarged a map of her counties on a board and put pins in various colors showing their status. She knew she had been effective. She had the ability to persuade people to her viewpoint and to take action. This was the same talent that others used to get customers to buy products or services.

She felt embarrassed again when it was evident that George Stillman was having trouble in Cedar Rapids and Waterloo, and she was assigned to take over Mason City and the surrounding area from him.

She continually analyzed what the essentials to success would be for the Daggett campaign in terms of issues. Iowa was a mixture. Her area was still mainly agricultural with hogs, cattle, corn, wheat, barley, and soybeans. Many people made their living by working the land

and family farms survived. As farms were automated, workers streamed into towns and cities. A momentous industrial development effort matriculated to Iowa to provide the people coming off the farms with places to work. This helped maintain the family farm. Owners of smaller holdings could still keep them provided they worked in a job in the cities. Wives worked in the cities or drove tractors while their husbands brought paychecks home. So in each town in her area there were factories. Sioux City was industrial and commercial. Gateway Computer had established in nearby South Dakota.

What should the Daggett agricultural policy be? How should they treat the debt and financial issues? Was there an Iowa angle to it? Would the aerospace policy be good generally or should they confine it to Cedar Rapids? The environment was an issue, but it often entailed keeping the government from restricting the use of fertilizers and pesticides. The modern farm economy was based on the abundant crops of chemical assisted production.

She argued for a speech in Sioux City recalling the DC 10 episode, and extended it to encompass Daggett's foreign and economic policy realities. She thought that would be good all over the state. She recommended a rally in Fort Dodge as being a good place to deal with realities in agriculture. She got a mall working on the schedule in Sioux City and visits to farmers around Storm Lake were added to the program. She had local media agree to cover Daggett, who would take questions from people in living rooms or Grange Halls which would be good press. As governor of Illinois, he would know how life in the small towns and villages centered around such gatherings. Her volunteers made the arrangements.

There was competition for the candidate's time among the territory coordinators and arguments ensued. Karen felt that she should ask only for what she knew would be productive. Melissa Rondo, who had Des Moines, Ames, and the Southwest, wanted Daggett every time he came. So did the others. The schedule filled in. At the end of the meeting Merrick asked Karen to see him in the morning.

That night she told Earl about the meeting and the arguments. Maybe she had done something wrong and Merrick was going to chew her out. Earl told her not to worry. Good performance attracted both praise and criticism. What if she had said something she shouldn't have said? That night she didn't sleep until late, trying to imagine what she did and then worried she wasn't getting enough sleep before the meeting.

When she came to Merrick's office, he told her to close the door.

She almost trembled. He asked her to sit down. "Of all the recruits, we thought you were the one we would have to support. It turns out you're giving the support. You are doing an excellent job. I get the reports from the old pols. They like you and they respect you. Some of them are old enough to be your great grandfather."

She was relieved.

"You're also a team player. You wanted Adrian for only enough time to meet your objectives. You were also ready with what he should say."

"That's my job."

He laughed. "Right now, I have a problem in our relations with headquarters. I need a permanent liaison. I was expecting more help. The candidate's time and money are key resources. I need someone to represent us there. Since you have been successful and your territory is in good shape, do you think you can help me in Chicago?"

The concept started Karen's mind running. She would pay a visit to the regional coordinator and his staff pleading the case for Iowa. "I can do it if you need me. I just want to be sure we don't lose momentum."

"With what you have done, we won't."

"What is the main issue with us and Chicago."

"We're Iowa. The first political event. Not the one most necessary. The way we are organized, we have to compete for the time and money. They keep the accounts and you have your budget reports. We have to revise the budgets as we need to and milk it out of the treasury. A lot depends on their knowing what we think is going on. I know for sure that you will do a better job in telling them."

"I'm flattered and a little scared."

"Things are happening fast?"

"Yes."

"It's always true in a campaign. There is no future unless we win and little time for decisions."

"What about George, Melissa, and Willis?"

"They have their hands full."

"I mean what will they think?"

"They won't like it, but you are the only one with a territory under control. I should have given you Cedar Rapids. I can take care of the shortfalls in Des Moines. We'll get ready for Chicago today. Plan to be there Monday and stay a couple of days to get acquainted."

That night Karen called Earl, excited. She made plans to meet him at Spirit Lake on Friday night. They would have to be in Sioux City for a party on Saturday evening, but they could have Friday evening and part of a day to themselves. The next day she made her appointments in Mason City, starting with dinner on Wednesday with the local chairman and his wife.

When Earl got to the Log Cabin Lodge at six and called from the desk, she was ready with a tray of wine and cheese on the coffee table. When she opened the door she was wearing a nylon robe. Earl saw a single queen-sized bed. "Welcome to Spirit Lake," she said, kissing him. "Will you accept a glass of wine instead of your usual bourbon?"

"Under the circumstances, I think wine is appropriate," He put down his garment bag and held her to him. He could feel she was naked under her robe. "What a nice surprise."

"I wanted to take the first step. You're a great gentleman, and I appreciate you."

He kissed her again. She stepped back and let the robe slip off her shoulders so it was held by the sash around her waist. The she started to undress Earl. After she slipped a condom over his erection she pulled the belt of her robe loose and let it fall. Her body was nearly perfect with high pointed breasts over a flat stomach and well-shaped legs. They fell on the bed. The first time he came too soon. She waited and then had her orgasm before his second. They made love a third time after eating steaks and salads delivered by room service. Afterward she snuggled against him thinking of her future and him. He knew he was in love with her and he knew it would be difficult.

The day at the lake was a delight. They kissed in the woods. That night she became Daggett's person again at the committee party in Sioux City. On Monday evening, she called Earl from Chicago.

THE AD IN *Variety* in New York said: "TV crew for off shore operations, one year assignment, plus add-on; line producer, camera, assistant camera, sound assistant, sound, light, assistant light, electrician, make up, costumes, and script, 3 PA's."

The employer of record was a production company called Bahamas Film and Video Limited with an address in Nassau. Payment for all of the equipment would be made in advance from an American bank. It would be loaded on trucks and taken to Melbourne where chartered vessels would load it to go directly to Harbour Island. Through one of the special arrangements with Bahamian government, import clearance would show it as delivered to Nassau. Considering the amount of money that POLACO was investing in the Bahamas and the liquidity it gave to the Bahamian banks the consideration was minor. Edgar brought Cybill Chubb, who was his second in command. She had military, as well as investigative training, and played the role of a semi-idle female who spent time listening in the upscale establishments for violations of the secrecy program. Carrie thought she looked a typical British colonial. She was older, but took care of herself swimming and training with the soldiers.

They all sized up the applicants and tried to guess who would fit in best. They hired seven women and seven men so as not to further distort the imbalance of the sexes.

At the same time Helene was in New York going through executive search channels to recruit creative talent for the communication group. She came up with Vicki Godecky as a director of television operations who had previously served as producer of TV commercials. As a condition of coming to Harbour Island, Vicki insisted on taking her regular assistant Pat Stabler. Both were in their thirties and divorced with no children.

Edgar was comfortable with all of their recruits except Pat Stabler. He saw in her substantial talent, but also substantial independence and a potential willingness to rebel. Vicki defended her as a multiple function person who could do all of the jobs on the crew and even act if necessary. On her resume and application form Edgar had seen modeling and acting credits. He sized her up as an underachiever who liked to do things, but didn't care for the responsibility and accountability, and on that basis he objected. Helene used the urgency argument on him. He compromised, and agreed to Pat provided he could bug her quarters from the beginning. Helene, respecting his judgment, agreed.

On the same trip Helene recruited Leigh Richards, an advertising executive who had won most of the awards in the advertising industry as an agency account executive. She was also fleeing a divorce and like Helene, with children in high school, was won by the salary offer.

The new artistic director for the Communication Group was Conrad Reed. Breaking the trend of recruiting the divorced and childless, he was an early age widower.

"POLACO Productions" as it was quickly named by Pat Stabler, was organized and put to work. The TV crew received their equipment from the docks at Harbour Island and construction began. The creative atrium group became a TV set with the computer workstations and executive offices around it. The projection system was fitted to serve as a background. All quickly adapted to the island life, working hard during the day and playing hard nights and weekends. The ambiance of the island stirred two romances and other, more casual relationships.

EVERYONE ON THE Daggett senior campaign committee had the sinking feeling that there wasn't enough time or enough money despite the large amounts they had raised. Viewing what had to be done in Georgia, Florida, Texas, Tennessee, Ohio, New York, South Carolina, and California, the first judgment was that Daggett could not be established. This led to an overriding objective of early wins in Iowa and New Hampshire. They believed that establishing his validity in those states, would carry forward to the big states, but it meant overspending candidate time and money in those two small states, when it was the larger states that delivered the delegates. They reflected on the Dole campaign of 1996 when he technically lost Iowa and in fact lost New Hampshire, but then came back to win because of strong organizations and planning where the votes lay. His opponents exhausted themselves trying to establish their validity and also exhausted their funds. It was troubling. All the hopes raised by the early successes were now subdued in "reality."

Terry Leelan called his senior staff together. Everybody seemed tense as they gathered around the conference table.

"I know you all feel uneasy now that we see how much we have to do, but remember, we have a much better candidate with stronger support on the issues than has ever been marshaled before," he began.

"That may be," said Dominick Kluczinski, "but in primaries the candidate has to get known to the people who are going to vote. Issues don't matter that much, except if they define the candidate."

"Maybe that's the answer," said Anne Russell, "the issues define Adrian as the much superior person."

"Dominick, we have to play the issues game as best we can and use as much time as possible to meet people," Leelan insisted.

Mitchell Fiddler objected. "We have only one chance at this, Terry. There isn't a second at bat. We can't be wrong and one way to be right is to follow the typical critical path. We're not doing that. In a primary, the candidate has to meet with as many groups as possible and I'm not sure we physically have enough time. Do you agree,

Alan?" he lowered his head and peered at Alan over his half-lens reading glasses.

"It would seem that we are rapidly gaining recognition with our positions on issues," said Alan.

"We also have a hell of a big unfavorable percentage. I don't like all of these positions. The more we take, the more opportunity our opponents have to criticize," Mitchell replied.

"It's taking our positions that has gotten us our exposure, Mitchell," said Anne. "We can't gain the ground we need to gain between now and next February by keeping mousy quiet and squirreling around shaking hands."

"I understand what you have done, Anne," said Kluczinski, "but, I believe we have done enough. What Mitchell is saying, and I agree, is we should keep to the regular primaries schedule and not expose ourselves any further."

Terry knew that differences in opinions were bound to arise among such a talented staff. He also knew that he would have to resolve them. "We can't all agree on everything, Mitchell. The strategy we followed so far with the reality campaign has carried us to the lead with a high 'Q' rating, and has brought us huge financial support. And I'm saying we have reached this position, so let's stay in it."

"I think you have to keep in mind, Mitch and Dom, that we have opponents who are not going to sit forever and let us take them apart. We have to do that to them until they're out of the game," said Adrian, recognizing that the fundraising was successful because of Mitchell and because of Anne and because of the combination of the two.

The discussion and dissent rambled on.

At the end Adrian went to Leelan's office. "Do you think we have maintained the momentum of the money raisers?" he asked.

"I think so, Adrian. They are here to rebuild our national political structure. Anne and Nancy have frightened them, but they will respond the same way as Alan did, when we get into a rhythm. In the meantime, they'll keep bringing in the cash."

"I really think the success in financing is a combination of Anne and Mitchell."

"It is, Adrian. Mitchell knows that. He's just conservative, and he's had the same seasoning in his life as Alan, but for a longer time."

"Do you feel in your gut that we are going to do this thing?" Adrian asked experiencing the periodic sense of the overwhelming magnitude of the effort.

"I feel that we are going to win the nomination and the presidency.

We may be short of time, but we are long on weapons. Think of it as a political blitzkrieg," Leelan insisted in a confident manner.

"That's the way I feel about it. But this is a new game to me," Adrian admitted.

"You ran for governor of Illinois."

"The people of the state of Illinois had to elect me because there was such a mess and the alternative was unacceptable."

"The people of the United States have to elect you too, Adrian, for the same reason."

☆ **Chapter 13** ☆

EDGAR SLAUGHTER, WITH a briefcase full of documents beside him, completed his reading in the comfortable first-class section on a Delta jet descending toward LaGuardia Airport. He was headed for the Lincoln Building across 42nd Street from Grand Central Terminal to visit Paul Melius. In his jacket pocket was a confirmation for a box seat behind first base at Yankee Stadium for a game that night. He would hear the New York Opera Company's Don Giovanni the following night and would go to a matinee at Carnegie Hall on Saturday and to the theater on Saturday evening. An old girlfriend would be his date for the weekend. He had called to find her unmarried. He thought about how she might have aged. She had been a vivacious red head with whom he had been intimate during the holiday periods. With Melius he was to hear the report on Adrian Daggett's background. While every campaign investigated every opponent, a job this thorough was probably unique.

In Melius' office, open windows let in fresh spring air. The noise of the city was a murmur below. It reminded Edgar that he was in New York, a place he liked ever since he was a West Point upper classman who could get away for Saturday afternoons and evenings in the city.

"What's the situation, Paul?"

"We haven't got a lot. We need to go over each report so that you can see for yourself. The five women he dated seriously have all had subsequent relationships. Three are married with families; one is divorced, and one is in a relationship that hasn't made it to marriage. She is a Professor of chemistry at Bowling Green. The one who is divorced is a marketing director of a hotel chain operating Holiday

Inns based in Chicago. Of the other three, one is a neurosurgeon practicing in Columbus, married to an Ohio State professor, one is with IBM as a regional sales manager, and one is currently at home raising her children, but is a trained musician. She teaches piano and plays the organ at the Episcopal cathedral in Chicago."

"None of them are going to accuse him of anything."

"I think that is a reasonable conclusion, Edgar," Melius laughed.

"He had affairs with five women of that caliber and didn't get married?"

"The report is that he just stepped back from family life. He was on the edge of the 'me' generation. Premarital sex was not only accepted, but expected."

"How many of these women did he live with?"

"Apparently two, the doctor and the IBM'er. The breakups were as amicable as they could be."

"Did he cheat on any one of them?"

"It's hard to tell," Slaughter pondered for a moment.

"Well then, Pamela must be something."

"She is. She is a scientist, a Ph.D., a beauty with brains."

"I know that, but she's a lot smarter than just being a scientist."

"We checked her out. She had two love affairs prior to Adrian. She broke them both off to pursue her career. She had men trailing after her."

Slaughter nodded.

"No indication of his cheating on her?"

"Rumors, but I don't think I can turn up anybody."

"No sexual harassment charges?"

"There were two. One by a known alcoholic and one by a woman who is now in a mental institution."

"Well at least you found that out," Slaughter smiled. "It's always nice to nail a guy like Daggett on straying from his marriage."

"If he did stray, it was probably with high powered women who would never admit it."

"Maybe we could arrange for him to be accused."

Slaughter sat back in his chair.

"All that will do is get you a libel suit, Edgar."

"What about the marriage?" he asked.

"We don't have a camera in their bedroom Edgar, but they take vacations together without the children. They went skiing last April at Steamboat in Colorado. The year before they went skiing in February at Stowe in Vermont. That April just after the children came back from Easter break they went to Acapulco and stayed at Las Brisas. They sleep in a queen-sized bed and they don't wear pajamas."

"How did you find that out?"

"Interviewed the maid."

"What about drugs?"

"There is no evidence of any kind that Daggett has ever been a drug user or even tried them."

"Alcohol?"

"He and Pamela usually have a cocktail or wine every night except when they are on a weight-loss program."

"You're full of good news."

"From Daggett's point of view it's good news."

"Taxes?"

"Every return we have been able to get was prepared by an accountant. The last 14 years by the same firm that now does it. He's had two disputes. Routine."

"Bribes?"

"He never did a lot with politics. His government relations people were always white hat. I think looking for something would be fruitless."

"Nothing in the computers, news items, court records?"

"Nothing."

"FBI file?"

"Nothing, except reports on the recent surveillance from the secret service."

"What about the company. Did the company do anything questionable while he was in charge?"

"There was downsizing. You could probably find employees who might not like him."

Slaughter wondered whether there was an afternoon game that he could go to. "There must be something."

"There were four union elections when Daggett was CEO," Melius said. "He won all of them. He successfully threw the union out of three plants and kept it from unionizing a fourth."

"That could be valuable."

"I think it might, but it has to be carefully handled, Edgar. Remember he won the elections."

They sifted through the papers and the reports and noted any possibilities of smearing Daggett in some way. The information about the unions was useful, but not decisive. Edgar decided that he had come up empty. His reputation was that he always found something. "Are we completely out of options?" he asked.

"It depends on how much money you want to spend," said Melius.

"Make your suggestion."

"I'll put an operative in the New Hampshire campaign and the Iowa campaign either salaried or volunteer and try to get close and see what is going on."

"What are you looking for?"

"It's non-specific," Melius said. "Some corners may be cut, Edgar, with respect to regulations and the law. He and Pamela may split up to increase coverage. Campaign sex could occur with either one of them. Maybe the operative could get into a position where she could accuse him of something or seduce him."

"A big long shot."

"That's where we are."

"Let's wait. Too much exposure considering what we have in place. Maybe somebody else associated with him will create a scandal."

"It might have to be somebody else."

THE ATMOSPHERE AT Daggett headquarters improved in the month of May as Adrian moved around the states to meet with Democrats, appear at fundraisers, and enlarge and explain his positions. The poll results made them all feel upbeat. He continued to gain, although the unfavorable percentage stayed with him. New polls showed him beating Hatford while Porter and the others would lose. Alan Jacobs, who lived by these numbers, called for an analytical meeting with the top experts of their polling firm, Rossberg & Janowski, whom he thought were the best in the business. Four of them flew out from Washington to Chicago so people from the staff could hear the dialogue. Alan invited representatives from the key states. Merrick Reynolds sent Karen Crezna. She was excited to be included and had her writing pad out ready to make notes.

They used the large conference room on the top floor of the headquarters building now decorated with framed photo collages of Adrian in his campaign. Coffee, bagels, and muffins were on a buffet. The windows were open to a fresh Lake Michigan breeze. Alan asked for 30 minutes on the numbers which Parker Lothan, senior vice president, of Rossberg & Janowski presented.

All went well until he recommended that the campaign step away from the strict reality positions and begin to tell people what the polls indicated they wanted to hear.

"I don't think there is much opportunity to change positions away from anything but the pure reality campaign. We have promised that," said Anne.

"But there is a point, Anne," said Alan. "We have accomplished a lot with the positions on world involvement, aerospace, paying down the debt, technology development, infrastructure, and the environment. Now maybe we need to do something else. We've got to look at these numbers very seriously."

"I sense momentum," said Anne, "in what we are doing."

"But, we haven't yet felt the competitive fire," said Alan.

"What do you think that any one of these opponents is going to be able to do against us?" questioned Anne. "They're boobs."

"They may be boobs, but they could get good consultants," said Alan.

"I agree with Anne," said Nancy. "For once we have a candidate who is charismatic, warm and genuine, and most important, knows what he is doing. He's telling people the truth. I don't think we should try to change him."

"All of the qualities that you have just cited are reasons why he is electable, and why he twice won easily in Illinois. You're not going to reduce his chances of being elected by telling people what they want to hear from this point forward," said Lothan.

"I wish I were comfortable with that," said Nancy. "Our numbers are demonstrating a problem and maybe we all sense it. But there is the question in my mind. If we start to soften the implied criticism of the political establishment, we are going to discredit ourselves."

"Nancy," Alan said judicially, "I think what our guests are trying to say is we have a first class candidate, one who is unique among presidential candidates in the last 40 years, since Kennedy, and that we ought to sell him as a man rather than sell his issues. It is true that issues can complicate an election."

"We've gotten where we are, in terms of recognition, with the issues, Alan," said Anne firmly.

"We are sitting here with the best polling firm in the country and they are telling us to lay off the issues," Mitchell Fiddler raised his voice.

"I don't think we are quite saying that," said Lothan. "But what I'm saying is tell the people what they want to hear more than you have done so far."

"I'm having difficulty understanding what you mean, Parker," said Anne. "I clearly see what your numbers are showing. I would rely on yours ahead of anyone else's. But I'm not sure of the analysis."

Christine Gallagher, the statistical director at Rossberg joined in. "We also think our statistics are the best you can buy. But we also have to offer the best analysis that we can give. We try to build a sense of the numbers. We look at them as they evolve."

"We're debating that judgment," said Anne, "because the decisions we make now are critical as to whether we storm away with the nomination or whether we struggle for it. You come up with the character issue being the key one. The recommendation that we mitigate issues positions I believe also mitigates Adrian's character. We have given people the opportunity to vote for a man who truly understands the world as much as anyone can, as complex as it is, and who can truly communicate based on his own intellect. The original concept of the campaign was to raise the contest to a higher level, to a level where our opponents cannot compete. This was to force them to deal with issues which they can't handle."

"What we need," said Alan, "is an idea of the effectiveness of the issues campaign in terms of building an understanding of the issues and an understanding of Daggett and what the reaction to him is regarding trust. Is it based on his positions or on the fact that he has a position or is it just a perception of his ability to problem solve?"

"We can get at that," Lothan said.

Anne Russell decided the more sophisticated the campaign, the less smoothly it went. "Until we see some tangible evidence to the contrary, we should stick to the game plan. We have an issues staff that is unprecedented."

That seemed to be a reasonable conclusion to the discussion. Everyone was anxious to avoid strife inside the campaign. They all knew that politicians and staffs who allowed that to happen were in the burial grounds of politics.

THE SHOOTING OF the police car at the Scottish Village remained unsolved. After weeks had gone by, it still bothered Alvin Carter because he couldn't tell Ian what had really happened. A van was found which had been rented in New York. It contained burglar's clothing, black hoods, sweaters, shirts, and slacks. Alvin bought it from the rental company, and had a free lance forensics team from Pittsburgh work it over. They found a few fingerprints, shreds of clothing, and hair, all of which were carefully retained. A gun was found by children chasing frogs in a swamp. It was of the same apparent caliber of the bullets used to shoot the windshield of the police car. Only a fragment of a bullet matched in a ballistics test. Roadblocks had been set up by the Pennsylvania State Police as far as 60 miles from Harrisburg on the main highways. No suspicious people were found traveling at the late hour. A re-check of the hotels showed no suspicious check-ins. Interviews with all night restaurants showed no unrecognized customers, and service stations reported nothing unusual. But then, professionals would not be detected this way.

Why professionals? Did POLACO find out that there was campaign activity at the village office? If that were true, there was a mole, and POLACO was aware of their involvement in the Daggett campaign or suspected it. Alvin put this into a confidential e-mail to Stephie, Tony, Nancy, Terry, and Ian.

THE DECISION ON the debate in the meeting with Rossberg & Jankowski fell to Adrian and Terry. They called together a working group of Anne, Nancy, and Alan with members of their staffs, the regional directors, and one representative from each state. Merrick Reynolds sent Karen Crezna again. The top floor conference room was crowded when Adrian and Terry came into the room. They all rose to applaud. Adrian went around the table and shook hands with everyone. Karen's heart leapt when he recognized her and said, "I see they have you attending strategy sessions, now."

He spoke briefly. "No candidate for any office has ever had the support that I have from this staff. When I despair of the short time we have to accomplish our goal and the difficulties before us, I think of you, and my mood changes. I want you to do the same. Think of us and our team and think of our mission. By our very existence we are changing the American political landscape, which for decades has needed the remedy we can bring. If we are successful, American politics will change. It will be given a new energy, and the power that comes from knowing and speaking the truth. This is a great mission, and you are the leaders of a great staff." They cheered and applauded. Anne Russell yelled, "Bravo!" Tony turned to see if the staff video was on and providentially they caught the whole statement.

"The purpose of this meeting is to consider what we have called the issues game," Adrian continued, "You are all aware of our strategy of presenting specific issues and using them to attack the present political establishment, which indirectly attacks our opponents. By our positions on the issues, we define ourselves as the reality campaign and prospectively as the reality government. I mean to tell you that I hope that all of you will be in that government, if that is your choice."

There was more applause and cheering.

"To prepare for this meeting we have an outline at your place which sketches our position on some of the issues. I'd like to sit as audience so I'll turn this over to Terry. He likes to lecture and he likes to be chairman."

"Thank you, Adrian," Terry said. "Set your watches to see when he takes over." They all laughed.

Karen Crezna thought to herself. I am 23 years old and I'm here experiencing this.

"How is abortion playing in Iowa, Karen?"

Karen blushed. She was surprised to be asked a direct question.

"So far it seems to be at least halfway paved over," she said. "I see acceptance of the idea to stop the debate. I do not feel people who are pro-life consider us to be pro-choice. It seems that a middle ground is being established and we are on it which, I understand, is our objective."

After some others had commented, Terry said, "If we compared the abortion movement to other great movements in American history, it does not seem important and may not be sincere. Do you think we could peel away some of its support? I mean to point out that compared to the feminist movement, the abolition movement, the civil rights movement and the environmental movement, abortion has little significance. Further, we could allege that leaders of the abortion movement on both sides are largely on a power trip or worse. This is not to say that the leaders of some of the others weren't too, but their original purposes were genuine."

"Not bad for a campaign manager," joked Adrian.

"See, five minutes into the meeting," Terry retorted. Everyone laughed.

"Sounds a little complicated to me," said Alan Jacobs.

"There is a ring to it," said Nancy. She sat next to Tony who had come in after the introductions, to keep his profile low.

"We've talked about another issue: religion and school prayer," said Emily Langdon from Tennessee.

Roger Bennett said, "Our intention was to keep this one until after the primaries and use it on Hatford in the general election. We are working on an initiative to permit teaching of religious history, philosophy, morals and ethics, and comparative religion in the public schools. The purpose will be to help reestablish morality."

"That is bold," said Emily. "That would dump everything over-board in Tennessee for a lot of reshuffling. The Christian Right wouldn't know what to do."

"That's where we want them," Roger said. "We thought that would appeal to their members and shift some to the reality side."

"Iowa, what is the situation there? Do we need to use it as an issue now?"

Karen found herself making decisions for the state of Iowa. "I think in Iowa that issue could be important. People in Iowa would associate it with education and teaching students morals and ethics."

Adrian paused. "Good point, Karen. Religion and education go together." She was 23 years old, she thought, and a presidential candidate called her by her first name. She felt a wave of humility.

Anne Russell looked at Karen as well. "If we launch this, it's going to be a national bomb shell and could conceivably create a lot of debate about church and state. Our issues team has carved out a very precise, simple, easy-to-understand proposal. We think religious people are going to favor it. The United States, although the churches are far from full even on Easter, is still a religious country. Does that make sense in Iowa?"

Karen felt perspiration break out. "On balance it is a good issue. It is something that political people have avoided. I think people in Iowa believe it needs to be addressed. There isn't anyone I know who doesn't think that our secondary schools and that the education of our children is a major problem. I think it would be positive." She hoped they wouldn't call on her again.

"Thank you. Bill Packet, what do you think, in Georgia?

"It would be great to bring this out in the general election and challenge Hatford with it. It's a great October surprise. Aside from the ultra liberals and the ACLU, I'm concerned about the Pentecostal churches. They might feel the teaching of religious literature, history, and philosophy would not be sufficiently Biblical."

"What about the reaction of the conventional institutional church-es?" asked Anne. "Would they fear that the teaching might be seized by the Pentecostal churches or by the Catholic Church? Who has some ideas as to how the Catholic Church would react, Dominick?"

"I could ask the Bishop, but they might have some reaction against the possibility of Protestant teaching. They might also think they provide all the Catholic Education needed."

"What about the Jewish community, Alan?" asked Anne.

"We are not all that religious," Alan joked. Everyone laughed. "There are more similarities than differences between the Jews and the Christians. You may want to consult the orthodox Jews. I would expect an argument."

"I think this group has come up with a good idea, Terry, and that is to bring up the religious education issue," said Adrian. "This has fascinating possibilities."

And they went on. They covered atomic energy, energy needs, and nuclear waste from both power plants and weapons production.

On the Civil Service they recognized that huge cost savings could be created by eliminating inefficient government employees. They set a goal to cut 1 million employees saving $50 billion by empowering supervisors to weed out dead wood with modifications in the Civil Service Act. Not only would costs be saved, but also productivity and employee attitudes would improve. Penalties for arbitrary actions against individuals would be stiff, and action against units or organizations that failed to meet reasonable performance standards would be severe.

The meeting generated new opinions and ideas. It lasted through a buffet lunch until late afternoon when Adrian and Pamela left with Anne, Nancy, and Terry to fly to Nashville to a dinner of the American Chamber of Commerce. Adrian was to give a major speech to launch reform to reduce litigiousness and re-build trust in commercial and financial dealings.

Anne gathered the press who, once came wondering, and now came anticipating. The television cameras were waiting. The subject had been announced. When Adrian and Pamela appeared there was sustained applause.

At the rostrum he began, "This is about the way we do business in the United States and how we will treat each other in our commercial relationships in the future. This is about litigiousness and the drain upon our society it creates. In advance, it must be said that within the legal profession, most are fine people who learn the rules by which we must live and help us live by the rules. There are prosecutors who seek to keep us safe and defense attorneys who seek to keep the system of justice safe. Agreement lawyers define and establish relationships between entities and create the vehicles through which major new commerce flows. There are government lawyers who create regulations that protect us sometimes from ourselves. But there are others who seek to gain unjustly by the system and exploit its weaknesses.

"It's impossible to tell the economic impact of unjustified lawsuits and awards. Reserves against settlements and insurance fees are significant percentages of product costs. Companies steer away from business investments because of potential lawsuit involvement. Some companies have dropped businesses or sold them because of the fear of litigation.

"Litigation is often times done with a total disregard for the truth. False claims are made and small out-of-court settlements occur because corporations and other businesses find it less costly to settle, rather than to struggle when legal fees will be greater than the settlement and the cost of time. Plaintiff lawyers, like suited vultures, wait with their clients for the arbitration of small matters with the appearance of prey assured."

He made specific proposals. One was that the plaintiff pays the cost of a successful defense with added payments for the cost of the defendant's time at the option of the court. He stated that his administration would propose a tax on legal fees to pay for the prosecution of perjury in civil cases where it is suspected. This, he said, would be a first step toward re-establishment of the truth of people's statements and toward the mitigation of lies now raining on lawful people and business entities.

He further cited the importance of reestablishing trust. He cited examples of productive, trusting relationships and the high costs of those in which trust was absent.

He was interrupted frequently for applause. At the end, people cheered. Pamela felt a lump in her throat and her eyes were shining. Adrian, acknowledging the crowd, held Pamela tight. Another reality initiative was mightily received. Those who crowded around the rostrum told them little stories of their experiences. Others said they could only hope that he would be elected to stop the nonsense.

At the press tables the reporters could scarcely wait for the speech to end so they could rush to tell the story. Reports appeared in all the major newspapers, in the national magazines, on network and cable television, and on radio. *Business Week* did a cover story, *Forbes*, and *Fortune* followed suit. *The New York Times, The Wall Street Journal,* and others editorialized favorably. Reporters ran over each other to get statements from the groups concerned. The Ralph Nader family took exception with other consumer organizations. The American Bar Association applauded it. The American Trial Lawyers Association was mute. The Small Business Association invited Adrian to speak at their national convention.

At the end of the evening, finally alone with Pamela in their suite,

Adrian collapsed into a chair.

"Was it that good?"

Pamela was at the table at the end of their sitting room slicing an orange from a fruit basket. "Yes, dear, it was that good."

"Jamie Crimmins wrote it. He's caught my style, and is doing very well. Mark him down as chief speech writer or better."

"You're not even nominated yet."

"I guess I expect to be; I expect to win in November. This is the high; the low is feeling inundated. What did you think of the meeting?'

"You have an extraordinary staff. Anne Russell says they are so much better than any she's ever worked with, that it's hard to anticipate a comparison."

"That's the way Anne would say it."

"Anne Russell never misses anything."

"They all contribute, and Terry is doing an extraordinary job."

"He's becoming a manager."

"This all could still overwhelm him."

"Not with the others there to help him, particularly Tony."

"It's too bad he can't be the official deputy chairman or something."

"We'll use him. We will need technology executives in government. I'll ask Ian to let me have him as under secretary of defense for research and development."

"He may not be available, because you are going to have to give Nancy whatever she wants. You won't be able to select two people from PENMET."

"Let's see what it looks like when the time comes. Are you having fun, Pamela?"

"I think it's a mission that I might prefer not to do, but I realize now what it all means."

"Can you tell me? I'm sometimes baffled."

"It means the whole of American politics has to change and start electing people like you."

She had kicked off her shoes. While he watched, she raised her skirt and pulled her pantyhose from her long, shapely legs.

"I get scared, sometimes. Can I really measure up? There's always someone better."

"If there is, let him come forth. I'll tell you who is not better; Porter, Perona, and Hatford, are not better than you."

"How can you tell?"

"Women can tell."

"You're the smartest woman I've ever known, Pamela, and one of the most beautiful."

"Why thank you, Mr. President-to-be. You're not busy," she said standing up, and coming to him. "Unzip me."

When she lifted her dress over her head he undid her bra and caressed her breasts. She turned to kiss him.

AFTER THE DAGGETTS left the meeting, Tony came to Nancy's office. She was transfixed, typing onto her computer.

"I thought other people were supposed to do the writing," he said.

"Once a copy writer, always a copy writer."

"Are you writing copy?"

"I had an idea; I want to get it down."

He watched her in silhouette. He wondered what she was like just coming out of school at the age when he married Jean. How did she feel as a Polish girl from New Jersey going out in the world with a degree in communication? She did well, he knew. She had faith and courage and was wise enough to select her objectives. He had always guessed she was very sexy, but never showed it very much.

"There," said Nancy spinning her chair toward Tony. "So what did you think of the meeting?"

"I'm glad I came. We have some good people on the state level. I wanted to hear their feedback."

"They are level headed, Tony, and they know what they are doing. We can expect them to be successful."

"What's the outlook?"

"The polls are good. Things are going well, Tony. There are obstacles, and there is the time factor, but we are going to win. You don't look happy."

"Does it show?"

"Has to be problems at home."

"The campaign's gotten in the way of the marriage," Tony said. "I'm on Jean's turf. She doesn't like that and she doesn't like our program. She is a perception person."

"Like most of the professionals. Anyway, brace up there, it will pass particularly when we win. Let's go get some of the state people and take them out to dinner."

"More talk."

"With the state people at dinner with us there won't be anything but political talk."

"I'd like a close-up look at them," Tony said.

Nancy called her secretary and had her beep Karen Crezna, Bill Packet, and Emily Langdon.

Karen couldn't believe the invitation. She was going to have dinner with Nancy Letersky and Tony Destito!

It was a great time. Nancy suggested Phil Schmidt's just over the border in Whiting, Indiana. She snagged a campaign car which Tony drove down Lake Shore Drive and over the Calumet Skyway. The restaurant near the lakeshore was 1930s art deco with lots of black, red, and silver trim with white tablecloths. They ordered a pitcher of beer and buttered and boned trout with all of the trimmings. Soon the table was piled with food which the young people enjoyed while they told their battle and intrigue stories.

Driving back to Chicago, the talk continued. Despite early morning flights, Karen, Emily, and Bill decided to continue the evening and headed for a disco by the river, near the Executive Plaza Hotel where Tony was staying. Tony invited Nancy for a nightcap. They took the elevator to the top floor bar. In the darkened room they could look over the gleaming northern part of the city and down at the canal where boats were moored beside the Tower Apartments, long a landmark of the city. At a table by the window Tony asked the waiter if he had Armagnac. "By all means," the waiter said. "Would you prefer the Papelory or the Marquis de Causade?" Tony selected the Papelory.

When Nancy asked him what it was, he told her and she decided to try it.

"This tastes like it is expensive," said Nancy.

"I'll charge it to Ian."

She raised her glass and smiled into his eyes. "To Ian, and to victory."

He raised his glass. "To all the victories."

She smiled into his eyes again.

"Have our opponents started to fight?"

"We're not sure they can."

"Where are you living?" he asked.

"I should have shown you. We drove right past the apartments down by 48th Street South. They're in two tall buildings. I jog on the beach every morning. Two blocks east there is a wonderful gymnasium with a swimming pool, so I joined."

"Has anyone in Chicago taken a fancy to you?"

"Only for my body," she quipped. "I couldn't tell if they had any brains."

Tony laughed. "I used to think I was good at handling high-powered women, but I'm not sure any more."

"It will pass, Tony."

"I have a bad feeling, that with Jean things may not be the same again."

She touched his hand to console him. He thought he'd better change the subject.

"How is it working with Anne?" he asked.

"Anne would be the best at whatever she tried to do. If she were a gun slinger she would be the best."

"I think you would be too."

"I'm a little clumsy sometimes, You just don't see it."

He remembered her perfect jackknife in the winter swim at Pheasant Run, and how she looked in her swimsuit.

"You're clumsy like a lioness."

"Nice simile, Tony."

They had found a parking place on the street. The area was brightly lighted. In the background sirens were screeching because a boat was coming down the river. The drawbridges were going up and down in sequence.

They walked across the street to the end of a small park on the embankment along the canal. She held his arm and pulled closer to him. He could feel her excitement at the spectacle. When the boat passed, they walked back across the street. He took her keys and opened the door while she stood in front of the car. He went to her; she took his waist as she normally would to hug him, and at the last minute decided to kiss him. He kissed her back. They kissed again, then once more. He whispered in her ear, "Goodnight."

She said, "Good night, Tony."

He stood on the sidewalk and watched until she was out of sight.

THE NEXT MORNING, spirits were high in the Daggett campaign. Adrian, Pamela, and their entourage took off from Nashville in pre-dawn darkness to fly to a breakfast meeting with the Kansas City, Kansas, Rotary Club. As the members arrived there was little else but talk of the speech of the night before. When Adrian entered with his escort, applause exploded into a standing welcome. He set aside his prepared text and asked if they wanted him to take questions about the lawyers. They answered with more applause. For 40 minutes he talked with them. When he left they stood to applaud again.

Ninety minutes later the campaign group was together in Chicago for a meeting of the Senior Committee. Roger Bennett and the issues staff were ready with the briefing paper, delivered to those to be attending by 9:30. Tony spent some time with Mitchell to see if the money was still flowing in. It was a happy meeting as the staff approached euphoria about the press response to Adrian's speech and the progress they had made.

Back in Iowa, Karen had checked into a motel room in Mason City to prepare for a meeting with the local volunteers. Her television was tuned to the local station. Her thoughts were interrupted as she caught the first words of a new commercial.

A woman's voice said, "Do you think we really need to pay more taxes to pay down the national debt? That's what I've been hearing."

Before it ended, she and a dozen others had dialed campaign head-quarters in Chicago. The campaign technicians in the communication control room ran it down and taped it. They phoned the conference room to say they would direct it to the video monitor. Everyone gathered; the screen flickered. The scene was a prosperous middle class kitchen with an island stove where "Jane" was cooking. Her husband leaned against the counter holding a tall glass of fruit juice. "Jane" was in her late forties, trim with brown hair. "Louis," a little older, was also trim with graying hair.

Jane: "Do you think we really need to pay more taxes to pay down the national debt the way we've been hearing?"

Louis: (exasperated) "I don't know why we have to pay more taxes. I thought Congress balanced the budget. That's what the big fight was about when the government was shut down."

Jane: "But it seems to have become a big deal again. What is so important about paying down the debt? We seem to be going along pretty well with things the way they are."

Louis: "We don't need to pay more taxes to the federal government. The more money we give to the Congress the more money they spend."

Jane: "And on what?"

Louis: "They always seem to be able to think of something."

Jane: "That's what is frightening, not the debt."

The scene shifted to an exterior view of the house, and the voice over said, "This is brought to you as a public service by the Southern

Conservative Coalition."

The television flickered off and the room was quiet for a few seconds.

"Ask them to play it again, please," requested Anne.

Terry picked up the phone. They watched it again. Tony felt butterflies in his stomach. The only people in the world who could have written that script and gotten it on the air so slickly were those who worked for Helene Courtney and Erla Younge. They also had the money to swamp them on the air with their message.

"Is it who I think it is, Tony?" Adrian asked.

"I would assume so," said Tony as he reached for a phone to call Alvin Carter.

"It appears that we have some competition," said Nancy.

"We will still win," said Anne.

"This is what I was warning you about," said Alan Jacobs.

TEN THOUSAND LETTERS of the first direct mail appeal for contributions to the Southern Conservative Coalition were timed to arrive at the homes of known conservatives and Republicans three days after the new TV ad appeared. Two days later Federal Express brought $20,000 of response. Letters then arrived with checks and $20 bills. Courier packs delivered larger checks. POLACO computers recorded the results and generated acknowledgment letters which went out from the SCC headquarters. Donor's names were added to a master list; those indicating they would help further were marked for telephone follow-up.

On Harbour Island, Helene and Warren Hatch monitored the success on computer graphs. A steady effort of continuous airtime opposing the reality precepts would respond to Daggett. They had an audience who would pay for it.

Helene flashed the "go" signal for media buys for the obviously successful "Jane and Lou" ad, and for letters to be mailed at a rate of 10,000 per day. The target was a million households and 40,000 contributors in the first stage and 10 million households and 300,000 contributions to sustain their attack. Helene and Erla were right about adapting the "Harry and Louise" formula without gimmicks or fancy visuals.

When the second ad was ready they watched the final cut. This time it was a younger couple, Norman and Cindy, watching television news when Norman turns off the sound and says angrily, "Cindy, I don't believe this business about the United States being the world's policeman."

"It frightens me, Norman. Who approved that?"

"Fortunately it's not policy, but some politicians are proposing to make it policy."

"My vote is for somebody that turns that off. I don't want my children fighting wars."

"And, I don't want to have to pay for them."

"Neither do I. Not with lives or money. We don't need to do that."

"Nobody can solve all the world's problems.Look what happened in Somalia when we tried to help just one country."

"Where do these ideas come from?"

"I hope the people that propose stuff like that recognize that people like us will vote against them," Norman said firmly.

"No one with ideas of America being the world's policeman should be allowed to hold office," Cindy added.

The scene faded and a voice over announced, "A public service of the Southern Conservative Coalition."

"Slick," said Helene.

"I think they played it well. Good set too; very appealing. How much money has come in?"

"So far almost a million."

"We're building the perception that Daggett is an irresponsible interventionist," Hatch smiled complacently.

"Seems to be working just fine."

SUNDAY NIGHT WAS the only time that Jean and Tony regularly watched television. In better weather they would normally be outside, but it was a rainy day. The order of business was *60 Minutes,* a mystery on PBS, and then *Masterpiece Theater.* At ten when the CNN news came on, Jean got up from the couch where she was snuggled beside Tony to go to their bar in the family room to get two glasses of port. When the ads finished she came back beside him and clinked glasses.

When it was time for commercials, the screen flashed to a logo in front of the American flag. The voice over said, "This message is brought to you by the Fulton Foundation of Leesburg, Virginia. Ladies and Gentlemen Congressman Darcey Granton speaking to the Mission Society of San Diego California."

Congressman Granton appeared at a red, white, and blue bunting draped podium with the applause just ending in the background.

"So the question of dealing with the national debt and balancing the budget should not shrink the paychecks of working people in this nation. Rather we should expand economic development by the application of conservative principles of low taxes and reduced government regulation to realize economic growth, to supply the revenues to government that will keep the budget balanced, and to pay off the debt. In so doing it is ultimately necessary that we further reduce government spending on expensive research projects, on expensive forays into space, and on unnecessary national defense. We must reduce expenditures in order to assure the important safety net of social welfare. On this matter there is a forthcoming national debate and those of us who believe in conservative principles must be prepared to win that debate."

There was loud applause which subsided.

"We must insure the economic health of America for our children and their posterity. Thank you." There was more loud applause and a pan to the audience which stood clapping madly. Then the voice over said, "The Foulton Foundation brings messages related to public issues to the American people."

"Looks like somebody else is after you," said Jean. "Early on in the game. Very well presented, very well written, just the right touch"

"That's got to be POLACO," said Tony. "Nobody else is that good." He took the glass from Jean and put it down on the coffee table.

"They sense your vulnerability," she said. "I told you they would come after you."

"How can people prostitute themselves to say something like that, something we have heard for the last two dozen years and which obviously won't work?"

"They know what people want to hear, Tony."

"I don't care what people want to hear. They have to focus on reality. Avoiding reality can destroy the United States with a financial collapse."

"Who understands financial collapse?" she asked. "Who believes in it? Who could picture what it does? Do you want to go around scaring people?"

"We may have to." He took a sip of the wine.

"Then you'll lose," she said. "People don't want to hear about the tough problems. They only want to hear about the easy issues. Abortion. That's easy, all you need is an opinion. Analysis of complex facts is not necessary."

"Don't you think that's the reason why the country is in such terrible shape, because politicians only want to deal with easy issues?"

"When are you going to realize, Tony, that you have to play by the rules?" she asked. "You can't change them." Jean glared at him.

"If the rules are wrong, we have to change them."

"Then you are going to go down and you are going to take us with you," she said. "What do you think is going to happen if the election goes south? If it is POLACO, they are going to come after PENMET."

"How can they?"

"By accusing you of being involved in politics, illegal contributions, of buying favors," she said. "They can come after us personally. Politics is a dirty business, Tony. You're going to lose your job, because there are going to be big changes at PENMET if it is attacked because of this political involvement, and I'm sure it will be. POLACO knows about you, Tony, and they're coming after you. Maybe it is already too late."

"I can't believe they found out," he said. "We've kept it so secret. Alvin Carter thinks it's a mole."

"Why wouldn't they put a mole in your organization? You don't think they have scruples do you?"

"We're looking."

"It's going to bring down the company and you're going to suffer. You could be president, Tony. I'd like you to be CEO of PENMET. Don't you want that?"

"Of course I want to be president."

"You have the organizational ability," she moved close to him and took his hand. "You have the savvy and you know the business."

He eyed her, waiting for her to continue, but she left it at that. "What do you want me to do?" he asked.

"I want you to resign from the campaign and concentrate on your job and bringing out the new Ceramalloy," she said. "Bring it out, Tony, and crush the opposition. Stay in the commercial business. Leave the elections up to someone else."

"My orders are to see that Daggett is nominated and elected."

"And if that is what you have to do, for God's sake, Tony," she raised her voice and let go of his hand, "do it the right way. Keep the campaign off this revolutionary kick."

"Somebody has to do it, Jean."

"Not you!" she yelled, got up, and stalked out of the room. Then she came back to the doorway.

"Tony, I married you because I knew you were good in your heart and in your brain and that you had the energy to go places and keep up with me," she said. "But I don't want to go down, Tony. You are 46 years old and you're worth $4 million. I feel like taking my share now so I can protect the kids."

She stalked out again. Where had it all gone, all the life of their marriage? He knew she would be proud of him if he were president of PENMET. It could all come crashing down, and she had just served notice that she would not stand by him if he failed.

☆ **Chapter 14** ☆

ADRIAN HAD BEEN scheduled to be in Chicago the next day for a training session and then fly to a fundraiser in Buffalo. Instead, he and Pamela were on the campaign plane with Terry, Nancy, Anne, Mitchell, Dominick, Tony, and Alan headed for a meeting at the MacAulliffe mansion. Ian's limousine was at the general fleet terminal and in 30 minutes they were ushered into the library by Francisco.

A Learjet at Teterboro picked up Stephanie Comstock, Alvin Carter, Denise Williams, and David Gibson. Tony brought them from the airport. They all sat around a large oak table, newly purchased for such meetings.

The first item of business was a report by Alvin Carter on his investigation of the "Southern Coalition" and how he had confirmed that POLACO was the destination of the returns from the "Southern Coalition" mass mailings.

"Once we traced the replies of the mail solicitations to their final destination at Harbour Island, we observed the pickup by a POLACO electric car we knew," he concluded.

"I'm glad you are working on this campaign, Alvin," said Adrian.

"So we assume POLACO is also the source of the Southern Conservative Coalition ads we have seen. We also assume they are responsible for the one that appeared Saturday from the so-called Foulton Foundation," said Terry. "Since we started, we have always been the organization with the superior resources in terms of both finance and talent. Not only does POLACO have immense resources, but also they are now raising money based on a media blitz, which is going to draw extremely well. Their message appeals to a lot of well-off people and not-so-well-off people who are also not so well informed. You can expect they will test these messages nationwide then target them in the key primary states. Porter and Perona will jump on them."

"We will have to discredit that message," said Anne.

"There is a larger issue here of strategy," said Ian, "The reason for this meeting is to determine our basic strategy."

"I have been arguing the need to rethink it for some time," said Mitchell with a thin smile.

"The situation has changed, Mitch," said Adrian. "We have to determine everything we can about the intentions and probable actions of POLACO."

"Why are they doing this? What's their problem? Aren't we running a very good man for president?" asked Gibson.

"It's not their man, David. We have to assume they know everything we are doing and we have to assume they know why."

"Now we have the company in danger," said Stephanie. "We have exposed it."

"How do you mean?" asked Nancy.

"They can accuse us of illegal political expenditures on one count after another. They can harass us. They can impugn the character of the management."

That was Ian's concern. His mind was racing ahead as he considered these contingencies. What had he gotten into? He spent most of his adult life building PENMET into the best example he could of free enterprise. Now this could be poisoned. He had made a determination affecting the company. But, he hadn't fully assessed the risks to the company and its employees. This magnificent asset to the United States and to the world could be crippled or even destroyed. Most of all he feared investigators and probing reporters. They would have to be very sophisticated to find them, but he had things hidden. Some that even Susan didn't know. He looked at her. She turned and their eyes met. She smiled at his attention.

"Ian," Gibson spoke in a clear, persuasive tone of voice, "consider what damage might be done to the companies that are participating in POLACO should they start that kind of action. They may also be guilty of illegal interference in politics, however that might be defined. We also have those confidentiality agreements. They can attack Tony and me personally. We have not only given our signature, but also our word and broken both."

Tony sickened as he thought of fighting a lawsuit to protect his modest wealth against the animal lawyers Ward Cowell could unleash.

"Denise?" asked Ian.

"It would surprise me if they did anything before the election, because I believe it would reflect badly on both sides. But they might attack, if they were losing badly and thought they had some angle. They have no agreement not to strike at us. I can see ways of replying that relate to 'reality.' Perhaps the reputation of PENMET would carry us through or at least they might fear it would. Sorry, I'm musing."

"That means that our future would depend on the mercy of the media. A lousy risk," said Ian.

"The jackals chew on whatever bodies are on the ground," Denise philosophized. "Ward Cowell is less vulnerable, but he has to think about it."

"They are not all jackals," Anne said. "They have responded reasonably well so far to us. Many newspapers and TV stations support our challenge to the political establishment. There are things that we can do both to defend the company and make an issue out of the accusations they might bring. We could leak it ourselves, and then reply." They laughed. Ian and Adrian appreciated Anne's effort to lighten the dark mood of the meeting.

"I admire your ability to deal with these people, Anne, Denise, but I fear their gang attacks," said Ian.

"Let's get back to the positive side," said Leelan. "We all came together months ago to examine POLACO and its potential effect. I consider myself privileged to work with you because you decided to risk your own money, and your company's, to stop a serious potential threat to the United States."

That was the point, Ian thought. He had not considered the risk to the company. "From what we are seeing," Leelan continued, "We know the threat is real. POLACO is now maneuvering against an honest and effective candidate to their own ends. They don't want the political structure of the United States to be restored and strengthened, because they prefer to have continued confusion and frustration with somebody like Hatford or Porter as President. They want to feed on that, Ian. That's their reality, and a great many people in the United States think of their own interests first and the country second. You are the reverse example. With God's help it won't be publicized. But if it is, in the end it could boil down to your being someone who cared more for the country than for his wealth." He looked to Ian and then to each person at the table.

Ian thought of the secrets. "But I am responsible for a corporation that affects the lives of tens of thousands of families throughout the world," he said. "Our employees, our vendors, our customers, our communities; we are participants in all of them. I have tried to build something that is powerfully good and I've risked it on a dice table called politics."

"Ian, after we have seen what POLACO has done, it is reasonably clear that they are going after American institutions including the Constitution," Terry said logically. "There is risk here, Ian, but we must defend the Constitution of the United States by pursuing the strategy we have adopted." David Gibson intuitively felt Terry was right. Nancy and Anne never had any doubts.

"What about my fiduciary responsibility?" asked Ian. "I have exposed the corporation, which I do not control, with a majority of stock. I could be sued by the stockholders."

"You have committed your own funds," said David. You're paying the salaries of Nancy and Tony. People in the company don't know that, but that is the record. The company is not involved."

"But I am."

A lawyer of few words, David Gibson could speak eloquently. "The only stake here is your job, Ian. You don't need it," he said. "If they decide to throw you out or you decide to resign if there is exposure, what is more important? We are dealing here with an internal enemy to the United States, one with a cleverly devised plot, hugely financed, to manipulate themselves into power. If they really wanted to restore American democracy they would support Adrian Daggett."

"You're convincing," said Ian. He took a breath and resumed his characteristic demeanor of calm resolve. He had considered backing out, now he recovered to his original faith in the decision. "Aye, David. We have set about a course and we have to continue. What do we do to reply to this artful ignominy of evil intent?"

Alan Jacobs came up with a core concept. This was to counter the planting of misleading ideas by debating them and directly attacking the ads which presented them. Adrian could name the foundations and strike back at them, but Alan suggested that was not enough. The background of debate had to be established and he recommended Nancy's idea as well as developing soft ads to reply to POLACO. Nancy had already asked Tony to join a presentation of the television debate in New York. Tony looked at her and thought about seeing her there. Anne realized that they could now focus the staff at

Chicago and Cleveland on the ads of the two foundations. POLACO had provided a target.

THE CAMPAIGN GROUP left at three for Buffalo. The staff went back to the headquarters on a PENMET jet to examine the polls on the reaction to the POLACO fusillade. Ian asked for some time with Denise, Stephanie, and David. Driving back, Tony's mind was full of different scenarios that might emerge from the private meeting without him. When he turned into the parking lot his car phone rang. It was his secretary, Joan. "Mr. Destito, Mr. MacAulliffe has just called and asked you to come back to the mansion."

Now what was it? He turned around and headed back, wondering what awaited him. Were they changing the structure? Were they backing down? Would he get out of this and placate Jean?

Francisco showed him back to the library. It was now after 4 p.m. Denise, Stephanie, and David were still there seated at the table. Ian was now behind his desk and stood up. "Have some refreshments, Tony." He went to the buffet of juices, sodas, and cheese and crackers trying to imagine what was happening. He selected a piece of cheese and with a wheat cracker to calm his stomach.

"Sit down Tony," Ian said approaching the table. "Forgive me for sending you all the way to headquarters and then calling you back and wasting your time."

"I needed some thinking time," said Tony.

"So did we, and we've come to some decisions. One of them affects you." Tony realized that was the reason he wasn't invited to stay.

"Tony, when you arrived at PENMET, Denise and David were already close advisors," he said. "Stephanie was promoted just a year or two later to the top job in finance. There were reasons that I had these advisors. On several occasions I took risks with the FTC, with the securities laws, and with banking regulations. In each case when investigators or prosecutors moved against us David and his firm held them off. When it was the media, Denise told us what to do to stop them.

"There have also been private and personal issues. I have invested twice in companies which turned out to be fraudulent and one time an attempt was made to develop the perception that I was involved in the fraud. After Evelyn was killed the children were young and I needed to be with them. But, I also needed some feminine companionship. I hired three women to occupy a house I bought in Siddonsville. The deal was they would be on call and I could visit whenever I liked. They kept their jobs and apartments or whatever. On Saturday nights we had a little party. Then I took the kids to church on Sunday. When I started dating seriously, this activity wound down. It stopped when I became intimate with Susan. Continue, David, its embarrassing."

Gibson took up the story. "After Ian, these girls became regular amateurs. They had earned extra money from Ian. They bought the house and continued to party for pay. Eventually it got in the papers. Denise and I had to act fast. We paid them each for a while and then set up a million-dollar annuity for each through a Canadian bank. The deal is if any of them break the agreement, they forfeit the annuity through escrow."

"The newspapers and the radio station were paid off, Tony," Denise said.

"We've used bribery in other instances," Gibson added. "I don't think we need to go into the details now. Suffice it to say we can't stand a lot of deep scrutiny."

They all looked at him gauging his reaction. The reason for this disclosure was suddenly apparent. Tony swallowed hard as Ian came to the point.

"We have never elected anyone to the job of corporate executive vice president," he said. "I don't believe in anointing a successor very far in advance of my own departure. But I am going to ask the board to elect you and make you the heir apparent, should anything happen to me or should I be forced to resign. These people could do things to us Tony, and make it necessary."

"No, Ian, I don't want to..."

"You have to Tony, unless you have a personal reason not to accept," Ian said. "If I'm forced to resign, then I want to be sure you take over so you can continue Daggett's support, and you can also defend the company from what you know to be the source of attack. I don't want anyone else involved in this. I expect this is going to be a permanent appointment if all goes well and that you will become CEO after me. You have the brains, the character, the knowledge, the spirit, the personality, and the wife that it takes. If serious shooting starts and I get hit, you will have time to take over quickly and set things right. Your election will be done quietly, but it has to be a board resolution. Before the board meets I'll call everyone personally. I don't believe many will disagree. We will have Nancy cool it, but there will have to be a press release. It will be substantial news on Wall Street. Congratulations, Tony."

Ian stepped toward him, he stood up to shake hands, and the others stood up and gathered around him. Tony felt David's hand on his shoulder. Denise added a hug and kissed his cheek. Stephanie did the same and for the first time Tony could remember, he felt her tears and saw her eyes were wet. Emotion overcame him for a moment along with the realization that he was one day to sit behind the big desk and work with the board, and make the final tough decisions. Jean would be ecstatic. He saw his future in flashes as he heard himself thanking each for their good wishes. He said, "I only hope that I can live up to the standards that you have set, Ian."

"You have everything in you to do that," Ian said. "Now let's sit down and talk a little further."

Tony went back to the buffet for a glass of water for his dry mouth.

"You know the POLACO people," Ian said. "How well are you acquainted with Helene Courtney?"

Good Lord! Could he ever tell him the truth about Helene?

"Do you know her well enough to ask her for a private meeting off Harbour Island?"

He felt the eyes of the others watching him for signs of unspoken communication. "We're friendly, Ian. I think I can do that."

"We want you to have a private meeting with Helene," Ian said. "You can tell her we know the foundations are theirs and that they are responsible for these ads. I want to set some mutually beneficial ground rules that there be no attacks on the corporations involved. They may feel they are in a better bargaining position since they have those confidentiality agreements, but they also have something to lose because they know we can leak this in a way that they would never be able to track back to us. Denise is preparing that weapon, but that will be our insurance for a deal to protect PENMET if you can make it. You decide the timing. There may be other things that Terry would like to negotiate. I leave that up to you both. Just keep Denise and David informed."

Tony tried hard to stay in the present and to concentrate on the ensuing discussion of an understanding with POLACO. His mind jumped from subject to subject. He felt the others watching him for signs of wavering or weakness. Did they know about him and Helene? Should he admit it to Ian? At the end of the discussion Ian walked them to the door as he normally did. A limousine was waiting to take David and Denise back to the airport for the quick trip to Teterboro. Stephanie hugged them both before she got into her Buick Riviera. Tony walked to his car. Ian followed and shook his hand one more time. "I've thought for a while, Tony, that this might happen as a normal succession where the board selected from several candidates," Ian said. "Now I have to force it because no one else can know about POLACO. I hope you can make an agreement to protect the company. You had to know the secrets. These have to be protected, but you have to be in on the planning to defend us should they be discovered. I will constantly pray for your success and for the continuance of this corporation. Godspeed."

Tony gazed at Ian, tears in his eyes. He hesitated and then embraced him realizing it was the first time he had ever done it. He could feel the warmth of him and smell him, a faint aroma of tension as well as cologne.

Tony drove away deeply thinking about the stunning turn of events. Jean hypothesized that the POLACO issue would doom him. Now it had thrust him into the position both he and she sought. He prayed that the circumstances which had elevated him to this lofty height would not also cause him to fall.

As Tony's car drove off, Ian looked at his watch. It was only 20 minutes after five, and a fine day close to the summer solstice with plenty of daylight left. As he had dressed casually, to play golf all he needed to do was to change shoes. He looked for Susan, but found she had gone to the village and then to a meeting in town and would not be back until after six.

He walked out to the clubhouse by the golf course where there were showers and lockers for his guests and got out his favorite clubs. One of the groundskeepers saw him, a young man nicknamed "Chippie" who asked if he could caddie. The son of one of the village workers, Chippie was born with a clubfoot and Ian's medical plan paid for the operations to repair it. The boy brought the bag out on his shoulder and handed Ian his driver. He teed up the ball and spiked a shot just to the left of the center of the fairway.

THE NEXT MORNING, Tony woke up early and left the house before Jean was conscious. There was no opportunity to give her the big news. In his office, Tony dialed Helene's cellular number. After a long delay, she answered a little out of breath. "Hello, this is Helene."

"And this is Tony."

"Hi," she said in a friendly way. "How are you, where are you? You know all of the questions."

"How's your back?"

"Recovering nicely."

"So you're back jogging on the beach?"

"Wrong guess."

"Something's got you out of breath."

"We're doing our training."

"To defend the island against its enemies."

"Something like that." He could hear anticipation in her voice.

"I'd like to see you."

"That would be nice."

"I'm not sure. We know that the ads are yours."

She paused, "Your intelligence work is good. Why do you want to meet?"

"Well I'd like to see you, but I also think we should establish some ground rules."

"I'd like to see you too. Ground rules about what?"

"About the forthcoming war we are going to have."

"Okay, I'll have to talk with Ward. I assume you have any permission you require."

"From the top."

"I'll call you. Good-bye, Tony."

"Good-bye, Helene."

TONY CONTINUED HIS busy day half concentrating on what he was doing and half anticipating the return call.

His friend Bernie Cheslin and his wife Midge, both excellent tennis players, were coming for doubles and a cook out. Lately he and Jean had not been playing singles. She was setting the table on the terrace. He dropped his briefcase in the den and walked through the French doors to greet her. She turned and pecked him on the cheek.

"I have something to tell you," he said. "Ian is going to propose to the board that I be made executive vice president."

She looked astonished. "What's this about?" she asked suspiciously.

"It's about my succeeding him."

"What brings this on so suddenly?" she asked coldly.

"He wants to establish a line of succession in case POLACO attacks us and somehow forces him to resign."

"You mean they would accuse you or him of illegal use of funds and so forth."

"Maybe not illegal, but they would cast innuendo."

"You'll go down with him, Tony," she warned.

"Well, help me, Jean, help me deal with this."

"I'm trying to help you, Tony," she said. "You won't listen. You've gotten into this thing about saving the world in your own way. I know the world needs to be saved, but you're not going to do it the way you're trying to do it." Her face was set in hard lines that almost destroyed its natural beauty.

"This argument never ends."

"It never will end until you understand what I am trying to tell you."

There was a pause. Tony turned his back on Jean.

"I think we'd better not talk about this now," he said walking to the door.

"I think you're right. We have guests coming," she said.

Tony went up stairs to change, incredulous and fuming. He found a tennis shirt and some shorts and threw them on the floor. He felt like spitting on the rug. He had just told his wife he was going to be Chief Executive Officer of the 20th largest company in the Fortune 500 and she hadn't even hugged him. After the tennis there would be an argument.

HELENE THOUGHT ABOUT inviting Edgar, Erla, and Warren to discuss the potential rendezvous with Tony, but decided to do it alone with Ward. "So they found out about us fast," he said, relaxed with his mid-morning coffee.

"It seems they did," Helene said, "and now they want to talk."

"I can understand why they would," he said. "I was right when I told Sadovan to lay off you and Tony. Every man who knows about your relationship is jealous of Tony. Take that as a compliment. I got your list of possible subjects they might bring up. There may be others, but I don't think it's worth the time of speculating. You have the authority to make any deal that seems reasonable. If you have any doubts, tell him you have to talk to me."

Helene smiled, pleased to be increasingly making the decisions.

"I think," Ward continued, "they probably want to protect themselves now that they know we are the opposition. You should agree to any mutual protection to avoid a battle of annihilation of our corporate identities and management. Keep them in the agreements not to reveal what they know about POLACO."

"They may try to get us to back off and support Daggett."

"That is not negotiable, Helene. You'll have to bring that one back to me and the board."

"I know, but it would be nice not to have a war."

"We're struggling for our survival; they are struggling to keep us from surviving so there isn't much we can do except fight," Ward said. "We have our commitments. Are you recommending that we disband POLACO?"

"It's an option."

"Helene, we can't possibly even think it," he said sternly. "Daggett is going to be another Democrat. We have no commitments that he is going to change the course of history the way we want to and serve the purposes you agreed to support."

"Daggett gives every appearance of trying to change the course of history, Ward," she said. He stared at her and she returned his gaze.

"Helene, has this guy Tony got you misfocused?"

"He certainly doesn't, Ward. I'm doing my job by giving you options. I'm just telling you that if we supported Daggett he would run all over Porter and Hatford, if a deal could be made."

"He would have to agree to not regulate the markets and not to come up with ideas like national health insurance or cost controls on health products and services."

"He has come up with some things we favor."

"He's preempting our issues. We're in a position of saying 'me too' on most cases."

"I realize that, Ward, but he's also telling people he means what he says."

Ward zeroed in on her. "I have to be able to trust you, Helene."

"When you can't, I will resign."

"I will rely on that. You are the commander in the battle. You have to win it."

When she returned to her office she phoned Tony and they made a date for mid-July at the Chateau Frontenac in Quebec.

ALAN JACOBS RECEIVED bad news about the opinion polls. The POLACO foundation advertisements had impacted in New Hampshire and in Iowa where they were initially concentrated. There was a three-point increase in the unfavorable ratings as the ads pulled support from the undecideds. In both states Findlayson had joined Porter in keying off the ads with their own versions. Their work was sloppy and not particularly convincing. Alan and Terry Leelan had discussed the matter privately with Adrian in advance of the Senior Staff

Committee meeting. Alan's position was to try to defend the lead by responding to the ads. Terry's position was to widen the lead by addressing more issues. They decided to do both.

Terry sat at his desk pondering the effects of the blind-side initial hit by the POLACO entry. He questioned whether he had blundered. They were being attacked on specific issues. POLACO had introduced a formidable counter theme from which Porter, Findlayson, and Perona would all attack Daggett. Not a pleasant prospect to deal with. The attempts by Porter and Findlayson to chime in on the POLACO themes might be clumsy, but they reinforced the perceptions that POLACO was fostering. He wondered if the Daggett campaign would have enough money to withstand a continuous bombardment between now and the general election 15 months away. The general election, he realized, would only be an issue if they won the nomination. He decided he'd better focus on that.

Alan was still uncertain about the arguments from Mitchell Fiddler and Dominick Kluczinski that they should adopt a more conventional campaign. If the favorable to unfavorable percentages didn't change, even if the undecided vote went three to one against them, they would still win. Alan now had to put together a coalition of interests that would nominate and elect his candidate. He knew that campaign managers had been doing this since the beginning of the Roman Republic. For an hour or more, he sketched notes on a pad. Some of them were about a deal with Richard Sandellot.

The issues expansion strategy was taken up by Terry Leelan at the Senior Staff Committee meeting.

"The issue now is to determine state by state, what issues we should open in order to continue our attack," Terry insisted. "I'll entertain debate on this, but I think we should continue what is successful, until it stops being successful."

"Terry, we've heard Alan say that we should revise our tactics," Mitchell prompted. "Let's get to creating impressions and perceptions rather than trying to be too specific. That is what the opposition is doing. Fight fire with fire."

"You can see we are now under attack," said Dominick springing at the chance to support Mitchell. "We need to reorganize, regroup, and rethink."

"I disagree," said Anne. "We are in the lead because of our reality campaign. We have taken their ground on some of the issues, which preempts them from using them." She became very emphatic and persuasive speaking as she rose from her chair. "I say NO. Now and forever NO to any idea of trying to be a campaign of perceptions, and I am an expert at creating perceptions. I say we go issue by issue, battle by battle, and be totally honest. If they are not going to raise any issues of their own, then their only identity will be as the anti-Daggett party. I think Terry will tell us all that no one has ever been able to win an election doing that." Anne sat back in her chair fairly glowing at Mitchell and Dominick.

The room fell silent. Adrian cleared his throat and spoke, "I respect all of you very highly. Mitchell and Dominick, without your contribution we wouldn't be here. It would be unnatural if we didn't disagree. I have one view of this. So far we have done what has come naturally, and raised issues in which we believe. I think we have to continue to do that. If we were to falter from that we would discredit ourselves; perhaps in the eyes of the people, and surely in our own eyes. If we are going to change American politics, we have to do it with the truth."

"Hear-hears," sounded around the table. Tony studied the faces. Nancy and Anne were smiling with Roger Bennett. Alan looked quizzical. Anne hoped that it was over and there would be no further discussion, but Mitchell interrupted her thoughts. "All right Adrian, I respect your judgment, but can we review this issue often, and can we keep in mind that it may sometimes be necessary to generate perceptions, even true perceptions about reality?"

"Only a fool doesn't constantly review decisions," Adrian reflected.

☆ **Chapter 15** ☆

SADOVAN AND GALLOSEY were in Helene's mind off and on all week. They had been pushing hard for the final policy regarding Edgar's punishment and interrogation program to be carried out. She had decided how to do it, and had committed to Edgar and Ward. She believed if only people who had gone through it could order punishment or interrogation, it could be controlled. It was an authoritarian state practice, and it had to be controlled or it would be abused. Such a policy would also help instill the integrity she believed to be an intrinsic part of an organization like POLACO.

Arrangements were made for a Friday afternoon. Carrie would be with her. No one else would know, but a videotape would be made of the process if needed for future use to intimidate others or to validate that Helene had been through it. She and Carrie were ushered into Edgar's office after the security routine. She was wearing loose-fitting slacks and a short-sleeved blue blouse. She had brought an old cotton robe. Edgar strode in before they sat down and went up to her.

"You shouldn't do this," Edgar said in a solicitous tone. "Let me stop the preparations."

"No. Let's get on with it."

"Helene," Carrie said with genuine concern, "you really don't need to do this."

"I do need to do it and if you think it through, you'll agree. How do you want to start Edgar?"

He gestured, "Come this way."

They went through one of the doors from his office and down a hall. The corridor led to three other sound insulated rooms. Each door was open. They entered one. The walls were solid gray cement block. There was a mirror on one side, which she knew was one-way glass. The lighting was dim. In the center was an apparatus looking like a cross between an exercise bench and an electric chair.

"This is a straddle," Edgar motioned. "We tie your feet first to the straps and you bend over the straddle. We tie your hands to the cross bar and pull tight. This is for punishment mainly, but can be effective for questioning. The pain is inflicted by these. He picked up a red metal rod about 2 inches in diameter which had a plastic handle with some dials on a crosspiece. It had a pointed end. An electric cord ended in an industrial plug. This leaves no residual marks so we can deny any accusations," he said. "The subject strips and steps here."

He pointed to the ankle rings and straps.

"Why strip?" Helene asked.

"Pain is always inflicted on bare flesh. The body doesn't remember pain, but everyone remembers being naked and completely vulnerable. You don't have to strip. You can just loosen your pants."

"No, I need to undergo the full treatment; both for my own understanding and the video record," Helene insisted.

There were two of Edgar's men and one of his women in the room wearing masks. One had the probe, one had the camera, and one was waiting to strap her down. All three were visibly nervous.

"Do you want to undress in there?" Edgar pointed to another room.

"What would the procedure be?"

"Here."

"Here it is."

Quickly, in a business-like manner, she undressed.

Edgar watched admiringly until Helen's body was entirely exposed. Her breasts were high and firm with large nipples. She was firm with no fat and a flat belly. Her pubic hair covered a small area.

"Please stand here," said the unencumbered masked assistant. She felt her ankles being strapped about a foot apart. He adjusted the straddle to her stomach.

"Okay, would you bend," said the assistant.

She bent over the straddle and he put her wrists in padded leather loops that he pulled tight. She was fastened down so she couldn't move with her buttocks in the air.

"Normally, punishment will be eight to twenty stings on the cheeks, thighs and back. Three would go on each cheek. Two or three on each thigh and the rest on the back or the sides. Now this is what they'll feel like. Edgar pointed to an area on her left thigh and the assistant touched the prod to it.

A point of pain like a bee sting hit her inner thigh and then spread and intensified. She flinched and tensed her entire body before forcing herself to relax.

"This will be on the right thigh," Edgar warned.

The assistant gave her two stings without any apparent reaction from her.

Edgar recognized her ability to force her body to relax, minimizing the pain she felt.

"That's it," said the one who tied her. He immediately loosened her arms. She stood up feeling residual pain burning the afflicted areas of skin. Then he untied her feet. Carrie held her robe which she pulled on.

"How long does the burning last?" Helene asked gingerly rubbing one of the inflamed spots which glowed red like a new sunburn.

"About 36 hours. Not like a strapping," Edgar said. "It will be red until the pain stops and then the redness goes away. It will be sensitive for a week or so."

"Okay, it's not that bad. I can understand that eight to twenty would be a deterrent."

"No doubt," Edgar nodded emphatically.

"And the stripping helps."

"The manuals say particularly with women."

"The interrogation," Helene prompted.

"It begins in this room," Edgar gestured toward the one she and Tony had seen on a tour of the facilities.

Inside was a table with another electric probe on it and several chairs. One was large and heavy and had straps to hold the legs and arms of the person sitting in it.

"This is a simple questioning scenario," Edgar said. "You will play a suspected mole and we will give you a date, place, and time for an exit boat. This is on the card. My interrogators know the information. When you give it all to them, we will stop."

He handed her a card on which he had printed: NEXT WEDNESDAY AT DUSK AT THE FISHERMAN'S DOCK. A WHITE BOAT WITH A BLUE LIGHT.

"Memorize this; it is your secret."

Helene scrutinized the card.

"This has to be really in you, Helene," he said, "take some time. Imagine it a very critical message about an escape."

"All right, Ms. Courtney," said one of the detectives in a voice, which belied the sinister appearance given by the black plastic mask he wore. "This is your next step. There are several beyond this, if you persist in resisting us. Sit down."

She was firmly guided toward the chair and pushed down into it. Edgar stood back while the attendant strapped her wrists and ankles in soft fabric restraints.

"Now you have one more chance to tell us when you were planning to leave. If you haven't gotten the idea, we are going to inflict pain. My colleagues will give you a small demonstration."

Helene knew the probe was hovering behind her in the hand of the attendant who stood out of sight behind the chair. His hand reached around and pushed her robe back. Then she felt a sting. She was relaxed for it and didn't flinch. She kept her body loose.

The probe touched her thigh with even more pain. She kept relaxed, watching the process and noticed the power had been doubled.

"Ms. Courtney you are disappointing us," said the interrogator. "We don't want to hurt you." He paused. "Ms. Courtney one more minute."

The assistant with the probe kept behind her, out of sight, as did Edgar, Carrie, and the other attendants. She felt hands behind her come down to open her robe. There was a pause. Then the robe was unbuttoned, lifted from her shoulders, and pulled out from under her. She felt a wave of helplessness overwhelm her, along with the first small doubt that she could fulfill the commitment she had made.

"Ms. Courtney, you have one more chance," the voice warned.

She saw the probe come out from behind her left shoulder and slowly, but inexorably approach her breast.

"One more chance Ms. Courtney," the voice drawled out as the probe inched closer to her nipple.

"Fuck you!" she said in defiance. An astonishing starburst of pain exploded in her breast as the probe made full contact on her nipple. An involuntary spasm demolished her attempt to relax her body and she fought to regain control, but again the probe made contact and again the starburst of pain. She barely stifled a scream.

"Why don't you give us a reason to stop, Ms. Courtney?" the voice reasoned.

She watched as the probe came slowly towards the other breast. She resisted the temptation to brace herself and tried to distance her mind from her body. A new pinwheel of pain in her right breast made a companion with the one still burning in her left. She yelled an obscenity to cover the suffering in her outcry.

"Tell us the secret, Ms. Courtney or you'll go to the next level.

What you've felt is only the kindergarten of pain. We can take you to high school or even to college if you insist on higher education."

The probe stung her left shoulder, her navel, and then her breast again. She cursed causing swift retribution as the probe found her lips, applying a searing kiss.

"Tell us," the attendant growled.

"No," she said.

"You'll be hurt much worse than this if you don't tell us, Why not end this? The next stage will be many times worse than this. All of us will hurt you. You will eventually tell us. Why not tell us now and save yourself? You could be having a nice dinner in an hour."

"You can't make me tell you anything."

Suddenly Helene was grabbed by her hair and her mouth forced open allowing the probe to find her lower gum line. The pain filled her mouth and teeth. The expletive again not quite marked the scream.

The interrogator grabbed her hair and jerked her head so her face was against his. "You'll tell us Ms. Courtney. You'll tell us. We'll take you to high school. You'll learn a lot." Helene felt her hands and feet being untied. She was pulled up and her arms were yanked together behind her. She felt handcuffs snapped on her wrists. She was pushed back into the chair and hobbles were snapped on her legs. "Now, Ms. Courtney, you insist on further education. This way."

She was pushed forward and could only creep in the restraints. In the next room she saw a long narrow table with cables attached to leather loops at each end.

"This is it, Ms. Courtney, your classroom. You will have several teachers just like high school but they will all be teaching the same subject."

Helene thought of what a real prisoner would feel and how her actual situation differed. She intellectualized despite the pain. She was determined not to allow it to stop her.

The second man knelt to take off the hobbles which had been put on mainly for effect, Helene decided. When she felt her legs free, she brought her knee up in his face hard as she had learned in the military training and then pushed him to the floor. The woman grabbed her arms and pulled her back.

"You little bitch!" the man swore, getting up. There was blood on his mouth.

"A grave mistake, Ms. Courtney." The interrogator nodded a sign. The man she had struck picked up a probe, and made a show of turning up the power. He then thrust it into her shin where it felt like a kick from a steel-toed boot. Helen let out a surprised yelp, then swore profusely.

With Edgar standing back, one of them worked the handcuffs off. They lifted her on to the table. First they fastened her wrists behind her head. She waited. When they went for her ankles she pulled her left leg loose and kicked the interrogator in the face. "You'll regret that, Ms. Courtney."

All three of them fastened her feet. Then she heard a hydraulic motor hum and she felt her arms being pulled. Another motor sound and her legs were out straight. Then both motors and the indescribable pain of stretching ached within her joints. "That's the beginning Ms. Courtney. You are naked and helpless. Now you must tell us your secret."

"Bullshit."

The motors whined and the pain worsened. "Ms. Courtney shall we pull your arms out of their sockets? Unless we know your secret, you will surely know more pain."

The stretching kept her from her plan of keeping relaxed. Her tormentors knew that. "There will be more pain, Ms. Courtney. Now," he said raising his voice, "what is it you can tell us?"

She was silent, concentrating on what she was going to do when they started.

"Very well, Ms. Courtney. First the offending leg."

She saw them with the probes; each had one. The woman went to the sole of her foot. She flinched, Then it was on the knee. The pain shocked through the nerves. Then her calf and then worked up her thigh to her crotch. She was ready to scream.

"One more chance. Ms. Courtney"

They paused to throw her off her thought sequence. She waited and watched. Then the woman slowly went for her left breast. She reached for the nipple and held it against the probe. Helene let out a cry of pain. The woman then seemed to measure from her navel to a point. When she touched it, Helene felt her stomach become a pool of pain. They hit her buttocks and then right on the navel; then her right breast; then her neck. Then they started one after the other on her stomach and along her sides. They were orchestrating a whole symphony of pain. Helene's consciousness exploded in galaxies of pain then drifted eerily over the scene. She could hear their entreaties to tell the secret, but they were talking to the body on the table which she viewed as a disinterested spectator. As each pain probe came down she wavered, then went back to watching. The pain filled her. She looked at the insulated ceiling and the cement block walls covered by padding longing for the blessed insensibility of inanimate matter. Sweat, nausea, and an almost irresistible urge to urinate pulled her back to body awareness where she found rampant surges of pure pain coursing and swirling.

"Stop," commanded Edgar. "That's enough." Helene heard, but was beyond comprehending. Where was she? Her stomach wanted to empty. She fought to control it. She felt her body go limp as the stretching was stopped. The ache in her joints went away. The searing burn of the prods remained at high intensity. Her arms and legs were free, she saw Carrie with her robe. Helene tried to get up and then fell off the table onto the floor on her hands and knees. She was panting and wet with sweat. The others gazed in awe at the pathetic figure to which the powerful, attractive woman had been reduced. But they were even more in awe of her ability to resist in the wake of the most intense interrogation ordeals modern technology could devise.

Edgar lifted her gently by her arms to standing and she fell forward into his arms. He picked her up and carried her from the room and down the hall to his office and laid her on his couch. Carrie put the robe over her.

"Helene, can you hear me?" he said to her in a conversational tone.

"Yes, Edgar, I'm okay," she said weakly. "I hope I don't throw up. It's awful."

"Most people would be screaming with the dry heaves after what you've been through."

"I need sleep, but it hurts too much."

Edgar was concerned. He hoped he had not affected the ability of this hugely competent woman to do her job. He could have stopped them sooner, but he succumbed to the curiosity to know how much she could handle. He found out. Edgar had the "treatment" when the probes had been first invented. Someone else had stopped it before he let out the secret. This would be a bond between them. He and Helene had outlasted the pain. He brought her water. "Take some to stop dehydrating and these." He handed her some pills, painkillers, and muscle relaxers. She swallowed them and lay back.

After a few minutes she said, "I can get dressed now." Carrie brought her clothes. Edgar left the room. When he came back she was dressed and sitting up.

"I think I can walk. I want to go back to my apartment." They helped her up. Edgar hung onto her arm feeling her weakness and waiting for her to collapse. Helene tried not to think of the pain, but it was all over her. She intellectualized that this was how victims of torture must feel. That is what it was. She tried to make her decision about it, but she couldn't focus.

In the elevator she leaned against Edgar. They took her to an electric cart and drove to the hotel residence. At her floor she stumbled out of the elevator. He held her. Then she stumbled again and he felt her weakening. He picked her up and carried her the rest of the way. She fumbled for her keys, and Carrie opened the door. Edgar laid her on her bed. Carrie fixed the pillows and drew a blanket over her legs. Helene passed out immediately and lay breathing deep and slow.

"She'll wake up soon, Carrie. Try to get her clothes off. She'll be more comfortable. Also, she'll need fluids. What does she like?"

"Any fruit juice. Let me see what she has." Carrie left for the kitchen and brought a tray with pineapple juice and some fruit bread.

"She may want something to eat," Edgar said when he saw it.

Helene groaned and opened her eyes. "I'm thirsty."

Edgar held her up so she could drink some juice. He left when Carrie took off her clothes. When he came back she was looking at him from under a light blanket.

"How'd I do?" she asked.

"Too much. I should have stopped them."

"I didn't tell them."

"You didn't."

"How many people tell?"

"Most."

"I understand. I felt like I would give in at any moment. Am I going to dream about it?"

"Maybe, but there will be no pain in the dream."

"Will I be able to sleep?"

"After you take some more of these and I give you a shot of morphine."

"Will you stay with me?" Helene asked.

"Carrie will stay." Edgar said.

"No. You stay with me. Can you?"

He did. When she was soundly asleep, Carrie made some salad and broiled fish for supper. He used her computer to read the news on the Internet. When he was tired he got a blanket and pillow and slept in her easy chair.

☆ Chapter 16 ☆

ON ITS SECOND afternoon, Adrian was scheduled to speak to the Amalgamated Metal Workers convention at Cobo Hall in Detroit. It was standing room only. In the balcony press box, Anne's operatives worked the reporters and local TV crews. The introduction was neutral in tone, but there was an ovation and Adrian stood at the podium waving. When it quieted, he thanked them for the honor they had bestowed with their invitation and cited the labor movement as one of the great movements in American history. The audience lustily applauded.

He then tried to explain the economic changes which the world had undergone and the change from American economic hegemony. He cited the time when the dollar was worth much more in terms of other currencies, but he declared the changes were necessary for world peace and economic growth. He cited the need for the Marshall Plan and the IMF. All of the nations aided, he pointed out, were now the best allies and trading partners of America.

Some clapping interrupted, but was scattered and died down quickly. Adrian continued with sincerity only he knew how to summon up. He was too focused on his message to notice the tepid reaction, however.

He described the transition of industrial competition since the Vietnam War and talked of the relationship of wages to productivity. His main point was a new role for unions in partnership with employers to raise the level of training, to cooperate in revitalizing industrial organizations, and to see to greater productivity producing ever better products at lower costs as a long-term effort. He spoke of the need for more union men and women to reach for professional goals. He asked for a national dialogue on the role of unions and related national policies. He spoke of industrial dislocation as a result of ill-advised collective bargaining. He said that unions must transcend to the new role to assure the prosperity of their communities as well as of their people.

It was America's destiny, he said, to lead in free trade and world competition. All of the industrial and financial resources, he said, needed to be focused on ever-greater improvement. America was the greatest nation in history and must take the role of the greatest nation in promoting growth and assuring peace. He asked that they not lose sight of the principle that the strength of America industrially and economically is the keynote resource of the nation.

There was applause and a few whistles, but it didn't last very long. Adrian knew he'd made a mistake. The president of the union shook hands briefly. He and Pamela waved and started to leave. With a smile pasted on his face, Adrian wondered if he had inadvertently ruined his campaign; it only took one large faux-paux.

As they were stepping from the platform someone shouted, "Mr. Chairman, I would like to make a comment on this presentation." The president of the union paled.

"And who seeks recognition?" the presiding vice president asked.

"Donald Wilson, from Butler, Pennsylvania, Mr. Chairman. We have just heard a former business executive arguing for lower wages for workers, and I think it was lousy for him to come here and give that speech about letting companies send jobs overseas."

There were cheers and whistles for that.

Adrian turned and went back toward the rostrum. "Mr. Chairman, may I reply?"

With Pamela standing beside him looking out at the audience, Adrian said, "Ladies and gentlemen, I have come here as a candidate for the Democratic nomination for the presidency of the United States. I have just told you what I believe to be the truth of the American situation and of the future role of this great organization and other unions. You can decide to go back to the old form of confrontational bargaining and milk what you can out of management. You will simply find yourself vulnerable to areas where workers will not unionize in order to get your jobs. I believe that a transformed labor movement can make a significant contribution to the economic welfare of the United States. It is up to you to decide what you are going to do with your organization. I plead with you to recognize the reality. I will come back if you would like to discuss it further, and I would be honored if you asked. Thank you."

This time there was more applause. He and Pamela waved and then left. As he escorted them out of the hall the president of the union, Clyde Witowski, came to him.

"I appreciate your message, Adrian. It is a hard one to get across," he said.

"Let me know if I can help you. I'll try."

"I don't know if I am helpable."

"Don't give up on it, Clyde. It is the real future."

"I know and I understand, but I have to be re-elected."

"Politics?"

"Politics."

Adrian saw he was dealing with managers of unions who were the same as the national politicians running for election by making promises. This was all going to be very difficult.

In the limousine with Pamela he said, "That was a dumb thing I did."

"You told the truth, and what you believe," she said. "Keep in mind it's the truth that people need to hear."

"But they don't like it. Mitchell is going to climb all over us."

He opened up his cellular phone and punched in the code for Terry's private line; there was no answer so he punched for Anne. "Get ready for some damage control. Take a look at the tape. We've messed up."

"We can't be right all the time, Adrian. What did the press section look like?"

"Like a dummy, I didn't look. Pamela thought she saw some activity."

"I'll beep Louise," Anne said. "Keep the faith."

"We will."

"Is she coming back with you?"

"She'll be on the plane to Des Moines."

"Keep faith," Anne repeated.

Louise Sczyniac was one of Anne's new recruits at Evans & Copeland assigned to the campaign. She had experience in political operations and campaigns with a Washington firm. One of the executive searchers found her and Anne gave her a nice boost. She was articulate, good at writing, but better at the combat around the press tables. A tall brunette with a warm smile, she could captivate. She was wrangling with the reporters in Cobo Hall when her beeper went off. She saw it was Anne and stepped aside, taking a cellular phone out of her bag.

"What happened?" Anne asked.

"We've tried a reality speech with people who don't want to face reality," said Louise.

"How widespread was it?"

"I think a good percentage of the audience favored what he said and understood it, but there are too many rednecks and too many union politicians trying to get ahead. I think this guy who asked the question may be running for something."

"Try to go and meet him," said Anne. "Find out who he is and what he is about. He could be from our friends in the Bahamas."

She realized Louise didn't know about POLACO. She repeated to herself that one mistake often begets another.

"What do you mean 'Bahamas?'" Louise asked.

"I'll tell you about that another time," Anne said. "See if you can find out where he is from and who he represents – and what his aims are."

"I'll do my best," Louise said.

It took Anne a few minutes to get the tape onto her computer and after watching it, she concluded it was a better speech for The Detroit Economics Club than for the Metal Workers. What metal worker had any idea of the price of currencies? It almost seemed like they had gotten their speeches switched. They had missed the politics inside the union. A half-hour later Louise called to say that Mr. Wilson was running for president of his local.

THE SPEECH WAS a hit on Harbour Island.

"Do we give the information about the union elections to Porter? Maybe he can turn the corner with that," Marsha suggested.

"Why not just give it to the unions? Let them noise it around their halls," said Warren.

"We'll still do that, but we should control how it's used and get the maximum political swat out of it," said Erla.

"This is a good way to introduce ourselves more personally to the Porter group," said Marsha.

"Not too personally."

The next day, Warren and Erla were on the way to Washington with Melius' intelligence about Adrian and the unions.

Adrian felt the effects of an attempt to label him as a union buster. Anne appealed to the press to ask the employees who had worked for him what they felt about him and his dealings with them. Finally, with a great deal of encouragement, a network news magazine show did a grudgingly favorable story on the subject. Most of the press simply didn't have the energy to check out the antilabor allegations. POLACO located and pointed out a few "disgruntled" former employees of Adrian. These people, whom Adrian had discharged because of incompetence, were greedy as well as spiteful, so it was easy to get them to complain.

HELENE POSTPONED THE meeting with Tony to early August. She stopped in New York on the way to Quebec; hurried through two calls and rushed to LaGuardia to wait an hour before her flight time. Quebec would be a different test from the interrogation. She knew Tony loved her, but he would be loyal to PENMET, particularly if the rumor transmitted from "Cynthia Reese" was true. The report was that Tony was promoted to executive vice president or would be. What she felt for him she made an effort to suppress. He was the enemy now in a vague sort of way, but still the enemy.

Tony's Lear taxied up to the general aviation terminal and he stepped off the plane dapper in a tailored gray Italian suit. She stood on the runway, wearing a blue summer dress with an open neckline. He smiled at her. The breeze rustled her hair. She hugged him and held her cheek to be kissed. In the limousine, she told him she had a suite and had gotten a separate room for him.

The limousine passed beneath the arch of the great main gate. Quebec was the only walled city in North America. Soon they turned into the courtyard of the hotel. The massive red brick structure with a plethora of pointed gables symbolized a proud French Provincial citadel looking down on the harbor. On top of it was a lofty tower, a quarter of the dimension of the building and twice as high. Their bags were quickly on a cart and were pushed in front of them through brass-bound doors into the lobby of dark oak paneling.

Tony went to his room which looked down on the courtyard. After the bellman left, he watched a car unload a gaggle of young people.

Helene had suggested he come to her suite near the top of the tower. The door was ajar. He pushed it open and saw her standing by the windows.

She turned to face him.

"Are we dining together or separately?" he asked.

"Let's make it a nice evening together. Take me to a good restaurant and tell me all about Quebec. I'm hungry for some French cooking. We don't get that you-know-where." She turned to look out. "It looks like the United States is projecting its power up here."

Well under the bridge to the Ille d'Orleans and crossing in front of the city was a line of American and Canadian destroyers, followed by two larger ships. Tony could tell immediately one was an Aegis cruiser. The second was another cruiser armed with large missiles.

"Probably a training exercise for ROTC or Annapolis cadets," Tony said. "They'll have a good time tonight."

"Let's you and I have a good time tonight, too."

They took the funicular from the wooden-decked promenade around the hotel down to the old city. It was a slanted elevator on the outside of the cliff. Looking out of its window they could see the roofs of the city approach as they descended.

They were seated by the maitre 'd at Le Marie Clarisse fully reminiscent of old French Canada with whitewashed stone walls, heavy, dark stained oak beams and small stained glass windows. Shelves were decorated with accessories of old Canadian glassware, chinaware, and pottery. Their two glasses of vodka with ice were accompanied by a plate with lemon and lime slices and bottles of Schweppes tonic water.

As they sat across from each other Tony saw she wore a pale green sleeveless dress which had a matching jacket she had brought for the cool of French Canadian summer evenings. He admired her brown hair perfectly coifed with natural waves over bright blue eyes with long lashes.

And she looked at him. She saw a hint of tiredness or sadness in his deep dark eyes. He wore an open collared polo shirt with a blue blazer. She wondered why it was he who was selected to be executive vice president, but couldn't ask about it unless he brought it up. He mixed their drinks and raised his glass to her.

"I don't know what we should drink to."

"That we are both happy at the outcome of the meeting, particularly in your new perspective," she said.

Tony wondered what she meant by that.

"What are the parameters of dinner conversation?" he asked. "Can I ask how your life is?"

"Twice a week we do the military things now," she said. "I'm getting very good at hand-to-hand combat. But I still hurt from Edgar's interrogation."

"You did it."

"Yes, I had to."

She told him about it. Thinking of her naked aroused him. The fact was POLACO might use such methods. The idea that those who ordered it had to have endured it was clever. Helene would come up that.

She told him about Sadovan and Gallosey and the executive committee and then seemed to realize she might be telling him too much. He ordered a Bordeaux St. Emilion to go with the salmon they had ordered.

Helene wanted to walk in the old city. Some of the old stone buildings were contaminated with tourist vendors. Other streets of a restoration project communicated an 18th Century feeling. Companies had offices in the old city and people resided there in replicas or restorations. The Church St. Marie Des Victores was open and lighted with candles. They spent a few 17th Century moments.

Coming out of the upper funicular station on the hotel promenade, they heard music. On the other side of the hotel, they found a band from one of the American ships in a free concert. White uniformed cadets danced disco with girls either recruited from the town or who had happened by. The number ended and the band started "Moon River." The chief in charge invited slow dancing. The scene on the promenade changed to couples. Helene said, "Let's dance Tony."

He took her in his arms and she moved close to him. He realized it was the first time they had danced together. They moved toward the railing where they stopped and looked out over the roofs and into the shining harbor. The night was velvet. The flotilla was anchored in the fairway with lights on the ships from bow to stern. She took his arm and suggested they get some Grand Marnier in the tower.

From her suite windows, they could see the ships in the river formed in a straight line. Tony poured the liquor and brought it to her and held his glass to hers. "Tony you are a good person," she said. "You do what you think is right. You have a high sense of morals and ethics. Why are we on opposite sides?"

"Maybe we won't be."

"I don't see that, Tony, unless you have a startling proposal."

"I hope what I have is acceptable to you."

"I very much hope so. I wish we didn't have to fight."

"It might not be inevitable."

"It is," she said. "I like to make love to you, Tony. But how can I make love to someone I am going to have to struggle with? If you lost you might be giving up a lot."

"I could go somewhere else."

"Not with what you have now," she said.

Tony didn't react. "It's a risk," he said.

"Why are you taking the risk to fight us? What's so important?"

He would have liked to tell her it was his country. Instead, he held her close, kissed her, and said, "Aren't we getting over the line of the parameters we set for this evening?"

"I think so," she said.

He looked into her eyes. "I'm as troubled as you are about being on opposite sides."

She smiled at him and they clinked glasses again.

"If you made love to me would it be what they call campaign sex?"

"I hope not."

"I hope not too." She turned her back to him. "Unzip me."

The dress fell around her hips. She wasn't wearing a bra.

After the second time, she asked him to leave and meet her in the morning at a conference room she had arranged.

AT 8:58 THE next morning, he knocked on the door of the meeting room. She opened it and smiled at him. The room, paneled in straw colored oak, had a single window looking over the harbor on the north side of the hotel. Helene poured coffee for him while he gazed out the window. They took their seats on opposite sides of the table and she handed him a hardbound notebook.

"We have to keep our notes in long hand of course. I thought you might want this. We can each write down the agreements we make and sign or initial. Then we can send the notebooks to our attorneys."

"I agree," he said.

"All right. I have a series of points and you have a series of points to bring up. Let's agree that neither of us will lie; that we will tell only the truth. But if we don't want to tell the truth, we will say that we cannot answer a particular question or give particular information."

"I'd like to be able to ask that a question be rephrased."

"I agree," said Helene. "All right, you open the first topic."

Because of the night before and because things seemed mellow, he decided to bring up the key issue of protecting PENMET from attack.

"We would like to agree that neither side will allege either publicly or privately, that the other is involved in political activity of any kind, legal or illegal, or is providing funds legally or illegally from the corporation, foundations, or personally."

Helene saw he brought up the key issue without surveying the negotiating ground. "Why should we do that?" she snapped.

"You have the same reasons not to be attacked as we do, and you have 23 companies to defend."

"I have 23 companies with an average price/earnings ratio of around 19. Your price/earnings ratio is over 35. You have a lot more to lose – half your market cap or more."

She meant it when she said the personal relationship was outside the business one.

"We'll agree not to attack any of your companies or POLACO itself," said Tony, "if you agree not to attack us with any form of innuendo, allegation, and so forth."

"Suppose someone is required to testify in court?"

The steel nerves on the tennis court were all part of her.

"We can save some time if you would tell me what you want in return," he said.

"I want to be sure that you will not contact any of our companies regarding any of your activities or ours," she said, "and that you will not tell anyone any information you know about POLACO."

"Isn't that covered in our confidentiality agreements, which are both corporate and personal?"

"I'd like to restate it here," she said. "I want you to promise not to cause anyone to reveal information to any of our members or suggest that to anyone."

"I'm not sure that I can agree to that."

"Come on, Tony, anyone under your control doesn't contact any of our companies about us, or leak anything related to us. Stop playing games and negotiate reasonably."

"You started the game, Helene."

"That doesn't make any difference. Let's stop it."

They went over the statement of agreement word by word. In two hours Tony believed he had the best protection from accusations he could get for PENMET. They agreed they would make sure the people in the campaigns understood that support of the foundations on each side would depend on the campaign not alleging influence by any private entity.

"You're up," he said.

"I want to expand the confidentiality agreements to your organizations to provide that no references are made to any of the participating companies and no contacts are made by you with any of the participating companies in any attempt to undermine our organization," she said. "That means you won't lobby with any of the existing members to try to influence them to withdraw their support."

"That might be hard to control if secrets are revealed by other parties."

"I think that you might have to agree to this regardless."

"I can understand this would be part of our agreement not to allege the political involvement," he said, "but I can't see if someone else has raised that question, why we should be bound?"

"We have to insist on your total silence on any matter regardless of third party revelations."

"That is certainly not common in confidentiality agreements."

"This is not a common confidentiality agreement."

Tony sat back in his chair and studied her across the table. "I'm concerned about our ability to control the campaign," he said. "I have to think about that."

Helene wondered if perhaps he had not considered this as a negotiation point, which was not the case. "Do you want to set it aside?" she asked.

"Please."

"You bring up a subject."

He glanced at his list, taking a moment to think.

"I'd like to bring up the concept of spending limitations," he said. "Each side would agree not to exceed a certain amount of spending on soft costs."

"How would you ever enforce that?" she asked.

"We would be willing to accept a pledge."

"We would not be willing to accept a pledge," she said. "In addition to that, we would be handing you information which could be used against us."

"We have already agreed not to allege political activity and inappropriate or illegal contributions."

Helene looked right at him. "We have more money than you have, why should we agree to spending limitations?"

"Because if too much money flows from either side, the media would notice and make it difficult for both of us to explain."

"Your funding is mainly by Ian MacAulliffe."

"But you have an organization which you are trying to keep confidential."

"We have already agreed not to allege misuse of corporate funds."

"I'm saying we should agree not to expose ourselves by too much money. Remember Clinton and Nixon."

"What amount did you have in mind?" she asked.

"$200 million."

"You're speaking of soft costs from POLACO vs. soft costs from your foundation or from MacAulliffe."

"MacAulliffe and whatever money we raise on the side would be included," he answered.

"I'm thinking more of $350 million."

"Total, or just from POLACO?"

"Just from POLACO," she announced.

She was tough. Tony tried to figure out what number she really wanted. The high number would allow a huge advertising campaign from the POLACO foundations.

"Don't you think that is a little too much."

"It's only about 15% of what Procter and Gamble spends," she countered.

"I'd like to see it at $250 million," he said. "There's a compromise."

"I don't think we are going to compromise," she said. "Your campaign may raise a lot more money than ours. You already have a great deal."

"Responsible people responding to Daggett."

She saw he had a genuine feeling about that.

"Let's put that aside," she said. "What else do you propose?"

"We would like to agree that during the course of the campaign there will be no personal attacks on either candidate, nor will either side use our resources to provide information concerning the opposing candidate to the campaigns," he said. "We also agree in the campaigns which we essentially control, we will not allow personal attacks."

Helene thought of Melius' full investigation of Adrian Daggett.

"It's possible for us to agree in our own advertising or publicity not to make personal attacks because that would not be allowed under regulations concerning soft money," she said. "I can't speak for the campaign since we don't control it. And, how will we know if you used your resources to uncover something about Hatford or Porter or others with a clandestine investigation?"

"If we say we won't do it, we won't."

"I don't think there's a point here, Tony. We don't control the campaign. I know that you are a lot closer with the Daggett campaign than POLACO is to your opponents' campaigns. Maybe you can speak for the campaign, but I can't."

She wondered if there was a weak spot in Daggett they hadn't found. Perhaps it had something to do with the family. She made a note.

"Our interest is an issues-oriented campaign that would benefit the American people," he said. "Major questions of integrity are okay, but Whitewater and Hillary Clinton's billing records don't belong in democratic practices."

"They certainly do if it reflects the character of the candidate," she said.

"Most of these issues had to do with the candidate's family or friends," he said.

So maybe they should investigate some of Daggett's friends, Helene wondered. But then he never ran a campaign that was short of cash. Scandals happen when a candidate has to rely on friends to keep a campaign going. She jerked her brain back to the present. "I still don't think there is an issue here."

Tony wondered if Helene had indicated the possibility of a mole in the campaign. Moles were his last item. He was thinking of how to approach it.

"Okay, let's set that aside and let me think about a few points. Your turn," Tony said.

"Breach. If either side breaches the agreement in the opinion of the other side, you and I will meet," she said. "We will discuss the breach and the required remedy. This meeting will take place on the shortest possible notice at a convenient location. If the breach is remedied, the agreement stays in force. If the breach is not remedied and it is certifiably a breach, then the agreement is terminated and all signals are off."

"Suppose you cook up a breach?" he said.

"Why would we do that?" she said. "We would lose protection."

"I think somehow there has to be some kind of arbitrator."

"Who could we possibly have? And why would we breach?"

"That's why we have provisions like this," he said. "If a third party reveals everything about POLACO, you might decide to create a breach so you could attack us."

"Why would we phony one up?" she asked. "We'd just go ahead and breach the agreement. I'd call you up and tell you the agreement was breached and we weren't going to remedy."

She paused and Tony waited. She tapped the table with a pen.

"Then there should be some kind of financial penalty," she mused.

"How could there be a financial penalty?" Tony asked. "We are not going to show this agreement to our boards."

"I think this agreement is a balance of terror."

"You're right about that."

"Any more issues?" she asked.

"I have one more which concerns moles and spying," he said. "We wonder about how you found out about our relationship with Adrian Daggett. Would you comment on that?"

"No, I'm not going to answer any questions about that," she said, "but what's your point?"

"I want an agreement that neither one of us will inject personnel into the others organization in order to get information," he said, "and also that we will not undertake any spying externally against each other. I'm referring to PENMET, POLACO, and the campaigns."

"Again, Tony, I can't speak for the campaign," she said. "You are much closer to the Daggett campaign than we are to either Hatford or Porter. We don't even know who our candidate is yet."

"What about exempting it for your high powered intelligence operation?"

"I don't think we can commit, Tony," she said. "We have to be able to have the flexibility to defend ourselves and know what's going on." She had been prepared for this possibility.

"Do you want us probing around Harbour Island and trying to insert moles into your underground? Do you want us developing information about you and the members? Somebody else might misuse it."

"What do you mean 'somebody else'?"

"You don't think we are going to do this ourselves, do you?"

Helene knew that it would be much more difficult for PENMET to insert a mole into POLACO, and she quickly thought about the possibilities of exterior surveillance. If anyone came on the island and stayed there, Edgar would surely know about it. POLACO had the power to deal with anyone on the island. She came to the conclusion that PENMET would never try it anyway. This was a distinct advantage because of the good luck they had inserting "Cynthia Reese" into Nancy Letersky's department at the top level of PENMET.

"Okay, let's put that into the hopper."

They chewed over each issue to define it. Salads came for lunch. By midafternoon, they had a very thorough, but inconclusive discussion. Helene asked if there was any possibility of playing tennis before dinner. Tony telephoned a tennis club on the St. Lawrence shore and in sub-standard French, made a reservation. They worked until 3:15 p.m. and then broke up to change. In the courtyard they slung their tennis bags into the trunk of a limousine.

The courts were beside the river at the base of the cliff that Wolfe's soldiers climbed in 1759 to lay siege to the city. They selected a clay court and Helene beat him 6-2, 6-2.

After they showered a limousine took them to the Montmorency Falls and across the bridge to the Ille d'Orleans. Tony kept the destination a surprise. It was La Noite, an original 16th Century farm house which had become a restaurant. At the parking lot their driver raised a flag. A few minutes later a horse pulled a carriage up a lane to fetch them. The costumed coachman helped them step high to the seats.

Helene squeezed Tony's arm when she saw the building. "This is wonderful. What a nice idea." She kissed his cheek.

The house was gray stone with fortress thick walls. The rooms were partially paneled in maple. Shelves of antique glassware, pottery, and pewter accessories added to the feeling of being back in time. They shared their French Canadian entrees.

In the limousine she held his arm and kissed him again. "Thanks for that," she said. "I wish I could expect more surprises like that with you. I have no illusions. What we said to each other in Vermont didn't count on the widening chasm between us."

"We're negotiating 'the Geneva Conventions' before the war begins," he said.

At the hotel promenade, the band was playing and the cadets and the girls were dancing under the lights, in the soft summer evening. Tony and Helene had a reprise of the night before. He held her while they slept and left when the sun woke them.

After breakfast in the conference room, the agreement slowly evolved. They agreed to no form of attack on the others reputation, that PENMET would not contact any members of POLACO and that neither side would attempt to expose the other by leaks or other indirect action. The spending limit was set at $275 million, a high number which Helene was not sure the Daggett campaign could reach. Helene prevailed on the penalty for breach. There was no conclusion regarding moles or other spying, as well as, personal attacks on the candidates. All of this was hand written into the two notebooks and they both signed each.

"I'll take your strong signature back to my executive committee," Helene said.

She sat close to him on the way to the airport, as though to get a last feel of him. On the tarmac, where two jets waited, she turned to him. "Maybe there is a way out, an unexpected endgame." When she kissed his cheek she whispered, "We'll see in God's good time."

On the flight back to Harrisburg, Tony was consumed with doubts about her and any future they might have.

☆ **Chapter 17** ☆

ACTIVE DAGGETT SUPPORTERS from all over Northwest Iowa came to a meeting in Sioux City. The campaign paid for one overnight, so they arrived before lunch, and left after lunch the next day. Here, Karen worked over the details of the strategy and use of Daggett's time. She called for a second candidate visit to Sioux City, and one in the Council Bluffs area which she had taken over. Everyone knew she and Earl were a pair, and at the dinner party they were teased. She was proud of him and he of her. She conducted a campaign like a veteran, talking with people and reassuring them and she was approachable in the warmest way.

She now stayed at his apartment when she was there on campaign business and on weekends. She felt the pace quickening. Merrick had told her to show up in Des Moines on Monday morning. On the weekend together, Earl took her to his offices at Gateway 2000 and showed her the plant. Then they drove to a forest glade where Earl knew of a swimming hole. They went skinny dipping in the heat. He took her to dinner at The Green Lantern and they spent the rest of the time in bed. She left early Monday morning, not wanting to lose a night of sleeping with him. She didn't stop at her apartment, but went directly to the office.

After getting a cup of coffee she went straight to Merrick.

"Am I in any kind of trouble?"

"Not the bad kind," Merrick chuckled. "You are doing very well, Karen. You have a career before you in this business. The problem is I am going to have to promote you. We are behind in Cedar Rapids and even here in Des Moines. I will handle that. You have to get on top of things in Cedar Rapids and Waterloo and maybe you and Earl can go back to his home down by the river in Davenport and make some things happen there. I'm going to turn over your territory to a new person coming in, Jennifer Riddie, who will be here tomorrow. You will have to take her around and introduce her, but I want to start hearing the same reports from Cedar Rapids, Waterloo, and Davenport that you send from Sioux City. You will be Assistant Director for the state. You'll also be on the traveling team when the candidate is here."

"Why me?" was all she could say.

"You have the energy, the sense of detail, and reliability." He said. "It's a question of intangibles. I know you have it abundantly, and I know the others don't have as much as you have."

She couldn't believe it. The 23-year-old assistant director wondered if it was because she had guts the others didn't have. She called Earl, excited. They scheduled a trip to Cedar Rapids, Waterloo, and Davenport. She would meet his parents and see where he grew up.

On Friday afternoon, Earl hitched a ride to Davenport on a Gateway plane on its way to Washington. Karen was at the airport and felt the thrill of his arriving on the company jet. They went to the big family home, a glorious white trimmed beige Victorian house on a street lined with great trees. The yard was large, with an alley to the garage. His father, a tall handsome man with a big smile, shook her hand and then gave her a hug. Then Earl's mother gave her a hug and kissed her.

"We never thought Earl would bring home a political operator as pretty as you."

The Hanleys had invited all of their Democrat friends, some Republicans they suspected would support Daggett, and the members of the local Democratic Committee to a barbecue Saturday. It was on the spacious back lawn off the terrace of the home, complete with a red, white, and blue striped tent. A "DJ" played. Ethyl and William Hanley wanted to help Karen, but they also wanted to show off the spectacular girl Earl had brought home. They hoped the relationship would be permanent. Neither could see how he could ever do any better.

Karen moved among the guests with her professional ease and winning way. She heard a few side comments wondering why the Daggett campaign hadn't sent her down before. Earl explained that she was just promoted and was assisting throughout the state.

After the last guest had arrived, Earl's father called the meeting to order.

"You didn't think we brought you down here to feed you without having something to say at a Class A political gathering," he said. "I'm not going to say it, I'm happy to tell you." He paused with good timing for laughter and applause. "Instead I'm going to introduce to you this princess of a girl, Karen Crezna, representing Adrian Daggett and his reality campaign. Reality is something that I've seen in business, as you all know. You know it too in your businesses. It's been a long time since we've heard someone talk about reality who wanted to go into government and particularly, to be president. I better turn this over to her before I make any mistakes."

There was laughter and applause.

Karen spoke for a few minutes talking about Iowa and Davenport and the promise of the reality campaign. She said the issues were complex and controversial, but at least for once, issues were being addressed that most politicians prefer not to discuss. She wondered if the crowd was now too lubricated to ask questions, but she took the chance and offered them the opportunity. They had fun talking with her. She had fun as she played the real campaign role.

After everyone was gone, Earl's father congratulated her. "What I get from these people is that your person down here was a touch on the arrogant side," he said. "We put some cards in your hand to play. These people will carry this county for Daggett if you show them how and then let them do it."

He was talking to her as an adult. The Hanleys were two people who had gone through very rough times, and had stuck together and toughed it out.

That night in the bedroom, which Earl announced he was sharing with Karen, they lay together naked on fresh new sheets.

"Has your dad always treated you like an adult too?"

"From the time I was 12 years old," he said. "He counseled instead of ordered."

"What a family. He seems to be more prosperous."

"He helped me buy that condominium to make up for the money they didn't have for college. Things are better."

"I really appreciate what they did today."

"They had fun doing it."

"Earl, I like what I'm doing," she said. "I've grown up so much in the last few months. It seems unreal that I met you."

"I met you by being a Democrat."

"This is not going to be easy. I love what I'm doing. Merrick has told me I will be hired for the permanent staff somewhere if not

Washington."

"Jeremy Reubin is the best."

"I know. This is a huge opportunity. But I really want to go into government if Adrian wins."

"Adrian is going to win."

"I hope so, and I hope I do well in government, but you're in Sioux City. Could Gateway find something for you to do in different cities? I mean would you ask them if you could come to Washington or wherever it is?"

"I can certainly ask," he said. "But I'm not going to sit in Sioux City thinking about you. I can find career opportunities wherever you go. There will be people who need computer people for a long time. I think part of my career is going to be making you happy."

"As soon as Iowa is finished I don't know where they will send me."

"I'll stay in Sioux City until you land somewhere and then we'll make plans," he said. "At least we will have a few months."

"I love you, Earl."

"I want you to have a career that you want and I want you to have my children."

"Our children."

"I want you to be fulfilled. You love politics; and I sort of like it. If Adrian is to be elected, we have work to do."

"How do you mean?"

"It won't be easy. Forces are gathering; these foundation ads are the first shots."

She was nearly blissful when he pulled her back to reality. They were talking about a tough future. She had never met anyone with the maturity he had or the good sense and character. No wonder he was rising quickly at Gateway. He was reliable, and he was committed. He had a view of the future.

"Can you sleep without making love?" she asked him.

"It would be hard."

"Well let's do it quietly," she said. "Your parents might be asleep now."

"Quietly."

ON MONDAY MORNING Earl left while his parents asked her to stay while she had meetings in Davenport. They gave her a key to the house, hoping she would keep it and have reason to use it.

The next week Earl drove to Cedar Rapids to see her struggle with more problems than she anticipated. She tried working with George Stillman. He resisted. There was no hope for cooperation. Earl scheduled a week off to be with her in the city to pull things back together and add strength to the campaign.

After being away more than two weeks, she had the experience of finding her apartment in Des Moines strange. She knew where things were, but felt surprised when she found them. In a private meeting with Merrick, they decided on reorganization. George would be transferred to an urban area campaign, and they would bring in a new recruit to work under Karen. She had a feeling they were piecing things together. He told her that all campaigns started that way. The ones that "pieced" the best, he said, won.

A week later she was in Sioux City with her bags packed to ride the bus with Adrian Daggett. At the airport reception she met Louise Sczyniac, in charge of the press and TV contingents. All through Northwest Iowa they had arranged meetings, some in homes, some in Grange halls, some in schools, and churches. It was three days of racing from one town to the next while appearing to be relaxed and casual. They had breakfast, lunch, and dinner with different groups and met others for coffee and soda. Each evening there was an after dinner meeting where dessert was served. Each morning before the breakfast and with not very much sleep, she joined the jogging party with Adrian, Pamela, Louise, and others on the traveling team.

At each meeting Adrian spoke briefly and then took questions. Sometimes before talking he would ask what the audience wanted to hear about. Karen saw he was a superior campaigner. Speaking of reality made him genuine and made her feel he would win. When the question of the foundation ads came up, Adrian took them on, toe-to-toe, pointing out the errors of the views and wondering who was spending so much money trying to drive the United States further into debt or out of world leadership. He asked what the world would be like if the greatest force for good was restrained by political bickering and the failure to recognize reality.

The three-day race ended late at night back in Des Moines. Karen saw the candidate safely to his presidential suite at the Marriott and took a taxi to the office and to her car. She drove to her apartment and crashed on the bed without unpacking. When she woke at six she called Earl and then hurried through her shower and dressed for breakfast with the Des Moines Rotary. As usual, Adrian received a standing ovation after he had finished speaking.

After the Rotary breakfast, 45 minutes was set aside for a meeting at the Iowa headquarters and hand shakes with the volunteers. Like most campaign offices it was in an old building where leases weren't necessary, just west of the downtown on Grand Avenue. This was at least a "Grand Address" in Des Moines for those who hadn't seen the building. It was a squatty three-story red brick structure of nondescript 1920s architecture. Most recently it had served as the headquarters of an entrepreneurial company building a chain of dry cleaners. With success, this firm moved on to better facilities.

There was a large open area on the third floor for secretaries. Coffee, muffins, and bagels were served and everyone was invited to meet the candidate. Merrick took Adrian around the room and introduced him with special remarks about each person. He had told him before that things were not going that well. Adrian took the cue and spoke to the group.

"Some people say Alaska is first; some people say Louisiana is first, but the reality is Iowa is first," Adrian said. "All of you are here for reasons related to bringing about a sea change in American politics by refocusing Washington on reality. That means refocusing politicians on reality.

"It sounds like something easy to do since all of us live with reality in our businesses, our jobs and our lives. Somehow or other, political people don't do it. It comes from the technique of trying to get elected. They focus voters on perceptions to create euphoria and ignore the critical issues. I can tell you squarely no nation can survive on perceptions. No business ever has. Our work is the foundation to our whole future.

"Much of our success will depend on what happens in this state. If we get the Democrats of Iowa to vote for reality in a big way, it is going to be a big boost; perhaps a decisive one. You are playing for high stakes. Most of you are volunteers. I want you to know how deeply Pamela and I appreciate all of you and I know all of the campaign staff and others supporting us share that feeling as deeply as we do. Without you it can't be done. With you everything is possible.

"God bless you all and may He keep you safe as you travel. I look forward to seeing you frequently and in February to be here at your victory celebration."

There was loud applause and whistles. Merrick apologized that they had to start a meeting and got more applause.

"Was that okay?" Adrian asked Merrick, as they turned toward the conference room.

"It was more than okay, Adrian."

The meeting with Merrick, Karen, Willis Gregeory, Melissa Rondo, Jennifer Riddie, and Amy Johnson, who was a volunteer working full time in a leadership role, was teleconferenced to Chicago. On the screen they could see Terry, Nancy, Anne, Alan, and several others. Adrian greeted them, "Good morning from Iowa."

Terry quipped back, "Is that where you are?" Everyone laughed.

There were quick reports from each of the quadrants. Merrick wanted his people to feel accountable and this was one way he could make a strong point. They were sitting in front of the candidate and on television to the campaign high command. They talked about their strategy and answered questions until Karen said it was time to get on the bus.

"Thanks for the time, Iowa," Terry said. The people on the screen waved and the people around the table waved back.

When they broke from the conference room, Louise was waiting with three television reporters and their crews, and two newspaper reporters from Cedar Rapids who were going to interview Adrian on the bus and cover the morning coffee at Grinnell College. After that, there would be a fundraiser luncheon at The Amanas at Zuber's. Karen felt refreshed after a night in her own apartment. She missed Earl, but was too busy to think about it. Most of the time she thought of the date in February. They scrambled from Cedar Rapids to Waterloo to Mason City to Monticello and then to Clinton and Dubuque. It was a wild ride, and she had to keep focused. On the bus she helped with press interviews, kept in communication with the destinations, and planned the next moves.

Earl flew to Chicago on business Thursday and to Clinton on Friday afternoon. He joined the action for a weekend which led them back in Des Moines with a major press event on Monday. Merrick and Karen regrouped and waited for the soundings of the first polls. This would be a test for Adrian. He would be back in two weeks for a tour of the Southern district from Des Moines to Ottumwa and down to Davenport.

She called the Hanleys. "You were so nice to me and had such a nice party. How would you like to do it for the next President?" She hoped Earl would be there. She asked if Adrian could visit Mrs. Hanley's high school.

IN A BOARDROOM overlooking Central Park, from one of the new towers on Third Avenue, Anne and Nancy made their third presentation of the TV debate idea to the second largest television syndicator in the country. At the head of the table, the long-term CEO watched their interaction with four of his people, two from programming and two from marketing and sales. At the foot of the table Tony Destito also watched.

According to Nancy's proposal, the content of the program would be provided by liberals and conservatives with known personalities who had a proven ability to speak on their feet with sagacious reasoning. These two groups of sparkling characters, as Nancy described them, would put on the show. They would use the Westminster style of statements, direct questions by opponents and also direct questions by judges. They would invite experts in the topics who could handle the format. In each show there would be a winner and a loser based on a "900" number vote. Charging $2 would pay for the 900 call and add revenue. Nancy had a producer work out the financials and prepare the treatment.

In their first pitch, they picked a cable channel, and were told that "nobody watches television debates," "The other debate shows all bombed," and "There is no hope for anything except PBS and probably no hope for that."

The second pitch had been to a network where they were told there was insufficient appeal. While the 8-9 hour was desirable for young people to watch such a show, the low response might damage the 9-10 and 10-11 hours.

They brought Tony to the syndicator in order for him to attest that production funds would be available for a venture to produce the show. They had visited the public broadcasting station in Chicago, which was noted for its excellent management and had received substantial interest in producing it if the market could be developed. That market in the public broadcasting system, however, depended on each of some 250 stations deciding on its own to pay for the show if that were necessary. Marketing to the public broadcasters was just the same as the marketing to the broadcast stations or cable channels in syndication.

They chose to make their pitch to this particular firm because its management was competent and sensitive. They thought there was more to business life than making profits. When Nancy finished, the Vice President for Programming said, "It's too political."

"It's too political?" questioned Nancy.

"I mean it's too political for television," he said. Anne felt emptiness in her stomach. Tony wondered what he meant.

"It's too political. Sponsors don't want to be associated with things their customers might disagree with."

"In this case both political viewpoints are shown. People hear what they think and what other people think," Nancy replied.

"Customers want to hear only what they think and they don't want to hear what other people think particularly if their team loses," said the Vice President of Sales.

"We thought it would add variety and spice to the show to have a conclusion," said Nancy.

"You can do that with history questions," said the programmer. "Or you can do that with geography; with any subject, but not politics. Advertisers are sensitive to politics."

"Why do they sponsor the conventions?"

"Because people watch them, and no one will criticize them," said the Vice President, Sales. "How am I going to sell advertising for a political show that not too many people are going to watch?"

"The British stations get good ratings for the debates in Parliament."

"They're meaningful."

"What about newspapers?" she asked. "They carry various points of view and the news."

"If you're reading a newspaper and you don't like it, you can turn the page to something else and still get benefit from your time. On television you have to listen or change channels and that's what we don't want to have happen. We don't want the channel changed," said the Vice President of Programming.

"Don't you have any consideration of the need for dialogue in the United States? Our public dialogue is miserable."

"We still do better than most countries where people get shot."

"The issue is not whether people get shot," Anne retorted. "It's giving people information and analysis that will aid them in making decisions in an infinitely complex world that is growing more so every year."

"Politics doesn't sell."

Nancy stood up.

"Why do you think people wouldn't like the show where they could compare viewpoints?" she asked.

"Ms. Letersky, people who would like this show probably don't watch television very much," said the Vice President of Sales.

Nancy thought there was good reason for that if people like these were managing the business.

"Did it occur to you, with a show like this you could spark a new market? With the proper promotions you could bring people back to television who have left it," said Anne. "We'll help publicize the show so that it becomes the best known new thing that has come across. I think I can call on Tony Destito to support that."

"We can fund the publicity of it," said Tony "through Evans & Copeland. I don't think you have many shows with that kind of support."

"That's a point," said the younger programmer, "I see it as a live broadcast from Chicago, 'The Midway Union.' It's 8:00 p.m. Chicago time, 9:00 p.m. in New York, 7:00 p.m. in Denver and 6:00 p.m. in Los Angeles and San Francisco. We use the 900 number idea and see what happens. PBS needs money, give them the "900" money and let it help pay. You publicize it: we'll sell it to the public stations."

"We'd become an extension of the Daggett Campaign," said the Vice President of Sales. "I don't like it."

"I like Daggett," said the red head. "The country needs something like this. I think we should do it. It's a good idea."

Nancy was glad to find an ally. She saw the CEO smile when the red head made her point. For the first time he spoke, "Nancy, would you and your colleagues, in addition to providing publicity support, also call on some of the largest markets with us to help train our people?"

Anne saw days disappearing into a time vortex. Nancy looked at her; she gave her a nod.

Nancy looked at Anne. Anne said, "We'll do it."

"Okay, let me call you," said the CEO. Two days later he phoned to tell Nancy he wanted to join in the effort to restore reality in American government. He said he couldn't lose money doing it and they must figure out a program where they might make some. He also said that he would contribute 10% of the gross profit to the foundation if that were permissible. He said he needed one show as the demonstration.

Nancy went into action; she gathered all of the prospective members of the debate teams who had been signed up. A lot of the production work was completed. They decided to call the show "The American Debates" and they decided to make it elegant.

It was presented as a black tie evening at the Conrad Hilton. The first scene was of limousines drawing up with police keeping the entrance clear. Elegant women were assisted to the sidewalk and through the doors of the main entrance with their escorts. Andrea

Grisham, the blue-eyed red head who helped make it happen, was in a gown on the arm of her date for the evening.

The next scene showed groups of people ascending the stairs to a gallery where long-skirted waitresses and waiters in white mess jackets offered champagne. The pace of the show was quick after the audience settled in. At seats around the debaters, the camera showed the CEO and the executives of the syndicator and financial supporters without identifying them.

The debate started quickly with the chairman introducing the speakers who would oppose each other on a resolution that the United States should provide full support to the United Nations in dealing with outlaw nations, genocide, and warlordism.

Those in favor argued for the nurturing of democracy, the protection of rights, and the maintenance of world peace. They cited the events which occurred without American resolve backing the UN which motivates men and women with evil intentions pursuing a personal agenda. Peace, they said, could only be attained when every ill begotten politician faced the determination of the United Nations to keep peace and order. They proposed an international tribunal to try warlords and terrorists and others for crimes against humanity and that they be sent to a UN island prison.

Those opposed argued that the effort was impossible and that the United States could not pay the costs of keeping world order in money and blood because it was not attainable. They resurrected the scene of the loss of 18 men in Somalia. They appealed to the test of American interests. Why should the United States try to stop genocide in Africa where it had been going on for centuries? Should the United States become involved in communal rioting in India or Pakistan? What was the limit? From their questions and points, fact, interpretation and logic of outcome were fired back and forth.

At the intermission the cameras showed the elegant audience having another glass of champagne with a few quick interviews. The program continued with questioning and questions by the judges. Following two rounds of rebuttal, the camera went to the scoreboard as the chairman announced it was time for the 900 calls to begin. Two panels burst to life with the audience vote. An avalanche of telephone calls commenced. The judges gave their verdict which was five to two for the team in favor. At the time of the sign off, the chairman declared the team in favor the probable winner with 133,000 votes to 105,000 for those opposed.

The next day, the television review sections were ecstatic: "DEBATE SHOW LIGHTS UP A TELEVISION EVENING — PBS DOES SOMETHING RELEVANT."

"NEARLY A QUARTER MILLION VOTES IN DEBATE."

The PBS rating for the time slot had never been higher in the cities which carried the program. The producing station and those who carried it shared just under $450,000. Anne and Nancy knew that would get everyone's attention.

☆ **Chapter 18** ☆

IAN SENT NANCY Letersky to Chicago as the permanent director of communication for the campaign. Dominick Kluczinski found her a furnished apartment two blocks from the elevated south of the city. She packed her clothes, some glasses and dishes, and many of her books. At PENMET the casual announcement was made that she would be on leave to pursue the public-spirited opportunity to participate in a national campaign. No one knew of the advance campaign work she had done except a small portion of the PENMET inner circle, "Cynthia Reese," and the POLACO senior staff. She remained an officer of the corporation and could return to her duties any time. She kept her condo in Harrisburg hoping it would be a while before she lived in it again.

DURING THE BLITZ in Iowa, Pamela separated from Adrian and flew off to the Lady Garment Workers Union convention in Atlantic City and to some other events which Anne's staff had scheduled to test her as Adrian's representative. Experienced at teaching and giving papers at technical meetings, she was a good performer on the platform. She knew how to command an audience and dramatize. When the Lady Garment Workers saw one of their own on the platform, slender, glamorous, and early middle-aged, there were loud cheers and a standing ovation. She told them the same thing Adrian told the metal workers, except she rewrote the speech for the women leaving out economic theory. She liked Amy Camisona, the president, and thought they would become friends.

A local service propjet took her to Washington to visit the National Organization for Women. The next stop was to Florida, to visit a Cuban Women's Organization in Miami, and to stop by to see her mother and father and Adrian's parents. She headed west to Houston and Dallas and met with local women's organizations, and on Terry's behalf, looked in on the Texas organization. Then it was to Des Moines to appear with Adrian at the big press conference.

ANNE BUILT THE press conference at the end of the Iowa trip into an event. Adrian and Pamela appeared with the leaders of the Democratic Party who had pledged their support. The initial statement referred to the response by Sioux City to the crash of United Airlines' disabled DC10 and the efficiency and effectiveness of the volunteer emergency services there, whose reputation led to the decision to attempt the landing at their airport. Adrian used the story of preparedness of the emergency volunteers and the feeling and warmth by which the community received those injured and those who were grieving to illustrate the frontier culture which was an American quality. He said Iowa was the essence of that.

It was a lively and intelligent conversation with all of the major newspapers, TV stations, and radio stations in Iowa gathered for the occasion. Every station in Iowa carried the story, every newspaper in Iowa wrote about it. They gave it more space and airtime than any other candidate had gotten so far.

A lunch with the Lion's Club followed and then an afternoon meeting with the faculty of Iowa State University at Ames. A jet was ready at the Ames Airport to take Adrian and Pamela and others back to Chicago with the national media when the meeting was finished. Anne played them with all of her skill. Some of them believed Daggett was the best candidate they would ever see. However, persistently there were questions on the issues brought up in the ads by POLACO's foundations. Questions by the Iowa reporters clustered around education as a key issue in Iowa which consistently led the nation in student and faculty performance.

Education took up half of the time at the Ames meeting. The faculty wanted to know what Adrian planned to do to bring better prepared students to college. They wanted to know how his administration would raise the consciousness of families of the needs of secondary education. They probed his views on morality, safety, gangs, and drugs all related to education.

As the wheels of the campaign plane were retracting, Karen was driving back to Des Moines. Part of her was accelerated and part of her felt like collapsing across her bed. She needed to preserve her sleep and her exercise. After three hours on paperwork and on the telephone she headed home. In a sweat suit she ran her two-mile course. It relaxed her and restored her perspective. She made a tuna salad, telephoned Earl, and went to bed to sleep for ten hours.

On the short flight back to O'Hare, Adrian talked with the wire service representatives. From the airport, a limousine took him and Pamela to Lake Shore Drive and their Chicago apartment. Pamela insisted on the occasional night off, to which Alan grudgingly agreed. In the limousine he put his hand on her shoulder.

"What's this, an evening alone?" he asked.

"You're tired, but pumped up."

"You've lived with me long enough. But we ought to talk about education. There were a lot of questions. I didn't like our answers."

"It's a big subject. What do you want for dinner?"

"I want to go to Rosario's and have a big salad and split a spaghetti and meatballs."

"No more than that?"

"We have to get a meeting together on education in Cleveland, a day, or maybe more," Adrian said.

"Your schedule won't allow you 20 minutes."

"I'll send you and Terry, our educator. What are the real bottom line issues? Keep it simple. Include the point of teaching religion. Some people will get riled up, but I think it will be favorable and I don't think our opponents will expect it. The whole idea of better education should be a means of rebuilding a sense of morals in the United States. But, we also have to concentrate resources on the kids."

"I'm not sure we should drop that religion bomb. There is too much controversy already," Pamela offered.

"Controversy has made us. I think it's good stress. Look at the money that is coming in."

"Is that the right measurement? I'm not sure we have it crisply defined."

"Your scientific brain."

"I thought you married me for it."

"I married you because I loved you for a lot of reasons and I wanted you to have my children. I think you did well."

"Is that all?" she asked, smiling.

He felt embarrassed by what he had said. "Not nearly all. You are my confidant and aide."

"Aide?" Pamela raised her eyebrows.

"I can't live without you. Sometimes I worry."

"No candidate's wife has ever been assassinated if that's what you're thinking."

"If my enemies knew how vulnerable I am to losing you they might try."

"Who, for heaven sakes?"

"We are in a high stakes game with a determined and not necessarily moral opponent."

Pamela had wondered if God would protect Adrian from an assassin: would He protect her too? "Tonight we have to relax. If you'll mix me a cocktail while I change, we'll go to Rosario's and then we'll make love."

Wearing casual clothes, they walked with two bodyguards to the restaurant. Emilio Rosario, the Daggett's favorite host, greeted Adrian and warmly hugged Pamela. He showed them to their favorite table and looked after the security people. Emilio fussed over them, brought out their favorite Chianti and took their order. They talked about family affairs, the media, and the children. They decided they would have a family meeting about it. For the time being the media was too busy covering all of the candidates to bother with the families. When Adrian emerged as the strong front runner, that would change.

They carried half a bottle of the wine back to their apartment. Adrian took Pamela's coat and after she poured the rest of the wine he turned her to him and started to undress her.

"My enemies must know how much you mean to me. The one event that I might not withstand is losing you. You are everything a wife can possibly be. I am an unworthy husband."

She put her finger to his lips. "We are a marriage, my love. I have been worried someone would kill you and I wouldn't be able to handle that. You are too dear to me. I believe God has blessed us with each other and He will protect us."

"I believe that, too." He touched her hair while she unbuttoned his shirt.

When the were naked she smiled sweetly, "Shall we finish the wine." They sat next to each other on the couch and began touching after they clinked their glasses. In the bedroom she reminded him how sexually sensitive each part of his body was and how absorbing a long foreplay could be. He responded to her body. They forgot their titanic responsibilities and issues. A good sleep followed.

THE NEXT MORNING Adrian asked Terry to hold a meeting in Cleveland to start work on a more detailed educational program aimed at improving the quality of primary and secondary education and at teaching moral values. He was, he thought, the next of a long line of politicians and candidates who had attempted that. Or had they really? Did they have the staff he had? Most likely not. The committees and commissions with some exceptions were made up of politically interested people or the special interests pushing selfish agendas. He would be different.

COFFEE WAS PERKING when Alvin Carter arrived at Tony's office for a meeting he requested. When Tony was ready he went to the desk, "I've heard some news," he said, as he extended his hand. Tony stood up and took it. "Stephie told me it's coming before the next board meeting. She wanted me to think about it. Congratulations Tony, you're the right guy. People in this company love Ian and they are going to love you. You're the leader for the next century."

"It astounds me, Alvin, and it troubles me."

"To be following Ian?"

"I suppose so, I wish he would be CEO forever. It's the way it came about. He was concerned we may be attacked by POLACO and that he would be forced to resign, but I think I have avoided that if Helene's signature is binding to POLACO."

"Agreements have a way of coming apart."

"There's too much at risk for either side."

"So you told us." He sat down and pulled out the notebook he always carried.

"Tony, I've tried to think through the attack on the village and I can come up with only one explanation. That is that we have a mole in the campaign."

"That's not unusual is it?"

"No, they're easy to place at low levels. My guess is that the mole some how found out who Nancy was and they probably had her tailed to the village. They went into the village office looking for proof of our involvement. It would seem, from what you have said, they got it."

"Isn't that a long stretch. How would they know to follow

Nancy?"

"Nothing else to try."

"I was going to call you. I can't be specific, but I think Helene knew of my appointment as CEO. Some things she said."

Alvin took a sip from his mug. "That would not come from the campaign, but most likely from a mole here. It seems we're under mole attack."

Tony laughed as he imagined a gang of Disney-sized armed moles charging across the parking lot.

"What's the counter measure, rat poison or cats?"

"I wish cats would work"

"They're easy to recruit." Tony laughed again as he visualized the moles warded off by Disney-type cat characters.

"There must be one here. How would that secret get out?"

"I don't have proof, Alvin. It's a feeling."

"This brings me to recommend something else we have to consider."

"What's that?" Tony asked.

"We need to consider, Tony, placing our own mole."

"I thought that would be very difficult."

"That doesn't mean we shouldn't try."

"What's your idea?"

"We get a woman pro or a woman writer, since there are so many women in the POLACO management. We establish her as a writer if we have to by financing publication of some of her work or we have stuff ghost written. We spend a little money on an outside firm to have those things publicized and then she takes a vacation to Harbour Island, likes it, and buys a home. She hangs out where the POLACO staff hangs out, meets people, gets to know them, and finds somebody who is not so happy and gets some details of what POLA-CO is doing. Maybe we can access documents. Maybe that person will tell us what's going on."

Tony paused. "Wouldn't there be jeopardy to this person? POLA-CO is the police power down there."

"It would be best to send pros."

"What about the campaigns?"

"We can send in volunteers or we can try to get somebody hired. As the primaries approach they'll start to hire more people if there is a chance of success."

"For Harbour Island wouldn't it be better to send two?"

"Could be. It doubles the exposure, but it also doubles the chances for success."

"That's what I mean," said Tony, about to authorize the first covert action ever taken by PENMET.

He talked to Jean about it. She said that since everybody does it, maybe he should. Information was the most valuable commodity in politics. The next morning he phoned Alvin and told him to start the project and draw money from the foundation to pay for it. He wondered if this decision might one day cause him to be fired by the board.

A FOLLOW-UP meeting on education was in a three-way teleconference between the headquarters' group, Adrian and Pamela in Des Moines with the traveling staff, and the educational issues team in Cleveland, with Roger Bennett sitting in. Pamela had gone to Cleveland to brief the issues team on the discussions with Adrian, Terry, and the senior staff. While other prospective first ladies often poured sand in the bearings of campaign machinery, Alan and Terry were delighted to have Pamela with her extraordinary intelligence and curiosity and her ability to present. On the campaign trail she dutifully stood behind her husband, but when acting independently, she was strong and forceful. Terry noticed she never failed to compliment people for good work or good thinking.

Three hours in the morning had been set aside. Adrian explained he had asked for this meeting to clear up some questions and to develop a policy that would respond to the reality of secondary schools in particular. He challenged the group by restating that he was not happy with the answers they had to questions about education at the press conference in Des Moines.

The discussion focused initially on the quality of teachers and teaching and the quality of management as the critical variable in success. The conclusion was that the quality of management related directly to the involvement of the communities. Communities with good schools and successful programs almost universally had strong community participation. A key obstacle to the quality of management was large bureaucracies in some states which often prevented anything new from happening.

In terms of teachers they ranged in life's bell-shaped curve from excellent to unsatisfactory. There was discussion of recruiting, evaluating, tenure, compensation, training, and strengthening the classroom. Then John Gutherie and Martha Lafferty of the Cleveland staff presented their idea. The most potent force in any community was business. The local ones and the divisions of multinational corporations had very similar interests. Improved education results were critical to long-term business success. The key initiative would be the promotion of business involvement in education through tax incentives and other means. People from all disciplines in the business would put their talents to work assisting in the classrooms. Businesses would invite the schools to their facilities not for tours, but to experience the inside. Teachers would intern in businesses related to their disciplines during the summers or on sabbatical leaves. This would keep them aware of their subject as it is really used and its significance to their students. Students would intern in the summers or at holiday times to get direct experience. Business personnel would connect the curriculum to the real world. A focus would be on showing students the reasons for education and the personal advantage of success in school. It would be a national program backed at the highest level. Reports of progress would be gathered and would be the subject of a quarterly report by the President to the people. It was a dramatic new proposal which had been attempted in various degrees by forward-looking jurisdictions. The staff discussions of this topic were lively and active.

"Maybe in this complex world all of us must be involved in the education of our children. We must mass our talents. The more the children experience the working world, the better they will understand how they must prepare themselves," Adrian noted.

"What about the influences on kids? I've heard that it once was home, church, and school. Now it's peer pressure, television, magazines, and home is fourth." said Nancy.

"We have a high dropout rate, a high failure rate, and we have students who are not fulfilling themselves," Martha pointed out. "A significant percentage of the families in the US are dysfunctional. They don't provide a positive background."

"Television is a huge problem," Gutherie said. "Too many students spend too much time watching it. Some of the things they watch may have knowledge to communicate. Children may see life situations in which they can partake vicariously. There may be some other things, but they would learn much more by reading about them."

"We have too much mindless and meaningless television," Nancy firmly stated. "That is a federal problem. More than regulations about violence on television may be needed. If we make cigarette makers put warning labels on their product, we should make television stations remind students that they are better off reading than watching the crap they have on."

There were "hear, hears" from the other screens and from behind Adrian. "So one policy point that we have come to is to do something about the television set and the content of the programs," said Roger Bennett.

"We could make the stations advertise good programs on other stations," said Terry.

"That would create the most expensive lobby ever seen in Washington," said Anne.

"Maybe we could use the foundation to produce TV ads to promote studying and not watching television," Nancy suggested drolly. Everyone laughed.

"That's an action point," said Adrian. "Everyone has known about the problem. No one has addressed it. We will. What about safety? When I was in high school nobody ever thought about safety."

"That's from the drugs, Adrian," said Martha. "We need to establish some additional courts and prosecutors to deal with some of this. Maybe it will soak up some of the lawyers we would like to put out of business."

"We should add a caveat to the business involvement idea and make sure that no lawyers appear in schools urging that students become lawyers," said Terry. Guffaws resulted.

"Or political consultants," said Alan to more laughter.

"How many of the dysfunctional families are dysfunctional because of the use of illegal drugs?" asked Terry.

"A lot," said Burt, "But also from the failure of education."

Roger Bennett added, "It is reasonable to say that fighting drugs the way we are is not going to be productive. Reforming education and accomplishing these objectives may be a much more important answer to the drug problem and to putting families on the right track."

The meeting ended after many more questions and remarks and with praise from the candidate and the campaign staff for the excellent work done by the issues staff. The Cleveland telecom screen faded to black, and an exchange began between Des Moines and Chicago.

"Get a speech ready on that would you please, Terry? That is excellent work."

"For the National Education Association?"

"How important is education in New Hampshire?" asked Nancy.

"They think about it more and more up there. They're becoming a 'high tech' state."

"I like this," said Terry. "We aren't talking about national standards. We're not talking about enforcement. We're not talking about spending more money. We're talking about something tangible to do. Something the federal government can do."

"Don't forget limits on television," said Anne. "Why not rate shows with respect to alternative related reading material or other activities?"

"That would be an endless struggle with the broadcasters and the advertising industry," said Alan.

"Maybe not," said Nancy. "A lot of parents would support this."

The conference ended and Adrian turned to the people who were seated at the table with him, "That was very good. I congratulate you all." He looked around the room. Pamela was there with Merrick and Karen. Louise had promoted a new person to the traveling staff to help her with the reporters and the writing. It was Michelle Proust, press aide and POLACO operative.

IN WARD'S OFFICE the windows were open to the sea breeze as the weather cooled.

"I think you've got the essentials we need," he said after Helene reported on the Quebec meeting. "Are they going to honor or are they going to play hardball in some way?"

"They may try something, but I believe they will completely adhere to the agreement. We don't need to worry about it."

"Good work. Did you have some fun?"

"Yes we did." She told him briefly about the Chateau Frontenac.

"Did you tell him about your episode with Edgar's people?"

"I did. He knows about our security and the possibility of forceful interrogation. I didn't see any harm in his knowing we might use it."

"You have it under control. I admire it very much and I'm grateful to you. Gallosey and Sadovan are satisfied even though you haven't ordered every fifth person to be interrogated, to find out if they were doing something wrong."

"A policy surely to increase employee loyalty."

Ward laughed, "You've set parameters. Who else is going to have to do it?"

"I'm moving Carrie over to head human resources so she would. I think just the two of us with Edgar, but Madeline has been talking about wanting to be able to send people down for punishment or otherwise as counsel."

"I don't expect her to do what you did. Edgar told me you're one brave lady. Did you get any other information from Tony?"

"Nothing on the company. I tried to draw out the relationship with the campaign, but he didn't say much. Should I keep the relationship going?"

"Only if you want to. Or maybe I should say I hope you want to. There could be value."

"I feel awkward about it, but I do enjoy him."

THE SUDDENNESS OF the invitation to join the traveling team temporarily kept Michelle from her regular connection. She sent an UPS overnight envelope to Florida asking for instructions. After the teleconference, she was in the possession of the most important information she had come upon. A week later when the chill of a morning in New Hampshire reminded everyone the time was approaching, she got a phone call which told her to pick up a Federal Express package at the airport in Manchester. She told everyone her father had sent her stock transfer papers she had to sign, and left to fetch the package.

In it there was delightful news. The way Helene and Edgar had decided to "run her" was to send Bill Haber to Chicago. He would become her boyfriend; then she could justifiably call everyday from the field. She was excited Bill was on his way and that he would take an apartment in a luxury building not far from where she lived and would join her health club. She would say she met him there. Through him she would transmit the information circulated internally in the Chicago headquarters which was faxed to wherever the candidate was. Further, she was in the big meetings in the field with Daggett.

What seemed like "the education bomb" went off in two parts. They revealed it to the NEA convention in a rousing speech. The press area was overflowing when Adrian and Pamela arrived. There were cheers and whistles as they came to the platform and when they were introduced. When he talked about slashing the educational bureaucracy, the delegates went wild. Most of them applauded while he described the plan for business involvement. They loudly cheered the idea of labeling TV programs.

In presenting his concept for the future role of unions, he called for cooperation of unions with administrators and the business community. He asked their support to raise American primary and secondary education and to be the best in the world to make America the most competitive nation with its education serving as a foundation.

At first there was some hesitation on the role of the union in the applause, but there was a standing ovation when he finished.

At the podium and waving with him, Pamela whispered in his ear, "This time you did it right."

"I can't believe it's a union."

"Most teachers really care about what they are doing. They will be front-line troops for us."

The union president joined them at the platform, shaking Adrian's hand and kissing Pamela's cheek. He turned to Adrian and said, "You are the first politician I have ever heard who I thought was really interested in education."

In the press box Louise was beset with questions.

"Does he really mean it?"

"You bet he does," she responded.

"Do you think the business community will respond?"

"They will. They have an interest."

"Do you mean to mitigate the power of unions in education?"

"We suggested a new role for them."

She answered each question about four times.

The story was featured prominently by all the media across the country. Network news carried it. CNN ran it on every newscast the next day. The full speech was on C-SPAN. The newspapers carried it. Education was a hot button in the United States. Now a major proposal had been made, a challenge to the business community of every school district. It was also a challenge to the broadcast industry.

In the days following, examples of how this had already been done started to appear. It was a great story. The response was better than Anne Russell even dared to hope for. The polls couldn't tell everything, but for years they had said that education was the number one issue in America. No political candidate really addressed it until Adrian did. Adrian would have to follow it up with business leaders. She would make it a point of getting him together with business and educational leaders. This would draw votes – very enthusiastic votes.

The broadcast lobby called screaming. They had profited from "lowest common denominator" programming and reputed any serious challenge to their practices. The Daggett campaign represented their first serious challenge.

MICHELLE PROUST'S REPORT through Bill got to Harbour Island a week before the NEA speech. Louis took it to Erla who called a meeting which included Helene. Looking at the calendar of events and considering how Michelle had been delayed, she guessed that the speech would be the announcement. Michelle confirmed that two days later.

"When are we going to stop getting bombed out of all our issues? He's going to take us out on this one."

"Do we have an educational policy?" asked Helene.

"Not one like that," said Erla. "We're focused on national standards, incentives for teachers and students, and improved liaison between the secondary schools and community colleges plus more money for buildings and computers."

"How big is this?" asked Helene.

"Could be big," said Marsha. "People may perceive this as something tangible. Daggett has a high trust rating. They will expect him to deliver."

"Education's still the number one issue. No one talks about it very much in specifics," said Erla.

"I wouldn't say no one said anything about it," said Warren. "I think if we check the dialogue we would see quite a bit."

"You'll see quite a bit of vagueness," said Erla. "We are for good education, we are for improvements, we are for better scores, we are for better discipline. What does it all mean? It looks as though Daggett has formed a real policy."

"What do we do about this intelligence?" said Helene.

"We could get on record before Adrian gives his speech. Porter or Findlayson could announce an unspecific plan to get business involved in education. That would preempt him and at the same time give us some policy development time," said Marsha.

"You have to be more specific than that to counteract," said Warren.

"Maybe not, Warren. If we just make the statement then we can develop something that is a little different and some other things that may be the great issues group of Cleveland didn't think about."

"If we give this to Porter and give him what to say, they may suspect the moles."

"Michelle's cover is very good," Edgar said. "She is using her name. The only giveaway is that her father is associated with one of the companies backing POLACO."

"They might not think of that."

"We can hope they won't."

Two days after the first reports rolled in on Daggett's educational policy, Senator Porter called a press conference to point out that two days before Adrian's speech he had begun talking about business involvement with education. He accused Adrian Daggett of having stolen some of his ideas. The Harbour Island staff thought his performance was less than exceptional. CNN broke the story at noon and once again the switchboard at Daggett headquarters lit up. Anne, trying to have a quiet lunch at her desk, heard about it and called for the tape. Nancy and several of her people came to watch. They also judged the performance to be weak.

"Shall we prod the press to come in and ask about this?" said one of her young associates.

"No, let's wait and see who asks. That'll give us an assessment of the importance of it. Then we'll respond."

"What shall we say?"

"Does anyone in the United States who knows the quality of our issues staff, possibly think we need to steal ideas from Senator Porter? We have been very effective campaigning without Senator Porter's assistance. Then we can hand out the study that Cleveland did."

Those present applauded.

"But," said Anne, "they have established their position, which is what they wanted to do. Now the question is, was this happenstance, or did they find out what we intended to do?"

Two days later Tony and Alvin Carter landed at Meigs Field in one of the Learjets. It was a subject that could not be discussed by phone. Terry Leelan picked them up and took them to the Conrad Hilton where Anne, Nancy, and Alan were waiting with Mitch and Dominick.

The meeting was called to order to review the facts and to estimate whether or not the statements by Porter indicated a leak. Willis Porter rarely came up with new ideas or confronted difficult issues. They decided that someone either in the Porter campaign or POLACO had access to Daggett planning information. There were two possibilities: a security leak such as someone riffling through the trash for un-shredded material, or a mole. The detective work would focus on Cleveland and would have to be delicate; the egos in Cleveland were large and sensitive.

TIME CONSTRAINTS TO establish sufficient name recognition for Adrian and to associate him with particular policies prompted the decision to forego participation in the Alaska and Louisiana pre-primaries. In the view of most of the state coordinators, there still wasn't enough time for Adrian to be exposed in their states to insure the results they wanted. Terry Leelan, however, acting as National Coordinator as well as campaign director, apportioned Adrian's time and he kept everyone to the schedule. Headlines and TV coverage went national on more than a dozen occasions. They were in a rhythm. New issues were introduced and old issues were validated and enriched. In each case Adrian was the candidate telling the people what he really thought and what the tough issues were. He put the onus on incumbent politicians for ignoring the tough issues and attempting to placate the public. Adrian called on the American people to face the future with courage and understanding. He developed that theme without stating it in almost every presentation. The American people must be prepared for the future, complex and daunting as it may be.

Parker Lothan continually tracked the response to this in each state. He reported unusual popularity in the future orientated states like North Carolina and Tennessee, Texas and California. Based on that, Terry reasoned that a foray into Alaska and Louisiana could pay off handsomely. Alaska was still a state with a frontier attitude where the future had to be faced. Louisiana was rebuilding its economic base on top of its extractive and chemical industries and rapidly becoming a nexus of culture and education in its major universities and New Orleans.

During the holiday period the primary campaign wound down usually for a two week rest. The thesis was that voters were too concerned with family activity and holiday plans to pay much attention to politics. Sensing an opportunity, Terry dispatched Dominick Kluczinski to visit the Democratic leaders in New Orleans, Baton Rouge, Alexandria, and Shreveport and sent Nancy to Juneau, Anchorage, and Fairbanks. His idea was an all volunteer mission. Five days before Christmas they would hit Alaska with a big rally two nights before the Holiday and work the malls on Christmas Eve. They would travel to Louisiana on a flight on Christmas day striking there six days before New Years with time for a major speech in New Orleans and activities in the other three main cities. The very able junior people would spread out to cover the small towns, to meet with the Democratic organizations, hold local press conferences, and make other appearances such as they might be.

Terry lofted the concept with Adrian and then asked him if his body could stand it. He knew there were plans for the family to gather at Christmas at Fort Myers. Pamela called the children and asked if they would like to go to Alaska instead. Dianne thought it was a great kick. Donald asked if he could bring his girlfriend. Linda needed to be persuaded. Since they were fond of the girl Donald was dating, they invited her.

The proposal was controversial in the senior staff committee. The reasoning was that all available time should be invested in the big states. Terry knew it would be lost in the Christmas rush in the big states, but the arrival of Daggett and his reality campaign would be an event in the Alaskan cities and towns. He felt the same about Louisiana. Regardless, the senior staff volunteered. Anne and Bob Russell brought their skis as did Alan and Lauren. Nancy brought her children and their skis. Terry and Annalee did cross country as well as alpine. Annalee said, "If you live in Ithaca, New York you'd better learn to do something with the winter or it will get to you."

Karen and Earl volunteered, although Karen much wanted to see her family and to engineer a visit with the Hanleys. Jack Wood and Louellen Parsons, who worked in New York, signed on with their current best friends of the other sex. Louise Sczyniac volunteered and brought a boyfriend whom she had barely seen in three months. Michelle Proust signed up to bring Bill Haber.

By the time they were celebrating the end of the junket on New Year's Day in New Orleans, the success of the foray was well on its way to being legendary in annals of American politics. The "Caribou Gumbo Tour," as it became known, would become a traditional part of future presidential campaigns.

Louise cooked up an exotic invitation for the reporters, television news producers, and their crews. The trip was portrayed as "A Holiday Honeymoon 'Vacation' to Some of the World's Best Skiing and Partying." They included photographs of the scenes of hotels and ski slopes and city sights of Anchorage, Fairbanks, and the Marriott in New Orleans.

There was enough of a crowd to fill "Reality One," the newly leased and gaily painted Boeing 767 parked at O'Hare. In the afternoon of December 19th, the media adventurers and guests flew from Washington and New York and other cities to O'Hare where vans met them to carry their equipment to where the party started. The press section of the plane was equipped with an open bar. They took off in the early evening when Adrian and Pamela and the staff arrived. Flight attendants served shrimp cocktail and Chicago rib eye steak. Over the Canadian Rockies the pilots announced a beautiful moonlit night and turned off the lights so the passengers could see the shining

pristine snow on the jagged peaks. After a few minutes mostly everyone was asleep.

When they came inside the Anchorage airport and saw its huge
light oak beams lacquered to a shine, they knew where they were.
After dawn from the hotel they were excited by the way the mountains surrounded the city towering above it. It was Alaska. Everyone
felt the excitement.

The first action was a speech to the combined service clubs. Adrian
brought up the critical issues: financial stability, education, environmental conservation, reduced litigiousness, world peace, and health
care. He received shouts of approval from the lusty crowd. In the
afternoon he worked a mall while Anne and Nancy worked the media.

Karen and Earl were detailed to fly down to the Aleutian Islands
stopping at every small town with an airport or a frozen lake. Their
plane was a DeHaviland Beaver turbo prop. Jack Wood and Louellen
Parsons were assigned the West Coast; Alan and Lauren flew to the
North Slope oil communities, and to the central area. Michelle
worked the press with Louise while the boyfriends worked the lifts.

Terry made his way to the University where he had been invited.
The fundraiser came up the first evening followed by a dinner speech
to the business associations, which was televised at campaign
expense. The next morning Adrian headed to Fairbanks while Pamela
went off to Nome and Point Barrow. There she drove a dogsled. In
the evening back at Anchorage there was a major press conference
and a dinner for the Democrats.

On their adventure down the island chain Karen looked cute in an
Alaskan fur coat wrapped around her face and down to her knees. Earl
wore bearskin with a fur hat. It was a mini-campaign. Four people and
two reporters came to the first press meeting. Karen spoke at a service
club luncheon and appeared on local television. The people of the little
towns were glad to see her and glad to hear her message. At Kodiak
they were given a sled ride through the town. Where they stayed
overnight they made friends whom they hugged when they left. Some
people hoped they would be able to return one day to America's Far
East where there is very little political bullshit in the business of life.

The evening before Christmas Eve there was a come one and all
Christmas party fundraiser for $50.00. A thousand people paid. The
media people made a story out of the reaction of Anchorage to the
candidate who appeared on TV news. On Christmas Eve they went
to Juneau for a luncheon of Democrats. Back in Anchorage, all the
staff, wearing special scarves, went to the main mall to wish everyone

a Merry Christmas. Karen, Earl, Louellen, and Jack were home to join them. When the mall closed Earl took Karen to church for the midnight service. On Christmas day there was a late breakfast, an afternoon of skiing, and a dinner flight to New Orleans. Everybody slept. Terry was concerned that he was exhausting his key people.

The staff and reporters alike stayed at the Radisson among the Tulane University Medical Center buildings on Canal Street. On December 26th, Adrian spoke to members of service clubs at lunch and for dinner. Democrats from all over Louisiana streamed in to Baton Rouge to meet him and hear him. At the Baton Rouge Marriott there was a huge reception. The staff worked the crowd. As they met people they brought them to shake hands with Adrian and Pamela. Health care was more important in Louisiana, Adrian stuck to that theme and after a few minutes he started to take questions. He saw they had read a lot about what he had said before he had met them. Major speeches were scheduled in New Orleans, Alexandria, and Shreveport.

A luncheon of the bankers association in New Orleans drew a big crowd from the Mississippi Valley and across Lake Ponchartrain. He talked of the issue of fiscal stability and his policy to protect American democracy. He also spoke of the need to be conscious of abuses on certain markets from which the public and investors must be protected. In Shreveport he spoke of environmental irrationality and in Alexandria he approached the education issue and the reality of the need for deep involvement. He worked several of the big malls in New Orleans and Pamela visited the Tulane Medical Center hospitals. They met with the St. Charles Parish Democratic leadership.

Karen and Earl, Jack and Louellen and two other teams used cars instead of planes. Karen drew the eastern fourth of the state and met with the county and city committees. From breakfast to dessert and coffee she appeared at little press meetings and at club luncheons and dinners, and in homes to talk with people. Small town newspapers came to interview her.

The last day of the year, Adrian traveled to Lafayette, Morgan City, and Houma to visit the new industries there. On New Year's Eve there was a fundraiser – come one, come all, at the New Orleans Marriott on the river. It was a huge success and was the precursor of a great party. Adrian and Pamela and the staff joined in the dancing and socializing. Pamela danced with 33 different men. Many of them kissed her hand; several kissed her on the lips. Karen was swept into the dancing with many cut ins. Earl kept an eye on her and saw her kissed several times. He finally gave in and asked some other girls to dance. At midnight he kissed Karen.

The New Year's Day brunch was at the Omni Royal Orleans with the chance to walk around the Veaux Carre, the French Quarter. The plane left at five.

Everyone slept.

☆ **Chapter 19** ☆

THE FIRST DEBATE of the Democratic candidates in New Hampshire was at the Sheraton Tara in Nashua. This was scheduled for 90 minutes on local public television, but was picked up on the PBS network for stations that wanted to use it. CNN carried it live. Each candidate had a podium and could use notes as well as make them. The format was two-minute opening statements and two-minute closing statements. In between, the candidates would question each other and audience reaction was allowed. Adrian drew the first round of questions and Governor Perona asked him if he really meant to increase taxes to pay down the national debt.

Adrian attacked, "My staff has not been able to identify any decisions, votes, or statements which you have made indicating an understanding of economics, much less high finance. No politician also, to our knowledge, has ever addressed the American people about the danger of our national debt, because of its size, or about the continued monthly balance-of-payment deficits that sees well over 150 billion dollars pass out of the United States each year. This is added to our national indebtedness and also to the dollar balances on deposit in foreign countries which constitute another major threat politicians don't discuss. There is a finite limit to how much of these deposits the system will hold, particularly in light of the new European currency. The interest on the national debt load is $4000 per household.

"We are a debtor nation. If anyone thinks these problems do not exist let him tell the people they don't. If anyone thinks these problems will go away let him tell the people that they will. I know the problems exist and I know they won't go away and if I am elected I am going to do something about them."

The audience broke into applause. Perona felt wounded.

Senator Porter was next. "But, why should you raise taxes?"

He got the next clawing: "I assume if you win the election, Senator, you will attempt to pay down the debt with tax cuts. The Republicans, after creating half the debt, struggled to balance the budget with tax cuts. All this did was add to the debt. We seem to be a nation that is beset with politicians who can only promise to cut taxes. That will not secure our future. The American people will pay higher taxes, if necessary, to assure the future does not include a fiscal crisis. I gather you would risk the crisis rather than raise a disagreeable issue. You all underestimate the American people. They do care. They do understand. They will spend the time to understand particularly if they and their families are in danger."

The audience applauded again.

Marilyn Findlayson asked Daggett if he was willing to risk the excellence of the American health care system by bringing on cost controls and national health insurance.

"I very much doubt, Ms. Findlayson, that you know anyone who does not have health insurance. Do you know what people who don't have health insurance do when they get sick? The answer is they consult a pharmacist for free and buy an over-the-counter drug until they get so sick they have to go to an emergency room. How much is that costing? Does anyone know? I wonder if the health care industry might be better off with higher usage and lower prices. If I am elected I am going to find out. The first order of business will be a comprehensive health care plan. We will have a national system like every other industrialized country."

Senator Porter jumped in, "Those countries don't have the quality of health care we have."

"No, Senator," Adrian answered. "Theirs is better than ours." He paused. "The reason is because all of the people have access. They have a lot fewer sick people. We don't even count them. We're afraid to because of the costs that will be revealed in lost productive time and in pain and suffering. I will not allow low-wage workers to go around sick"

There were more applause and whistles.

"Are you going to require the government to select physicians?" Findlayson responded.

"That people would have to stand in line for an unknown doctor is health care industry propaganda. The system will allow people to go to their own doctors. The essential to good health is to have your own doctor who knows you and your body."

There was more applause.

Robert Ramsdell saw that Adrian was dangerous and gave his question a build up. "You have said in your remarks that you would fully support United Nations initiatives in dealing with overseas civil wars, genocides and famines. I predict this will lead to another tragedy of Vietnam proportions and to ignominious embarrassments of Somalia."

"I disagree with the statement, Mr. Ramsdell, but what is your question?"

The audience laughed and applauded.

"America's mothers don't want their sons and daughters to be wasted in foreign adventures which you apparently will pursue."

"Still no question?"

The audience guffawed.

"Do you intend to make the United States the world's policeman?"

"The United States is already the world's principal policeman. If we reform the UN and then mass America's resolve behind it, the United Nations will become the police force it was intended to be. There has to be a policeman. When tyrants and despots are guaranteed that they now will be tried for crimes against humanity, the crimes will eventually stop. If the UN is not placed in that role then it will automatically fall back on the United States, with help from Britain, France, Canada, and others in NATO. The main issue is peace and the proliferation of nuclear, chemical, and bacteriological weapons. Shall we stop having peace and shall we not seek security from weapons of mass destruction? Peace has a price. Freedom has a price. The greatest weapon against the proliferation of big weapons is peace. There must be peace, and we must pay the price for it."

The audience cheered.

Richard Sandellot asked Adrian why he would increase expenditures on aerospace and defense. Adrian told him the investment in aerospace assured the technological superiority of American arms and continued the American defacto industrial policy of investing in aerospace and defense to spin off the newest and latest technologies to all types of industries.

When it was Adrian's turn he asked both Senator Porter and Governor Perona how they would provide for the health of all Americans. The answers were vague and Adrian pointed out the vagueness. The audience applauded that.

He asked Marilyn Findlayson to justify why America should continue to be a debtor nation. She stumbled, not ready for him.

He asked Robert Ramsdell if he could outline his foreign policy. Adrian concluded that it was essentially isolationism in an increasingly interdependent world and suggested that Ramsdell would favor protective tariffs to drive the world into another depression.

He asked Richard Sandellot if he would seek regulation of certain markets. Sandellot answered that he would investigate the need.

CSPAN rebroadcast the program several times.

IN THE UPSTAIRS conference room at Harbour Island the POLACO staff watched Daggett bloody everyone except Sandellot. Edgar sat next to Helene. She felt his maleness until she became absorbed in Adrian's performance.

"This man is a terror," Ward said at the end. "Can we do anything to stop him?"

"There may be no stopping him in the primaries. We'd better concentrate on the general election when the Republican resources will be with us," Helene answered.

"His opponents can't handle him, Ward," Erla Younge added.

"Anyone want to bet there won't be another debate?" Marsha asked.

Warren Hatch was clearly impacted by Daggett. "I agree with Helene. We have a lot of work if we want to keep this man out of the White House."

Ward's secretary appeared with a note. "Sadovan is calling," he said. "You'll have to excuse me. Let me know when you want to talk."

The room emptied as though everyone wanted to distance themselves from the phone. Helene and Edgar stayed and let Ward know they were there. After a few minutes he waved them into his office

"Sadovan has appointed himself Chairman of the Board, to look after me, the CEO," Ward said. "Unfortunately he has the support of the others on the committee. He wants us to smear Adrian Daggett and has suggested Radion Gallosey's consultant on dirty tricks to help with the job."

"And, who is this consultant?"

"Joseph Drago & Associates," Ward said.

"We know of them," Edgar said. "Melius uses them to do things he won't do. They're not consultants. They're operators."

"Sadovan insists we must make people question Daggett's reputation. He demands we attack him."

"How does he want us to do it in view of Melius' findings. Bribe someone to make allegations?" Helene asked.

"That's what he recommends; 'Let Drago handle it,' he says. Humph."

"Very dangerous, Ward. What angle? Sexual harassment?" Helene postulated.

"He thinks that even if the allegations on that subject are proven false that people will remember them."

"That may be true of a less dynamic candidate," Helene said. "Daggett is a different matter. He is personally powerful and he has monumental backers in terms of influence."

"We have to go forward, Helene. Let the Drago people do what they can. If it works, then we are rid of Daggett. If it doesn't, maybe we are rid of Sadovan and Gallosey."

"What about the other candidates?"

"They can truthfully say they are not involved."

"What about us?"

"The payments will be covered. At worst the Conservative Coalition will get blamed. At least that's what Sadovan expects."

"Who's talking to him?"

"It's him and Gallosey. They're fighters. They want immediate action."

"How do you want to handle this?"

"You two. No one else should know. We will pay through a law firm."

"Ward, I have a bad feeling about this," Helene protested.

"So do I, but we can't say 'no' at this point. If it doesn't work then you can say 'no' as often as you need to. If it works, everybody gains," Ward explained.

"We should advise against this. I'll take a strong position that this is a dangerous diversion from our central mission. We should let Daggett win the primaries and get ready to beat him in the general election."

"I can't prevent you from giving Sadovan your opinion."

"He will remember it." Helene assured both herself and the staff.

BY THE TIME Alvin Carter had recruited two females for the Harbour Island penetration, he and his operatives had made a full covert reconnaissance of the island and the POLACO facilities. Daphne Poltrac, an elegant blonde woman of 42, was an established writer of magazine articles and had published a sophisticated novel. There was no need to establish a false identity. This ensured that Daphne's background could withstand POLACO's most intense scrutiny. She could afford to establish a winter home on Harbour Island. Both she and her character had survived Alvin's thorough evaluation before she was offered the assignment. The salary was $10,000 a month plus a luxuriant winter cottage and all expenses. A first right to the story, with PENMET retaining final approval, was a key incentive to her engaging such extraordinary and possibly dangerous duty.

As her partner they selected Sharon Gilling, one of the first African-American women to be trained by the CIA. After resigning in the midst of the deterioration of that agency, she went to work for a publishing company, and did extremely well as an assistant editor and then as an editor. After another deep background check, the allure of intelligence work, the righteousness of the cause, and the salary Alvin offered brought her onto the team. She was 38 and divorced with two children.

Daphne also had two children. She had lost her husband, a construction engineer, in a fluke accident. The children were in college. Insurance payments and her success in writing had made them comfortable in a townhouse in Greenwich Village and in a farmhouse in Vermont, near Ludlow, which served as summer retreat and ski lodge. Daphne had been a basketball star and a cum laude student in English at the University of Indiana. At 5'10" and lanky, her fluid movements still made her an exceptional figure at basketball and skiing. Sharon was two inches shorter and buxom. She was a softball and soccer player as befitted her compact, powerful build and on the pistol range could outshoot all but two or three men in the CIA. In the two, Alvin had one tough trained agent, and one intelligent and savvy journalist with an impeccable background. Both were logical plants, perfect for socializing and making contacts with the POLACO staff.

By Thanksgiving, Daphne and Sharon were settled into the elegant four bedroom Victorian home. Alvin then could only wait and wonder whether Edgar Slaughter would catch his moles before they became productive.

FLASHING LIGHTS AT the campaign phone center signaled a

major event affecting the Daggett candidacy. Opportunistic media people wanted to try to reach principals first and get the scoop of the reaction. Friends of the staff also called to make sure the news was known.

Anne's phone rang at 11:10 a.m.; 12:10 in New York. Louise Sczyniac's voice said, "Tune in CNN. Somebody's accused Adrian of sexual harassment." Anne half expected something like that; they were doing too well. It might appear that the only way of stopping Daggett was by impugning his character which was viewed increasingly positive even by those who didn't care for his policy options.

The anchor made it sound like a natural disaster or an invasion. "To summarize what we know so far: a former employee of the State of Illinois has accused Adrian Daggett of sexual harassment. This employee is supported in her statements by at least four others who have lent their names to the action. The complainant, Annabelle Mayberry, has filed suit for recovery of costs and emotional damages resulting from having to leave the state government. So far there are no statements from the Daggett campaign or from Adrian Daggett himself."

"Is this a set up?" asked Louise.

"I have to believe it is. Where are you? I forgot the schedule," Anne asked.

"In the other Springfield."

"Massachusetts?"

"Where we will speak to the Massachusetts leadership conference at 1:30 this afternoon. I was having a sandwich when I saw it."

"Louise, tell Adrian. We'll need a teleconference before the speech."

"Poor man never has a relaxed lunch."

"We have to move fast." She saw Terry at her door waving her to the conference room.

When the telecom circuits were completed to Springfield and to Harrisburg where Tony, Alvin, and Stephanie Comstock participated, Terry read a statement, which had been faxed by a friendly reporter.

"Annabelle Mayberry was employed by the Illinois Environmental Protection Agency. During that time, she regularly attended meetings of the Governor's Cabinet as an advisor to the Commissioner of Environmental Affairs. She had been widowed by a private aircraft accident in which her husband, an executive with a utility company, had been killed. Adrian Daggett had been at the wake. According to Ms. Mayberry's account, Governor Daggett began making advances to her several months after. These advances became so insistent as to make Ms. Mayberry decide she had to leave state government. She indicates a number of other women were similarly harassed by the governor and has given the names of four of them who will support her testimony. She has filed suit for compensation for losses incurred in the sale of a home in Springfield, for the costs of moving to Belleville, and emotional damage. She is now an environmental consultant with a major national firm working from their office in Clayton, Missouri, a suburb of St. Louis. She also taught environmental sciences at the University of Southern Illinois in Carbondale. She is a resident of Illinois living in Belleville. Ms. Mayberry would have liked to continue her career in state government, but felt that she could not as long as Adrian Daggett was Governor."

There was silence. Terry asked as casually as he could, "Do you know her, Adrian?"

Adrian began slowly, "Yes, I do. What she says about attending the cabinet meetings is correct. I did indeed see her at the Christmas parties. I recall hugging her when I wished her Merry Christmas a couple of times. I recall hugging her at her husband's wake. I knew him. He was ten or twelve years older than she was. She's an intelligent woman, but I've always had an inkling of doubt about her character."

"Is any of this business true about your seeing her often or harassing her?"

"Nothing like that happened," Adrian stated firmly looking straight into the camera.

"We are going to find that she and these other women have been paid to make this accusation. The question is whether or not we can prove it," said Alan.

"I'm sure that's happened before," said Terry. "We need an investigation and we need it quick."

Alvin Carter was already on the phone.

"We also need to decide on how to respond to this," said Anne.

"I think I should threaten to sue this woman," said Adrian.

"That's one possible approach," said Anne. "If we're absolutely sure this allegation is not true, we have to deny it and we have to prove it's not true if we can."

"Do you want to have a statement from Pamela?" asked Nancy.

"Let's all think just a minute," said Anne. "What's your reaction, Adrian?"

"I certainly will sue this person. There are grounds to do so. But it sounds to me like this has been carefully crafted."

"It probably has been," said Tony. Alvin was still on the phone.

"We're now four and a half weeks from New Hampshire," said Alan.

"That's the reason they did it now; enough time to let it sink in, but maybe not enough time for us to respond," said Tony. "It's three and a half weeks to Iowa."

"I think you're right, Tony, as to their reasoning. But the response has to take care of this matter quickly. We can't depend on an investigation," said Anne.

"Reporters are likely to ask you questions about this when you go out of your hotel door, Adrian. I think you should say something like, ' there is no substance to the charges. I do know Annabelle Mayberry, but she is accusing me falsely. I'm having my lawyers investigate and we will take whatever action is indicated to be appropriate.' You can say you have seen her and spoken with her at parties associated with the governor's office; that she has attended cabinet meetings as an advisor to one of your commissioners, but that the charges are absolutely false and are a gross misrepresentation of the facts."

"I think we should refer this to our legal people," said Terry. "Adrian, we'll brief them on it. We'll limit your contact with them to their calling you to ask you specific questions."

"That's good. We're very busy," said Adrian.

"Let's keep things moving along everybody," said Terry. "Do we all agree on Anne's advice concerning how to answer the reporters?"

"I think we should wait until we have talked to the lawyers," said Alan.

"To hell with the lawyers," Adrian exclaimed heatedly. "I'm going to follow what Anne said. We should have a release on this. Can you get something ready and get it out to Michelle or shall I have her draft it?"

"Why don't you and Michelle draft it and send it back to me. This is the first time we've had to deal with anything really negative about you personally, Adrian, be sure to keep your temper." Terry knew that even a consummately reasonable person like Adrian could react over-emotionally when his personal integrity was impugned.

"We know you're tough, Adrian," said Nancy soothingly. "Just remember all you have to do is stare down the jackals, they won't bite."

By two o'clock Michelle Proust had prepared an excellent press release which everyone immediately approved, increasing her perceived value to the campaign.

ALVIN HAD THOUGHT part way through an event like this. Within 90 minutes, Broderick Rose was on a charter jet from Jacksonville flying to St. Louis with three of his key operatives. Marylou Michaels was on another chartered jet to Springfield.

Before leaving, he and Alvin activated their contacts in the investigative and information business. By 5:00 they had the resumés, work histories, and other information about all five of the women involved.

At 5:00, Alvin sat down to study them. Annabelle was born in De Kalb, Illinois. A fast check on the family indicated that her father was a successful general contractor. He built highways and bridges, dams, and buildings. More than half of his business was with the state, so he was intimately involved with state politics.

Annabelle had been an honor student in high school, a cheerleader, and an accomplished dancer with leading roles in three successive years of the school's musicals. Upon graduation from the University of Illinois at Champaign-Urbana in environmental science, she began a career in environmental consulting, water remediation, ground water testing, air effluent testing, and developing anti-pollution measures. After completing her Master's Degree at the University of Chicago, she went into state government where her father's connection landed an appointment in the Daggett Administration. Her marriage to an executive of a utility company in Springfield made the government job convenient. They had one child, a son, when her husband was killed in the crash of a chartered plane which took a chance with a thunderstorm.

Alvin wondered what type of personality she was. Would she be amenable to a bribe? Children of wealth usually aren't unless there had been reversals such as the death of a well-salaried husband.

He pushed the button on his phone to call his lead analyst.

"Do you have the name of Annabelle's father's construction company? I need as much financial history as you can get quickly."

"Her maiden name was Linden. Give me five minutes." In the time frame one of the junior people brought in a D & B report on Linden Company, General Contractors. It showed a downward trend. Employment had fallen from 78 in 1985 to 23 in 1993, and then to 11. The payment record had fallen as well from the very best rating to one that was mediocre. There were clear signs of financial stress. It added up. POLACO had found someone they could buy. Alan would need access to bank accounts, credit reports, and personal habits. To get at that information they had to get a criminal investigation started.

On the plane Marylou Michaels had received faxes of information about Veronica Torblad, one of the supporting Daggett accusers. Currently, Torblad was head of research for Cantwell Associates, a lobbying firm in Springfield, which had a good regional reputation. Marylou telephoned the Cantwell office as soon as she deplaned.

"Cantwell Associates," a man's voice answered.

"May I speak with Veronica Torblad please?"

"I think she's left for the day, miss," a man's voice answered.

"I have some information for her, and I also want to meet with her."

"I suppose this is about the Adrian Daggett sexual business?"

"I'm investigating it, that's correct."

"Well, I'm sorry she's not here."

"You're in lobbying?"

"Yes, we primarily represent people in Illinois and we do public relations."

"Would you mind if I ask you a few questions?" asked Marylou.

"Well, yes, I suppose I have a few minutes."

"Is 'Torblad,' Emily's maiden name? I thought she was married to a professor at the University, but I don't remember the name."

"She was married, but now divorced. Her ex is a lawyer. His name is Eric Torblad."

"Did she leave state government because of the Daggett business?"

"I don't know. She applied for a job here and we thought she would be a good person for us. The first we heard about the Adrian Daggett thing was this morning."

"Does Veronica know Annabelle Mayberry that well?"

"I believe they were friends."

"Do you know Annabelle Mayberry?"

"I met her a couple of times. She was an environmental scientist. We represent the Illinois State Foundry Association."

"What was Mayberry like to work with?"

"She's a bureaucrat regulator. I don't know how much she really understood of what we were trying to tell her. What's your interest in this business?"

"We're an investigating firm."

"Are you working for the Daggett campaign or for Daggett?"

"I'm afraid I can't tell you that."

"I know you can't, but if you are working for him, tell him we think this is a bum rap. Somebody's playing games. When he was governor women chased him! Did Veronica ever say anything about Daggett in the office?"

"No, that's why we wonder about this. We've never heard about it before. Will you want to see her?"

"Yes, that's why I'm calling. I hope you don't mind if she spends some time with me tomorrow?"

"Not at all."

They exchanged names. He was Albert Spahn, a partner.

She immediately sat down in a chair in the airline terminal to make notes.

WHEN SHE ENTERED her suite at the Hilton, Marylou called the Torblad residence. Veronica answered. Marylou told her, assuming the role of a legal investigator, that she needed to talk with her before any reporters reached her. It was 5:45 in the evening; she asked Veronica if she'd had dinner yet and since she hadn't they decided on Marylou's suite at the Hilton.

"Sounds good," was the immediate response.

At 7 p.m. in her suite, Marylou had a seafood salad with a bottle of Missouri white wine chilling and a Beaujolais Village waiting to be opened. The door buzzer rang. Opening it, Marylou saw an attractive, thirty-something woman with a soft, classic figure. She smiled as they greeted. Marylou began.

"Come in, and thank you for coming over."

"Thank you for the invitation for dinner. It gets boring eating alone," Veronica admitted.

"I'd expected you would have a family."

"No children."

"A not-so-happy divorce?"

"Not so happy."

"Is he in government?"

"No, his family owns a fuel oil and heating business. He's a lawyer. He does all right in his practice, I guess. It's bad being married to a lawyer. If you ever get divorced, they drag you over all the sharp stones."

"Naked." They laughed.

Marylou decided she was dealing with one very educated lady.

"Would you like a cocktail or wine?"

"Wine is fine. I see it's Missouri."

"I was introduced to it in St. Louis a couple of years ago," Marylou said.

Veronica added enthusiastically, "It's good wine, Missouri is the third largest state in wine making. Problem is, the people in Kansas City and St. Louis drink it all up."

The fact collection proclivities of the professional researcher were evident.

"And, what is your connection to the Daggett business?" Veronica asked.

"I'm an investigator. I'll leave it to you to decide what my purpose is," said Marylou hoping that would pass and that Veronica was not legally sophisticated even though she had been married to a lawyer.

"I guessed that when you said you wanted to talk before I met any reporters. Does that have to do with reserving testimony?" asked Veronica with a deceptive air of innocent curiosity.

"Could be."

Marylou thought quickly to choose the right approach. "Why don't we sit down and enjoy this lovely salad and you tell me where you're from and where you went to school. I'm from Jacksonville and went to Florida State. The army put me through law school. It was the only way I could get there."

"Well it's nice you have that advantage. I'm from Willamette. I went to Wellesley and I did my Masters Degree at Boston College. I'm working on a Ph.D. at Champagne-Urbana. My ex doesn't pay me enough to go to school full time, so I still have to keep my job. I did economics and political science. I love research and I took a lot of technical subjects. They pay me well enough."

"Do you do political research?"

"That's the most fun."

"I thought you'd say that. How did you meet Annabelle? Tell me about her and the Governor."

"I met her when she came to work in the Illinois Environmental Agency. We provided research services for them and we did a lot of work together. She was friendly. I wasn't very happy in my marriage so we got along."

"You weren't happy in your marriage?"

"No, my ex was screwing a client's ex-wife. He was proving something."

"I hope he didn't give you anything."

"I tested okay I never saw any of what Annabelle described in her statement. The only thing I can tell you is there used to be parties. Democrats, you know, have parties. Adrian was the Governor; that meant some women had a crush on him. He was such a great guy and by all means good looking. If he told me of a bedroom somewhere and that I should go up and take off my clothes and he would join me, I might well have done it."

"Did he ever ask you?"

"No."

"Did he ever approach you in a threatening or harassing way?"

"No. Once in a while when I saw him we would hug. I liked the feel of him, but I guess that's not what's supposed to happen anymore."

"Some people can twist things. We have to make sure this is a legitimate claim. Can you vouch that it is legitimate?"

"All I know is what Annabelle told me."

"When was that?"

"About two weeks ago she telephoned and told me what she was going to do and asked me to back her up with a description of parties and anything else I had seen that might support her."

"What did she offer you in return?"

"Why, nothing."

Marylou saw hesitation and a look away. She guessed Veronica would not pass a lie detector test with that question.

During the call to room service, Marylou planned a move at the end of the dinner. She returned to the subject of the department where Veronica worked, and about the relationship between her, Annabelle Mayberry, and the rest of the personnel in the environmental unit. They talked about Veronica's research work.

When the bottle of white wine was half empty, and Marylou opened the Beaujolais, there was no protest about saving the wine. They each had one glass while eating. Then Veronica poured a second. "You do know," Marylou stated, "if you are taking money from Annabelle or from somebody supporting Annabelle in this matter you are exposing yourself to a horrendous law suit from the Daggett's."

She watched closely and saw evidence of destabilizing.

"What do you mean?" Veronica asked, her voice wavering slightly.

"Did you ever see Adrian Daggett actually harass Annabelle?"

"Not unless hugging her at a Christmas party is harassment," Veronica recovered. "I told you all the women liked to be hugged by Adrian Daggett. It's nice when you can do that. Now, because of harassment, nobody touches anybody. Guys don't even ask you for dates, particularly the desirable older ones that are single. The higher up they get, the less they'll play in the office. If you give them a signal some of them get scared."

"At these parties did the women usually approach Adrian to be hugged?" Marylou asked assuming the investigative role again.

"Oh yes, he was openly warm. I think he likes women. He certainly has enough working for him."

"Maybe there is another way to look at this," said Marylou trying to find another way to apply the pressure. "Do you know about any facts directly or by hearsay that would indicate to you that Adrian was having any affairs either with people inside the government or outside of the government?"

Veronica thought for a minute. "I don't think I ever knew of any facts, as you say, but there were some rumors."

"Would you call those rumors gossip?"

"That's what I always thought they were."

"Can you recall any of them?"

"The chief speech writer, a very talented and very pretty woman named Audrey Henkens was recently divorced. I think she might have been 35 or 36. She traveled a lot with Adrian. Pamela didn't always go with him. I heard talk that maybe Audrey relieved some of the tensions of being Governor once in a while."

"Were they close, Adrian and Audrey?"

"A speech writer has to know how the elected official thinks and feels."

"Were there any rumors about Annabelle and Adrian?"

"I never heard anything."

Marylou decided on a more direct approach. "Does it seem strange to you that after nearly five years, when Adrian is running for president, Annabelle suddenly accuses him of sexual harassment?"

"It might take that much time to think it over," said Veronica with a sideways glance.

"Why do you think you've never heard anything about this until now?"

"Maybe Annabelle didn't want to tell me."

"And you heard nothing about anyone else complaining?"

"No."

Because she was a researcher and accustomed to reporting facts; this woman was used to telling the truth, however, Marylou thought she was shading the truth. She watched Veronica pour herself another glass of Beaujolais. "One reason we're investigating is the possibility this charge has been instigated against Adrian by his opponents since he is running away with the primaries."

"I don't know what you mean," said Veronica. Another wrong answer. Veronica wasn't dumb. She knew exactly what the question meant.

"In order to embarrass a candidate, schemes are set up and money changes hands. Many lies have been told about prominent people for money which originates from their enemies. If this is a lie about Adrian Daggett do you know how much it is worth?"

"I would have no idea."

"Take a guess."

"I'd rather not guess."

Another deceptive answer. "I can't guess." or " I don't know where to start thinking about this," is what non-involved people would say.

"It could be two or three hundred thousand dollars plus the guarantee that any suit would be defended and any judgment paid," said Marylou.

"Who would do that?"

"Someone running for the presidency. It is very valuable you know."

"People don't get rich being President."

"When they leave office they rake in the money from books and the lecture circuit. So do their colleagues. Then there is the patronage and the ability to influence legislation, regulations, and to set policy. You certainly realize what a reversal of certain environmental policies would mean to certain industries?"

"We used to deal with some of those issues. I never thought of it in that particular way. I mean about the value of government action to some companies," said Veronica.

"How did Annabelle approach you about this?"

"Well, she called and said there was something she hadn't told me. She told me her story. Then she asked if I would support her and if she could use my name. I asked her why she needed my name. She said that her lawyer told her that she needed the names of people that could talk about the Daggett administration and what he was like in general toward women."

"What did you say?"

"Well I didn't know what to say, but then I said it was all right."

"Were you friends in the sense that you shared feelings and secrets?"

"We talked, we went out together, we shopped; the things women do."

"Did you talk to her about your marriage?"

"I guess so. You have to talk to somebody."

The answers didn't fit. Why would an intelligent lady like this let Annabelle, even if they have been quite friendly, use her name without knowing the specifics, or did she know the specifics?

"Were there others with whom Annabelle was friendly with?" Marylou asked.

"There were two or three others. We were sort of a group for a while."

"Were they also professionals?"

"Oh yes. We all had good jobs. We all needed to have some fun and we needed somebody to do it with."

"When Annabelle called you, can you recall just how the conversation went?"

"She said that she wanted me to know something that had been going on for a while that she hadn't told me about. She said she thought it was necessary for her to speak out now that Adrian Daggett was running for President. We chatted and then she told me she might need some help. I asked her what kind, and she told me that she wanted some names to give to the media when she made her announcement. Then we talked some more and she asked me if I would support her."

Marylou was now convinced money had been offered. There were too many inconsistencies. She wondered what the strategy was. Perhaps it was to get Veronica thinking and talking so much about Adrian and his exploits, that the whole matter would be exaggerated. Eventually the allegations of harassment would gain credence as imperfect memories were subtly manipulated by the onslaught of false information. This process had been researched and used mainly by practitioners with sinister ends. It was closely akin to the "repressed memory" techniques used in several famous abuse cases in which both the "victims" and "perpetrators" remembered horrible crimes which, in fact, never occurred. She didn't see that she would get a lot further tonight and that challenging Veronica would serve only to warn the others. Best to leave it where it was. She thanked Veronica and left it open that they would resume the discussion the next day.

As Marylou made her notes, she reinforced her conclusion that Veronica was getting a monetary reward. Veronica needed money, and was accustomed to it. At least she didn't demonstrate frugality about other people's wine. She was lonely and apparently wanted to change venues, but didn't have the cash. She was vulnerable. She probably needed money for debts. She was smart and educated, but naive. Marylou felt that Veronica Torblad could be the loose thread that could unravel the fabric of the deception.

Marylou wrote down the specific questions and specific answers she had gone over with Veronica and then called Broderick. It was a long conversation until after eleven. It was now late. He said they would talk again in the morning. She piled all the room service paraphernalia on the cart and pushed it through the double doors of the sitting room into the hallway. In one minute she was hanging up her dress and in one more minute she had peeled off the rest of her clothes. In something of a daze, she laid out her running shorts and a sweatshirt and drew back the covers of the king size bed and fell into it. She thought she had scored with Veronica. But now they needed proof that money was the reward for the attack.

THE FOLLOWING MORNING after the banks opened, Alvin Carter was headed to St. Louis on a Learjet and Tony Destito to Springfield on a Cessna Citation. Each carried one hundred fifty thousand dollars in cash. Ian had authorized bribes for the truth. He withdrew the money from his personal accounts after arranging a loan for quick payment. He told the president of the bank exactly what he was doing with the cash. Neither of them knew whether it was legal to offer a bribe to turn states evidence to somebody who had already accepted a bribe. It was, however, the best way to expedite a criminal investigation which would get at bank records of those involved. Alvin Carter had told them that if they could tip over one of the five people, the other four might come tumbling down.

Back at PENMET, Ian sat back and surveyed his elegant, dignified, and proud office. The question came again; would he be required to resign all of this in disgrace? Would Tony Destito soon sit in this chair at this desk because of his decision to oppose POLACO in a risky involvement in politics? He imaged headlines, TV stories, and whispers. He and his father owed much to the United States. He was now giving something back, part of his fortune and possibly what the founders had called "sacred honor." He knew of businessmen who liquidated their honor twice a week in semi-fraudulent deals. He had kept his full reserves of honor. The prospect of dishonor and disgrace terrified him. He told himself if American democracy was saved for the future at the cost of his honor and his fortune it would be worth it. He was in the position to oppose a sinister group attempting to undermine the Constitution. He accepted the challenge, but the risk of damage to his reputation and legacy weighed heavily upon him.

MARYLOU DROVE OUT on the tarmac to the PENMET plane. In thirty seconds, Tony carrying his new briefcase, was seated in the car. He called Broderick Rose who was at Lambert Airport waiting for Alvin. Tight coverage had been arranged for all five women. From the operatives assigned to tail Annabelle Mayberry, they learned that reporters had been waiting outside of her apartment and television interviews had been arranged. Reporters also approached the two other women who lived in St. Louis. Their immediate concern was Veronica. They invited her to lunch at the suite of the Hilton and she accepted for 12:30.

The local agency they hired in Springfield called to say reporters had been in touch with Veronica and might follow her to the luncheon. Tony ordered six top security persons to get to the hotel quickly to manage the situation. One would be stationed outside of the door of the suite, two would be downstairs, one would float, and two would be inside the suite. Marylou called Veronica and said, "We understand you may have some people following you. Don't worry about it. Just come to the suite. We'll handle them." Room service brought salads, sandwich makings, and soup to the kitchenette in the suite and stocked the bar with soft drinks, fruit juice, beer, and wine.

When Veronica approached the hotel, the downstairs guards reported two local reporters and two TV camera crews following her. She strode into the hotel from the parking lot. At the elevator the reporters caught up. Two security people moved in to keep the television camera men back, but the reporters had got on the elevator with her and the floating guard. They started to ask whom she was visiting. The guard moved the reporters away from her, but the questioning persisted.

Finally at the suite, Veronica was greeted and introduced to Marylou's friend "who wanted to meet her." They suggested some lunch first, however. They helped themselves to the food while Marylou asked questions about the reporters, trying to find out what they had been told.

They talked about other peripherals. When they finished their food, Marylou began, "We have something we'd like to show you Veronica."

Tony got up from the table and moved over to the coffee table to the new brief case. He looked Veronica in the eye. Marylou continued, "We know, Veronica, that you have taken money from Annabelle and people associated with her in return for allowing them to use your name in support."

Veronica whitened and then flushed. "I don't know what you mean," she stammered.

"We know that money is being deposited into another bank under an assumed name and that you signed a signature card for that assumed name which Annabelle gave you along with a false social security number. We also know that they have promised to pay your legal expenses should any be involved and that they have already provided you with an attorney should you need one."

Veronica looked at them incredulously. "How did you ever find out?"

Tony sighed inwardly with relief.

"We can't tell you that," Marylou continued, "You know that this is a civil and possibly a criminal offense. You have exposed yourself to being sued by Adrian Daggett. If the matter is turned over to a prosecutor, I am sure the District Attorney's Office will investigate." She paused to let it sink in. "We have, however, Veronica, another option for you which will solve your money problems and also get you off the hook with Adrian Daggett, as well as protect you as much as possible from the prosecutors." She let that sink in.

Tony opened the briefcase and in it were thick bands of $100 bills. There were fifteen of them.

"You can give back the money they gave you. We'll give you this money to replace it."

"Why would you do that?"

"Give it a little thought, Veronica. We'll give you more if you will repudiate the people who got you into this and if you will repudiate Annabelle Mayberry by making it known that she solicited your cooperation with an offer of a payment."

"She asked me not to tell anybody."

"You changed your mind once you realized you had done something wrong."

"But I don't know how I can do it," Veronica pleaded.

"It's very easy, Veronica. You take our money; we'll give you a lawyer who represents you. We'll pay his fee. We'll pay any other lawyers' fees that you might need."

"But what do I do, what do I say?"

"Our people will prepare a statement for you. There will be some other things I want you to do. No one will ever know that you have this money from us. All you have to do is earn it by telling the truth." Marylou's speech was soothing and convincing.

"Suppose I don't do that?"

"You won't get our money and you're going to get sued. We're going to go to the authorities with the evidence we have. You won't have any of the money they gave you left by the time this is over. You will have to put a lot more of your own into your defense. You'll be further in debt then you are now."

"I need money."

"We know that, Veronica. You're essentially an honest, hard working person, but you happen to need some money and Annabelle found you at a weak moment. You might even say something like that."

"I can just give them back the money?" Veronica asked incredulously.

"Yes. You can give them back the money and you can tell the truth."

"How do I tell the truth? My firm will be furious. I'll lose my job."

"I don't think you will. If you do lose your job, we'll see that you get another one."

"How can you do that?"

"How did we find out what you've done?"

Veronica put her head in her hands. "Oh, why did I ever do this? I've never done anything like this before."

"That's true, that's why you can still save yourself by telling the truth," said Marylou giving her more reasons to accept their offer.

"How do I know I can trust you?"

"We'll give you three cashier's checks for $25,000 to put in the bank where we opened an account for you. You can invest the money through the bank or buy bonds and use the interest to pay off your debts."

"How much would I have?"

"If you do everything we ask it will be $100,000."

"A hundred thousand?"

"Yes, a hundred thousand dollars."

She paused. Tony wondered whether she was scared, bargaining, or confused. "Then there's something else," he said. "I'm prepared to offer you a bonus. We'll give you a signing bonus of $5,000 and we'll give you a performance bonus of $45,000, if what you do totally repudiates this false accusation against Adrian Daggett. With $150,000 in good grade corporate bonds, that would be about $8,000 a year in income."

"You work for Adrian Daggett."

"More or less," he said. She looked at Marylou.

"More or less," Marylou agreed.

"What happens next if I decide to do this?"

"We'll leave by a back entrance to the hotel in a limousine to the airport. A private plane is there which will take you to Chicago or a town near Chicago."

"To Chicago?" she asked, puzzled.

"We'll probably go to St. Charles, Illinois."

"But I don't have any clothes or my things," she objected.

"You won't need them. We'll buy you all you want."

"You'll do all of this after what I've done?"

"We're talking about what you are going to do. What was your true opinion of Adrian Daggett?"

"I'm going to vote for him."

"So are we. Were also going to ask you to stay with us until the time of your announcement and we want you to take a polygraph test."

"What do you mean 'stay with you?'" Veronica asked.

"It's up to our public relations director to decide when you reveal the truth."

"I don't see why he would delay."

"It's a 'she' and she decides."

"What am I going to do about my job?"

"We will talk with Mr. Spahn after you're on your way to the plane."

"Does he know?"

"Yes, he does," Marylou lied.

"Oh my goodness. I'm such a dummy." Veronica put her head in her hands, on the verge of weeping.

"We all make mistakes. Will you help us to clear Adrian Daggett? Just say you'll come with us."

She paused, thinking of the options and whether there would be a way out if she changed her mind. "I'll do it. But somebody has to take care of my cats."

We'll have one of our detectives do that, if you will trust us with a key to your apartment."

"I'll trust you. Just make sure who ever feeds them also pets them. They are very friendly. They'll come to anybody who will give them some affection."

"Help us do a good job, Veronica and you and your cats will have everything you need."

Veronica was starting to feel at ease as Marylou called security to have the reporters removed from the hall in front of the suite door. When that was in process, a limousine backed into the hotel loading dock. When the reporters were in the main elevators with the guards they took Veronica down the service elevator to the loading dock. She was away from the hotel with two security guards before the reporters figured it out. At the airport and in the airplane she was secure; there was no way the media or anyone else could reach her.

Before take off, Tony and Marylou headed for Spahn's office. Marylou cell-phoned him to make a quick appointment. Tony called Anne Russell who said they would wait to see how much the story percolated before they would introduce the contrary evidence. She didn't want the contrary evidence to be the only thing people heard about. It was best everyone be aware that Adrian was charged before they proved it false.

At the Cantwell office, Marylou explained the situation of their employee. Spahn wasn't surprised that the charges were bogus. He was worried about the adverse publicity and said he thought he would have to discharge Veronica. Tony asked if Spahn had an engagement letter form. Spahn asked Tony why he wanted it. Tony handed him his card. He authorized a $25,000 stand-by retainer for the services of Veronica Torblad. Spahn said he would see that she was made available. PENMET would be an important name on their client list.

They landed in St. Charles after chattering on the cellular circuits. Adrian was due back in Chicago in two days. Veronica had to be kept hidden some place where she would not be recognized. At The Pheasant Run Resort Tony booked suites for Veronica, Marylou, and himself. Marylou took Veronica shopping for the things she would need and some new outfits using nearly $3,000 of the cash.

When they returned with a cartload of parcels, Tony was on the phone with Anne and David Gibson. A statement had been agreed upon and sent to the private fax in Tony's suite. On television news programs the story was rapidly moving with fresh interviews of the support cast and Annabelle Mayberry. Also in the news was the report that Adrian was now clearly the Democratic front runner. He was shown brushing off questions about the accusations. He said an investigation was on going and he could not prejudice that by any further comment.

The character assassins among the reporters of newspapers, the newsmagazines, and television and radio savored the moment.

☆ **Chapter 20** ☆

AT HARBOUR ISLAND, Daphne and Sharon could tell whether a normal day had passed or whether special issues had arisen based on the appearance of the senior people on the tennis courts. If Helene, Erla, Edgar, Madeline, Ward, Marsha, Warren, and Harold were out playing by 5:30 p.m. it was probably a normal day. If they weren't around until 6:15 or 6:30 something had happened. If they didn't appear at all, important events had occurred. Daphne and Sharon confirmed this at their encounters with POLACO staff people whom they had come to know. They made sure to pass the tennis courts before 6:00 p.m. each day to take a look. They included what they could see in their reports.

By 6:30 on the day after the Annabelle Mayberry attack was launched, Helene finished a singles match with Edgar winning 6-2, 6-2. With an operation by Joe Drago going on, Edgar couldn't concentrate on tennis. The first hours seemed successful with the story accelerating across the country keyed by television tabloids, and then taken up by the regular TV news, which seemed to affirm it. The newspapers carried it and joined in speculating. Elaborate and expensive preparations seemed to be producing results.

At the courtside table where fruit drinks were served, the talk was how well the story was received. They knew this would be followed up by an attack on his opposition to unions. Maybe Adrian Daggett could be stopped. The Porter campaign had negative ads out in New Hampshire and Iowa. Findlayson had made her own negative comments. The modern law of politics was when nothing else works, go negative. POLACO, with its resources, had developed a big negative story for the Democratic candidates to exploit. Next week there would be another one.

Ward and Madeline appeared a few minutes after Edgar and Helene had finished their match and asked for a game of doubles. They decided to play some more. Edgar was always happy to play with Helene to whom he was increasingly attracted. He couldn't resist her. Playing from mid-court they won seven straight points when Cybil Chubb brought a fax from the Drago firm which came over a secured line. Its message was that Veronica Torblad had disappeared.

"What do you mean disappeared?" asked Ward.

"Disappeared?" asked Madeline.

"Edgar?" Helene said asking him to offer his opinion.

"It means they have either broken Veronica Torblad or she has gotten spooked and has run off. It's not a good sign."

"Damn," said Ward.

"I thought this was suppose to be air tight," said Madeline.

"We told you the risks."

"Sadovan and Gallosey are not taking the risks. We're taking the risks. Damn them," said Ward. "Edgar, I thought this was going to work."

"We don't panic here," said Helene.

"Where could she be?" asked Erla.

"Anywhere," said Edgar. "Somewhere where she thinks we won't find her."

"Can't we trace her?" asked Ward.

"Let's see what we can learn from the news media," said Edgar. They went to the clubhouse and turned on CNN *Headline News*. The third story was an interview with Annabelle Mayberry and one of her supporters. Afterward the anchor added that Veronica Torblad had seemingly disappeared from Springfield and had been last seen at the Hilton Hotel.

"Is that a lead, Helene?" Ward asked, grasping at a straw.

"You better believe it is," said Edgar.

Helene rose and smiled, "We can use my office."

They worked the telephones and called the news desks in Springfield. It soon became evident that reporters had tracked Veronica to a suite at the Hilton and that they had not seen her leave. They found out there were security guards involved who kept reporters away. They confirmed that Veronica had been spirited away and no one knew where; she wasn't at her office or apartment.

Edgar ordered a stakeout on her apartment. Drago was one step ahead. He had already done that and had a report that Veronica had not been back to it. Someone had entered it, however, and left shortly after.

"I think we can come to the conclusion that the lady has not gone off by herself in remorse for what she has done," said Edgar. "We need to find out where she is and, if possible, get her back."

"You mean our opponents may have her and, as you say, 'broken her?'" asked Helene.

"By various means of persuasion or bribes she is going to come out and tell the truth. If there's been any sloppiness in handling the money they will trace it to us."

"If it's a Daggett operative and it probably is, they will do it right," said Erla.

Helene was in full crisis management mode as she thought about the geography of the situation.

"Can we find out who had the suite in the hotel?" she asked.

"We'll certainly try," said Edgar.

"And if they flew her out in a private plane, we might be able to find out where she went. We all need to get to St. Louis," Helene said. "That's where the action is going to be."

AT 2:00 A.M., an elegant man dressed in a gray suit with a tie that matched the stripes in both the suit and his colored shirt, and with perfectly polished shoes and perfectly cut gray hair entered the Hilton Hotel in Springfield and walked smoothly to the desk. The night manager was sleepy. The elegant gentleman asked for a favor to see the list of registrants for suites during the previous day and the day before that. The night manager explained it was against hotel policy to give out that information.

The gentleman handed the night manager an envelope. He kept one hand on it and showed the manager that the other held a 38 caliber automatic. He asked him to look in the envelope. In it were five hundred-dollar bills. He stayed by the counter while the night manager had the computer make a printout. When the elegant gentleman left, he took his gun and the printout. Shortly after, Edgar had a fax from Drago saying there was only one possibility which was a single woman who ordered a suite and had seemed to eat only in the suite with room service. Her name was Marylou Michaels.

An hour after dawn, the senior staff of POLACO boarded the

Gulfstream jet and in a few minutes were headed toward St. Louis. Once on the plane, Helene started a conference. They planned their action against different assumptions, but focused on Veronica Torblad telling the truth in a manner engineered by Anne Russell.

Edgar received word from Drago that his operatives obtained access to the air traffic control records from Springfield for the previous day and found one flight of a Cessna Citation from Springfield to Dupage County Airport near St. Charles. On the plane's Internet computer he pulled up the travel information on St. Charles and its environs and saw that there was one major hotel resort, Pheasant Run. He phoned them and asked for Marylou Michaels and found she was registered. With that stroke of luck he began to think about what to do and what to propose to the group on the plane. It was a good bet that Veronica Torblad was in that hotel.

AS ANNE, NANCY, and Terry, along with Quentin Locksley – an attorney from Adrian Daggett's personal law firm – approached the Pheasant Run tower suite entrance, they encountered a wiry security guard with a mean expression and a giant "45" on his hip. He knocked on the door to announce them. Tony, who had arrived earlier, got up from a desk chair and greeted them.

Marylou led them to a sitting area. Veronica was nervous and appeared to be unraveling quickly. Anne and Nancy tried to soothe her woman to woman.

"It's far better you tell the truth regardless of how embarrassed you might feel, Veronica," Nancy told her. "If you ever have to tell your children about this you'll be able to do it honorably."

"But you have given me money, too."

"Only to help you through a tough time. The offer made to you was illegal. We're giving you funding to tell the truth and guarantees if you're attacked in any way."

"Attacked!" Veronica started, "What do you mean attacked?

Anne realized she said the wrong thing. Never say more than necessary. "These are guarantees to show our good faith," said Nancy. "We want you to know that you don't have to worry about anything in terms of your finances. We realized you were tempted into this by Annabelle because you needed money. We've made you an offer to keep you harmless."

"But I don't want to be involved in anything legal."

"We know you don't want to be involved in any legal actions, Ms.

Torblad," said Quentin Locksley, "But, I also have to remind you that you and Annabelle and the others who have lent their names to this fraud are already at risk for any action my client might take. You could be a defendant in a multi-million dollar lawsuit if you hadn't decided to recant. I will excuse you from this lawsuit, but it's only my duty to advise that you implicated yourself in this when you agreed to lend your name for compensation. We offered you a way out. Now you have to take action to save your reputation and what assets you might have. You are more fortunate than the others are in that we have offered you protection of your assets and very likely an increase. We can always withdraw that offer."

Anne hadn't expected anyone named "Quentin" to be that tough.

"I suggest we order some food before we get to work," said Tony.

After the meal they talked for nearly two hours to define all of the facts and to coach Veronica about how to handle the difficult encounters with the media that she would face. They prepared a statement that Quentin approved. He also brought an affidavit form for Veronica to sign. The papers were ready when there was a knock on the door and the security guard slipped in leaving the door slightly ajar. "I have a Mr. Wurtmann here. He says he's here to see Ms. Torblad."

"Who is he?" asked Terry jumping out of his chair. Tony was behind him. "How did he know that Veronica was here?"

The door was pushed open and Wurtmann stood in the doorway. He was a large man, well over six feet tall wearing a trench coat. He said in a loud voice, "I'm an attorney and I have a message for Ms. Torblad. 'We know where you are and what you are doing.'" The guard, almost a foot shorter than the intruder, tried to push him out. "Think carefully about what you are doing Ms. Torblad." Tony rushed the intruder with Terry and the guard joining. The three of them overpowered Wurtmann and wrestled him to the floor in the hall. Marylou found a gun in a shoulder holster and held it on him with the safety off. The guard cuffed him on the floor and held him there. Terry came back into the room, closed the door and set the lock.

Veronica went hysterical. "How did they find me? You told me they wouldn't know. How did they find me? I want out of this," Veronica sobbed. "I want out and I want out now."

Anne saw her earlier mistake exacerbated the intrusion.

EMPLOYEES OF THE Missouri Trust Company's main branch at Clayton, Missouri followed the Annabelle Mayberry story with special interest. Annabelle was a long-term customer of the branch. Sandy Gordon, the branch manager, wondered what this threatened scandal was all about as she eased her Chrysler LHS into her reserved parking slot beneath one of the new Clayton office buildings. Clayton was "the" office center satellite to St. Louis, one of the early ventures of this type. The city that was a lazy partial suburb became a nucleus of buildings up to 25 stories high, made of white brick or stainless steel and glass and was the cream location for business in the area. Clayton had upscale shops for upscale people, and Sandy Gordon had the upscale bank.

Once inside her office, Sandy sat down facing her workstation and brought up Annabelle's account. Her curiosity was aroused by vague reservations about the character of her customer and now increasing notoriety. She looked at her savings account first, and saw nothing unusual. The checking account was a startlingly different matter. Yesterday afternoon a wire transfer for $10,000 had arrived which was immediately transferred out again. Using her codes she checked the source. It was from the Cayman Islands. Sandy sat back in her chair looking at the screen, her heart pounding. In front of her was information of extreme importance to the next president of the United States, yet professional ethics and the law both forbid her to reveal it.

Sandy had been president of the Rotary Club. She was vice president of the Chamber of Commerce and would be president for the next two years. Her salary had steadily increased as the bank's business had increased as a result of her civic and commercial activities. Her branch had won every award mainly because of her.

Sandy considered her situation. She was a highly successful professional woman, who at 48 years was a solid, established community leader. As a banker and a graduate of the University of Missouri in economics and history, she understood that the issue of the federal trade deficit one day had to be faced. She also knew of the excesses of speculation in currency markets; she handled some accounts which bought and sold currencies. As an account rep., she had been successful. She paused to have her family and came back to work in the branches. Now, she had the plushest branch of them all. But, what would happen to her career if anyone found out what she had done?

She clicked her screen back to her menu and got into the wire service log to be sure the transfer was from offshore. Why would

Annabelle Mayberry be receiving money from an offshore bank? She wrote down the bank numbers involved and then clicked on the tracing block window and entered in the number. The transfer was indeed from a U.S. dollar account in the Cayman Islands in someone else's name. Why would Annabelle Mayberry receive money from the Caymans? It probably wasn't from the Caymans, but from another Caribbean nation or Europe.

She waited until after closing time when there was no one in the office and then printed out a copy of Annabelle's account and the routing. At her house before 6:00 p.m. she called Chicago information and asked for the number of the Daggett Campaign. She dialed the number and asked for Terry Leelan, the only name she knew. After ten minutes dealing with protective staffers, she got through to Dominick Kluczinski. She asked if there were any senior representatives of the campaign in St. Louis working on the Mayberry question and explained why she wanted to meet with them. Dominick thanked her and gave her a phone number to contact Alvin Carter or Broderick Rose at the Airport Marriott Hotel. Dominick asked her to call back to him if she could not connect. When she called the hotel she got the mailbox pitch, but she declined to leave a message. Instead she drove out to the airport.

In the spacious lobby, she found the house phone and asked for Mr. Rose. Sandy explained why she was there and was invited to come right up. Maybe they weren't really there, maybe they wouldn't be interested. Sandy had begun to wonder as the serious implications of what she was doing struck her again. The two imposing African-American men were very interested. One was tall and husky: the other of average height, but very fit. They introduced themselves as Alvin Carter and Broderick Rose. They asked her to sit down on the couch while they sat opposite her after getting some beverages.

"Mr. Rose," Sandy started, "I am risking my career and a very nice salary by bringing you some information. But, I feel that Annabelle Mayberry has wronged Adrian Daggett and I might be able to help you prove it. I'm her bank manager."

That got everyone's attention. Sandy handed over a copy of the account statement. "This morning $10,000 came in to Annabelle's account from a bank in the Cayman Islands."

There was silence. "Why are you bringing us this?" asked Broderick.

"As I told you, because I think Mr. Daggett has been wronged. I think that he should be President. I feel strongly about that and I think this whole accusation is phony."

"We have a lot of questions to ask you about Annabelle," Alvin said.

VERONICA TORBLAD MADE her first public appearance at a press conference at the Hyatt Regency on the lake. Reporters and cameras filled one of the largest rooms. The national networks, CNN, CNBC, and the local stations were there. The media circus was about to be introduced to the second act.

When everyone was seated, Anne, Veronica, Quentin, and Alan Jacobs appeared on the dais. Anne stepped to the bank of microphones. "My name is Anne Russell. I am a senior vice president of Evans & Copeland, the Daggett campaign public affairs consultants. I'd like to introduce to you a young woman who has come forward to us to recant a certain statement that she has made in support of the allegations of sexual harassment on the part of Adrian Daggett." The room audibly buzzed.

In their hotel suite in St. Louis the POLACO staff huddled around the television to watch.

At the podium Veronica paused and looked at the cameras and the people and then said, in a soft, wavering voice, "My name is Veronica Torblad. I am going to read a prepared statement which will be distributed to you. After that I will take questions for a few minutes.

"I have recently lent my name in support of Annabelle Mayberry and her allegations of sexual harassment on the part of Governor Adrian Daggett. I greatly regret this act on my part. I undertook to lend my name in support of Ms. Mayberry in return for the payment of $20,000, which was deposited in an account in a foreign bank. Other compensation, contingent on the nature and magnitude of my future involvement, was promised.

I acceded to this under the pressures of a recent divorce and financial strain. I'm an employee of Cantwell Associates where I am a senior researcher. Previous to that I did similar work for the State of Illinois.

By lending my name in support of Ms. Mayberry's allegations, I involved myself in a situation where a fraud is being perpetrated, in my judgment, on the people of this nation by parties unknown to me. Ms. Mayberry contacted me, renewing a friendship, and told me of incidents of sexual harassment to her by Governor Adrian Daggett. I took it upon myself to believe the incidents. Ms. Mayberry asked me to lend my name in support of her allegations indicating I might have other information about the governor. I hesitated to do that when she said she could make it worth my while to enter into an agreement. I understood at the time that this involved the receipt by me of money. Ms. Mayberry asked me if I would accept $20,000 immediately deposited in a bank to my account in the Cayman Islands and an additional $10,000 at an unspecified date when the affair was substantially over. She further said that if I was a party to interviews on television that I would receive $5,000, for each interview and, if the print media interviewed me I would receive $1,000 for each interview. I was not to solicit these interviews or offer my services in any way, but was to comply with requests by the media. This I understood to be a conspiracy to defame Governor Daggett.

I have accordingly signed an affidavit of the truth in this matter and have sent a letter to Annabelle Mayberry asking her to take back the $20,000 that was deposited and to make no payments of any kind to me. In the affidavit I indicate that I know of no incidents or facts that would indicate that Governor Daggett ever sexually harassed anyone. All of my knowledge of the accusations made by Annabelle Mayberry are from her. I never saw Governor Daggett in any kind of compromising position with women.

I am deeply ashamed of what I did. I ask for the forgiveness of Mr. and Mrs. Daggett and their family. I ask for the forgiveness of the people who have been misled into doubting the character of a blameless man. I am deeply sorry. Thank you."

A rash of hands flew up in the room, and reporters noisily vied for attention. Anne stepped to the podium and pointed to one. "Please state your name and your affiliation before your question so a transcript can be prepared."

"Martin Orgood, Chicago Tribune. Do you know, Ms. Torblad, who gave the money to Annabelle Mayberry?"

"No."

"Have you seen any of the checks or financial documents?"

"No," Anne pointed.

"Linda Backos, CNN. Have you ever heard rumors or reports of Governor Daggett sexually harassing anyone?"

"No, I did not."

Tears started to appear on Veronica's cheeks. She was trembling slightly. Anne pointed to another reporter.

"Dennis Gaverra, NBC. How did you come here, Ms. Torblad?"

"I was flown here in a chartered plane from Springfield."

"Did you ever touch Adrian Daggett?"

"At parties I danced with him once or twice. I know him and he would shake hands or sometimes hug me when we met."

"Isn't that sexual harassment?"

"Everybody liked to be hugged by Adrian in our organization. Nobody felt harassed."

Another question was shouted out. "Has anyone paid you any money to come here and to say this?"

Anne stepped to the podium. "I think that's enough questions for Ms.Torblad. I will answer that. Gifts have been received from donors who prefer to remain anonymous to pay the expenses of Ms. Torblad. These donors are attempting to hold Ms. Torblad harmless from any attacks or legal action from those financing this defamation conspiracy. This concludes our statements for today. Anne patted Veronica on the back and led her offstage.

VERONICA TORBLAD GAVE only the first press conference on the story that day. The second one was in St. Louis. Another gaggle of media and cameras crowded a room at the Adams Mark downtown. The great arch looming over the city and scenes of the Mississippi lent impressive import to the video ambiance. At 3:00 p.m. central time Annabelle Mayberry flanked by two attorneys and two main supporters with one attorney each stepped onto the platform. A tall, gray-haired, gray-suited man with Annabelle accepted the microphone. "My name is Evan Rampart, I'm with the firm of Bailey, Rampart and Wicker. We were asked to represent Ms. Mayberry. She will read a statement after which I will take questions."

He stepped aside from the microphone, and Annabelle stepped forward. She smiled shyly at the cameras and the reporters as she had been coached and began reading.

"Thank you for coming on such notice. I thought, however, that it was very important for you to hear the truth about the transaction between Veronica Torblad and myself.

As you may well know, it is not easy to find support for any action against almost any defendant regardless of how heinous the offense might be. If any of you have ever been in a traffic accident, tell me how many people come forward and volunteer as witnesses. Justice could only be done by those who know the truth and who will also support the truth.

It is I who owe an apology in the matter of Veronica Torblad because I agreed to her request for money in return for her support.

Fortunately, I have had some support financially which I could offer and agreed to give to Veronica Torblad. It was the wrong thing to do, but I did it out of desperation for support. I should not have done it. I'm ashamed that I did. I intend to pursue a redress of the wrongs done to me. I ask your forgiveness for this transgression. I hope for the support of right-minded people who will pursue the truth with me. Thank you."

Each reporter shouted a question at once. Evan Rampart stepped to the microphone and said, "One at a time please," and pointed.

"Have any of your other so-called supporters asked for money?"

"No," said Rampart. He pointed again.

"Who are the benefactors?"

"They have asked us not to reveal their names at this time," he pointed.

"How much have the benefactors contributed to Ms. Mayberry?"

"I can't give you an exact figure." He pointed.

"What's the purpose of this money being given?"

"Some people want to see justice done." Again he pointed.

"Why can't you tell us who the benefactors are?"

"I said it was their request."

"What is the money they have given being used for?"

"Obviously there are expenses and legal fees."

"Are you working pro-bono?"

"Our compensation is a matter of lawyer-client privilege." He pointed.

"How many of the others involved received funds from any bene-factors or will they?"

"For the same purposes as Ms. Mayberry." He pointed.

"How much money do you think will be actually supplied by these benefactors?"

"I think these questions are getting repetitive. Thank you for coming."

ANNE WAS ON the phone when Nancy swung into her office to tell her the news. Ten minutes later the staff gathered in the conference room to watch a tape of the second performance.

"Stonewalling," said Nancy after they had seen it twice.

"A good job of it," said Anne. "We have to reply. Do you agree Terry, Alan?"

"Shouldn't we wait. Hasn't there been too much in one day?"

"No, I think this has to go now. We still have a chance for the denial to be on the evening broadcasts and in the morning papers."

"I agree," said Alan. "We started it, we have to deny it."

"Should it be Veronica?" asked Terry.

"Let the lawyers do it. They like to see themselves on TV."

"Let them earn their money," said Alan. "What do we do about this?"

"Other than denying it, there's not much we can do," said Anne, "Except we have to catch them in a lie or at least in an embarrassing or unsavory situation."

"That's up to Alvin Carter and Broderick Rose," said Nancy.

"And don't forget the bank manager," said Anne.

Tony watched all of this with a knot in his stomach. The morning tracking poll had showed Adrian off seven percentage points. A crucial poll tomorrow would reveal how many believed that Adrian was still guilty after Veronica Torblad's statement and the response. He found himself partially caught up in the day-to-day, hour-to-hour maneuvering of the political campaign as opposed to the aggressive, but measured pace at PENMET. In politics sometimes the strategy was hour-to-hour and the tactics minute-to-minute.

When the TV screen flicked on connected to Des Moines, Adrian was sitting alone. "They're trying to bury the Torblad statement. Are we issuing a denial?" he asked as the staff entered the room.

"As soon as possible," said Anne.

"I've got the information about the finding from Mayberry's bank. We've got to thank that person in a very special way."

"Appoint her to the Federal Reserve," said Alan.

"No, I think we want her around," said Adrian. "She's loyal to the cause and has guts. Now how are you going to exploit the facts about the $10,000 in Mayberry's account?"

"It's more difficult now that they have admitted that Mayberry has anonymous benefactors."

"What we have to do is to find out exactly where that money came from, and document it. If it's tainted, which I'm sure it is, we can completely discredit Mayberry."

THAT EVENING MICHELLE reported the information about the bank statement to her live-in relay. The following morning, Louis telephoned Helene in St. Louis with the report. Helene called Erla, Edgar, and Marsha together.

"It's absolutely impossible that anyone has found out anything about the bank transfers," said Edgar.

"How was it done?" asked Helene.

"From an anonymous account in Switzerland to a bank in Cannes, to a Cayman Islands bank where they opened an account for Mayberry."

"How much did we put in that?"

"$300,000 US dollars," said Edgar.

"We better think about what this means," said Helene.

"It could be a feint, trying to get us to react. That would mean they know about Michelle."

"If they knew about Michelle, they wouldn't have her on the traveling staff," said Edgar. "They might try to misinform her, but they would transfer her back to headquarters."

"Where she'd be happy sleeping with Bill Haber," said Erla.

MARYLOU MICHAELS AND her beau/colleague Andrew, and another couple who freelanced went to Grand Cayman. Broderick and Alvin headed for Paris to await confirmation of the next bank in the chain. They sent Marylou and Andrew posing as a couple and each carried $9,900, in $100 bills. Broderick and Alvin also carried the same amount. They intended, if necessary, to pay for information in cash.

The two couples, looking like they were on a long weekend, checked into the Holiday Inn Resort. They enjoyed a swim, played doubles, had cocktails and dinner, followed by dancing under the stars of the tropical night and went to bed reasonably early.

In the morning, after a light breakfast of tropical fruit and some feta cheese, Marylou headed for the target bank, posing as Annabelle Mayberry and carrying the necessary counterfeit credentials. She asked at the teller window if she might see her account and have a print out of the transactions. There was some delay and then the assistant manager, told her that they were sorry, but they had just received instructions that no one, including Annabelle, was to see the activity in that account. The instructions were from the bank that made the deposit.

Marylou protested and was shown the message which came from The Banque Nacional branch in Cannes. It was in French, which Marylou easily read. She left the bank and walked back to the Holiday Inn where she used her cell phone to report this strange occurrence. Broderick and Alvin had checked into a hotel near Roissey and were delighted to hear that a city had been identified, even though the news also meant there was a leak. Someone in the group who knew about their possession of the bank information was in contact with POLACO. This was the only way to explain the sudden and unusual clampdown on Mayberry's access to her own account. The leak would have to wait. He told Marylou to do what was necessary to get the information and to call him at the Carlton Hotel in Cannes.

Marylou and Andrew waited to just before closing time at 3:00pm to go back to the bank. At the teller's window in the furthest corner, Andrew explained that "Annabelle" needed her financial statement because a special financing program was underway. He hunched over the window and put a $100 bill in the tray. The teller looked at it; Andrew saw curiosity and then understanding in her eyes. He put down two more bills, which she quickly scooped up.

"I'll give you a bunch of these," he said. "I need the transfer document of the initial deposit."

"That's very difficult," the girl said frightened.

"Can you get it if I were to give you $2,000?" The girl paused, "Come back tomorrow morning just after ten."

"Why not now?"

"You have the $2,000?"

"I have it." He brought out a wad of bills and showed it to her.

"It's too late, they're closing. I'll hand them to you tomorrow at 10:00 a.m."

"I think it should be now for $3,000," said Andrew.

The girl looked even more frightened, but $3,000 was very important to her. Who would find out? She could print the statements with the screen print button and no record of her action would exist. She thought quickly. "Tell them you're waiting for me to convert this money to Swiss Francs." Then she disappeared.

A few minutes later, the assistant manager came out and saw them. When she locked the door, turned the sign to show the bank was closed, she noticed "Annabelle" seated in a lounge chair and reading a magazine.

"Somebody is helping you?"

"Yes, thank you." Marylou pointed to Andrew at the window. "I'm with him."

The assistant manager was in a hurry to pick up her daughter. She gave the matter no further thought.

Broderick Rose was getting ready for bed when Marylou called with the news that the amount deposited in the Cayman bank was $300,000. She reported she had a copy of the transfer from Grand Cayman to St. Louis.

In the morning he and Alvin went to the main office of Banque Nacional and asked for the manager. A short, slightly stocky balding man came out; Broderick showed his credentials as an American investigator. In good English the manager asked what that meant. Broderick explained that they were tracing some funds used, which they found had been transferred to the bank in the Cayman Islands.

"Cayman Islands? My curiosity is aroused, gentlemen. Please join me for coffee." He escorted them into his office and called an assistant to serve them. "We do a large amount of business with Americans here in Cannes, but not during the off season. Large transfers, especially to the Cayman Islands, are very conspicuous at this time of the year. Tell me, is it a large amount?"

"$300,000 US dollars."

"You know, of course, that the information you say you need is confidential and I am not allowed to tell you. You were prepared to offer an amount of money?"

"Yes, we have cash," Broderick said. He glanced at his briefcase.

"Is your client in international corporate business?"

"No, this is a political matter," Alvin responded.

"Does this involve the presidential primaries?"

"Yes." Both men, Alvin and Broderick, replied at once.

"The Mayberry affair. I don't believe that woman." The Frenchman pursed his lips.

"Neither do we. We believe that she received a payoff of $300,000," Broderick responded.

"Then you're working for Adrian Daggett."

"Yes."

The Americans were impressed with the Frenchman's knowledge of current events.

Picking up the telephone during the cafe-au-lait ceremony, the manager spoke in French for a few minutes, then turned back to his guests. The computer printer started to hum.

"Don't open your briefcases, gentlemen." Putting the document in an envelope, he continued. "I cannot personally provide the information you require. He wrote "Mayberry" on the envelope and placed it prominently on his desk. "I must excuse myself. If you like, finish your coffee. I'll be back shortly."

Alvin and Broderick watched him leave. In the envelope they found the transfer authorizations. When the manager came back he told them how to use the codes. He identified the clerk and manager who took the deposit and the main Geneva branch of the Banque Union d'Suisse.

They asked what they could do for him. "When you see Adrian Daggett, please give him this Frenchman's very best wishes. I'd like to vote for him, but obviously can't. He would be best for America, best for France, best for the world. This Frenchman is happy that he could do a little something."

After preparing a fax, Broderick and Alvin had time to catch the 5:00 p.m. Air France 747 from Roissey to New York.

FRANCISCO RODRIGUEZ BROUGHT the fax to Ian and Susan at their customary early breakfast and sent a copy to Tony. Time was ticking away toward the Iowa vote. Knowing what was available from the Cayman Islands and now from Cannes, Ian and Tony decided on a strategy. He first phoned his friend, the senior Senator from Illinois to arrange a special meeting in his office. The Senior Senator agreed on Ian's guest list and postponed appointments to accommodate him. Ian then called the White House. The deputy chief of staff phoned back in ten minutes. After that he called the Justice Department and several other officers.

Broderick and Alvin, staying at Kennedy Airport, got the word to fly to Washington. Marylou and Andrew were summoned. When it was time, the Citation took him from Harrisburg to Reagan National Airport in twenty minutes where a limousine, which had picked up Alvin and Broderick was waiting for him. Marylou and Andrew, who had already arrived from Jacksonville, were in another car looking smart and primped. They went to pick up David Gibson on his way from LaGuardia.

The limousines swooshed Ian and his party to Capitol Hill. In the ornate, high-ceilinged room where the Senator received his guests, Ian and David gathered the original documents, testimony, and other information on the Mayberry affair. This had now been sent to the FBI, the Secret Service, the cognizant committee staffs on Capitol Hill, and the inner group in The White House. The invited soon arrived; the deputy director of the FBI, the deputy director of the Secret Service, the chief of staff of the Senate Judiciary Committee, the chief of staff of the House Judiciary Committee, the deputy chief of staff of the White House himself, and the deputy Attorney General. David Gibson reviewed what they had and then asked that investigations be started by all cognizant elements of the government to determine whether a crime had been committed. He cited the legal authority for the action he requested. Congress would investigate to determine if legislation would be required to enable law enforcement and the courts to better deal with such situations in the future. He asked for an immediate announcement of the investigation by 4:00 p.m. that afternoon.

The deputy director of the FBI objected, looking directly at Ian. "Why should we do this for you? We have to complete a preliminary review before we start an investigation."

"We have done your preliminary investigation for you," Ian replied. "Here you have a clear case of suspected bribery to impugn the reputation of a candidate for the highest office of this land, probably the most qualified and able who has been a candidate since Roosevelt, Truman, and Eisenhower. You know as well as I do, that this town is riddled with nonsense and the only hope of straightening it out is to elect Daggett president."

"We don't deal in politics, Mr. MacAulliffe."

"If that is your position I will seek a writ of mandamus."

"Mandamus for what?"

"We have that figured out. It will happen this afternoon. You will be named."

"Well, suppose you do. Maybe it's not an FBI matter," the deputy director asserted.

"I'm asking you to investigate whether or not it is an FBI matter, and to make that determination today."

"Well, suppose I decide not to announce it."

"Then you get mandamus."

"I'm also concerned at the speed that you're asking us to act," said the deputy director of the Secret Service.

"I've already explained why we have to act quickly. I want you to know gentlemen, that if you delay this 24 hours by forcing me into court, I will make the action of mandamus the most publicized in history. Both of you will be named. Your bios will get national attention and the editorials are not likely to be favorable."

"Gentlemen," the senior Senator intervened, "I think it is very easy to announce an investigation, and publicize the information that is available in order to assist Mr. Daggett in shunting this attack. It seems to me a clear case of bribery for defamation of character. Surely an investigation should be undertaken to determine whether a crime has been committed. The Senate committees will be ready to start hearings. I can tell you that those before the Senate Judiciary Committee will start soon. There are members of Congress who believe the country is in danger. Apparently you don't."

"I don't like to be pressured by an American corporation and do an investigation which I'm not sure is properly a matter of the FBI," said the secret service deputy.

"You understand the question is Adrian Daggett and taking action to save him from this well-timed, well-engineered, undermining attack with an overt paid-for-lie."

"I'm not sure this information is valid."

"I'm asking you to investigate it," Ian said firmly. "You will find out it is valid. If you don't, I will see that you two are embarrassed out of your careers. If I go after you two, it will be for ignoring your duty, not to your agencies, but to your country. Do you think the Constitution of the United States is safe in the hands of the politicians that now are playing with it?"

"Maybe we should investigate your role in this campaign. There seems to be a lot of interest," the FBI deputy threatened.

"Investigate all you want," said Ian looking the man square in the eye. "But if you make one questionable step that in any way affects my company or myself, I will pursue every available avenue of redress, including seeking a judgment against you personally, and anybody else involved."

The deputy director was accustomed to intimidation, but not as the recipient. MacAulliffe had some powerful friends. The easy course of action was to do what MacAulliffe wanted. The Secret Service Director felt the same way, but he recognized that what MacAulliffe wanted was in the best interest of the country. It was likely some federal judge in the District of Columbia, or an adjoining state would sign a writ of mandamus. It might already have been arranged. Judges liked the opportunity order a government official to do his duty.

"All right, I agree to investigate," said the deputy director of the Secret Service.

Presented with a fait accompli, the deputy director of the FBI agreed. At that point, it was a matter of arranging the most unusual press conference ever to be held on Capitol Hill. The Senator from Illinois used his staff to call in the press. Notices were passed out in the pressrooms of the Senate and the Capitol. At the White House briefing room, the major media were called for an announcement of a development in the "Annabelle Mayberry Affair." Portions of the conference were carried live on all networks with extended coverage on CNN and the news channels. PBS produced a segment for the news hour.

The CNN announcer explained that the press conference called by the senior Senator from Illinois was to be attended by the deputy directors of the Secret Service and the FBI, the deputy Attorney General, and the chairmen of each Judiciary Committee. As the live-feed started, the senior Senator from Illinois was at the microphone. "Ladies and gentlemen, we appreciate your gathering on such short notice, but extremely important information has been made available to me which I have now shared with the Federal Bureau of Investigation, the Secret Service, the White House, the Justice Department, and my colleagues; the Chairmen of the Senate Judiciary Committee and the House Judiciary Committee. They have been given, through private sources, information that Annabelle Mayberry transferred $10,000 from an account in a bank in Grand Cayman in the Cayman Islands, to her account at the First National Bank of Missouri at the Clayton, Missouri Branch. This money was traced back to a transfer from the Banque Union d'Suisse branch in Geneva, to Banque Nacional d'France in Cannes. We have evidence the total amount of the original deposit was $300,000. The documents concerning these funds indicate the payments correspond to the time frame of Ms. Mayberry's accusations against Adrian Daggett. I have therefore, called for an investigation by each of these agencies and the committees of Congress to determine if a crime has been committed and if legislation is needed to prevent such occurrences of false claims against any political candidate in the future or to enable law enforcement to pursue justice.

"It has also been evident that the claim by Veronica Torblad in support of Annabelle Mayberry's was false, and was promoted by Ms. Mayberry. Ms. Mayberry has denied that and indeed, attempted to impugn the reputation of Ms. Torblad by indicating she solicited funds from her, rather than Ms. Mayberry offering them. It is now evident that other funds were offered to Ms. Mayberry. One could guess the guarantees that went with them. This is a matter that has to be investigated. We have documents from each bank which evidence the series of transactions."

The senior Senator then gave the microphone to the Secret Service Deputy who indicated the direction of the investigation would be to validate the evidence and determine all relevant facts. This information would then be turned over to the FBI to investigate further, and determine if a federal crime had been committed outside of the jurisdiction of the Secret Service. Both committee chairmen indicated their interest was in determining if legislative action was required; either with respect to the statutes or the responsibilities of the investigating agencies. The Senator from Illinois and the others took questions for twenty minutes.

THE ACTUAL EVENT was going on before Helene heard about it from a Washington source. After watching a tape Louis Fischer's people made and wired up to her powerful portable computer, she called a meeting with Marsha, Erla, and Warren for 5:30 p.m. when Edgar was supposed to be back. Ten minutes into the meeting they reached a conclusion that there was not much they could do. With a federal investigation going on, they had to avoid telling any further lies. Marsha felt she had been checkmated. Helene tried to think of something that might save them.

Somehow bank records had leaked. Somehow the tracing had been done. It's possible that there had been a penetration of the Swiss Bank where a corporate law firm had been retained to open a numbered account and make the initial deposit. Immediately after the network evening newscasts were completed at 6 p.m. St. Louis time, Helene's beeper rang. The message was to call a phone number in Chicago. She excused herself; Tony Destito answered. He wanted a meeting that evening at a conference room in the McDonnell Douglas Division of Boeing on the opposite side of Lambert Field from the terminals. He suggested that she bring one person with her. He told her he would bring Nancy Letersky.

Helene and Edgar arrived at McDonnell Douglas/Boeing after dark. The architecture was modern and dignified, befitting the character of the company, which had accomplished so much in American aviation. The building was adjacent to historic Lambert Field, St. Louis' major airport. Their car followed a security guard who parked and ushered them up to the main doors. In the reception area they were greeted by a security sergeant who asked for identification and then took them to one of the executive conference rooms. Caterers were carrying in a buffet supper while Tony Destito and Nancy Letersky were waiting.

Tony shook hands with Edgar and introduced Nancy. He then

introduced two local private investigators who would sweep the room for bugs. Tony invited Edgar to check their credentials and inspect their equipment. Edgar cast an expert eye upon their technique as they probed around the walls and ceiling. Two white-jacketed waitresses put tossed salads at each place and Tony invited everyone to sit down to eat. It was difficult to make small talk, but he brought up a number of subjects, including Nancy and her background, and her role in the campaign. Helene and Edgar were already familiar with the information.

When they finished their salads, grilled trout was served accompanied by stuffed potatoes, and a vegetable medley. Bottles of mineral water were placed on the table. One waitress indicated where four pieces of key lime pie could be found, and coffee was brewed. They also left cookies, cheese and crackers, and fruit and drinks in a cooler in case the meeting was late.

When the four diners were alone, Tony began. "This meeting is to discuss the effort that someone has undertaken to smear Adrian Daggett's name in a fictitious sexual harassment scandal. We know the accusations made by Annabelle Mayberry have no foundation. We have evidence that Annabelle Mayberry was paid $300,000 to make those allegations and we assume she has received certain other guarantees to be held harmless from civil suit. As you saw at the press conference on Capitol Hill this afternoon, the matter is now being investigated by the Secret Service, the FBI, and two Committees of Congress. These investigations were initiated on the basis of these documents. He handed Helene and Edgar each a light blue envelope, the PENMET color.

After a minute Helene asked, "How did you get these?"

"A noble bank manager risked her career to give us this information about the money passing into Annabelle's account. She gave us the numbers that you see on the wire transfer. We went to the Cayman Islands Bank and bribed a clerk to give us the source of the wire transfer, which was from the Banque Nacional d'France branch in Cannes. The bank manager there handed copies of what you see to our investigators, with his best wishes to Adrian Daggett."

"I don't see anything from Switzerland," said Helene.

"We thought that you might prefer that we didn't go there."

"I can't understand how foolish Annabelle was to draw the money to her account. What was the reason?"

Apparently, she thought no one would notice. She could have opened another account in the US, but her name would be known.

The same thing would have happened."

"You were very lucky, Tony," said Edgar.

"Face the facts, Edgar. We got to Veronica before anybody else did. We didn't follow up the other possibilities because we had enough evidence."

"That bank manager should lose her job," Edgar muttered.

"She took a big risk, but she did it for a good reason. That's more than you can say."

"That's not for you to judge," said Helene. "What is it you want, Tony?"

"This has to be cleaned up, we want Annabelle to admit what she did."

"And, if she doesn't"

The investigation will continue and Adrian Daggett will file suit against Annabelle. The facts about what happened will come out one by one. I have two agents in Geneva who will shake down the Swiss bank tomorrow morning. That's a few hours from now. We have the name of the clerk who opened the account and the name of the officer who authorized it. The French bank manager phoned Geneva and shared these with us. We have until 2 a.m. or they will start their operation. With the American investigation underway we will call in the French Secret Service, the Swiss police, and Interpol to assist."

"You can't do that, it would violate the agreement we have Tony," interrupted Helene.

"No one is attacking you or exposing you, Helene. I offered you an agreement not to do this sort of thing."

"I don't see that you have very much."

"When we get finished it will be obvious. We haven't been to Geneva yet. And, the Feds and the Eurocops have the right to see all of the bank accounts."

"All right, Tony, what is it?" Helene surrendered defiantly.

"We require that Annabelle Mayberry confess that she lied and was bribed. We will give her a release from all civil liability and we will not pursue the matter further. There has to be a total and complete recantation. There can be no doubt, and we want to approve the statement in advance. We want similar statements from the others who had lent their names to this. We will accordingly give them releases from civil liability if they wish them."

"You know damn well there is no deal without releases."

"Further, I want an agreement that there will be no further financed accusations against Adrian Daggett, and we will agree to the same, which we would never do anyway."

"How can we give assurance of that in the campaign?"

"You know what I mean. You know exactly what I mean," Tony insisted.

"And if we don't agree to this?" Helene asked glaring at Tony and disdainfully tossing the blue envelope across the table.

"Then you'll have to deal with a law suit from Adrian Daggett with endless discovery. You'll also find yourself dealing with Interpol," Tony glared back at Helene.

"We'll see about that."

"Be reasonable, Helene. You perpetrated a false accusation against Adrian Daggett. You got caught. You tried to lie your way out of it, and you got caught again. You're in quick sand. We're offering you a way out."

Helene realized POLACO was at a grim disadvantage. PENMET had skillfully raised the stakes by involving federal investigators. They stopped short of moving on the Swiss bank, but they had gotten that far and might well be more successful if European investigative agencies joined in. Once a criminal investigation started, the cash could be traced to withdrawals from Southern Conservative Coalition accounts. Now everything was public and they had given it the highest possible profile. They did that, of course, for a reason. She could guess what the poll results would be. Daggett would fully recover and probably add a point or two of sympathy votes. She needed to end the affair and get it out of the news.

"If we were to agree to this, what guarantees would we have that you won't attempt to investigate further and identify us?"

"We want it to end, too," Tony assured her.

Helene didn't answer. "Give me some guarantees."

"We can't guarantee against any press involvement. You took a risk of investigative reporters."

"You can mitigate it by disinterest."

"We'll agree to accept Annabelle's statement that indicates the charges were illicit, and we don't care to speculate or pursue any further who undertook this."

"You have Anne Russell come up with something better than that," Helene said.

"You know my gist."

"I want to have the right to approve the statement that Adrian is going to make."

"I can't agree to that. We won't have time."

"We have fax machines and computers now, Tony."

"Okay, I'll agree, if you'll agree to make the approval in four hours, but I want the overall agreement that there are no more paid accusations against Adrian Daggett or anyone associated with him or his campaign."

Helene was disappointed that he included the broader concept because of the possibility of attacking others associated with Adrian. "I want to be sure you don't pursue an investigation, and that you use your influence to call off 'the Feds.'"

"We didn't start this, Helene. You thought you could get away with this, and you probably would have if it hadn't been for someone taking a serious risk."

"We'd like to know who did that."

"I'm sure you would, and I'm sure Edgar will find out, I want your assurance that you are not going to pursue that person in any way, and I want your assurance that Annabelle will not pursue her."

"How can we give assurances for Annabelle?"

"You bought her. Tell her what to do," a note of exasperation had entered Tony's voice.

"You're asking too much, Tony."

The iciness of Helene's demeanor was devastating. Tony had started to fall in love with this woman and still liked her and wanted her. Edgar's interest in Helene did not escape his notice. " I think we should start writing," he said.

"I'm not coming to any agreement tonight."

"Helene, we're not going to let this go. You know as well as I do, this has to happen. You have to end the ordeal. At 3:00 a.m. Eastern Standard Time our investigators will move on M. Surnet at the Banque Union d' Suisse in Geneva. Tomorrow the press conference will be from Paris."

She realized she couldn't bluff him. "All right."

Was he bluffing her? Probably not. They'd keep the investigation expanding to continue the publicity. It could implicate Porter or Perona and maybe Hatford. It would come up in the general election.

"No one is happy about this, Helene, particularly us. We were the victims, remember?" Tony stared sadly at Helene, trying to find a glimpse of the warm companion he knew behind the cold professional faÁade. He then thought of Nancy. He looked up at her and for a moment their eyes met.

And so they came to an agreement. The following morning a draft statement by Adrian was faxed to Helene at her hotel. An hour later the recanting statement was faxed to Tony. At 3:00 p.m. Annabelle Mayberry appeared before another crowd of reporters and a bank of TV cameras at the Adams Mark. Guarded by a flying wedge of lawyers, she admitted she lied and that she had been paid. A barrage of questions were screamed at her. Her lawyer's answers were slightly more than nothing.

At 4:00 p.m., Adrian Daggett held a press conference, where he regretted that Ms. Mayberry had succumbed to the temptation of the money from whatever the source was. He said that with her full admission, he had no further action to take in the matter. Alan Jacobs watched tracking poll results. Adrian quickly gained back the 7% he had lost, and 3% on top of that. The undecided total fell by that amount. That he had lost no more than 7% indicated an unshakeable baseline of trust in his character. Alan commented to Tony that if there was anybody in the United States who hadn't recognized Adrian Daggett, they surely did now.

Helene came to the same conclusion looking out of her office at a projection of Harbour Island's pink sands. She wondered if Sadovan and Gallosey would take the blame. The ordeal had cost nearly a million dollars and the reputations of four women.

This was the price of failure. She feared the price of victory would be much greater.

☆ **Chapter 21** ☆

WITH TEN DAYS to go, Karen Crezna was filled with anxious expectation. She had been on the job for more than a year and a half preparing for one climactic event. Success or failure would determine her future career and perhaps the rest of her life. It would also determine the future of her country. She thought only of one thing; victory for Adrian Daggett, launching him toward the ultimate goal of the presidency. This would also be a victory for the people who truly cared about the country and for a "reality government" in Washington that would make profound changes in the course of politics in the United States.

The holiday tour through Alaska and Louisiana was delivering results. Alaska had already gone to Daggett with 42% of the vote. Perona had 30%, and the balance was scattered through the other candidates who did not go to the state. Perona had spent eight days in Alaska, Adrian four. Louisiana would be decided this weekend. Adrian was there with the final campaign effort. After, he would be in Iowa and New Hampshire for the last mad blitzes. Merrick, Karen, the coordinators, and their volunteers had arranged rallies in Cedar Rapids, Davenport, Sioux City, Ames, and Des Moines. Iowa City clambered to get on the schedule with a rally at the University, and Karen struggled to arrange it.

Volunteers now poured into the Daggett offices to man the phones to get voters to the caucuses to fold and mail letters, and to make literature drops. People were needed to help at the rallies and coffee klatches and to be present at the caucuses to verify the votes. The organization swelled five-fold. Porter and Perona were in the state, and so was Findlayson, trying desperately to win back votes. Porter and Findlayson had openly questioned Daggett's character based on the Mayberry accusations. Perona was smart enough not to comment. Only Richard Sandellot announced that he did not believe the accusations and suggested early that they would be found to be false.

After the recanting by Annabelle Mayberry, Porter was accused of creating the ruse. He denied involvement and said he still was not sure what the truth was. He left it to the investigators to determine what happened. In this manner he tried to delay closing the issue by implying there was more information to find. In fact, the issue was closed by the way it was handled.

Porter had invested nearly a month in Louisiana, Adrian hardly a week. In the polls, Adrian was leading with just under 50% of the vote. Adrian appeared at rallies and other affairs in New Orleans, Baton Rouge, and Shreveport and bus-stopped into the bayou country. He won with 47% of the vote to Porter's 35%.

Karen and Merrick felt over-committed with events going on in every city and in the major farm counties. They feared they had spread their resources too thinly. Consolidation of the anti-Daggett vote on Porter caused Perona and Ramsdell to fade along with Findlayson. Porter gained and flaunted it in his speeches. He claimed to be the natural choice of the Democratic Party to lead the national government because he had the most national experience. He started to go negative. Adrian Daggett was a businessman, a Republican who would not serve the traditional liberal causes of the Democratic Party. He tried to exploit the labor issue. He alleged Daggett was a rich man, who made money as a corporate leader in the rich days when corporate presidents were paid 30 and 40 times as much as their line supervisors in manufacturing. On other issues he keyed off information supplied by POLACO.

In the final days, the battle of the advertisements began. Porter went entirely negative focusing on two issues. In ads, talking heads suggested that Adrian Daggett was a man who wanted to increase taxes and send Iowa's sons and daughters to foreign wars. The Daggett campaign replied with positive ads. Daggett was the man who would assure the financial stability of the United States. He would lead the United States into a position where it would act as guarantor of world peace through the United Nations. Another ad listed the specifics of the education program so important in Iowa. Porter claimed Daggett had stolen his education plan. The Chicago staff produced an ad which showed all of the staff papers and pictures of the staff who had developed the Daggett program. Porter pounded on the theme in his speeches, saying, "a vote for Daggett is a vote for reduced paychecks," and "a vote for Daggett is a vote for body bags." Because Daggett was for increasing military and aerospace spending, Porter charged that Daggett was also a cold war warrior out of touch with the modern world order and a war monger.

The Daggett reply was an ad that propounded the message that Adrian Daggett would see that the United States maintained its leadership in industrial technology and in weapons technology to assure the safety of all democracies in the world. Porter screeched that the cold war was over, and that defense funds should be redirected to reducing taxes and increasing social welfare programs such as Medicare and Medicaid.

Alan Jacobs and his people tracked the numbers daily. Impact from the negative ads added to the already substantial unfavorable total, but Adrian was still ahead with a well received, positive campaign. The final speech and rally in Des Moines was televised statewide. In a jammed municipal arena, Adrian reiterated the positive programs and spoke of the American spirit which, with reality in view, could lead the world to peace. He promised to return a sense of reality and truth to American government, and real debate to the national dialogue. He said he would lead the United States back to greatness with the American spirit restored, and with America facing the real issues, "not because they are easy, but because they are difficult."

There were wild cheers and a standing ovation. Adrian and Pamela were waving to the crowd while Karen reminded them that there was still one more stop that evening for coffee and dessert at a retirement home.

The television cameras were waiting there. Adrian talked to the elderly residents about the speech they had seen and listened attentively to their comments. One veteran said, "That's the kind of country I fought for in World War II."

An elderly woman chimed in, "That's the kind of country my first husband died for. You have to bring it back to us."

"We need you, Mr. Daggett, to tell us what it all means. Our politicians don't do that no more," said another woman. There were about 50 people in the room. Daggett spoke to each of them, personally.

One lady joked, "If you hug me it won't be sexual harassment." He touched and hugged them. Karen, exhausted, found tears running down her cheeks. She was embarrassed, but she saw Pamela wiping glistening eyes. She prayed that night beside her bed for the first time since she left grade school and asked God to give the people of Iowa the wisdom to start this man on the course to America's leadership.

The print ads climaxed in the newspapers on Sunday before the caucuses and the Daggett campaign took full-page ads in every newspaper in the state, all positive. Their opponents took full-page ads portraying Daggett as a quack doctor prescribing medicine for America. The negative ads saturated the airwaves the day before the caucuses. In the final meeting in Chicago before they all left for Des Moines, Terry Leelan said, "We are now coming to the first battle of political good versus political evil."

THE NIGHT BEFORE the caucus day, Adrian, with Karen directing, helicoptered to Ames, Mason City and Fort Dodge, then spent the final hours at the headquarters in Des Moines making phone calls to each of the local headquarters. As the time for the caucuses arrived, all of the campaign staff returned to Des Moines and gathered at the Marriott. Unlike elections, there were no exit polls from the caucuses. The networks couldn't call an early winner. The Iowa campaign would listen to their own returns from their own reporters.

At the hotel, they found the ballroom jammed with television equipment. Beside the podium, an orchestra was warming up. Reporters milled about a buffet, or pecked furiously on portable computers. Louise, Anne, Nancy, and others from the campaign staff from Evans & Copeland mingled with them. Opposite the reporters' table was a giant white board where the returns would be posted. Each county was listed, and under each county, each city and a miscellaneous column. More than a thousand meetings in Iowa would impact the future of the nation and the candidacy of Adrian Daggett.

Karen's heart was pounding when she saw Earl arrive. They went around the ballroom, and greeted the people she had recruited and managed in the campaign. She squeezed his arm every once in awhile as a gesture of affection and a plea for moral support.

Merrick, the old pro, had been through it many times before, and wondered how much time he would have off before the next political crises would dominate his life. This time he was certain of victory. The question was by how much. His wife, Marianne, whom he very much wanted to see, was on a plane from Washington to share the moment. Karen, who was a whirlwind of activity, checked the buffet, the band, and instructed the banquet manager who was overseeing the event. She checked the podium and looked at the electronic equipment. She stood back watching while Anne, glamorous in a mauve cocktail dress, was interviewed by CNN. When Anne saw Karen, she reached into her portfolio and brought out an envelope marked, "Karen and Earl." Anne smiled as she handed it to Karen and complimented her arrangements. Inside the envelope was a hand written note from Pamela Daggett inviting Karen and Earl to join them in the Governor's suite. She stared at it, and again her mind went through the same theme. "I'm 24 years old and this is happening?"

She led Earl into the suite where she saw Mitchell Fiddler, and Dominick Kluczinski huddled with Anne and Tony Destito. Nancy Letersky was on her cell phone sitting beside a table. Pamela and another attractive woman, beautifully dressed in red, were with Alan and Lauren Jacobs. Terry and Annalee Leelan and two local couples from the Democratic leadership were talking with Adrian. Karen went to greet several others of the leadership people from the party, and introduced Earl to those who hadn't met him. The atmosphere was tense, exciting, animated, and hopefully joyous. Karen, feeling hungry, but unable to deal with the mechanics, wondered how she would be able to maintain her momentum until the end of the night.

The suite doors opened and a tuxedoed Maitre'd strode in and asked Nancy if they were ready for the buffet dinner. This was rolled in on tables with silver chaffing dishes flickering in candlelight. Adrian Daggett, looking around the room, spotted Karen and immediately came over to her and Earl.

"Earl Hanley," said Daggett, "if I thought of it we could have had you and Karen drive a dogsled around Iowa."

"We missed a play. We could have offered rides," said Earl. They laughed.

"And you all worked like sled dogs. I'm deeply grateful for all you have done – particularly giving up the holidays. I don't think I've thanked you for that."

"We won," said Karen, hardly believing she was talking to the probable future President.

"Let's hope we'll be celebrating another one soon. Let's get some dinner to fortify ourselves in case we aren't celebrating."

Karen marveled at the man, ready to calmly accept the worst. Terry greeted her. Merrick and Marianne arrived. Karen feeling she was surely the youngest person in the room, took Earl's arm as they went to the buffet. They sat to eat with Nancy Letersky, and were introduced to the woman in a dark red dress who was Susan MacAulliffe.

Tony Destito joined them and sat beside Susan. Nancy looked up at him and smiled.

After dinner Karen excused herself to go back to the floor and greet the volunteers coming in from their caucus meetings, and to check and recheck all of the arrangements. These people deserved a nice evening. On the elevator back to the suite she started worrying "what if we lost?" In the suite seven television sets had been turned on. All were muted except for CNN. One was a direct feed from a camera focused on the posting board in the ballroom so they could see the latest direct tallies. Nervously, everyone watched CNN as they opened their coverage.

"The first returns from Iowa with less than 1% of the caucuses reporting are a surprise. Senator Porter is leading Adrian Daggett at the moment with 752 votes against Daggett's 430. Marilyn Findlayson is trailing with 97 votes, with the others scattered. So Porter starts to an early lead in the Iowa Caucuses. He has promised an upset."

"They said that just to attract viewers," said Nancy.

"Where were those numbers from?" asked Merrick looking at the board.

"From Decorah," said Karen, looking at the board.

"Our weakest area. The farmers only vote their pocketbooks up there."

They watched as Porter continued to lead in the next few returns.

"Where is Sioux City?" Karen remarked. "Where is Des Moines? Where is Cedar Rapids?"

"They're coming," said Merrick. For the next ten minutes the chatter on CNN rumored an upset based on returns from the smallest caucuses. Porter had a lead of four thousand votes to Adrian's three thousand.

CNN switched to their analyst. "What do you make of these early returns showing Porter with an upset in the making?" asked the anchor.

"It's too early to tell. Iowa is now an urban state, and we're seeing returns from the heavily agricultural districts."

They chatted on about Iowa voters. One analyst said the reality campaign of Adrian Daggett was difficult to analyze and might establish new lines of voting.

Then the anchor said"We have word that the returns from the cities and the northwest and the south are being delayed by heavy turnout at the caucuses. Who do you think that favors?"

"My guess is that it favors Daggett because his organization is strongest outside of the Northeast quadrant. I understand because of early difficulties in their organization, they more or less conceded the area east of Mason City north of Cedar Rapids and Waterloo, without serious effort. These early returns are mostly from there. We'll have to wait and see what happens in the cities."

CNN went to commercials. All eyes in the room turned to the board. An audio link was established with the volunteers posting numbers on the board. One said, "We've just received the early results from Mason City, Daggett is leading two to one."

Cheers rang out filling the room.

"That's the way!" said Merrick, pumping his fist.

When CNN returned to the program, the anchor reported the Mason City results which brought Daggett up even with Porter. More cheers filled the ballroom.

CNN showed totals favoring Porter again, and shifted to the Porter headquarters at the Holiday Inn near the airport. The correspondent spoke to Porter's campaign director, Steve Zimmer.

"We certainly are encouraged, we certainly expect to win. We knew from our own polls that the Daggett lead was exaggerated."

"What did your polls actually show?" asked the correspondent.

"A tight race, as we've been saying all along. There has been a lot about the tax policies, the so-called bitter medicine that Americans would have to take to pay down the debt, and the aggressiveness in foreign involvement. We believe the people in Iowa are going to reject those views and the so-called reality campaign. There is nothing wrong with American Democracy. Our system works better than the systems in any other country as Senator Porter has been saying. We expect him to be nominated."

"What about the surprising results in Alaska and Louisiana?"

"That was a function of the money Adrian Daggett is spending. His staff undertook the holiday campaigns, and big public relations, advertising and staff expenses, with the large injection of soft money used on his behalf in those states."

"Well, what about the assistance you're receiving from the Southern Conservative Coalition and the Foulton Foundation?"

"We of course, appreciate that assistance, but this is not under our direct control."

"Don't you believe you benefited from the anti-Daggett saturation campaign in Iowa and the various ads talking about the issues?"

"We're not sure what the impact of those is. We think this vote will reflect the will of the American people. These are Americans out here, you know."

"We know that. We've just seen the returns from Fort Dodge come into our broadcast center. We understand that the vote in Fort Dodge has gone 59% for Daggett, and that Daggett is now leading in the over-all totals. What do you have to say about that?"

"I'll have to look at the numbers and the source of the numbers. We've been all over this state. We have a good organization and we're going to have a very good showing tonight."

"Thank you very much," said the correspondent. "Back to you."

The anchor took over and immediately switched to Daggett head-quarters. A correspondent appeared on the screen next to an obvi-ously jubilant middle-aged woman. "Here at Daggett headquarters there is excitement, and expectation, but it's been muffled by the early returns. Merrick Reynolds, the state coordinator, is still in the suite with Adrian Daggett and the other senior campaign officials. We have here one of the senior volunteers, Amelia Johnson. Ms. Johnson are you looking to come out of this with less than you anticipated?"

"Certainly not. We have positive results in the caucuses which are still going on in Des Moines. We know they are still going on in Cedar Rapids and Waterloo and other cities."

"What's your view of the farm vote? We don't seem to see the farm vote supporting Adrian Daggett."

"I think it's too early to tell that. The returns are still coming in from the Northeast, which was not our best area."

"Which was your best area?"

"We are going to carry the Northwestern area by a majority and in the Sioux City area, we will be at least two to one over all the others."

"Can you confidently predict that?"

"Let's wait and see."

"Back to you." The anchor came back on and went back to the analysts.

"We've just heard from a senior volunteer at the Daggett cam-paign, and the coordinator for the state at the Porter campaign: both are saying they are going to come out of this with a victory. What's your take on this Professor Bricken?"

Harry Bricken, Professor of Political Science at the University of Iowa, removed his glasses and spoke directly to the camera. "If Adrian Daggett does not get a majority of the votes in Iowa it will be considered a Porter victory, because the polls up to this time have shown Daggett polling at least 55% of the total."

"So you believe that if Daggett gets less than a majority and Porter shows more than 35%, Porter can claim a victory?"

"Something like that."

CNN went to commercials.

In the suite, spirits fell as the vote from Ottumwa came in, showing Daggett with more votes than the other candidates, but with a total of only 43%.

"Not our best city," commented Merrick, dryly.

Karen opened her cell phone and dialed her regional coordinator in Sioux City. He told her not to be concerned, they were still counting.

CNN went back to the analysts.

"What city do you think will be the most significant for this race?" asked the anchor.

"Sioux City, because of its size and make-up of the community," said the second analyst. "Adrian Daggett has been to Sioux City several times. There has also been concentration from the early days in Cedar Rapids where his aerospace policies should be popular, and in Des Moines, of course, because of its size and also its make-up. An early signal might come from the returns from those three main cities."

"The vote continues with Porter slightly in the lead, with approximately 11% of the caucuses reporting."

Each minute seemed like ten to Karen. All that she believed in and all that she had done was at stake. They stood and watched. Network coverage would begin in 45 minutes. They would have to go down to the ballroom. It was down to the last 45 minutes. Would she have a chance to go to Washington, or would it be law school?

There was cheering in the background from the ballroom. The volunteers posting the numbers said Davenport was coming in. It was a record vote with Adrian carrying it with 64%. When that happened, Alan Jacobs phoned Parker Lothan. Lothan said that he was about to project, but needed two or three more results from Des Moines, Sioux City, and Council Bluffs. He said, however, "Alan, Davenport is telling you what it is going to be."

"I hope you're right," said Alan.

"I am right," said Parker.

Adrian and Terry, standing together, were looking concerned when Alan gave them Lothan's word. Then they heard wild cheering over the audio from the ballroom. They saw that in Sioux City a record number of votes were cast and Daggett took 68%. The Daggett total jumped into the lead on the CNN board. Adrian told Merrick, "I think it's time you went down stairs and let them talk to you. Anne and Nancy went with him. In a few minutes Merrick faced CNN camera. "We've just seen the results from Sioux City. Merrick, what's your comment on that?"

"It's an area where we knew we'd be strong. It's put us in the lead, and I think we are going to stay there. In fact, I think that lead is going to build. We have a great candidate and a great staff."

Excitement started to brew in the Daggett suite. Of the total vote count, over 27,000, Adrian had over 14,000. Porter's total was 8,000 – less than a third. CNN switched to the Porter headquarters, and the correspondent spoke. "We're back at Porter headquarters where the mood is subdued. I have with me the campaign coordinator, Steven Zimmer. Were you surprised by Sioux City?"

"No, we knew that Daggett is strong there, and that a lot of money and time was concentrated on that area."

"Did you consider yourself to be strong in Sioux City?"

"We knew that was our weakest area. We're still confident that were going to come out of this with a strong showing."

"Did you mean 'strong showing' or 'victory?'"

"A strong showing, as I told you before is a 'victory.'"

"How much effect do you think the sexual harassment scandal has had in this election?"

"I think it's added to the concerns of voters. A lot of people think where there's smoke, there may well be fire."

"Even though the accusation was proven to be false?"

"I have to go take a look at some numbers, if you'll excuse me."

Into the camera the reporter said, "The optimism expressed earlier this evening in the Porter camp seems to be diminished. Back to you."

They switched directly to the Marriott ballroom. "I'm here where the jubilance of the Daggett supporters is growing. The first returns have come in from Des Moines showing Daggett taking nearly 60% of the vote. This is less than the Sioux City totals, but there seems little question here that the Democrats of those cities are looking to Adrian Daggett to lead their party to victory in November. Back to you."

Daggett ran nearly 60% in almost all of the caucuses in the Northwest quadrant. In Des Moines he was at 58%. Then the totals came from the manufacturing center of Cedar Rapids, where Daggett polled 63%. As this unfolded, the network coverage came on. NBC interviewed Merrick. "What's your analysis now Merrick? Do you think this pattern has shown that the more sophisticated voters are going to vote for Daggett, or do you think this is due to your organization's concentration on the cities and on the northwest and southern tier of Iowa."

"I believe we got a great response from the agricultural caucuses in the Northwest and in the south, where we were able to tell our story effectively. In the cities, of course, there are other voters, but this is an endorsement for the reality campaign."

"What's your view of the negative issue ads that were run by the Southern Conservative Coalition and the Foulton Foundation?"

"At the beginning they hurt us, but we thought in Iowa they would backfire, and they may well have. It's possible the Porter forces might have done better if these foundations had not intervened." Merrick hoped the foundations and the Porter campaign would believe him.

"Congratulations to you and to your staff. This was a magnificent performance for Adrian Daggett in Iowa."

Karen's feet didn't touch the floor. She was smiling and beaming, when Adrian came to her and said, "I want Merrick and Marianne and you and Earl to be on the platform when I give my victory statement. You can stand behind, then I'm going to invite you to come forward."

In the ballroom, the crowd cheered each new result posted on the board as Des Moines, Waterloo, Cedar Rapids, Davenport, Council Bluffs, and the Sioux land cities fell into the Daggett column. The agricultural cities were less prone to vote for him, but in the northwest and the south they carried every caucus. Anticipation hushed the ballroom, as the senior volunteer, Amelia Johnson, stepped up to the microphone on the platform. She thanked the staff and volunteers for all their good work, and then introduced the candidate. To wild cheering and the band playing "Columbia the Gem of the Ocean" Adrian and Pamela came from the side, followed immediately by Merrick and Marianne and by Karen and Earl. Terry, Nancy, Anne, and Alan stood behind the two who had delivered the vote in Iowa. Pamela and Adrian held hands and waved, acknowledging individuals whom they spotted in the excited crowd. The cheering went on, and Adrian was unable to stop it for more than three minutes. Cries rang out, cheers sounded "Daggett, Daggett, Daggett." Then they changed to "We Want Daggett, We Want Daggett."

On the platform Pamela took his arm and kissed his cheek. He turned back and kissed her lips. She whispered in his ear, "This is only the beginning, I love you!" Daggett waved to quiet the crowd, and with all of the cameras on him, said," I thank you all for your great work. You've bravely embraced reality for the first time in many years of American politics, and just look at the result." A great cheer went up, and those standing behind him applauded.

"In every campaign there are heroes, and in this one you are the heroes. This is a record turnout and a record vote in Iowa. We are going on to New Hampshire and we're going on to all the other states, and we're going to build on what you've done here." There was more cheering.

"I particularly want to thank the people who were the leaders here. Merrick Reynolds and Karen Crezna. Merrick is accompanied by his wife Marianne. Karen is accompanied by Earl Hanley, an Iowa volunteer whose political partnership with Karen seems to be progressing to something more serious. "There was laughter and applause." The four of them stepped to the platform and waved to the crowd. Karen couldn't believe she was being seen by millions of people watching on television. She did not know that more TVs, in more households in the United States and worldwide were tuned in to an Iowa vote count than ever before.

Adrian personally greeted as many people as he could with Pamela. Merrick and Karen said thanks to everyone. At the edge of the room Tony Destito and Susan MacAulliffe who couldn't resist being there, sat at a cocktail table. When a waiter passed with champagne, they each took a glass and clinked it.

Later, as the hall began to empty, Terry came to Karen and asked if she and Earl would come back to the suite. There he told her she would leave with Merrick in the morning for South Carolina. Karen hastily left instructions with Amelia Johnson to clean up her office. She had to go home and pack and make love to Earl. They wouldn't see each other for a while.

A few minutes later Tony's phone rang. He thought maybe it was Jean. It wasn't. "Hi, Tony. Your old buddy here."

Tony smiled. "Hi, Wes." The Harrisburg Patriot News had robbed him of a tennis partner, Wesley Corbin, who had covered the Pennsylvania state legislature, but was promoted to Washington correspondent. "Tony, I need to talk to you. When will you be in Harrisburg? I'm in town until Friday. Can we have lunch?"

"Sure Wes. Tomorrow, at Harry's Tavern?" He wanted to see his old friend. "Do you want to interview me? I have no comment," he joked.

"Make it the Gazebo, Tony – we don't need to run into all the politicos at Harry's." He was serious. "Tony, did you know that Jean is working actively on the Porter campaign?"

Tony was stunned. He couldn't reply.

"I really need to see you, Tony."

"Tomorrow at 12:30 at the Gazebo," Tony said on autopilot. "Thanks Wes, I'm heading back to Harrisburg now."

How much would this explain about Jean's attitude and her absences from home when he called? What else was his friend going to tell him? He knew there was something more important from the tone of Wes' voice.

MERRICK AND KAREN arrived at Columbia, the capital of South Carolina, the next afternoon, still needing sleep from the climax in Iowa. Jack Wood and Louellen Parsons, Alaska – Louisiana volunteers, who were from South Carolina were already there. Mark Morris, the coordinator from Jeremy Reubin met them at the airport. Their mission was to find a way to win the primary in that state, which Porter was heavily counting on to spark the resurgence of his campaign. To defeat Porter there was to potentially knock him out.

At the headquarters in Columbia they reviewed strategy. Porter and his campaign hammered hard on the issues of taxes, foreign involvement, and health care. He was using his Iowa materials and abstracts from the POLACO foundations for his ads. Merrick sensed a mistake and ordered some special polls. It turned out that a majority of South Carolina people influenced by retired military professionals and veterans, favored a more aggressive world presence for the United States. On health care many agricultural and day laborers and share-croppers were not covered. Conservatives of both parties favored the Daggett program to protect the United States from fiscal weakness. Regrettably, racism still undermined the good work done in the South. With this in mind they would concentrate on the cities and the coast to which many Yankees had relocated and where many African-Americans lived. They would need all of these votes not only in the primaries, but also in the general elections to counter the rural vote which would inevitably go to the Republican candidate.

With Morris and his staff, Merrick made the assessment that with the right campaign they could throw Porter back. Merrick assigned Jack and Louellen to Greenville, Spartanburg, and the North, and Karen to Charleston and the South. They would visit and support the local staffs. Merrick would stay in Columbia to give Mark authority to make the changes that would be necessary.

ON THURSDAY AT the Gazebo, a fashionable restaurant in Harrisburg, Tony found Wes Corbin waiting. They embraced as was their custom. Before Wes was relocated to Washington they saw each other at least once a week. They played tennis often. Once Wes and his wife, Megan, joined Tony and Jean on a vacation to Colorado for a week of skiing. When Megan was dangerously ill with a meningitis infection, Tony spent many hours with Wes at the hospital.

At a corner table Wes first asked questions about PENMET. After they ordered, Wes came to the point. "Am I correct in concluding that you and Ian are in heavy support of Adrian Daggett?"

"You are. But, I hope that can stay off the record."

"This whole conversation is off-the-record. It is because your wife is not only working on the Porter campaign, but she is also having an affair with Malcom Cummings."

Tony put his hands to his face for a moment. "How do you know?"

"They were in Washington last week at the Willard. It was a meeting of the Porter Group from the Democratic National Committee. I saw them coming out of the elevator twice. I had a friend check the registry."

"She wasn't registered?"

"I'm afraid she was not."

"Maybe it was a mistake."

"I had her followed, Tony. She was staying with him."

Tony felt the floor give way underneath him and he fell forward into space.

"It was last week?"

"I called you as soon as I was sure."

What do you say when a trusted friend tells you your world is about to change? Wes supported him through the first hour of this new reality. They talked about what it meant and what he should do. Tony remembered that he was just as guilty.

KAREN MADE A three week deal with the Holiday Inn in Charleston and then scrambled around her new territory in a leased Chevrolet van. Her first week was a blur of meetings, meals, and driving. Each afternoon she felt a little more exhausted, but carried through the evening. Each night she called Earl, and looked forward more to his coming for the final weekend and for the vote.

In her hotel room with a room service dinner she watched the New Hampshire voting. After a few returns were posted, all of the networks and CNN projected Adrian Daggett to be the victor with 55% of the vote, based on exit polls. She called Earl all excited. She watched the whole of the proceedings including the triumphant entry of the candidate.

At the end of the NBC broadcast the anchor summarized, "The Daggett reality campaign has now captured four straight states. In the New Hampshire primary he has overwhelmed his opposition. While there are allegations of huge amounts of soft money coming to the Daggett Campaign supporting the largest issues staff ever employed in American politics, from this base he has expounded on critical issues to create the 'reality campaign.' The time has come when the American people must understand the reality of the world. They will understand it only when they are told clearly about it. That, Adrian Daggett has set about to do. Goodnight from NBC News."

THE NEXT DAY, Karen left at dawn to drive to Columbia for a meeting with the campaign staff and state leaders who had declared their support for Adrian. On the way she heard on the radio that Perona and Ramsdell had dropped out of the race and that Richard Sandellot would cease campaigning. They decided to ask for three full days of the candidate's time. Jack and Louellen based in Greenville would plan a day there, Merrick and Mark in Columbia would plan a day in the mid-state area and Karen would set the schedule in Charleston. Terry sent Nancy to direct the media campaign from Charleston and to be there to help Karen.

With Nancy in Charleston, the following day there was a teleconference between the South Carolina cities and Chicago. Terry, Anne, and Alan were seated in the headquarters studio. Terry started, "I want you all to know, we recognize you're standing down there in front of an onslaught by Porter and his people where they must win. If you can win for Daggett, it will end Porter's campaign or at least his credibility. We see some of the things going on, why don't each of you take five minutes and tell us what you observe."

Karen gave the report for Charleston. She cited the frequency of the ads for the Porter campaign and also from the two foundations. Every hour of the day, either the foundation ads were on, Porter's ads were on, or the two were joined together. The others told essentially the same story.

Alan interrupted at one point, "How strong is the local leadership support of the party decision to back Porter?" Each group gave the names of local Democratic notables who were supporting Daggett.

Terry summarized, "All right we have a situation in which the Porter campaign is putting all of the time they can and all of the money they can to showing a primary victory. The SCC is pouring in all the money they can to saturate the state with foundation ads. We have limited candidate time because we can't risk our leads in the Super Tuesday states and the primaries that still follow. Our job is to figure out a way to stop Porter in South Carolina. Who has some ideas how we can do that?"

"It's particularly important," commented Alan, "because now the Porter group has announced they are going to win in South Carolina. If we could just beat them by one point, I think it would be fatal to them."

"I've looked at the campaign ads down there," said Anne. "I don't see any great improvement in the quality. How are the coalition and foundation ads playing?"

"There are various reports on the response to Porter's. We have no direct measurements of the effectiveness," Merrick told her.

Karen had one idea. "I know that the campaign money is limited, but are there funds for soft money advertising down here?"

"That's more available than campaign money," said Terry.

"Most of the ads they are using down here," Karen analyzed, "are the speech ads from the Foulton Foundation. Do we possibly have time to prepare some speeches by prominent South Carolina Democrats who favor us, and to put them on to counter the ads from the foundations? We would then have local people answering the slick national ads."

"That's a neat idea," said Nancy. "We record talks or speeches to present the Daggett viewpoint contrasting the Daggett view to the opposing view.

"We can't get too close to naming a candidate in a soft fund ad," said Anne. "The speaker has to prefer a policy or an idea."

"Okay, but you get the idea. That's a good one, Karen," Nancy told her.

"We don't have time to arrange speeches, Karen," Anne said, "but can you recruit people who would do it fireside-chat style?"

"What style?" Karen asked.

"Franklin Roosevelt used to have what he called fireside chats. He was sitting beside a fire and talking, but that was on radio so nobody could really see. We can do it on TV," Terry explained.

"Why not do it in a variety of environments according to the person talking?" asked Nancy.

"Do we have the resources to get this going?"

"Don't worry about the resources, Terry, you get permission to use the soft money," Nancy said enthusiastically.

"All right let's get this started. The three South Carolina groups will discuss with each other who might give these presentations or 'fireside chats.' Nancy you have the production experience. You're in charge, take over and get it done."

IN HARRISBURG, NANCY usually used crews from Washington. There was no time to deal with a strange crew, and the DC people were accustomed to political people and producing political pieces. She enlisted "Cynthia Reese" to arrange for two cameramen, a sound operator with his equipment, two production assistants, a grip, a script person, and a line producer to fly down to Charleston on a company plane for a week's work. She explained to "Cynthia" that the purpose must be confidential in the office, but it was to produce some emergency T.V. spots to be used associated with the Daggett campaign in South Carolina. She then thought that it would be a good idea to have "Cynthia" come along. She asked her to arrange a plane for the evening which could stop at Dulles or BWI to pick everybody up with their equipment.

After a long hiatus, Cynthia had some intelligence to report to Harbour Island.

Karen found herself suddenly involved in television production. She inspected two studios, found one to be shabby, the other to be reasonably well equipped, but with only a limited setting. To add ambiance to the visual component, she and Nancy decided to shoot on location.

The South Carolina leadership meeting quickly determined they wanted to have at least one African-American Democratic leader, and at least one woman. There were only thirteen days to go. They had to complete at least three ads in three days in order to have a full ten days of airtime before the election.

Nancy gave Karen a list of local equipment to get: trucks, generators, lights, vans, and hundreds of yards of electrical cable. Karen found a volunteer who knew what it was and where to find it. They rounded up leaders who supported Daggett; a former congress-woman and now the African-American chairperson of her county committee; a former congressman and onetime gubernatorial candidate, now an elder statesman of the party; a lawyer and long-time Democratic Chairman in Greenville county; a professor at the medical school who was on the Charleston City Council; a professor of history at the university in Columbia who also was Majority Leader of the state legislature, and an African-American entrepreneur who was active in Democratic politics and had established an export-import business in chemical products.

Karen drove to the entrepreneur's home in the South-of-Broad section, and found it to be a delightful old house. She decided they would televise him in his comfortable and well-decorated study. He would also be joined by his wife who would also comment. She was a matronly professor at the local community college. They were an appealing couple; Karen hoped all of the others would be as good.

At the Planter's Inn she got some ideas for scenes and found the management sympathetic to Adrian. They let her use public rooms in return for booking the political talent who would do the ads. She found herself imagining how things would look on TV.

In the midst of the hectic phoning and planning she sped to the airport to greet "Cynthia Reese". The arrival was announced and presently an intelligent-looking blonde wearing slacks and a tweed jacket, carrying a briefcase emerged from the jetport, standing out among an ordinary group of travelers. Karen stepped up to her and asked, "Are you 'Cynthia Reese?'"

"Yes, and you must be Karen Crezna," "Cynthia" smiled delightedly.

At the Middleton Place restaurant on the Ashley River, over she-crab soup and stuffed flounder, Karen briefed "Cynthia." They discussed the issues positions they wanted the leadership group to take, and prepared a plan to interview the leaders first and then write for them or take dictation. Nancy would then direct the shoots while the next scripts were prepared. They would all help with the editing.

When Nancy arrived they were ready with the outline of the program. She reviewed, revised, and approved their plans. It was nearly 11:00 when they finished, and "Cynthia" took her first opportunity to telephone to Paul Melius. Five minutes later he was taking down the details.

THE NEXT MORNING, the mural in the executive atrium at Harbour Island showed an outside scene of blowing rain. Edgar strode up to Helene's office carrying Melius' message. He admitted to himself he felt like seeing her. She was in her morning briefing with Louis and some others. Edgar gave her the fax.

"It's been a while since we had a 'Cynthiagram.' This makes up for it." She buzzed for her secretary, and had copies made for everyone. They adjourned to a conference table.

"Good for you, Edgar, moles do work, but there isn't much time."

"It's nice to work for people who tell you what your opponents are going to say and who is going to say it," said Erla who arrived with Marsha.

"It's nice to have the intelligence. What do we do about it?" asked Helene.

"Should we notify the Porter people?" asked Harold Smalley.

"It will impress them," said Louis.

"It'll also let them know we have a mole close in," said Edgar.

"The Daggett group won't necessarily be sure of it if the reply comes after the attack. They might suspect, but they won't have evidence. They will have evidence if something leaks before the attack," Edgar counseled.

"Any other inputs?" Helene asked. "Marsha, we need a task force to counteract this as best we can. You're in charge. Louis, Erla you're on it. Why don't you each pick one of your people to join in? We have a couple of days to get something really good done. Edgar?"

"Call me if you need me."

The others started talking. Helene walked away from the table toward her office with Edgar following her for a few steps. "I still have quite a bit to untangle in the Mayberry affair, and we want to preserve the attack about unions," she told him.

"I understand. Try to make sure they keep in mind what their actions might reveal," he said.

Inside her office, Helene turned and looked at the table of people starting to make notes and plan their work. It was her job to make such assignments, but she had a flash feeling of a smell of the game. What was she really doing, other than making money and perfecting her ability to run a high-powered organization?

FOR ADRIAN'S FULL day on the coast, Karen and her volunteers set up rallies in Charleston and in Myrtle Beach, followed by press conferences and then a big dinner and fundraiser in Charleston to give local business people a chance to meet the candidate. Adrian and Pamela toured the navy yard, one of the medical equipment manufacturers, and the newest paper mill by chartered helicopter, on which Karen rode with them and did the last-minute briefing. A briefing book was sent FedEx in advance with information about each place they would visit, with the names and brief bios of people they would meet, all done to Karen's standards.

THE PLAN FOR the fast-track shooting of new soft ads worked. When the scripts were ready, they rehearsed and then the takes were made while other interviews were conducted and more scripts were written. By the time the second ad was ready for its shoot, the first was in editing. Each of the guests from out-of-town were asked to enjoy the hospitality of the Planters Inn for an extra evening, while they made sure everything was correct. The shooting took a long time with each subject because they made a thirty-second, and one-minute version of each spot. It was getting crowded at prime time. Stations had some spare space where they could take out their own program ads and put in a paid political ad, but the ad had to fit.

They started on Thursday and worked nearly all night. On Friday, after the second subject was completed, Karen said everyone should take the balance of the evening off to start fresh at seven thirty in the morning with another set up at the Planters Inn. She asked Nancy, "What is it I'm doing?"

Nancy said, "Karen, you are the producer."

All of the production crew except Karen and Nancy had left for dinner and some relaxation when Nancy put the first tape into one of the VCR's. It was the Charleston businessman and his wife. He sat at the desk in his study, his wife stood beside him. He wore a blue blazer with a white shirt and a checked tie. She in a shirt dress with a scarf.

"If you are watching this presentation, you've already most likely seen television ads from self-proclaimed conservative foundations raising questions about some of the great issues of our time. One of these concerns foreign policy and attacks the resolute use of American power to defend democracy around the world. These ads play on the fear of American involvement. But we have much more to fear from the consequences of American disengagement from world affairs. Franklin Delano Roosevelt said, 'We have nothing to fear but fear itself.' This is true in any democratic government, because the people of a nation rarely become evil, but it is evil individuals who establish autocracies. In a time when there is trade in atomic weapons, nerve gases, and bacteriological weapons we can't stand by and allow such governments to go unchecked. We also cannot tolerate ethnically motivated mass murder killing. Our liberty and world peace has a price. People of all races and backgrounds in the United States and other free nations have paid the price. I'm from South Carolina, and I don't believe America should shrink from world involvement. We have an overwhelming force for good and should always use it whenever evil threatens to crush a helpless and innocent people."

His wife added, "I don't want our sons and daughters in the armed services to be put in harm's way, but I recognize that all Americans must take risks. If these risks are not taken, then the world becomes less safe for all countries and it becomes a less moral place in which our children will live."

"That timed just about right. We may have to crimp it a little," said Nancy. "Nice setting, nice scene Karen, It looks super."

"How are white people in South Carolina going to respond to an African-American businessman?"

"It depends on the individual. I think most of them will listen. The racist element will tune it out. But, we're dealing here with ideas and foreign policy, neither of which holds much interest for most racists. Now ask me about the black people in South Carolina."

"Okay," Karen said, "what about them?"

"They're going to love it. Is "Cynthia" around? I'll buy dinner and we'll get some sleep."

"Let me call our line producer to make sure that the crew doesn't stay out all night. We gave them time off to rest, not to party."

On the way from the Holiday Inn Cynthia asked if they could stop at the Federal Express office. She said she had forgotten to pay a bill. Neither Nancy nor Karen suspected her package contained their media schedule and the scripts.

In the morning, they took the majority leader to the harbor where she made her statement wearing a Burberry trench coat as the great bridge loomed in the background. Her point was that both the military and the financial strength of America had to be maintained. She pointed out that America had passed from being the world's greatest creditor to the world's greatest debtor. She declared that it was undeniably necessary to maintain the fiscal strength of the United States to provide a stable world economy, and to afford the military expenditures necessary to defend the country, as well as to maintain peace in the world.

Karen arranged for the medical professor to discuss the national health insurance program at the entrance to The Medical University of South Carolina, as familiar to most people in South Carolina as the bridge. This message was that America needed the full strength of its people to compete in the international economy and that the full strength required maximum health. He questioned the current system, in which those who could least afford it were often saddled with the bulk of medical care cost.

The first ads appeared on Saturday night. The Mayor of Charleston and the Governor both had doubts about their allegiance to Porter and their associated patronage deals. After conferring on Sunday, the Governor called Terry Leelan. He wanted to talk, but it had to be face to face. Terry was heavily engaged in the final push in the primaries, and Tony Destito once again found himself in the role of an emissary with the authority to contract important business. Tony had intended to spend the weekend at home with his children, while Jean was traveling to a party event from which she would not be back until Sunday evening. Fortunately, his son, Martin, had his driver's license now so the kids would not be marooned. Martin drove him to the airport where he embraced his son and then dealt with his feelings as he watched his Buick Park Avenue depart with the new driver at the wheel. Five minutes later, he was airborne with the nose of the plane pointed toward Columbia.

The Governor's office was an arche-type of the South with high ceilings, tall windows of the pre-war style, and glassed bookcases. A couch and two chairs of green leather surrounded a coffee table. Two other green leather chairs faced the massive desk, behind which there was a green leather chair flanked by the flags of the state and the union. The Governor was standing and Tony was shown in by the gracious, gray-haired woman who had greeted him, calling him Mr. Destito and welcoming him to the state and the capital.

The Governor stepped forward to shake hands. "I see you Yankees move pretty fast. Welcome to South Carolina."

"It's a pleasure to meet you, Governor."

"Do you understand that I was elected to this office with the cooperation of many of the Democratic leaders that are now backing Senator Porter, and I have verbally given my support to the good Senator?"

"A briefing paper was faxed to me when I was on the way down."

The Governor was youthful in appearance despite the silver hair at his temples. Dressed in a blue pin stripe suit of the latest style, he radiated energy. When they sat down Tony saw that he was wearing black loafers which were surely Bally's.

"Then you know something of the history. I'm prepared to switch sides, because having met and heard your candidate when he visited my state, I believe he is a better choice."

"We're delighted Governor," said Tony waiting for the quid-pro-quo.

"You understand, of course, that if I were to do this, I might be risking the bitter enmity of those people who have been supporting Senator Porter."

"I can understand that," Tony said.

"You understand of course, that if I'm not Governor of South Carolina, I'd like to be assured of gainful employment."

Tony wondered if he would accept being Ambassador to The Republic of the Congo. "Governor, we make no promises for any offices in the federal patronage, because we feel we can't until we are elected. We do, however, stipulate that we will remember who helped us."

"I don't think you've got as much help so far in this primary campaign as I'm about to give you, if we can make a deal. If Willis Porter loses South Carolina, he is finished. I think I can give you South Carolina."

"What did you have in mind Governor?"

"Since we have this very large nuclear facility in our state, Savannah River and the Barnwell radioactive waste repository, I have acquired a strong background in the management of energy resources. I thought that Secretary of Energy might be a good career move."

"I know the United States deeply appreciates the fact that the site has been established, and does not hesitate to pay the extremely high taxes that you have levied on waste coming into the state," said Tony.

"We had to have a good political reason to make that the site, Mr. Destito. If we didn't, I wouldn't be talking to you here in this office."

"I obviously have to talk with the campaign about this and also with Adrian Daggett. I assure you I will get back with you before the end of the day."

"You can be sure of my cooperation and my loyalty and allegiance once I pledge it. But you understand, I have to look out for my future. Going back into business here or lawyering or lobbying would not be the same."

"I quite understand, Governor."

THE LIMOUSINE THAT brought Tony to the State House sped back to the airport. He raised the center window and called Joan on his cell phone to find out where Nancy was and to tell her he was coming. He also needed to have a teleconference arranged between Charleston and Chicago, wherever Adrian was. From the plane Tony phoned ahead to rent a car and booked a suite at the Planter's Inn.

Outside the Inn, he saw a generator truck and a support truck with cables leading into one of the windows indicating that the shooting of the ads was still in process. A bellman took his bags to the desk; when Tony had registered he gave him $5 to take them to his room. He followed the cables and found Nancy, Karen, and Cynthia Reese. The writing was done, so they were helping in production, with Nancy directing. She was enjoying the chance to do television. When she turned and saw Tony, she was surprised, but also pleased. "Hi, what brings you here?"

"A special mission."

"A mission to Charleston. You came down to make sure we were working?" Nancy laughed. Tony greeted Karen and "Cynthia" and asked them to meet in his suite. By the time he had his bags half unpacked and his jacket and suit hung up, they knocked at the door.

He let them in and then got soft drinks from the refrigerator. "What I have to say now has to be kept entirely confidential. It is something we would normally keep within the high level of the campaign, but you people are here on the ground and we need to make a very fast judgment. I've just come from the governor of this state who has been a luke-warm supporter of Senator Porter. He has offered to come over and support Adrian but he wants a deal to become Secretary of Energy. I think we can probably bargain him down to a guarantee of a job not-less-than, but the question is, does that cinch the win in South Carolina? That plus the advertisements that you are apparently exhausting yourselves to produce."

"If a high profile personality like the governor who is popular," said Karen, "switched over to us, it would be a big opportunity. We could key on the reasons for his doing that. It would also be a huge blow to Porter to lose the governor's support. Our foundation ads are refuting the negative ones from the SCC. The campaign ads would trumpet his coming over. More media interest would be created. That would probably cinch it."

"Cynthia?"

From my experience I agree with Karen. It's a great opportunity to gain a lot of media points. It would be awfully hard for Senator Porter to explain."

"It would also hurt the Republicans wouldn't it?" asked Karen "The media could start positioning Adrian Daggett as unbeatable."

"It's way too early for that, Karen," said Tony. "But we could deliver the coup d'grace to Porter. He has been forecast to win South Carolina and the reason we sent you and the other political commandos down here was to stop that from happening. You, "Cynthia," are a commando reinforcement. By their nature, commandos don't get reinforced very often. I've heard you're both doing a super job. Now let's talk to Chicago."

Five minutes later using Tony's portable computer, they were able to get speaker phone connection with Chicago where Terry and Alan were gathered with Anne. Nancy excused herself saying she was too busy with production and let Karen brief the South Carolina situation in the telecom.

"That's good what's going on down there, Karen, and we appreciate your help, 'Cynthia,'" Terry said opening the conference. "Okay, Tony tell us the story."

Tony reiterated his visit with the governor.

"He might not make a bad Secretary of Energy," Terry observed. "He certainly has enough Department of Energy activities in his state."

"Politically there would be an advantage. He would be the representative Southerner from the deepest of the deep South," added Alan.

"I agree with that," said Anne.

"Obviously Adrian will make the decision, Tony, but what's your recommendation from down there?"

"If we want to knock Porter down now, it looks like the thing to do."

"Good, we've all got battle fatigue," said Terry.

"You're still going to have to run the rest of the primaries," said Tony. "I'm not particularly fond of making these kinds of commitments."

"They're pretty fundamental to politics. We've been lucky so far to be able to deal in general promises, mainly because we're believable. This guy, however, has to take a big chance and he's going to be very specific."

"I understand the chance he's taking. What do I do?"

"Start planning your presentation to him and figure out how you're going to make sure he does what he says he's going to do. I'll talk with Adrian. We recorded your statement about what happened. We'll get back to you, but I'm going to recommend we go with this."

"Thanks a lot, people, this could be a big break," said Terry as he signed off.

Karen went to find Nancy and they headed for the Holiday Inn to do the editing. "Cynthia" went to her room to call Paul Melius with some more very critical news.

Twenty minutes later, Terry called back to Tony to say that Adrian agreed. Tony immediately called the governor and made an appointment for 9:30 in the morning. He then spent some time making notes and planned to come back to Charleston. Tony's emotions were more confused than ever. How could they not be? Nancy was here, Helene was at Harbour Island, and Jean was in Harrisburg; perhaps with Malcom Cummings. He had a hard time deciding where his heart was.

A WHITE CADILLAC drove on to the tarmac at Columbia. In fifteen minutes, Tony arrived at the state capital where a state trooper immediately opened the door. "If you'll just wait here, Mr. Destito, the governor will be down," was all the trooper said. Two minutes later, the governor was striding toward him. He barely stopped to shake hands, before he plunged into the back seat. Tony got in after him. The governor was visibly upset.

"Where to, Governor?"

"Head for the country club," the governor said to the driver, "and please put up the window." The window between the front and the back seat rose. When it was closed, the governor turned to him, "I don't know who you told about what I said yesterday Mr. Destito, but I got a most disturbing phone call last night – most disturbing."

"A disturbing phone call?"

"A very disturbing phone call. I was threatened, Mr. Destito, by someone who knew what I said to you. I swear that I never told anyone else but you, not even my wife."

"Governor, I have no idea what happened. I telephoned Terry Leelan, Alan Jacobs, and Anne Russell. They, in turn, called Adrian who approved the arrangement. I spoke with our attorney David

Gibson, and two more staff people here in South Carolina. I didn't even speak with the chairman of our campaign in South Carolina. One of those staff people was actually from my office and the other is with Jeremy Reubin. We want to win this state, Governor. We wouldn't do anything to jeopardize your confidence."

"I know you do, Mr. Destito, but there is no way I can cooperate now."

Tony searched his mind for an argument. "What were you threatened with, can you tell me?"

"I told them I wouldn't tell you anything more about it. Just let me say that it was more than a political threat. I was threatened with an investigation to be specific. There are a few things that might be found out by a determined opponent."

"Things that will keep you from being appointed Secretary of Energy as we intend to do?"

"No, nothing like that. Just some things I don't want my wife to find about. Do you understand?"

"I understand, Governor. Few of us are in any position to cast stones," he said thinking of himself and Helene. He wondered if the threats were really limited to sexual exploits. South Carolina's "good 'ol boy" system, was notorious even in the south.

"In politics there is too much temptation and too much giving in to temptation. That's why your opponents thought they could get away with the accusation they made about Mr. Daggett."

"I think I understand all too well, Governor."

"In any event we can't go forward. I'm terribly sorry I did this. I hope possibly you might consider me simply on merit. I needed to talk with you in a place where there were no bugs. The state police sweep my office every month. Unfortunately, I can't have them come in and do it until regular time, unless I can think of a good reason."

Back on the plane, Tony pondered what had happened. Somebody had leaked something to the opposition about the governor's possible change of support. He knew whom he had told, the question was whom had anybody else told? He phoned Chicago and found only Anne available. He told her what had happened and asked if she knew of anyone else who had learned of the Governor's prospective action. She told him that she had called Roger Bennett in Cleveland for material for the governor's announcement."Cleveland?" Tony asked.

"Oh my God," said Anne. "I'm a fool. I hate it when I do dumb things."

"We all do. In this situation, we all can't remember everything. I'll get Alvin on it right away."

"I'm sorry Tony, I blew it. I blew South Carolina," Anne lamented.

"Not yet, work on your publicity, your ads, your arguments. We can still win," Tony reassured her. He was not able to reassure himself.

"I hope so, Tony," Anne said.

Tony told the story to Alvin Carter, who was angry with himself because he thought he might have missed something in the investigation in Cleveland. There was no evidence of anyone in the Cleveland office who would possibly be passing information to the opposing camps. He'd look again, but he had gone over this thoroughly. Then Tony mentioned that Karen Crezna and "Cynthia Reese" also knew because Tony had asked them about the impact of the governor's shift.

"I can't imagine either of those two being an informer. They are both doing excellent work."

"The best moles are the ones who do excellent work. We'll have a look."

"Cynthia" knew that after her report she would be closely scrutinized. It would all depend on how good her cover was. She would have to be extra careful.

THE FIRST INSERTIONS of the ads that the team had written and taped, were into the basketball games on Saturday afternoon. They continued around the sports events on Sunday and then on to the Sunday evening news shows. Monday morning they punctuated the morning news shows, and continued through the noon news, the evening news, and prime time.

There were enough ads to avoid monotony. They could be scheduled over the remaining days, so that people who watched the same programs in the evening could see all of them without annoying repetitions. There was a quick result. By Wednesday, the South Carolina tracking polls showed Adrian gaining. Karen heard positive comments as she traveled the coastal area. The ads and the candidate's visit energized the local organizations. More signs appeared, more press was garnered, as the campaign engaged in a fierce battle with the Porter forces. The Porter Campaign went negative on the pocket book issue and world involvement. All of the Daggett ads were positive. All of the foundation ads were positive.

Tony stayed in Charleston where he and Nancy supervised the final editing of the ads with Karen and the line producer. The program produced excellent material and when the last of it was finished on Tuesday evening, Tony invited the entire crew to dinner where they all sat around a big table at Sticky Fingers with pitchers of beer. Tony raised his beer glass to the group and pointed out that they had conceived these ads only one week before, and now six excellent political advertisements were circulating on television and radio. They cheered and whistled. Soon the waiters piled the table with southern barbecue and catfish. When they were finished Karen pleaded exhaustion and returned to her room at the Holiday Inn. At the hotel, she called Earl who said he would be down for another victory celebration. She told him not to count on the victory, but she would love to see him. He said he was confident she would win her battle of the ads. She snuggled under the covers and was asleep thinking of Earl coming to see her before her mind got turned to any of the problems she had to face.

The crew, buzzing on the beer and sensing accomplishment, hit the streets of Charleston ready to succumb to any temptations the big city could offer. Nancy turned to Tony and said, "I feel like getting drunk."

"You better not. You still have work to do, and you don't need a headache."

"I need to get back to Chicago, but I think I should stay here for now and help with the media. This is a hugely expensive effort. Come to the Planters Inn with me, let's have a night cap."

Tony knew there was no lounge at the Inn, and that the nightcap would come from the service bar in Nancy's suite. He debated for a moment. "I'll take you there."

THE PREMIUM ROOMS in the Plantation Inn were rebuilt in the fashion of wealthy planters and merchants prior to the struggle of the succession. They were finished with light cedar wood panels. There was a pleasant smell, which thwarted the attack of termites and wood eating worms. The interiors were small with high ceilings that were efficient to heat in winter, but had the coolness of high ceilings in summer. The couch and chairs in Nancy's sitting room were plain dark red. On the walls were pictures of the old South, buildings of Charleston, the houses, and people, and one of the harbors full of sailing ships with bails of cotton lining the decks. Tony was far from relaxing in ante-bellum luxury as Nancy fished out the tray of liquors from the cabinet underneath one of the chimney lamps. She offered him Courvoisier, Tia Maria, Drambouie, bourbon, or scotch.

He made a weak attempt at flippancy, "No Grand Marnier?"

"Drambouie will have to do. I'm going to have some bourbon." She cracked the ice trays and filled the glasses with ice. She handed Tony the bottles; he twisted off the caps and poured the drinks. He was trying to decide whether to sit on the couch beside her. He chose the chair opposite.

"What a week, whose idea was this any way?" asked Nancy.

"How do you like campaigning?"

"I love it, Tony. I believe it's the most worthwhile thing I could be doing. The decisions we make affect history."

"More than you probably think. We have to win this."

"For us or for the country?"

"Both. They've been negative, we've been positive and we've won. It's very important that a positive campaign based on the real issues put Adrian Daggett in the White House."

"That was some job you did on the investigation."

"Alvin and Broderick Rose did it. It wasn't me."

"You're the one who started it. You were aggressive. Nine executives out of ten would find some reason not to make the decision and wait for more information. They would have blown it by wasting time."

"We were lucky. Sandy Gordon is a courageous woman."

"What will happen to her?"

"Adrian met her and liked her. She'll be in the Daggett government if we win."

"We're going to win Tony, I feel it."

"The general election is a lot different than the primaries with POLACO in it. If we win South Carolina their face will be bloodied. They will come at us."

"As long as they don't have more than three times as much money as we do to spend, we can handle them."

"You're feeling gutsy."

"You saw what the team did. Karen got the idea a week ago about these television ads and now they're on the air."

"That's what you have to do to win. Are you connected in Chicago yet?"

"I'm too busy Tony, and you?"

"It's not getting any better."

"You're the optimist talking: does that mean it's not getting any worse?"

"I wish it were true." He decided not to tell her the latest news. She got up from the chair and went to the couch and took his hand and pulled him to his feet. "Kiss me, Tony."

"I'm executive vice president, Nancy."

"You're also a man, and I'm not going to bring a sexual harassment suit against you. Do you want me to sign an affidavit?"

"You know I like you, Nancy."

"Yes, I know, and I like you too, Tony. Now come over to the couch. I want you to kiss me and maybe make love to me."

She took his hand. He sat on the couch; she sat beside him and then turned herself so she was across his lap facing him. "I'm waiting," she said.

They spent some time kissing, and making small talk, then they went to the bedroom.

They came away with jumbled feelings. Tony's brain was full of concern about his position and starting an affair with a senior employee. He crowded out his feelings by thinking of Ceramalloy, Adrian Daggett, and the great mission Ian MacAulliffe had been set upon and summoned him to join.

Nancy thought of the vacancy in her life without male companionship, and how well Tony would fill it. But, he was inaccessible now, ever more vulnerable to rumor and scandal. If he were to divorce Jean, she would have to leave the company to marry him. Perhaps she was getting way ahead of herself she thought. She started thinking about an election to win and an office at the White House beckoning to her.

☆ **Chapter 22** ☆

THE BATTLE OF the ads enjoined. Each side maneuvered with its other weapons. The Daggett campaign found South Carolina ideal for emphasizing its environmental stance. Much of the shore of South Carolina was salt water wetland, which nurtured the sea as a spawning place for fish and other aquatic life. An environmental speech and press conference was organized in Charleston.

A plane was chartered for reporters and television crews from Greenville, and Spartanburg, and buses fully equipped with refreshments of all types went to Columbia, Sumner, Florence, and Myrtle Beach. A small plane picked up participants from Rock Hill. Tony picked up the leaders of the environmental associations in Greenville and Columbia in the PENMET Learjet.

Karen met the candidate at the Charleston airport, after arranging an arrival event for which her volunteers on the telephones brought out the Daggett faithful. The Sheraton-Charleston ballroom had been reserved for a luncheon of community leaders, environmental organizations, and others from the coastal area. The media took notice as Adrian entered the ballroom with Pamela, escorted by local dignitaries. They encountered a standing ovation. After lunch, the president of the local Industrial Roundtable, who had won the right to introduce him, put aside the Evans & Copeland script and spoke off-the-cuff. He said he agreed with Adrian on the role of the United States, in its position in the world, that it should use its strength in both military and economics for the good of all mankind. There was enthusiastic applause. Nancy and Karen were seated at separate press tables. Their eyes met in mutual acknowledgement. The ads were working.

Adrian bestowed the ritual "thank yous" and immediately got to the matters of the environment. He spoke of the key issues of grand-fathering power plants, and trading pollution rights; of the wetlands development and the plethora of permits granted by the US Corps of Army Engineers. He complimented the environmental movement and cited its main accomplishments. He then made some direct commit-ments. He would ensure the introduction of legislation that would stop the trading of permitted pollution. He drew laughter and applause saying, "The idea of creating a market for permission to pollute the atmosphere of the world is about as intelligent as selling permits to speed or run stop signs." He criticized industrial resistance to the clean air act and complimented the many corporations who individually recognized their responsibility. He asked, "If technology exists to stop pollution and we, through our inaction, harm future generations in terms of their health or their livelihood, how can we possibly face them?

"On the matter of the wetlands issue, it is within the power of the President to take significant action. I know of the pressures upon the President to allow the development of wetlands for residences and resorts. I know of some fine examples of good work in these areas and how many people love the seashore and the tranquillity it brings. I also know there is relationship between the wetlands and the sea. The sea nurtures us with food and with oxygen. Wetlands are the spawning grounds of fish and sea birds. There may be other values, which we don't yet understand. No one is entirely certain of the value of the wetlands, but I am aware that political pressure to develop them must now be resisted. In this matter I can tell you what action I will take. If I'm elected, executive order number one will forbid the further development of any wetland in contact with salt water in the United States until a thorough scientific determination can be made. Then all responsible parties must agree on the extent of additional development that can be allowed." He was not allowed to finish the sentence. The audience rose, wildly cheering and applauding.

Adrian and Pamela stood at the podium waving to the audience. Behind the rostrum a practiced eye could see a conversation going on between the chairman and the Mayor of Charleston along with sev-eral county officials from the coastal cities. The Mayor of Charleston asked for recognition. He came to the podium and shook hands with Adrian and kissed Pamela's cheek and then turned to the audience. "Ladies and gentlemen, as you know, I have supported Senator

Porter's candidacy for the nomination of the Democratic Party. I have
to tell you now I have reconsidered." Applause and cheers broke out.
"I have always been faithful to our party leadership, and I've sought
to cooperate to develop this state and deal with its problems. I know
now we have in our presence a very special kind of candidate and a
very special kind of man. I apologize to the South Carolina leadership
and to those who may have anticipated my support. I have to tell you
now I'm for Adrian Daggett, and I'm for this environmental position.
I want this man to be our nominee and our next President. Thank
you." There was another standing ovation.

WITH ALL SIX of their new TV ads released, along with radio versions which Nancy placed during the commuting hours in the main
cities, the tracking poll continued to move. Inexorably the gap
between Porter and Daggett narrowed. Karen spent the final Friday
in Beaufort, which was noted for its large contingent of "old-line"
Democrats. She was interviewed by the newspaper and attended two
meetings where she spoke and took questions about Adrian Daggett.
In retirement country there was evident interest in national health
insurance. Many were retired or ex-military people who recognized
the need for risk and sacrifice. She often got discussions going with
the people exchanging ideas with each other. Driving back to the airport to meet Earl, she was so tired she felt heart pain. The cell phone
rang. It was Merrick.

"How was your day?"

"Good, I think. I'm glad they eat dinner early in South Carolina
and serve fried fish instead of fried chicken."

"We're not so lucky up here. I thought you would be interested in
the latest track. The gap is narrowed to 2%, we are inside the margin."

"I'd like to say we'll beat him, but it would take too much of the
energy I have left to get to the airport."

"Well let's see; it's 8:15 a.m.. What time does Earl's plane arrive?"

"Just before 9:00 p.m.."

"Well it seems to me it won't take more than a half an hour to get
to the Holiday Inn. You and he can take the rest of the night off and
get some good sleep."

"Thanks, Merrick." A warm feeling came over her thinking of Earl
and of falling asleep naked with his arms around her.

"How's the rest of the team, Merrick?"

"You are the one that should be the most tired after producing those ads. It was a great job, Karen. You are the kind of person who fills voids. That's the most important thing in a team member. Is your schedule full?"

"Nancy and I invited a bunch of reporters to lunch tomorrow, Saturday stringers. We are going to show them the ads and invite them to comment and hold sort of a press conference for the people who don't get to go to the real ones. It should be good for some copy. Tomorrow afternoon we have a couple of parties and tomorrow night the big doo-dah Daggett dance. It's dress up. I have to be a Southern Bell. Why don't you come down? When is Marianne coming?"

"Not until tomorrow morning. That means I have to wait until tomorrow night to make love."

"Who's making love tonight?"

"You may be bone tired, but I know what's on Earl's mind."

"Men. That's all you think about. Will you be down tomorrow?"

"Marianne would enjoy a dress up. Buy me a couple of tickets and I'll send her out to get a costume. Am I supposed to look like a Mississippi gambler?"

"Same as a political consultant."

As she turned into the airport access road she saw a Delta plane landing. She was at the gate when Earl came striding up the jetway carrying his garment bag, his briefcase and a copy of *Primary Colors*. She stood against the wall opposite the entrance. He came up to her smiling, but not saying a word. He put down his luggage and then grabbed her and hugged her. She felt his lips on hers and she returned the kiss. "Hi," he said. "You look beat."

"Does it show? I'm bone tired. I can't drive another mile or answer another question."

"You don't have to. Let's go."

He handed her the book and picked up his luggage. "I hope you don't talk like the people in that book. The language is filthy."

"People who become arrogant with power talk that way, others mimic them."

"What's our schedule?" he asked.

"We are going back to the hotel; then I'm going to take off my clothes. I've collected little bottles of body lotion. You will use them when you massage me. While you massage me I will appear to be in a deep, fatigue induced coma. But I will be fully conscious of everything you do."

"I hope you don't mind if I molest you."

She was holding his arm, and put her cheek against his shoulder.

"You can have your sex tonight. Tomorrow, I'll make love to you."
He looked down into her eyes grinning. "Sex is all I came for."
She hit the muscle of his arm.

He didn't push himself on her even though she saw his erection as he climbed into bed. The massage took the tension out of her. After half a hamburger, some salad and a glass of beer she went to sleep with him holding her as she had anticipated. She awoke refreshed and lay beside Earl thinking of the schedule and the events up to and through the day of the voting.

THE LEARJET AFTER delivering the new TV personalities who lived in Greenville, had headed north. Tony needed some time in the office and to deal with the situation developing in his marriage. He wanted to see Jean and the children before they left for a visit to Florida with Jean's mother. He hadn't decided how to handle the affair she was in or the one he had probably started.

Ian saw him late in the day.

The pleasantries were brief. Ian got right to the point. "That's a good job that's been done, Tony. The American people are responding to Daggett and what we have presented to them. I'm increasingly concerned, however, about the effect on the company."

"The numbers that I have seen so far look good Ian."

"I'm concerned about the intelligence that we are getting from those girls on Harbour Island. They are getting into conversations with POLACO people. Alvin tells me there is a division in POLACO management and that Ward is being pressed to do things he doesn't want to do by his sort of executive board. There are reports that Ward and Helene didn't want to fight in the primaries to conserve their energy for the general elections when the consolidated Republican organization would be their ally, but these others made them do it. They argued that if Daggett wasn't nominated they wouldn't care about the general election."

"Not unless Sandellot won."

"I hope we are in touch with him."

Alan has had one conversation with him. Daggett will meet him and their staffs will meet. He is as good as Daggett."

"So I understand. Maybe a vice president?"

"We don't know whether the country is ready for that yet. After the primaries we'll add up the constituencies and see. I think he'd be a hell of a Secretary of State. That would signal the focus on African affairs."

"How is the senior campaign staff holding up?"

"They are fighting a hell of a battle in South Carolina."

"Do you think we will win?"

He told a brief story of the ads.

TONY'S RESOLUTION TO attempt a patch-up in his relationship with his wife was shaken with her very first words that evening.

"How is America's most political corporation?"

"Sales and profits are rising and our candidate is winning," Tony replied in a conciliatory voice.

"So I am told."

"What we are doing seems to be working."

"This is the primary, Tony, not the election. You've been lucky."

"Adrian made the decision not to change the reality campaign. We are going to address the issues in the general election, as many of them as we can."

"You ran on trust against Porter and Findlayson. Primaries partly are about trust."

"You said we were going to lose the primaries."

"You won them, Tony, and I congratulate you, but I'm telling you the general election is going to be different."

He wondered whether that was rationality or spiteful ill will. He found himself thinking about his wife as he would think about an employee. In the past he could sense how she was the feeling. Now she was sleeping with Malcom Cummings.

"How are things with your campaigns in Pennsylvania?"

"There are not many challenges in the primary, it depends on whether your man Daggett is far enough ahead to hold off Porter."

"Your people are going to have to take on our campaign themes."

"They won't, Tony."

"You mean you won't support the national candidate?"

"We're trying to get our Congressman and Senators elected. I am going to be in one hell of a position on the committee if your involvement leaks out. Can't you stay out of it?"

"I had to go down to South Carolina, Jean. Something happened." He told her about the governor.

"That's just the kind of trouble you're going to get in if you stay involved in this campaign. You should get out of it, Tony. Let Terry handle that stuff."

"There aren't enough high-level people to do it. Besides I have the authority to commit foundation funds."

"What do you mean?"

"We can loan money to the campaign temporarily if somebody has to be bought off. We had $300,000 in cash ready to deal with Annabelle Mayberry."

"Did you use it all?"

"We used some." He wondered why he was telling her this.

"Tony, I don't want to argue politics with you. I can't convince you so why talk about it."

"Let's talk about something else," he said.

"Why don't you come to Florida with us?"

"I can't handle your mother right now."

"My dad is going to be there."

"I'd like to see him, but I don't think with your mother"

"She's the only one that will be happy when she finds out you are throwing away your career. She relishes every story I tell her if we have fights."

"I wish you wouldn't tell her."

"Whom do I have to talk to, Tony?"

"Your mother is as bigoted as any person I have ever met. I wish you wouldn't have the children around her."

"I keep the conversation away from that. I have discouraged her."

"I still wish you wouldn't have the children around her so much."

"She is their Grandmother."

"She's a witch."

"And fuck you, Tony. She's my mother, and just maybe she was right, maybe I shouldn't have married you."

That night lying in bed beside her he pondered something he knew about himself. He had to have the support and love of a woman behind him in a marriage. He needed a warm place to come to when the world grew stormy and cold. Jean had done that for him for a long time. He'd come home from a troubling meeting or situation and they would talk. She'd make suggestions. Then she would hug him; often they made love and all the bullshit would get into focus.

TONY AND A spare crew flew back to Charleston in a Citation. He found Nancy in her suite at the Planters Inn looking over the final media schedule and preparing the media buys for the soft ads. Tony asked her if she was ready for the ball tomorrow night. She said she hadn't had time to get a costume and she didn't want to be a wall-flower. When Tony told her that he was ready to go, she allowed him to convince her to go shopping.

She wasn't a quick shopper and tried on seven outfits before she picked one. He reminded her she was only renting it and she reminded him there was only one ball and if she was going to go to it she wanted to be as perfect as she could be. She was stunning in her hoop-skirted off-the-shoulder gown of mauve covered with an overlay of white lace. He found a costume which gave him a passing semblance to a merchant.

In a soothing Southern drawl she asked if the gentlemen mer-chantman was going to call for her and escort her to the affair. Tony stepped back and bowed and said it would be his honor to do so, embarrassed that he hadn't asked. They went to dinner and talked about the campaign.

In her suite she went into the bedroom and tried the dress on. She came back wearing it. It had to be taken in a little at the waist. She showed him how to put in the pins. When she turned for him to unbutton the back, she stepped out of it naked. The years had been very kind to her. She had full, firm breasts with enlarged nipples that turned up a little. Her hips were full, her stomach flat and her thighs and buttocks firm. She smiled her dimpled smile at him and then kissed him. "I've read that the ladies of this era used any excuse to get out of their encumbering clothing."

ON SATURDAY MORNING Tony put the plane at the disposal of Merrick and the Colombia campaign staff and suggested he use it as he might want during the day, but bring people from Greenville down to the affair. A number had been planning to drive down; Merrick was able to offer them the convenience of the plane, a great gesture to the party leadership on whom he would depend to get out the vote on Tuesday.

The ball was about getting out the vote, and rallying the troops. Nancy entered clinging to Tony's arm. She saw the tables around the dance floor decorated in white with candles. There were electric can-dles on the chandelier and the light was at a low 19th Century level. An orchestra of violins and woodwinds started to play a waltz and Tony politely pulled her to the floor. "One before we start politick-ing." He whispered in her ear. She held her cheek on his. They danced until the music ended. As they applauded they found Karen and Earl just in front of them. Karen wore a white brogue dress with a hoop. Earl was in the flashy black and gold of a river boat gambler. Tony saw his vest pocket bulged with a pack of cards. When Nancy asked what the drill would be, Karen fluttered her eyelashes behind her fan and said, "Why, darling, we just have to talk to everybody." And they did, except Tony insisted on passing the bar and buying everyone a drink first. Nancy ordered bourbon and so did he. When the others weren't looking he turned around and looked into her eyes and held up his glass to touch hers.

Merrick arrived wearing a red and black gambler outfit and blond Marianne was a dance hall girl in a low-cut red dress with black net stockings. Cornelius Lawlor, the businessman who recorded one of the issues ads, wore a federal period waistcoat and his wife wore a long gown. They were free blacks, they told everyone. Other African-Americans came as preachers, lawyers, doctors, gamblers, and chicken fighters with their women costumed to match them. Several African-American students came as Union soldiers; their girlfriends were union spies.

They danced, they talked, and they sat at a table with Merrick and Marianne, the Lawlor's and two African-American couples who were dressed as minstrel show performers. The dinner was roast chicken with cornbread, deliciously delicate and not too expensive. A wine cask dispensed South Carolina wine; a keg of beer had been tapped. There was a brief program where Merrick and Mark spoke. A tape of Adrian was shown on a big television screen. There was applause and cheering, and in the hall, Tony could sense there was expectation and confident determination.

The orchestra played the old traditional "Goodnight Ladies" for the last dance. Tony swung Nancy onto the floor. She stood back from him while they danced and said, "And what would you like to do after this dance, Mr. Merchant Man?"

He whirled her around and then stopped and said with a slight bow, "I'd like to have a drink or two with this lovely lady."

She curtsied, "This lovely lady accepts, with pleasure."

They danced until the music stopped and the applause ended. The crowd started to leave. Some couples headed off toward the bar. Tony saw Earl holding Karen's coat for a trip back to the Holiday Inn. The coat check line was quick and soon he was holding Nancy's coat. As she slipped into it he squeezed her shoulders.

In Nancy's suite at the Planters Inn, Tony looked in the service bar and found a Sonoma red wine. He poured it into the two glasses which they clinked. She came close to him and held up her face to be kissed. He obliged. They had to put their glasses down to continue the kissing. On the couch they struggled with her hoops. She stood up for him to undress her. He started to feel her warmth, warmth that he needed from her essential character. She understood his business and probably understood him more than he knew. With all the intellect, energy, and high-powered personality there was tenderness and lovingness.

Sunday morning before setting out on the scheduled agenda of visits to surrounding cities, Nancy asked Tony to take her to mass at the Episcopal church, one of the old buildings just off Broad Street, red brick with white trim and a white steeple. They spent the day in Karen's room. Tony marveled at Karen's energy and enthusiasm. He felt they accomplished a lot with those who were critical to the election on Tuesday. They stopped to visit those who didn't come to the big city parties. People in the little towns of Monks Corner, Marion, and Georgetown were excited to meet Nancy. Having a person from the national campaign call at their homes was almost like having Daggett himself.

Tony saw that Karen had the will to win and a talent by which she infected others with the same will and desire. The whole day Earl drove while Karen talked on the phone. While they were parking back at the Planter's Inn in Charleston she called Merrick for the latest poll and squealed with delight. She said out loud, "We're even!"

Nancy said, "That means were going to win."

"You better believe we're going to win," said Karen.

When they left Karen and Earl, Nancy took Tony's arm. "We've been cooped up all day, how about a walk South-of-Broad?"

"As the lady wishes," he said assuming his character of the previous evening.

They strolled down the street past the houses with the doors to the porch, all of which had mysteries of the families that lived in them. They were of the people who first established the colony and built its economy and then destroyed it by promoting secession and Civil War.

In Nancy's suite after he took her coat and hung up his, she turned her back to him. "Unzip me, I have to get out of this dress, it feels clammy."

"You don't look clammy."

She shivered out of it, picked it up from the floor. She was wearing a half-slip. She bent and pulled down her panty hose and gave a sigh. I don't wear much when I'm at my apartment. I guess I don't really like clothes.

When they were naked in bed, pangs of guilt attacked Tony as he remembered the nights at the same Inn with Jean so many years ago. With that came the inhibitions to having sex with an employee even though she was an officer of a giant corporation. Would she ever threaten his career? He answered his own question intellectually. Nancy said, "You're feeling something."

"Guilt and all the other things," Tony admitted.

"Tony, if Jean gave the support you needed to do your job and face the decisions and the risks you wouldn't touch me. I know this is not about sex. You need support just as I do. You need affection and I need it too. I could face the world by myself and I have, but it's a lot more fun when there is somebody there sharing it with you."

"I don't know what's happened to her, and what's happened to our marriage. I'm on her turf when I'm in politics. She must resent that horribly." He couldn't bring himself to tell Nancy of Jean's affair.

"Politics breed things, Tony. Have you ever thought she's involved with another man?"

"No I haven't," he lied. He just couldn't tell her.

"I believe you haven't, because you have ultimate confidence in yourself and what you can do, and in your own character. You can't imagine anyone competing with you for a woman successfully. But it may have happened, Tony, because Jean wants some things that you can't give her. Or maybe Jean is in that stage of life where she doesn't know what she wants only that its nothing she already has. Maybe she's trying to prove she's still attractive. When women are over forty, Tony, they're not the center of attention they once were. I cried on my fortieth birthday. I was alone."

He touched her cheek. "It's unfair."

"No it isn't Tony. I chose unwisely. I knew he was a big-time party boy, but I thought he would grow up. He didn't. I thought he was mature enough to face the fact that I would have a strong career, and he couldn't. It must wrench him horribly to think of me and what I'm doing, and how much money I'm making."

"How does he know about that?"

"Because I pay his rent, Tony, on a two bedroom apartment in St. Mary's. He has a nice apartment because the children go to see him. I want it to be decent. We send him gifts of clothes for his birthday and for Christmas. I pay his phone bill so he can talk to the children."

"Are the children all right?"

"They are as well as might be expected given the circumstances. I was too career oriented. Their childhood's weren't bad. I gave them love, so did he. He never abused them. He wouldn't be alive if he had and my brothers found out about it. It's not too bad. We have a big family. The kids enjoy their cousins. Most of them have gone off to college. Oh, I'll tell you the family story another time."

"You're some woman. He didn't know what he had."

"Yes, he did, Tony. He didn't like it." She smiled. "You have only two more nights to help me with my sexual frustrations. You're a wonderful man Tony. I fantasized about you. I've always wondered if you fantasized about me, but I thought not."

He pulled her to him. "You look wonderful and you are wonderful. Someone who appreciates you as much as I do will show up."

She wanted that, certainly. She also wanted to be the press secretary of President Adrian Daggett. She knew that would be the best opportunity she would ever have.

In bed she was hungry for him, but even though urgent and erotic, there was a special feeling to it, tenderness and an intimacy. He thought of her tenderness and her dimpled smile as he fell asleep.

The Cessna Citation took off from Charleston headed from Columbia in the half-light before sunrise. Aboard were Karen and Earl going up to pick up Merrick, Marianne, and Mark and on to Greenville to get Jack Wood and Louellen Parsons. In Greenville and Spartanburg they visited locations where telephoning had already begun, and then zigzagged around the state to appear at as many places as possible. They wanted to see if there were enough volunteers, and to help with last minute developments.

NANCY ARRANGED A private dining room at the Planter's Inn where they could have dinner and watch the final televised appeals of the Daggett and Porter campaign. Both campaigns had purchased eight-minute segments preempting advertising on each of the major networks at different times. In the dining room there were television sets tuned to each network. By agreement throughout the state the stations would put the same candidate on at the same time. Porter got the slots at the top of the hour and Daggett those at the half-hour. Porter started at 8:00 and Daggett was last at 10:30.

In Porter's first segment, speaking from Columbia, he appeared tired and haggard. The speech sounded almost like that of a Republican. He cautioned on foreign involvement; he cautioned about reforms of health care; and rejected the need for Americans to reduce their paychecks to pay for a debt reduction. He dared to be cautious. It was well done and compelling despite the un-dynamic appearance of the senator. Nancy quietly said to Tony, "Five will get you ten that was written in Harbour Island."

"I'll keep my five," Tony answered.

Speaking from Greenville where Merrick, Louellen, and Jack made arrangements, Daggett thanked many supporters by name including the Mayor of Charelston. He summarized his case: the United States being a force for the good of the world; support for the UN to achieve world peace; national health insurance to assure access to the great health care system to everyone; control of health care costs; and the need for financial responsibility avoiding risks in the international markets. He defined what a reality government would be and what a reality campaign would be in the general election. He repeated his environmental promises concerning the wetlands and used that as an example of what decisions reality would bring.

Porter had two different message formats which Nancy was convinced were done by the POLACO staff. He skillfully referred to the Daggett issues and then hammered relentlessly on paychecks and foreign deployments. He accused Adrian of not being a true environmentalist. In his final segment he spent the entire time painting Adrian as a tax and spend liberal who would be rejected by the American people.

Nancy and Alan had one more surprise, which had been kept a top secret until earlier in the day. The PENMET plane had picked up the mayor of Charelston and his wife and flown them to Greenville. In the 9:30 slot instead of Adrian Daggett alone, the Mayor and his wife, and Pamela were with him. The Mayor of Charleston addressed the people of South Carolina from the Daggett Headquarters with Daggett standing beside him giving the reasons for his support of the reality campaign. The young people around Nancy's table applauded everything he said.

At 10:30 Adrian responded to the accusations. He accused the Republicans of "borrow and spend." He said the time had come to pay the lenders. He made the key points: peace in the world with American resolve backing the UN; a stable, healthy world economy, universal health care, eliminating the cost of irresponsible law suits, and making sure the environment was safe for the future. "One reason for speaking from headquarters," Nancy said to Tony, "you have your best people around you to write a quick response. Neat!"

After the 10:30 segment Merrick said, "Okay, you guys, one more day to go. You got to get out the vote. In her suite, Nancy poured two glasses of port and handed one to Tony and smiled at him. "To victory! We're going to do it." They clinked their glasses.

The next day Nancy and Tony joined Merrick, Marianne, Mark, and his wife on the plane zigzagging again to appear at the headquarters locations. Their primary night celebration was to be in Charleston, since the Mayor there had made his move. By noon time they learned that voting was heavy. By 4:00 p.m. back in Charleston when Merrick and Mark made their appearances at the telephoning, the news was that there would be a record turnout. Did it mean a surge for Daggett or a backlash against him?

The plane was dispatched to bring the leaders from Greenville and Spartanburg. Those from Columbia drove down, once again, to the ballroom at the Sheraton Charleston. The Charleston volunteers put together a summary board which added to the excitement of each election night. The national media crammed the room with television cameras and reporters swarmed, sensing a news night. Merrick and Nancy were interviewed and a *World News* reporter from CNN got hold of Karen. She did so well, the interview was repeated several times on the headline news segment and on the prime time news and then again as CNN started its coverage of the voting.

In their command suite, with all the television sets turned on, Merrick, Jack, Nancy, and Tony watched. The campaign plane was on its way with Adrian and Pamela and more reporters. A group of state leaders were at the airport. Earl, Karen, and Louellen stayed down on the floor where the volunteers began to arrive. In the room there was a buffet with dinner selections of baked fish and chicken which they hardly touched. Someone had to be available to be interviewed. Merrick let the reporters have Karen, Louellen, and Jack.

As the returns started coming in. He sat with his face serious beside Nancy and Tony. CNN shifted to its coverage. The local network stations preempted their programs. One of the television sets showed the totaling board in the main ballroom. CNN opened its broadcast from downstairs in the Sheraton with a reporter standing with Jack Wood and Louellen, asking them questions on how the people in the campaign personally felt. CNN then switched to the Porter headquarters at the Holiday Inn in Columbia where a reporter said Senator Porter was in his suite waiting for the returns, and interviewed Steve Zimmer, the national campaign director. Viewers found out that the Senator and his campaign leaders were confident of a victory despite the deluge of expenditure that the Daggett campaign had made in the final weeks. When asked his opinion of the heavy vote and reports of lines of voters still waiting to cast their ballets in Greenville and Charleston, Zimmer had no comment.

After a few minutes, scattered returns from the rural areas began to show on the board. These solemnly favored Porter. When the votes from Florence appeared Daggett was behind with 40%. Porter was ahead in Myrtle Beach which gave Tony, Nancy, and Merrick that sinking feeling, but 20 minutes after 8:00 p.m., CNN projected Daggett to win. During the next two hours, the totals built up. The remainder of the coast and the inland cities were solidly for Daggett. At 9:00 p.m. the network news programs broke in with reports from South Carolina which CNN had been carrying all along. Adrian Daggett was the clear winner.

Before his supporters in Columbia, Porter vowed to continue to fight. There was applause and cheers. In Charleston at the Sheraton, Adrian, who had arrived, brought Merrick, Louellen, Jack, Nancy, Karen, and others to the platform. The room went crazy. He made his victory statement. People came forward to shake hands with him. Soon the dais was crowded while the applause and cheering continued.

ANOTHER GROUP WATCHED on Harbour Island in the upstairs conference room where the windows were open to a cool Bahamian night. Everyone wore a sweater of some kind, nibbled on finger sandwiches, and drank tea. They watched the CNN commentator anchor sum it up. "Adrian Daggett has won again; this time defeating Senator Porter in a primary which Porter had vowed to win. There is little credibility left in the Porter campaign. He has declared a fight to the end, but there may be some reflections tomorrow morning. How much further can Porter go without winning something? He is not leading in any of the "Super Tuesday" states and that is one week away. Adrian Daggett has beaten him. He has to face the facts."

"And we have to face it too," said Helene. "It was a mistake to use up our ammunition."

"We'll have to make more," said Erla.

"General elections are a lot different than primaries," said Warren Hatch.

"They'd better have different results," said Ward. "I think, Helene, we are going to have an very unpleasant meeting with Sadovan and Gallosey and their like-minded directors. But, this time we'll tell them what the reality really is."

"Reality," laughed Helene. The others joined her in a chuckle.

"There is something to be said for it," said Ward.

IN NANCY'S SUITE, after they had joined the other leaders in greeting everyone, she turned to Tony and put her arms around his neck and leaned back and looked in his eyes. "Is this the savory moment of politics, the victory?"

"I think that's what a lot of people look for, the victory and the patronage."

"Patronage, the spoils of democracy."

"The awful spoils of democracy."

"Then what is the victory?" She turned and signaled for him to unzip her dress which she pulled over her head.

"I guess it comes at the end of the term. Have you accomplished what you set out to do? And was what you set out to do worth accomplishing?"

"That takes a lot of emotional maturity and maturity of viewpoint."

"Not too many people have that."

"Let's talk about that sometime, but tonight's the last night," she said as she slipped off his jacket and started unbuttoning his shirt.

At the Holiday Inn, Earl and Karen didn't know when they would see each other again or where. They undressed for long slow lovemaking. She sat on top of him while he was inside her. She looked down at him at his eyes and said, "We won, we did it."

He cupped her breasts in his hands and tickled her nipples. "Is that all you can think about?"

"You know how much it means."

"Yes, I know."

"Do you know how much you mean?"

"I know that too. I hope you know how much you mean to me."

"I think we'll have a life together, Earl. There's a lot to work out, but we can do it."

"Is that the sex or feelings?"

She reached and pinched his nose and then swung herself down on top of him flat and kissed him.

THE TELEVISION NETWORKS, news channels, and the newspapers were full of it the next day. What would Porter do? First there were excuses. There was too much money spent. The Daggett campaign couldn't continue to spend at that pace. Their arguments were spurious; they ran a hidden negative campaign. Earl and Karen listened to it while they took a shower together and dressed. Tony ducked down to his own suite to leave Nancy the space she needed to get ready. He watched it. Nancy watched it while she prepared for a meeting she had called for 10:00 a.m., after a conference call with Terry and Alan so she could impart their instructions. They hadn't won yet.

Merrick and Marianne missed some of the chatter with early morning lovemaking before they took a shower together. They too were not sure when and where they would see each other again. Louellen and Jack woke up in the same bed, a little embarrassed. They turned on the television and started focusing on the next steps in the campaign, while Jack pulled on enough clothes to leave for his room. He hoped nobody would see him.

Nancy had coffee and some pastries ready when they all gathered.

"If there were medals given out for these battles you have fought you would all receive high rewards," said Nancy to start. "No senior staff could ask for better people than you in the field. These last three weeks in South Carolina were a pitched political battle with hand-to-hand combat, and you won. You won with your energy, your personalities, your enthusiasm, and with your innate ability and innovations. You all have a great sensitivity for people and are hugely suited for what you are doing. We probably knocked out Porter, but he hasn't given up. Even if he does, we're still going to press forward to Super Tuesday and the other major primaries.

"Merrick, during the election, assuming the nomination, you are going to be National Field Coordinator. We want you to go back to Chicago and organize an office. you're going to have to go to every state, meet the people, look over the organization and its suitability for the general election, and decide who stays and who goes on the salaried staff. Your job will be to recruit people we need and help them to organize their own operations and see to their training.

"Mark, for the next week you'll be traveling with Adrian as special coordinator for the Super Tuesday states. Then we want you in Chicago until Merrick decides where he wants you.

"Jack, you'll take over as state coordinator wherever Merrick needs you, but until we complete the primary program you're going up to Columbus. We'll drop you off on the way to Chicago.

"Louellen, we are having some difficulties in Missouri. There are not enough people to cover the state. You'll be on your way to St. Louis. The only advice I can give you is don't try to recruit Annabelle Mayberry for our organization." The tension broke into laughter.

"Karen, the Texas leaders like the idea of producing soft ads for Texas for both now and in the general election, so you're headed for Houston. You'll be a full-time producer. Show them how to do it, and help them in any other way they ask.

"All these assignments are temporary, except for Merrick. Once we have the nomination secured there will be vacation time. All of you are invited to a meeting in Vail two weeks after we win, in which we'll spend an unknown number of days planning the general election campaign. We want everybody to be fresh for that; we all know how tired you are right now. Earl, there's a seat on the plane for you up to Chicago. I thank you all so much. It's been great fun. We did it. God Bless You!"

There was applause and "hear hears." Merrick and Mark thanked everybody personally. In a few minutes the room emptied.

"Nice job, leader," Tony told Nancy when they were alone. "You're going to be a hell of a press secretary."

THEY ALL RODE to the airport together. Karen kissed Earl good bye beside the PENMET plane. She and Louellen were on the same Delta flight up to Atlanta. In the gate area, they saw CNN continuing to talk about Porter and then suddenly there was a press conference. Smartly dressed, but clearly tired, Senator Porter came before the reporters who had been waiting for him and announced he would cease his campaign. He went through the "thank yous." In the questioning he blamed the loss on the huge amount of money spent to elect Daggett, on hidden negative campaigning, and on an obfuscation of the reality that Daggett purported to represent. When he asked if he would support Daggett in the election, he declined to answer.

In Chicago Anne said, "Clearly a beaten and bitter man."

"Until we came along, he was the front runner," said Terry.

"He had dreams of how he would run for the White House against Hatford, win it and then sit in the Oval Office which he has, of course, visited many times," Alan added. "This is victory. We have beaten him. We won."

"Let's wait until the total is official," said Mitchell Fiddler.

Terry smiled, always the precise one. "We'll wait, then we'll have everyone in here for one hell of a party. We'll get everyone out for a real rest and then we'll concentrate on another Senator by the name of Hatford. Hatford's had a little trouble. He hasn't won every state, but we will have and we'll have the political momentum."

Adrian Daggett rolled forward, and indeed they did win every state. But they didn't wait to start their vacation and their planning. When they had the required number of delegates pledged at the convention to assure the nomination, Adrian continued a reduced schedule.

The victory party was at the Palmer House. In the great ballroom the band mixed disco and slow dancing. The tables banked three deep around the dance floor were lighted with candles. Around the room were the flags of the states in which they had won primaries. Adrian and Pamela, Terry and Annalee, Alan and Lauren, and Nancy went to each table to greet and congratulate. There was a short program with a speech by Adrian. The old guilded room rang with cheers of "Daggett, Daggett, Daggett." Only the campaign TV was allowed.

The Falcon spun up from Harrisburg with Susan and Ian, Alvin, and Tony. "Cynthia Reese" was invited recognizing her contribution to the knock-out punch in South Carolina. Earl flew in and danced cheek to cheek with Karen. During the slow numbers Michelle Proust danced cheek to cheek with Bill Haber with mixed feelings. She was a spy celebrating the opponent's victory. How should she feel, she thought? Bill said they needed to go on and do their part of the celebration. Nancy introduced "Cynthia Reese" to a number of the campaign people, one of them was Michelle. Neither Michelle nor "Cynthia" knew of the other's duplicity.

Ian and Susan and the others from Harrisburg mingled mainly with the senior people. Ian liked parties and he also liked victories. To avoid attention, the Harrisburg group left before the party ended and flew home to sleep in their own beds. One conversation that Ian wanted to have, however, was with Anne Russell, and Anne's husband Robert. The MacAulliffe's offered Anne and Bob the use of their townhouse in San Miguel. Ever concerned about key people and their welfare, Ian sensed Anne was straining her marriage. He thought ten days in San Miguel might appeal to her and it did.

They accepted the gracious offer and two days later were on the Continental flight connecting from Houston and to Leon. Anne had never been to San Miguel and once she was there her thoughts of the campaign began to fade away. On the second night they had dinner at the restaurant Baranquilla and then walked all the way across the town past the square and the cathedral, and up their street. Anne was lovely in beige slacks and a white and rose sweater. They sat in the courtyard and had a glass of sweet wine. They then went up the outside stairs to the balcony to the master bedroom. Bob called Anne to stand in the moonlight while he undressed her. As she stood naked and Bob started his lovemaking she felt the world come back into focus. Each day they went to the club for tennis and golf. Each night they selected a restaurant. They talked and they made love. When the limousine came to take them back to the airport each felt they needed more time.

Karen wanted to see Earl, but she also wanted to see her family. She flew to Cedar Rapids. Her mother and father met her and took her home for her favorite dinner; pot roast, and buzzing excited talk about her being on national television. She had to tell the stories of the campaign and all that she had done. Her father was hugely proud of her. She was good Iowa stock and was his daughter. Her brother and sister were awed. She called Earl at 10:00 p.m., went to sleep and did not wake up until just before ten in the morning. That evening the aunts, uncles, and cousins came over to a party: they all had questions about her life.

The next afternoon with her skis and boots, briefcase and luggage they took her back to the airport. Earl met her in Des Moines and they connected on to Denver and Vail. Since that was where the meeting was to be, they thought they might as well enjoy themselves before getting back to business. They skied, they swam, and they talked about their future.

Nancy went to visit her children at their respective schools. Terry and Annalee headed for Martinique. Alan and Lauren and two other couples flew to Virgin Gorda for five days of sailing on the Caribbean where it was impossible to be interrupted by telephone calls. Adrian and Pamela, who were unable for political reasons to leave the United States on vacation, headed for Naples and time with their parents. Adrian realized, as he grew older that he grew happier each year that his father and mother were still alive and found a great comfort when the old man's arms went around him.

In high school in the depression Hugh Daggett couldn't visualize college. He got his diploma and then, reasoning that war would soon break out in Europe, he joined the U.S. Army. In a year he was a Sergeant and married his high school sweetheart. Adrian was born and then his sister Jenna in the months after Pearl Harbor when his father was jungle fighting. Hugh was among the first to leave for

Australia and the New Guinea campaign. He came home from the Philippines as a master sergeant three years and seven months later. He went to work in a small fabricating firm where he became essentially an engineer and an operating executive. His company built and installed custom machinery and then developed its own product line. Money was set aside for Adrian and Jenna who were star students and school leaders. Adrian's mother, Eleanor, became a department manager at the regional office of Aetna. Jenna went into the Peace Corps after college, came back to medical school, and became a medical missionary in Central America. She came home with malaria and then joined a hospital staff in Fort Wayne. She married an executive friend of Adrian's and had two children.

When Hugh was 55, he went on a part-time schedule at his company and enrolled at a community college with Ellie's enthusiastic support. He traded in a 4.0 GPA for admission to Case Western Reserve where he completed his degree in psychology in three years. Still with a 4.0, he entered Pittsburgh Theological Seminary. He served the Presbyterian Church as a temporary minister and a hospital chaplain. His family was there for his first sermon and his first serving of communion. When he was 65 he became the permanent minister of a nearby church. He retired after 10 years, but continued working at the hospitals, nursing homes, and with mentally ill people for whom he became an advocate. The family joke was that the state legislature of Ohio dreaded the warm weather when Hugh and Ellie Daggett returned from Florida, and the Florida legislature breathed easier. He told anyone who would listen about the mentally ill, the ignored people.

After three days of golf, tennis, talk, and some good home-cooked food, Adrian and Pamela also headed to Vail for some skiing before the meetings began. Pamela's parents came for breakfast and they all rode to the airport in a big limousine. The morning air was cool, but they were warmed by the sun as they said their good byes. The two sets of parents had become friendly and saw each other on the occasions of televised events where Adrian was starring.

Standing in a circle Adrian's father put an arm around Adrian's shoulders and another around Pamela's waist.

"We are all so proud of you and what you are doing and how you are doing it. You live a grand life. You have your own plane, and the trappings of power. If you win, immense power will be yours. I can only say remember you have a God, Adrian and Pamela, and that He has certain purposes which we must try to understand. Think of what is really important to Him. Freedom and truth are gifts from God. I believe hungry people, people without opportunity or a means of hope, young people who have no sense of their role in society, people who are sick and without proper care, and old people who are alone are the most important people in God's eyes. Try to figure out what God thinks needs to be done. If you do, you can be a great President, Adrian, and Pamela, you will be a great first lady."

Pamela's mother kissed her and held her cheek and told her, "We all love you and Adrian, my dear." She stepped back, "We talk a lot in our church about the morals of America. You hear your political friends talk about them too, but they don't say anything. There is only one answer for immoral people, Adrian, and that is to take them back to God and back to a religion focussed on morals and ethics. They have pushed God out of our schools and out of daily life. We will not have a peaceful society until we bring Him back. God be with you both and protect you."

They hugged, then the four parents stood and waved while the sleek jet, engines whistling, taxied out to the end of the runway. It turned slowly and after a pause gunned into its take-off roll to its thundering leap into the sky. It left behind the most poignant scene of Adrian's life.

☆ **Chapter 23** ☆

ADRIAN CUT OFF his skiing early for an afternoon meeting with Mitchell Fiddler, which Mitchell had requested. He left Pamela on the slopes and, following lunch, headed for his suite with the entourage of bodyguards. After a shower he was fully relaxed and was pulling a sweater over his head when the secret service agent knocked on the door and showed Mitchell in. He was glad to see him; they shook hands. "How is our store of cash, Mitch?"

"It's rebuilding nicely," Mitch said, "and, of course, the Federal funding will be dropping in. I think I can tell you we have plenty of money for the campaign. The job now is to raise soft funds to dilute Ian's contribution as much as possible. The fundraising isn't over."

"It's never over, I've been in politics before," said Adrian. "What's up?"

"I want to talk with you about the general election campaign. You know it's going to be different from the primary campaign. This is fought across the country in every state, but it's the big states that count. Each one becomes a battleground of sorts."

"I think Anne will play the national media well, off the issues campaign," Adrian said. "We'll get the jump on them as best we can in the speeches scheduled in states which still will have primaries."

"Adrian, I have raised something over $65 million for the primary campaign, enough so we could spend freely without the constraints of taking the federal funds."

Mitchell saying that he had raised the money stretched the point. He did a good job by direct appeals, but there was something good to sell.

"My concern is that we'll have more limited funds in the general election to do a bigger job," he said. "Bigger by half or more, and with more focused and worthy opposition. I will continue to raise funds, but it is going to be difficult for me to continue this work if the campaign is going to be continued to be run the way we ran the primary campaign."

Adrian saw Mitchell was making a move early, before the plans were set, before the staff meeting.

"I recognize that there is a huge amount of talent in Anne Russell and Nancy Letersky along with a high measure of enthusiasm for you," Mitchell said. "I have huge respect for Alan Jacobs. At his young age he is an able political strategist, among the best. But I cannot continue to work with Terry Leelan and Roger Bennett and this herky-jerk, shotgun mode which defies all the principals of political campaigning. They play this "issues game" which they have sold you on, and it is not the way elections are won. We have to get back to a much more conventional campaign philosophy. I am here to try to rescue your presidential campaign. It comes down basically to this. I want you to appoint me as campaign chairman where I can utilize the great talent we have to win the election."

Adrian felt anger welling within him, "Isn't that sort of like firing the coaches that got you through the playoffs and hiring new ones for the Super Bowl?"

"We haven't been in playoffs, Adrian. The primaries are pre-season. There's a whole bunch of games coming up that are a whole lot tougher than anything we've done so far. I want to call the shots in this campaign from now on, with your consent, of course."

Adrian crossed his arms in front of his chest. "Mitchell, you can have any job you want in the administration, but I want you to stay in charge of finance," he said.

"Adrian, you have to recognize that Terry Leelan and Roger Bennett are idealists who are practicing something that is hardly practical and has never been proven."

"You've got to get specific, Mitch."

"The American people when they go to the polls have two or three issues in mind, Adrian. The most you'll ever find anyone will comment on are maybe six. Three of them are their own issues and three of them are issues that were developed in the campaign. You're talking about a dozen or more issues. I heard there were 20 on Terry's list. You can't talk about 20 issues in a campaign, Adrian. They won't stick."

"Maybe the problem with American Democracy, Mitch, is that politicians don't talk about issues at all. They don't talk about solutions to problems. They talk vaguely about the problems and vaguely about what should be done. They don't deal with any of the tough issues at all if they can avoid them. They focus on partisan banter."

"They may know something about being elected, Adrian. You can't talk through 20 issues and get elected President of the United States. The people aren't interested. You have to create an impression of who you are and something about what you are going to do which is what every other successful politician does. You can't do anything until you get elected, Adrian. I know you have some specific objectives. I support most of them, but you've got to get elected."

"I thought what we might do is figure out what we are going to do if we get elected, tell people and let them decide."

"That's how it's suppose to be, but it isn't. People do what they have to do to get elected. They tell the people what they want to hear. They wait until after they get elected to tell them the bad things."

"We've already said what you think are bad things."

"Only in the primaries, Adrian. People have short memories. Whatever we do now will be forgotten before the Fourth of July."

Adrian thought that there was still hope to salvage Mitchell since he hadn't said he would resign if he wasn't appointed. "Mitch, we can't change a winning organization at this point," he said. "We can only change it if it starts to lose. But there is a dichotomy in our philosophies. I want to change the way Americans campaign for president. I want issue staffs like the one we have in Cleveland to hammer out the policies as best they can and to bring them to the American people. I want a clear understanding of what this administration intends to do if it gets elected. You realize that 45 people are going to sit together until we beat out our strategy. All of them are going to be in high positions in that administration mostly in the White House. You are one of them. I happen to think the campaign we put on had a lot to do with the money that came in. People want a truly issues-oriented Presidency and an issues-oriented campaign for it. People want to be told what's going on."

"Adrian, since 1974, the people have not believed the government," said Mitch. "They don't believe what you say about issues. We are living with a legacy of Richard Nixon who lied to the American people. A case can be made that Harry Truman was the last president to tell the people the truth. Eisenhower and Dewey started using spin-doctors. I don't think Terry Leelan understands that."

"It could be that Terry Leelan understands that American people want somebody whom they can trust to tell them what is really happening."

"Adrian, one reason that campaigns don't take these issue positions is that if they voice something people don't like they suddenly become vulnerable. They can't take it back. You've got to be careful of what you say. George Romney destroyed himself by saying he was brainwashed in Vietnam. Gerry Ford lost the election in the debate when he said Eastern European countries had certain freedoms of choice. It looks to me like you're going to climb out on 11 different limbs and all they have to do is get one."

"Mitch, we're trying to develop an offensive here. What's the best defense? We had Porter, Perona, and Findlayson going in circles and coming back with blatant generalities."

"Adrian, there are other people who share my opinion."

To hear that Mitchell was politicking upset Adrian. He didn't want to have a publicized major reorganization, particularly in campaign finance. It was best to keep it together.

"All right, Mitch, if we can't come to a clear program in the meetings that start tomorrow, I want you to speak out," he said. "I want you to challenge the issues theory in open debate. I want you to bring in people to support you whoever they may be. I will invite them. Dominick I know is one, and then we can hash it out. But for now I want the issues-oriented campaign to bring the people into the game. We have to have the support of the people, Mitch, and hope that they elect a Democratic Congress so that we can do some of these things we're talking about."

"Do you appoint me as campaign chairman if we decide to change the direction?"

"We'll give the orders to Terry and his group, and if it doesn't work out I will indeed replace him. With whom I don't know, but I do know that we've got to have a specific strategy and we have to have the resources to accomplish it. If we don't have specific goals and objectives well known in advance we'll lose."

When Mitchell left and the door was closed Adrian said "damn" out loud. He resented Mitchell's discussing their strategy with contributors, which was probably what he had done. He was also troubled that Mitchell had some good points. They were in a different game in the general election and they needed to think their way through it. But, he believed passionately that the American people had to be involved in general elections and not just observe them. He loved the debate show Nancy had come up with, which continued as a monthly event on PBS. He wanted to tell people what the issues really were, but he also wanted to win. Were the two goals compatible? Regrettably it was a valid question. Pamela came in red-cheeked and young looking from the skiing. He kissed her, and then started telling her what had happened. As she undressed and took a shower they talked about it.

THERE WAS ALSO discord at Harbour Island. There were no vacations after Adrian's total went over the top. The vacation week for the Daggett campaign was a week of preparation for an Executive Committee meeting. Gallosey kept telling Ward how he could not abide failure. Helene and her staff prepared a very careful presentation which set forth the facts of the case. A central point was that the staff recommended no further action in the primaries and Sadovan and Gallosey had insisted on doing more. They had a rehearsal session where Helene gave the presentation and Harold Smalley played the part of Gallosey and Sadovan.

It was Sadovan who called to say he would bring everyone in his plane from Miami. Helene and Ward went to the airport to meet them. Standing beside Ward she felt tense and she could feel tenseness in him. He did not like adversarial meetings he could not control and he did not control POLACO the way he controlled American Carbon Products.

The initial greetings were informal and casual. The baggage, golf clubs, and Sadovan's tennis bags were unloaded into the cars. The mood was cool as they crossed the bay to the island. Helene wondered if Sadovan recognized his mistake in forcing the primary battle or whether the others had criticized him during whatever conversation they had prior to coming to Harbour Island. Helene noticed he had lost weight and looked very fit. Radion seemed more morose or threatening than Sadovan.

The first business was a tour of the completed intelligence center. By 11 a.m. they were up the elevator to the upstairs conference room, where they would meet and have lunch.

Helene gave a report of the struggle in the primaries with facts and figures, polls and vote counts. She showed how the POLACO intervention had been staged with shaded maps indicating the states in which the foundation ads were circulated and where there were other activities. It was a precise description of how the resources of POLA-

CO had been deployed. She analyzed the Annabelle Mayberry affair showing the effect on the polls. Then she answered questions.

"I still don't see how the Annabelle Mayberry thing failed," Helene said.

"There must have been a leak of some kind," said Ryan Keeley.

"We have absolutely no evidence of that. We do have evidence of a very rapid response by PENMET, who had their investigative people from Jacksonville moving to St. Louis and Springfield so fast they got to Veronica Torblad the evening of the announcement. They were effective in convincing her to retract her statement. Then there was the information from the banks which was decisive."

"You couldn't stonewall it?" asked Radion.

"Not with federal investigators involved. Ian MacAulliffe did that. He used his political clout. Then they offered to stop everything if we would have Annabelle recant."

"There was a deal. How did you get to that?" asked Radion.

"Tony Destito called me, we had a meeting in St. Louis." Helene frowned. "It was my judgment we had to stop the business or they would drag it on, releasing bits of information at a time to get the maximum effect. Then there would be a lawsuit by Adrian Daggett against Annabelle Mayberry and a process of discovery assisted by the federal investigators. We had to keep that from happening."

"Did you agree with this Ward?" asked Radion.

"I did."

"Were you consulted in advance?" asked Radion.

"No, Helene has the authority to make these decisions."

Helene waited for an accusation that she was incompetent to do so, but she didn't hear it. Instead Ryan said, "There's no question that was the best judgment. I congratulate you, Helene, for taking advantage of the chance to deal."

"How are these agreements recorded?" asked Bernt.

"In handwriting, we have a copy, they have a copy," said Helene.

"Is there anyone who questions this judgment?" Ward asked.

"I fully support it," Alex Peterson declared. "We'd done a foolish thing against Helene's advice and the advice of her staff and she got us out of it without any exposure."

"With minimum exposure, Alex," Helene intersected. "My guess is there are two or three investigative reporters working on the question of where the money came from."

"Are they going to be able to find anything out?" asked Ryan with a slight twinge in his voice.

"PENMET stopped after interviewing the bank in Cannes," said Helene. "Tony Destito told me he had the names of the clerk and officer that opened the account in Geneva. They went through these banks like a bowling ball through pins."

"Aren't we going to take any action against these bankers?"

"We don't see that we'd get anything from it, and we'd reopen the issue."

"I think we should take the job of that woman down in St. Louis who spilled the beans about the money passing through Annabelle's account," said Radion.

"We won't do that for the same reason. The issue is closed. This whole process has ended. I advised against it. Now we must martial our resources for the real fight."

There was a pause. "Mendos, you haven't said a word," said Ryan.

"I wanted to see how this woman handled herself under your questioning," Mendos replied. 'I think we should respect her judgment and her ability to accomplish our objectives, and I think we had best not overrule her judgment again. It's always nice, Helene, to savor the victories, but you also have to deal with the defeats. We tried something and it failed. In my judgment you kept it from wrecking us."

"Thank you, Mendos," said Helene.

"I do have a couple of questions about your meeting with Destito. Where was it?"

"At a conference room at McDonnell-Douglas/Boeing."

"You were in St. Louis?"

"That's where the action on Annabelle Mayberry was."

"Who was at the meeting?"

"I took Edgar Slaughter. Tony had Nancy Letersky with him."

"Did you sweep the room for bugs?"

"Tony had a local private detective and an assistant there. He allowed Edgar to approve their equipment and their results."

"Mr. Destito thinks of things."

"He does. He's a good person, but tough minded."

"Did you sleep with him on the trip?"

That hurt Helene. The question was half an accusation, and it reminded her that it was over; that it was unlikely she would ever kiss him again, that "God's good time" was a fantasy. "No," she said.

"Then I think we should get on with the future," he said.

Helene recovered her composure. "Marsha has prepared a situation report," she said, "which we can all look at. This assesses the strengths and weaknesses of the opposing organizations and gives the intelligence about the senior people. Keep in mind that we have two well-inserted moles. One was on the traveling staff during the primary campaign, and the other was in the public relations department at the corporate level at PENMET. During the South Carolina primary fight she was temporarily assigned to assist in the production of advertisements which replied to our ads. She was able to tell us that the governor of South Carolina had contacted the Daggett campaign about shifting his allegiance from Porter. We were able to stop that."

"I won't ask how," said Ryan.

Helene showed the television ads which the Southern Conservative Coalition had used and tapes of the opposing ads that the Daggett campaign had produced. Then she crisply laid out the plan, giving them diagrams of the issues as they planned to respond to them and the issues they would raise. She showed them the things they would use in each of the states in their anticipated relationship with the Hatford campaign. There was dialogue and discussion as she went through the program. Ward chipped in with his support.

At the end Mendos said, "I said we should not overrule you in any decisions you make, Helene, but we also have to direct you to accomplish certain generalized objectives. You've got to stop Daggett from being elected because he and MacAulliffe were smart enough to recognize the one way they could destroy us. You have described the beginning of a well thought out campaign, but I don't see decisive strokes. There must be something that cuts Daggett down to size so that he can be beaten with reasonable certainty. I haven't heard that yet."

"A lot happens in the course of a political campaign, Mendos," said Ryan. "A strong good effort like this should help Hatford very much because you have to remember that Hatford is not Porter. He has the full weight of the Republican Party behind him and massive funding. We are the leveraging factor because we can concentrate on the issues that Daggett wants to stand on. Every time he opens an issue and we choose to refute it, we can attack him. With resourcefulness we should win."

"I agree with you, Ryan," said Sadovan, "that we should win. But I want something decisive. The stroke, the surprise attack Daggett and his advisors don't expect. That's what wins it."

"Whatever kind of stroke can there be?" asked Bernt. "There are limited options in politics. We have tried the dirty tricks, as you call them, and they almost blew us up."

"A blow from which Daggett has difficulty to recover," said

Sadovan.

Ward held up his hand to halt the conversation. "Tell him about it, Helene," said Ward.

"We are going to try to force Daggett into a defensive position on his major issues," she said. "Paying down the debt which requires raising corporate taxes and forgoing tax cuts will make a pocketbook issue. We agree with his policy of maintaining the investment of the aerospace industry and perhaps even expanding it to maintain a wide margin between the American nation in military and any other technologies. But on the matter of foreign involvement, while we agree on the use of American power, we can, if this board agrees, start an organization, Mothers Against Wars. We can call it "MAWS." It'll be a catchy name. This, by the way, is a product of a conversation between Erla and Marsha, when I asked them the same question you asked. It's their idea, we have to make a judgment. Is it more important to defeat Daggett or is it more important to have our way in foreign involvement which he happens to agree with?"

"Regardless of what we do," said Ryan, "congratulate your two people for a good concept."

Sadovan noticed Helene had credited those who came up with the idea. "Tell me more about how you'd organize this."

"After Daggett's first major speech on the subject when his people start pumping the issue we'll fund another entity which will start MAWS. Erla and Marsha have people picked out to do it."

"I don't like the idea of arguing against foreign involvement in the United States," said Bernt. "This is a serious issue in Europe, particularly in Germany since we can't use our forces outside the country, and the same for Japan."

"It's a choice," Helene said. "I've asked the same question of the staff. The answer I get is that MAWS could simply be folded up after the election if we beat him. If he wins, it can stay in place as an advocate group."

"I could only agree to this," said Bernt, "if the organization is disbanded regardless of the outcome of the election."

"We assume your success, Helene," said Sadovan looking her in the eye.

"Nothing is certain, Mendos," said Helene. "When we are against people like Anne Russell and Nancy Letersky. We've all felt the impact of their effectiveness. We had to win South Carolina, and we couldn't."

"What are you going to do about the coastal development restrictions? We have big developer customers who are very upset," said

Alex Peterson.

"We are getting some consultants together on that, Alex, and we'll have a scientific opinion of the need for restriction of wetlands development."

"They argue scientifically, Helene," said Alex.

"The science will be based on the percentage of the wetlands that have actually been developed," Helene said. "Our polls indicate substantial support for the Daggett position. It may be difficult to refute. Hatford might not want to resist it. We may have to use the foundations to soften it."

"All of the financial members will be concerned because they have huge business with coastal developers," said Radion.

"What's the position concerning education?" asked Ryan.

"The response to Daggett's proposal has been very favorable according to Hirsch. We may not be able to resist that directly. However, we will draw up a list of probable expenditures and wonder by how much he is going to have to raise taxes in order to pay for all he wants to do. We'll have economic consultants work on that and add the caveats that the markets remain free. The whole idea of restraining speculation on the currency market has got some support. A lot of people are thinking about it."

"You have to stop that, Helene. Do you have any idea what the fees on currency speculation are? What the profits are? There must be argument for all types of free markets. Once some damn liberal like Daggett gets a hold of market restraint he will over apply it," said Radion.

"My take of Daggett is that he is a substantial businessman and he understands markets," said Sadovan. "You have been doing too much on the currency markets and you should stop it Radion. In fact, perhaps it should be the policy of POLACO to voluntarily restrain the currency markets."

"Absolutely not," said Alex. "We must have no markets restrained. You have to agree to that, Mendos."

"What kind of thinking is that, Mendos?" Radion asked.

"Too much greed, Radion, it draws attention. You got into the headlines with Thailand and hitting the baht. You didn't care what you did."

"The Thai government was stupid. The market disciplined them."

"Since when is shorting a currency in concert with other speculators called 'market discipline?'"

"The market invited the action."

"Manipulation is not part of market discipline."

"There should be no regulation," said Alex.

"I will agree we will close on the restraint of markets," said Sadovan. "We can continue at dinner or tomorrow. I would like to have the honor of a tennis game, Helene, while these others go swing their sticks. I hope you will all walk so that you get exercise instead of taking carts."

WHILE SHE CHANGED in her apartment, Helene wondered what she was seeing in Mendos Sadovan. Was there in addition to the intellect and understanding, a willingness to admit the mistake of forcing the confrontation in the primaries against her judgment? Did he have a sense of fairness in dealing in the markets? Did he have feelings for her, or sexual attraction? She guessed he couldn't have accomplished what he had as a corporate leader without admitting mistakes. His staff was loyal to him. That usually meant good communications, frankness and fairness.

To speed the tennis games and to forward community relations, Helene had allowed the local school to use the courts for tennis instruction up to 4 p.m. each afternoon, after which they were cleaned and smoothed for the staff players. The boys and girls stayed on to chase balls, for which they were hired at generous wages. Edgar assigned a security agent to watch the people on the courts, to see that they did no more than use the bathrooms and snack bar. He agreed it made POLACO look less forbidding and secretive, but at the same time he wanted it no less secure.

When Helene arrived at the courts, Sadovan was warming up with a Bahamian boy they knew as Kevin. Sadovan stopped when she arrived. When the students saw there was going to be a match, five of them crowded around asking to be chosen. They decided to have two. Sadovan selected a tall girl who volleyed with Helene for her warm up. When she was ready, she met Sadovan at the net. "What should the stakes be?" he asked.

She smiled at him. "Your choice, Mendos."

"I'm glad the $1,000 you won the last time we played put us on a first name basis."

"Of course."

He looked at her in her two-piece tennis dress which showed her midriff when she served. Her arms and legs were perfectly formed, smooth with muscles underneath. He had felt the conditioning. She was a powerful woman with a beautiful face, an attractive body, and a superb intellect which made her utterly desirable to him.

"To have the same stakes as last time is like paying you a fee."

"You thought I was just another helpless girl."

"I want to see you play as hard as you can play, the same as last time, but with a side bet. One thousand dollars that you can't win a love set."

She gave him the balls to serve and immediately saw that he had been practicing and taking some lessons. He was able to hold his serve three times, before she broke him to win 6-3.

"Is this the love set?" he asked.

She smiled, then tossed the ball for the first serve of the second set. She bore down, thinking of nothing but the game and beating him. She concentrated on her groundstrokes and serves, and on her footwork. He tried to ace her with his strength and succeeded twice, but she had timed his serves and returned them to score. He served at love-five. "My last chance," he said across the net. She grinned. She knew he had not been concentrating in the beginning, but now he would to save a $1000. He served and she returned it, and they rallied until she got a passing shot. It was deuce. He got an ace and an advantage point. He missed on his next serve, and she hammered the second. At deuce, she returned a hard serve into the ad court and went to the net to take the advantage point. She returned to his backhand corner and saw that he couldn't get his racquet on the ball. She ran forward again to smash the ball past him to the base line. He came to the net, and took her hand. "I've learned my lesson," he said. "I will not play again for money. Let's rest." They went to the verandah for lemonade. "You play so very well I wanted to see how good you would be when you really concentrated," Sadovan said. "You would be ranked in the top hundred."

"I love the game," she said. "I love studying it; practicing it and I like to beat men in singles."

"I gather you do."

"You've been practicing, I can see that."

"To try to beat you, but that will never happen unless you injure yourself."

"So for you the game is more than just exercise."

"I have three passions: My business, women, and tennis."

She took that in and scrutinized his face. "Why did you join POLACO, Mendos?"

"Ward's idea was a good one. Democracy has become untrustworthy.

It used to be essentially a government, now it's essentially a power game. We're in a good position to win the power game. When most of the people don't really care what happens, making laws becomes a matter of who has the most influence. Now we have Ian MacAulliffe and Adrian Daggett. The future is not so certain."

"What do you expect to get?"

"Free markets, defeated liberals; a stable conservative government; and, if necessary, a corporate state."

"Do you believe that democracy can be reformed?"

"I believe that if POLACO is successful it will be good for the country, and the world. Business has to have more power in Washington than the single interest groups. I don't understand Ian MacAulliffe's motives. He should be on our side. Sometime I would like to find out what he really thinks."

Helene, for all of her intellectual curiosity had been too busy to consider that. Or, was it that she didn't want to think about it? Why examine details of the motives of the enterprise that was making her rich?

"If for some reason POLACO is found out and it fails, which I don't think would be your fault, you must come to work for me," said Sadovan. "There are so many things that we could do. For one thing you could probably run one of my companies."

"Is that because you think I'm good, or you want me around?"

"I would like to have you work with me," he said. "But I admit I'm jealous of Tony Destito."

So he had finally signaled it. "I think that affair has ended," said Helene.

"How did you bargain effectively with Tony when he was your lover."

"Easy. He made some mistakes."

"How did he get to be your lover?"

"I chose him, when I knew he was interested," she said. "He's an extraordinary man."

"And you are an extraordinary woman. How do extraordinary men get 'chosen?'"

"By practicing patience."

She couldn't turn him off. She wasn't sure she wanted to. That was the best thing to say. Getting involved with Sadovan might be like getting involved with Napoleon.

IN THE MORNING session at the boardroom they reviewed the decisions. Adrian Daggett would be denied the Presidency and the full weight of POLACO would go in support of Senator Hatford. Independently POLACO would start the MAWs organization at a time to be determined for maximum effectiveness. The program for the development of Congressional candidates would be accelerated to have as many candidates as possible ready for the off-year election in the event that Daggett might win, despite all the best efforts.

Sadovan made a strong point of internal security to be sure that the secrets were kept. They complimented Helene for adding a unit to the security forces which also had extra benefits. They also agreed with a plan of contacting the Hatford Campaign through the Southern Conservative Coalition of which she, of course, was the executive director. They talked about other initiatives that POLACO might take.

At the end, Sadovan, still the leader of the pack, said, "I think this is a good plan, Ward, and the resources that we have are going to accomplish it. I recognize the skill of the opponents. Accomplishing these objectives will require the attention and concentration of everyone. You know what they say about winners: they find a way to win because they hate losing. I hate losing. We came under this arrangement with you, Ward, because of the objectives established. We suffered a setback because of MacAulliffe. He changed the game on us. We've got to be successful. Your personal credibility is at stake. We have marshaled a lot of money here."

Ward didn't like that. He hadn't envisioned board meetings with tough questions. He was going to be a kingmaker. That was the up side, now he was on the down side and had to scramble back, or better, power his way back.

Helene recognized the challenge to her. There was more she had to prove. She wasn't sure if she would rather have Erla's job, but she was there. They paid her very well. Where else could she make $30,000 a month?

WITH BOTH ENJOYMENT and apprehension, Adrian watched Terry run the meetings on the national campaign. He also watched Mitchell Fiddler and Dominick Kluczinski. He had to decide if he could still trust them and whether or not he should tell Terry about his conversation with Mitchell. Terry had proven himself to be a motivating leader of high-powered people and had also demonstrated that he could manage money. He collaborated with Mitchell Fiddler in a businesslike way and he kept arguments about minor issues from becoming major ones. Terry rarely needed to follow up; his staff was superb; he could fully rely on them.

The aspect of Terry, however, that most impressed Adrian was his concentration on the campaign with a total refusal to think about what would happen after the election. He was the obvious White House Chief of Staff, yet he, like Adrian, wanted to demonstrate a political campaign based on issues and debate and to establish a new level in American politics.

The first task was to form a national campaign organization. Each state had to have a chairman. Some were chosen from the original clutch of Democratic supporters. New ones needed to be named. There had to be an effective campaign manager in each state to organize and direct work at the local level through party channels. One absolute essential was getting Democrats to vote Democratic on Election Day. The organization was as important as the rhetoric and the fancy national publicity and advertising. Polling by state had to be organized, so campaign managers and leaders would know clearly where they stood. Parker Lothan was at the meeting.

On the second day they went through the states one-by-one, starting with the most important, California, New York, and Texas. They looked at the latest polling data, at the primary results, at the issues sensitivity and at media relations.

On the third day, they began to talk about how they would organize and operate as a team. There were some new members, the six salaried professionals from the Sandellot campaign. The senior people were George King and Tom Haynes, mid-thirties, African-American men with bright eyes and eager faces who both had Capitol Hill experience on committee staffs. King had experience as a public official in Georgia where he was elected mayor of a small town. Haynes had a Ph.D. in political science and economics and spent four years with the Joint Economic Committee.

Adrian and Pamela invited the new group for dinner with their wives and were impressed. They particularly were taken by Lucile Cush, a graduate student for a Ph.D. in political science at Duke where she also helped coach the track team. Light skinned and lithe, she was attractive and dressed like she had a fashion consultant. The army had provided her access to education. She was over thirty, had a reserve rank of Captain and an offer that any time she wanted to come back in military intelligence she would be welcome. Lucile had much higher ambitions.

Alice Lofton was impressive as an administrative person. A petite, demure, dark skinned woman in her '50s, she had handled all of the tasks of the central office for Sandellot. She had campaign and staff experience in Congressional and Senatorial contests. Calvin Ripkin, a chubby live wire and the public relations and speechwriter for Sandellot, was already in Anne's group with Harris Winthrup, who did the press work for Sandellot.

Merrick and George King liked each other when they met. They sat together at the meetings. Good chemistry seemed natural between Karen and Lucile. Terry and Alan watched who got along with whom during the first two days and on the third day they started making proposals. Louise Sczyniac would continue as the chief press coordinator, assisted by Winthrup, and would utilize her primary staff including Michelle Proust who received compliments when her name was mentioned. Alice Lofton would take over the central advancing support.

Merrick, as national coordinator, and George King, assistant national coordinator, were responsible for the state, county, city, and town offices. A flying squad working for them would undertake commando duties where organizations needed to be boosted. Jack Wood, Louellen Parsons, Tom Haynes, and Karen Crezna were named to the spread along with Lucile. Tom was designated as the field commander. Each would have offices at the headquarters where they could carry out assignments in Chicago and where their messages could pile up when they were away. Nancy designated Karen to focus on the soft ad video production with Lucile assisting with the writing. Nancy pointed out "Cynthia Reese" had been very helpful in the effort in South Carolina and would be available in the event of an emergency.

The fourth day, Terry, Nancy, and Anne began the issues discussion. Adrian watched Mitchell and Dominick for signs of strain. They covered each major issue which they had opened and then planned which issues they would try to steal from Hatford. They went through them all.

No one there could exactly recall, when Mitchell Fiddler interrupted. "These are too many issues, we can't explain them all. In fact, we shouldn't explain too much about any. Can't any of you see that we will overwhelm the voters? They can't absorb all of this."

Anne and Nancy felt a pause.

"Mitchell," Anne said. "We won the primaries in five straight. We embarrassed our opposition in the New Hampshire debate. The money has poured in; Republicans are joining our constituency. The people want issues and we're giving them issues. We are destroying perceptions which were reality, and were wrong. People want to hear the truth and they want us to face it."

"Who says we monopolize the truth?" Mitchell asked. "We are going to crash with another truth and they'll sink us on one issue. Look what happened to Dukakis."

"His staff couldn't seem to solve the problem of the anecdote, about the man who was let out of jail by flooding the country with anecdotes of hundreds, who were convicted of crimes on faulty or false testimony or evidence," Nancy said loudly.

"Who are you to think you can handle any problems that might come up?"

"Mitchell," Anne said. "We have the best issues staff ever, we'll use them."

"We'll also take Hatford apart in the debate," Nancy added.

The middle level and junior people fell silent and listened. Nancy was frightened by the acrimony.

"This is an issues campaign," Roger Bennett said quietly. "We are good on the issues, the real ones. We out-played the opponents."

"Do you think you're going to out-play Hatford and POLACO?"

"We'll risk losing the confidence of the people if we change," Anne stated.

"The polls show we're on the right track, Mitch," Alan said. "It's hard to argue for change."

"What risk will we take if we just use the polls, to tell people what they want to hear, and attack our opponent like every other campaign does?"

"A big risk," said Terry. "A risk of the trust of Adrian. That trust comes from our telling them what we really believe. We'll be just another candidate with money."

"Mitch," Adrian addressed him, "We made a deal, you have to show how an opponent could exploit us on any position in a manner to which we can't respond."

Mitchell leaned back on his chair and looked at the ceiling. "It's so risky. No one ever does it this way."

"We won!" Nancy exclaimed.

"But we're now in a different war. All of the Republicans and POLACO are arranged against us."

"Everything is a risk, Mitch," Terry said. "What every other politician does will eventually ruin this country. It is implicit on democracy that the government must speak the truth. If it doesn't it is guilty of manipulation. That probably is the reason for the failure for most democracies."

"You are challenging public opinion," said Dominick.

"The public can't have a right opinion if it doesn't know the truth," Terry said. Adrian brought it to a close. "We're here Mitchell, Dominick, and any other who accepts your position to make a professional change in American government, through the means set forth in the Constitution. I don't know of any other way to do it. We'll continue until we see tangible evidence that we're wrong."

"It may be too late," Mitchell worried.

"You and Dominick must give us the warnings," Adrian challenged hoping they would accept the assignment and not resign. "Let's take a two minute recess."

Louellen was seated next to Nancy. "What's POLACO?" she asked.

"I'm not sure I heard what he said," Nancy answered.

On Saturday, before lunch, Terry and Adrian called a halt. They suggested everyone go swimming or skiing and then come to a party for dinner in the evening. They would resume with a brunch meeting after church on Sunday. Terry said he'd like to give everybody the whole Sunday off, but there were 211 days to go to the election.

The Daggett's hosted the party and called for casual dress. Everyone sipped cocktails and munched on Colorado smoked pike and a large wedge of cheese. During dinner of a salad, sautéd trout or roast beef and baked potatoes, a DJ set up his music. Adrian made sure he danced with all of the females and Pamela made sure she danced with the males. The DJ and his assistant mixed disco with slow and added a polka, a rhumba, and finally called square dances. It was like an office Christmas party with the spouses excluded except for Pamela. Terry, Alan, and Merrick also danced with all of the women. Dominick did get an extra drink into Mitchell Fiddler so that he followed him to the dance floor. It was a time of touching and bonding. They were going to go through a lot together in the next 211 days.

On Sunday the brunch buffet started at noon. 45 minutes later, Terry started the meeting. Everyone was refreshed for the toughest topic. In the United States increasing numbers of families were dysfunctional, increasing numbers of children were wayward, increasing numbers of adults were lost. It was a hard question, and a big issue that politicians rarely approached. America had to be the melting pot of cultures. It was a complex value system. In the earlier days, family and religion held it together. Then came television, two car families and prosperity; then two job families.

However, the teaching of values in schools was controversial. Court action took prayer out of public schools. Now the possible need was to put religion back. Back in the form of teaching the history of religion, the philosophy of religion, morals and ethics, and comparative religion. Terry had seen a quotation from The Reverend Wendy Heinz, a Presbyterian Minister in Western New York, who asked from her pulpit one Sunday, "How can we teach our children about truth, if we don't teach them about God?"

The following day, after some discussion of what their opponents might do, Terry, Anne, Nancy, Alan, and Merrick gave everyone their assignments. They put the organization in gear. Each had a clear view of his or her role, and they now had to make up their own specific plans. During the discourse on the issues, Nancy and Anne made notes of ideas for speeches and ads. In Anne's fantasy it was no longer a tournament field of medieval knights charging at each other, but a large scope of modern war with every conceivable electronic weapon focused on developing and communicating ideas.

HELENE WENT ALONE to Washington to meet with Hatford's campaign manager, Randall Dustin, and political consultant, Ross Chamberlain. She had with her some very substantial material. She had dispatched a package by Federal Express after she had made the appointment to let part of her message sink in before arriving. Normally she would stay at the Hay Adams or the Jefferson, but on foundation business she chose a less auspicious hotel, but one of good quality, the Canterbury, which offered a quiet neighborhood of townhouses on "N" Street.

Like most political campaigns Hatford's rented space was in a lesser building. It was on upper Connecticut Avenue. Helene decided she would get her exercise walking there, so dressed in a gray wool suit and a green plaid silk scarf, she put her pumps in her bag and wore her favorite running shoes for a two-mile trek. It was cool in Washington, she was glad she had her Burberry trench coat with its liner.

The receptionist smiled as she changed shoes. She had just finished and was looking at the Hatford posters when Randall Dustin and Ross Chamberlain came into the room. Randy was of medium height and build and Capitol Hill-looking with close-cropped graying hair over a pleasant smiling face. Ross was taller and somewhat younger with his blond hair long. Both wore gray suits. They greeted her warmly and showed her to an elevator. In the top floor conference room, Ross took her coat, noted the brand, and hung it in the closet. A coffee service was waiting.

After they sat down Randy said, "That was quite a package you sent." In it he had received Paul Melius' report of the investigation of Adrian Daggett, the special report on Daggett's resistance to the unions in his former plants, the scripts of a half-dozen new ads on the key issues and a business plan for a non-profit corporation called Mothers Against War.

"I hope you've had the opportunity to look at it."

"I've read every word."

"I came alone so we could talk about policy matters between us," Helene said. "You know there's a good staff behind this."

"We see that," said Randy. "We never thought that there would be an opening to seriously appeal to the union vote. An idea occurred to us; we can say 'what is the reality of the reality campaign?' and then name the union issue with the suggestion there may be others which have been hidden. We can play off the reaction he got in the Metal Workers Union, and make an issue out of it."

"How's the Senator's position with the unions?" Helene asked.

"The Missouri unions have always supported him because he's been fair with them and backed union issues on critical votes," Ross said.

"We haven't studied that," Helene said. "Maybe you can share a voting record with me."

"We have some disks." He made a note on the side of his pad.

"Can you give us a little more information on The Southern Conservative Coalition?" he asked.

"I'm sorry," Helene said, "I forgot to send that along with the other documents." She reached into her portfolio and pulled out two copies of the non-profit corporation filing which made no mention of POLACO and a brochure which Harold Smalley had done to solicit contributions. It was called "The Conservative Voice of the South."

"To whom do you report?"

"To the chairman."

"And everyone else reports to you?"

"That's correct."

"Were you involved in the Annabelle Mayberry affair?"

"I can't give you any information about that," said Helene.

Both men understood immediately what she meant.

"We have a question on what we should do about foreign policy. Senator Hatford has always been somewhat aggressive," Ross said.

"The argument against Daggett is the United Nations taking over the American foreign policy," Helene said. She watched them for a reaction.

"We would emphasize something on that to make a clear distinction between us and Daggett," Randy said. "Then you can start your Mothers Against War and make all kinds of noise. Who is going to start 'MAWS?'"

"A group of political professionals who can get it going. We have the right people to develop it. Some of them have political ambitions of their own so they might use this as their cause."

"I'm not sure letting this thing loose is a good idea. That's populism," said Ross.

"We'll kill it when your Senator is elected by cutting off the funds."

"You'll have to have private fundraising in order to legitimatize the thing."

"We'll see that the budget is bigger than the private fundraising."

"I'm still concerned," said Ross. "These things can develop a life of their own."

"Ross, let's get your man elected and we'll worry about MAW's after the election."

"I'm sorry, I don't like it."

"Let the polls speak for themselves. You're behind," Helene proffered.

"How would you go about sensitizing the unions?" asked Randy.

"I would feed it to the National Labor Council when it meets to endorse a candidate."

"I think the staffs should meet," said Randy, "and cooperate together. You're additional soft support. We need more information on the union situation than you've shown us."

"I think that we should meet every once in a while, to talk things over," said Ross.

"I'd be happy to," said Helene. "You can come to our headquarters in Jacksonville except the warm weather is coming. We'll fly here instead. That will save you the travel time."

"I look forward to that."

After the meeting, Helene took a stroll and reflected on the Hatford campaign. Her immediate reaction was that the staff was too

academic. She visualized complex policy discussions in the office
without action and decision. They certainly couldn't tell her what the
Hatford campaign strategy would be. She would decide about them
when she found out what they could do, but she thought they should
be farther along than they were. Didn't they recognize how hard the
job was to win?

She stopped at a park bench to put her running shoes on when her
cell phone rang. It was Ward. Sadovan wanted her to arrange a meeting with Ian MacAulliffe so he could attempt to persuade him to stop
supporting Daggett. She had to call Tony.

A MAJOR FOREIGN policy speech was scheduled for Adrian in
Stamford, Connecticut at the Stamford Forum for World Affairs.
Formed after World War II and associated with the possible locating
of the United Nations in the town, it became an ongoing organization
patronized by a broad spectrum of the community. The campaign
accepted the invitation to appear and publicized it as a major foreign
policy event. The normal format of the forum allowed questions and
discussion after the presentation which Adrian loved to do.

At the Stamford Marriott, a special dinner attended by dignitaries
was given by the Governor welcoming Adrian to the state. The
amount of media attention brought excitement to the ballroom. The
official party entered to a standing ovation as the governor escorted
Adrian and Pamela to the platform. The president of the forum
enlarged on Evans & Copeland's draft, making it obvious that he was
a supporter.

Adrian began the speech by keying on the issue of the resolve of
the United States to support the United Nations. He reflected that this
was significant to this audience since in the late 1940s Stamford with
Greenwich had asked to become the home of the United Nations,
locating it in a rural setting at a place called Mianus Gorge near the
New York border of the small panhandle of Connecticut. He postulated that perhaps a rural setting isolated from urban pressures would
have been more productive, since in the complex of world affairs,
people need time to think rather than be constantly wired to the
diplomatic and lobbying circuits of the city. He then reviewed his
worldview.

He criticized those who advocated that the ethnic problems in
Bosnia and the rest of the former Yugoslavia were unsolvable, having
been ongoing for centuries. He said none of these problems were

unsolvable, and that the key issue was the inability of the United States and the United Nations to react to the purposeful fanning of the flames of ethnic hatred by the leadership of Serbia. He reminded the audience that the world had pledged no repeat of the persecution of the Jews by the Nazis. That brought long applause.

He cited the analogy of the failure of France to send its army to destroy the Nazis after the occupation of the Saarland in 1935, which could have been done without serious fighting. The French, still traumatized by the horror of World War I, refused to move. The United States in the Bosnia situation was impacted by the memory of Vietnam and also refused to move. German General Staff papers subsequently showed the intention of the army to arrest Hitler on the challenge from France and to restore the German Republic. World War II might not have happened.

Vietnam, he said, was a terrible concept of a war fought with irrational constraints on the military services. Further, and worse, it was to support a government which was in no way democratic and did not deserve support. He pledged that as President he would never place restraints of that nature on any deployment of American forces. The objectives would relate to the nurture of democracy, the prevention of genocide or the prevention of suffering by large numbers of persons as a result of civil war or lawlessness. He was interrupted for applause.

Adrian said he would strengthen the United Nations' ability to deal with international terrorism, including the right of arrest and transfer to trial before an international court. He would add to that the ability to arrest war criminals, and warlords and others for crimes against humanity. He further recommended the establishment of an international penal colony where terrorists and war criminals would be sentenced to hard labor. He emphasized that the system would be structured under an international rule of law based on British common law. He also said that he would support the forming of a permanent United Nations force for rapid deployment to troubled areas.

As a policy for Africa, the Balkans, and the Middle East, separate units of the United Nations would begin to resolve the ancient tribal rivalries and establish an economic basis for peace among the nations. He laid out a plan to accomplish this, which drew long applause.

He said important objectives were to contain nuclear proliferation and to extend United Nations authority to investigate activities by outlaw nations. He indicated as a final step, the organization of a United Nations force that would deal with nuclear threats by outlaw nations against any individual nation.

"I do not foresee countries surrendering sovereignty to an international government for the next several centuries," he said. "However, a measure of international cooperation and resolve is absolutely necessary for world peace. Anyone who denies this ignores history and the modern context. A number of nations have terror weapons. The only way for the world to be safe from them is to have peace. The new century must see the end of hatreds. These have exacerbated relations between peoples for more than three millennia. It will take time and effort. There will be failures and successes. But the hatreds have to be expunged from the world for the human race to survive. Thank you."

The speech was received with a standing ovation. For the first time in a long time, an American politician who had the power to potentially do something about it spoke of the issues of the world in the future in terms of reality and understanding. Pamela joined Adrian at the podium. The applause and cheers continued.

The forum president went to the podium, called for order and said, "We have informed our guest in advance that questions were customary here and that they would not be easy ones." He pointed at one of the more than a dozen hands that were raised.

A glamorous woman stood and asked, "Isn't the United Nations so imperfect in its organization that we cannot give a pledge of unqualified support?"

"The United Nations is like any organization based on democracy. It's imperfect," Adrian answered. "But with resolute support from the United States and the industrialized nations plus India, Indonesia, and others capable of giving support, it could be successful in endeavors like Somalia and in keeping the peace. We have to have an international organization to keep the peace. There is no substitute for it."

The president pointed at another hand. A lady rose. "How can you justify sending American boys and girls in uniform to these crazy countries where there are hardly any interests of the United States at stake?" she asked. "In Bosnia, you make the point about the French failing to take action against the Nazis in World War II. It was obvious that the Nazis were becoming a threat and were rearming Germany, and therefore they made a mistake. But, what earthly harm could a nation like Serbia, Bosnia, or Croatia ever be to the European powers or to the United States?"

"The issue is starting fascism and fascism overcoming democracy," said Adrian. "Slobodan Milosevic took power in Serbia and fanned the flames of ethnic hatred to do so. Now suppose we do nothing and Slobodan Milosevic undertakes the conquest of one country at a time. Suppose we are unable to contain him? And where is the next vile potentate or thug going to appear who fans racial hatred to gain power? These things have to be stopped if there's going to be a peaceful world. We have to have a world that forgets its ancient hatreds. We have to have a world where every nation is democratic with a legal government."

The president pointed again, and a short man with a shiny bald head said, "These positions which you have espoused are so new and so far off the mainstream of American thinking, I fear for your candidacy when they are made known as they will be tomorrow."

"The purpose of the reality campaign is to elevate the hard issues which politicians have avoided or used in a populist way to forward their reelection," Adrian said. "Nations cannot be managed by avoiding the reality of tough issues or by telling people what the polls say they want to hear. I'm bringing the reality to the American people and I have faith in their innate understanding. They will not be fooled." A cheer erupted.

The president pointed to another hand and the questioning continued.

They made headlines and TV news broadcasts. There were favorable comments and shrieks of protest. There were editorials in the newsmagazines and in the national newspapers. Some spoke against the concept of a Pax Americana. Others supported Adrian's reasoning that for the world to be a peaceful place nuclear proliferation must be stopped and international laws protecting basic rights must be developed and enforced. Others supported popular pressure against use of military resources.

The Hatford campaign was queried by a media looking for an argument to start. They got a substantial dose of "not allowing the United Nations to set American foreign policy." Asked to comment, Adrian said he found the Hatford concept to be "a provoking perception."

To preempt any Hatford initiatives on litigation, the Daggett group decided on another major speech on limiting lawsuits. A convention of the Pharmaceutical Association at the Dallas Convention Center was selected because the support of that organization for national health insurance was important. They would speak about that and then offer support against the lawyers. The evening banquet was oversold. Anne flew down and joined Pamela with a number of glamorous women from Dallas and the industry at the VIP reception. Many were doctors or scientists. Adrian had a good time talking with them about recent discoveries. With the anticipation that Anne and her troops had built up, there was spontaneous applause when Adrian and Pamela appeared with the officials of the association at the head table.

After the dinner and the introduction, which the president himself had prepared, Adrian stepped to the microphone. He thanked the audience for the first welcome. He said he hoped the message would be one that would get a similar response. The audience laughed. He complimented the industry on its many achievements and he called it a keystone of American health care in terms of the marvels it had created.

Health, he said, is an important contribution to productivity. The national health insurance proposal, he said, was motivated by the fact that there were millions of Americans who did not have health insurance. They did not have preventive care. They became emergency room cases when their illnesses got bad enough and early deaths with all of the associated costs.

There were natural concerns about government entry into any industry, he admitted, but there were other considerations. Costs of health care had skyrocketed in the United States. He cited the statistics. Some costs, he said, were possibly justified; others, he said, were probably out of control. Adrian said he believed in free enterprise and markets and in the importance of incentives, but he also believed in fairness as a vehicle to the success of any industry. Health care was too important as a national asset to be ignored by government. The reality was that it was part of the social contract. He would support certain reforms to assure that all Americans had access to an excellent system. He quoted a doctor who maintained that the American system was inferior to Europe's in that it did not give access to all. He suggested that every other industrialized nation in the free world had access for all. While he abhorred socialism and welfarism, in health care, he said, these other nations may understand something that America had missed.

He said he recognized the huge risks on research which the industry took. He said the new system would be fair to those who were fair. He believed, he said in fair profits. He did not believe in obscene profits. Those companies who do, he said, usually live to regret their avarice.

In the aggregate, he told them, he could not see how the industry could not benefit with more customers. He promised them a voice that would be heard. He also promised another benefit, that he would do away with predatory lawyers. He reiterated his pledge to the American Chamber of Commerce. With whatever legislation it took and however long it took, there would be "loser pays." For the benefit of the medical industry, there would be limits on judgments. He wondered if that might result in enough cost savings to justify no further interference. Rich executives, he said, and rich shareholders benefit all; rich lawyers in the plaintiff practice do not.

"There are many aspects of American life that we may find personally distressful like crowded highways, meaningless television, inadequate schools, air pollution, and unsafe city streets," said Adrian. "Among all of those, the lack of trust and fairness in our dealings with each other is the worst and potentially the most harmful to our society. Democracy has to be based on truth, fairness, and trust. By various insidious means, the philosophy of relativism was brought into this country. The truth, ladies and gentlemen, is not relative. Trust, Ladies and Gentlemen, is not relative. Fairness is not relative. We must reestablish all three in the United States. I pledge to you that if elected to your highest office I will do everything I can to see that it happens. Thank you."

Surprisingly they stood and applauded for a considerable period. Adrian stood waving, as the applause went on and gestured to Pamela to join him. When the applause died down, the president stepped to the microphone and said, "We have allotted 20 minutes for questions. I'm sure there will be many from this group. Pamela will you also accept questions?" Pamela smiled. The President pointed to an older lady in a pillbox hat. "I have two questions for Mrs. Daggett," she announced. "Do you agree with the idea of national health insurance and cost control?"

Pamela coolly answered, "There are a lot of situations I could relate. We know the number of Americans who have no insurance. My daughter, Linda, has a friend who is working her way through Columbia as a waitress. Her father works as a short-order cook. Her mother is a day-care worker. They have no insurance. One day in the kitchen she bumped her knee. She got an infection from it which made her sick. She kept hoping it would go away, but it didn't. She collapsed one night and was rushed to the Emergency Room. She almost died from anemia and was in bed for weeks. A short course of antibiotics would have cured her. How many times is that story duplicated? Even if we don't care about the individuals, what we are doing is expensive. But, in this country, we care about people and we want them to be healthy and productive."

A man stood and interrupted, "What about the costs? You understand research."

"Research is expensive and represents a risk," she said. "Businesses take the research risk to stay ahead and to grow. The pharmaceutical industry has a high research risk. The key is fairness. When the auto industry raised prices in the United States after a voluntary quota for the import of Japanese cars was negotiated, the outcry against them was justified. Your industry is one of our great national strengths. Practice fairness, and the public and the government will respond fairly. At least the government my husband runs will. If it doesn't, let me know." There was laughter and applause.

"I didn't ask my second question," said the woman still standing. "What's he like to live with?"

"He's busy," Pamela smiled. "We try to budget time for each other and for the children. When he was governor I was disappointed that we had to send the kids away to private schools, because it's so hard to be the child of the governor when you're in his state. I respect him, I love him, and he is my best friend."

The president pointed to a tall gray-haired man. "This is for whichever Daggett wants to answer," he said. "In this proposed legislation or Constitutional amendment or whatever the combination might be, how will you limit damage awards?"

"We will consult with you on that and also with other advocate groups," Adrian said. "Statutes may be necessary. Our feeling is that the institution of 'loser pays' will deal with 90% of the problem. That is the first objective."

"I have to disagree with you Mr. Daggett because certain juries are willing to award our money generously. I think limits will be necessary."

"We will consider anything you wish to propose, and will look forward to the dialogue."

The president pointed to another distinguished man. "Mr. Daggett, you've been a business leader. You know price competition. We are in a situation where firms that take the research risk face so-called generic producers. We have to earn high margins to pay for the research while we can. How does your concept of fairness apply to that?"

"I have not thought about that and I apologize. Fairness can apply; we will have to work together to determine how."

A raven-haired lady was recognized. "Mr. Daggett, do you think you might be another business executive of great competence who is headed for the meat grinder of Washington where such people are turned into hamburger that quickly spoils?" There was laughter.

"I've been a governor of a major state, a state with a lot of the problems the country has," Adrian said. "I've been in those problems as a politician, not as a business executive. I recognize the difference between politics and business. Pamela and I look forward to Washington with the staff we have gathered. As far as interest groups and advocacy groups on a national scale are concerned, I will offer them the opportunity to participate, but this time they are not going to stand in the way. We will debate; we will not exchange platitudes. If we have to fight, we will fight. I have a clear purpose to dispel the perceptions these people live on and to bring to the public facts, logic, and reasoning. Businesses that allow themselves to be managed on the basis of perception are not generally successful."

Pamela said so he could hear, "You're rattling."

"My wife tells me my answer was too long," Adrian said. "Let me say that we have returned all checks from The Trial Lawyers Association."

They continued with Adrian's best medium, Q & A. There was another standing ovation and then people began filtering down forward to the rostrum to shake hands. Adrian was relieved. With this industry's support or neutrality there was great hope for his national health program.

In the limousine headed for the presidential suite at the shiny silver Hyatt, long a landmark of downtown Dallas, Adrian asked Pamela and Anne, what they thought.

"I think intelligent people favor you, Adrian," said Anne. "These are sophisticated men and women who have ideas of what's wrong with the country. They know you are telling them what's wrong. They know the country needs you. Some will support you even if they think you're bad for their industry."

"You think they are that objective?"

"Good people have always subordinated their interest to the interest of the country, Adrian. You're not threatening their industry with extinction. You called for fair profits. Any sophisticated businessman understands fair profits. You admitted you hadn't thought about the question of low price competition and offered to consider it."

"The lobbying by this industry is horrendous."

"They have a lot of issues, dear," said Pamela. "Research is expensive. People don't understand how expensive it is. Maybe we have to tell them that."

"If we announced regulation of pharmaceutical price, the bottom would fall out of their stocks."

"We've met a lot of pharmaceutical executives, dear," Pamela said. "I don't get the impression these people are thieves. They are sophisticated, they understand biochemistry, which is complicated, they understand pharmacology, and they understand finance. They are going to understand you."

"How many more speeches do I have to make? How many more dinners do I have to go to?"

"There are 173 days to the election," Anne said. "There has to be enough time off to rest your voice and your brain, but we have to go all out. My guess is you'll have to give 170 speeches, including an acceptance speech. Do half as well as you did tonight and you'll get elected. The issues campaign is going to work."

The Secret Service agent following the limousine watched as the Hyatt doorman opened the door. Two lovely ladies came out first, each attracting admiring glances from a crowd leaving a party, and then got smiles as they saw Adrian and recognized Pamela.

In their suite wearing the terry cloth bathrobe supplied by the hotel, Adrian stood while he watched the news, which made the arrival of people at the Convention Center look like Academy Awards Night. The cameras focused on the well-dressed wives of the industry leaders and the Dallas-Fort Worth elite. There were interior shots at the dinner and then shots of Adrian at the podium with inserts from his speech. Pamela joined him wearing her robe and took his arm. "They did a good job," he said.

"You did a good job, darling, you were wonderful. It's true what Anne said, people who care about the country will elect you."

"I hope we get it done for the right reasons," he said. "I want to do this, Pamela, but it seems never ending. If we win this election what kind of life will we have?"

"I've thought about that, dear," she said. She hugged his shoulder. "We'll have to take some time for ourselves, as much as we can. But, you will be the leader of the free world."

"I want to minimize the effect on the kids."

"They'll handle it. Let's you and me keep the marriage in mind." He took her in his arms and kissed her.

They usually slept naked. Pamela liked to go to sleep in Adrian's arms. With his head on her pillow smelling the sweetness of her hair, he knew the marriage would survive because of her.

THE NEXT WEEK in Chicago there was a regular meeting of the Senior Staff Committee to review the issues session and to start the plans for action. Tony stopped by Karen's office to congratulate her and welcome her to the big city. Her face lit up when she saw him. She got up from behind her desk and they hugged. "I hope I'm able to do this job," she said.

Tony smiled. "Never doubt whether you can do a job," he said. "Find the objectives, gather the resources, and accomplish them. We have every confidence."

"I love making those commercials," she said. "Maybe I should have gone into television."

"You belong in the political business, where you make a real contribution," Tony assured her. "How's Earl?"

Karen's face brightened even more. "He's great," she said. "He went to Des Moines and closed up my apartment. He packed everything in my car and drove here and found me a place almost with a view of the lake."

"Sounds like he sees something in you."

She grinned and shrugged her shoulders.

At the meeting other staff members were invited, including Michelle Proust. They discussed a number of the items from the Vail meetings during the morning. Adrian talked about the platform. He suggested a main statement be a list of critical issues and then the action the campaign proposed in easily readable language. Nancy seconded that. The phone rang, Anne answered and then said "We've got some news coming in, everybody. Sabrina Sellkirk has called a news conference on Capitol Hill to announce a formation of an organization called 'Mother's Against War' or 'MAWS.'"

"Corny," said Tony.

"Effective," said Anne. The big screen TV set blinked on and Sabrina Sellkirk appeared before them in the Ways and Means Committee Room in the Rayburn Building. She rebuked Adrian's foreign policy initiatives and called for mothers throughout the country to band together to vote against him to save their children's lives. She promised a 'mother's test' would be announced by the organization for any adventures of a military nature. She railed against sacrificing our children, the young men and women of America, in dubious interventions in which the United States would become obsessively mired. She invoked the memory of Vietnam and the 55,000 names on the Vietnam Wall. She called on mothers throughout the country to send in contributions of $10, or whatever they could, to bring this message to the American people as a matter of debating foreign policy. Her partisans in front of her applauded each point, and she took the questions of reporters anxious to start a controversy.

"That's POLACO," said Alan Jacobs. "She doesn't have anyone on her staff that could write a speech like that. She couldn't."

"Let's see how she does with the questions," said Anne.

The first reporter asked, "When did you decide to start this movement?"

"When I first heard of Adrian Daggett's aggressive positions," Congresswoman Sellkirk said. "We cannot have a president who is going to have our sons and daughters killed for no essential reason."

She pointed to the next reporter. "Where is the initial funding for this organization coming from?"

"I have a number of friends who have been willing to help get it started," she said. "Mainly I want it to come from the mothers of America who are concerned about their sons and daughters who might join the military, and other people who sympathize with those who have sons and daughters in the military. I have a son who, as you may know, is an Air Force pilot."

She pointed again. "What are going to be the main activities of the organization?"

"We're going to develop a newsletter," she said. "We're going to try to get together money to produce advertisements for television. We are going to be an issue organization and the issue is we don't want America to be the worlds' policeman and cooperating with, or encouraging misadventures of the United Nations."

She pointed. "Who are the other major supporters of the organization?"

"I'm the founder of the organization," she said. "I have several friends who are going to join me on the board. We formally incorporated yesterday. We have a handout that lists the others involved."

She pointed. "What will be your alternative policy?"

"We are directly opposing Adrian Daggett," she said. "We will support a foreign policy which does not put our children in battles in which we have not even a remote interest."

Anne said, "Well rehearsed, don't you think?"

"She certainly is not a politician rambling on with her answers. She's been coached," said Nancy.

"A sitting Congresswoman, a Republican from Colorado," Anne said. "Utilizes her position to start an organization to oppose Adrian's views on foreign policy. We assume she is financed by POLACO, by small checks coming in from various accounts and various banks of various individuals. I wonder if she has been paid a sum of money to do this?"

"Would that be illegal?" Nancy asked.

"I don't know, we have to ask," Anne said. "If she's been paid enough she'll resign her seat to campaign against Adrian, and my guess is she'll wind up in a cabinet post should Hatford get elected."

"What does this look like?" asked Adrian.

"It's a well-thought-out method of publicizing the argument against our foreign policy. It's going to stir up emotions. It will be scathing in its attacks and if POLACO's involved it will be well funded and well executed."

"The first torpedo," said Anne.

"Maybe we can steer away from it," said Terry. "Let's think about it, and what we can do."

"I think it would be a lot of fun to invite them to the debate show," said Nancy.

"We should do that," said Terry.

"Maybe we have to turn this into a national debate about whether it is better to avoid conflict or to meet it for the long-term safety of our young men and women," said Anne.

"Let's use Karen's idea and have local people speaking out against the Mothers Against War," said Alan.

"Let's have a battle of anguishing mothers versus logical mothers," said Terry.

"That's it," said Anne. "We have the mothers do it."

"Mothers of Veterans," said Alan.

☆ Chapter 24 ☆

SADOVAN GAVE THE meeting with Ian full treatment as a corporate summit. After more than a dozen calls between Helene and Tony, the Athens Hilton was selected as the site. Helene was to attend with Ward and Madeline. Ian and Susan brought Tony and David Gibson.

The Cowells and Helene enjoyed Air France's First Class service from Miami to Paris where they had scheduled six hours to connect to Olympic Airways to Athens. Leaving Ward snoozing in the airport hotel, Helene and Madeline taxied to the Rue Fauberg d'St. Honore where the shops still had an ample supply of spring designer fashions.

Ian used his Falcon's intercontinental capability and, after fetching David at Teterboro, headed across the North Atlantic. The steward and stewardess served malt scotch and broiled haddock. Everyone slept well. Their scheduled stop was at Linate airport in Milan. Susan preferred Italian fashions and Ian took her shopping with David, while Tony used a limousine to visit the Duomo and the very old church on the south side of the old city which had been started in the eighth century. In each building, he wondered which of his ancestors might have been there and thought of how far back the history of Italy went.

At the hotel the next morning, Sadovan had two meeting rooms reserved. In one he served a buffet of rolls, pastries, fruit, cheese, and coffee. In the other, a long table was set up with mineral water and glasses in place. While having coffee, Ian, Susan, and David were introduced to Helene. Ian felt her vibrations and understood why he suspected Tony was attracted to her. David met Madeline for the first time, to size her up as a legal opponent. After the preliminaries, they sat down on opposite sides of the table and Sadovan began. "Not too far from here, near the Acropolis is the Hill of the Pynx. I'm sure you know about it, Ian. It's the place where the Athenians came as early as the Sixth Century BC to debate the issues of their city. One man, one vote. A simple form of democracy. Votes were taken on bits of broken pottery. Sometimes the issue was public worker expenditure; sometimes it was to declare war. There were arguments, I'm sure, about the size of the navy: sure the troops in those days were mostly under universal unpaid military service.

"Those were simple days, Ian, and yet people attempted to have enemies ostracized since it only required a majority vote. The population of the city-state of Athens was 300,000, about the size of Toledo. Democracy failed in Athens. Pericles took over and stopped listening to the debates. He consulted the citizens only a few times when he wanted money and made the unfortunate decision to fight Sparta one time too many.

"The Roman Republic endured for more than 700 years with representative democracy. Senators were elected at large. The Patricians compromised with the Plebians for their collective security. In the end rivalries killed it.

"I'm aware of this Mendos," said Ian. "This was all precursor to the development of democracy in England and in America. The American Revolution started something unique."

"Not so unique, Ian," Sadovan replied. "The federalists looked for the establishment of a republic. The Jeffersonian Democrats had some other ideas."

"And they prevailed," said Ian. "The Americans broadened the franchise."

"'The Rise of the Common Man,' Ian, meant that we bought votes with whiskey or with populists ideas."

"Nothing is ever going to be pure, Mendos. No institution is pure. We should always try to make it pure. Every system and every institution has imperfections."

"The imperfections of modern democracy are too great, Ian."

"Structure has a good deal to do with it, Mendos. So does the ability of most of the people to put the interest of the country ahead of their own interest."

"Nobleness is rare in modern politics," said Sadovan.

"That's why I'm backing Daggett."

"You're backing one man with a specific motive," Sadovan said. "We think that is to prevent us from establishing our program. Our program is to build a political system, Ian, which will protect multi-national business as long as it can be maintained. What you do with Adrian Daggett only delays things. We need to put in place a large number of people who are competent and dedicated and loyal."

"Loyal to whom?" asked Ian.

"Loyal to us, and loyal to America."

"I'm not sure of the loyalties," Ian responded looking Mendos Sadovan squarely in the eye.

"The question is why are you, Ian, head of the largest company in your industry, opposing the establishment of POLACO?"

"Because I don't believe POLACO will be wholesome for American Democracy for very long."

"We are trying to preserve it from its ultimate collapse," said Sadovan. "How long do you think it will last with the type of people who run for office? Where is the nobleness? You have to go through some process to find it."

"I don't believe American Democracy needs your interference, Mendos. I do believe that it needs to be restructured."

"How would you propose to restructure?" Ward intervened.

"I would stop the entrepreneurial candidacies," Ian said. "I would establish standards by which people would judge politicians on the basis of their service to the country and not their constituencies or some other agenda."

"You want politicians who are not political," Sadovan said. "Impossible if they have to be elected by a broad franchise. As long as there is a broad franchise there is a propensity for low common denominators. You can elect your noble Daggett, but when an ignoble opponent appears, the fight is on his level."

"That didn't seem to happen in the recent primaries, Mendos."

"Very few candidates can afford the amount of money spent on the Daggett primary campaign," Ward said. "When most people run for office there is very little money and very little they can talk about."

"We raised the level of the dialogue," Ian said. "Our national dialogue is dismal."

"There is no hope, Ian, that American Democracy can survive," Sadovan said. "POLACO is going to take it around the next bend in the road. Even if we had nobleness and even if we had competent leaders, how are we ever going to explain modern life to essentially uneducated or poorly educated people who have the right to vote?"

"It is the essential duty of everyone in government to inform the people of the truth," said Ian.

"Too often it's in the interest of the leaders of government or their challengers not to inform the people," Mendos countered. "Another question is how do you do it? How do you teach people who may not understand college-level concepts of chemistry, biology, and the scientific method about technology? How do you teach them to identify lies, lies that beget the interest of the prevaricator?"

"How would you restructure, Mendos?"

"A council of business leaders elected by the heads of corporations approves all major policies. The candidates for President and the Congress are chosen from a list approved by the leadership of each party and they meet certain standards set by the Constitution. The vote would be by limited suffrage."

"How would you limit suffrage?"

"First by denying it to anyone who hasn't voted in the last three elections and anyone who isn't registered. That establishes clear intent not to participate in the democracy. We would have an examination of voter's for certain basic intelligence issues and some knowledge of historical and current events. Any voter who fails the test would be able to repeat the test until he passes. Everyone would be required to take the test every ten years."

"And how pure would the democracy be that monitors all of this?" Ian asked cynically.

"As honest as the Federal Reserve banks."

Ian paused and then looked at Ward, Madeline, and Helene. "You are speaking of fundamental changes in the Constitution," he said. "How do you propose to implement them?"

Sadovan glanced at Ward. "By electing candidates to Congress," he said, "and the major state legislatures who adhere to the doctrines we advocate. We are confident we'll find enough candidates through Rollin Tinton and the Recruiting, Training, and Election Group to fill the key slots. In 15 years, we will control the major committees of Congress and will have elected the President. Within 25 years, we will have appointed the members of the Supreme Court. It's a long-term thing, Ian, but that's how it will be done. We have the very best people working on it. You should support this, Ian, a calm but resolute revolution to preserve freedom."

"How can there be freedom if there is limited suffrage?"

"We had freedom in the United States with limited suffrage," said Ward. "The same in England."

"We can continue the premises of English common law," Madeline added. "You don't have to have screwy policies at the apex of government in order to have common sense common law for the people at the level of their communities."

"Ian, it is far better to protect British common law and the essential freedoms of the Bill of Rights by having POLACO take America forward than by having democracy collapse and some fascists do it."

"What is the difference between a POLACO government 25 years from now and fascism?"

"We will design the POLACO government," said Sadovan. "You have to join us in this. And that government form will spread around the world in a quiet revolution. The alternative is the chaos the present politicians will bring us to. We have to take the lead, Ian, people like you and me."

Ian already had thought through the leadership he had taken on. "Why are we taking these initiatives?" he asked.

"Because it is only we who can afford it, Ian," Sadovan said.

"The most good is going to be served, Ian," said Ward, "if business takes over. At least with business the greatest good for the greatest number can be realized."

"Who would enforce the legal constraints on this new form of government that would protect liberties?" asked David Gibson.

"A system of courts devoted to enforce the laws," said Madeline.

"Then what happens if the government decides that the laws need to be changed?" Susan MacAulliffe asked.

"That would go through a legislative process."

"Of this government's legislature?"

"There would be the constitutional guarantees of the Bill of Rights and of English Common Law," said Madeline. "That's more than we really have today."

"I still believe it is incumbent upon all of us to reform Washington by electing good leaders," Ian said.

"The time for that has passed, Ian," Sadovan said. "There are too many bad ones there. You may temporarily reverse the trend with your Daggett. The outcome is inevitable. American Democracy becomes fascism or it becomes what we want it to become. You belong on our side."

It was indeed an attractive alternative. It sounded good, but there was an inevitable flaw. It was complex, and Ian knew he would be hard pressed to explain it. It had to do with one person or group having too much power. He could see how the process would evolve in small steps. Each step would be a step of opportunity and it was impossible to forecast the end result. He wondered about Rollin

Tinton. This man would find himself on top of a significantly power-ful group if they were successful. Hundreds of elected officials would owe allegiance to him.

"This is too complex for us to settle at one meeting, I will consider your arguments which you have expressed very clearly," Ian said. "If I decide that we are going to continue on the present course, we will resign from POLACO."

"We don't want you to leave POLACO, Ian, you belong in it," Ward said.

"Even if I'm struggling to elect Daggett in order to stop you from doing what you're telling me?"

"We don't want to have to explain this to our members," Ward said.

"How do I explain $45 million and $10 million a year?"

"We'll overlook the ten; you'll get a good yield on the deposit."

"I will abide by your wishes," Ian told him.

"We hope you'll join us, Ian," Ward said. "As opposition you may play into the hands of those who may already be looking to under-mine the American democracy and wrest freedom away from the American people."

"One of the results that you need to keep in mind from your action, Ward and Mendos, is civil conflict," Ian said. "I think that I can assure you that civil conflict will result if anyone tries to take free-dom away from the American people."

"It depends on the terms, Ian," said Sadovan. "So many of them don't care and I'm not sure you can make them care."

"It's not something that's done overnight. I agree the damage has been done by crass political forces, but I'm not sure I'm ready to give up on the American people just yet," Ian said signaling his probable conclusion.

They were powerful arguments that Sadovan gave to take America "around the next bend" and there was definitely a next bend. The shoddiness of the political structure in Washington made that inevitable. Political structures didn't heal themselves like biological organisms if they became sick. Greed and personal agendas seemed ever to ascend over the public or national interest. Was that the inevitable destiny of freedom? History seemed to indicate it was.

The self-appointed new leaders of the movement for a new America offered him a leadership role. If he turned them down, how soon would it be before secret police knocked at his door? Or would they bother to knock?

The meeting went on through a buffet lunch and ended in mid-afternoon in time for Ward and Madeline to reach the airport for a flight to Moscow. Ian and Susan took some exercise walking in The Plaka, the "Greenwich Village" section of Athens. Tony and David Gibson drove out to the site of the Battle of Marathon. They came back over what was supposed to be Phidipides' route.

That evening Ian took them in a limousine to Piraeus for an excellent fish dinner. Driving back, they saw the Acropolis gleaming in its lights. Ian told the driver to take them up to the top, where on a warm moonlit night, they looked out over the city from the Parthenon. The adjacent Hill of the Pynx was also lighted and there they saw the natural white marble stage where the government of ancient Athens stood to face their constituents who held the power. Susan held Ian's arm while they strolled toward it with David and Tony following. After a moment Ian turned to them. "It all began here," he said; "Washington, Jefferson, the French philosophers, the British philosophers, and the people, from the Venetians to the Americans. The idea came from here. The concept of the rule of law and the power resting on the citizens and freedom under the law is an essential part of Western civilization. I don't believe there can be a rule of law that will be meaningful for very long without democracy and constitutional government to assure it. We're doing the right thing. It's not going to be easy."

WHEN THE COWELLS left, Helene and Sadovan agreed to play tennis, but she also wanted to swim. The Hilton boasted the largest swimming pool in Greece. In Paris, she had bought a one-piece suit and a bikini of the latest fashion which showed as much of her body as she wished. She wouldn't wear them around Harbour Island, but here was a chance. Besides, the water would be warm and the one piece would feel clammy. The Hilton supplied a beach robe which she wore to the pool.

While she was swimming laps, she saw Sadovan walking alongside. She surface dived over to see him.

"The only court I could get was at 4 p.m.," he said.

"That's fine," she said smiling at him from the water. "I'll finish here in a few minutes."

"Don't tire yourself out. I want a good game," he smiled.

She dove away from him and then pretended to blow water out of her mouth at him.

She dried off and changed into her favorite tennis dress and met him in the lobby. A limousine was waiting and in 15 minutes they were at a tennis club which accepted people from the hotels. A red clay court was ready with a teenage boy and girl to warm them up and to shag the balls. Beside the court there was a tray with a pitcher of lemonade and four glasses. Sadovan remembered his employees.

At the net, she faced him and smiled. "Is there a chance for me to win another $1,000?"

"I said I would never again play you for money," he said. "Only for the pleasure and to try one day to beat you."

She smiled and told him to serve. He was still involved in the meeting with Ian, and she, too, had strong emotions over what had occurred. She felt a sense of failure, which to her was alarming. It was clear; not only had POLACO lost Ian MacAulliffe, they never really had him in the first place. Not only that, the tone of the discussion with Ian disturbed her, as if it indicated something was missing in POLACO. Something they never had and ultimately, human rights were involved.

Not only that, if Ian was gone, seeing Tony again on anything but an adversarial basis would be out of the question. She won 6-1, 6-3. After that, she said, "You played well."

"Not well enough, Sadovan said."

She saw that he really wanted to defeat her, just as he had wanted to persuade Ian MacAulliffe. "I can think of a reward," she said holding up her face to be kissed. He put his arm around her shoulder and obliged.

"That was very nice," he said. "Let's follow it with dinner. I promise a good one. Can you be ready in an hour?"

"Easily."

"Come to my suite for a cocktail."

As she pulled off her tennis dress in her suite, she wondered if she had in a weak moment kissed Napoleon.

Toasted crackers, feta cheese, and smoked calimari were waiting with a chilled bottle of Demistika.

"Forgive the Greek popular wine," Sadovan said. "But I like its flavor when it's ice cold. If you would like something else, we have the service bar."

"When in Greece..."

"How do you read the meeting?" Sadovan asked.

"We gave him something to think about," Helene said. "I thought you described POLACO well. Ian is not going to easily part with the concept that democracy requires universal franchise."

"I thought he might agree to a limited franchise since half of the electorate give up their right to vote anyway."

"Ian is going to object to their giving it up permanently."

"It is very complicated," he said. "Governments must get things done. Governments must establish policies. They can't do it if there's going to be a political storm every time something doesn't work. I'm not sure the political scientists understand."

"They probably do, but most of them would say it's an issue of leadership," she said. "Mario Einaudi used to repeat constantly that the executive should run the government with the advice and consent of the legislature. He objected to the legislature's initiating laws. He thought they should all come from the executives."

"I forgot you were a political scientist. A published one. I'm impressed by everything about you."

She smiled at him.

"Do you think there is any chance Ian will stop supporting Daggett? You know how that started?" Sadovan continued.

"Ian has a high-powered executive staff and high-powered advisors. He's concerned about the constitutional issues we raise. He probably agrees with our goals, but disagrees with the method."

Sadovan tapped his fingers on the table and sipped his wine. "They figured out the one decisive intervention and actually embarked upon it to elect somebody like Daggett as President," he said. "Daggett is supremely confident, has excellent character, extraordinary background, deep beliefs, a fine family, and is about as well connected as anyone could get. He has a vast network in industry, finance, and in government and what connections he doesn't have, Ian will have and they both know how to use them."

"You mean he will produce an exceptionally good administration?"

"He will, and few of them will be politically motivated at the high levels."

"But what can one administration accomplish?"

"If they stay in office eight years, they can change the American political scene. They will set new standards which the people will start to expect, and they will gain control of the media in the sense that they will focus them on the real issues rather than the peripheral. If the media started being mainly fact-based and the government started explaining the world to the people..." He paused. "Then again Daggett could make mistakes," he said. "And the opposition could close in or possibly the opposition could force mistakes."

"If the opposition attacks constantly and on every issue, it could destabilize even the best people," Helene said.

"That is also true."

The limousine took them as close to the restaurant in The Plaka as they could get, as most of it was a pedestrian mall. They strolled past a variety of shops until Sadovan gestured toward a door in a pastel blue and yellow facade. The Maitre'd escorted them to a stairway to the basement room which continued the Mediterranean colors. Their table was in a corner against a leather bench. The Maitre'd seated Helene to Sadovan's right. He then lit two tall candles and poured mineral water and white Demistika into glasses.

"This is your formal welcome to Athens," said Sadovan raising his glass. They clinked.

"I appreciate your hospitality in the oldest city in Europe. Is that correct?"

"Rome and some of the Italian cities may be older," he admitted. "Historians have difficulty sometimes dating."

The waiter came and addressed them in French and proceeded to hand out the menus and discuss them in that language. Sadovan ordered the seafood selection as an appetizer with a special salad. Helene wanted to go ahead and order lamb. He told her in French, "You can only order one course at a time, otherwise they bring it all at once."

"You realize the waiter paid you a great compliment. He thought you were French. France produces the most beautiful women in the world."

"Maybe that's why I studied French, so to be mistaken for one."

"You are not only superbly talented, Helene, but you are also beautiful." Sadovan brought his deep dark eyes to bear on her.

She smiled at him and held her finger to his lips. "Don't try to seduce me Mendos, I choose."

"What man could have ever let you get away?"

"He was weak, Mendos; talented, but weak. He couldn't handle my making more money than he did. Tell me about your first wife."

There was a pause while he decided to answer the question. "She was like you, attractive and powerful with dark hair and beautiful blue green eyes. Her smile could light up a room. She was an architect and designer."

He still loved her she guessed. "But what happened?" she asked.

"It was me, I was too busy," he said. "There was another man, a real estate operator, and she left me for him."

"How does that make you feel toward him?"

"He's a very lucky man. It was my fault; I lost her."

Only a real man could admit that, she thought. "When did this happen?"

"Three years ago." He paused for a few seconds and picked up his glass. "To the future, the past gives us lessons, let us heed them." They clinked glasses. "What is your future, Helene?"

"Immediately it is to go to Senlis and spend a few days. It's a town north of Paris near Chantilly."

"I know it. A 14th Century church? Very beautiful."

"And a hotel-restaurant where you go in the back door from the modern intersection and out the front door into the 17th Century. I eat their marvelous cooking, go to the bakery, and then I run it off along the country roads. I speak French, read a book in French, and every evening I drive to Paris to the theater or the opera. I like to feel as though I am French for a few days."

"As I said, you can play the role."

She smiled.

"What do you think is going to happen to France?" Helene asked.

They talked of the country they both enjoyed.

There was much more in Sadovan. The conversation turned to children, schools, and sports. Sadovan had a son, Theodore, doing graduate work at Yale and a daughter, Justine, two years behind at Smith. He showed Helene their pictures.

After dinner he said, "Would you like to walk around The Plaka and possibly visit one of the bars where there will be dancing or would you like to go to the Acropolis?"

Helene tilted up her chin and said, "Both."

The limousine took them to a small hotel. In Greece, traditionally the men dance, but women's liberation had interfered. At first he was shy and they danced only to the Western slow music. It was the first time she had danced with him. She realized how hungry she was for a good man. Later the music began to infect them and they joined in the folk dancing which he knew well. Greece, she found, had been his exit point in the flight of his father, mother, and sister from the onrush of the Red Army. He told her the story. The family was from Montenegro, where his father taught physics at the university. He had served in the resistance movement against the Nazis, but was not welcome in the communists' fold. With careful planning, he escaped in 1947 when Sadovan was two years old. Sadovan had started school in Greece. She asked how he learned such excellent English and he told her the family never spoke anything but English. When they finished with the dancing, a limousine took them up to the Parthenon. It was magical, bathed in light showing off the whiteness of the marble. He stood watching as she took his arm. "What was this?"

"The Temple of Jupiter, Zeus."

"What did they do here?"

"I think they came at festivals. I've never studied that much. Over here is something more important." He took her hand and they walked to the edge of the cliff and looked down. She saw the lighted ancient theater. "The Greeks started theater, poetry, writing," he said. "Without the theater and poetry we would be jungle animals with computers."

Helene looked down and imagined the theater crowded with Athenians and the stage filled with actors and a Greek chorus. Beyond the park immediately around the Acropolis, the city was a sea of light.

She turned to him and held up her face to his. He kissed her tentatively and she returned the kiss and they stood kissing for a long moment.

"What a superb place for a first kiss," Sadovan said.

"I thought the same," she smiled. "We won't count the one at the tennis courts." They kissed again.

"So I have told you to ignore the gods and honor the theater. Do you want to see the Hill of the Pynx?"

"Yes, since we are here." She took his arm.

They stayed only for a minute then went back to the Plaka.

They strolled around the streets. In the antique shops Sadovan pointed out paintings that interested him. At one jewelry store he commented, "This one sells real Rolex watches."

"How do you know?"

"I bought one and had it checked."

"Just for that purpose?"

"No, I gave it to my son-in-law to be."

"A generous father-in-law."

"I couldn't allow him to know only my business reputation."

She could see he was a man with many reputations to uphold.

"Shall we have something to eat or drink?"

"Let's have room service," she said, "in my suite."

He smiled at her.

She gave him the key to unlock the door and he held it for her. She turned and waited for him to kiss her again. She was now hungry for him, Napoleon or not.

"Why don't we both change into the bath robes provided," she said. "I'll go first and I'll order some Demestika and some cheese. If you would like brandy, there is some in the service bar."

In a few moments, she was back wearing her robe and carrying the second. In Greek style, the room service arrived quickly. She sat on the couch and motioned for him to join her. He poured the wine.

"Salute."

"No, you should always drink to something."

"To more evenings like this."

She smiled and raised her glass.

The first time a couple makes love there are little embarrassments and some clumsiness. Helene organized most of that away. In the morning she awoke remembering how she went to sleep snuggled in his arms and how she found him to be gentle and passionate.

When he heard her move, he came into the room with a tray of juice, coffee, rolls, cheese, and smoked fish. He smiled and handed her the juice as she sat up. He noticed she did not pull up the sheet to cover her breasts.

"How nice," she said.

"I will order anything you like," he replied.

"No, this is fine." He sat on the bed and put the tray between them and poured coffee and hot milk and served her a cup. He then got up and brought her a robe and held it while she slipped into it.

"You have planned your vacation in Paris and I can understand the attraction, but I have an offer."

She knew what it had to be and started thinking about being on a boat with him.

"I see you think you know what my offer is?"

"To cruise in the Greek Islands on your yacht."

"I would be honored."

She smiled at him. "Where do you propose to go?"

"That would be decided when you look at the chart on board."

"And who would be with us?"

"I have a crew of fourteen. Seven men and seven women. They are all highly trained."

"I suppose they are paired?"

"It makes for reduced turn over. There is a captain and first mate; his wife is also a watch-keeping officer. The captain's wife is my secretary and the communication officer. There is an engineer; his wife is the chef. The others handle the duties of helmsman, dockhand, waiters, steward."

"What kind of accommodations do I expect?"

"There are two main state rooms, you may have one, I will take the other"

When would she have the opportunity to sail the Greek Isles on a yacht with a crew of fourteen owned by a man who was obviously interested in her?

That afternoon they chartered a jet to Kavalla. A limousine met them at the general aviation terminal. Sadovan showed her the old town with its Roman aqueduct and they drove out to the ruins of Philippi along the old Roman road to Constantinople, the Via Reggia. At the airport a yellow and pink helicopter already had their luggage loaded and off they went toward the large island. In twenty minutes he pointed to his vessel anchored in a harbor. There was a helicopter pad on the stern where they landed. He showed her around the yacht and introduced her to the crew.

On the bridge she selected the destinations. Two nights later she fulfilled a fantasy and jumped naked into the warm moonlit water. He watched her and was ready with her robe when he helped her back onto the fantail. As he draped it around her shoulders she kissed him. She pushed herself close to him as they walked across the deck to the hatch leading to the companion way toward their staterooms. She led him into hers and turned to him. "I've always fanaticized that."

"I'm glad you did. You look like you just sank Daggett's campaign ship"

"That pleased? But it's because you are here." She pulled his shirt over his head.

He touched her hair and kissed her. She pushed down his shorts and massaged his erection. She shook the robe off her shoulders and stood naked before him.

He led her to the bed and laid down first and then guided her alongside him. The sex became wild.

☆ Chapter 25 ☆

THE NATIONAL CHAMBER of Commerce convention invited both Adrian and Hatford to speak on successive days at luncheons. Being conservative, they scheduled Adrian first thinking that Hatford would come out ahead. Anne's group rallied the media to come to see him face a hostile audience.

The president of the association used the Evans & Copeland script in his introduction. Adrian received polite applause as he took the rostrum. He gave the usual compliment to the organization and then began with a story.

"About ten years ago, in one state, a major corporation initiated the program for permitting a glass container plant. The siting involved the usual reviews and an air permit for emissions from the glass furnace. A series of questions were asked by the regulators from that state, and answers were given. Then more questions were asked and another round of answers were given and then yet a third round of questions and more answers. The process continued for a period of a year when the company announced it would not continue the project. Ladies and Gentlemen, according to the Statistical Abstract of the United States there are 752 factories in this country that already are making exactly that same product the same way."

He felt the audience warming.

"One way to cause harm to the American economy is for government to engage business in extended dialogue and processes about regulations which essentially set the same standards the companies would set for themselves. I have personal experience with this problem. We had an air pollution policy which was exactly the same as that required by the U.S. Environmental Protection Agency and the environmental agency in the state in which we were located. It still took almost six months to present this in order to obtain a permit to expand our plant, and add several hundred jobs. I can tell you, ladies and gentlemen, 80% of the people that took those jobs were unemployed or under-employed before those jobs were created."

That got some applause.

"Crippling effects of over-regulation have been felt by the nuclear power plants, pharmaceutical companies, medical establishments, and research universities who all generate certain quantities of radioactive waste. The amount of radionuclides in some wastes is minuscule. None-the-less, the waste, if it has any radiation, must be called radioactive. It is not difficult in the United States to get a permit to dispose or process low-level radioactive waste and there is one place where it can generally be disposed at a very high cost. It is somewhat more difficult to get permits to process hazardous wastes and to stabilize them and recycle them, but this is available in the United States.

"However, when confronted with low-level radioactive wastes mixed with other hazardous wastes, no regulatory body would accept the responsibility. For years the industries generating them had no choice, but to store them. The regulatory legal mechanisms of the national bureaucracy and state bureaucracies ground to gridlock over a relatively simple problem from the scientific point of view. It was so bad that portions of the waste were sent to a firm which had a permit to release 20 curries of radioactivity annually into the atmosphere. They charged a fee to burn this waste which allowed the curries to escape into the air to the limit of their permit. Companies that were desperate to dispose of the waste because of bulging storage facilities and other OSHA requirements limiting the amount they could store, had to pay dearly for the privilege of having this firm burn the materials that were burnable. The regulatory system stood by and watched this happen. Because of the uncertain regulatory climate there were no private sector initiatives. Industry couldn't tell whether anyone in government was available to determine whether any process would be acceptable and they refused to risk the costs of developing one.

"Why in hell are we paying regulators to struggle with or stymie each other? I know the tricks they play to extend tasks. I will not tolerate that. The government in a democracy is supposed to serve the people and not itself."

Applause erupted.

"In regulatory matters reality and science must be the ultimate determinants. We cannot afford to have bureaucrats create regulations that create jobs for bureaucrats. We cannot afford to have regulations that add unseemly costs to our manufacturing research, academic, and medical processes. We have to stop it and the reform is going to be traumatic. If elected President, ladies and gentlemen, I am going to administer the trauma."

The audience rose.

Adrian went on to say most companies are environmentally responsible, care about the health and safety of their employees, and conform by policy with all labor regulations. Because they are socially responsible, he said, a large majority of companies don't need to be regulated the way we do it today. He suggested government should not treat all businesses as though they represented organized crime.

He described what he called "self-permitting." He said companies which had proven themselves to be responsible would be required only to give notification of intention to construct particular facilities with engineering descriptions and all the details showing that they would conform. They would be required to consult with their communities to show what they're about and that they are operating within the spirit and letter of the laws and regulations. He said the government would inspect and review records and the companies using this procedure would take the risk of being shut down if they were not operating within regulations. He said this would be a "one strike" situation in that once any company was found to have taken advantage of the procedure, they would be required to seek permits for an undetermined period.

The audience interrupted him.

Adrian said he wanted a new relationship between business and regulatory agencies of consultation and review. He pledged there would be no permitting process that would review technologies over and over again. He said he would start with a blue ribbon commission of experienced regulators working with experienced businessmen challenged to create a better way. He went on to warn mean-spirited businesses that there would be severe penalties for violating regulations.

"At one time in one of our major industries a major corporation took a huge environmental initiative in order to process a waste stream," he said. "They invested tens of millions of dollars and many, many thousands of hours of engineering and management time and consulting fees. It took them four and a half years to obtain a permit before an operation that would materially contribute to the reduction of a burden on the American environment could start. I tell you, if I am elected, that will not happen again. Science and rationality must prevail.

"This is a pledge to the public that we are going to radically change the system of regulation in the United States. It is going to be simplified. The responsibility is going to focus on the corporation rather than the regulator, and we are going to realize material increases in productivity and a reduction of corporate costs. We are going to make it easier for entrepreneurs to form new businesses and for corporations to undertake new innovations and operations.

"We are also going to reduce the cost of the national government by the cost of carrying those who cannot do their job or won't. Much has been accomplished to make government personnel aware of their missions. Many have responded. But, the final step of the reform of the civil service legislation must be taken. Responsible supervisors must have the capability to remove unproductive or unresponsive employees. This is too complex to describe here, but please know I will do it.

"It is a daunting task to bring about reforms like these. However, I accept the challenge to make these changes. There is another challenge. That is to you to make them work."

Cheers and loud applause echoed around the hall.

As she almost always did, Pamela joined him. The chairman asked him to take questions. The chairman pounded his gavel and hands shot up.

The chairman pointed to one.

"Do you really believe, Mr. Daggett, there would ever be self-permitting for air permits or other environmental permits in the United States?"

"I can tell you no government regulator knows more about the technology of a pharmaceutical company, a metals producer, a glass producer, or a chemical producer than the company's good people," Adrian said. "Who can better judge whether or not a process is environmentally or occupationally safe? I challenge the members of the Chamber of Commerce to be your own judge and weave that good judgment into your planning. There has to be a change in the structure, there is too much growth; the technologies are too complicated. We can't limit them by cumbersome and uninformed procedures."

The applause echoed again.

The chairman pointed to another hand, "But how are the companies going to know what the regulations are that they have to conform to? There are volumes to these things."

"Part of the agency responsibility will be to determine the applicable regulations and to deliver interpretations. In the self-permitting process, the companies are going to have to understand these regulations and be subject to inspections. The idea is to accomplish the transmission of information and all of the other functions of a regulatory agency, but without the delay of the permitting or the expense of the application. This accomplishes the same thing. The company is obligated under this mode to understand and obey the law. There is no less force of government enforcing the law."

The Chairman pointed. "What about the burden of regulation on small businesses?"

"Small business is very often burdened more by the states with reporting requirements and tax management requirements that should not be imposed on companies with fewer than ten employees. I will seek a national policy which allows entrepreneurs to start businesses without undertaking withholding taxes and social security payments and such other things on behalf of their employees until they get themselves organized. In particular, one individual working as a consultant or engineer or in other pursuits by himself with a staff of part-time people should not be required to report as though he had hundreds of full-time employees. If as a national policy we cannot get this accomplished, then I will seek statutes or laws necessary to lift the burdens so small companies will be more efficient and their entrepreneurs less harassed."

The chairman pointed. A thin man rose.

"Mr. Daggett, your business experience has been at a high level. Are you aware that there are regulators who like to use their power and cause as much delay or other trouble as they can? What would you do about them if they don't work for the federal government?"

"I assume you recognize such people would get caught in our sweep of the federal level," Adrian replied. "There are probably more of these types at the state level. If the state is enforcing federal laws, as in the case of most environmental regulations, the federal government can set standards of treatment of business and enforce them by publicizing incidents and by withholding federal funds."

The questions went on for a few more minutes. Adrian and Pamela left to another standing ovation.

In the limousine the cell phone rang. It was Terry. "That's one more issue Hatford won't use."

There was no need for Anne Russell's skillful persuasion to get the media attention for these new proposals. Adrian had started a national discourse. There were screams from the environmental fringe that no company and few governments could be trusted to protect the environment. To thoughtful people they sounded hollow. Cries of anguish arose from the government employees unions that Adrian had proposed abrogation of a historical covenant and the return of gross patronage. Terry replied, at a press conference, that no one who did a good job and was interested in doing it better need fear anything except promotion; that job skills requirements would be enforced; that hiring practices would be under constant examination; and that the reviews of individuals would begin with those who had maxed their sick days during the past three years without evident illness.

There were many editorials and TV news reports; almost all were supportive. The constituencies, however, would resist.

HELENE RETURNED TO Washington with Erla and Warren to meet with the Hatford campaign. This time Randy Dustin brought his issues director, Daune Yaeger, and his chief political strategist Emmett Lawson. Daune came from a competitor of Evans & Copeland. Lawson was a political consultant, a former Capitol Hill staffer, and White House fellow who formed a company with three associates; The Political Relations Center known as "PRC." They had grown with success mainly in promoting Republican candidates in congressional and senatorial elections.

After the introductions and talk about the Southern Conservative Coalition, which Helene, Erla, and Warren officially represented, Randy began. "This meeting is confidential and its purpose is to give information to the Southern Conservative Coalition about the strategies we will follow to elect Senator Hatford. As a beginning, I want to make the point that we consider Senator Hatford and Mr. Daggett to be comparable candidates. Our candidate is an excellent speaker, as is Adrian Daggett, and we consider them to be equal on that point. In terms of trust, Daggett has a higher rating, but that, we believe, is only because he comes from outside Washington. This is something we have to overcome. Their platform appearance is about equal. Thus the strategies are the critical variable."

Randy paused to let his statement sink in. Helene wondered where these perceptions came from.

"At the present time there is a lot of soft money available to the

Daggett group that has been used to create a strong issues staff," he said. "In the primaries they opened a large number of issues full of details of what they intend to do with very strong commitments. We expect the same to continue. We intend to wait until these issues are largely laid out with the exception of the ones I've mentioned, and to attack them on specifics. Increased taxes is a basic pocketbook question, and rarely popular. It's possible to develop the perception of the United Nations dominating America's foreign policy and dictating it. We will make the United Nations appear to be irresponsible which is not difficult considering the behavior, disarray, and blatant behavior of its bureaucracy.

"On the matter of national health insurance, we have seen the Southern Conservative Coalition use the "Harry & Louise" approach indicating selection of health care providers will be dictated by bureaucrats. We will inveigh generally against any market interference as government meddling. We'll organize all of this program into a climax which rationalizes that the Daggett plan will not balance the budget and Daggett is in fact a 'tax and spend liberal.' If we allow Daggett to take the lead in the campaign issues, he will afford us opportunities to entangle him in his own statements and cripple him."

"We also have arranged," said Emmett, "a series of substantial speeches by Senator Hatford which will affect the campaigns in each state. These will, of course, be supported by our direct campaign ads and those you contribute for which we are most grateful."

"I haven't heard anything about big government," said Erla. "You got preempted on that and if you don't occupy the ground on other issues that are positive on your side, I can assure you the same thing will happen. It's hard for you to take a strong defense posture without agreeing with Adrian. What's your stand on crime and drugs?"

"They didn't do Bob Dole any good," Emmett said.

"Why would you say that?"

"He lost," said Emmett. "Besides the polls show this is a diminishing issue."

"If you don't take a position on crime and drugs you might get bombed again the way you did on regulation."

"I don't think we got bombed on regulation."

"Then what do you call it?"

"We have no reason to propose a reform, such as Adrian Daggett has, in our program."

"What were you going to do?" asked Helene.

"We haven't worked that out as of yet. It seems regulation might not be an issue in this campaign. It doesn't show in the polls."

Helene wondered how they had lost their perspective. Daggett was making the issues and setting the "rules of engagement." Most likely campaign politics with everyone jockeying for position for the victory spoils had diverted them from the real task of figuring out how to win. She was fully aware that the Daggett staff was highly focused on winning.

"Don't you think it might be a good idea to take some issue initiative rather than rely entirely on counter punching?" she asked.

"We have thought about proposing tax cuts, but with an opponent proposing a tax increase we wonder if it's necessary."

"What do your surveys show?" asked Erla.

"We see a confused pattern as a result of some of the Daggett pronouncements."

"Including the loss of Republican votes to Daggett?" asked Erla.

"I'm not sure if that's anything more than temporary," said Emmett.

"It also appears to me," said Helene, "that we are behind in the polls."

Randy shrugged.

"The polls before the conventions are probably not meaningful," he said. "We see no cause for concern. We have yielded the initiative to the Daggetts to let them make mistakes."

"Suppose they don't make too many mistakes?" asked Helene.

"They already have," said Emmett. "They have a large unfavorable percentage. That's the critical signal. That will grow to well over 50% as we develop our total story on Daggett, which shows that he can't pay for what he wants to do without substantial tax increases. We will indicate that the increases are for much greater on spending and not for deficit reduction."

"What are going to be your identifying issues?" Helene asked, still looking for their theme.

"We're certainly going to be different from Daggett on debt reduction and on foreign policy. We're going to go strongly negative against him on those. We're certainly going to oppose him on national health insurance. That's always been a bad issue for the liberals. We're going to go against him on his refusal to propose tax cuts with a budget surplus. We'll postulate that he intends to spend the surplus. We will win with those issues."

"I asked you what your theme issues are going to be," said Helene. "Everything you've mentioned so far is a counter punch. What's your theme issue?

"We're traditional Republicans; everyone knows we're against big government."

"But you got preempted on one big government issue."

"We're going to portray Daggett as a big government, big spending politician who is not going to really pay down the debt. Negativism works, Helene. You can help us by refuting him on the higher taxes and involvement overseas."

"The Daggett campaign has a theme; reality," said Helene. "It's the 'reality' campaign to elect a 'reality government.' How will you oppose that?"

"I've just been telling you that. We are going to question everything he says on key issues."

"I think what Helene is trying to say you is have to tell people what you're for as well as what you're against," said Warren.

"There has to be something positive that you propose," Erla said.

Daune, a heavyset Swedish woman, cleared her throat.

"The reality is," said Daune, "they have taken away the big government issue by saying they are going to shrink government by one million employees, partly with their new model of regulations." Emmett looked angrily at Daune.

Helene observed what was going on. Daune was sending her a signal. The senior staff of Senator Hatford was obviously not ready for this meeting. "What's your constituency strategy?"

"We're aiming at the middle class and the upper class and we will appeal to union voters through the mechanism of the information you shared with us. There will be some good speeches on that."

"What about states?"

"We are going to focus Hatford on the must states, California, Texas, Ohio, New York, and Florida. We'll concede Illinois to Daggett. We'll certainly win Indiana. I don't see Daggett getting anywhere in the mid-south or in Michigan; his no tax cut posture will do him in there. After promising to dismiss government employees, Daggett conceded Maryland and Virginia. Maybe we'll win in the District."

"But he's saying that he'll cut the capital gains tax."

"A rich man's issue," said Emmett.

Helene excused herself and gave an eye signal to Erla to continue the discussion. She saw the Hatford campaign was wallowing in political mud. They probably didn't want help, particularly. They all wanted to be heroes in the eyes of the boss. Only Daune was thinking the whole process through. Not easy working alone.

On her cell phone, she called Ward's office and set up a meeting for first thing in the morning. In the plane on their way back, she, Erla, and Warren talked through the meeting and their strategy. Erla, Warren, Harold, Marsha, and Edgar gathered with Ward and Madeline. Helene summarized the meeting in Washington.

"All of this indicates, Ward, that these people don't have the ability to operate a national campaign. They can't foresee the things that can happen that are overridden by a central theme. They can counter punch but, unless they are exceptionally effective, the reality theme will smother them. While it may be possible to get people to vote against Daggett they also have to vote for Hatford, otherwise they might not vote at all. There is a whole bunch of dynamics that nobody fully understands or can measure. Their idea of adding up all of the things that Daggett wants to do and calling him a tax and spender is a good one, but the numbers have to come together. They have to be convincing. The Daggett story sounds very good, particularly from a man who sounds like he is going to do what he says. With these people in charge there isn't much hope."

"What do you propose, Helene?"

"Look at the opposition," she said. "Terry Leelan was selected apparently by Ian MacAulliffe to head the primary campaign. Ian and Terry formed the issues staff under Roger Bennett which has produced some highly competent work and many detailed fresh ideas. We see that in the new model of regulations. They have probably got three or four other things ready to drop. Michelle has reported one or two of them that we don't understand yet."

"Thank God for our moles," said Ward, looking at Edgar.

"We face a team that has Nancy Letersky, a top flight corporate type, running the communication. Anne Russell is among the best if not the best at press and publicity relations. Alan Jacobs is among the best and comes from the best political consulting firm. We can match them with our human resources, but the Hatford campaign can't," said Helene.

"Well?"

"Warren Hatch has to become the head of that campaign, so he can rely on us and use us as he needs us the same way Terry Leelan can bring in the resources of that issues staff and PENMET."

There was silence. Warren started to feel his heart pounding.

"Why Warren?" said Ward.

"Because he is a well-known conservative activist," she said. "The decision would not be questioned."

"How are we ever going to possibly accomplish this?"

"You and Mendos, Radion, Ryan, and others are going to have to come up with a connection. We'll prepare a paper on a proposed strategy and theme for their campaign."

Once again there was silence.

"Is there anyone who disagrees with this position?" asked Ward.

"It's pretty bad, Ward. They are relying on going totally negative against a highly positive and effective campaign. They have no theme," said Marsha.

Ward looked at Warren a little skeptically.

"Warren, can you handle this?" He asked.

"I can," Warren said. "If I have support from all of you here."

"All right, I think we have to have a meeting of the executive board, but we'll do it in Washington," said Ward.

He understood what Helene was saying. There had to be a careful presentation to the senator and his inner circle to tell them what they need and to get them to do what Helene proposed.

"If anyone has connections to the inner circle it would be Ryan because of the large factories they have in St. Louis and Kansas City," he suggested.

"I think that is the best place to start," said Helene.

RYAN DID INDEED have access to the inner circle and with one phone call arranged for Helene to give a private briefing to Carolyn Masiac, the senator's administrative assistant. This was set for Ryan's private conference room in his headquarters building in New Orleans. She loved the French Quarter and came the night before the meeting to enjoy a stroll down the Rue Royal, looking in the galleries for something that might catch her eye. In the morning she went running on the levee, conscious of the attention of several longshoremen who had slept off drinking bouts by the river.

Wearing a blue Gucci suit, she arrived early and was greeted by Ryan who showed her to a small conference room. A coffee service with muffins and beignets was on a small buffet table. They chatted about developments in the campaign. Shortly after, Carolyn arrived and Ryan gave them each a little background on each other. He told Carolyn that Helene worked with the Southern Conservative Coalition as executive director and also with another group that several corporations had formed to provide assistance in soft costs.

Carolyn knew that Helene had met with Randy, Daune, and

Emmett from the campaign. Ryan told Helene that Carolyn had been in politics her entire adult life. He didn't say that Carolyn believed she was headed for a top White House job and real power, but Helene came to that conclusion on her own.

They each had a cup of coffee at the buffet and looked for a moment at the view from the top floor of the Mississippi Chemical Building of the great crescent of the Mississippi dotted with ships and river barges.

"Did you arrive last night?"

"I stayed at the Royal Orleans. I can't resist the galleries on the Rue Royal."

Carolyn stiffened and Helene wondered if she took going shopping and the use of the French name of the street as a sign of softness. Carolyn didn't know Helene was cooped up on Harbour Island and was almost fluent in the language.

"You said you had something for us?"

"Yes we do," Helene said. "It's a paper I had drawn up after I met with the campaign staff. Also you will find an intelligence document which summarizes the Daggett positions which I had our special staff prepare."

She passed the papers across the table and pulled out her own copies.

"These papers indicate to you that based on the present plans of the Hatford campaign we are going to lose," she said. She saw no change in the skepticism in Carolyn's eyes.

"Let me see how you come to that conclusion," Carolyn said without changing her expression.

Helene went through the items point by point by the polling results.

"You do your own polls?" Carolyn asked.

"We use the Hirsch organization."

"Hirsch?"

"Yes."

Carolyn was impressed with that, but Helene still read skepticism.

"What is it that you want?"

"We very much want Senator Hatford to be elected and we are prepared to substantially aid the campaign."

"But you have already communicated that to the campaign, and I assume coordinated your activities and advertising with theirs."

"We have, but we see that more is needed."

"Our strategy is simple," Carolyn said. "We wait for Daggett to make his mistakes, we already have some."

"I agree that simple strategy is best," Helene said. "But we've found no theme to your campaign and no issues that you are going to assume."

"Perception is reality, Helene. We are going to create perceptions of what Adrian Daggett will do when he is president which a majority of the public aren't going to like."

"You may think you're going to do that, but Daggett has an able staff; far better than the one running your campaign."

"How can you say that?"

"They haven't told you of the need for a campaign theme. They haven't told you that you need your own issues. They plan only to amalgamate the case against Daggett by adding up the costs of all of his issues and then assess him as a tax and spend liberal."

"That's what he is."

Helene looked her in the eye.

"I'm afraid that's not the case, Carolyn. He's a real candidate. We oppose him for reasons of the issues he has raised."

"So will the public, as we define what he means."

"You may define what you want people to think he really means," Helene said. "You can do it issue by issue. But, without a theme to your campaign, you're going to end up like Bob Dole. His theme, if anything, was anti-intellectualism, which destabilized a lot of voters."

"The Dole campaign was incompetent," said Carolyn. "We have the best people we can get our hands on."

"From political circles, you are probably correct," said Helene, "but Daggett has a team of top professionals. So far you have lost the issues of legal reform, regulatory reform, and downsizing government which should be Republican issues. It seemed to us the campaign staff took too long a vacation."

Carolyn leaned back in her chair and thought for a moment.

"I'm interested in what you say about theme."

Helene reached into her briefcase and pulled out two files passing one across the table to Carolyn. On the outside the words "Assuring Freedom" were printed in large letters. Inside there was a one-page summary of the key points.

"Carolyn, by going negative under a positive theme of "Assuring Freedom" you double the impact, plus you could also pick up some related issues. This way your overall perception is positive. You need to persuade people that the Hatford candidacy assures freedom that embraces the pocketbook issues, 'freedom of the pocketbook' which replies to Daggett's opposition to tax cuts. You need 'freedom of choice in health care' to create perceptions about national health insurance. 'Freedom from the United Nations' could add perceptions concerning the foreign policy. It all comes together in a master theme. This is the main thing I find missing."

Helene paused to be sure Carolyn understood; she did. She was genuinely competent and smart, and was probably one of the rare people in politics who did not think she knew everything and admitted her mistakes.

"Who did this?"

"My staff."

"Your report says you met with Randy and his staff in Washington last week?"

"That is correct. We worked over the weekend."

There was a pause. One of the problems Carolyn had was not being able to get the right people in the campaign on the phone after 6 p.m..

"I see what you mean, Helene. What do you propose?"

"One of the people that we have retained to work with us is Warren Hatch."

"So that's where he disappeared to," Carolyn observed.

"He's done a lot of the fundamentals, which you have seen."

"The foundation ads are very well done."

"Thank you. We propose that you appoint Hatch as the overall director of the campaign so we can integrate this staff with the present campaign staff."

"I don't see how we can afford that."

"We'll keep it within the definition of 'soft costs.' All you have to do is pay Warren."

The powerful paper on the campaign theme had impressed Carolyn and made her re-think the campaign situation.

"Tell me more about this staff, Helene."

"This is related to the Southern Conservative Coalition. The staff is funded by contributors primarily corporations interested in promoting the conservative viewpoint. We are, as you know, based in Jacksonville."

"Is it possible for the Senator and myself to meet with them so we can exchange some ideas?"

"We will bring them to Washington or to wherever you want."

"That is very thoughtful of you. Time is now the key commodity."

"More important than money," Helene said.

THE FOLLOWING WEEK, a Gulfstream jet zipped over Florida and across the Gulf of Mexico with Helene, Erla, Marsha, Ruth Farrencolt, Harold, Warren, and Louis. They landed in Houston where Senator Hatford was scheduled to speak and checked into the University Hilton where Hatford would be staying. Helene took them all to Papasitos Mexican Restaurant in the University area for dinner to get them in the Texas frame of mind. When they returned to the hotel, the presence of the Secret Service indicated Hatford's arrival.

The following morning, it was easy to find the meeting room from the agents standing by the door. Helene and Erla were the first to arrive. They found a room with a conference table and the precise number of seats needed. The walls were decorated with paintings of Texas scenes and a buffet table on one side offered coffee, juices, fruit, and rolls. When everyone was present, the Secret Service phoned Carolyn. Five minutes later she came in the room with the senator.

Helene immediately tried to size him up. He was tall and graceful with graying hair and very thin lips. He smiled as she introduced him and Carolyn to each of her people. After Carolyn brought coffee to the Senator at the head of the table, he asked everyone to be seated.

"Thank you all for coming over to Houston. I hope you had a good evening," he said. I had to give a dinner speech." They laughed. "Carolyn has shared the excellent paper you did after Helene met with Randy. We are interested in your proposition, but obviously you can understand I wanted to see you in the flesh. Warren, it's particularly good to see you."

Warren smiled, "And to see you, sir."

"We appreciate the opportunity, Senator," said Helene. "I think maybe the agenda has given us a number of questions you would like to discuss and we are ready to do that."

"I congratulate you all," Hatford continued, "on your great idea of 'Assuring Freedom' as our campaign theme. It seems to me it off-sets the 'reality campaign' so that we are talking 'reality' against 'freedom.' That makes a nice contrast."

"Thank you," said Helene. "We've been thinking about this a little longer than since last week."

"I can see you have," said Hatford. "After reading your memorandum I can see that you knew we needed to re-think some things. This morning, I will speak a few minutes on my reaction to your memorandum and on some philosophies I see entering the program. Then we should chat for as much time as we need to get to know each other so you can do as much as you can for us."

Helene thought he gave a good synopsis of his personal philosophy and the way he would respond to the Daggett issues. He seemed to have fully grasped the ideas that they had put forward in their memorandum. Daggett's message, she realized, was reality, but scattered all over the issues map. She assumed the issues campaign was going to bank on triggering responses from different constituencies and she imagined correctly that Terry and Alan had organized those constituencies into a master plan.

The response to this had to be a simpler and more cohesive plan such as Ronald Reagan's, "The problem is not in the government; government is the problem." Empty and meaningless as it was, it created perceptions. The reality campaign might hinge on whether or not people took the time to understand the reality issues or whether they preferred to be guided by perceptions. In recent years, there had been an obvious preference for the simple answers. Helene foresaw that "freedom of the pocketbook, freedom from the UN, and freedom to choose health care" could win out. She would make the voters choose perceptions.

At the end of the discussion the Senator got up and walked over to Warren and said, "Okay, Mr. Hatch, you're hired. Give us some time to arrange the announcement and move yourself up to Washington."

Warren rose to shake hands and said he looked forward to joining the Senator as soon as possible. The Senator didn't know that Warren would continue to draw his retainer from POLACO while he also received payment from the campaign. Warren was also turned on by the high profile of running the campaign and prospectively being in the White House or one of the agencies. He would, of course, prefer the White House and might insist on it. The performance of the POLACO staff would make him look good.

WHILE THE HATFORD campaign stumbled, the Daggett staff looked for another issue to steal. It was Anne's idea to combine gun control and crime. Her colleagues embellished it from there for the annual convention of The National Association of Chiefs of Police.

When the staff of the association heard what Adrian wanted to say they were delighted to make a place for him. The program was extended on their second day so Adrian could speak at 3:00 in the afternoon. As the conference was in Minneapolis, it would be four o'clock Eastern Time, fresh news for the evening and early enough to win live coverage. Anne would see to the proper arrangements. The opportunity to visit Hubert Humphrey's state would also be used to schmooze the Minnesota Democratic organization with 14 electoral votes.

The president of the association called a mid-afternoon recess to order, and when everyone was nearly in their places, Adrian and Pamela entered with an escort of association officers.

Adrian greeted them and thanked them for making a place for him on the program. Then, reflecting on the protests against his foreign policy because of putting young men and women in the armed services at risk, he reminded them that uniformed personnel put their lives at risk everyday in the law enforcement and fire fighting services.

"It's customary in the United States, that Honor Guards consist of enlisted men of the United States Army, Navy, Airforce, and Coast Guard," he said. "If I am elected president, I will add to all Honor Guards an American policeman and an American fireman also of enlisted rank. You deserve that recognition and I shall see to it."

Loud applause lasted for nearly a minute.

He then spoke of the incredulous argument about the banning of the sale of assault weapons. Despite the profound objections from police associations, he recounted the fact that many members of Congress and senators were persuaded to oppose and mitigate the measure. None of those who voted against that ban, he said, had any concept of reality in the streets when a gunfight between police and criminals erupts.

"Chiefs of police, like military officers consider every life for which they are responsible to be precious. No one ever wants to see a policeman gunned down in a hail of bullets because he can't match weapons in the hands of criminals. We can't have that in the United States and we won't. As a government conscious of reality, we are going to limit not only the sale of assault weapons, but the sale of all weapons that are unnecessary in the hands of the civilian population."

The audience clapped and cheered.

Adrian continued to say concealed weapons and all automatic weapons previously purchased would be registered. He said this would not include bolt and pump action guns or any type of single shot repeaters nor would it include collector's vintage guns.

"Whenever the subject of gun control comes up, the gun manufacturers lobby makes statements about the legislation that are far beyond the intent of those proposing it. The reality is that huntsmen will not be affected unless their aim is so bad they must have Uzis. Sport shooters will also not be affected. Shooting at a target with an AK 47 is not a sport. The various so-called 'militia' organizations readying themselves to defend against various imagined threats should become sport riflemen or pistolers. No one has the right to demand that weapons be sold to them which might harm our police."

The audience rose and there were cheers

Adrian continued by complimenting the substantial progress in reducing crime in certain key cities. He promised to bring forward legislation that would further strengthen the capabilities of police forces to deal with robbery and assault in particular.

He suggested a national dialogue on the marketing of illicit drugs. Selling drugs to minors, he said, was not an insignificant crime, rather it was in many cases a kind of murder, because it destroyed life.

Adrian pointed out that street gangs were another reality with which the police and society must deal. He recognized the problem as complex and that police might need assistance. He said that the possibility of conducting sweeps with the National Guard should be considered. Rehabilitating young men from gangs with military type training and schooling, he said, should be considered. He recognized there were a huge number of people dedicated to protecting their neighborhoods. He knew the police could not allow gangs to control streets; strong measures were needed. He said his administration would see that the needs were met.

"All of you have philosophized about the real meaning of police work," he said. "It is an over simplification to say your job is to enforce the laws. It's far more than that. Your job is to inspire people to respect the law; to serve as role models to young men and women; and to aid education in its major function of producing good citizens. You are in many respects the backbone of democracy. Without the rule of law, democracy is meaningless. The responsibility for maintaining democracy is partially in your hands. You play a key role. I shall look forward to the expanded Honor Guards. Thank you for the invitation to come here."

His audience rose cheering to a standing ovation. All at the head table crowded to shake hands. Pamela joined him at the podium. The president of the association asked if there could be questions. The Daggett style of dialoging with the audience was well known. The president tapped his gavel and offered to answer a few questions. A number of hands shot up as the audience sat down.

"Do you believe you would propose a constitutional amendment to repeal the right to bear arms?"

"I no longer think we need 'a well-ordered militia,'" Adrian replied. "That segment of the Bill of Rights probably should be repealed. We're going to stumble over it in the future if we don't remove it."

The president pointed again. A large man rose. "In the matter of drug marketing, would you favor making the sale of drugs a capital crime?"

"I don't like capital punishment that much," Adrian said. "There are over-eager prosecutors. I would favor long-term imprisonment possibly off the US mainland at hard labor."

The questioner, Adrian could see, had not heard what he wanted to hear.

The president pointed. A young man stood up. "You are the first politician I've heard mention the problem of the marketing of drugs. I agree with you that we must take every possible step to stop the marketing, but why not use the military and its technology for interdiction?"

"It's kind of dumb not to use any kind of capability we have to stop drug use," said Adrian. "We have to assess that. Perhaps faced with a greater interdiction capability and other barriers traffickers would be discouraged."

"One last question," the president said. He pointed. A tall gray-haired woman stood.

"We've heard a lot of this before from political people," she said. "What will you do if the National Rifle Association successfully lobbies or intimidates Congress to prevent or repeal automatic weapon legislation?"

"We will raise the issue a level to nationalizing the gun manufacturers," Adrian said. "There is precedent for the government to own and operate arsenals. That will bring all the facts into public view."

"Do you mean that?"

"Vote for me and find out."

The audience rose again to applaud as he and Pamela left with the group that had brought them into the hall. The next day the newspapers and television news were full of the speech. Many people were happy to hear that somebody was thinking about a long-term effort to mitigate the use of illegal drugs and guns. Many of them lived on streets often controlled by gangs, where drug selling was in the open and where gunfire was often heard.

The executive group of The National Rifle Association convened an emergency meeting. After deliberation they decided to have another meeting which their sponsors would attend.

☆ **Chapter 26** ☆

WHILE WARREN HATCH prepared to leave to take over as head of the Hatford campaign, Helene put the Harbour Island staff onto 14-hour days to give the biggest possible boost and to gain back time lost. She asked for a skeleton plan for the campaign, for a theme and doctrine, for print and TV materials, and for background information and up-to-date intelligence.

Marsha and her Political Analysis Group, aided by Fischer's Intelligence Group, developed a constituency plan and prospective strategies in each state. Erla and her Doctrine and Intelligence Group enlarged and enhanced the theme of "Assuring Freedom." The Communication Group wrote prospective speeches for the Senator and cranked out advertising copy, press releases, and position papers. They wrote and produced TV ads. For seven straight days everyone started early and worked until they couldn't focus. An immense amount was accomplished. Warren carried away briefcases full of documents and tapes.

Daphne saw her role as external mole more clearly when she could report that for seven days none of the senior people had played tennis, there were no other games, and no one from POLACO was at the bars in the evening. The whole POLACO staff was obviously occupied on a most important project. It was her job to find out what it was, but she would have to wait until they reappeared.

Most mornings, Daphne ran past the POLACO compound or took a walk at lunchtime. She spent some time on the inshore beach at the Romora Bay Club with a view of traffic to and from the airport and the POLACO dock. When she thought there might be action, she worked on her portable computer on the beach.

Sharon did the daily shopping around 11:00 in the morning and went past the docks downtown. She did her running in the afternoon along Bay Street and looked at the parking lot of the Landing to see if anyone had come out early with a POLACO vehicle. Between 5:30 and 7:00 p.m. either Daphne or Sharon would walk or ride past the tennis courts. When tourists or others stopped to watch, they mingled into the group.

Daphne wondered why there was no concealment of the tennis courts. Originally they were part of a tennis club which wanted to advertise their courts and offer passers-by the attraction of watching a game. No one in POLACO had thought of what they might reveal.

During the evenings, Daphne went to the posh bar, Valentine's, which had a hotel, yacht club and dock, and where the background music was classical or Broadway. Sharon was a regular patron of The Landing, which had a hotel and no dock, where the music was calypso or reggae.

Daphne used her reputation as a writer to become part of a regular group which included POLACO staff. The conversation was usually light, but could get philosophical. She avoided asking questions that might signal her professional curiosity. Others asked her about her writing and she was able to discuss her projects, telling the absolute truth. She invited them to parties at her house. Sharon did the same. Friendships evolved from these and some information had been sent back to Alvin Carter.

Sharon developed a relationship with a local businessman whom she saw on weekends. Daphne started a liaison with a recently widowed aerospace executive from Atlanta who owned and rented out three homes in the town. He came every third or fourth weekend. They used his 40' sloop which slept six and was docked at Valentine's for day sails. He promised her a trip down Eleuthera Sound to the Exuma Keys. She didn't tell him that she would not be able to do it. Both men served a purpose at the bars to make things look as natural as they could.

Monday evening, after the full week of no tennis, Daphne suddenly found the courts full. Volleyball was going strong and there was even a coed soccer game for the overflow crowd. Walking on farther toward the beach Daphne saw other POLACO people swimming. Everyone was outside. Whatever had occupied them either was completed or an intermission had been declared. She saw Helene, Ward, Madeline, Harold Smalley, Erla, and Marsha all playing.

Walking quickly back to her house Daphne planned the evening. She and Sharon would be early at their respective hangouts to eat dinner. That way people would gather around them and join them.

At Valentine's, Daphne picked a table that would normally hold four and six squeezed together. She had just taken two sips of a gin and tonic when Laurie Pinta, POLACO's computer whiz, and Preston Martin, who she thought was in intelligence, came in.

"Where have you all been?" Daphne smiled. "Sharon and I have been drinking alone. The last two nights we drank together."

The established line was that Sharon and Daphne didn't go out together during the evening because they worked and lived together.

"We've been busy. All of a sudden a big job came down from above," said Laurie.

"We were congratulated today that we did two months work in a week."

"It sure feels like it," said Preston.

Laurie and Preston were proper nerds. Daphne didn't think she would get much out of them. "Whatever were you doing?" she asked. "Was it some kind of campaign?"

"It was something like that," Preston said guardedly.

"We've decided to call a perfectly legitimate candidate a racist," said Laurie.

Daphne didn't blink, but her heart started pounding. This could be the break she was waiting for.

"Nobody is a racist in politics anymore," she said innocently.

"This man certainly isn't," Laurie said, "but we're going to accuse him of it."

"Laurie, we shouldn't talk about this," said Preston.

"I'm sorry. I'm a little mad about it," Laurie said. "We should deal in issues not in accusations. His lack of family values? What nonsense."

"Our assignment is to win an election, Laurie," Preston admonished.

"I don't know why we're opposing this man."

"Opposing who?" Daphne decided she could ask.

"Adrian Daggett," said Laurie. "He's the best man who's run for president in the United States since Harry Truman and maybe a lot better."

"Hi, you guys," said a woman's voice. Daphne turned and felt even luckier as Ruth Farrencolt joined them. Now she had intelligence, the computers, and Marsha's right hand. The waitress came with menus.

Ruth said, "Set a place at the end of the table. Jimmy's coming."

Jimmy Cooper was Ruth's steady boyfriend.

"You look upset, Laurie," Ruth observed.

"I don't like opposing Adrian Daggett."

"I suppose I don't either, but we have to do it. That's our job," said Ruth.

"I think our job is not to talk about this," said Preston.

"What are you doing opposing Adrian Daggett?" Daphne asked to keep the conversation on the point. "I thought you were a political research foundation like the Einaudi Institute."

"We're a good deal more applied than the Einaudi Institute," said Ruth. "We work directly on political issues in the United States. Some of our sponsors apparently don't like Adrian Daggett and they're sending Warren Hatch, our political director, to be his campaign manager. So I guess we're going to be involved."

Preston gave her a "you're talking too much" look.

"I may not even mind campaigning against Daggett if we did it on the issues. This idea of attacking him as a racist and an anti-unionist is pathetic." Laurie, who was generally genial and quiet, was riled up.

"It's politics, Laurie," Ruth said.

Daphne smiled.

"That doesn't mean I have to like it," Laurie responded. "I also think the theme is kind of mushy." She turned to Daphne. "Suppose a guy's running for president and his theme was 'Assuring Freedom.' What would you think?"

"It sounds Republican," Daphne said.

"No, what does it mean to you?"

"It means maybe reducing the size of government, pushing back the bureaucracy."

"Well, that's close," said Laurie.

Jimmy Cooper, a tall, sandy-haired advertising writer came up behind Ruth and reached under her brown hair to massage her neck.

"Oh," Ruth groaned. "I went seven days without that."

"I went seven days without sex," he joked.

She swung her arm in his ribs as he sat down.

"That hurt. Remember you're in military training."

Now Daphne had four bright young people sitting at her table. Preston, light-haired with white skin, medium height, an introvert; Laurie, shorter, slender and demure with shoulder length dark hair and a serious look about her eyes; Ruth, tall with light brown hair, attractive; something of a klutz, but gaining confidence in her military training. Jimmy, in love with Ruth, a creative extrovert.

"You guys are talking politics, I guess," he said.

"I just asked Daphne if she understood 'Assuring Freedom' and I think maybe it's not so bad," Laurie said.

"Of course, it's not so bad, we're the group that thought it up," he smiled.

"I think we're not supposed to talk about this in front of Daphne," Preston said.

"We have to try ideas on somebody outside sometime," said Laurie.

"Okay, Daphne, what do you think about 'Assuring Freedom' as a campaign theme?" Jimmy asked.

"She said it sounded Republican, but then she came up with reducing the size of government and chopping at bureaucracy," said Laurie.

"Laurie wants an issue-oriented campaign," said Ruth. "I don't think there has been an issues-oriented campaign since the Civil War."

"There were a few things like hard money versus soft money," said Daphne.

"Politics is perception," said Jimmy. "What you hear and see is not what you get."

"Well that's what I'm arguing about. Adrian Daggett is trying to change from perceptions to issues," Laurie pouted.

"Issues are too complicated for most people," said Jimmy, "but they still want to vote. If Daggett wants to deal in reality, he has to recognize that most people are not going to know what they're voting on."

"Very few people understand the key issues," said Ruth. "Therefore, political campaigns create perceptions. It's the only way they can communicate about their candidate."

"The candidates themselves are perceptions," said Laurie. "They have to read their statements, and we have to work together to find solutions to the problems. Most of them don't know what the problems are."

Ruth grinned.

"Senator Hatford will know what all of the problems are and he will have perceptions of how to overcome them," she quipped.

They laughed.

"Daggett," Laurie insisted, "is an environmentalist. He has promised to stop the development of coastal wetlands which he can do without the approval of Congress. He's the first presidential candidate to come up with something tangible to do about education other than talk about it and spend money. Local involvement is the thing; that's what'll wind the clock. He's fiscally responsible and will take no further chances with the markets. He's got a worldview of how to achieve long-term peace and stability. Other than not liking his idea about interfering in the currency markets, what's the big deal about Adrian Daggett?"

"I totally disagree with national health insurance," Daphne said. "The American system is the best in terms of quality of care that is offered. Most of the other systems are inferior." She wanted to avoid seeming to be an observer.

"And what's so inferior in Sweden, Switzerland, Germany, and Canada?" asked Laurie.

More came out over dinner. When they were finished with their meals, both couples seemed eager to head for an apartment. Daphne told them she was glad to see them that evening because she would be away for the next two days in New York.

She had not expected to go to New York when she sat down at the table. Now, judging from the information she had gathered, she fully expected Alvin would want her to come to Harrisburg or would meet her in New York. All of the time she had spent philosophizing with the young people of POLACO, entertaining them at her home, and bonding with them had just paid off. She had a reasonably detailed outline of POLACO's program to defeat Daggett. And there was the startling news that Warren Hatch would take over the Hatford campaign. He would be the obvious tie with POLACO and would be the conduit of POLACO resources into the general election battle.

She walked back to her house thinking through the conversation and the key points. She phoned American Express and booked the morning flight from North Eleuthera to Fort Lauderdale, then on to Newark. Then in her studio she began writing pages of notes reaching back in her memory for every detail from the beginning. She was nearly finished when Sharon came in. "Did you confirm Warren Hatch is going to take over the Hatford campaign tomorrow?" Sharon asked.

"I did," said Daphne. "Except he's going to do what Helene tells him."

"What else do you have?"

"POLACO's Communication Group is going to write campaign ads working with the intelligence section and the ideological section and then send them to Warren to be produced. The rumor is that Helene is taking over the campaign and Warren is a figurehead for her."

"I don't think Warren would be a patsy to Helene. He will assert himself. His ego will make him do it."

"There is a rumor that he's never run a campaign before, but that Erla and Marsha have so they will make a lot of the decisions or at least very strong recommendations. The Communication Group will also work on a lot of new radio and TV ads for the foundations in order to refute Daggett on the issues.

"You'd better sit down at your desk and write everything down," said Daphne. "Get every detail you can and then we'll compare. With whom did you meet?"

"The computer people Jeff and Julie Spencer, Norma Wilder, the writer, and Pat Stabler from the video production group. Everyone was working day and night. Last week they actually produced some four different ads."

Sharon then gave a rundown. They were "Harry and Louise" type ads with professionals and their families. The snatches of dialogue they had related to her were tantalizing: "How can there be a fiscal crisis if we're in the largest economy in the world?" "How is Mr. Daggett going to pay for his new programs and also pay down the debt?" "How much of this is reality?" "What is reality?" "Maybe the reality is tax and spend." "Freedom of choice, freedom of enterprise, and freedom from big government."

"Get it all down in writing, Sharon. Think of every detail. I'm going to New York tomorrow. I'm not going to file this report by telephone from here. I'd like to take you with me, but I think you should stay and keep listening."

While Sharon started her notes, Daphne packed. They compared findings and asked each other questions until they were both too tired to talk.

In the serene light of the late spring morning and after a sleepless night, Daphne took off from the airport. She sipped coffee and nibbled on a piece of fruit bread as she watched the clear blue water slide beneath the plane. She took out the combined notes and began to digest them into a memorandum on her portable computer.

In Fort Lauderdale she phoned Alvin who was in his office concerned that he hadn't heard from her. When he found out what she had, he complimented her for booking herself on the next flight to Newark. He told her to meet him at the Continental Airlines Presidents Club at gate 78.

When Daphne arrived and asked for Alvin at the desk, she was ushered to a conference room where she found both Alvin and Tony

Destito. Tony had brought a portable printer so they could all review the document she had finished. There was silence in the room as they read what she had written.

"This is unbelievable, Daphne," said Tony. "From two conversations."

"No, not from two conversations, but from months of conversations and a bonding process. It happened last night. We set up the means by which people we knew suddenly talked to each other and to Sharon and me about what was going on."

"There is more here than just facts," said Alvin. "We have two people, Laurie and Pat, who are disenchanted."

"It feels like more than disenchanted," Daphne said. "Pat wants to leave, but their contracts won't allow it. There are also strict confidentiality agreements which they broke last night by talking in front of someone from the outside. At my table Preston Martin didn't contribute. He admonished the others to stop talking. It could be a problem for Ruth and Jimmy or for Laurie if her relationship with Preston breaks up. He's a stiff neck, very proper."

"We know they have the means for interrogation and for punishment," said Tony. Then he realized Daphne hadn't been told about it.

"What do you mean?" she asked.

"Edgar Slaughter has set up an interrogation center which uses electric probes as a means of encouraging people to talk and also as punishment for people who disobey the rules."

"They have that?"

"Operations like this have to have some form of discipline beyond the usual discharge of employees. Edgar is a pro, he knows it."

"Electricity?"

"What they use leaves no marks so they can deny using it."

Daphne wondered what would happen to her and Sharon if they were ever in Edgar Slaughter's hands.

"We could sit here and have fun interpreting all of this, but there is another question," he said. "How do we get this communicated to Chicago?"

"We could have Nancy come here or meet her at Cleveland," said Alvin.

"I think it's best if the senior staff people meet Daphne and we dissect this with them."

"I don't see any risk," Alvin said.

"Let's go to Chicago," said Tony as he reached for the phone.

A limousine fetched them at O'Hare. By 3:30 Chicago time, they were at the Executive Plaza, where Tony had booked a suite for one of his regular visits. A few minutes later, Tony introduced Daphne to Terry, Alan, Anne, and Nancy. They sat down around Tony's sitting room, which was bright and cheerful with light colored furniture and walls. Alvin started the meeting.

"You all know that we've been concerned that we have two moles, one at PENMET and one at the campaign who are giving information to POLACO," he said. "There is convincing circumstantial evidence. I am pleased to tell you Daphne Poltrac is our mole at Harbour Island."

That got everyone's attention.

Daphne told the story of how she and Sharon had worked. She described Harbour Island and how they observed POLACO, including the tennis and other sports. She described the evenings at the bars, and the special parties and get-togethers. Then she told what had happened in the last nine days.

"These are," she said picking up a stack of stapled papers, "the summaries prepared from our notes of last night. These include every fact that we learned and the conclusions we reached. I thought maybe you should read this to better understand what we have found."

"How long have you been on Harbour Island?" asked Terry.

"For six months."

There was silence while the senior staff read the paper.

"What a neat job," said Alan.

"More than a neat job," said Nancy. "Incredible."

"So this is what intelligence is all about," said Anne.

"This is the winning strategy," said Terry, "if it wasn't against us."

"The theme 'Assuring Freedom' has a ring to it. I see what they could do with that," said Anne.

"A lot of potential damage," said Nancy.

"One big bombastic speech trumpeted around the country," said Terry," then repeated and repeated and repeated."

"I would have never guessed a theme like this," said Alan. "Freedom from big government and freedom from bureaucracy."

"As you can see they said freedom from a lot of things. I think health care is involved in it by freedom of choice," said Daphne.

"The attack points would be on foreign policy, the taxes, the pocketbook issue, national health insurance, and perhaps atomic energy," said Nancy.

"I'm not so certain about that," said Daphne. "Somebody named Sadovan, I hear, has to be consulted."

"'Sadovan,' is correct. Mendos Sadovan," said Tony.

"They will attack us accusing Adrian of being anti-union and racist," Terry mused.

"That's what one of the young people was so much against," said Tony. "She listed all the things that Adrian was for that were good, and asked why they should oppose him."

"That in itself was interesting," said Terry. "It is not clear that the people in the lower ranks know what is actually going on."

"That's likely, Terry," Alvin said. "They won't trust very many with the secrets. Maybe Helene really doesn't know the ultimate objectives."

"Once someone gets accustomed to earning as much as they pay, there won't be a lot of questions," Nancy speculated.

"There will always be some who question," Alvin replied. "Those are the ones we might work with."

"I'm glad our work accomplished something," said Daphne.

"Do we know very much about the polling they're doing?" asked Alan.

"We only know there is a lot and information is fed into their intelligence center."

"They probably have estimated that using the atomic energy issue will exploit perceptions already created," Terry said. "Hatford only needs to say he'll maintain the status quo, when we really need to be thinking long-term about energy options and developing an energy policy."

"Which every other nation in the free world has," added Nancy.

"How did they produce four videos in a week?" asked Anne.

"They have their own production unit," Daphne said. "People were recruited from New York. Sharon mostly sees them. One of them, a very intelligent woman, Pat Stabler, is unhappy with her contract."

"Was there any discussion of our taking their issues?"

"Sharon picked up on the slow pace of the Hatford campaign in occupying the issues ground which has particularly allowed Adrian to take the regulatory reform issue. That was one reason for a meeting between Helene and somebody very close to Hatford to get Warren appointed."

"Does Hatford and his staff know about POLACO?" asked Alan.

"They wouldn't tell them about it," said Tony. "There will be some kind of screen."

"Probably the Southern Conservative Coalition," Terry offered.

"Our problem right now is racism," said Nancy, "and anti-unionism.

Why have they picked those subjects?"

"Maybe we're vulnerable because we haven't talked about it," said Alan.

"That's easily remedied," said Terry.

"That may be it," said Anne. "We've had only one speech on race. They think they have an opening to attack us. Is something ready?"

"There's not a lot of strength in Cleveland on this," said Nancy. "Some people are working on it."

"Where could we give a good speech on racism after a publicity build up?" asked Terry.

"We'll check the schedule," said Nancy. "I bet we have a good chance to defuse that one. I wish we could do the same about anti-unionism."

"I hope we can find out more about it," said Anne. "Now that these subjects have come up and we know it, Sharon and Daphne can ask the occasional question."

"It will be helpful to know what they've got or what they think they have," said Alan.

"We'll try," said Daphne.

They talked with Daphne until about 7:00 in the evening. Tony went down with everyone to the hotel lobby. Anne, Alan, and Terry each took taxis while Nancy waited in line for the fourth. When he was quite certain no one could see Tony got into the cab with her.

Nancy's apartment was modern with modern furniture decorated with campaign posters and campaign photographs. She made little changes every few days; the feeling was livable and comfortable. There were two sofas and a large screen television in the living room; a glass table for four in the small dining room; and a bar in the kitchen for breakfast and other meals. The bedroom had a chest of drawers, a dresser, and a queen-size bed. The bathroom was spacious with both a tub and a shower stall and two basins. When she showed those to Tony, she said, "This reminds me every morning that I live alone."

"It bothers you, doesn't it?"

"I intellectualize in a way saying I have a chance to be press secretary in the White House, and I don't want the entanglement. But then emotionally I feel I'm getting older and I'm alone. I'm not trying for sympathy, Tony."

"I know. If we win this election, you'll be fighting them off."

"I just hope one of them is as nice as you with brains, and feelings."

He couldn't answer that. In the kitchen she brought out a bottle of port and poured two glasses.

"Is Daphne in danger, Tony?" she asked.

"Some, but Helene has that punishment interrogation business under control," he said.

"What do you mean by that?"

He told her about Helene's policy.

"Have you reached a conclusion about Jean?"

"I think you're right," he said. "It must be another man. She has an excuse to be away most evenings. When I'm traveling she leaves the house. There's someone to feed the cat and walk the dog. For a long time we made love every night. Now, she's on her side of the bed and I'm on mine. She tries to avoid making love to me."

Nancy put her hands on his cheeks and kissed his lips lightly and said, "I won't."

She turned so he could unbutton her blouse while she dropped her skirt. She leaned her back against him. He fondled her firm breasts and caressed her nipples and stomach while he kissed her neck. She turned to him and slipped off his jacket and loosened his belt.

"I feel lonely and you feel empty." She unbuttoned his shirt while she kissed him.

"It's a new feeling," he said. "It's as though nothing makes sense any more."

She took his arm and moved him toward the bedroom. He lay down and pulled her on top of him. "You make sense, Tony. It's all important."

He had felt emotionally empty. She gave off her energy and her courage that brought her from the working class to near the top. How similar yet how different she was from Jean. Nancy made the world make sense again. Thinking of her filled him.

Ever since Charleston she'd felt it was more than sex with Tony. But what was it? Maybe she and Tony made sense.

ANNE RUSSELL FELT a compelling urge to strike hard at the accusations that POLACO was planning to make about Adrian's racism. She mobilized her staff and some extra resources from Evans & Copeland to make an appearance at the Human Resources Executives Association convention into a national event even though it was organized only ten days in advance.

The association was delighted that Adrian would speak. The annual gathering was at the New York Convention Center, which gave Adrian an opportunity to meet with Democratic leaders of this important city. Anne arranged a special dinner for the senior people of the association with Adrian and Pamela the night before at the Cornell Club so he would have a feel for their views. The New York media committed. The networks sent crews along with CNN.

At the convention, Adrian congratulated the human resources profession of the United States for forwarding the cause of civil rights. He said that while there were notable exceptions, the achievements went substantially unheralded. He recited these in terms of companies that had become racially integrated. He also spoke of companies who had published policies by which racial harassment or racial slurs were punished. He said there was no place for that in American business. Good businesses, he said, focuses on obtaining the quality of people who can contribute and expand their productivity and effectiveness regardless of race or sex.

Then he spoke of the shadow racism still cast in the United States. "In our political system and our democracy we may be faced with one inscrutable challenge and that is to become truly the melting pot, the nation where every person regardless of his heritage has an equal opportunity to realize the American dream. If America fails to become the melting pot, if race is allowed to divide us, we will not be successful. Martin Luther King is celebrated with a holiday as are Abraham Lincoln and George Washington. George Washington saved the foundling nation with his leadership and Abraham Lincoln saved the established union from division with his. Martin Luther King saved this great nation from a scenario of violence and dismemberment. For that we must forever be grateful to him and we must never allow his 'dream' to fade back to the paranoia of racial feelings. There are also other heroes in this effort who have accomplished great things in their companies and in their communities. These are men and women who have shared this view that America must prove itself as a multi-racial society.

Reality is that there are still people who would desecrate Doctor King's memory and who would maintain segregation as it was between the Civil War and World War II. We know that there are executive offices where there is no intention to treat minority people fairly and where language offensive to our African, Hispanic, and Asian Americans is used. I can tell you that when I am president of the United States and I receive proof of such language being used or of racial incidents within these corporations, I shall by executive order punish them by denying them federal business."

There was applause. Adrian then suggested that the association bring forward recommendations for government action to further equalize opportunities and extinguish racial bigotry. He touched the role of education, spoke of EEOC, and the other initiatives individuals can take. He ended:

"On this issue I ask for the support of this organization. You, of this organization, are the key to business and institutional involvement. America must be a nation of races that achieve much together. There will always be apostles of hate, and advocates of racial wrong. They must be refuted in the workplace. If they are, they will gradually disappear and our society will step to its position of unending glory. Thank you for inviting me."

There was a standing ovation.

The CNN commentator turned to face his audience. "You have just heard Adrian Daggett make an unusual statement about civil rights. He spoke of the reality of bigotry in the United States and asked the National Association of Human Resources executives to take a part in this eschewing it from our society. He pledged as President to exclude from government business, companies who were reported to allow racial incidents and racial slurs. He urged the executives to do the same in their businesses."

All three national networks carried the speech story. All the local stations of New York carried it. CNN *Headline News* had it on all day. A political analyst interviewed by CNBC remarked that Adrian Daggett knew that in most of the affairs of the United States, not too much happens until business gets involved. It was hard to find a newspaper or television or radio station in the United States that didn't run the story and a huge number commented editorially.

Two days later, reviewing the reports Anne Russell was satisfied that they had blunted any attack that might be based on inattention to the issue. She called Cleveland to thank the issues staff for a top-rate job in getting ready so quickly. That staff was her idea. She even told herself it was a good one.

☆ Chapter 27 ☆

MICHELLE PROUST TOLD Bill Haber of the insertion of the speech to the National Association of Human Resources Executives on civil rights into the schedule and of the plans for hyping the appearance. Yvonne Sperling, a senior analyst, realized the significance. She was a husky African-American political science Ph.D. from Georgetown. She carried a copy of the summary her group had prepared to Louis' office and waited until he finished a phone call.

"Something you need to look at boss."

"Good news?"

"No. Something suspicious." She laid the report on the table in front of them. "We had the final meeting with Warren giving our report to Ward on Monday last week. Notice on Thursday, Michelle reports a change in schedule with a speech on civil rights. Now the Daggett campaign is hyping the hell out of it. The question is, is this happenstance or was there a leak? Did they find out we were going to attack him as a closet racist?"

Louis turned a little white and looked up at Yvonne. She was not the most likable young woman on the staff. She was intellectually competent, but sometimes arrogant. Louis was uncertain among high-powered women, even if they worked for him. He reached for the phone and called Erla and explained that she, Helene, and Edgar should be at the intelligence center for a briefing on a potentially important matter.

Two hours later, Yvonne gave a computerized presentation on the big screen of the information correlated with the publicity bursts around the country. She showed the trumpeting announcement release which Michelle sent, and projected a graph of the pick-ups of comments by the Daggett people. Merrick Reynolds had mentioned the speech four times in four different cities. Nancy Letersky spent two minutes talking about it on an interview show and made a point of it at a press briefing. Terry Leelan also mentioned it in an interview with *Newsweek*.

"That's the scope of it," said Yvonne. "A major effort on civil rights is under way and started three days after we concluded our campaign planning and decided to attack the weakness in his civil rights record."

"Do you have any evidence of a possible leak," asked Edgar. "Anything that anyone has said that might hint they were ticked off. Any communication to anyone on the outside?"

"So far nothing. We can go over the papers again with that in mind, maybe something will trip," said Louis.

"It's a hell of a coincidence to see a hurry-up program going on like this. It's obviously a big-time effort," said Erla.

"Good work, Yvonne," Helene said. "I think we need to wait and see what Daggett says before we make any decisions."

"No question," said Erla, "but I will suspend the racism attack."

"I agree. Don't do anymore work on it for the moment," Helene told her.

"The staff would be happy."

"I know, but we don't want to attack a well-fortified position," said Helene. "Let's be sure our issue bombs don't explode in our faces. Let's first see what he says."

"I don't believe what he says will make much difference," said Edgar. "We have to consider the possibility of a leak, and we have to investigate."

This was a complication Helene didn't want. They would have to report it to the executive committee. It would take time. Although Edgar's investigators would be careful, the fact that they were looking for something could not be kept secret. The morale of the staff would be affected. Worst of all she might have to use Edgar's interrogation methods or punishment.

THE MANAGING EDITOR of *Explicit*, the leading supermarket tabloid and also publisher of *Details,* the salacious gossip magazine, carrying similar material offered a cold diet coke to an elegant gentleman with whom he had an appointment in his cluttered conference room. On the table were 8"x 10" photographs of five women who had past relationships with Adrian Daggett. The man opposite him was tall; dressed in a dark brown suit and colored shirt with a tie that blended perfectly. His strong muscular hands were perfectly groomed; his slightly graying hair was perfectly brushed. The document beside the pictures was obviously the work of a sophisticated investigative agency. Beside the document was an envelope containing a check for an advance payment of $20,000.

The editor was accustomed to paying for such stories. "I assume your motive in offering this to us has something to do with getting Senator Hatford elected."

"We believe the public has the right to know the full background of Adrian Daggett. Could the reality campaign object to your bringing up realities about his sex life?"

"But all of this was before he married."

"It's still going to be a luscious story for your readers and will gain you some notoriety among other media."

"You are absolutely sure all of these facts are correct?" the editor asked. Checking the validity of information was not one of his publication's strengths.

"Our advance payment will enable you to engage an independent investigation to check them without any expense on your part. If you find that any of these facts are incorrect, you may keep the twenty thousand and forget the story. Keep in mind your mission is to sell newspapers and magazines with editorial content that will excite your readers."

"This will excite them all right. I just don't want to be sued by someone with the legal power Daggett has."

"I have provided the funds with which you can check the facts, I have told you my proposition."

"What else is going to come out about Daggett?"

"There may be other stories."

"Don't forget about me."

"I assure you, we won't."

ANNE NOTED THE marked improvements in the Hatford campaign immediately after Warren Hatch was formally announced. The Washington Press Corps and the news services wrote articles about him and the campaign. Randy Dustin resigned; Anne expected more would follow him. The speech language seemed to get simpler and avoided the clichés and slogan phrases popular in recent elections. She wondered how the interface of soft cost and campaign cost was being handled with POLACO apparently writing the speeches. That, she thought, would make an interesting investigation.

Soon the new ads appeared. Anne asked the engineers to collect them and invited Nancy to watch with her.

On the screen a scene faded in of two executive-looking women having lunch at an executive-looking restaurant.

One said, "What do you think of not getting tax cuts now that there is a budget surplus, and that there may be tax increases to pay down the debt?"

"The theory, is that we will save on the interest payments. Except to save one dollar in interest, we have to pay $12 in debt reduction."

"That's why the taxes have to go up? Do you think there is any real danger of a fiscal crisis?"

"How can there be a fiscal crisis if we're the largest economy in the world? Every nation has debt. We won two world wars and the cold war with it."

"I have to agree. Economic growth will pay down the debt the same as it balanced the budget."

"The main thing for the government to do is to keep its hands off the economy and let things work."

"Discipline."

"By both politicians and the people."

"I agree; don't rock the boat."

"I'm not sure of the problem anyway – the threat of 'the international markets.' What do they have to do with what happens inside the United States? I think it may be economic fear mongering."

"If 'the international markets' misbehave, we should cut them out."

"We definitely should."

The scene faded to gray. A voice over said, "This message was brought to you by the Southern Conservative Coalition as a public service."

"That's pure propaganda if you define propaganda as lies," Nancy said. She thought she would involve Tony in the response.

"It's effective," Anne said. "It gives people a reason not to believe the truth."

"Which is what the stock traders want them to do. That is to protest against any move toward regulation. Why don't they mention what Daggett believes? The soft ads haven't mentioned his name."

"They don't need to because everyone knows Daggett promotes paying down the debt and regulation of the exchange markets. It's classier to deal only in the idea and also avoid questions about the soft funds."

The next ad was a speech type. On the screen a professional-looking younger man stood beside a series of graphs. "The so-called 'reality campaign' you've been hearing about from Adrian Daggett may in fact be something other than what he says it is. In most of his positions, Mr. Daggett seems to intend to spend more money; then he says he is going to raise taxes to pay down the debt. Taxes are important to every American. Let me show you this." The video highlighted the graphs as he spoke of them.

"This represents the deficit and the recent years of our receipts being less than our expenditures. We added up the total of what Mr. Daggett wants to do, such as increasing defense expenditures, increasing expenditures on aerospace technology, and developing a national insurance program. You can see the totals of each. We think without raising taxes the deficit is going to be something like this. The graph showed higher totals than the previous years. How is Mr. Daggett going to pay for his new programs and also pay down the debt? The answer is he has to raise taxes to keep the budget balanced and the debt repayment scheduled. Is it tax and spend liberalism? You're paying for it. How much of it do you really want? How much of it is reality? Maybe the reality is that this is tax and spend." A voice over said, "Paid for by the committee to elect Hatford."

"Slick," Nancy said.

"A core argument. That one we have to answer. This will blend with the 'assuring freedom' theme versus 'reality.' Damn those people are smart."

"We can handle them," said Nancy.

Senator Hatford himself faded in on the screen. "Assuring freedom is essential now to the nurturing and continuation of American democracy. Freedom is what democracy is all about. If we lack freedom in any way, we will not enjoy as individuals or as a corporate body the total benefits of democracy, the democracy for which many American men and women gave their lives or suffered battle wounds to preserve. I will assure the continuance of American freedom, freedom of choice, freedom of enterprise, freedom from big government, freedom from oppressive taxation, and freedom from unnecessary military service which may result from foreign entanglement. These are the blessings our forefathers worked for and achieved. They are our heritage. Join me, and we will assure them together."

The voice over said, "Paid for by the Hatford for President committee."

"That's a neat quarter minute," Anne said.

"They're good over there aren't they?"

"See how difficult they made it to answer that," Anne said as she thought about how to reply.

On the screen a scene of a family picnicking on a seashore appeared. A teenage son and daughter and two younger siblings, a boy and a girl, were with a youngish graying father, and a slender, fit-looking mother. "Dad," said the daughter, "is it really true that we have to sell federal lands for development in order to pay the national debt? Is it that bad?"

"I don't think selling federal lands for any reason is a necessary idea," said the father.

"Mom?"

"The federally owned lands in the United States are a birthright to all of us dear. That's a birthright to everybody and no one should ever speak of selling them."

"But is it necessary to do that in order to keep the country safe?" asked the son.

"The United States is the biggest economy in the world," said the father. "It has been for a century and I don't see the danger that we need to panic into action that would affect all of the generations of this country for the future. We don't need to sell this seashore for example. There has to be someplace where people can enjoy God's great outdoors."

"I hope they don't take this away from us," said the daughter. "Where would people go? Teens don't have enough to do now. What's better than camping or picnicking at a place like this? The alternative for some kids is drugs."

"And out here there's necking," the father joked.

"John," said the mother.

The youngest asked, "What's necking?"

"This was a presentation by the Foulton Foundation," said a voice over.

"I hope these don't get any better," said Nancy.

"They did that just right. It's not corny and not preachy."

"There's one more."

The screen faded to a serious-looking political-type anchorman. "Beyond the issues," he said into the camera, "concerning the reality campaign of Adrian Daggett are questions about Mr. Daggett himself and his moral standards. We have not heard in the reality campaign any statements concerning the needs in America for high moral standards to be represented by America's leader. We've heard nothing in discussion about morals. So there had to be a question. What does Adrian Daggett believe? We have a few hints. He was forty years old before he married a substantially younger woman. We know he has sent his children away to school and at an early time started to break up his family. What kind of a family was it? What kind of family man was Adrian Daggett? Questions? Is he suited to lead the country in which our family values are so critical and so deficient? What kind of example will he set? What kind of sensitivity will he have for the needs of families in the moral sense? Does he care? Has he cared? What secrets are hidden in his past?"

A voice over said, "Paid for by the Committee to elect Hatford." Applause broke out.

"There is the family values pitch," Nancy said. "Seems like a weak case."

"Some people might respond."

Both of the Daggett communication leaders realized the challenge Helene had issued.

THE ELEGANT GENTLEMAN arrived by limousine and checked into the Mayflower Hotel, on Connecticut Avenue in Washington. He used a credit card which did not bear his true name. In a small suite subtly furnished in traditional style, he placed a list on the desk by the phone. He took off his jacket and hung it up. The suitcase, which the bellman brought, was packed as though he was staying several days, but was unopened. He worked his way through the list, giving the same message each time he dialed. He used a prepaid calling card through an "800" number which bore the false name. The Mayflower telephone system could not record the numbers he called. He wrote down the names of the people he talked with if they were different from those on the list.

Pleading a sudden change of plans, he checked out that afternoon. The Mayflower graciously charged him for only a half day. The doorman saw him to a taxi to Reagan Airport, but he redirected the driver to Union Station, where he bought a first class ticket to New York on the four o'clock Metroliner. He got off the train in Philadelphia at 30th Street Station and walked to a parking lot. He drove out in a blue Mercedes convertible. Smooth travel on I-95 to Trenton and then on the New Jersey Turnpike brought him to Manhattan through the Lincoln tunnel. He stopped at a corner in midtown to use a public phone. Back in the car with the top down he let the feeling of Manhattan please him as he made his way down 7th Avenue to a garage in the west village where he had a permanent stall. He walked two blocks among young people in shorts enjoying the early summer evening and up the steps of a townhouse. After he opened the door, an elegant lady also wearing shorts, kissed him on the lips and poured a drink for him as he carried his luggage upstairs.

In a dozen cities, selected employees of Paul Melius and Joe Drago carried bags of packages to Federal Express offices and paid for the shipments in cash.

THE FIRST CALL came to Anne at ten minutes after eight the next morning from an old friend who had been with his newspaper for as long as she could remember.

"I hope you're calling to tell us you're doing a big-time story on the Daggett family."

"We may very well, Anne. *Explicit* magazine has a front-page story about Adrian Daggett's love life before he married Pamela. I want to know if you can comment."

"This is the first I've heard of it, Irv, can you fax it to me?"

"If you'll promise to comment exclusively to me."

"You know I can't do that."

"What's the fax number in your office?" The fax rang and spewed out six pages of copies and photos. The headline was "The Five Loves of Adrian Daggett." Underneath the headline were photographs of five attractive women with their names identified. The story spoke of Adrian's affair with each of them giving the approximate dates. Included were two with whom he had lived and the dates of co-habitation. In typical tabloid style the article begged some questions as to who terminated which affair and whether Adrian was capable of true love. Anne picked up the phone. "I have it, Irv. How did you get this?"

"It came on Federal Express."

"Who sent it?"

"Your opponents, I guess! There was no letter. Just a phone call yesterday."

"We have no knowledge of the details. We consider this to be an imposition, if it is true, on the lives of respectable, competent, contributing women who have associated with Adrian. We have no understanding as to how this could reflect the quality of his family life. He is devoted to Pamela and his children. I assume you called *Explicit.*

"Yes we have."

"What did they say?"

"They swear on the heads of their children and by all that is holy, that this is true."

"Did they tell you where they got it?"

"They claim a confidential source of high reliability. They say they checked it out."

"Do you have to comment on this, Irv? Do you have to carry it?"

"The people's right to know, Anne. If these are facts, and they have been released to the public, we can carry them."

"We didn't release them. We don't know if the reports are true. Quote me."

"I will." said Irv.

She hung up, "God damn it to hell," she swore aloud, seething in anger. She got up from behind her desk, turned out of her office and bumped into Nancy who was coming to see her. "You know? I just got a call from CNN."

"Irv Fleischman called me."

They stepped back into Anne's office. "What do you think?" asked Nancy.

"POLACO."

"Some attack. Where did they ever get that information?"

"From private detectives. They spent a lot of money on it. We should have anticipated that."

"The good news is they think they need to smear our candidate in order to win," Nancy speculated.

"Exactly. The bad news is we have to deal with it."

"Let's get ready. There are going to be a lot of calls."

"Did CNN say how they got the information?" Anne asked

"They got a copy of the paper by Federal Express after a phone call."

"Same as Irv."

"Let me get Karen, Lucile, and Bennett," Nancy said.

"I'll call Merrick for Jack and Louellen. I'll assign Tom Haynes to direct this."

"Sure. That will be enough."

The selected seven people squeezed around Anne's conference

table. She closed the door and explained the problem. Copies of the fax were passed around. Terry was in Cleveland. Alan was with Adrian. Anne finished her briefing.

"We assume all major media were alerted including newspapers around the country. Probably major TV and radio stations. They're going to be on us like a pack of jackals. We have to reply to their calls now. I tried to keep Irv Fleischman from running it. It's certain everybody else will."

"Is it true?" asked Bennett.

"We have to assume it is. They wouldn't risk outright fabrications after the Mayberry debacle," Anne replied.

"Is this investigative reporting?"

"We're not sure. It doesn't make much difference."

"Would the women have any recourse of law like invasion of privacy?"

"I don't know," said Anne. "Probably not a solid case."

"Have any of them volunteered information?" Nancy asked.

"I don't see that any of them are quoted in the article."

"I'm sure they're being solicited, even as we speak," said Nancy grimly.

"Okay, what do we say?" asked Louellen.

"We hugely regret the intrusion on the lives of productive people who have a right to privacy. We deplore the attempt to impugn Adrian Daggett's family life by raising this question. Adrian Daggett is devoted to his family and loves them deeply. He is devoted to Pamela," Nancy offered.

"Just about what I said to Irv," said Anne. " Use your best judgment in each circumstance. Tell them we'll have a statement in an hour or so. Get the fax number and name and we'll send it. Anybody got anything better?"

"The phones will be ringing," said Nancy. "We'll tell the operators to hold the calls from the media and to pass them to the next available person among us. We won't approach the media or anything like that. We'll give the initial reaction. Karen, get this out to Adrian."

Karen ran back to her office and brought up the campaign itinerary on her computer. Adrian was speaking in Raleigh. Michelle Proust was the cell phone contact. Karen dialed her number. She answered.

"Karen Crezna, Michelle. How are you doing?"

"We're doing well, thank you. It's hot."

"We have lousy news. There's an article in *Explicit* that you have to show to Adrian. You got your wireless fax?"

"Yes I do. What's it say?"

"It names five women that he dated or lived with prior to marrying Pamela. We think it's engineered to attack him on family issues."

"What he did before he married Pamela is irrelevant."

"We're trying to control it, but we need to have Adrian look at this and then give us any further instructions. We assume it's true, and that it's the work of a private detective or a group of them probably."

"Send it on. He's busy right now, but he'll be finished in about a half hour."

"Ask him if he wants us to let Pamela know about this right away."

"Expect he will."

Michelle felt sure that the folks at Harbour Island already knew of these developments, but they still would be interested in the reaction. She would be first to inform Adrian and would report his response. She read the fax and then printed out a copy which she dropped into a folder in her briefcase.

ADRIAN CAME OUT of the hall where he was speaking to a regional Lions Club convention looking fresh and bright eyed. Alan Jacobs followed him out. There were handshakes with the local officials and the conference leaders at the limousines. Alan got in first, then Adrian, and Michelle slipped into a jump seat.

"How were we?" Adrian always asked of the first person he saw after a speech.

"B+ to an A-," said Alan.

"I'm sorry to give you this Adrian, I really am sorry," said Michelle. She handed Alan the copy she had made. It took a minute for him to read it.

"Oh my God," said Adrian. "Who the hell did this?"

"I just got it from Karen Crezna. They have a special task force answering the phones in Chicago."

"How did they ever do this?" asked Adrian. "Why involve these women?"

"They've got to try to tarnish you, Adrian," said Alan." They'll do anything they can."

"I know. I know we responded to the race thing. That took a huge effort, but this?"

"Is it true, Adrian?"

"Oh yes. Everything is the truth."

"Five affairs in fifteen years. I don't think there is anything abnormal about that," said Alan.

"It's these questions they ask, Alan. Am I capable of true love? Is Pamela the one? Does she know about my past?"

"I have to call, Anne." Alan dialed the code and handed Adrian his cell phone.

"Anne Russell," she answered.

"Adrian."

"Hi. Have you got this thing?"

"I've got it, where did it ever come from?"

"We don't know, Adrian. Confirm or deny?"

"It's all true, Anne. Every word. Names are correct, photos are correct. How did they get this? Why did they bring these women into this thing? They all have their own lives going now. I think they're all happy, maybe with one exception."

"All I needed to know was whether it was true. Somebody spread it around."

"You mean called the media about it?"

"Oh yes, and sent copies."

"Can we find out who did it?"

"I think we can be reasonably sure Edgar Slaughter was involved. If the report were a lie, and we could find out who spread it around we might have something. But if it's true, I don't think it's worth it. I have seven people manning the phones. The calls are swamping us. Whoever did it to us, did a good job. Every major newspaper, all the TV and radio stations, and the news services have it in detail."

"I have to contact Pamela. Can you get someone to reach her and have her call me."

"I want to talk with her too. She's in New York and they're going to be all over her."

"This weekend is the Blair graduation. They're probably out buying a dress and other things for Dianne."

"I want to get to her before the New York scorpions do. I need to talk with the kids."

"So do I."

"Let us organize that for you, Adrian. We'll call back." The conversation in the car ended. Michelle Proust made a mental note that POLACO was immediately suspected.

At 5:30 that evening Adrian spoke to his children by conference call from his hotel in Cincinnati. Donald was in Chatham,

Massachusetts on Cape Cod where he was working as an assistant manager for the summer at one of the local hotels. Linda was visiting a friend in Middlebury, Vermont before returning for her summer job as an intern at an airline office in New York. Dianne was with her mother in a suite at the Waldorf Astoria. After graduation she would work on the campaign and stay at the apartment on Lake Shore Drive. When the operator announced everyone was on the line Adrian spoke, "Kids, I want to talk about the story you must have heard."

"You don't have to explain anything to us, Dad," said Donald.

"I just want you to know, because you will find out if you marry as late as I did, that there will be flirtations and affairs. In my case there were. But I married your mother, I love her deeply, and I have been faithful to her since in every respect."

"Dad, we know that," said Dianne. "You love us all."

Linda was a little teary. "Daddy, you don't have to say anything. We know how you feel."

Adrian felt his emotions overcoming him. "Being my children hasn't been easy for you I know. I love you, I pray for you. I hope this in no way embarrasses you or your mother. I truly love her. She is the best thing that has ever happened to me along with you three. I would give up everything if I had to for you all."

"You don't have to give up anything, Dad," said Donald. "The country needs you like the State of Illinois needed you."

"Dad, stay in there and fight," said Dianne. "Don't let these people hurt you."

"Only you could let them hurt you, Dad," said Donald.

"I'm scared of what they might do," said Linda.

"Don't be, honey," said Adrian. "Anne Russell is going to have a conference call with you to tell you what to do when the reporters come after you. Keep in mind they're not all bad. Unfortunately, some can deliver a nasty sting."

"When will she call?" asked Linda.

"As soon as we're finished," said Adrian. "Is there anything you want to ask me?"

"We know that you married late, Dad. We know that you are a particularly good-looking and successful man. What else do we expect?" said Dianne. "We're glad you're our father. We don't have any questions."

"I don't, Dad. I'm old enough to understand it now," said Donald.

"I love you, Daddy," said Linda.

"I love you," said Adrian.

"Don't worry about us," said Dianne.

"I'll try, kids, God bless you. Stay put and Anne will be right behind me." Adrian hung up the phone and paused for a minute.

An AT&T operator connected Anne.

"How are all the young Daggetts?" she asked. "I hope you have your armor polished."

"What's going to happen?" asked Linda.

"As soon as reporters find out where you are, you're going to be chased. We've added additional security to you, Dianne, with your mother. Donald, I don't think anyone knows you're in Chatham and, Linda, I'm not sure I know where you are. When they find you there are some rules of engagement. We'd like to kill this story off as soon as we can, and I think it means you have to just affirm to the reporters that your mother and father and you three are a solid family and that you always have been. Have any of you felt cheated by your father's career?"

"I suppose we would've liked more time with him," said Donald. "He still took me to ball games, and he took me on Boy Scout trips and he watched me play little league. I always knew that he was busier than other fathers. He couldn't be there all the time."

"My parents never went country clubbing. My father gave up golf when we were little so he could spend more time with us. I remember lots of nice Saturdays," said Linda. "He and my mom came to as many games, affairs, and events as they could. Let's face it, we had to go away to school. That was the best thing," said Dianne.

"Okay, just be honest with the reporters the way you would with anyone else. They may try to get you to say things you don't want to say. Just say 'No,' and point out to them if their questions are misleading. They're going to be especially mean with your mother. But you can count on expressing some meanness also."

"We can handle them," said Dianne bravely.

"I wish I could stay in Vermont," said Linda.

"If you want to, why don't you stay there a little longer, Linda. I know you'll be coming back to New York to work in the city for the summer, but maybe you'll want to stay there until the heat's off."

"I'd like to," said Linda

"I'll speak with your Dad. You're coming down to the graduation, right?"

"That's what's suppose to happen," said Linda. "I'm going to drive directly to Blair."

"Why don't you do that. We'll have security at the hotel there. You can drive back to Vermont if you like."

"I think I might like to do that," Linda said.

Michelle Proust surmised that POLACO would want to know where Pamela Daggett was. She plugged her portable computer into the data outlet in her room in the hotel in Cincinnati and accessed Pamela's schedule. She called Bill Haber to get the word off to Harbour Island that Pamela and Dianne were at the Waldorf Astoria.

The New York media already knew. Anne's staff couldn't resist publicizing a mother-daughter jog in Central Park for which the secret service gave permission. Anne detached Louise from the campaign in Cincinnati to fly to New York. Tom Haynes hustled to Cincinnati to take over the campaign press. Delta got Louise to LaGuardia Airport in New York in time for a late evening briefing in the Daggett suite.

They decided to keep to the schedule and jog in the park. Phone calls from Southern Florida, which Erla instigated, made sure everybody else in New York knew where Pamela was. By the time Pamela and Dianne returned from the exhilarating exercise, reporters and television crews were pushing their way into the lobby. The Secret Service agents led them to a side entrance and snuck them upstairs where Louise arranged for a press conference and invited the reporters to set up in an available meeting room. She ordered coffee, bagels, and fruit as a gesture of good will. The earliest possible time was 10:00 EST. The engineers in Chicago arranged for CNN to feed into the campaign circuits. Adrian was hopping between breakfast in Louisville to lunch in Milwaukee and would watch in the jet. Louise's one regret was the reporters would have more time to prepare their questions. In the meantime she and Pamela had to finish and publish a statement.

The hotel couldn't provide a large enough room on such short notice. The reporters and cameramen bulged out into the corridor munching on the baked goods and drinking coffee. Microphones were set up on a rostrum against the back wall. There was no place to sit.

Louise entered from the door at the rear of the room followed by Pamela and Dianne precisely at 9:58. They wore impeccably styled conservative dresses and looked very much like the wife and daughter of a first family. Louise stepped to the podium and the room quieted.

"My name is Louise Sczyniac. I am field press director for the Daggett campaign. Mrs. Daggett will now read a short statement and then we'll take questions."

Pamela stepped to the microphone as Louise left it, straightened her back, looked at the crowd and smiled gently. "Thank you all for coming this morning. No need to tell you this is in reference to the tabloid article by *Explicit* concerning my husband's liaisons prior to our marriage. I believe this is a despicable invasion of the privacy of these women, all of whom are high quality women who are leading productive lives. Adrian and I are concerned for them and the impact this may have on their lives. We wish that somehow we could have prevented this action by a publication whose very name indicates its appeal to prurience. This tabloid's intrusions on the lives of worthy people is not a worthy contribution to the national dialogue or culture."

Some laughter frittered around the crowd.

"We are uncertain how this publication acquired this material. All of the facts are correct as far as Adrian and I know. The manner of use is despicable. It is clearly evident that the intention was to cast doubt on Adrian's personality, character, and his sense of morality. Anyone who knows Adrian knows the truth about how abundantly he possesses the best of these qualities. Adrian was one of the earlier people to marry at a later age, as is so much more the practice today. He was nearly 40, I was 26. I was interested in activities and topics of discussion and maturity, which was hard to find in a 26 year old man twenty years ago. As our relationship grew, he told me he wanted to start a family life as he knew it with his parents and he wanted to do it with me.

"Adrian thinks he was a better father for teenagers in his 50's, even though he was occupied with his business and subsequent political responsibilities. Adrian took specific time off for an excellent family life. He gave up golf to play with his children. There has always been and continues to be romance in our marriage. I trust him, and we are each other's best friend."

"Mrs. Daggett how do you feel about this report. Does it threaten you?"

"In no way. I've addressed that question in my statement." She pointed.

"Would you have married Adrian had you known everything about all of these women?"

"Of course." She pointed.

"Did you suspect any of these involvement's before you married, Mr. Daggett?"

"He was nearly 40 and a remarkably attractive person. What do you think I suspected?" She pointed.

The man was medium height, clean-shaven, but had uncut disheveled looking long hair crowning a long thin face. "How do you feel, Mrs. Daggett, when you think of Mr. Daggett making love to these other women?" he asked in a provocative tone.

"I don't think that is pertinent." Wrong answer.

"Mrs. Daggett, how does it feel to be merely the last in a series of conquests by a compulsive womanizer?"

Dianne released her grip and stepped in front of the reporter. Louise and Pamela watched, stunned as Dianne's right hand slashed across the man's face. He fell backward over some television equipment into the crowd. There was a hushed silence of disbelief. Looking down at him, Dianne pointed her finger at his face and exclaimed in barely controlled anger, "That's enough of this bullshit." She turned and stepped back toward the rostrum.

"Excuse me, Mom." She took a deep breath, composed herself, and faced the microphones and cameras. The lump in Louise's throat almost choked her. "My father is a great man, and he is a great family man. He loves my mother and he loves the three of us, me, my brother, and my sister. We're a great family. This whole thing is happening because somebody spent a lot of money investigating my father to try to raise questions about his background and our family. All of you have questions. Whoever did this wants you to ask them.

"My father is running for President because the politics of this country are a mess. It's a mess of perceptions created by the candidates, the campaigns, the politicians, their public relations companies, and the interests supporting them. My father doesn't believe in perceptions. He believes in reality and that's what he wants to bring to the government of the United States. My father is trying to change the future like you've heard him say. There're a lot of people who don't want the future changed because of their own selfish interests, not the interests of the country or the world.

"Now let me tell you about my father as a father. My mother is his best friend. She's his confidant; he tells her everything. He tells her because he needs her advice and because he wants her to learn. My father never does anything without consulting my mother. You would think we kids have a lot of trouble because we're Adrian and Pamela's children, but we don't. Our parents taught us that life is about contribution. What did you guys contribute today? Asking my mother how she feels about my father making love to other women and saying he is a womanizer. That's bullshit. That's what the people who paid for this investigation of my father wanted you to do, and you did it.

"My father really did give up things so he could be home with us kids on weekends. He used to belong to The Torch Club. That only took one night a month, but he still gave it up so he could be home with us because he was away so many other nights. He gave up all of his own activities so he could be a good father, and he is. Before my father decided he would run for President, we had a family meeting. My mother and father flew from Chicago. The meeting was at the Marriott Hotel at Newark Airport. We all decided the country needed my father. He consulted us first.

"My father and mother are moral examples to everybody, but particularly to us. I have never heard my father swear. We've always gone to church, we've always prayed before our meals. When something happens like somebody is sick or dies we hold hands and pray for them. That doesn't mean my father isn't tough, and that doesn't mean we're not tough. Mr. Sleazeball reporter just found that out. We're a tough solid family. We love each other, we love being together, we love talking to each other, and we love playing with each other. It's a great feeling to be in a family like this."

"Now has anybody got any real questions? Because this is the last time anybody in the Daggett family is going to talk about this."

Louise felt her throat loosen. Pamela looked on in admiration. What a child they had created and raised. One hand went up, Dianne pointed.

"Why do you say there will be no more questions?"

"Because everybody knows what this article is about. Everybody knows it was planted. Why don't you investigate how *Explicit* got this information? Why don't you investigate who investigated my father? That might be a real story for you."

Another hand went up.

"Did you really have a meeting at the Marriott Hotel in Newark to discuss whether your father would run?"

"That's what I said, didn't I? It was at the Marriott at Newark Airport one Sunday." She pointed.

"Do you think your father would have not run if you kids had not wanted him to?"

"That's why we had the meeting. We couldn't imagine anybody who would make a better President."

"What happened at the meeting?"

"My dad explained what he wanted to do for the country. Then it was mostly about how it would affect us."

The reporter whom Dianne slapped said, "I'm going to sue you."

"For what? You were harassing my mother!" There was laughter. "Or for your being a jerk and a sleaze? More laughter ensued. "Go get a lawyer and tell him you have a neck injury because a 117 pound girl slapped you." The laughter became guffaws. The reporter retreated.

"Okay. That's it," said Dianne. Those holding cameras, notebooks, or pencils and pens put them down so they could join in the applause.

Louise almost felt sorry for the man Dianne slapped as it happened that night in 50 or 60 million households watching TV news. Millions more saw him in the newsmagazines and the newspapers. *The New York Daily News* gave him the front page under the headline: DAGGETT DAUGHTER DECKS DETRACTOR.

It played very well. A daughter defending her mother against a lascivious reporter and then telling him reality.

AT HARBOUR ISLAND Helene and Erla and their staffs watched as Adrian's youngest child blew a gaping hole in their carefully constructed attack of innuendo. They had, however, planted the seeds of doubt. These could still be cultivated, but there would be no media overreaction. The slap at the reporter and the subsequent exposure of the real purposes in the sincerest language by a young girl who was just about to graduate from prep school became the symbol of media irresponsibility. Whenever anyone questioned Daggett's character most people would remember Dianne's touching defense of her father.

People reading and watching began to understand that perceptions were as phony and dishonest as the process of developing them.

☆ Chapter 28 ☆

KAREN JOINED THE others to watch Dianne's performance and then returned to her new life. She was now the producer of the "soft ads" and time was filled with phone calls and decisions. She organized and coordinated activities, communicated with state people, and made the first contacts with prospective minor celebrity talent. She decided who would appear in the TV ads, the issues they would talk about, and the settings in which they were taped. Her life became a relentless cycle of flights to interviews and shoots, nights in the editing room, and meetings to prepare and review budgets.

In the beginning, the campaign had been a new adventure for Karen. Now, as with most competent workers in successful campaigns, there was still a sense of adventure, but she was overloaded beyond belief. In Chicago she arrived at the office before 7:00 in the morning, after running two and a half miles from her apartment on the near north side. On nice mornings she enjoyed the marvelous urban setting of the Chicago Lakefront in the early light.

Providentially the executive offices had showers. She negotiated to use one and kept outfits, underwear and nylons in her office. Vending machines in the cafeteria provided whole grain cereal, milk, and fruit which she ate at her desk. Her hair was short and easy. By 7:15 she was working with it still wet. By 7:30 the office was full.

A health food deli put on a buffet in the cafeteria for lunch. There was little time for chatter. Everyone took the lunch back to his or her work. Some forgot to eat it. She found she was best at administrative work in the morning and creative work in the afternoon, so she tried to schedule her calls and her meetings accordingly. The office was full until 8:00 p.m. every night. Normally she left about 8:30 after the phones quieted down. Saturday was a full workday until early evening when groups would form to go out for dinner and some drinks. Sunday afternoon, the office was usually half full. When she was in Chicago, Earl arrived Friday evening; she took Sunday off if she could.

The critical part of her job was to collect the best possible people to appear on camera. She telephoned some to ask if they would support Daggett with an issue-orientated fireside chat. She had to judge whether people were good prospects over the telephone and then visit them. Others called in volunteering. A response had to be made to each of them. Most were positioning themselves in the party, or seeking patronage. She learned about brazenness.

It was touchy when she had to tell most of them that they were not going to be on television. She usually said there were only a few slots left and she wasn't sure exactly how the "producers" would use them. In fact, the decision was largely left to her. Nancy trusted her judgment. Her immediate goal was to build up thoughtful and appealing presentations by Democratic leaders and ordinary people to refute the slick, deceptive ads of the POLACO foundations.

At 10:30 each evening she talked with Earl. On her bedside table was a reading file of campaign materials from their opponents, internal memorandums, reports, newspapers, and newsmagazines. She worked on these in bed until she couldn't focus and went to sleep.

Nancy and Merrick selected Karen to join the floor team at the convention to interface with The Platform Committee. The assignment to one-on-one contact with the delegates excited her, and she would be in Miami a week longer which meant that Earl could maybe be with her a week longer. She missed him. When he came to Chicago she was so focused on her work she feared she didn't communicate with him except through lovemaking. She desperately wanted some time with him to talk, to hug him, to feel him, to cook for him. She felt the strain of the campaign on their relationship. She intellectualized that if Adrian Daggett became president she would have plenty of choices, but she loved Earl and wondered if she would ever find any man like him. She hoped she would have an ocean-front room at the hotel in Miami Beach where they would live for three weeks. It would be nice not to pack a bag and head for an airport for a while.

THE MEETING OF the National Labor Council in the ballroom of the Cleveland Hilton looked like a UN Security Council meeting. The members sat at a "U" shaped table. Each president of a national union had three or four staff people behind him. Around the room Amy Camisona saw a mixture of women, African-Americans, and Hispanics amongst the staff. Only Carlos Himenez, president of the Agricultural Workers Union represented a minority in the front rank. Amy, as president of the Ladies' Garment Workers' Union, was the only woman.

At a table across the top of the "U" was the council staff. Jorge Carraballes, the staff director, sat beside Olaf Jenson, the chairman. Behind him were his directors of public relations, government relations, community relations, and employer relations. Jorge was formidable and directed the action when fights broke out with The National Association of Manufacturers. The brilliant Mexican-American from San Antonio commanded respect from both sides.

The meeting concerned the endorsement of a presidential candidate. Amy had met Pamela Daggett personally and studied the Daggett positions with her staff. She argued in favor of the endorsement of Adrian Daggett. Carlos Himenez was staunchly in favor of Daggett on the grounds of the national health insurance program since the members of his union often had little or no health insurance. The president of the Aerospace Workers Union, John Hendrick, supported Daggett and his strong position of technology development.

Three of the others argued strongly in favor of an endorsement of Senator Hatford based on information which had been shared with the board. They argued that Adrian Daggett had actively opposed union elections during his business career and succeeded in keeping unions out of several of his company's factories. They also ridiculed Daggett's view of a changing role of unions. Amy personally thought the role of unions should change. She looked forward to talking with Adrian when he came to their annual convention to follow his wife's excellent presentation the summer before. If the National Council voted to endorse Senator Hatford, she wondered how he would take it.

Amy leaned back in her seat and whispered to her political director to count the votes. In five minutes she was handed a paper which showed her it was even. That meant the chairman Olaf Jensen, who was president of The Lumber and Paper Workers Union would cast the deciding vote.

Olaf also had a count done and considered the opportunities the role of tie-breaker presented to him. After the next speaker, mid-way in the afternoon session, he called a half-hour recess and leaned toward Jorge.

"You're sure of the count?"

"Yes sir, 7-7."

"Have you been in touch with Warren Hatch?"

"He said that you'd have a prime time spot at the convention on Tuesday night."

"Anything from the Daggett side?"

"They would like to meet with you and any other members of the council, to talk about labor policy. Their convention plans, they say, haven't crystallized since they have the later convention."

"That's an excuse. The question is, what is the right political move? We could get things out of Hatford. Daggett is going to talk to us about productivity and the changing world of unions. What do the polls show?"

"Daggett is still 6 to 10 points ahead."

"Before the conventions the better opportunity for favorable legislation is Hatford. If we back him and he wins, fine. If he loses, we can still send our political commandos up to Capitol Hill," Olaf seemed to reason.

"If Daggett wins it might well be a Democratic Congress, but we're not going to get anything from Daggett that doesn't make sense," Jorge counseled.

"What will we get?"

"The things he's talking about. He'll try to do national health insurance."

"We have to support that unless it's too expensive."

"I think they'll do it right," Jorge advised.

"I think we're better off with the Republicans. Daggett is going to stumble somewhere. We'll end up with nothing to show for risking our careers."

"They tried to smear him a couple of times and you've seen what's happened," Jorge reminded.

"Yes, but there are issues lying out there. There's going to be a big battle if the Republicans do it right."

"I'm not impressed with their campaign staff."

"That's why they brought in Warren Hatch."

"I'm not sure how much of an improvement he is," Jorge said.

"There's a lot of support from those foundations. Hatch didn't just happen."

"In that case, you may be right if the campaign is reorganized and themed properly."

"Okay," said Olaf. "Call the Democrats one more time. Signal me if there is any change."

Jorge wondered how much of the decision would depend on whether Olaf would get moving at the Republican or the Democratic Convention.

At the end of the day they voted. There was a tie. Olaf called for a recess and announced that he would give his decision in the morning. He then set his public relations machine in motion to announce the decision in favor of Hatford. Amy placed a call to the Daggett campaign headquarters and asked for Pamela Daggett to call her back.

In 15 minutes her phone rang. "Hi, Amy, I thought you were in a big meeting," Pamela greeted her.

"I am; that's what I'm calling you about. I'm not supposed to. A report has been introduced at the council indicating that Adrian successfully opposed unions in elections in his factories four times. He's being portrayed as anti-union."

"Most business men are, but you know the mitigating view we have."

"And I agree with most of what you say. There's been a long argument about endorsing Adrian. This report has the Hatford people all over us. The vote, this afternoon, came out a tie."

"Oh goodness, we're counting on union support. Where did this report come from?"

"It was introduced by the staff. Is it all true Pamela – the story in *Explicit*?"

"I'm afraid it is."

"Someone is investigating you very thoroughly. I didn't think the Hatford campaign had the guts to do that."

"Someone is supporting them, Amy, in a big way."

"I feel big money on their side."

"I believe your feeling is consistent with... reality," Pamela joked.

Amy laughed. "There are a number of people who agree with you that unions have to change their role, but it's going to take some time.

"Time is something we may not have."

"I understand. Is there anything you can do," Amy asked, "to sway Olaf Jensen who will break the tie tomorrow? There's a lot of pressure on him from the Hatford side."

"I'll have to make some calls. Someone will get back to you."

"I can encourage Jorge Carraballes to call someone in the campaign. Who should that be?"

"Alan Jacobs, Amy. Thank you, I appreciate your calling."

IN HIS OFFICE, the Chicago Headquarters, Alan considered Olaf Jensen's polls in recent elections indicating that union members voted the way they wanted regardless of what the union or the National Council suggested. But, union endorsement particularly at the level of the National Labor Council was not trifling. It was particularly important for the Democratic candidate to have it.

His phone rang and Jorge was announced.

"Good afternoon, Mr. Carraballes."

"Hi, Alan."

"What's happened that Pamela Daggett tells me you'll call?"

"A tie vote on whom to endorse. Jensen will decide. Amy Camisona suggested I let you know about this confidentially so you could respond appropriately."

"I appreciate that, Jorge."

"I'm a supporter of reality in government, and your ideas about the changing role of unions. But change comes slowly in the union business. We need a lot more dialogue. I hope your candidate will provide that during the campaign and during his presidency."

"We're very interested in a dialogue on the role of unions."

"I agree with that, Alan. I think it's important to escalate it to the national level with the President involved. That would make it possible for some of our union leaders to focus on the longer-term future."

"Can I ask you which unions support us?"

"I really can't tell you. You can guess where the aerospace workers are. The national health insurance program is important to another."

"Our polls show union workers are interested in America's being a force for good in the world."

"Unions are a hot bed of patriotism. The question is what can you offer to sway Jensen. He wants to be on TV at a convention."

"I understand. Can I call you back in about two hours? Where can I reach you?"

Jorge gave him his cell phone number.

Alan contemplated the problem looking at a picture of his lovely wife. His mind wandered to a vision of her in his arms kissing him. He was tired. Ten minutes later he was beside Anne, Nancy, and Terry in a teleconference with Roger Bennett and his labor group headed by Jack Krasti, a distinguished professor of labor relations from the University of Indiana. After Alan had described the conversation with Jorge, Terry asked, "Is there anything we can do?"

Krasti, an acerbic individual with a generous measure of cynicism, said, "They're looking for goods. The Republicans will offer something on the minimum wage and something on job-related benefits and security. The big unions don't give a damn about minimum wage, but they have to look like they care. Our proposition is the national dialogue on the future role of unions. The rank and file won't understand it without an effort to inform them of their long-term interests. A lot of people running the unions at the local, regional, and national level will understand it as a threat to their power and will reject it. The only way we are going to accomplish anything is to get the members educated and involved so that support can be marshaled for the progressive labor leaders willing to abandon the old confrontations union ideologies. Global competition is not the only issue. We need to address retraining, secure retirement, the retirement age, and continuing education.

"Olaf Jensen asked for the recess to deal. He'll look for the maximum exposure he can get. He has to be reelected too, you know. If the council at Olaf's decision endorses Hatford we have a chance of prying some of the unions away to take a separate position. We have the national health insurance plank, that will help the agricultural workers and the garment workers. That union has good leadership focused on retaining jobs in the United States. The aerospace and airline unions are the most progressive. They probably voted for us.

"Our opponents will trumpet Adrian's role in defeating unionization in four company elections. Too bad he wasn't President of an already unionized company. Who's drumming up all of this information about Adrian's background?"

"We assume it is one of the foundations, probably The Southern Conservative Coalition, spending money on investigations," said Terry. He knew that POLACO could not be revealed in this conversation.

"It may boil down," said Krasti, "to what kind of exposure Olaf Jensen is being offered at the conventions, or otherwise. He will enjoy doing the press conferences helps his own job security. I don't see any useful outcome to offering anything more than we have. We've offered national health insurance, a lot of investment to increase jobs and the national dialogue on the future."

"What do you think the Republicans have offered?" Terry asked.

"Probably a prime time slot at their convention. They'll write the speech, then they'll get Olaf some speaking engagements and see that he gets paid for them."

"Aren't there any other cards we can put on the table?" asked Alan.

"Most people in the unions are not going to understand what a national dialogue is about until we explain it," said Krasti.

"Couldn't we some how get across the idea," Roger Bennett interrupted. "A national dialogue could lead to a consensus of labor, management, and government and the community at large as to the modes of coordination with the newly constituted union dynamic."

"Graduate students in political science might understand," Krasti quipped.

Anne listened intently. The brains of the senior staff were crammed with issues and problems. It was hard to respond quickly to this one. "Can we try to separate out the unions who favor us?"

"Under the rules of the council they are allowed to make separate announcements on critical issues."

"Olaf's a publicity seeker," Jack added. "I'll bet they offer him a slot at the convention."

"And, subsequent speeches," scowled Bennett.

"And, TV ads from the Foulton Foundation about anti-unionism," Nancy added.

"There must be something we can do," said Alan. "Can we threaten to come out against unions or to force changes if we are elected?"

"It's awfully hard for a Democratic candidate to be successful without support of the unions," said Terry. "We're for the dialogue and we'll try to explain it. We're for national health insurance and we're for some other union issues. But, the fact is Adrian defeated a union in plant elections."

"This wasn't an issue in Adrian's governor race in Illinois?" Nancy asked.

"The unions supported him heavily in Illinois," Krasti responded. "The plants where the elections were held were in Ohio."

"That distinction escapes me," said Terry.

"That sounds like a purely political matter," said Alan. "Let's treat it politically. We'll offer Olaf a slot at the convention. If he doesn't take it, he can't say we ignored or snubbed him or union concerns."

"I see that point," said Terry.

"That might be a way to handle it," said Jack.

"We can give him some reasons why they should support Daggett despite the Ohio plants," said Anne thinking out loud.

When Alan Jacobs dialed Jorges Carraballes cell phone he knew that the arguments were tentative and incomplete. Alan had to wait while Jorge found some privacy and then presented the offer.

JORGES CARRABALLES LAID out all the arguments to Olaf and some of the others. Democrats were the traditional friends of labor. The national health insurance program, and the national dialogue on the future of unions would protect and revitalize unionism. Olaf chose the publicity and the honorariums. He announced the decision at his council in the morning and brushed aside opposing arguments. A press conference was called for 1:30 p.m. to announce the endorsement. There was no difficulty getting the media to attend.

The campaign engineers projected the scene in Cleveland on the big screen in the main conference room where Terry, Nancy, Alan, Anne, Merrick, and many others brought their lunch. Before the broadcast they could see a serious faced Jorge Carraballes watching the set up. Behind him was Olaf Jensen and about a half dozen union presidents.

"See who's not there in that group," said Alan.

"I don't see Amy Camisona, and I don't see Carlos Himenez," said Nancy.

"There must have been some more arguments this morning," said Terry. "Who do we have there?"

"George and Louellen," said Alan.

"Call George."

The anchor came on and introduced Jorge who spoke, "Ladies and Gentlemen it's my pleasure to present to you the President of The National Labor Council, who is also the President of The Lumber and Paper Workers Union, Mr. Olaf Jensen."

Olaf stepped to the microphone and laid some papers down on the rostrum.

"I have a short statement and then I'll take questions," he said. "Before the beginning of the deliberations of the council meeting, the most important business of which was to endorse a presidential candidate, we were given some information which is of paramount importance." He then described in detail the four union elections in Adrian's former company.

"With this information the national council was forced to come to the conclusion that the Democratic candidate to be does not support the union movement. Indeed, his record as a businessman stamps him as a union buster. Since he is not a sitting member of congress or the senate we have no national voting record. We do know the voting record of Senator Hatford. There has been extensive discussion and the council has voted to endorse Senator Hatford for the presidency of the United States."

There was a hush.

"We believe that by working with Senator Hatford we will be able to pass legislation which is important to the union movement concerning employee benefits, job security, and related issues. The Daggett campaign has proposed that organized labor accept some vague new role in the future. But we know our role and have known it for over 100 years. Therefore, the labor movement has to come down to fundamentals. Is the president in favor of unions or is he not? Senator Hatford has demonstrated past support. Mr. Daggett has demonstrated past opposition. Thus, the endorsement goes to Senator Hatford. Thank you."

One question was shouted above others. "What was the vote?"

"The vote of the council was a tie. As chairman I broke the tie."

He pointed to a reporter. "This is obviously not even close to a unanimous decision."

"It's still the decision." He pointed.

"What unions voted in favor?"

"Each union will make its own position known to its members." He pointed.

"Do you think the other unions will support this decision?"

"I expect our member unions to present a united front." Anne left the room and called Pamela who was touring the Marine Corps Air Station in Cherry Point, North Carolina with Adrian.

"Pamela, the National Labor Council has just announced a split decision to endorse Senator Hatford. We should try to organize a press conference for those officials who voted in favor of Adrian for later this afternoon. Can you get in touch with Amy Camisona?"

"I can try. I'll ask her to call you."

"Tell her that we will make all the arrangements through Evans & Copeland. All she has to do is gather as many as she can."

A few minutes later Anne's phone rang. After the conversation, she called a staff meeting to start in five minutes. She also called her Cleveland office and had a task force on the way to the convention hotel.

THE REPORTERS GATHERED again at four thirty in the afternoon. Positioned around a rostrum with a bank of microphones were Amy Camisona, Carlos Himenez, John Hendrick of the Aerospace workers union, Arthur Tremor of the Airline Union Conference, Bill Odemsky of the Petroleum and Chemical Workers union, and Eden Wilkes of the Metal Worker's Union. Amy Camisona was the first to speak.

"It would be unfair to the American public and its view of the labor movement not to clarify further the decision of The National Labor Council to endorse Senator Hatford, the presumed Republican nominee for the presidency. The people you see here along with myself supported the endorsement of Adrian Daggett, the apparent Democratic nominee, for a number of reasons. Last year Pamela Daggett came to speak to our convention in Atlantic City and began discussions about how we can work together to develop a new concept of the labor movement that would fit the future economy of the United States. I greatly respect this whole concept of a national dialogue about the labor movement which Mr. Daggett has proffered. We need unity in this country – unity of thought among the communities, laboring people, union members, management, and government about what the role of the modern union should be. This is an over-riding consideration in my judgment to protect the interests of the members of my union and accordingly, with the assent of our delegate assembly, I voted in favor of endorsing Mr. Daggett. I'd like to introduce Carlos Himenez, president of the Agricultural Workers Union."

Carlos came to the microphone and began speaking with a slight Spanish accent. "The people in my union are not middle class like the people of the trade unions of the Middle West and the North East. My people are often migrants with no permanent homes. My people work for low wages with no benefits. Mr. Hatford cares little about my people because they can neither deliver a large vote nor finance support to his campaign. I represent, Ladies and Gentlemen, people to whom every sickness or injury is a potential disaster. Many have never seen a doctor in their entire lives because they do not have the money. Those who need operations live shortened, crippled lives until they die of neglect. Their children's growth is stunted and their bodies weakened and disfigured for want of health care. You people who have health care, think about how important it is to your life. I speak for my people who don't have it. Hear me! I believe Adrian Daggett will see that we get it."

John Hendrick spoke of the interest in an American industrial policy to allow all unions the opportunity to plan for the future. Arthur Tremor spoke of the need of ongoing training, and continuing education and cooperation. Eden Wilkes summarized the arguments and focused on long-term competitiveness and economic strength. But it was Carlos Himenez's impassioned plea for the welfare of the poorest worker and his deeply felt conviction that Adrian Daggett would do the right thing that the nation would remember.

AT HARBOUR ISLAND, Helene, Ward, and the management group watched the tapes over coffee.

"Olaf Jensen gets high marks for his statement and his answers to the questions, but it was sure blunted in part by the second press conference."

Louis Fisher asked, "Who did it?"

"Anne Russell and Evans & Copeland."

"I wonder what they paid?" Ward asked.

"Maybe nothing," said Helene. "Or, maybe a promise to consider someone for Secretary of Labor."

There was a pause while each considered how much they gained by the initiative as opposed to what they had expected.

"They have taken some of his sting out of the National Labor Council decision by quick action. They were on the inside with someone," said Helene.

Later at her desk in the atrium office, Helene heard her phone politely hum and glanced from the papers on her desk to see that a secretary had answered. A polite beep came told her that Mendos Sadovan was calling.

"Mendos, how are you?"

"I'm fine Helene, I hope you are as well."

"As well as anyone doing what I am doing could be," replied Helene.

"I finished reading your plan to defeat Mr. Daggett. I'm impressed. If this doesn't work, nothing will. What are the possible failure points in execution?"

"Our candidate himself, I think, Mendos. It depends on whether he can carry the speaking load and put the message across. As you can see, we've simplified it a great deal."

"I think you've got the hook issues needed. As I look at them I believe opposing Daggett's position about expanding nuclear power may be important to us to defeat him."

"More so than the United Nations or choices in health care?" Helene asked.

"People tell me it's possible for him to make 'the time has come' approach for those issues and escape the gibbet. We're starting to read that the idea of raising taxes to pay down the debt is not so obnoxious."

"I think after the people see the way we've attacked it, Mendos, with the freedom theme, they might feel differently. So far the polls and all of the analysis indicate that we should go ahead and attack his atomic energy policy and try to make it a pivotal issue. A lot of people are sensitive to it."

"You asked me to approve opposing Daggett's views on the expansion of atomic energy," Sadovan said. "In the interest of defeating Daggett we leave it up to you. This is an emotional issue. There is a substantial constituency that is against nuclear power and trying to destroy the industry. So perhaps Senator Hatford should take a status quo position and let the anti-nuclear lobby have their way as virtually every politician in the United States has done. There might be some way you could see that the anti-nuclear groups cause Mr. Daggett a good measure of trouble."

"Do I see a vision of protesters at every Daggett rally with death heads and mushroom clouds following Daggett around the country?"

"That occurred to me," said Sadovan. "Fear and ignorance are powerful allies. In this case it's fear of the unknown, postulated by the anti-nuclear lobby and ignorance of the population on matters of science and engineering. This is exacerbated by the popular distrust in the government and almost anyone in authority."

"That makes it very hard to refute the claims of danger and disaster."

"And what claims we will make; explosions, radiation poisoning, mutation. Let me know if I can help further. I hope we'll see each other again soon."

"I hope so too, Mendos."

She remembered she'd slept with the man...on a different continent.

NANCY'S CONCEPT OF television debates materialized to a program produced by the Chicago Public Television station with the financial assistance of one of the PENMET foundations, and with the guidance and official aegis of the University of Chicago. The program was called "The Midway Society Debates." The setting was the ballroom of the Conrad Hilton amidst its historic grandeur, almost unduplicated in the United States. TV cameras were pointed out from the balcony around the whole room. A "press gallery" was advantageously positioned. The rest of the space was crammed with audience.

On the ballroom floor, cushioned benches behind a podium faced each other across the neutral ground dominated by a speaker, who sat in an elevated, high-backed leather chair. Two clerks and two pages were at desks around the speaker at floor level. Opposite the speaker, the Sergeant at Arms sat at a desk where two pages were also available. Behind the benches were chairs for members supporting one side or the other and tables where documents were sorted and exhibits prepared.

Around the rest of the floor between the camera positions were chairs for the audience. A special box was set aside to the right of the speaker for those who made special contributions for the production of the show. Occasionally they were introduced to the speaker.

The program was ninety minutes long. Opening statements from each side were condensed into four minutes. The balance was questioning and open debate with each side having equal time. Thirty seconds was allowed for a question and one minute for an answer. Two of the clerks beside the speaker were timers. There were five judges who had a brief time on camera when they asked a question, at their option, of each side. The last three minutes were for summations and then the TV audience would vote on the winner.

On this occasion, the debate was to be on a motion which called for the society to urge the government to take initiatives to expand nuclear energy facilities and restrict construction of those burning fossil fuels. Orrin Egglington, president of The Center for Resistance of Expansion of Atomic Power (CREAP) looked over notes with Maxine Marshal, president of the Women's Movement to Stop Nuclear Pollution and Josh Smitton, vice president for nuclear power issues at the Center for Environmental Recovery. Orrin knew that like himself, Maxine and Josh had both agency and Capitol Hill experience. Orrin and three associates formed the organization he represented. One of his colleagues was experienced in mail order marketing and telephone soliciting. They had gathered a constituency to which they faithfully presented newsletters and briefings on the doings of the electric power industry in Washington. Maxine and some others had separately formed a women's organization which at first concerned Orrin and his associates, but their money continued to flow in and so did Maxine's. There was demand for their publications and their members sent in their dues and subscription money. Each of them drew nice salaries and had adequate expense accounts and even retirement funds. Their organizations had cash reserves. All they had to do was to keep the issue alive until they wanted to retire.

It was important to them to take issue with everything the nuclear industry did, and push it under as much scrutiny as possible. For this they utilized relationships with Capitol Hill committees. Orrin's public affairs associate was reasonably good at getting media attention and produced news releases provoking fears that the earth was threatened by nuclear contamination.

The Midway Debates, now going into the fifth month, proved to be the most popular television show on PBS and gained momentum with each broadcast. The fact that they were invited by the producers was publicized. The show was of such stature that it became almost impossible to refuse.

Each side was allowed four persons who would speak in the debate. The industry had Mark Klippstein, President of the Nuclear Power Association, Robert Ross, former chairman of the House Committee on Science and Technology; Professor Wilma Westcott, chairwoman of the Department of Environmental Sciences at Rutgers University; and Julia Manilla, chairwoman of the Association for Minority Economic Development. Orrin knew what their arguments would be. He knew the points were valid, and he would have to counter them with the fear he traded in. He had his staff prepare the best opening speech they could, making it sound as science-based as possible and filling it with pseudo-scientific references. He saw that there were at least a dozen people behind the industry bench preparing exhibits. There were rumors of a surprise that would be wheeled into the room. They were no rules of discovery in these debates. Surprises were possible. He was to speak first.

Mark Klippstein was known for his speaking ability. Before his retirement, the congressman was known as one of the best orators in the House. Orrin knew his own ability and Maxine wasn't bad, but John was almost wooden reading his scripts. The line producer smiling, to get everyone relaxed if possible, gave cues for them to take their places. Orrin put his notes on the podium and sat down at the bench. He knew he had to make the opening work. He kept thinking about it as he heard the speaker announcing the show and then introducing him. He stepped to the podium.

"Mr. Speaker, over this discussion or debate, over this entire dark subject; over this entire industry of nuclear power world wide, there looms a dark specter. This specter profoundly expresses the fears of the people of the evils of radioactive energy, radioactive particles, loose radionuclides and the potential of the nuclear power industry to poison the earth. This specter has a name. Its name is Chernobyl." Orrin continued painting his picture of nuclear power and its threat to life on earth.

When he finished, applause rippled through the audience. "Magnificent," Maxine said in his ear. Mark Klippstein, recognized by the speaker, rose to his podium. "Mr. Speaker, the nuclear power industry in the United States has a record of safety and effectiveness which places it high among the technologies which have been brought forward by science and industry to the huge benefit of mankind. While our opponents have conducted their campaign of fear mongering about this industry in the name of the environmental movement, they have in fact overtly allowed damage to the environment which could have been avoided by the construction of more nuclear power plants. The essential point, Mr. Speaker, is that the fossil fuel generation of electric power has created one of the most monstrous environmental phenomena in the history of the world. And this phenomenon is no imaginary specter. This phenomenon is acid rain."

He cited the data concerning acid rain and the annual damage it did. He pointed out that this was tangible and the threats of damage by nuclear power plant waste had never materialized because the waste was minute and controlled. He said that in the U.S., the annual increase in demand for electricity would increase the pollution of the air, lakes, and rivers. He noted the example of France which would soon be 100% nuclear and had both clean air and a clean safety record.

The room was filled with polite, but enthusiastic applause. The speaker rapped his gavel. "The side in favor has the first question."

The former congressman rose and stepped to the podium. "My question concerns the so-called specter of Chernobyl. You make the huge point of one disastrous incident, but what caused it? Please tell me your belief as to the causes."

Maxine rose to the podium on the opposite side. "It makes no difference what the cause is, Mr. Speaker. First we must concern ourselves with the fact that it happened. Chernobyl spewed radioactivity for thousands of miles from the site of the incident."

"Point of order, Mr. Speaker. I asked for the opposition's understanding of the causes, and we are getting a repeat of the effects."

"Will someone answer the question please?" said the Speaker.

"The question is irrelevant, Mr. Speaker, to the point of the motion. The fact is that Chernobyl did indeed happen."

"I have sustained the question and it should be answered."

"We believe there was faulty design, there was inadequate training, there were mistakes by the workers. These could happen anytime, anywhere."

"I would like to clarify the point, Mr. Speaker," said Klippstein. "The design indeed was faulty and there are no reactors of that design in the United States. Those that are still in operation in the former Soviet Union are being closed down. The design was inadequate. Mr. Speaker, the standards of operation and design in modern nuclear plants entirely preclude this event. That design was never licensable in the United States."

"Those opposed?" asked the Speaker.

"How can you be sure that these conditions will never repeat themselves again anywhere in the world?"

Mark Klippstein stepped back to the podium. "Years before Chernobyl, at the very beginning of nuclear utilities, we in the United States, established design and operation standards and procedures which we enforce absolutely. An important factor is recruiting the right people, training them the right way, and supervising them with modern systems."

"Mr. Speaker," protested John Smitton, "There is no one who can possibly give us all of the insurance of the safety of any nuclear power plant. Once we have seen Chernobyl, we know what can happen. After that accident, we realize that it was ultimately necessary that evacuation programs be established for a radius of at least 20 miles around the area of a nuclear power plant. Technology is not perfect and cannot prevent horrendous accidents involving the power plants themselves or their wastes."

"Those in favor?" The Speaker indicated.

"We would like to ask, Mr. Speaker," Professor Westcott proffered, "how often our opponents fly in airplanes? We'd like to see the hands of anyone who has flown in an airplane less than 20 times."

"We hardly see that as relevant, Mr. Speaker," Smitten protested.

"It goes to the point of the effectiveness of technology in preventing accidents."

No hands were raised.

"Then I assume that those in favor have reasonable trust of aircraft technology, air line technology, and FAA technology to make flying reasonably safe. Flying, in fact, is the safest form of travel because it is strictly controlled. In nuclear power plants, Mr. Speaker, there are an immense range of controls. Technology is able to take aircraft flying through the air at close to the speed of sound through storms and through the night and land them with the degree of safety that those in favor of this motion will accept. Nuclear power plants don't fly. Controls and instrumentation in place are immensely more substantial and effective than those traveling at aircraft speeds. The logic does not hold, Mr. Speaker, that nuclear power plants can't be built that can operate safely."

Orrin asked, "What happened to your safety systems at Three mile Island?"

Wilma answered, "They worked. Damage was restricted to the facility. There was no explosion, meltdown, or any significant release of radioactive materials. No one was harmed."

Orrin said, "That's not what we believe."

"The amount of radioactive energy released was approximately equal to one day's exposure from the sun," Wilma stipulated.

"Are you suggesting we use sun block to protect ourselves from nuclear wastes?" Maxine taunted.

There was laughter.

She continued, "Those are government and industry statistics and we don't believe them. The government has lied and so has the industry. Many people were affected."

"Point of order, Mr. Speaker," said Wilma. "Our opponents refuse to believe the government which is the only entity capable of gathering the data. We insist that government data be recognized as a valid source."

"The government has reason to cover up, Mr. Speaker."

"Our opponents refuse to believe the truth, Mr. Speaker, because it proves them wrong."

"I rule that the government data is admissible unless specifically proven to be inaccurate or deceptive." said the speaker.

"There's no time for that, Mr. Speaker."

"Then there should be a debate about the truthfulness of the government data. Let us go on. Those opposed?"

The speaker turned to those opposed.

"I believe, Mr. Speaker," said Maxine at the podium, " that our opponents forget that hundreds of square miles of soil have been irrevocably contaminated with radiation. The generation of dangerous wastes cannot be avoided by the nuclear industry. It generates the waste and ejects it into the environment. Last year, Mr. Speaker, the nuclear industry put nearly two million cubic feet of waste containing 111,000 curies of radioactivity into the environment. Mr. Speaker, that's where it has to go when it comes out of the nuclear plants. Do those opposed to the motion deny that?"

"I see you do accept government statistics," said Julia Manilla. There was laughter.

"Where was most of this waste deposited?" Maxine asked.

"At Barnwell, South Carolina," said Julia.

"And what was it deposited in?"

".A landfill."

"What kind of landfill?"

"Mr. Speaker, this material was placed in a hazardous waste land-fill built with stringent specifications carefully researched to determine, prior to its licensing, that the wastes could not migrate from the landfill during the course of their decay. This facility is guarded so that unauthorized people can't approach it. This waste is radioactive to a limited measure, but it is in a controlled situation. Mr. Speaker, the wastes emitted by fossil fuel plants burning oil and coal are not controlled. They gush gasses into the atmosphere, tens of millions of tons a year creating uncontrolled havoc. Future historians will wonder about our sanity."

The speaker rapped his gavel, "Those opposed?"

"Mr. Speaker, those in favor have ignored the point I made of the contamination of hundreds of square miles of American land with nuclear waste. This has happened. The Columbia River has nuclear waste in it as a result of the damage done by those who operated the Hanford site," Maxine ranted.

Former Congressman Ross stood, "We have heard time and time again recitations of the sins of the people who managed Hanford, The Savannah River Site, Oak Ridge, and White Sands. I must remind you, Mr. Speaker, that at the time of those activities the nation was in a race, first with Nazi Germany to develop an atomic bomb, and then with the Soviet Union to out-produce them in terms of numbers and quality of nuclear war heads. These were crash programs to develop and produce weapons, not electricity. The environmental damage is regrettable, but truth remains that no member of the public has ever been harmed by peaceful nuclear operations.

"The turn of those opposed," said the speaker.

John Smitton got up, "You have made the point that the waste of nuclear power plants is safe in the environment. There are scientists who disagree and say that radionuclides can migrate into ground water and through the soil. Do you have any proof that the radionuclide containing waste can be rendered safe in the environment?"

Julia Manilla and Wilma joined at the podium. "Mr. Speaker, we react the radionuclides into almost insoluble glass. We can encase them in additional glass which guarantees that there is no radioactive waste interfacing with the environment. The glass enclosure system is placed in a sealed steel container. The containers are stored in engineered facilities which are constantly monitored. Compared to the wastes of fossil fuel plants the quantity of nuclear waste is minute and controlled."

John protested, "Mr. Speaker, we have no assurances that these assertions are true. We don't believe the industry and we don't believe the government. They have mutual self-serving interests. The nuclear industry, in particular, by ignoring public opinion, proves that it doesn't care about public safety."

Wilma replied, "Mr. Speaker, the industry has invested nearly half a billion dollars on the scientific research necessary to prove the retaining of radionuclides in glass. We'd like to present that as evidence. We know of no single peer reviewed paper that refutes in any way these conclusions which are the result of carefully conducted research in universities and other institutions. With your permission..."

"The time will be charged to your side," grumbled the speaker.

Down the isle from behind the seats of the team opposed came three people, one pushing a cart, and two carrying a table. The cart was full of technical papers. Wilma continued, "Mr. Speaker we have thirty four papers on the research of the solubility of this glass in all types of conditions. The key point: if the radionuclides are reacted into the glass in the manner these papers describe, they are captured and wherever the glass is, they stay. These papers indicate that the radionuclides will not leave the glass.

"Disposal facilities can be constructed to hold these waste forms and can be instrumented to warn of leaks which can be repaired. The low-level wastes of the nuclear power industry can be safely disposed. If my opponents are now going to question us about the fuel rod wastes, I refer to the technology of the disposal developed in France and now being undertaken in the United States. France has pioneered this technology and has demonstrated its material effectiveness. Much of the spent fuel rod material can also be reclaimed for reuse."

The speaker spent a moment looking at the pile of papers. "Those opposed?"

"Mr. Speaker, point of order," Orrin protested. "We were not informed of the presentation of this evidence in advance and therefore we are not in a position to respond to it. Our opponents have brought forth a very technical issue."

"Mr. Speaker," Wilma responded, "the earliest of the papers on that table was written in 1981. I have in my hand a publication of the

National Low-Level Waste Management Program which fully describes this technology written in 1993. Mr. Chairman, our worthy opponents tell us they are representatives of the interests of the people of this country and their relationship with the nuclear power industry. But now, Mr. Speaker, we find out that our opponents are not aware of the technologies which are available to deal with nuclear wastes. How can they fulfill their obligations to their constituencies if they are not technically capable and literate on the subject of the means of treating and disposing of radioactive wastes?"

The speaker looked at Wilma and turned to the group in favor and said, " That sounds like a reasonable question."

"I don't believe it is germane to this debate, Mr. Speaker. We are not debating the capabilities of our organizations, we are debating the motion and we insist that these papers not be admitted as proof of any point, because we cannot confirm or deny their validity."

"Mr. Speaker, the motion concerns the acceptability of the nuclear industry to the environment and these documented analyses of methods of nuclear waste control are utterly germane to that question," said Julia.

The speaker paused for a moment. "I find the evidence admissible, provided there is peer review. I also find the question of why you have not read these papers to be germane. I think it is highly relevant."

"Mr. Speaker, I think the question is out of order, but I would appreciate its being rephrased."

"The question will be repeated."

"We asked how you can adequately represent your constituency when you are not able to debate the effectiveness of this classic technology for nuclear power plant waste." Julia repeated.

"We're not going to answer the question, Mr. Speaker, because it is nothing but a rhetorical question. We have read enough literature on the subject to support our position," Orin defiantly proclaimed.

The speaker rapped his gavel, "I rule that those opposed be penalized one question for not answering the question pending. Those in favor?" The association president rose up to the podium.

"I would like to know if our opponents are aware of the quantity of waste the present nuclear power plants will produce in the U.S. annually?

"Mr. Speaker, the exact quantity is not our concern. It is the danger that it poses," protested Maxine in a strident voice. "A tiny amount of that material on the loose can wreak terrible damage especially to innocent children."

"Point of order, Mr. Speaker. We asked for a specific number."

"Do you mean the 2 million cubic feet?"

"Mr. Speaker, we expect the United States will dispose approximately 100 tons of waste per week or approximately 5,000 tons of waste per year. This compares, Mr. Speaker, to the millions of tons and billions of cubic feet of uncontrolled greenhouse gases and other materials that fossil fuel plants generate. Further, the new form reduces the waste in volume to where each week it could be carried in six eighteen-wheel trucks."

"Those opposed?"

"It seems in discussing the waste issue Mr. Speaker," Maxine said, "that our opponents, while they are complaining about uncontrolled pollution from fossil fuel power plants, deny that there is also uncontrolled pollution from nuclear power plants. There have been a multitude of incidents in which radioactivity has escaped from nuclear power plants. These incidents are sometimes reported and sometimes covered up. Our duty to our constituency and to the people is to publicize these incidents and to make people aware of the dangers."

Klippstein approached the rostrum, "According to the Nuclear Regulatory Commission, Mr. Speaker, the total radiation released accidentally from nuclear power plants in the United States is equal to a fraction of one day's natural radiation from the sun. The environmental damage potential of such leaks is minute compared to the enormous burdens of sulfurous and greenhouse gasses that are placed in the environment by the burning of coal and oil."

In summation, Maxine reiterated the litany of risks and dangers with Chernobyl as the centerpiece and touchstone of their vision of nuclear energy's past and future.

The Congressman rose to the podium on the opposed side, "Mr. Speaker, perhaps the most insidious and politically dangerous phenomenon in Washington, where I worked for so many years, are the single issue groups. These are groups that are totally motivated by one issue and will tolerate no argument or differences of opinion, nor will they consider views or interests other than their own. They will sacrifice the general welfare and the welfare of entire future generations on the altar of their narrow self-interest. In order to force their issues on Capitol Hill, these groups threaten Congressmen with an active voting segment in each district which will vote as they direct against any politician who dares to disagree with him. Single-issue groups essentially gather power by their ability to influence votes and they use that power to promote their issue.

"The single issue group that is the focus of this debate is the one that is attempting to eliminate nuclear power as a source of electricity which is utterly irrational without any basis in science. These groups depend on their ability to twist the emotions of individuals and win them to their cause by brokering fear. Fear of the unknown, fear of the dangerous, fear of the technological, and fear of the new.

"We have presented in this debate the facts and essentials of the case that proves that atomic power plants are environmentally beneficial in many ways and are essential to continued economic growth, simultaneous with reduced air pollution. We are learning as a result of the global warming that our island home, the earth, is not limitless. Its resources have to be preserved. Nuclear power does not pollute and does not consume depleatable fossil fuels. It can be engineered so that it does not consume depleatable resources. The plants and technology we have now are the precursors of the technology to come which will be even more resource efficient. The issue of nuclear wastes is one to which we have responded. We have shown that nuclear waste can be contained and safely disposed beyond any reasonable risk or doubt. Mr. Speaker, the motion must approoved."

It was.

The Daggett staff had gathered in the eighth floor conference room to watch. They appropriately cheered.

"That's one way to put the cards on the table," said Nancy.

"We have to key on that," said Terry to Anne. "Can we get ready for the speech tomorrow night in Seattle?"

"We can, sir." Jamie Crimmins, now the key speechwriter, felt his stomach sink. He was exhausted. So were his people.

Adrian called in from the plane to speak with Nancy. She took the call and asked if he could go on the speakerphone.

"Okay, boss, you're on the speaker."

"Hi, everybody," said Adrian. "Great job they did on the nuclear antis." Everyone applauded. "I suppose somebody's already suggested we use this tomorrow night in Seattle."

"I already have the assignment," said Jamie.

"Keep writing them the way you're doing it," said Adrian. "I feel a lift in every sentence."

"Thank you, boss," Jamie said.

"How are the polls, Anne?"

"Terry and I are going to talk with Parker in more detail tomorrow," said Anne, "but Dianne got you at least five more points."

"Don't tell her that," said Adrian and everyone laughed.

"It's close to 60 to 40."

"Does anyone sense they have not begun to fight?" asked Adrian.

"I think many of us do, the convention is coming,"

"And then we will know," said Adrian. "Thanks to all of you, I know how hard you are all working and I know also that it's going to pay off."

"Pay off with what?" Terry asked with laughter in the background.

"We'll sprinkle a little patronage here and there."

"We've got to do better than ordinary patronage," said Anne.

"You will all be pleased," said Adrian, "but, we've got to win first."

There was more applause.

The audience was a large Chamber of Commerce awards dinner. It had been planned long in advance, every seat was taken in the large ballroom of the Hilton Hotel. Adrian spoke about the debate on nuclear energy and asked, "Where does all of this stuff come from? What kind of country is this where the government and political people allow this nonsense to be perpetrated on its citizens? I'll tell you," he said, "it comes from a failure of government to face and understand reality. It is a failure of government to communicate reality to the public. It is a failure of government which allows the people to be misinformed. Government and political people deny the public the facts upon which they can base a judgment. What do you suppose happens in a democracy where that goes on?

"If I'm elected we're going to deal with reality, the real stuff, the real issues, the real facts, and to make them known. I pledge that before God."

The audience roared its approval.

☆ Chapter 29 ☆

THE PLANNING FOR the Republican convention began before Warren Hatch left Harbour Island. After he moved, Helene met with him in Washington on Fridays, sometimes with Erla or Harold to deliver materials and to make sure the planning was on track. Each weekend, Helene went on to Westport to see her children.

During the two weeks prior to the convention, around the platform committee meeting, there were a series of press conferences and media events as the heavyweights of the party arrived. Each was given a briefing and speeches were prepared. These were based on polling data which identified what the public wanted to hear from Senators, Congressmen, and Cabinet members. Their comments flickered into television programs around the convention. The media focused on the obvious sound bites provided by the Republican accusations and awaited the Daggett campaign responses. The Republican platform committee procedures were an especially rich source. Sound bites from its hearings formed the leitmotif of the media symphony which Helene, Erla, Marsha, Harold, and their groups composed, the campaign staff played, and Warren Hatch conducted.

Under the Banner of the Southern Conservative Coalition, Helene, Erla, and a few staff people were headquartered in a trailer in the parking lot of the convention hall. The Foulton Foundation, with Marsha and Harold nominally in charge, was located in an adjoining trailer. Both were in frequent contact with Harbour Island.

John Chin in New York with Ken Hirsch, and others of the firm, kept up daily tracking polls of attitudes on different issues. Their purpose was to find out what people believed they thought about particular issues, and about Adrian Daggett. This information was used to reinforce negative beliefs about Daggett. Speechwriters made last minute changes according to the responses of the questions.

The PBS debate on atomic energy and the publicity surrounding it posed a challenge for the POLACO campaign staff.

"Paxson Bartholomew and his Environmental Coalition wants to blast out against atomic energy," Erla remarked to lead off a meeting in a room above the convention hall where a group was gathered to meet with Warren.

"This is a key item on the agenda," said Helene thinking of Mendos Sadovan. Her private opinion was that the fringe environmentalists were totally wrong. "That PBS debate was a setback. What do the polls say?"

"John Chin asked a series of questions about atomic energy. There's a big increase in the 'don't knows' and a big increase in the percentage favoring further development."

"What do we do about that?" Helene asked.

"In our constituency model, we're banking on the nuclear-antis who will certainly not vote for Daggett, but we have to be sure that they vote. If we don't trumpet our anti-nuclear song, a lot of them might just stay away from the polls. Single issue groups behave that way," Marsha philosophized. "The antis have been infuriated, and we need to keep them that way."

"We need to focus on the antis and not the public," Erla cautioned. "The debate will affect public opinion, but not enough to affect their votes. The wild-eyed antis are a force. It's their religion, ill founded though it may be. Their religious fervor can sway a lot of undecideds."

"Good morning," said Warren as he entered the room followed by Carolyn and Ross Chamberlain. Two other staffers arrived to sit at the table. Helene got up to get some coffee and brought a cup back to Erla as Warren said, "Okay, Ms. Younge and Marsha, what is it the people want to hear today?"

"I think we're on track with our constituency plan," said Marsha. "On the major issues, America being a force for good in the world is tugging at the approval of Mothers Against War. The support for the anti-war movement has probably not been lower for three or four years, but it's still a majority opinion."

"Good," said Carolyn. "That leaves us with our issue for our constituency."

Ross looked to Helene as though he did not agree. "I wish we could focus on the irresponsible foreign adventure and support the idea of adding American resolve and reform to the United Nations."

"Do they deserve support?" asked Warren. Helene sensed his ego had been fertilized by an increasing number of television and press interviews.

"What about atomic energy?" Warren asked changing the subject, "I hear Bartholomew wants to make a big thing about it in his speech." The question was eventually directed at Helene.

"We have no objection," said Helene. "The Coalition is in favor of expanding use of atomic energy in order to allow economic growth without increasing environmental pollution. However, we recognize the need to elect Senator Hatford and we recognize the need for the nuclear-antis to vote for him, so let Bartholomew make his statement and put it in the acceptance speech."

"The polls?" asked Warren.

"The antis are still there, Warren. They won't change. What's changing is the public view of them."

"Is there some risk to us?" Carolyn asked.

"It could flashback on us."

"Then why did they take on atomic energy?" asked Ross. "The polls show that people prior to the debate favored the antis."

"No American politician has ever taken a constructive position," said Helene. "But, Daggett did. Keep in mind, Warren, Daggett is not going to tell people what they want to hear. He will tell them what he believes."

"He looks at the polls," said Warren.

"Not the way we do, Warren," said Helene.

"We're doing it the old and proven way. What about values?" Erla questioned.

"The Dianne Daggett press conference took the media out of that issue. Our polls show a majority of people see no reason why Adrian Daggett can't be a good family man even though he had five love affairs before he married Pamela," stated Marsha. "It still helps us with the religious right to keep them solidly in favor of Hatford. They disagree with cohabitation of any kind."

"Are the candidate's wives to give speeches?"

"A majority of people, like 67% want to see that."

"The final death contraction in the political dominance of male chauvinism," commented Helene. Everyone laughed.

"Are there any other changes?" asked Warren.

"I don't see anything that would change it materially," said Erla. "We have values, taxes, and national health care on the first night.

Laws, foreign policy, and health care on the second night, and the third night we have Barbara Hatford and the three that Hatford defeated in the primaries in seconding speeches each requesting that their name not be put in nomination. The fourth night we have the acceptance speech. All of this will be woven together as we had planned. We will make last minute adjustments as needed."

Helene was uncomfortable not being able to review the speeches. All of the first drafts were prepared on Harbour Island and were delivered to Warren.

"What are the stats on health care?" asked Warren.

"We have polled it several ways," answered Erla. "The support for the system is softening. People are concerned about those who don't have insurance."

"What does that tell us?" asked Warren.

"We are unalterably opposed to nationalizing health insurance," said Helene. "It tells us we have a problem and we'd better deal with it."

"This could be improving the present system without being specific," said Ross. "We are going to claim that American health care is the best in the world. We have the most publicized medical people in the United States doing ads for us."

"It would be nice to be leading the charge against government regulators," said Carolyn. She looked across at Helene signaling with her eyes that she was grateful for the restructuring of the campaign that Helene had led.

The assistance from what they thought was the Southern Conservative Coalition made Helene and Erla popular among the Hatford campaign speech, release, and position paper writers. They were delighted to be able to refer questions to the Coalition staff which were answered by Louis Fischer. They found this an amazing resource for supporting data. They could request editorial assistance and get answers in the form of speech texts or other copy. Their results and focus materially improved.

EDGAR BECAME CONVINCED that any espionage action that might have tipped off the Daggett campaign to the planned assault by POLACO on racism came from the outside. There were now 179 employees. His staff checked each one thoroughly. It was not difficult to make a census of tourists and visitors with the check in and check outs at the major hotels. There were also the dockwatchers who made detailed notes of arrivals and departures. They focused on POLACO employees in particular, but no one entirely escaped their attention.

Daphne and Sharon readily made the suspect list. Edgar was eager to meet both of them. The timing of their arrival was suspicious in itself. It was after Tony's meeting with Helene where no agreement concerning moles or spies was reached. The cover was ideal. As best he could tell, they were both legitimate, Daphne the somewhat celebrated writer, and Sharon the respected editor. He instructed Cybill Chubb to have both of them watched for two weeks to see if there was something to learn.

If they were moles, he would need to find out who was running them. He suspected Alvin Carter, the senior security person at PEN-MET. Edgar valued every piece of information about an opponent. Finding the suspect was simple. Proving involvement was difficult. He was glad to have the interrogation resource available, but he knew that Helene would be loath to use it. While he could order an interrogation, he would not do so without her consent.

IT WAS CONVENIENT to have the conventions on the West Coast, because it meant that the delegates would get more sleep. Prime time began at 5:00 p.m. in California and lasted until 8:00. This also meant there would be less time to fill if the convention opened as it normally would at noon on either coast. The rebroadcasting of the prime time began as soon as the live broadcast ended, so that the West Coast was in fact covered twice.

As in most televised events, the anchors immediately took center stage.

"What have you seen so far in this convention, Matt?"

"Bill, I think this may be an excellent start for the Republicans. The convention has been going on now for five hours. There were a number of powerful statements today in the beginning of the platform debate. The themes are evident. The Republicans are going to challenge the debt payment program of Adrian Daggett. They're going to challenge his health care initiatives and they are going to challenge his own character and values. The story from *Explicit* magazine was answered by an incredible and spontaneous public relations coup. I refer of course to the 'slap seen round the world' delivered by Adrian Daggett's daughter, Dianne. But, the Republicans are determined to resurrect it. I know that the Southern Conservative Coalition and the Foulton Foundation are both here with staffs. The foundations are not in the publicity spotlight, but their presence is telling."

"Thank you, and now down onto the floor and the podium."

At the podium, the temporary chairman pounded the gavel, bringing the convention to order. He proceeded to introduce the first speaker, an African-American Republican Congressman who, in a strong and lusty voice, spoke heartily to labor and the middle class. He told them not to be fooled by the reality campaign, which was reality as Adrian Daggett perceived it. He told them not to be fooled by the health care initiative that was an empty promise too expensive to carry out. He told them not to be fooled by Adrian Daggett's reality environmentalism. He asked them if they wanted to send their sons and daughters to foreign wars, and if they wanted the United Nations running the American foreign policy. He focused briefly on the freedom theme and called all Republicans and all voters to rally around a candidate who would assure that Americans retain their freedom, particularly the freedom to be Americans. He got a rousing ovation.

AT THE CHICAGO headquarters, the 7:00 p.m. start of prime time meant that most of the day's work had been done and the staff could order up food and sit in the main conference room on the top floor and watch the big screen.

"This speech summarized their main themes," said Nancy to Anne.

"They'll hammer on these issues throughout the campaign," Mitchell Fiddler said. Dominick Kluczinski nodded.

The second speaker of the evening for the Republicans was a well known multi-term Congressman with a reputation for dramatic oratory.

"They're firing off their big guns early on," said Terry to Nancy.

"It's the right way. That first speech grabbed the audience."

"Our polls tonight will tell how much."

The Congressman started slowly with a dialogue about American family values and how they reflected the raising of American children. He spoke of the importance of values to the family and values to the country. He spoke of the importance of family to the country and to its success. He asked a question, "What values does a man display when he marries at age forty after five love affairs? What was Adrian Daggett thinking when he was in those affairs? What was his motivation in bedding all those women? Did he show any concern for them as persons – any respect? The personal character of a President is critical to the country. What kind of character is this Daggett?

What kind of marriage can he have? What kind of family man is he? He is certainly different from most Americans."

"Lay it on thick and neatly, that issue is back on the table," said Anne to Nancy.

"I see POLACO's paw prints all over this," Nancy replied.

The third speaker for the convention was Olaf Jensen. He originally had negotiated for the second night, but was persuaded that more people would be watching him the first night if he came on about 9:00 p.m. Eastern and 8:00 p.m. Central. He agreed.

Few in the hall had ever heard a union speech before. It was something between a rock 'em, sock 'em talk by a coach to a football team and "repent-for-the-kingdom-of-heaven-is-at-hand." He affirmed the labor council's decision and related the details of Adrian's opposition to unionization at the factories his company controlled. There were boisterous cheers when he finished as the delegates embraced the labor issue, a first for many of them.

"That was a solid hit by a well-aimed torpedo," said Terry.

"Close the water-tight doors," said Alan. "They are doing very well. We may be behind in the morning."

Terry couldn't believe that. They always led in the polls.

The main speaker of the evening, coming on at 9:30 p.m. for a half-hour speech, was a distinguished Senator with a background in economic policy. He questioned whether or not the reality campaign used reality in its fiscal planning. How was it going to keep the budget balanced and pay down the debt? How was it was going to expand aerospace investment? How was it was going to increase military capability? How was it was going to provide jobs and training for workers coming off welfare? How was it was going to provide national health insurance? How was it was going to step up environmental investment? "Tax and spend, that's how spending goes up, taxes go up. That is the Democratic equation. When Democrats are in power, government employment increases. There was nothing real about the reality campaign except that the Democrats really will increase taxes," he concluded. The audience shouted and hooted their approval.

The Daggett staff looked on helplessly.

"I'm not sure I've ever seen anything this good," Nancy said to Anne.

"We have to beat them," said Anne. "No matter how good they are."

In the morning, the tracking poll indicated that Hatford was leading by two points. Helene was jubilant. It could be done. Daggett could be beaten.

AT NOON THE following day, Pacific Time, the ceremonial changing of the gavel over from the temporary to the permanent chairman took place and then further discussion of the platform continued. Pro-rights and pro-life speakers came to the podium. The platform committee voted on compromised language which the following morning everyone forgot. On prime time the commentators commented.

"No one anticipated the sudden reversal in the polls with Senator Hatford now leading Governor Daggett," said the anchor. "Last evening was a masterpiece of convention planning and strategy. The Republicans brought out their leading figures and, with extraordinary prose, they smashed into the Daggett reality campaign. Since the first poll Adrian Daggett has led Steven Hatford until today. What do you think is happening?" he asked his colleague. His colleague, an older woman with long experience in political coverage responded.

"It was a question of getting the best talent together. Steven Hatford can thank Warren Hatch for his first lead. Hatch has brought to the campaign what it obviously needed, a central theme for good communication and disciplined leadership. The uniqueness of Daggett's message and character provided him with the early momentum. He rolled over his opponents in the primaries, largely because they were unable to respond effectively to his reality themes. Now an opponent has replied."

"How do you rate the Daggett campaign staff?"

"They are a very good staff and they have a good candidate to sell."

"Do you see this as a real battle emerging now?"

"It is clear there is going to be a close battle. Steven Hatford has brought in the resources he needs to win the Presidency."

"Do you believe that Warren Hatch is essentially responsible for this turn around?"

"There haven't been any other changes. Hatch is the architect of this convention and you can see what it is accomplishing."

There was no let up in the prime-time barrage. On Tuesday night, a well-known, pro-labor governor attacked the Daggett record on labor and insisted that Daggett was against the right of labor to organize.

The second speaker that night was a president of a medical school, well known for her writing and commentary and one of the first women to ascend to such a position. With gray hair framing a stern face, she was an imposing figure whose intelligence was evident in every word she spoke. She struck at the heart of the Daggett argument about national health insurance which she said would destroy the finest medical system in the world. She recited its accomplishments. The capability to invest, she said, was absolutely critical to continued advancement of American health care. She stated unequivocally that Daggett proposed a socialist system of medicine that was wrong and that had already been proven to be unsuccessful. Nowhere in the world has health care advanced as it has in the United States. She warned that we change the system at our personal and societal peril.

The third speaker of the evening was an Asian-American Republican politician, a newcomer to the House of Representatives. A graduate of UCLA, and a member of the Committee on Foreign Relations of the House, he was very well spoken. He attacked the Daggett foreign policy as dangerously unrealistic. He spoke of the United Nations as incompetent. He decried the potential waste of the young lives of men and women in the American military services. He shouted that no man with such extreme interventionist ambitions, ideas should be allowed to exercise the mantle of power.

Just after 9:00 p.m., the keynote speaker was introduced. She was a former Cabinet member, now in her sixties, medium height, a little plump, with a shock of dark hair perfectly coifed. Her eyes glinted as she spoke. She introduced the theme of assuring freedom. She spoke passionately of what it really meant and chided liberals for never understanding it. To have true freedom was to have freedom of choice, freedom from government intervention, freedom from high taxes, freedom to work. The speech followed the theme with carefully convincing eloquence.

She was followed by another new Congressman, a short, bushy haired man, who thundered the Republican work ethic, which he contrasted to the Democrat's "welfare ethic." Americans, he said, have forgotten one essential to life and that is work. He dwelled upon the theme of dedication to one's life pursuits and hard labor of either mind or body or both to make those pursuits become reality. "The reality is, Mr. Daggett, that America has to be dedicated to working hard. We can't have any people who are not carrying their load or pulling their oar. The willingness to work," he said "is the great difference between people. It determines those who can do well and those who can't do so well."

There was a tumultuous applause.

There was no applause at the Daggett campaign headquarters as the staff watched the performance.

"One way to have a good convention is to write all the speeches," said Nancy.

"I agree," said Alan. He felt tired and frustrated. He wished his wife would be with him that night. There was still a mountain to climb.

"How much further behind will we be?" asked Anne.

"Another three or four points, I think," said Alan.

"We're going to regain it. We'll gain it back. We can do just as good a job. This is just a normal 'post convention bounce,'" Nancy rationalized, hoping it was true.

At their home, Tony watched alone, while Jean was out, probably with Malcom. When it was over he phoned Terry and he heard Alan's guess. He told everyone on the speakerphone that they would do better because they were speaking about the real issues and the truth. A special Senior Committee meeting was scheduled for Friday immediately after the Republican convention and Hatford's acceptance speech.

The Wednesday night performance included only two speeches before the nominations, seconding speeches, and the roll call of the states. The first was by the leader of the conservative wing of the party who spoke eloquently of the return of tax and spend liberalism and socialism in the form of the so-called reality campaign. He delivered a beautifully packaged set of the main points of the POLACO philosophy.

Barbara Hatford delivered a similarly well-packaged description of her husband as a family man with emphasis on his values. "I was his first and only love," she emoted convincingly, "and he was mine."

The nominating speech and the seconding speeches for Steven Hatford focused on him as an individual and sought to counter the trust that had been built up for Adrian Daggett. Then came the roll call of the states with each presenting a hokey little promotion. "New Jersey, the Garden State, casts all of its votes for the flower of the Republican party, Senator Steven Hatford. Montana, the Treasure State, treasures this opportunity to cast its votes for..." And so it went with Hatford easily capturing the nomination as expected. After his nomination, Hatford came to the convention to receive the great ovation. He then announced he would ask that former Secretary of Energy, and former Congressman Clayton Thomas, of California be nominated as Vice President.

"So, it's Hatford and Thomas versus Daggett and yet-to-be-determined." said Anne.

"They chose someone from California otherwise we would have definitely taken the state. They think that with Thomas on the ticket they have a chance," said Alan. "He's far from a heavyweight. Energy was a mess when he left."

"The ads from the coalition and the Foulton Foundation are going to resonate off this convention," said Anne. "They've covered everything perfectly."

"We have to do better," said Terry, "and we can. There hasn't been a lot of substance here. We can hit them with substance."

The next night prime time began with the nominating speech for Senator Thomas and the seconding speeches and another roll call of the states with promotions or gag lines. Thomas, who had been chosen only at the last moment, gave a modest acceptance speech in order to avoid upstaging Hatford. When he finished, he had his moment of glory with his family coming to the platform to receive the blessings of the convention.

The American political process halted for an extended period of television commercials before the introduction of the Presidential candidate by the convention chairman. It was rousing, resourceful, and dignified. Senator Hatford came forward to the platform to the traditional long-standing ovation. When it was over, he introduced his theme.

"All of you here in the hall and you patriots watching from your homes, your businesses, and clubs have participated in a great tradition of democracy in support of continued freedom, the most priceless possession of any woman or man. We are fortunate in our nation that people look to America as the shining example of what it means to be free. Never has the idea of freedom been far from us as we rose to world leadership, and as we fought wars to retain our freedom and to gain it for others. This nation is described as the beacon of freedom. Our pledge in this election is to preserve, protect, defend, and expand freedom in all of its manifestations."

He touched on them all. Freedom from excessive taxes. Freedom from conscription and the risks of war. Freedom of choice in health care. Freedom to bear arms. Freedom from excessive government regulation. Freedom of the use of property. Freedom to seek and gain an education. Freedom from excessive police power. Freedom from perverse arrest. Freedom to invest. Freedom of entrepreneurism...

"What's he talking about?" asked literal thinking Nancy.

"He's setting us up," Anne said. "Whatever he lists is a perceived threat from us. This is excellent work. I've never seen a rhetoric so effectively used."

"Oh, I think there are some precedents," said Terry.

"When?" asked Alan.

"In Germany and Italy between the wars."

The thought of fascism invaded Anne's thoughts as she made the connection between Hitler's demagoguery and what she was now seeing.

After the stirring acceptance speech, the traditional visits of people to the platform began. First Clayton Thomas stepped up to the cheering audience to hold Hatford's hand high as if in victory. Their spouses joined them, Cindy Thomas, youngish and blonde, exuding the health of a California girl, and Barbara Hatford stately and poised kissed their husbands on the cheek as they waved. The candidates' families filed in. Steven Hatford picked up his youngest grandchild, a blue-eyed, blonde-haired boy who gazed out into the audience and waved to them drawing a great squeal of delight from the crowd. Hatford smiled; he was leading in the polls.

FOR THE DAGGETT campaign staff, fatigued but game, it was another challenge. Plans were well along for the Democratic convention, but they called together a special crisis committee. This consisted of the usual members of the Senior Staff Committee. Tony brought Susan MacAulliffe, Stephanie Comstock, Reeves Fullka, and John Asheville, President of Jeremy Reubin Associates. A Learjet went to Teterboro to pick up Denise Williams, David Gibson, Parker Lothan, the account executive from the advertising agency and his creative director, and two others from Evans & Copeland. To put some younger people in the deliberations, they selected the three that were decisive in South Carolina; Jack Wood, Louellen Parsons, and Karen. They gathered on the Saturday following the Republican show in a large meeting room at the airport Hyatt in Chicago. They had one day to polish a convention and other aspects of their campaign to win back the lead. They started at 8:30 in the morning and finished at 10:30 in the evening.

CYBILL CHUBB AND Edgar Slaughter carefully planned the

course of action to identify what information had been released. They identified the staff members and with whom they dined the first night after the intense eight days of work for Warren Hatch. The list of contacts that evening presented ample possibilities. Sharon and Daphne were at the top. As for the staff, Julie and Jeff Spencer were married and keys to the effectiveness of the computer operations. Laurie and Preston were a recently formed pair. Preston was an intelligence analyst and Laurie was an expert on computers. Her functions were systems administration, technology insertion, and applications software evaluation.

Ruth was Marsha Fox's right hand. Jimmy worked as a writer and an analyst for the Communication Group. Pat Stabler was the critical pin in the television operation. All had been recruited at a considerable expense and brought to Harbour Island. It was not easy to recruit to Harbour Island. And, they were in the middle of a critical campaign.

"Who is likely to tell us the most?" Edgar asked Cybill.

"I think Preston. He's very proper, possibly over disciplined as a child. He's frightened of authority. He's twenty-seven years old and he probably was a virgin until he met Laurie. He's something of a klutz athletically, and with girls, I think."

"Is he bright?"

"Very. He's making a significant contribution."

"Let's see where we get with him. He had dinner with Daphne at Valentines."

"I think we should try Julie for the first interview. She and her husband have about the same personality, but I think she's more loquacious. She doesn't care what she says or is at least not careful about it."

THE HEADQUARTERS HOTEL was the Sheraton Balharbour in Miami Beach. After the flight and renting a car, Karen and Earl were ready for a swim. A tropical wave had kicked up surf so they used the Olympic-sized pool to swim laps and then went out on the sand to play in the breakers. Karen raced him into the ocean. In their room, their skin felt cold when they made love. He took her to Frank Gordon's for a sinful slab of swordfish cooked to perfection. The window by their table looked out over the darkening blue of Biscayne Bay, the reflection of the glass showing the red tablecloths in the wood-paneled room.

"Have I told you how much I've missed you enough times?"

"I need one or two more."

"You won't complain if I don't see much of you."

"As long as I see all of you."

"You're bad."

"Just horny. When a guy has a girl like you to think about it affects him."

"I hope it's my brains, personality, and hard charging that turns you on."

"It's the hard charging I like best."

"There's going to be some here. Porter's announced that he wants to amend the platform concerning national health insurance. Perona wants to revise support of the United Nations and Ramsdell wants to limit the scope of the changes to the government regulations policies. Porter says he is livid about the reduction of government employment and the amendment of the civil service act. Steve Zimmer is still coordinating for Porter."

"He was the campaign director?" Earl asked.

"Yes. They hate us. Porter was the front-runner until we showed up. Steve, I'm sure felt he was going to be a White House power."

"Why don't you just invite these guys to the platform at the end?"

None of them have said that they would support Daggett, particularly Porter. He's still angry. So is Zimmer. I imagine the whole staff," Karen told him.

"Then you'll have to lobby against them."

"Some people are sympathetic because we crushed them so badly. Their proposals might draw a sympathy vote."

"Maybe it becomes a question for members of the committee. Are they for Daggett or aren't they?" Earl suggested.

"We can't be arrogant. We have to deliver the platform. We have to concentrate on that. Terry and Alan want the platform they submitted. They don't want any tinkering with it." Karen glanced away from him and looked at the bay.

"Porter, Perona, and Ramsdell want to make their mark on the convention by changing the platform."

"I love you, Earl."

"I love you, Karen."

"Let's talk about that," she said.

They did for a while, but then the conversation soon returned to how she would handle the platform committee.

AT THE DAGGETT task force meeting the next morning, Karen refused to give up on Steven Zimmer. With the committee's knowledge and approval she called him for lunch. He was surprised enough to accept. His ego desired the stroking that a meeting with the nominee's staff would afford. His libido desired to explore an opportunity to connect with this high powered, attractive woman who was a rising star in the Daggett group. She took him to The Crab House so they would be away from the gaze of members of the committee.

"Tell me what you would like to see happen, Steven," Karen began.

"What I would like to see happen is for Adrian to declare an open Convention and let us fight it out to see who should get the nomination."

Karen was not sure how to reply. "In every election there is one winner and several losers."

"You drowned us in money, Karen."

If he felt that way why did he come to lunch? "We drowned you in good ideas, Steve."

"Okay, so it was ideas. What do you want from me?"

"I asked you what you want."

She obviously had read the submissions that he and his limited staff had prepared, so he correctly interpreted the meaning of the question.

"We want to be remembered as participating in the primary process. We want to be remembered when the time comes to hand out Washington jobs. We want to be remembered if you don't get the opportunity to hand out the Washington jobs."

"We'll have the opportunity, Steve. We're going to win."

He interrupted. "The general election is a lot different from the primaries. You're not going to be able to win it with your money."

"We don't intend to win it with money. We intend to win it with ideas and a superb candidate." She looked him in the eye.

"You've got a lot to learn, Karen. So far your experience is only the primaries."

She suppressed anger. "All right, so you want a job in Washington. Is that the bottom line?"

"Maybe it is."

"How do you expect to get it by opposing us in the platform committee?"

"Maybe you'll offer me something."

"It is Senator Porter who is nominally doing this isn't it?"

"It's complicated, Karen. Porter, Perona, and Ramsdell want what they want. We want you to compromise with us and give us credibility. I told you what I want."

"We have a policy, Steve. No patronage promises, except to remember you when and if appropriate."

"Well, I'm a different case, Karen. I'm an experienced and tough opponent and I'm going to get what I want in the form of publicity out of this platform fight because that's what it's going to be."

"What would it take to get you and Senator Porter to back away from this?"

"I've already told you what you need to do for me, but I have to fight you if you can't do anything for the Senator."

"The Senator will have to tell us what he wants."

"He's not going to tell you, Karen. The Senator is only going to speak with Adrian Daggett or Terry Leelan."

Karen felt she was in over her head. "How can I persuade you to support our platform?"

"I'm not sure that you can, Karen. I think I'm dealing at too a low level."

Karen felt herself turning red. She had made a mistake in contacting him and trying to handle it herself. She stayed in character.

She called Jack after the meeting. "I made it worse, Jack."

"We took a risk," said Jack, "He wants a job."

"You got it," Karen said.

"How about Deputy Commissioner of Indian Affairs for Northern Alaska?"

"Based there?"

"At Fairbanks, of course."

BACK AT THE Balharbour that evening, in her bra and panties, Karen was pressing her outfit for the next day while Earl read the newspaper and the newsletter published during the convention.

"Why are some of these people such snots? Steve Zimmer is a reasonably competent guy, why doesn't he just sell himself on his own merits?" she asked.

"He may not believe he has enough," said Earl. "He may feel inferior or he has fears. Therefore he feels that he has to get his way with negotiation or conspiracy of some kind."

"Or by being nasty."

"It's called intimidation, Karen. He tried to intimidate you."

"I think he was successful."

"Don't ever let anyone win by intimidation. See it for what it is."

"But we have to keep peace. We don't want a floor-fight at the convention."

"I understand. We don't want anything the media will hook onto, but they will have their time speaking on C-SPAN before that platform committee. You just work the committee and answer people's questions and do the same things you did in Iowa to get them to vote your way."

"These aren't Iowa people, Earl."

"I know that. Work 'em Karen, you can do it."

"I hope so. I thought this was going to be fun."

"It is, isn't it?"

"Maybe it is, but it's stressing. I feel inferior."

She unplugged the iron and she stepped around the board and he grabbed her. "Don't wrinkle my dress."

"Put it down and come back."

She went to the closet, hung it up, and came and sat down beside him. He unhooked her bra.

"I love you, but not now. We have to have dinner with Amelia Johnson and her friend, Grace Jurizuck."

"You don't have to lobby Amelia."

"I want Amelia to do some lobbying for me."

He realized she was focused on the dinner and how she would approach Amelia Johnson. Lovemaking would have to wait.

CYBILL HAD ALREADY met Daphne and was prepared to introduce her to Edgar. They took a chance on a Friday night. Edgar, Harold Smalley, Erla, and Marsha went to dinner in Valentine's dining room and then adjourned to the bar full of POLACO people mixed with tan summer tourists. Cybill, following the script, engaged Daphne in conversation when Edgar drifted nearby.

"Here are some people, Daphne, who would like to meet you." She turned and introduced each of them. Edgar was last.

"You're the famous writer? I don't believe the photographs on your book covers do you justice."

"You're very kind, Mr. Slaughter."

"This is Harbour Island. I think we can use first names right off."

"Very well, Edgar. Are you all with the foundation?"

"As of the last count," said Erla.

"I guess you all come down here to do your work, just as I've come to do mine."

"What drew you?" asked Marsha.

"I can stay focused for a long period of time. It's not easy to do in New York or even in Vermont. In Vermont, the weather is a problem."

"Are you a skier?" Edgar asked.

"I love it and it interferes with my work."

"You can't work all the time," said Erla. "I see you running and playing tennis."

"And swimming, but I take my computer to the beach."

"I really enjoyed your last book," said Smalley.

"Thank you."

"Is Harbour Island going to be the subject of one of your novels?" asked Edgar.

"It's tempting. There are interesting characters here."

"What are you working on now?" asked Edgar.

"I have two articles going and a novel."

"May we inquire?" he asked.

"Writers prefer not to discuss their work until after its published."

That's what she should have said, Edgar realized. "How often do you get back to the mainland?"

He knew she had flown off to Miami, seemingly without a lot of preparation.

"I have to see my publishers and I have to see my children. The publishers want to see me. The children are in college and they don't. Once in a while is okay."

"I would imagine they would want to visit you."

"I've only been here since the first of the year. This summer they're both working. They think Harbour Island would be boring."

"You must miss them?" Edgar asked looking her in the eye.

"I do, but I can miss them down here as well as in Manhattan or in Vermont."

"Why did you come here?" Edgar pressed.

"I had no idea I was moving here a year ago. I came on vacation and I liked it very much. There is some civilization, but not much of it. I have no social obligations. If I want to deal with those I go back to Manhattan. Life is quiet. I can focus. In order to live in the style I wish, I have to work quite hard."

"Sharon is your associate?"

"She has to work, too. Sometimes I feel as though I shouldn't have brought her down here, but we grind it out. Many writers and artists have a hideaway."

"But not one in which they spend so much time."

"Writing takes a lot of time. I think, Edgar," Daphne said, "that you've asked enough questions."

That's exactly what she should have said, Edgar thought, which did not relieve his suspicions. It seemed to him that she played her role too well.

"I apologize, would you join us for an after-dinner drink?"

"I would be happy to."

At the bar the conversation lightened to current topics. Daphne made sure that she did not show too much knowledge of or interest in the Daggett campaign. She had heard about Edgar Slaughter and knew fully well the probable significance of the conversation.

☆ **Chapter 30** ☆

THE SECRETARY OF the Convention received requests from delegates for items to be put on the agenda. She answered most indicating a need for certain action prior to the convention. One letter, however, was a point-of-order from the California delegation. The secretary faxed it marked "very urgent" to Terry Leelan and Alan Jacobs. At the Sheraton, Terry paged Alan who was on the convention floor with the lobbying team.

"We have a letter from California saying that they want to put the names of Porter, Perona, and Findlayson in nomination."

"Bullshit."

"They say they will make an issue out of it on the floor if we do not agree."

"Bullshit."

"You've got to be careful of California, Alan."

Alan Jacobs took a deep breath, "I know, but we can't have this," he said. "Nobody won any states in the primaries but Adrian. The Republicans had people who did win states who were not nominated, so that they would appear unified and acting under the same format that we would use. This sounds like Steven Zimmer."

"Can you see him?"

"With pleasure."

Alan went back to the meeting, took Karen aside and asked her to run down Zimmer and bring him to a meeting room they had rented at a small hotel near the convention center. It was in the delightful restored "art deco" section of Miami Beach. Karen wished she had time to enjoy the ambiance.

The hotel staff managed to get a tray of fruit juices into the room as Karen arrived with her quarry, tall, but paunchy Steve Zimmer. Alan followed a minute later.

"We're going to cut the crap, Zimmer," said Alan.

"What do you mean?"

"I mean about having Porter and the others put in nomination."

"It is the only gentlemanly thing to do."

"It will use up too much time. We need to talk about Daggett, or do you want him to give his acceptance speech at 2 a.m.?"

"If Karen has done her job, you know what I want."

"You might have gotten it honorably, but this way, no way."

"I thought Karen told me you would deal."

"No deals. Your credentials for the convention are revoked."

Zimmer's jaw dropped. "What do you mean 'revoked?'" he asked.

"It means that you are not going to be able to come into the hall," said Alan. "Whatever damage you do will have to be done outside."

"You can't do that."

"Try and stop me. Try and get into the hall. I'll have the television cameras record your being thrown out."

Karen had never been in a meeting like this before.

"Why don't you be reasonable Alan, all I want is a job," he said. Zimmer's face went blank.

"You didn't come over and offer to help us," Alan replied.

"Porter forbid it."

"I'll have to hear him tell me that."

"You won't believe me?"

"Not after what you've done."

"I'll have him call you."

"Just have him write me a note."

"If he does, will you give me something?"

"I shouldn't."

"Alan, we've known each other a long time."

"If I were to consider this, what is it that you want?"

"Under secretary of the treasury."

"No way. You don't know anything about finance, all you know is politics. Besides you can't have any visibility. Ask me for something that doesn't require confirmation."

"Then make me a counselor to the President on domestic policy."

"I don't want you in the White House," said Alan. Zimmer smiled. Alan had telegraphed he was going to give in.

"Why don't we get you on the Special Executive Service?" Alan said. "If you want a job why not a permanent one?"

"Make me an offer."

"Make a suggestion."

"Inspector general at interior."

"Maybe. I'll promise the equivalent in terms of salary."

"I want to know the location."

"Washington. Now you back off this nomination shit and you back off the amendments to the platform."

"I can't back away from the amendments; they're already filed."

"Well, see that you don't support them. Disappear."

"Can I have my credentials back?"

"If you behave. One word about nominating these guys or one word from you about anything and the deal is off."

Zimmer made a move to shake hands with Alan.

"We're not going to shake hands, but you have my word and you have a witness."

"I want to shake on it with both of you," said Zimmer.

"All right," said Alan, "but it's best if I don't see you up close again."

When Zimmer left, Alan looked at Karen. "That's part of a post-doctoral course in political science."

She smiled. "Why did you give in?"

"I probably shouldn't have, but we're spread thin, Karen. We can't suddenly have to focus on someone like him. The amendments have to be defeated. You're on the team that has to make sure that happens. We've neutralized him. After I simmer down, we'll see if I can find someplace where he'll be useful."

The platform committee began its hearings. Karen started a new notebook and carefully wrote down everything she thought she might have to remember. Amelia introduced her to a number of members who recognized her as a key Daggett person. Amelia gave a description of her work in Iowa each time she introduced Karen. At each phase of the meeting, Karen would talk with someone and bring up the subject of the Porter, Ramsdell, and Perona amendments. In the absence of pressure in favor, the platform committee voted them down. The question was, would anyone propose them on the floor?

THERE WAS DISAPPOINTMENT at Harbour Island. Helene had authorized the payment of Steve Zimmer's expenses plus a stipend to go to the convention through Paul Melius. Doris Hill was sent to visit

Steve at his apartment in Washington. She reported that Zimmer was disappointed in the defeat of Porter and the disruption of his plans for a position of national power.

AT NOON ON Monday, the opening gavel sounded through the convention hall which was hardly half full. Because the platform debate would begin after the procedural motions, Karen and the lobbying team were marshaled underneath the podium at a special table close to the recording secretaries. In addition to their cell phones, they each had special pagers, an earpiece, and a tiny microphone connecting them directly to Alan who was perched behind the podium at a desk hidden from TV camera view.

The temporary chairman pretended to bring the convention to order and began introducing the officers of the convention appointed by the Democratic National Committee. Looking out, Alan saw that the California delegation was substantially full. In her earpiece, Karen heard Alan's voice. "Karen, Jack, Louellen, head for California." On her way she heard, "Merrick, if you are on the floor, California."

At the delegation, their badges set them apart. The chairman came over to them. "And to what do we owe this visit?" he said.

"We hope you're not planning on doing the thing that Steve Zimmer suggested," Karen said.

"It wouldn't be appropriate," Jack added.

"Let me tell you all," said the chairman, "this delegation has caucused and we've decided that we want the name Willis Porter put in nomination."

"What would that accomplish?" Karen asked brightly.

"There may be some delegates here that would like to vote for him."

"You know many?"

"Well, I think I do, young lady."

"And I know a lot of people who are not happy to hear about such a motion," said Alan coming up.

"I just told this young lady that this delegation has caucused and we have decided to move to have the name of Willis Porter placed in nomination," the chairman said. "We are all interested in Porter and we know some delegates who would like to vote for him. We are more than ten percent of the United States, you know."

"And you also have 65 percent of the aerospace industry," Alan said. "The candidate you should be supporting, Adrian Daggett, has promised to increase expenditures on aerospace technology. I hope you want them increased in California."

"If aerospace expenditures are increased, they're automatically going to come to California."

"Not necessarily," said Alan. "Do you have any idea why the Johnson Space Center is in Houston?"

"Because Lyndon Johnson wanted it there."

"That's correct. Do you have any idea why the Jet Propulsion Laboratory is in Burbank?"

"Well, that's where it was built."

"And that's not where it has to stay. That activity could be moved to the Johnson Space Center. You'd better think of what companies get the new contracts that are coming out," said Alan. "Maybe you'd like to reconsider."

"I don't think it's your place to come over here and threaten the California delegation after it has made a decision," the chairman proclaimed.

"Your decision is threatening the success of this party, Mr. Chairman," Alan said through half clenched teeth.

Karen turned to the other delegates, "You really don't want to do this kind of thing to mess up the convention, do you?"

A number of them assumed the naughty child look and nodded.

"And while we're on the subject," Alan continued, "Don't you think it would be a good idea for Willis Porter to give a seconding speech for Adrian Daggett or would you like us to write him a nominating speech?"

"I can't speak for the senator," said the chairman.

"Well, then maybe you will have someone who can speak for him call me," said Alan. "We'd like to discuss his possible participation."

As he walked away, he switched on his microphone and said, " Karen, Jack, Louellen, stay there until the agenda is approved."

THE FIRST PRIME-time night of the convention was to focus on the needs for reality in policy-making and the victims of the absence of reality. Ten speakers were scheduled for brief presentations. The presenters would make one critical point. They were not necessarily going to be national figures. Two of them were from Karen's inventory of party leaders who were outstanding individuals. The group was introduced as a panel and then the chairperson of the panel introduced each person and called for an intermission of network advertising.

One by one the networks signed on, and their anchor described the events of the day, which had been broadcast by C-SPAN and PBS.

They reported that Senator Porter, Governor Perona, and Robert Ramsdell had all appeared before the platform committee and had sought to change the Daggett platform. They related the rumors that the agenda would be amended to call for all of the candidates to be nominated. They also conveyed that California had decided to nominate Porter, but at the last moment had declined and that observers attributed the change in heart to the work of the Daggett campaign.

A network anchor turned to his commentator, one of the news department's snowy-haired elder statesman, and said, "Is there anything you would like to add about the apparent disunity in this convention?"

"Well certainly there has been no overt effort by Willis Porter or Governor Perona, Robert Ramsdell, or Marilyn Findlayson to support Adrian Daggett," the older man said. "Willis Porter particularly was the front runner and the probable nominee until the Daggett blitz overwhelmed the professional politicians. There is ill feeling and a question as to how much this will affect this convention and the candidacy."

The cameras then focused on the convention platform as the program began. The chairwoman of the panel was the chairwoman of the Democratic National Committee well known for her speaking ability.

She immediately took control and introduced the speakers. The first presentation was by a state senator from Tennessee, an African-American woman elegant in both appearance and style. She captured the convention with her opening lines and with her story of being raised in a family where the cost of going to the doctor was a paramount consideration. She told the story of her brother who was hospitalized with an unusual pneumonia in his preteen years. She told of the damage the disease had done to his lungs which could easily have been averted with proper care. She asked a question: was this a mistake by her parents? Should the opportunity for proper care have been available? Should her father have had insurance?

The second speaker was a business executive who spoke elegantly on the issue of difficult government regulations. He related a story of obtaining air, water, and sewage permits for an expanded factory that would employ 380 persons. He told of the struggle for approval despite the fact that this factory performed exactly the same functions as another already permitted in the same state.

The third presenter was a professor of environmental science who listed the needs of the environmental program and mounted a defense of the Daggett position that nuclear energy should be a resource of the future.

When the delegates were given a brief recess, the anchor turned back to his older colleague, "Do you get the impression that these three speeches were similarly written?"

"I think the Republicans set a precedent," the commentator said.

The next speaker was a distinguished educator, well known to the convention. With illustrations, she raised a series of questions about the effectiveness of the nation's schools and the price that was being paid for not paying enough attention to them.

A retired law enforcement official made the important point that many men and women have become criminals because they couldn't read. He also discussed reducing the access of weapons to criminals.

A doctor called attention to the cost of malpractice insurance and the escalation of health care costs. He said that these costs resulted from the predatory actions of irresponsible attorneys and the leveling of large penalties by irresponsible juries which were ultimately paid by the American public.

A mother told the story of her son who joined the gangs and rejected education and how he was reached by a social worker. Then a working man spoke about how he was on welfare because of an illness that was not treated because of the absence of health insurance.

The speaker after that was well known, the foreign minister of an African country who spoke of the need of the United Nations for American support and the need of emerging democracies for the same.

Finally, a respected Republican banker appeared on the platform and spoke of his concerns for fiscal stability and the need for permanent policy change.

Merrick and Marianne; Alan and Lauren; Anne and Bob; and Adrian and Pamela watched from the presidential suite at the Sheraton. Alan prepared the tracking poll. They all wondered how it played. Was it too much to attempt to pass over the messages without big names doing it? Was it faulty to have the messages even sent in this way? There was applause, but no show of huge enthusiasm.

Earl watched from a seat in the very back of the stands where he tried to locate Karen and listen at the same time. The results seemed subdued. He asked people around him about the program. They seemed to understand and were listening.

In the anchor booth the commentator asked, "Do you see any sign of reduced enthusiasm here?"

"It was not a night of rousing speeches," the commentator averred, "but I wonder if something is going on inside the Democratic Party. Was the rush of Adrian Daggett too fast? Are people now pausing to reconsider particularly those in the leadership? Is there a constituency in this convention that does not favor the Daggett candidacy? Is this convention going to crystallize that movement? These are the questions. This doesn't seem like a particularly good night for the Democrats."

Karen found Earl on the floor after adjournment and grabbed him and hugged him. "I'm so tired," she said. "Did we bomb?"

"I don't think so," Earl said. "People were listening to the speakers."

"I couldn't tell," she said. "I was working on tomorrow's platform vote. There were some people I had to see."

"I saw you scurrying around."

"There were more people than me scurrying. We want this to run smoothly."

"What's keeping it from going smoothly?"

"Some of the delegations keep talking about these amendments and what happened to them."

"Are they admissible from the floor?"

"It would be the chairman's call."

Earl nodded. "Can I take you to dinner?"

"It's too late to eat."

"You have to eat something."

"Okay, soup and a little something in the suite. Is it too late to swim?"

TUESDAY MORNING KAREN and Earl were up for the group jog, but first she called the information line for the latest poll results. A voice told her they showed a significant gain. "Good for the Americans," she thought.

In her shorts and halter and running shoes, she was buttonholed by a CNN reporter who knew her for an impromptu interview. She asked for a minute to regain her breath, which gave her a chance to think about what he might ask.

"I'm with Karen Crezna, the Daggett staff member who was assistant director in Iowa and was active in the campaign in South

Carolina. She has produced some of the advertisements being used on television. Karen, what's your opinion of last night? It was unconventional."

"It was intentionally unconventional, Phil."

"But it didn't seem to rouse the audience."

"It was not supposed to rouse the audience," she said. "This is 'the reality campaign.' This was a description of the problems. Beginning tonight we will start to talk about the solutions. A lot of people think it is a good idea to define the problems and priorities before you start to solve them."

"Thank you, Karen."

"Always my pleasure."

As they stepped away, Earl said, "That was nifty."

Karen grinned. "I could get used to that," she said. "It will look nice."

"They were shooting you from the navel up."

"Two years ago I would have been embarrassed."

DURING THE AFTERNOON, the first order of business was the transfer of the gavel to the permanent chairwoman Ida Young. She was a senior congresswoman from the party and an early supporter of Adrian Daggett. She was also known for running meetings with firm guidance. She prepared to receive the report of the platform committee and for rulings in a possible floor fight about amendments.

The earpieces and microphones were invaluable. Karen and the others assigned to the floor rushed about meeting with people and carrying out orders from Alan, Merrick, and Terry, who were all on the floor with trouble on their radar scopes.

Alan Jacobs concluded that delegates in the Michigan delegation, Porter's home state, had persuaded the California delegation to support them in attempting to put across the amendments. Certain delegates and the delegation chairmen in particular would have their moment of fame. Allowing this could also be perceived to be a weakness on the part of the Daggett forces. If the movement was allowed to propagate, the convention would become confused and there would be embarrassment at the least.

Alan said in a low voice into the direct-talk microphone, "Louellen, make sure of South Carolina, my regards to the governor. Keep in mind what he asked for. Tell him we remember what he offered. Karen get to Iowa. See if you can find out what is happening. Make sure they're all right. Jack, see what the senior senator knows at the Illinois delegation and meet me in California."

Karen, who was in the California delegation, made her way to the Iowa area and found Amelia Johnson.

"Who's lobbying the amendments?" she asked.

"Some Michigan people came here. We told them we want this to go smoothly for Adrian."

"Any problems?"

"I told them to scat when they started to argue," said Amelia.

"Call me if you find out anything more."

Karen gave her a card with her convention phone number. The word came in her headpiece to check any other delegations they could. She stopped at Colorado and Connecticut. Both had agreed to support the amendments. She wanted to ask the one question she couldn't, "What did they offer you?" She realized that she could ask Amelia to help with that question and went back to Iowa.

"Do you have friends in the Colorado or Connecticut delegations or anywhere else where you could find out what is happening?" she asked.

"I think I already know, they are trying to reject the Daggett platform and thereby open the convention."

That frightened Karen. "Isn't that a little silly?"

"Somebody's trying something, Karen." When she related this to Alan, he had already heard it.

"Everybody get to California right away," he said for all of his floor operators to hear.

"What do you expect to gain by this?" Karen asked one of the California delegates.

"We don't want to be ignored in the Daggett count," the delegate, a tall man with a mustache replied. "He won the state primary and we're here to vote for him. We know that he is in favor of expanding aerospace technology, which benefits us, but we think he treated Senator Porter very badly and there should be some recognition here for what he wants."

"You think this is going to help Adrian Daggett get elected?" she asked.

"We'll support the platform, if it's amended."

"We don't think it'll be amended, Mr. Mitten," she said reading his badge.

"Call me Norman, please."

"Norman, I think this is going to endanger California's position."

"How do you endanger California's position?"

"Certain people from California are going to want patronage, which may benefit other people in California."

"You've got to give patronage to California. We're too big."

"We may have to give patronage to California, but that doesn't say to whom. We know that what you are doing is embarrassing Governor Daggett and the campaign. It's probably the objective of the people in Michigan, who we understand started it."

"Well, that's not what the real objective is," Norman said looking away from her.

"That's what we assume it will be," said Alan, who had come to support Karen. "You don't want to put California in a position of embarrassing Adrian Daggett considering his intentions for the aerospace industry. He's promised support for expansion, but it doesn't have to be in California. This delegation should caucus again."

"I can't call a caucus."

"You can request it and vote for it."

Alan punched a code into his cell phone and spoke directly to Chairwoman Young on the rostrum asking for a half-hour recess immediately on completion of the next person recognized. No one was paying any attention to the speakers anyway. After arranging the recess, he spoke into his microphone, "Karen and Jack, get to Michigan. Talk to the chairman. Louellen, get back to South Carolina and bring the governor over to help."

Karen heard her orders and she was after the chairman with Jack. Alan was presumably staying with the California delegation. When they reached him, Jack introduced Karen.

"There is going to be a recess for 30 minutes in just a short while," he said. "Do you have authority to withdraw the amendments or do you have to caucus?"

"Why should I withdraw the amendments?"

"If you want any hope of a job in the Daggett administration other than inspecting latrines in national parks, you'll make sure all this is forgotten," said Jack.

"We don't want people looking at this convention and thinking the normal idiocy is going to go on," said Karen. "If we want to win the presidency we've got to make people understand we really are going to do things in an orderly, rational way. Not based on polls or political position."

"What do you have to offer? I heard somebody else got offered something."

"Do you like being party chairman of Michigan?"

"Don't threaten me."

"No offers on the positive side," said Jack. "On the negative side there will be zip if you don't stop this amending."

"What's so important about amendments to the platform?"

"You know what it is. It's a challenge to Daggett."

"The American people are tired of this kind of nonsense in the political process," said Karen. "We should stop it for that reason."

"Will you call a caucus?" asked Jack. "I want to speak to your delegation."

Louellen arrived with the governor of South Carolina who knew the chairman. After an effusive greeting, the governor said, "My friend, Louellen, here, tells me there is a dispute going on between you and the main campaign. I can't imagine why anything like that should happen."

"We have our reasons," the chairman said.

"I don't think they are very good ones, at least not good enough to cause you to offend the Daggett Campaign," said the governor. "I certainly wouldn't do that after what they did in my state. This man is very electable against the distinguished Republican opponent."

"Senator Porter's people requested me to offer these amendments and to try to have them passed. I have to act on that request."

"I think Senator Porter was misguided to make that request of you sir, but I'd like to give you another perspective. Why are you throwing away your political career?"

Karen saw that the man was confused.

"I'd just like to ask something of Jack, Karen, and Louellen here," said the governor. "If my good friend were to deliver Senator Porter to give a seconding speech, what do you suppose that would be worth?"

Jack knew that Senator Porter and his allegiance to the Daggett Administration would be vital on Capitol Hill. He could, if he wanted, cause Daggett a lot of trouble and was signaling that intention. The amendments to the platform and the lobbying of the California delegation and other delegations was just the prelude.

"I'll have to ask Terry Leelan and Alan Jacobs, but my guess is that this would be a job as assistant secretary or a deputy administrator or maybe something in the Congressional liaison office," Jack speculated.

Also aware that fences had to be mended with Porter, Karen said, "I think the American people would greatly appreciate Senator Porter's support of Governor Daggett. The best place to show it is right here at this convention."

"May I talk to my friend from South Carolina a moment alone please?" asked the chairman.

Karen and Alan backed away and joined the others talking with the delegation.

"I just don't like being pushed around by these thirty year olds who think they know everything," the chairman told the governor.

"They know a lot more than you do and their connections are better than yours," said the governor. "Get off the opposition to Daggett and get Porter to send them your resume. If you don't, they will eventually get you and you'll only have yourself to blame."

"How am I going to convince Porter? He's so pissed off at Daggett, he can't stand to say his name."

"He lost. He has to accept the loss and do the best he can with it. The best thing he can do right now is to second Daggett's nomination."

"But he was the front runner. We were all going to Washington with our senator."

"Well, you can only go to Washington if you are a friend of Daggett's now," said the governor. "If you don't withdraw this amendment thing, you better become a Republican."

"What's so important about this platform?"

The governor arched a well-trimmed eyebrow.

"It doesn't make any difference," he said. "If Daggett thinks it's important, it's important."

At that point the gavel came down and the recess was declared for thirty minutes.

"Now call your caucus and call Porter," the governor said. "Let's you and me meet together with him and see if we can get him out of this hateful mood he's in."

The caucus was called. Jack spoke before it. He regretted the defeat of their candidate from their state, but there was much that they could contribute and much that the senator himself could contribute. Alan arrived. He spoke on party unity and pointed out that they had nothing but perceptions to gain and a great deal in reality to lose.

The chairman asked for a motion to withdraw the amendments. It was carried by a voice vote. Nobody asked for a count.

ALAN WAS ALREADY late for a meeting with Adrian, Pamela,

Terry, Anne, Nancy, Alan, Tony, Alvin, Ian and Susan MacAulliffe, and Stephanie Comstock on the matter of the Vice President. Ian asked to be included, although the choice was to be Adrian's. Adrian invited Stephanie since she was in on the program from the beginning and could provide special insight on the effect of a decision on the markets. To keep PENMET in low profile, a chartered plane had brought the Harrisburg participants to Opa-Locka from where two limousines had carried them to the hotel. No curious reporter would find a PENMET plane near the convention.

They met in a private suite at the Sheraton and set up for a conference. Adrian sat at the head of the table.

"Welcome to this unrecorded meeting which everyone here will know took place, but of which no one will ever find a record," he said. "In the past sessions, we have established criteria, Ian. In order of importance: Whomever we select has to be a person we can trust to handle the government. We must know that if something happens to me, the White House will be left in the control of someone who understands the world and government. He or she has to have the political savvy, a sense of history, and has to be financially and scientifically literate. We'd like someone who will continue the reality program. The third criterion is to be from a large state and fourth, to have good connections.

"Who is on the list?"

"Richard Sandellot, who you know is a former cabinet officer, former Congressman and presently a university president; Congressman Leonard Hart of Connecticut, who is a former multinational CEO now in his fourth term. He will support our program, but will not bring in, obviously, a very big state. Also, his connections are limited.

We have Bud Lough, former secretary of defense. He is a strong speaker, former Congressman, and former businessman. He is from New York and he has connections.

Mariano Grasso, a former mayor, a former Congressman, a former Ambassador and also an entrepreneur. He has operated his own business for a considerable period of time. He is, of course, an elder statesman. Currently he is a professor of government at Texas A&M. A number of polls have indicated that there are no objections to voting for Richard Sandellot on a national ticket. Dr. Grasso is somewhat less known."

"And, there is Senator Porter," said Adrian. "We all know him rather well.

"So race has no part in this," Ian interjected.

"It's totally out of it," said Alan. "No strong signals."

"That's good news," said Adrian.

"The absence of signals, Adrian," said Anne, "doesn't necessarily mean racism won't be there. People may not have answered the questionnaires with their real feelings. However, it's from Parker Lothan. We've asked him to test it as fully as he can in the major states. We wanted to look especially at Georgia, Florida, and Texas."

"We're going to have to make a decision," said Adrian. "Who wants to open the discussion?"

"To whom can we entrust the government who will also carry out our program?" asked Nancy.

"It's probably sure," said Terry, "that Sandellot would carry it out. I suspect that Grasso would try to, but while I know he can handle the government, I'm not sure about our program. Bud Lough would try to do his own thing; the others the same."

"How many names were there to start off with?" asked Susan.

"We had more than 70."

"Did you have Governor Perona among the seventy?"

"Yes, but not Findlayson or Ramsdell."

"Sandellot is probably the best in terms of handling the government. He's the best in terms of continuing our program. He comes from Ohio with 26 electoral votes. He will influence that. He was born and raised in North Carolina with 14. Mathematically it adds up to him," said Alan.

"Are we absolutely certain there are not going to be any flaws?" Tony asked. "They would be disastrous."

"Has he ever been under financial pressure?" asked Stephanie.

"He has," said Alan. "There was nothing to indicate any tax problems or anything like that. We've asked him all the questions. The man is completely honest. He also married late and had two prior love affairs. His wife is the former Martha Crockett. She is a professor of history at The College of Wooster. They have two children, a boy and a girl, both into their careers and both in marriages. There are three grandchildren in whom Richard and Martha delight. They play golf and tennis. They take vacations by going places they've never been to before."

"Some help on education from Martha," Adrian commented.

"What kind of church life?" asked Susan.

"They are Episcopalians. They attend church regularly to promote the idea to their children and grandchildren."

"Where have the struggles been?" asked Ian.

"In the early years, they were poor students who had to work their way through school. They both built up and paid off student loans."

"Net worth?"

"Not much over $350,000. There will, however, be some pension flows and social security."

"Who else has questions or discussions?" asked Adrian.

"What does his family look like?" asked Anne.

"Martha is well preserved, thick in the middle, but not too much. The son and daughter were both athletic in their college careers. They still are. I think both of their spouses are the same. Everybody is in good shape and their grandchildren are absolutely darling," said Nancy.

"Tony?"

"I think it sends a message, Adrian, that you are serious about the race issue."

"Does that extend to the whole of the reality message?" Alan asked.

"In my opinion, it does," said Tony.

"Alan? Judgement?" asked Adrian.

"I go by the polls. Parker can't seem to find any objections. I agree with Anne. There will be a lot of good press about it."

"What about the hidden feelings that aren't showing up in the polls?"

"There are going to be some," said Adrian. "It is a risk. Racism is still there, but it also has the effect of bringing in the African-American vote. That could more than offset."

Adrian called on each person, and asked each for rankings on the main criteria. There was a long discussion. More questions were leveled at Alvin who directed the FBI and other background checks. Five of the last 12 on the list were rejected because of the checks. The remaining people were clean.

"Does anyone else have any comment, concern, or objection?"

There was a long pause. Adrian understood what it meant. He understood the risks. He sensed it was the right thing to do. The scoring for Richard Sandellot for handling the government, were two fives and the rest fours. The next best was Bud Lough who averaged three and a half. The others averaged three.

"Let's break for something to eat," said Adrian. "I'd like it if Ian and Susan, Tony, Stephanie, Terry, and Alan could come up to my suite."

Pamela darted for the door and hurried up to the suite to order refreshments and a seafood salad, which would serve as a meal if necessary. She was just off the phone when the buzzer sounded. She opened the door looking slightly startled. There were Ian and Susan.

"Don't be frightened, Pamela, you're going to be First Lady," Susan said.

Ian smiled, "Aye, and what a First Lady she will be. No more elegant or beautiful lass has had the job."

While they were still chatting with the door open, Tony and Stephanie stepped from the elevator. Pamela was serving soft drinks from the refrigerator when Adrian opened the door and brought in Alan and Terry.

When they were seated and everyone had something cold to drink, Adrian began, "This is the final meeting on the short list, but I felt that Ian, Susan, Tony, and Stephanie should have an opportunity to question you Alan, about the political judgment of selecting Richard Sandellot. While I think we all agree he is the most qualified candidate we have considered, it would still be the first African-American to run on a national ticket. It represents a risk of something popping up in the form of subdued racism, which has been mounting again to some measure in the United States, possibly with pressure on the lower class jobs. I recognize, Ian, that your agreement accedes this decision to me, but you have risked hugely in this effort to deal with this POLACO group."

"I understand the risk," said Ian, "I appreciate your asking for our advice. I want the best person for any job. We have a mere slip of a woman as corporate vice president of finance of a giant company." Everyone laughed. "Alvin Carter is the best there is at his job. I have Japanese and Chinese Americans, Pacific Islanders, and many African-Americans in top management positions in our divisions. One of my directors is an African-American professor at MIT, possibly the most brilliant man I know," he paused, "other than you, Adrian." They all laughed. Ian knew how to relieve tension.

"Alan, why have other running mates been chosen?" Susan asked.

"There are many reasons for picking Vice Presidents," Alan responded. "Bill Clinton chose Al Gore to strengthen his ticket. Dan Quayle got it because he wouldn't outshine Bush. George Bush was probably chosen as someone who would not outshine Reagan. That is a bad cycle.

Everyone laughed.

Bill Miller ran with Barry Goldwater because nobody else would. Franklin D. Roosevelt may well have thought Harry Truman would do the right thing and was essentially honest and devoted to the country.

"Alan, review what you think?" Susan asked.

"I go by the polls," Alan said. "Too many polls have shown the same thing. The question always is who comes out to vote? The African-American community will come out to vote for Richard Sandellot, not only because he's black, but also because he happens to be very good. The racist community will vote against Daggett anyway, as African-Americans would tend to vote for him, so it depends on who votes. It is a risk, but I think Sandellot on balance will help the ticket. There is something convincing about selecting a highly qualified black man."

"Why is he so highly qualified?" Stephanie asked.

There was more discussion to which Adrian listened. Then he said, "I think I sense cautious agreement with the proposition,"

"The best decisions are made that way," said Ian.

Adrian picked up the phone. "Let's see if he can join us," he said. There was applause as he dialed a number.

"It's Adrian Daggett, Richard. Are you sitting by your phone?"

"We were just going out," Sandellot chuckled.

"I have some people whom I would like you to meet. Could you come up to my suite?"

Sandellot agreed and Adrian gave him the Secret Service number to call. After the moment of the decision, the conversation quieted while the event absorbed the people who accomplished it.

A few minutes later the buzzer rang. Pamela went to the door. She greeted Richard and Martha, the loving woman who was Richard's soul mate. She wore a calico sundress. He wore a blue blazer with a white shirt and tie over light colored tan slacks. Adrian went to him and shook his hand.

"You and I talked about your being my ambassador at large to Africa," Adrian said. "I want to take that off the board."

Sandellot looked a little shocked. Martha's eyes turned quizzical.

Adrian allowed a dramatic pause and then said, "Instead, I'm going to ask you to run for Vice President. You are by the judgment of all concerned, the best man for the job. When we do your first performance review I'll show you how this was scored."

Sandellot showed a second of disbelief and then smiled. "You mean you're going to have a black man on your ticket instead of a woman?"

"We have lots of good women," said Adrian, "and some of them have said that you can handle the government better than anyone. Based on your campaign rhetoric we also think you might carry out our program."

"You know I would do that, Adrian."

"God bless us all, Adrian," said Martha. "You do us a great honor."

"Well, I think it might be a good idea if you were hanging around the rostrum tomorrow night. I'm supposed to be nominated. When that happens I am going to announce the choice. Until then it's a deep secret."

"Yes, sir," said Richard. He thought of how his life would change.

"You'll be nominated Thursday night. I'm going to ask Andy Young to come to do it. I'm going to have Jesse Jackson and Raul Perona second you. Just try not to outshine me in your acceptance speech."

"No one does that easily, Adrian."

THE DEMOCRATIC CONVENTION sparkled on prime time with speeches that projected solutions to the problems that were presented the evening before. Jesse Jackson rendered the keynote address. He smote the Republican enemy on all the issues and welcomed the reality concept which he said was too long in coming.

Then Carlos Himenez, the unassuming president of the Agricultural Workers Union, delivered an emotional plea on behalf of his members for national health insurance. He described the plight of individual families and the only possible solution. He spoke slowly and humbly and with obvious sincerity. When he thanked the convention for the privilege of appearing before them, they gave him a standing ovation.

The next speaker was fellow labor leader, Amy Camisona, who spoke of the realities of modern economic competition. She declared that the role of unions must change. She said Adrian Daggett had a view of that change. She quoted Peter Drucker, who said that the essence of good leadership was to present a view of the future which is achievable. She reflected that Adrian Daggett would provide such leadership.

"The future is not in collective bargaining, but in joint security and joint efforts," she said. "The future is not in politics, but in reality. American politics a long time ago lost a sense of reality and we must bring it back. The reality is that the National Labor Council chairman made a political choice. I have made a realistic choice. Fuzzy perceptions to win votes is no substitute for a solid policy and a solid view of the future. Politics based on perceptions can never be a basis for good leadership. That is the likely reason for the essential failure of our recent presidents. Great leadership will deal with reality and Adrian Daggett will go down in history as a great leader."

The audience leapt to its feet and cheered.

Shortly, Carlos Himenez came back to the platform with his wife. Amy's husband stepped out and then they were joined by the others in opposition to the Labor Council's endorsement. A loud speaker thundered through the hall. "Ladies and Gentlemen please welcome to our convention Mr. John Hendrick, president of the Aerospace Workers Union and Mrs. Hendrick; Mr. Arthur Tremor, president of the Airline Union Conference and Mrs. Tremor; Mr. William Odemsky, president of the Petroleum and Chemical Workers Union and Mrs. Odemsky, Mr. Eden Wilkes president of the Metal Workers Union and Mrs. Wilkes; and Mr. Emil Troudik, president of the Rail Transport Workers Union.

The union presidents came to the podium in the order by which they were introduced. The delegates thundered their approval of the evening's ending with seven union leaders on their platform receiving the acclaim of the convention.

At the Sheraton, Adrian Daggett said, " Looks like it was a very good idea, Anne."

"It was surely unexpected," Nancy added. "That will neutralize the effect of the Labor Council. Now the Republicans look phony along with the Labor Council and Olaf Jenson."

"There are still three months to go," Terry cautioned.

"How do you view this second evening of the convention?" the anchor asked of his political consultant.

"It is a rousing response to the Republican convention," the consultant said. "They are presenting the case for the program of Adrian Daggett. The climax was a clever reinstitution of the traditional support by organized labor for Democratic candidates. Hatford needs the support of labor very much. The Daggett campaign this evening has given workers around the country reasons to ignore the National Council recommendation and to vote the way they usually do. The Daggetts know that when labor steps away from a Democratic candidate that it is difficult for the Democrat to win. Ronald Reagan won twice with strong labor support. Steven Hatford will not have that support."

A half-hour later Karen and Earl were with the Daggett gang in the Sheraton bar. The group needed time to unwind and to pay attention to their spouses. George King, who with Merrick at the control desk, came over and hugged Karen and introduced his wife, Bernadette. Lucile hugged Earl and introduced her boyfriend, John Nattair who had come down from Durham, where he was in a Ph.D. program in economics. Karen liked him at once; Lucile would not go to bed with a dolt.

"How about a swim?" George suggested looking at his wife.

"Fine by me," she said.

"Let's do it," said Karen.

"Last one to the pool has to buy the drinks," Lucile declared.

They laughed and paid their checks and headed for the elevators. They met Merrick and Marianne coming into the bar and quickly persuaded them to come along.

At the entrance of the pool they found secret service agents. They were told that the pool was closed while the Daggett family was swimming with their friends. George asked the secret service agent to ask Mr. Daggett if some of the staff could join them.

Adrian himself came out of the water dripping wet to see who was there. An agent behind him seemed ready to draw his gun while Adrian greeted Merrick, George, and the others and then invited them in. Bernadette King met the rugged looking presidential nominee in his swimming trunks while she wore a bikini.

"I should hug George's wife but I'm dripping wet," Adrian said.

"Why don't you do it anyway," said Bernadette. "I'm going to be wet in a minute."

Adrian proceeded to hug her and Marianne, Lucile, Karen and Louellen to be sure they felt welcome. On the warm night the wetness didn't matter. The pool water felt delicious and soon everyone was swimming and chattering. Anne Russell and Bob had been with the Daggetts and Alan and Lauren. Nancy climbed out of the pool to speak with the secret service to arrange for room service to deliver an assortment of drinks. Linda and Dianne Daggett had invited boys to come to the convention who were sharing a room near the Daggett suite. Donald had established a slender blond girlfriend with whom he wanted to share the moments the convention would bring. She was a Communication major at Trinity College working her way through as a waitress. He saw her reading on the beach one day near Chatham and fell in love. Karen saw the two kissing under the water unfazed by the great people with whom they were splashing.

AT THE FOUNTAINBLEAU Hotel where the Pennsylvania delegation was housed, Malcom and Jean were able to get to Malcom's suite without being seen. The hotel had a feature of turning off the phones to the message boxes. Anyone calling Jean would think that she was asleep.

"Twenty-four hours from now Adrian Daggett will be the nominee," said Malcom as he inserted the key into the magnetic lock and opened the door.

"And 90 days from now Steven Hatford will be the President-elect," said Jean.

"It's too early to predict that, Jean. The Daggett staff is powerful. I agree that exposing themselves on the issues so profusely is dangerous, but I see a lot of capability to respond and they are aggressive. After this convention, Hatford will be back on the defensive."

"It's the people, my dear," said Jean. "The people are going to decide in a democracy. You have to do whatever you have to do to get them to decide your way. That means understanding the polls and telling them what they want to hear."

"You may be right."

"We have to direct our state candidates," said Jean "to stay away from the Daggett line and concentrate on a few key issues. We have to decide which choice ideas are going to work for us and use them."

"And we stay silent on the fiscal and foreign policies issues?" asked Malcom.

"We should stick to the balanced budget deal and show concern for the policy of reforming the United Nations and the aggressive foreign policy if it comes up. We'll run ahead of the ticket if we do it right," said Jean.

"I hope so."

"Now that we have politicked with our delegation this evening, can I get you a drink?" he asked.

"Check the wine," she said.

She saw him stoop down to the liquor locker and pull out the tray. He was a strong-looking man with graying hair. His stomach was flat and the rest of his body hard. He was chairman of the Pennsylvania Democratic Committee and chairman of the delegation. He knew how to turn the wheels of political power. His family was three generations of wealthy lawyers and who had established the long-time leading firm in Harrisburg. Three years ago the family doctor told him his wife of 23 years had a difficult cancer. After many months of struggle she ordered her treatment stopped, except for pain relief and came home to die with Malcom at her bedside.

Jean Destito was his first flirtation. He trusted her. It had started the summer before at a meeting of Democrats from the northeastern part of the state at Pocono Manor. He had worked with Jean since she came on the committee and had much respect for her communication skills and her political judgment. She was effective in guiding the party communication program using polls to understand the thinking of the electorate. She appealed to that thinking. With her help the number of Pennsylvania Democratic congressmen and state legislators steadily increased. She crystallized the party's thinking around the key issues that the polls told her were paramount to the voters.

Malcom opened a bottle of Merlot and poured out the glasses. "I guess we're lucky that Tony was told to stay away from the convention," he said handing her a glass.

"I don't advertise that I am Tony's wife around the committee," she said.

She wore a light blue sundress that set off her blonde hair and tanned shoulders. While he kissed her he unfastened it in the back. She shimmied out of it over her slender hips.

"There are women of 25 who wish they looked like you."

She smiled into his eyes. "They don't have stretch marks."

"They would trade for them to be able to look like you."

She unhooked her bra, "No sag in the breasts yet, but remember that I have brains and character."

"You have personal power," he said. He put his hands on her waist and felt the toned muscles of her stomach and her back. She kissed him.

"I'm falling for you, Jean."

She held her fingers against his lips and started to unbutton his shirt.

"We like each other Malcom. We enjoy each other. We have mutual needs. Let's keep it that way until we can see the future more clearly after this election."

THE WEDNESDAY MORNING news shows reported the morning polls with Daggett slightly ahead and twittered with speculation on the vice presidential choice. Each anchor team interviewed various experts on the political process and between them came up with 27 possibilities, none of which included Richard Sandellot. Two or three of the wisest ones then told their hosts that he might be the choice. On the convention floor at noon the rumors started to fly. It was definitely going to be Lough; a deal had been made with Porter. Two hours later the word was that Porter had accepted and Findlayson would nominate him. The next rumor was that an unexpected choice would be made: Judy Messer, a fourth-term congresswomen from Los Angeles to offset Clayton Thomas.

While the whispers continued, Anne Russell was introduced to the convention in the afternoon session to present the visuals of the Daggett program that had been developed so far. All of Karen's TV ads were projected for the convention and the national audience. The campaign brochures and other materials were circulated.

Prime time Wednesday was the peak of the buildup on Adrian. Chairwoman Young called the convention to order for a showing of a film about him. It spoke about his business career and about his success in building a company and saving another from disaster to assume its industry leadership. It showed him doing the same for the state of Illinois. It pictured him as a vital, powerful leader who had a vision of the future which was achievable and which he could communicate. It showed that he epitomized teamwork where teamwork meant unselfishness. It showed him as an achiever and it showed his family side. A segment composed of home videos pictured his children growing up along with the often-repeated shot of Dianne Daggett knocking down the reporter asking embarrassing questions of her mother. Then it told the story of Pamela, her home, her education, her work, her successes, her failures, her marriage, and her love. When the lights came on again, Pamela was at the rostrum. Chairwoman Young said, "Ladies and Gentlemen, here she is."

The audience shouted and cheered. Pamela was almost embarrassed, but she kept smiling and waving.

Alan had carefully positioned her as a contrast. Barbara Hatford was the homemaker and the companion; the mother who did mostly volunteer work. Pamela was presented as a truly professional woman who had delayed her marriage and who needed a man of the caliber and ability of Adrian. Her speech was about issues that related to women and families. She discussed the national health insurance program and the education programs and touched the subject of values. She said it was a societal responsibility to see to the moral education of every child if families failed. She pointed out the reality of families that did fail. Her presentation was cool and reasoned and she lent it just the right amount of her charm and charisma.

Pamela smiled when she said thank you to the audience and received her first solo standing ovation. Donald came out and hugged and kissed his mother. Linda followed and when Dianne Daggett appeared, a special cheer came up. She grinned shyly and waved. Around America thousands of young women watching recognized a role model. Others, older, prayed that Pamela and Adrian were as real as the issues they presented. Chairwoman Young called for a short recess and then returned to pound the gavel, "For what purpose does the great state of Illinois wish recognition?"

The deputy chairman took the microphone, "To nominate a great American as the next President of the United States."

Chairwoman Young introduced the senior senator and chairman of the Illinois delegation. Tall and courtly, kind and thoughtful, the senator under his logo of white hair and tanned face received the applause from his colleagues for what he was about to do. He was brief.

"While the economy of the United States is well off, there are deep-seated problems that relate to justice, domestic tranquillity, peace and freedom," he said. "History is full of the stories of democracies who have faltered and failed because of the inadequate leadership. What a travesty it would be for this great nation if the same fate were to befall it. The leaders that produce only perceptions, and those who read only opinion polls to reach their decisions, are the kind of leaders who bring about ultimate failure. If the United States fails, ladies and gentlemen, the world will fail.

"We are in a time of great transition, which many families in America feel. In this convention we have enumerated the problems, the tough issues. Part of our educational system is not working. There is no strategy in our foreign policy through which world peace can reasonably be assured and the proliferation of terror weapons mitigated. There is a massive overhang of national debt. Our health care system has unsatisfactory access and high costs. Certain markets, particularly in foreign exchange, threaten world economic stability and growth. We have no national industrial policy to guide our future. We have no national energy policy to meet the needs of our economy without increasing environmental pollution. We have stifled our industries in regulations and rendered them less competitive. These are the tough issues. They are the ones which perception and poll reading politicians will never tackle. They are also the ones which can destroy the United States if they are not managed.

"You have heard from the campaign so far what the candidate

plans to do about them. You have not heard a shrill cry for tax cuts as a means of winning this election. Rather you have heard a call to action to assure the long-term future of this nation. I am proud that this call comes from a son of my state who will accept the challenges. I pray that Almighty God will be with him as he traverses the path of leadership. I am grateful to have the opportunity to put before you the name of Adrian Daggett of Illinois."

The hall erupted in a loud cheer and the senator stepped back from the podium. After a few moments, while he composed himself from the deep emotion he felt, the senator came back to wave. His eyes were wet. He disappeared once again and returned with his wife whose genuine affection and intrepid support of her husband and the party over the years had earned her a special place in the hearts of many party members.

Chairwoman Young pounded the gavel. "For what purpose does the great state of Michigan seek recognition?"

"To second the nomination of Adrian Daggett." Willis Porter appeared at the rostrum. A shout went up with applause. He waved and enjoyed it. With his speech, he pledged his support through the reality campaign. He acknowledged his disappointment in the results of the primaries. He hoped and prayed for a productive association with the next President of the United States. The speech got a warm reception especially from Michigan and California. His wife joined him to wave good-bye and a few moments later Chairwoman Young pounded the gavel again. "For what purpose does the great state of California wish to be recognized?"

"For the purpose of seconding the nomination of that great American, Adrian Daggett."

Judy Messer was introduced. Her speech touched on the importance of maintaining American leadership in all aspects of technological and economic development. There were two more brief seconding speeches from Texas and Alaska and a final one from a congressman from Iowa.

The convention proceeded with the roll call of states. Each gave its little commercial. Each delegation chair had his or her moment on national television. When the secretary reached Rhode Island, the camera suddenly shifted to the activity at the Sheraton Balharbour. Adrian in a crisp light gray pinstriped suit with a slightly darker designer tie was striding through the lobby in the center of a phalanx of secret service agents. Three limousines awaited him with a motorcycle escort for the drive to the convention hall. Cameras flashed and people applauded from behind barricades as he came out. The nomination ground forward. The final state, Wyoming made its report and the secretary certified Adrian Daggett as the nominee of the Democratic Party. The cheer went up.

The family box was now full. Adrian's father and mother, Pamela's father and mother and brother, the children, uncles, aunts, and cousins were now there. There was a bustle of activity behind the platform all carried by the television screens. Chairwoman Young turned to the convention and announced, "Ladies and gentlemen, the next President of the United States," and Daggett came forward. He looked out from the podium and wondered how much more shouting their lungs and throats could stand and how much more clapping their hands could do. They yelled and clapped and waved to him and he waved back. This went on for almost five minutes. The chairwoman whispered something in his ear having to do with the television schedule. He raised his arms and tried to quiet the audience by starting to say, "Ladies and Gentlemen" several times.

"Ladies and Gentlemen, my fellow Americans, I thank you from the bottom of my heart for your reception for my family and for my wife earlier this evening. Pamela is a great lady and a great friend. I am not going to let her down, ever." His voice broke; he paused. There was applause and cheering.

"My kids are great kids and I love them. I love this country. I love the truth and I worship Almighty God. I thank you for all that you have done.

"We face many challenges as the senator from Illinois so eloquently conveyed to you. In facing these challenges there has to be a vice presidential candidate in whom you can have the utmost confidence. The vice president has to be someone to whom the government can be turned over with ultimate confidence in his ability to manage it. The vice president also must be willing and able to carry out the program that we present to the American people. He or she must be a person of the highest character and must be able to participate in this government in a full and meaningful way in order to be prepared should something happen to the president. For many weeks now a group of my staff and I have pondered this problem of who this person should be. We believe, and I believe we have selected the very best person we could. Tomorrow night the chairwoman will call on the state of Georgia to make the nomination. Ambassador Andrew Young will be on the rostrum to nominate Richard Sandellot."

A huge "Yeow!" went up from the audience. George King turned and embraced Merrick and raised his hands in the air. Lucile Cush jumped up and down and then hugged Karen. The television cameras converged on African-American delegates in the various states. Adrian stood at the rostrum not finished with what he wanted to say. When the noise quieted he said, "I pray to God that Richard and I will conduct a campaign that merits the confidence of everyone in this nation and that we will achieve the mission you set us upon, and that God will encourage us, protect us, and inspire us." He turned and Richard came forward. The two of them stood talking and waving. In his booth, the anchorman said to the commentator, "This is a riled up convention now, energy is flowing."

"It is," said the commentator. "It's historic, a historic convention for the platform and the candidate that is nominated and now, of course, for the first African-American to be on a national ticket. Richard Sandellot, in my judgment, is ahead of the others who were considered. He is a man who is able to carry out the Daggett program and he is a man who will carry the story. He is also from Ohio with 26 electoral votes."

In the presidential suite, Terry asked Nancy to summon the floor team.

Twenty minutes later Karen and Jack, Louellen, Merrick, George King, Lucile Cush, and others arrived at the door with the secret service; Adrian, Pamela and the children.

Terry greeted his staff and congratulated his candidate. Then he gave everyone a copy of Adrian's acceptance speech to go over.

"Let's take a break to notify spouses, boyfriends, and girlfriends."

The cell phones popped out.

AT THE FOUNTAINBLEU, Malcom Cummings looked at Jean in his suite while they sat at a table.

"What do you think of that?" he asked.

"I know that Sandellot is a good man," said Jean, "but I would have thought that Renee would have been a better choice."

"There aren't too many women who measure up to him," he said. "What's the effect?"

"The effect is that Daggett is putting his ideas on the line," she said. "Why? He told the convention that Sandellot is the best man and everyone knows that he is a risk. So it looks like he's telling the truth."

"My conclusion too," he said. "Daggett made a good choice. I'm sure that they polled it."

"I'm sure that lily-white Tony and Terry Leelan looked at the polls. There is more at stake here than you know," said Jean.

"What do you mean by that?'

"Something I can't tell you about right now."

His curiosity was piqued, but he didn't pursue secrets.

Jean was troubled. Part of her wanted Tony and Adrian to lose. Part of her knew that it was terribly important that they won. In the lovemaking that followed she was able to temporarily set aside her dilemma.

IT WAS 1:00 a.m. when Karen opened the door to her room and found Earl on the bed reading.

"Last night was a fun night. Tonight was a late night. You okay?" he asked.

"Yes," Karen said slowly. "We had to determine if we needed more in Adrian's acceptance speech to make it a real climax."

"It might not be a bad idea," Earl admitted. "Things were pretty exciting today."

"They sure were," she said, "starting with Pamela. She was almost too good and then having the children come out on the platform, especially Dianne. It was incredible."

"Then having Adrian name Sandellot."

"Yes," Karen grinned, "Sandellot."

She backed to him and sat down on the bed so he could unbutton her dress. She stood and pulled it off over her head. "Thank God they don't make us wear stockings."

"It's hot all right," he said.

Karen sat down on the bed in her bra and panties. "I'm sorry we didn't have some time tonight," she said.

"You're busy making history," he smiled.

"You shouldn't have waited up."

"I don't like to go to sleep before you're here. I like to know you're safe when you call me in Sioux City."

"It's going to be like this a lot," she said, "if we win."

"You're going to win."

"It worries me," she said. "I sat at that meeting thinking about the speech and thinking about you."

"I am preparing for life with you." He raised the book and showed that it was a biography of Margaret Thatcher.

"I'm not that good."

"You're very good, Karen. You're only twenty-five."

"I'm twenty-four."

"Today's your birthday."

She closed her eyes, "I forgot."

"I guess you were preoccupied," he said. "He reached up and unhooked her bra. "Keep in mind even in this age of women's liberation, I think you're sexy."

She twisted toward him so he could see her breasts and then lifted herself so he could slip down her panties. She pulled off his undershorts and she rolled on top of him.

"I love you, Earl."

"I love you," he said before he grasped her hair and tilted her mouth to his. He paused, "Oh, I almost forgot, too." He reached behind the pillow and swung out a small gift-wrapped box.

"No card?" she asked.

"No card," he said. "This doesn't require a card."

She slowly opened it and inside she found a ring box. In it was a two-carat diamond. She kissed him. "I know it won't always be romantic like this," she said hesitantly. "I know what's coming, but I love you. I want to be your wife, but I want to be other things, too."

"I know," he said. "I know what you want to be."

Instead of sex they talked until she fell asleep with her head on his chest. He gently slid from under her and turned her on her side away from him so he could go to sleep holding her.

THE FINAL MORNING of the convention, the campaign staff met with the state chairs. This was an intensive briefing on the campaign plan and what was expected from the opposition. Terry made the point that the Southern Conservative Coalition and the Fulton Foundation had both made a presence at the Republican Convention and that substantial activity from them could be expected. Anne talked about countering sudden negative attacks. Nancy presented some other information about campaign literature. Alan gave his constituency analysis.

At noon, the final opening prayers were said. The Star Spangled Banner was sung. The chairman gave his remarks, leading off a series of lesser speakers whom, none-the-less were broadcast by C-SPAN and PBS.

Watching, but hardly listening, Adrian started thinking about

POLACO, the real reason he would give his acceptance speech and run against Steven Hatford. Even though he had made personnel selections and at the highest levels, and decisions involving hundreds of millions of dollars both as CEO of a corporation and as governor of Illinois, and although he had played the politics as governor, he still felt formidable opposition. But when he thought of the opposition, he also thought of his own people.

Ian and Terry had put together a staff that was the best, perhaps in American history. Anne, Nancy, Alan, and Terry were the best of the warrior race which fought these battles. They were supported by the powerful issues group under Roger Bennett. And they were even more formidable in that they had large amounts of money for the soft ads to promote their reality views.

Mitchell Fiddler had been proven to be correct. POLACO also used soft ads to attack on the issues. They had a lot of money solicited through their foundations. The Republican Convention had been a near perfect job after which Hatford had taken the lead. And, they also had 25 giant corporations who could encourage contributions by tens of thousands of employees. Contributions under the limit would go to the campaign and those over the limit would go to the foundations. The initial flush of contributions into the reality campaign from Republicans had dwindled. Big money from the Republican side was going into the POLACO foundations and the obvious strategy to defeat the truth.

Increasingly, it appeared that everything would hinge on the debates. Two were scheduled. Otherwise they would develop the best ads they could and try to refute POLACO with the quality of their message rather than with their frequency. Beating POLACO in quality was not easy. They would have to fire all the ammunition they could develop.

If he lost, how would that affect Ian MacAulliffe? Would POLACO abide by its agreements or would it seek to destroy Ian, who had sought to destroy it? He could visualize the well-orchestrated attack that Helene Courtney and Erla Younge would mount some months after Hatford's inauguration. If Helene Courtney and Ward Cowell and their Executive Committee were willing to bribe Annabelle Mayberry, what would prevent them from establishing an "informer?" There would be a dance of "unconfirmed reports" about PENMET. The media attack on PENMET and its management would be orchestrated. They would wait until the fall of Hatford's first year.

By spring there would be a crisis.

He thought about his staff: Anne, Nancy, Merrick, Tony, Terry, Jack, Dominick, Mitchell, the young girl from Iowa, Karen, and the ones from South Carolina, Louellen and Louise. The kids that came over from Sandellot, George King, Tom Haynes, Lucile Cush. They were all so powerful, they were all so determined. How could they lose? In his mind he paraphrased Winston Churchill, "it is our policy to wage a massive struggle to save American democracy and defend the American Constitution. The aim is victory. For only by our victory might the United States survive, and what would the world be like without a United States as the primary democracy?"

He prayed for God's help.

☆ Chapter 31 ☆

WHEN THE NETWORK anchors on Thursday night prime time turned to the convention rostrum, Chairwoman Young pounded the gavel and yelled, "For what purpose does the great state of Ohio seek recognition?"

The state chairman took his microphone, "To nominate a great American and a son of the great State of Ohio as Vice President of the United States, Ohio yields to the great State of North Carolina."

North Carolina claimed the nominee as his birthplace and yielded to Georgia. The ambassador appeared on the platform to an ovation and began the process of the nomination of the Vice President.

When the call of the states was over and his nomination certified, Richard Sandellot appeared alone. The crowd settled into a long spin of clapping and cheering. It was his moment. It was also a moment for all African-Americans. The band played its music and on cue changed to signal to end the greeting. The noise quickly receded as the delegates waited to hear from someone who had briefly been on the national scene in the early primaries.

Richard said America was a nation of races which were individually proud and which had molded a great nation together. He said he looked for African-American patriotism and dedication to keynote the unity of the American races.

African-Americans, Hispanic-Americans, Chinese-Americans, and Native-Americans, he said, have contributed in every way to building the new nation on its farms and in its factories, constructing its roads, railroads, and buildings. He congratulated those of the minority races who had seized the opportunity to move upward and to serve their country and their fellow Americans.

"All of the races of America contribute to the nation. All should be respected for that contribution. All of the races must be proud of this nation. There has never been a nation like it in history. There is no replacement for America. It is our task to make it work as a nation of respected, proud races, all of whom are Americans. The essence of racial disharmony and hatred is perceptions. Perceptions destroy nations and societies. This nation can fail if it does not find the leaders that will deal with the real problems and communicate reality to the people. This nation can fail if it falls into the pit of racism. It must not fail. Our campaign is critical to is success." There was huge applause and cheering.

"Let every American, and let the citizens of nations around the world look at this campaign to see that we stand for reality and we stand for truth. We reject the simplicities. We will tackle the tough problems. I am honored to be in this campaign as your candidate for Vice President. I shall serve to the best of my ability. We are going to win for the United States. We are going to win for democracy all around the world. Let us rejoice as we proclaim truth and expose the irrationality of our opposition. We are going to win." The audience rose and began to clap, some in unison.

"Let truth ring out in the land. We are going to win. Let the light of reality shine on this political process that we may reform and nurture our nation in its role of greatness on the stage of human history. We are going to win. I am a man of African origin, but I am an American. We are all Americans. Let us pray for our nation and let us proceed forward and seek victory. Victory. Victory. Victory. God bless you all. God bless America and may we be blessed in her service."

There was an outburst of cheering. He stood for a moment at the podium looking at the audience and was transfixed. Was this really happening? He waved and turned for Martha to come out and join him. He held her and kissed her and they faced the audience. A quarter minute later their children came onto the stage and then their grandchildren. Richard picked up his five-year-old grandson and turned him to the crowd. The handsome little boy waved as his grandfather and father waved. Their daughter Lisa had contributed to her college expenses by modeling. Her husband was a rising executive with a major steel company. Their tall son, Franklin Roosevelt Sandellot, smiled with his wife, Marguerite, whose family had come only one generation ago from Haiti.

The cheering went on and then suddenly burst yet louder and more intense as Jesse Jackson and Andrew Young joined the group on the podium. Bruce Smith, Hank Aaron, Evander Holyfield, Ernesto Sosa, and Mariano Rivera came out and there was yet more applause. Oprah Winfrey, Whitney Houston, and others joined them.

While the delegates were given the chance to recover from the emotions Richard Sandellot provoked, the networks ran an extended period of advertising. Then the anchor appeared. He asked the commentator, "Do you know who wrote the speech?"

"Oh, it was him," the commentator said. "I was privileged to hear him before. He is very good."

After that the world waited for Adrian Daggett. Chairwoman Young introduced Clarence Taylor, Chief of the Sioux Indians. Taylor, handsome and gray haired, developed the concept of the nation of races and then presented a stirring biography of Daggett, citing his accomplishments. In his own rhetoric he described the critical issue of political reform. At the end he called out, "America, we bring you the second Lincoln, the next President of the United States, Adrian Daggett of Illinois!"

A roar shrilled out of the audience, the official greeting of the convention to the candidate. Adrian came to the rostrum and waved while the band played the Illinois Fight Song. The chairwoman and the Indian Chief stood with him. Adrian embraced both of them and then they left him alone. As he stood in front of the television cameras and microphones, he wondered if he was worthy of the task. He wished he could tell the full story. He would at least hint at it.

After several minutes the music changed and stillness came over the hall and over 400-million households in the Western Hemisphere, Europe, Africa, and Asia where the TVs were tuned to watch.

He thanked Senator Porter for giving the seconding speech and also thanked Governor Perona and Marilyn Findlayson. Each name drew applause. He said he hoped they would all join in the movement to reform, re-nurture, and remake the American political system and to base it on understanding reality. He was interrupted for applause.

He spoke of the danger of government-by-perception and called it a product of "government-by-public relations" or "government-by-spin doctor." He spoke of the need to reestablish trust in the word of government leaders. This, he said, would be a long task, but it would never be accomplished without a starting point. There was extended applause.

The reality campaign and the reality administration, he said, would start the process by telling the truth and by tackling the hard issues. He said there must be communication between leaders and the people for there to be an effective government. It does little good for the government officials to tell the people what the polls indicate they want to hear. Many changes were necessary and he would focus on them.

The most important change, he said, will be the development of real debate based on facts and reliable opinion. The diatribe of single-issue constituencies, he said, had to be challenged. Political leaders have to do it regardless of risks. Debate was the means. Many differences of opinion, he said, were related to the advocates of various splinter segments who leave key facts and concepts out of their spurious arguments. He spoke of the need to establish mechanisms by which people of high quality appeared as candidates in every campaign. He imposed that as a responsibility of party organizations and pledged in the course of reform, the re-establishment of party authority. He was cheered loudly.

"Let us stop for a moment and consider the politics of perception. Perception of what? Perception that a politician means something when he means nothing, that he is doing something when he is doing nothing. My opponent wants to 'assure freedom' by doing nothing. Many of the ads against me on the television are simply lists of reasons for doing nothing and many of those reasons have nothing to do with reality.

"By not paying down the debt or establishing national health insurance, freedom will not be assured. The result will be the ultimate collapse of our democracy.

"Ladies and gentlemen, we must bring this era of pretending to an end."

The audience rose to its feet as one person, and the ovation lasted so long that Alan signaled the band to play a few bars to calm it down. This, the band did three times before it began to work. After the hall was quieter, Adrian continued.

"Fundamental to everything American, our prosperity, our social justice, our opportunity, and our personal liberty is American Democracy itself. This is so fundamental that many of us overlook it. We have overlooked the unwinding of this Democracy that has been going on for a number of years. You cannot assume the United States is immune to processes that would undermine our system. Much of this is based on creating perceptions which this campaign is so fundamentally against.

"Every one of us has to nurture the Democracy. Every one of us has to be conscious of each other's rights. Every one of us has to be conscious of each other's needs. Every one of us has to acknowledge and be conscious of the issues that surround us and threaten our institutions. The democratic process has to be genuine. It must be based upon views of reality.

"The American nation is the greatest nation to appear in human history. What nation has accomplished what we have accomplished? What nation has had the influence for good in the world that we have had?

"I believe that American Democracy is the greatest institution of the world except for those founded by God. Today that institution faces a subtler crisis than it did in 1860, but one that is no less compelling and threatening. Our campaign will transcend the perceptions of past campaigns and lay the facts and the reality before the people for better or for worse. Our campaign will call the people of the United States to participate in their democracy as fully as they can. Our campaign will call for many new approaches to reduce regulation, reduce litigousness, and reduce government costs, which we have outlined. Our campaign will advance policies of fiscal stability that will ensure the economic prosperity of this nation and of the world far into the future. Our campaign will promise to establish the United States as a reliable leader of the world that will reform and support the United Nations and achieve a lasting world peace. Our campaign will affirm to Democratic nations everywhere the friendship and support of the United States.

"We will initiate the concept of the United States as the nation of races unified in their advancement of the nation. We will call the American people to rally to the support of their country and the support of a government that is truly based on the consent of the governed. It's going to be a tough road. There are going to be obstacles and opposition unprecedented in electoral politics, but we will win." The great applause started and the audience rose again.

"This nation and its democracy are priceless to all of us. Let the call to understanding reality be proclaimed through the land. Let every politician who is worth anything heed it. God bless America and long live American Democracy. Thank You."

When Adrian finished, tumultuous cheers burst out. A cynical feeling passed through him as to what percentage of them really understood what his campaign was about. He smiled and waved. Pamela came to hug and kiss him. She was a trooper, he thought as they received the acclamation, a politician herself, and potentially a great first lady. Adrian turned and beckoned to Martha and Richard Sandellot who came forward and the cheering welled up. Sandellot raised Adrian's hand in victory. The audience cheered.

The Daggett and Sandellot children came out. Again there was a special cheer for Dianne, who smiled her special way and waved. Adrian hugged Martha. Richard hugged Pamela. Adrian looked up into the gallery for their parents. He pointed them out to Pamela. They both smiled and waved. The TV cameras showed them together in their box.

Adrian turned once again and the senior senator from Illinois joined him along with Jesse Jackson and Andrew Young. The senators and congressmen who had endorsed him early in the campaign then came forward. Then, with renewed applause, Senator Porter, Governor Perona, and Marilyn Findlayson appeared. They stood between Adrian and Richard and raised their joined hands in the gesture of unity.

Adrian looked toward Terry and Annalee, Anne and Bob, and Alan and Lauren. Nancy, alone, stood and clapped with the crowd and the music. When Alan saw that Adrian was looking his way, he flashed the thumbs up sign. It was a very good speech delivered with authority and sincerity. It had said something.

With the convention winding down, the anchorman consulted the commentator. "The Democrats have replied to the Republicans. How well did they do?"

"I think, extremely well," the commentator said. "The Republicans have really challenged Adrian Daggett with a surprisingly effective convention. They put on the best of the television presentations, but the Daggett campaign has replied with a superb convention of their own."

"We're out of the gate, do you think with both sides equal?"

"No. Daggett is clearly back in the lead by five or six points."

"Why was there so much discussion of American Democracy in Daggett's speech?"

"He believes that democracy is threatened by shoddy, overly intense politics and also by exploitative media reporting and the like. He is going to strike out at single issue constituencies and resist them."

"It almost seemed as though there was some implied threat to American democracy."

The commentator pondered a moment.

"He sees the amount of money in American politics possibly as a threat to the fundamental principles."

The anchor turned back to the floor cameras so that the audience could watch the cascade of the balloons. The floor interviews began. One was with Amy Camisona. The reporter asked her what she thought about the ticket.

"I'm delighted because both of these men have come to the American people saying the same thing," she said. "I think they are both potentially the leaders we have been looking for for a long time who will avoid politics and stick to management. Maybe democracies are like any other human enterprise, when there is too much politics, they fail."

AT HARBOUR ISLAND the senior group was seated around the table in the hotel conference room watching on a big screen. "There is a pacing," said Erla. "If we do well, they'll do better."

"He really drew a line in that speech. I thought he was going to mention POLACO and accuse us," said Harold Smalley.

"I wonder how our friends in Washington feel?" said Ward.

"I'll call you tomorrow evening," Helene said. She and Erla were due in Washington in the morning.

"What do you think the score is?" Ward asked.

"We put on a convention that was the best probably ever. Our opponents have shown the ability to do the same thing. They saw what they needed to do, and they executed to do it. They will be farther ahead tomorrow, but hopefully by no more than three or four points over for the margin of error. We are going to spend a lot more money on issues advertising between now and the election. Hopefully we will defeat Daggett with his own weapon."

THE MORNING AFTER their national convention most campaigns take the weekend off. On Friday, two chartered 737s left Miami International at 9 a.m. carrying the Daggett staff back to Chicago. Terry convened a luncheon meeting with Anne, Nancy, Alan, Merrick, Mitchell, and Dominick. Each brought up to three staff. Karen, who had sat with Earl on the plane thankful for the three weeks and wondering when she would see him again, was with Nancy.

"You're all mavericks of various colors and stripe patterns and you did one fantastic job at that convention. I applaud you," Terry said clapping his hands and everyone joined him. "Now, let's reassess where we are and figure out how we are going to capitalize on the convention to bring home the prize."

"With the debate," said Jack Wood.

"Not to win it, but to pulverize Hatford," said Louellen.

"We certainly have to concentrate on that. What I'm looking for," said Terry, "is the extra things we can do. Things that will gain for us or confuse and surprise the "hatfords.""

"We still have the religion bomb," said Nancy.

"We are thinking about scheduling it for a particular location in October," said Alan.

"Is that the October surprise?"

"We might call it that, it will keep Hatford busy for a while trying to deal with it. That's October; what do we do about the saturation of issue ads?" Terry asked.

"That's what I warned you about," said Mitchell Fiddler. "Now we are the ones being speared on the issues. They are overwhelming us."

"What's the ratio?" Asked Terry.

"It's about 5 POLACO ads to about 3 of ours," Nancy answered.

"They are doing more advertising," said Mitchell. "I warned you about this issues campaign. They found our weak spot."

"I don't think that issues are our weak spot," said Anne seeing the monster again. "It's issues that make the difference for us. Without them we'd be smothered."

"We are getting smothered the way it is. This is the way we could lose," said Dominick.

"We should reorganize this campaign into broader perception, Terry," said Mitchell. "Something that the opposition cannot so directly refute."

"Mitchell, we could all agree on that, but Adrian Daggett wouldn't allow it to happen," said Terry.

"That is because you have him brainwashed."

"I haven't brainwashed anybody, Mitchell. You know how these decisions were made."

"It's still your idea to do this issue nonsense which has everybody confused."

"I don't think the American people responding to these polls are particularly confused," said Anne.

Alan watched the argument develop. He saw Terry getting angry.

"Isn't there some middle ground here?" said Nancy. "How can we respond effectively to these POLACO foundation ads?"

"We had a lot of people on the platform during the convention," said Karen, hoping it was a contribution to unity. "Why don't we use them in the soft ads. Personalities that would be easily recognized."

"Would they volunteer? We can't afford to pay them," said Anne.

"Somebody greater than I will have to call them to ask them," Karen joked.

"I think we should start doing some soft ads that image our candidate the proper way," said Mitchell.

"I'm not sure that soft ads are allowed to do that," said Alan.

"They can take positions on issues which are not so precise," said Mitchell.

Terry's face grew red. He fought to keep his composure.

"We have just completed a very successful convention, Mitchell," he said. "We are now back into the lead coming up to a debate in a month when Adrian is going to shake Hatford like a dog with a rag doll."

"Suppose Hatford wins the debate?" asked Mitchell. "You're banking everything on the debate. Don't you think that POLACO is going to be prepare Hatford?"

"I think this meeting has lost its productivity," said Alan.

"I agree, I think the campaign has lost its productivity," Mitchell said. "We may be ahead now, but we are not going to stay ahead when the advertising is 5-3 against us."

"Mitchell, why don't you help Karen with her idea," said Alan. "You make the calls. See if you can line up some people who would go on for the foundations to help Adrian."

"I don't know whether this is going to do any good," said Mitchell.

"It certainly cannot do any harm," said Anne. "You owe it to us and the campaign to help us."

"I disagree with the whole idea," said Mitchell, "and I am going to talk to Adrian about it."

"I would like to talk to you about that, Mitchell," said Terry. "We don't need this kind of disunity."

"I think this disunity, as you call it, is critical to the campaign," said Mitchell. "I think you're right, the meeting should end."

"I don't think the meeting should end," said Terry. "I think you should leave, Mitchell."

"I will not leave until the meeting ends," Mitchell said hotly. "I am the Finance Director."

"We'll see," said Terry.

"All right you guys," said Alan. "The way we can throw this election is by having this fight. I don't understand, Mitchell, what it is you want us to do."

"Tell people what they want to hear," Mitchell said.

"That is not what Adrian promised to do," said Anne.

"I don't care what Adrian promised in a damned campaign speech. Tell the people what they want to hear. We are too controversial!"

"It would seem to me that this controversy has brought in a lot of contributions," said Anne.

"We have to continue to function as a cohesive staff," said Alan. "The way we have so far."

"I think we need new leadership," growled Mitchell, "and I'm going to tell Adrian."

"Go tell him," said Terry. "Now will you leave the meeting please?"

"I will not."

"All right, I'm going to ask Adrian to ask for your resignation," Terry loudly announced.

"You two have got to stop shouting at each other," said Nancy. "We're embarrassing our younger members."

"So let them be embarrassed," said Dominick, "there is a point to be made. The campaign is failing."

"Damn, it's not failing," said Anne. "We just gained 12 points. What would make us fail is going back on our word."

"I think the meeting should end," said Alan. "I'm leaving."

He picked up his papers and motioned for Jack and Louellen to follow him.

The meeting broke up.

Terry called Alan, Anne, Nancy, and Merrick into his office.

"I am going to have a showdown with Mitchell, but I want to make sure it does not interfere with the rhythm of the campaign. Consider the various options, the religion bomb is one. What else can we think of?"

"I like Karen's idea," said Anne. "Let's get some personalities to the soft ads."

"The opposition may protest."

"Let them protest. If the protest succeeds, we'll take them off."

"I'll make the phone calls," said Terry. "Tell Karen she has more work to do."

"She can take it," said Nancy. "How will we prepare Adrian for the debate? Bennett is working up the questions and he has everybody on the issue staff focused on it and in particular areas. We need to spend some time on their questions and answers and maybe we ought to get them into Adrian's head."

"Are we going to do a Chautauqua-type thing?" asked Anne.

"That's probably the best approach."

"Should we take a poll to see where he should go?" asked Nancy.

Everybody laughed. They needed it. They decided to go to the Wyndham hotel next to the convention center in Charlotte where the first debate would be staged. For two days the staff would act as reporters asking particular questions. The senior senator from Illinois volunteered to serve as Daggett's opponent.

PRESTON WAS DESPERATE to find a way to re-establish his relationship with Laurie. He had never been particularly successful with women. One reason he had come to Harbour Island was to perhaps find someone with interests like his. The women outnumbered men in POLACO and many of them were attractive and high powered. He and Laurie didn't exactly match. She was an athlete and he was a klutz. Their common interests were reading and music. She liked his classical collection.

The first time he had invited her to his apartment was to hear music and she wound up getting tipsy on wine and started kissing him. A week later, they found themselves making love. For him it was the first time in his life on a bed with an attractive, almost beautiful girl. He fell in love.

In a screaming fit, she broke off the relationship when he confessed to her he had told Edgar of the dinner with Daphne. She went into a feline rage at him and told him she never wanted to see him again, or hear of him. He was crushed. His work suffered, his body suffered, and his ego suffered all because of a sense of duty, which he already realized, might be a mistake.

Weeks passed and he didn't dare approach her. Finally, he couldn't stand it anymore and he called her and asked her to dinner at the Romora Bay Club. To his astonishment, she agreed. He took her there instead of Valentine's or The Landing so he wouldn't be embarrassed if she got up and walked away from the table. Instead he found her with something she wanted to talk to him about.

"How much do you know about the way that POLACO was founded?" she asked him after they sat down.

"What do you mean?" he asked.

"I mean have you ever seen any documents about POLACO and how and why it was started and by whom?"

"You don't want to know, Laurie," he said. "He knew he should have told a lie, but he didn't want to lie to someone he loved.

"What do you mean?" she asked.

"You should forget it."

"Why should I?"

"I'm telling you, you don't want to know."

She eyed him curiously.

"I do want to and you know something, don't you?"

"I know enough to tell you to stay out of this."

"What do you know?" she asked, anger creeping into her voice.

He stopped for a moment. "Laurie many people have died because of this."

"What does that mean?"

"That means you don't want to know anymore."

"I do want to know more," she said. "I want to bring these people down. I'm not sure of the full story, but it's smelling more and more like an attempt to manipulate American politics."

"You can't do it, Laurie. It's too big and powerful."

She eyed him again. This time in a different way, promising him with her eyes her affection if he would only tell her.

"How did you find out?" she asked.

"I found some disks which I think were left by one of the people they murdered so they would be found."

"Why didn't you turn them in so you would be a good boy?" she half taunted him.

"They scared me. I put them back."

"When was this?"

"I had been here a month and was setting up my station and my office."

"And what happened?"

"In a file of disks I found one which didn't match any software. I looked in all the hard drives until I found a custom program and tried it."

"What was it?"

"It was a contract of the original founding of POLACO four years ago."

"You have that?"

"Laurie, there was a meeting; a contract was drawn up in advance.

Ward worked on it here. He had a computer specialist; a man named Mikla Almasy. He was a Hungarian whose family had escaped when it was still communist. Ward's assistant was from Cleveland. A woman named Sheila Thompkins. She was attractive and divorced with teen-age children. There was also a Bahamian secretary named Elma Patter. She was from the island, but went to high school in Nassau and to a community college in Florida."

"Why are you telling me all this?" Laurie asked losing patience.

"Because they all died within a month of the signing of the contract."

"What? Ward would never do that!"

"Maybe it wasn't Ward."

"Did you look at the agreement?"

"Yes."

"Well, what did it say?"

`"You don't want to know!"

She looked him in the eye again, "Yes I do, Preston."

There was no denying her. "That agreement was for the long-term changing of the American Constitution."

"To modify the democracy?"

"Yes."

"To what?"

"To a 'corporate state.' Limited suffrage; approval of candidates by party committees; approval of all laws by a special council; reduced freedom of speech and assembly; guarantees of common law; new rules for the congress; limits on the courts regarding judicial review; limits on law suits; a bunch of stuff like that."

So that was what she needed.

"I want a copy of that disk," she said. "Do you have it?"

"No," he said. "And, you don't want it."

"Preston, do you know where it is?"

"Yes."

"Then I want you to get it for me."

"No."

"What do you mean, 'No?'"

"Sheila Thompkins was found raped and murdered on the beach on Eleuthra. It looked like she was swimming and got attacked by some gang. Elma's house exploded and she was killed with her husband and two children. Mikla realized he knew the document because he had to program the special software to encode and decode. He knew he would be killed. I think he left the disk to be found. He was a sailor and owned a yacht. He probably tried to escape with his girl-friend from the mainland. The yacht was found after an explosion had wrecked it in the Exumas."

"So, there's no proof," she said.

"What more do you need?

"I WANT THE DISK!"

"No, Laurie. We'll both be in danger."

"If you don't agree to get the disk for me," she said. "I'm going to leave the table. I thought you cared about me. I thought you were a man."

He never expected anything like this. "I have the one with the con-tract," he said. "I erased the software so no one would know I saw what was on it."

"That will do," she said. "I can work out the program." She actu-ally thought that the FBI would be able to do it.

"No."

She got up and strode toward the door. He stood and watched her pass through it. He signaled the waiter who had served only the appe-tizer and salad. Preston paid the check and found Laurie waiting by the car. He drove her to her apartment.

☆ **Chapter 32** ☆

JUST AFTER LABOR Day, Alvin Carter drove through the familiar Pennsylvania countryside resplendent with the deep dark green, almost blue, of late summer on his commute from his home to PEN-MET headquarters. He only partially noticed the rolling hills and sunny valleys. His brain was consumed by the problem of two operatives in Harbour Island who were now in danger of being caught by an adversary. A powerful intuition, supported by subtle clues, told him an investigation was going and that Edgar Slaughter had focused his attention on Daphne and Sharon. He expected Slaughter to quickly connect Daphne's sudden trip to New York to the subsequent rapid development of the racial policy speech. Joan Curz showed him to the conference room and brought coffee when Tony arrived. Alvin told him his suspicions.

"We need to think about getting those two women off that island, Tony. We can hear the hounds. I wondered if your friend in Spanish Wells might help."

"Ansell Monroe?"

"He might be able to tell us how to approach the island by boat and perhaps we could use his facilities in Spanish Wells as a base."

"A base?"

"I don't think Edgar Slaughter is going to let Daphne and Sharon leave. If either one of them tried even to get into a water taxi, he might detain them or have the police do it. Same with any boat."

"You mean he would sort of arrest them?"

"He would have virtual custody. There would be no getting them out of the POLACO compound, at least not without air cavalry."

"What can we do?" Tony asked with the same feelings of ultimate responsibility he had when he gave the order to place the moles.

"I propose to use mercenaries, Tony. I want to hire a squad to go in there and get them. We have to assume they're being watched, so going in with just two or three people probably won't work."

"What's happening there?"

"Daphne and Sharon are continuing their routine at Valentine's, at The Landing, and other places. They have to be able to insist they are legitimate and they may still deliver more information."

"So the time has come to get them out?" Tony asked.

"We should finalize the details of the exit operation and then execute the plan."

"The plan?"

"We send in a squad of mercenaries or military professionals for hire. They arrive during the afternoon on a large pleasure yacht, which docks at Valentines. They monitor the POLACO activities as much as possible during the day and after midnight they move in the house and get the two women out. There will be two or three minutes to pick up papers and any other important items before Slaughter's agents can respond. It happens at night with night vision equipment. We depend on surprise."

"How far is it from Valentine's to Daphne's house?"

"It's about a quarter of a mile. If all goes well, the operation will be on shore eight to ten minutes. As soon as the women are safely aboard, the yacht leaves for American waters."

"Are you sure this can work, Alvin?"

"I think it will. If we meet any resistance from Slaughter's agents we can overwhelm them quickly and probably take them out on the boat."

"Okay, get this started. I'll contact Ansell."

THE FINAL ITEM on the agenda of the regular Friday meeting between Helene, Erla, Warren Hatch, and his staff was the preparation for the presidential debate.

"It would seem to me, Warren, that we should come up and meet with you and Senator Hatford to prepare for what may be the critical night of the campaign."

"I recognize the importance of the debate, Helene, but I think we can do that here."

Helene hoped Warren's ego would not compromise their success.

"We have to concentrate all our resources on this one, Warren. Steven has to be prepared for anything."

"We can prepare him, Helene. It's better that you and your staff spend your time on the creative efforts that are whittling away the lead."

"If you lose the debate, Warren, the lead will be impossible."

"We won't lose the debate, Helene."

Warren wanted to be the hero of the debate and Helene realized that if she pressed the issue she would risk the relationship. "We are going to send you the debate questions we prepared anyway, but we would like to be in on the briefing."

"I don't think that is necessary, but I would like to have your questions."

Helene decided to let it go at that. There were other problems she to deal with.

THE NEXT DAY on Harbour Island there was a knock on Daphne's door, just after 12:30 p.m.. She opened it to find Pat Stabler in running shorts and halter.

"This is a surprise, come in."

"I decided to take a run instead of lunch."

"Let me get you something to drink, step into the parlor." Pat sat down on a wicker chair. When Daphne brought iced tea and sat opposite her she leaned forward and looked into Daphne's eyes. A quizzical smile came over her face, "For some reason I think you might be very interested in some copies of files about the founding of POLACO." She paused.

"What makes you think that?" Daphne asked. She wished Sharon were there.

"It's just a series of events I've noticed."

Daphne saw in Pat a bright and talented individual who did only enough to get by and live the way she wanted to live. Both she and Sharon had heard praises from the television crew of Pat's ability to tweak the script, the camera angle, the set, or the talent. She could also act and with shoulder length blond hair and green eyes, she was photogenic and telegenic. She was well shaped, but short.

She smiled her quizzical smile again. "When I met you I wondered why you and Sharon came to this desolate place. I noticed that the evening after the 'week of the fourteen-hour days,' I had dinner with Sharon at The Landing with Julie and Jeff Spencer and you had dinner with Laurie, Preston, Ruth, and Jimmy at Valentine's. Laurie tells me that she sounded off and I know that I talked too much about what POLACO is doing. I know the others made mistakes, except for Preston. He may have turned us all into security."

"I thought he was in love with Laurie," Daphne interrupted trying to stop the flow of reasoning.

"That might not stop Preston. The next day I heard you left for New York. I asked Laurie if you mentioned that you were going to New York. She said you hadn't."

"Then I noticed that nearly every evening, you or Sharon take a look at the athletic area. Then I heard a rumor that a company called PENMET, which is a member of POLACO, is in fact backing the election of Adrian Daggett. I heard they're trying to stop POLACO by putting a good heavyweight in the Oval office to replace the skimpy featherweight politicians who have messed up the United States."

"That's a rumor I haven't heard, Pat," said Daphne speaking the truth. She was shocked that it had gotten out. How? Who let that loose? Probably someone in the intelligence group.

"Let me tell you what I am prepared to do. I'll come back in a couple days. Laurie and I think that if I seduce Louis Fischer, I might get enough information out of him to allow Laurie to access the secret files."

A complex of concerns and reactions to the proposition flooded Daphne's mind. This woman had spotted her so she had to guess that Edgar Slaughter had as well. This could very well be a sting. But, if this offer was genuine, it might be an opportunity to bring POLACO down. Would Pat be smart enough to succeed? Did Louis Fisher have access to the secrets?

"It might be interesting as a journalistic proposition, Pat, but I don't see that you need to go and seduce anybody about it."

Pat looked steadily at her with an impish expression. "The proposition is that Laurie and I will deliver a disk or document. We think that POLACO, if not treasonous, is surely up to something with interests counter to those of the people of our country. We'll do this to escape. If you are who I think you are, you can get us out."

"Pat, if you did get out, don't you think they would pursue you if there was some reason to?" After she said it Daphne realized it was an admission of her suspected status. She didn't try to cover it.

"Laurie and I are both concerned about who we're working for. We want to find out what they are really doing. When we heard the rumors about PENMET we realized that something could be very wrong with POLACO, and that we don't want to be involved in it." Pat stood up and did some stretching exercises. "I've got to work up a sweat on the way back so the security won't get suspicious. I think you've told me what I want to know. We'll talk when you are ready."

Daphne stood. "Well, it was nice to see you, Pat." She went over to the door with her and watched as she stretched a few more times and then took off at a slow pace in the midday warmth.

Sharon came in a few minutes later. Daphne told her what had happened.

"Pat looks very casual and even hippyish. I think she's a free spirit, but moral," Sharon said. "She'll try to get the information because she thinks it's the right thing to do."

"This is the opportunity we've been waiting for. People from the inside who want to cooperate, just as Edgar Slaughter has spotted us and is probably investigating."

"What's he going to find? What does he do about it if he finds it?" asked Sharon.

"I told you they have some sort of punishment and interrogation capability."

"So we take a risk. Pat and Laurie are taking a risk too, but they don't know what they are dealing with. We do."

"Do we let them do it?"

"If we could deliver a certifiable copy of signatures," Sharon said, "of a document that indicates treason or the suborning of treason, it would be the business scandal of the decade and would be on the inside pages of tabloids for a year. That's what we're here for. We would've accomplished our jobs beyond anybody's wildest dreams."

"We've already contributed," Daphne protested.

"But, this is big. If they could find something with signatures on it and that talks about changing the Constitution."

"They're amateurs."

"But, they have access, Daphne. We don't."

"You're right. We should try," Daphne concluded.

"Pat Stabler is a professional in her work and she knows how to handle herself," Sharon said.

"PENMET is restrained from making accusations about POLACO?"

"Who said PENMET is going to make the accusations? Anne Russell will take care of that."

"Okay, let's do it," Daphne said. She wondered what accusations they might face from Slaughter and how they would deny them.

CYNTHIA REESE DID not like to have her picture taken. When the National Newsletter group asked her to sit for a new employee photo session, she declined. Alvin knew that there were at least two moles; one in the campaign and one at PENMET. After investigating the new employees, he had a hunch that "Cynthia Reese" was not who she said she was. It was necessary to snap a series of pictures of her over a period of a few days using long lenses. She was photographed leaving her car, entering the building, coming into the department, sitting at her desk, standing in line at the cafeteria, and relaxing on the executive gallery getting a tan on her legs. The spread of pictures was used by two operatives Alvin hired who fanned out from the city looking for hotels and motels where someone might recognize her.

At the Strasburg Inn they found several people who remembered her on a particular weekend. Alvin Carter conducted the interviews the next day. Even though it was some time ago, Liz Daley was a good enough looking blonde to have attracted sufficient male attention to piece together the activities. They tied her to a man who they thought was an operative. He used a false name and paid cash two weekends before the attempt to break into the Scottish Village offices. They also learned she had been there before to visit a suite, thanks to a room service waiter with an appreciation for feminine mystique. He even remembered the suite room number. They came back and interviewed him again and he was certain. They showed him pictures of different women and he picked Liz as being in that suite with a man who used a credit card with a false name. This was substantial proof that Liz Daley indeed was an operative herself. There was one more item to be checked.

The next morning Alvin connected from Harrisburg to Newark to Hartford and rented a car to visit the academy which "Cynthia Reese" had attended and from which he had transcripts of her grades. At the library, he asked for the yearbook of the class of 1979 half expecting she would not be listed in it, and she wasn't. Her University degree was from a well-known college in New England, 150 miles away. By mid afternoon he was there, but the yearbook for the class of 1983 didn't show her. It was now reasonable to conclude that the records were planted and "Cynthia Reese" was someone else. Fairly deep cover for a civilian mole.

Alvin wrapped it all up and sent it to David Gibson and to the Pennsylvania State Police. Gibson referred it to a criminal law firm for their opinion as to what charges could be made while his staff researched what civil remedies there might be against whomever was running her.

Alvin had kept Stephanie up to date. They brought the information to Ian and Tony and then they told Nancy. "Cynthia?" she asked, "'Cynthia' or 'Liz' is doing a good job on the corporate history." With Ian's assent they decided to take no immediate action.

LOUIS FISCHER'S PROBLEM in reporting to women, was not his only problem with them. Always the small, un-athletic figure among his high school and college friends, he found his release in books. He was profoundly afraid of approaching a woman. He felt a strong urge to do so, to touch, to feel, and to hug, but it was hard for him to initiate any contact. His mother had ruled the family and had totally dominated him and his brother and sister. He ruminated about this often and was thankful he hadn't turned gay.

He was never successful with any woman whom he thought met his standards. Still he noticed the women that he might someday muster the courage to approach. Pat Stabler seemed perfect to him. He was attracted to her small, athletic body. He noticed, with pleasure, that she sometimes didn't wear a bra and that she smiled a lot. She was different from any other woman who had not brutally rejected his timid advances. Pat had noticed his interest and imagined the possible opening to find out what POLACO was really about.

Louis was in a meeting with Yvonne and some of Erla's people working on the preparations for the presidential debate. They were trying to get as much information as possible from Michelle about the Daggett intentions so they could prepare Hatford. Heavy soft advertising deftly countering Daggett on his own issues was eroding Daggett's post-convention lead. Their analysis indicated Hatford only needed a stalemate in the debates to win the election. That was not necessarily an easy task. Helene focused the senior people on it. Because he was the senior person at the meeting Louis saw no reason why he shouldn't take Pat Stabler's call when his secretary said that she wanted to talk with him.

"Louis, this is Pat Stabler."

"Hi. Pat."

"Louis, I would like to talk to you in some detail about our television ads. I think we are missing something, but I can't get anybody to pay attention unless you can come up with some research poll-wise. I'm also interested in what's going on in other countries in political advertising. I am busy now, but if you're free tonight, I'll buy you dinner."

"I'd be happy to help if I can. You don't have to buy my dinner."

"We're frantic over here, there really is no other time to talk. I hope you don't mind."

"Oh no, I don't mind," said Louis. He sure as hell didn't.

"I'll meet you at the hotel at...when?"

"Seven o'clock okay? That will give you time for your soccer."

"No time for that these days, but I'll see you."

She drove to the hotel in one of the electric cars and picked him up. She suggested the Romora Bay Club where they could talk. When they came out to get into the car, she handed him the keys. At the club he held open the door for her and at the table he held her chair. Pat realized he was treating her like a lady. They talked business for a while and then about personal interests. Louis would collect television ads from campaigns in England, France, Germany, and Japan. He would also present some ideas on how to test the ads for effectiveness.

Pat shared a house with other members of the television crew on the bluff overlooking the ocean. On the way he asked her if she was available for dinner on the weekend at the Coral Sands. The answer, she said, depended on her work commitments.

He was full of hopeful anticipation. She called Friday before he had left his apartment and informed him that the crew was starting early so they would finish early. He asked her if she wanted grouper or lobster. She chose the lobster. At seven o'clock he came to her house with his electric car wearing a blue blazer and an open white shirt. She dressed in a gray, blue, and yellow slack suit.

THE BLADES OF Tony's chartered helicopter stirred the waves of water from Nassau towards the position given by Ansell Monroe for the Norma. After about 25 minutes, the Norma appeared at anchor at the head of the Exuma Sound pointed into the prevailing southeast wind. On the lee side, the helicopter crew dropped a raft and then lowered Tony onto it in a boatswain's chair. The helicopter backed away to land on the water. A line attached the raft to the helicopter now fifty yards away and another was coiled in the raft. Tony saw the men diving into the water off the Norma, but one swam toward him whom he recognized as Lance Wallens. A bearded face with blue eyes and dark hair popped up over the gunnel.

"Good to see you Mr. Destito. But where is your fancy yacht?"

"I'm at your mercy, Lance," said Tony.

"Aye," Lance replied.

"You'll be wanting a tow to the boat. I'll swim the line over and let them pull you in."

On the stern Ansell Monroe greeted Tony with a great bear hug and then kept him from falling into the ocean when he slipped on the deck wet with sea water and fish juices. The fish were filleted as soon as they were brought aboard.

Ansell closed his cabin door. "And what is this mysterious visit at sea?"

"Thanks for letting me come out, Ansell, I needed to see you."

"Aye, Tony, and I wanted to see you."

"You did?"

"Aye, Betsy and I have talked about her visits up with Juthrie where she has met Jean."

Tony guessed what that was about.

"But let's tend to your business first. Thank you for all you have done for us, the help with Juthrie," Ansell said.

"It's been a pleasure, Ansell."

"You look like you need a long sailing trip," Ansell said.

"Many strange things are happening, Ansell. I came, about one of them. Do you know the legend of the caverns on Harbour Island?"

"Aye" he said. "Not a legend. When I was a lad my friends and I found them. All the seeming entrances along the surface were just caves, but we found one under water, big time divers we were."

"What was it like?"

"The air was bad, but we looked around or should I say we felt around, only a small amount of light filtered through the water. We went back to try and explore with torches. We walked a little way, and then saw some chains. We ran, scared we'd find a skeleton which would come to life like in The Seven Voyages of Sinbad."

Tony laughed with Ansell.

"Last time I went there was when Betsy wanted to see them. We sailed to the island when we were first married. I looked for the place we'd marked by blazing a tree. Sure enough I found it and we swam in. The caverns are very large. Betsy and I walked a long way with a fishing line to lead us back."

Tony could also imagine that adventure. "Let me tell you what they are now being used for."

Ansell listened intently while Tony described the POLACO compound and the reconstruction of the caverns. He also told Ansell what was happening in American politics.

"I thought there was much coming and going for a research institution," Ansell said when Tony finished. "There's too much money over there. We hear rumors."

"Now there is something more that I have to tell you about moles. When it became apparent that POLACO had planted moles in our organization, we returned the favor."

Ansell listened to the story of Daphne and Sharon and the plan to extricate them.

"Why did you send lasses on such a risky mission?" Ansell asked.

"It's because so many of the management personnel at POLACO are women."

"That was quite a lady you brought over two years ago."

"She's the boss," Tony said to stop any personal inquires concerning Helene.

"A woman boss?"

"It's becoming fashionable, Ansell."

"So I read, but being a simple fisherman I don't understand."

Tony knew that Ansell was in fact fairly well informed. One of the few copies of the New York Times and the American news magazines that came to Spanish Wells were for the Monroe household who preserved them carefully for the library and the school after using them.

"We need some surveillance of the island," Tony said. "We thought possibly that you could help us with that by standing off for your fishing, but keeping an eye on them with powerful telescopic glasses with infrared night vision which we will supply. We know that you won't be able to do this all the time. We also need a staging point if things go wrong. I would like to be able to instruct our people in the attacking group and the girls on the island to make for your house if they have to."

"By all means," said Ansell. "We'll supply refuge and we'll answer the questions."

"There's one other thing, Ansell. We need a guide. How well do you know the waters around Harbour Island?"

"I live and work on them," Ansell said.

"Our plan is to take a large yacht with the mercenaries on it into the harbor by daylight, and make a beach landing by night."

"Best you have some moonlight," Ansell said. "This will be with lights out?"

"If possible."

"With GPS."

"We are also looking for help with a support ship, a fast cruiser which would have one or two of our mercenaries with some weapons to stop any advanced pursuit. It would also serve as an alternate escape craft."

"I'll be your guide and command your gun boat," said Ansell.

From his pocket he gave Ansell a cellular phone. "It's programmed to reach me, otherwise you have to punch numbers. The instructions are in the booklet. We assume that Edgar Slaughter can tell what frequencies are being used in the area. We don't think that he can monitor all the cellular conversations on the island, but there is a chance that he can. Speak carefully."

"Aye," said Ansell nodding his head solemnly.

"Be very careful." Ansell laughed. Then they talked of what Betsy had told him of her meetings with Jean.

Two days later as they were making for Nassau and the market, Lance Wallens watched the captain outside the pilothouse talking on a phone with no wires.

THE FIRST PRESIDENTIAL debate was to be held in Charlotte, North Carolina at the new convention center. The Daggett contingent moved into the concierge floor of the Wyndham Hotel two days before the event. That evening they inspected the great hall and stage that had been specially prepared for the event. Adrian and Pamela and the others marveled at the seemingly timeless architecture of the building. Straight gleaming white columns were brightly lighted before a background of arches and windows. Adrian thought it was the best new building he had seen. He commented, "This one will be around for a while."

They went to the stage and practiced the blocking. Adrian looked out into the audience from his podium and at the chairs for the three reporters who would question the candidate. "Let's practice," he said.

Terry slipped into the moderator's chair and pounded his fists on the table. "Let's have no violent gesturing or intimidating looks in this debate." Everyone laughed heartily.

Alan, Anne, and Nancy took the chairs of the reporters.

"Now that we have reviewed the rules of the debate," said Terry, "we'll have the first question from the distinguished reporter from Evans & Copeland, Anne Russell."

"Reporter?" she said. "I'm a senior vice president."

"I beg your pardon, Miss Russell."

"Governor, in your speech to the National Association of Human Resources Executives recently, you called for the United States to become a nation of races. Isn't that in itself a racist remark and totally conflicting with your statement that America must become the melting pot?"

"I consider that to be a typical media question aimed at generating groundless controversy," said Adrian. "Both statements are fully compatible. A nation of races is a melting pot."

They all smiled and applauded hoping their candidate would be as quick on his feet in the actual debate.

"The distinguished representative of the firm of Jeremy Reubin Associates."

"I'm also a senior vice president. Please get the introductions right, Mr. Chairman."

"I beg your pardon."

"Governor, hundreds of scholars, maybe thousands, have been trying to add up the total cost of the programs that you have put forward. It is said that you cannot possibly undertake the expansion of aerospace technology, provide national health insurance, make infrastructure improvements, keep the budget balanced, and also pay down the debt."

"That's a serious question, we'll work on that one. I pass." They guffawed.

"Very well, Governor Daggett, we will now hear from the distinguished representative and reporter of the PENMET house journals."

"Can't I be more important than that?" Nancy joked. "Governor Daggett, during your campaign, aspects of your personal life have been questioned and an issue has been raised about your personal values. Can you comment on this?"

"If I were the usual candidate seeking the office for the usual reasons, would I base the campaign on values of truth and reality if I didn't believe in them in my own personal life? Would the issues staff exist if I didn't believe that I had to present the issues to the American people?"

"What about your family values?"

"Talk to my family."

"Good answer," said Terry.

For the next two days they worked non-stop except for their morning jog and evening swims in the hotel pool.

As the time approached, 8:30 p.m. Eastern Daylight Time, the make-up and other procedures were underway. After the hours of intense grilling by his own people, Adrian was calm and superbly prepared. As he left the make-up room he had a moment with Pamela. She kissed him on the side of his head careful not to disturb the foundation on his cheeks. He embraced her and thought of the deep love they shared. She and Barbara Hatford would be in the front row. He was embarked on the most critical hours of the campaign. He knew the staff anticipated he'd win easily and win big. He knew that his preparation was thorough and effective, but mistakes and misstatements were always possible.

Roger Bennett had the chairman of each staff section of the issues group sit behind Pamela and the senior staff. The moderator gave the audience some detailed instructions of do's and don'ts. When the hour came, the pool TV director gave them the cue. The Chairman gave brief introductions and then by draw Senator Hatford was to be first.

Before the national audience that would watch the debate, Warren, and Ross Chamberlain decided to attack the three key issues and to add the value question, which they thought would help raise doubts about Daggett's legitimacy. They had hoped to go first in order to put Daggett on the defensive from the start.

Senator Hatford greeted the moderator, the reporters, the audience, and thanked the City of Charlotte, the sponsors, the television stations, and the networks. Then he cited four critical issues of the election. He spoke of the need to relieve the tax burden on the middle class in the context of a balanced budget. He spoke of the need to avoid foreign entanglements that are unproductive in the United States and not critical to its interest. He spoke of the prospective destruction of the American health care system by wanton government intervention. He concluded with a statement based on his theme that the national set of values that had so long sustained the United States must be re-established to rebuild the moral fiber and essential strength of the country. He cited freedom as one of those essential strengths.

Watching at Harbour Island, Helene was relieved. It was the best performance that she had seen Hatford give. The moderator turned to Adrian. He greeted the participants and the audience, thanked the sponsors, and then leapt at his opponent like a mountain lion with claws bared.

"Ladies and Gentlemen, you have just heard a list of contrived perceptions that are the very essence of the technique which I believe must be cleansed from our politics if we are to survive as a nation. It's this kind of fuzzy thinking that contaminates American politics with the potential of wrecking havoc on our democracy. Let me take the points backwards. The Senator has offered the view that America needs to have its values restored. The perception is that he and his party are going to restore them. The reality is that he and his party have not made a single proposal that would lead to the restoration of American values or even the definition of American values. Values are the goals the country is willing to work and sacrifice to achieve. Strong leadership cannot function if the governing principals are perceptions. To be led by perceptions is to be led by a mirage into a moral desert. Leadership, to be effective, needs a base in reality and I intend to bring it to Washington." There was applause and the moderator turned scornfully to the audience.

"The Senator's health care policy is based on the perception that challenging the costs of health care will destroy the system. The health care industry and its allies have dominated Capitol Hill perpetuating the view that the American system is the best in the world and should not be changed. Name one institution that has not been changed for the better in its history. The reality is that we have to challenge the health care companies and the health care institutions to justify their policies. Also, the Senator failed to mention the extremely important cost, which is malpractice insurance to protect doctors and hospitals against irrational lawsuits by predatory lawyers. Rarely does one hear a Washington politician speak of that issue, much less make a proposal. Whatever billions the plaintiff's lawyers put in their bank accounts is paid ultimately by all Americans through risk sharing with insurance and higher fees. That is reality." The audience couldn't restrain themselves. The Chairman scowled at them.

"The Senator criticizes foreign involvement based on the perception that we can choose when to be involved and when not to be and always avoid putting our forces at risk. The reality is the United States cannot be effective in foreign affairs without firm, immutable resolve to support the United Nations and NATO. Indecision and reluctance to lead by the United States, the inability to formulate and implement sound policy, and the opposition to support of the United Nations and NATO will result in war and chaos throughout the world. If I am elected President of the United States I will use the armed forces of our country as prudent and necessary to assure lasting peace. I will promote international cooperation and reforming and strengthening the United Nations." There was more applause in defiance of the obvious displeasure of the moderator.

"Finally the question of taxes and fiscal reform. Past governments have propagated the perception that the budget can be balanced with tax cuts. Has anything ever more ridiculous passed the American scene? The debt is not going to be paid down by tax cuts; it is going to be paid by down-sizing the government, and by all people, including the wealthy, paying their fair share of the tax burden. The perception further is that balancing the budget is the only step needed. The reality is that we are a debtor nation and we currently owe billions of dollars in interest on the government's loans and we continue to sustain our import surplus and balance of payments deficit in the current account. This means we cannot pay down the debt merely by balancing the budget. We need a substantial surplus over many years to do that. We are a great nation stumbling in excessive debt and toward a fiscal crisis. I will not allow that to happen. I reject the perception that with the budget balanced we can enjoy tax cuts."

The timer interrupted. Applause and some yells broke out. The moderator turned to the audience in one more futile attempt to restrain them. Steven Hatford was shocked. He was in a duel for this presidency against an informed and skillful opponent who did not engage in the traditional polite exchange. He had been seriously challenged before the first question.

The moderator recognized Bill Phillips of the New York Times who asked, "Senator Hatford you have in the past supported a number of foreign involvements, but you now indicate that you favor the policies promoted by Mothers Against War. Can you explain this change?"

Hatford answered that he could not support the Daggett programs of full support of the United Nations and yielding the authority of the United States to an international body.

As a response Adrian said that neither the Senator nor his party understands the need for a new international system to achieve a lasting peace and protect the United States from weapons of terror. He then gave a brief explanation of the reality of the international scene.

Senator Hatford in his rebuttal made the main point that he would not send American kids into senseless wars like Vietnam, adding gratuitously that it was the prime example of a Democrat's war and had needed Republican leadership to end it.

The next question was asked by Jessica Hoyt of National Public Radio. "Governor Daggett, you have proposed a solid effort to pay down the debt, but you have also proposed a number of programs such as increasing expenditures on aerospace technology, establishing national health insurance, and establishing a modernization program for the nation's infrastructure. How could you conduct all of these initiatives if you were elected and still have a budget surplus in your first full year?"

Daggett answered that he had proven credentials as a cost cutter and a down-sizer and as a manager of successful large corporations. He said that the government could be decisively downsized and that had never really been attempted. He said that health care costs could be substantially cut, particularly if legal action against doctors was restrained. He cited the government procurement policy as one that could be changed from buying at the lowest price to buying at the best value. He described bureaucracy to be cut away and the down-sizing in regulatory agencies as critical not only in reducing costs, but in increasing revenue as new businesses are established with regulatory interference reduced to the minimum.

Senator Hatford took on the issue of government downsizing and said that government downsizing was impossible because government employee unions would not permit it.

Daggett responded by saying that his campaign had returned contributions from government employee unions and would accept none because their intent was to remove from the government all employees who were not truly serving the people and interested only in their own retirement. He said he would start by reviewing every government employee who had 'maxed' his sick leave over any three years. He said that it was his experience that bureaucracy tended to create bureaucracy, and he knew how to stop it.

Applause broke out again.

The moderator, after once again warning the audience to restrain their reactions, recognized Trevor Witowski of NBC news. "Senator Hatford do you believe it is safe to allow tax cuts, and do you believe that the debt need not be paid off by the sale of national assets which is the only other option if tax cuts are the policy?"

Senator Hatford indicated that a budget-balancing program had been adopted by congress with the support of both parties and that the program was satisfactory. Daggett responded, "History tells us in its economic cycles that the world is in jeopardy and that the system is in jeopardy. The United States is a focal point of the world and the United States must be fiscally strong and healthy to protect its own citizens and to protect the citizens of the world. If anyone in Washington believes differently they don't understand the international financial system. We need people who do understand it and that does not appear to be my opponent."

Hatford then responded by saying that he couldn't allow more taxes on the middle class, as the Daggett campaign recommended.

Daggett, in a point of order, said that such taxes had never been recommended by the Daggett campaign or the Daggett issues staff and that the Senator was attempting to peddle another perception. Applause burst out.

Now the moderator became resigned to his lack of control. The questioning went back to Bill Phillips who asked, "Governor Daggett, how will this health care proposal that you have made really work?

Daggett asked if there was anyone who believed that health care costs could not be controlled. He said he would identify where the money was going and then eliminate excess costs from the system. He would work on legislation to restrain frivolous medical malpractice lawsuits as well as exorbitant fees. National health insurance would also be a priority.

Hatford followed his line that National Insurance would destroy the fundamental values of health care in the United States, which is the very best system in the world.

Daggett in his rebuttal quoted a letter from a doctor in Western New York who said the American health care system was not the best in the world because everyone did not have access to it. He said access was denied because there were powerful interests that wanted no government supervision or participation in the health care industry except to pay bills. He reflected that he did not have to remind anyone that many of these bills had been proven to be fraudulent. More applause broke out.

Jessica Hoyt next asked, "Senator Hatford, in developing your environmental position you have indicated or at least implied that you are against nuclear power. In the past you have supported nuclear power development. What is really true?"

Hatford answered that everyone has to recognize the fears of the people concerning nuclear waste and understand that the people were sovereign in the matter of such policies.

Daggett responded that the fear had been propagated by unprincipled advocate groups fanning the flames of ignorance and mistrust. "The people have been misinformed," he stated. "I am going to inform the people about the truth, the truth about the safety of nuclear engineering and the safety of nuclear wastes. I will make them aware of the environmental pollution by fossil fuel generation. If I'm elected President," he said, "I will find a way that the people can once again trust their government." There was applause again.

In his rebuttal Senator Hatford said the government personnel cannot be trusted and there must be constant oversight and review. Adrian Daggett shrugged his shoulders in a "there he goes again" gesture and the audience laughed. Senator Hatford broke out into a profuse sweat. His face began to shine. The moderator turned to the audience and scowled a warning.

Trevor Witowski posed the next question. "Governor Daggett, government employee unions for years have stood behind the civil service act and prevented any substantial downsizing of government or reduction of employment. Do you really think that you can downsize government even though you don't take contributions from these unions?"

Daggett told the audience he had informed the executive staff of those unions of his intentions to re-write the civil service act and dismiss the useless civil servants who created costs of government. Applause broke out.

Senator Hatford responded by saying that there were many people who nobly serve the government and the public and who deserve all of the benefits which the civil service act confers.

Adrian said that his policies would promote those people to jobs of greater responsibility and give them the authority to discharge unproductive workers. He said he would also give the supervisors a dictum that such discharge may not be done for their personal reasons or political reasons in which case they would be discharged. Applause broke out. The moderator turned and scowled at the audience. The applause increased. Daggett was in charge.

The next question from Bill Phillips. "Senator Hatford, your positions on education are not easy for me to understand. What are the clear policy points?"

Senator Hatford said that he favored the expanded tax cut initiatives to make college more affordable. He said the United States has the best higher education in the world and that makes us productive and efficient.

Daggett responded by saying that Republicans have always opposed public education and denied the resources needed to improve it. The problem with education, he said, was not related to higher education, but was in the secondary schools, which are free and guaranteed to every American. "The fact that these schools are deteriorating and producing less-qualified students for the colleges and universities is a crisis of the future. It is also a crisis of the future to turn out students from these high schools who will not go on to college, but will be successful otherwise in life either in their own businesses or as reliable and effective employees. We cannot continue to turn out students who, unable to read and write, become criminals. We have to make hard choices." He reflected on his community involvement program and said the choices would be substantial restructuring to make every community a learning community. There was applause.

Senator Hatford responded by saying that our education and our finances are not as deteriorating in condition as Governor Daggett would have us believe. He said that Governor Daggett was a purveyor of the myth of American malaise and that there is no such malaise. The audience audibly laughed at him.

The moderator recognized Jessica Hoyt. She asked, "Governor Daggett, what is your response to that statement?"

Adrian said, "I'm from corporate life where all progress is based on change, change that is programmed and financed. The planning is rational and based on reality. When I had enough of the weak decisions and absence of decision in our government I determined to enter this race. Corporations don't operate on perceptions. My opponent evidently does." The audience laughed and applauded.

"If I'm elected I'm going to work on finance, I'm going to work on lasting world peace, I'm going to work on education, and I'm going to work on the environment. I am going to restructure government so that it responds to reality and rejects perception; and so that the politicians are elected on the basis of the reality of their positions rather than the perceptions they create. The process is not going to be painless, but the results are going to serve the American people. I ask everyone, is endless debt the right reality for the United States? Is 19th Century diplomacy the reality policy to develop a lasting world peace? Is our health care structure based on the reality of our health care needs? Is our educational structure based on the reality of our educational needs? These all can be improved by change - change that is planned and rational, and I will bring about that change." More applause broke out.

Senator Hatford replied. "I disagree that fundamental changes are needed as Governor Daggett has put forward. We do not have a national malaise. The United States is a strong country of which we can all be proud and this country has solid, working finances. Governor Daggett overlooks all the progress that has been made by government in the United States." Adrian made a note on his pad. There was a scattering of applause.

Daggett's reply was, "I'm sure Herbert Hoover felt the same way." There was laughter. "The organizations that don't make changes when they are healthy become unhealthy when the changes are overdue. The perception that my opponent would like to create is that we are healthy and happy and vibrant and that nothing needs to be done. The reality is we won't stay that way unless we recognize reality and make the changes it indicates to be necessary." Strong applause broke out.

Trevor Witowski asked, "Senator Hatford, we need to discuss your environmental positions and particularly the issue of Governor Daggett's allegations that governments have stood by and watched the development of saltwater wetlands to the alleged detriment of the ocean biosystem."

Senator Hatford responded, "You have correctly stated that these threats to the ocean ecology have been alleged, but not proven. No studies have established the fact that we cannot use our shore line for human development." He continued to use up his time.

Adrian responded, "Here is another instance where the Republican Party spins a perception that the problem will go away as does my opponent. Does my opponent and his party deny the impact of industrial civilization on the world environment? Do they deny the impact of population? I don't care if there are no studies that indicate that wet lands on the salt-water shores should not be developed. I am going to stop the development until there are studies that prove that the development is beneficial. We are going to deal in science and not in perception. If the Daggett administration takes over next January, we are also not going to ignore global warming. We are going to seek the cooperation of industry to reduce the production of green house gases. We are going to sign and ratify the relevant international treaties. We are going to be the leaders of the world along with our allies in protecting the environment and ensuring that the air and water will serve us and human civilization in the long term. I will take those steps." He made a few other points. There was applause.

Senator Hatford said that Adrian was scrambling to please the environmental constituency with knee-jerk reactions and proposals.

Bill Phillips asked, "Governor Daggett, your opponents have raised the question of your personal values and whether or not you are truly suited to be President of the United States. You have not denied the issue of your five love affairs before your marriage to

Pamela. Would you comment?"

Senator Hatford was relieved. Finally a question to turn on Daggett.

Adrian said, "My daughter has dealt with this. The investigative reporters have not yet gotten to the source of the report, which was published in that eminent journal Explicit. What do I value? I value truth, facts, ambition, confidence, morals, and religion. I will bring them to government. Family values are a fuzzy concept launched by the Republicans against Bill Clinton as a result of his extra-marital trysts. I recall that he won the election."

Senator Hatford in his comment said, "The question remains and the reality is," he paused, cleared his throat, and this time got an genuine laugh, "Adrian Daggett had these affairs, I can tell you that my values are well known. I have been married to Barbara, my first and only love, for 38 years and we are devoted to our grown children and our young grandchildren."

Daggett responded in his rebuttal, "The question remains, who undertook the attack, who did the investigation? And I can also ask another question, who paid Annabelle Mayberry?" There was applause. "I will make you a promise that I am going to address the moral issue."

Hatford felt the full weight of the mismatch. Was it reality or only Daggett's skills as a debater? A powerful combination of both, he decided, while contemplating just walking off the stage.

There were a few more questions with which Adrian did the same exposure of perceptions and then the time came for the summations. This time Adrian went first delivering a well-crafted speech summarizing his reality theme and punctuated with a few effective ad lib comments. He mentioned more perceptions and took them apart with reality. One was the idea that "governments create jobs." He said this was largely untrue and that businesses create jobs. He referred to monetary and fiscal policy and regulation. He promised to eliminate all of the regulation possible. He promised truth instead of perceptions and defined "reality" essentially as "truth." The audience reacted with whistles and cheers above loud applause.

Senator Hatford, speaking almost with his teeth clenched, did not deviate from a memorized script that attacked Adrian as a purveyor of a false doctrine of reality. He said the government of the United States was successful: it would continue to be successful and that no essential changes were needed. He related this to the theme of assuring freedom promising to rely on their judgments that they had made in the past. The real issue was assuring freedom and the continuance of American Democracy. He urged people to recognize that their freedoms were precious and he pledged to preserve them. The audience gave a scattered response.

The moderator turned around to the audience and smiled as he got up. Adrian stepped across the stage, Hatford came toward him and they shook hands. Adrian looked confidently into his eyes. Hatford looked angrily at Adrian. The moderator shook hands with both of them. Pamela hugged Adrian and they turned to the reporters. When they went back to the center stage to meet the Hatford's the Senator was guiding his wife away. Pamela then hugged Adrian and kissed him. The Daggett children and the senior staff filtered forward to occupy the stage presenting the nationwide audience with a scenario of attractive, competent appearing men, women, and children all looking to Adrian Daggett with a potent mixture of admiration and respect.

"Stay on stage you god-damn fool," Marsha shouted at the television screen in the hotel conference room at Harbour Island.

"That was an unmitigated disaster," said Erla.

"Warren Hatch is an absolute ass. I asked him to let us help with this," said Helene.

"We're going to be down at least four points tomorrow, probably more," said Harold, grimly.

"How can we ever recover from this?" Louis asked. He had brought Pat Stabler to the conference room. Helene noticed she had a pleased cynical smile.

"We have to recover from it!" Helene pronounced.

"Let's listen to the commentary," Marsha said as NBC finished its ads and brought up the post-debate analysis show. Guests from journalism and politics sat around a table with the political consultant who conferred with the anchor in Charlotte. On cue the political consultant introduced his guests. Then he asked, "Who won, and by how much?"

"Daggett by a wide point count in every round."

"Daggett, a TKO"

"Daggett, by a knockout."

"Daggett, but not by as much as you think."

"Is that the first time we have seen a real presidential debate?" The consultant asked.

"I think so. It was a debate. Adrian Daggett savaged or embarrassed Senator Hatford on almost every question. Hatford appeared unprepared and incoherent."

"Daggett pummeled Hatford with his reality program. I can't believe that Hatford wasn't ready for the punches."

"About the only thing that Hatford did well was his summation. He may have gained back a small part of the lost ground, but Daggett attacked the first thing he said."

"Hatford was embarrassed by having the audience laugh at him."

"I think Daggett drew a clear distinction between himself and Hatford. It has been clear for a long time, but now it is tangibly clear. Anyone that doesn't understand that by now won't be voting anyway because they don't care."

"Hatford made the mistake of leaving the stage and allowing Daggett to claim a victory visually. Hatford was angry that he had been so poorly prepared, and I'm sure that his staff is going to hear about it tomorrow."

"Helene" said Ward. "I want you to call Warren Hatch first thing in the morning and read him out. That was the worst performance that I have ever seen anybody give."

"It wasn't entirely Hatford," said Marsha. "Warren and his staff prepared Steven for the last debate and the last campaign - the usual wishy-washy exchange. They didn't prepare him for Daggett with the powerful staff and his real world experience."

"Hatford looked like he couldn't handle Daggett," said Erla.

"Good God," said Ward. "Daggett made every point that he wanted to make and he stamped it on Hatford. Hatford might as well have been carrying a 'We Want Daggett' poster."

"Okay people, let's get to bed and we'll meet in the morning. This will sink in, I don't think we'll need transcripts of this awful thing."

"I think we do," said Edgar. "There was one clue. Daggett said he was going to be doing something about the morality issue. We've got to alert Michelle to look and see if she can give us a lead as to what they plan."

"How do we alert Michelle?"

"By phoning Bill Haber."

"Poor Bill, lonesome and winsome in Chicago while his love life is skittering around the country."

"He'll get her back," said Smalley.

"I hope undamaged," said Edgar.

Everyone left. Edgar stood by the door waiting for Helene who was the last to come out after picking up some papers she had been working on while watching the preliminaries. She put her hand against his shoulder and laid her head against his arm. He turned and hugged her. "We've worked so hard, Edgar, to be defeated and embarrassed. We've lost. It's Warren's fault for not letting us participate in the debate."

"It's not lost, Helene. Tomorrow we'll organize the counter plan."

"I know, but right now I need a double bourbon. What kind have you got?"

"Tennessee sour mash and I have some mint."

"That's it, music and mint juleps."

Helene had not been to Edgar's apartment on the ground floor of a house right over the security area. She joked that he should have a fireman's pole to slide down. He told her he could get to the office in fourteen seconds. They enjoyed Haydn and the drinks. When she left an hour later she kissed him several times. They agreed it was not a time for anything else.

THE SENIOR STAFF and the traveling staff were ecstatic. All manners of dignitaries arrived at the Wyndham to ask if they could visit the Daggett suite. The Secret Service called up names. Several CEO's of local firms and their wives and members of the faculty of Davidson, Chapel Hill, Duke, Wake Forest, and North Carolina State who knew Pamela or Adrian or one of the staff called. Louise Sczyniac, Michelle, and others were all smiles. Anne and Bob were with the reporters. Terry and Annalee were in the suite with Merrick and Marianne, Alan and Lauren, and Nancy.

In Chicago cheers rang out in the main meeting room with the big screen. Karen was ecstatic. Jack Wood ordered champagne and when it came Lucile Cush jumped on the table and shouted, "To victory!" Once everything quieted down Jack reminded everyone, "We haven't won yet."

In the small auditorium in the MacAulliffe Mansion which offered a large screen TV where the MacAulliffe's entertained with films or videos, Ian and Susan had watched with Francisco and Lucinda and other members of the staff.

"We're going to win dear," said Susan. "They will not recover from that."

"I'm very pleased that this is happening," said Francisco.

"I also Mr. MacAulliffe," said Lucinda.

"It's not over until the votes are counted. The deal is not done until the funds have been wired. We probably have the most skillful opponent in the history of the United States. They will not give up."

"Well dear, they certainly did not win the debate."

"No, Lass, they didn't."

HELENE CALLED THE meeting for 6 a.m. so they would be able to tell Warren Hatch what to do. They met at the hotel conference room. Edgar and Erla were there when she arrived. Marsha, Louis, and Harold were a little late. From the head of the table Helene asked. "Question number one is what spin do we put on last night?"

Marsha spoke out first. "We can rely on the famous old chestnut of bias by the media against Republicans."

"Hatford started sweating, maybe we can say he was sick," added Harold Smalley.

"The media would interview the doctors."

"Media bias, and a flu is our best bet" said Erla.

"Media bias also gives us a reason to cancel another debate," said Erla.

"That's the next question," said Helene. "Okay, media bias and a brief illness is our focus. I don't think it's going to convince very many people."

"It won't," said Marsha. "But we have to have a reason. This is the best one because we can't risk another debate."

"Don't you think that if Hatford was prepared properly he would be able to handle Daggett?"

"One time in ten would be the best you could expect," said Marsha.

"What did you others think about it?" Helene asked.

"Maybe more often than 1 in 10, but not often enough to risk another encounter," Harold said.

Ruth Farrencolt joined the group. "I wouldn't do another debate." Ward came in. Helene told him the issue before them.

Yvonne Sperling, newly promoted in the intelligence section also came in. "No more debates, she said. "No matter how you brief Hatford, Daggett would be too much for him." Daggett was considered the winner of the debate by a margin of four out of five. 77% found him to be the winner, 12% found Hatford to be the winner and 11% didn't choose."

"How much did the track change?" Harold Smalley asked.

"By 7%, Daggett jumped up to 61%."

"Good God," said Helene. "After all of the time and money we blow seven points in one night." she paused. "Next question, how do we gain it back? We need to have a task group on this; Marsha, Erla, Harold, Louis. Why don't you each bring in your top people and put them on to it. There is not a lot of time, but there is enough that if we move quickly we can reorient Hatford."

"I would like to suggest another task group," said Edgar. "One that is aimed at finding out what the opposition is going to do. We have that possible clue that they have an October surprise."

"Isn't that why we have Michelle there?" Helene said with a level voice.

"The campaign is nearly over; we can take a risk."

When the meeting ended, the sense of urgency pulsed in the air. Helene went back to her office and put in a call to Warren Hatch. She used his private number. A pleasant voice answered, "Mr. Hatch's office."

"May I speak with him, this is Helene."

"I'm sorry he is in a meeting."

"Then get him out, tell him I'm calling."

"I'll tell him, Miss Courtney."

Helene was at least glad there was a meeting going on at 7:30 in the morning.

"He can't take your call, Miss Courtney. He is in the middle of a discussion of the debate."

"Tell him that I have input for that discussion."

She waited. The plan of dealing with the press was turning over in her mind.

"He says that he will call you back in a half hour, Miss Courtney."

"I want you to give him the following note. Type it and print it out and give it to him: If you don't want to risk being dismissed for incompetence, you will talk to me immediately. Give that to him right away."

"Yes, Miss Courtney," was the nervous response.

When Warren received the note during the meeting of his staff his face whitened. He paused and then said, "Helene Courtney is calling with some input, let's put her on the speaker phone."

Helene saw the ruse when she was connected. She said, "I'm sorry to disturb your meeting, but I needed to talk to Warren privately. Take this in your office please Warren."

While Warren recessed his meeting Helene began to think of how she and her staff would have to become more directly involved. It was obvious she had to go to Washington and probably take Erla,

Marsha, and some others.

"What do you mean sending me a note like that, Helene, when I'm with my people? How will I explain this to my secretary?"

"I had to get your attention, Warren. That was the worst performance last night by a political staff that I have ever seen."

"What do you mean the political staff?"

"Your candidate was not prepared for the debate. He was left beaten and bloodied."

"What do you mean? I didn't think it was that bad."

"Warren, you lost at least 7 points, probably more. You let them re-establish their issues one by one. We had some momentum. You lost it."

"Helene, I don't see how I could have prevented it."

"I told you I wanted to be up there to participate in the debate briefings and you blew me off. Now, Warren, we're coming up there and we're going to participate in everything."

"What do you mean coming up here?"

"Exactly what I said. Find us some offices. That's your first assignment."

"I don't agree with that."

"It doesn't make any difference what you agree with, I'm giving you a direct order. I'll stop your retainer today; tomorrow you'll be fired as the campaign chairman and with good reason."

"I think this is grossly unfair."

"You didn't prepare your candidate."

"My candidate couldn't handle Daggett."

"That's obvious, but he could have done better. How do you propose to answer the questions as soon as the reporters have finished their morning coffee?"

"We are going to say it was media bias."

"Okay, we agree with that. What specifics are you going to give?"

"We are not going to give any specifics. We'll let the people decide it for themselves."

"That's not good enough, Warren. All of a sudden the campaign turned real specific again."

"What do you mean? "

"We have to come up with a solid reason that we are not going to participate in any more debates. No matter how you prepare Hatford, Daggett is going to beat him, He'll never handle Daggett because Daggett is too smart, too competent, and too aggressive."

"What do you mean about specifics?"

"I want you to cite specific questions that demonstrated media bias and explain how they did. We'll announce that we are withdrawing from the debates after this dies down. Now what plans do you have for recovery."

"We are just talking about that."

"What's the talk?"

"We think that we have to increase our advertising and keep struggling with Daggett's proposals."

"You will be struggling if you follow that course. You have to come up with specific proposals. Have you got any?"

"Why do you want to get specific now?"

"Because, you pompous ass, we got clobbered because you weren't specific last night." Helene realized she shouldn't have called him "a pompous ass." He wasn't all that pompous.

"I'm not sure that I agree with that."

"I don't care what you agree with, Warren. We are coming up there. We'll be there in the morning so make sure you find some office space. We'll need three large private offices, three small private offices and a work area. Try to get it in the building you're in."

"How could I do that?"

"You're bringing in reinforcements. Make sure somebody arranges the furniture and the phones, televisions, and the computers. Get it done by tomorrow morning."

"I don't know whether that is possible."

"Get it done, Warren, or I'll have somebody fly up there this afternoon to do it."

"How am I going to explain this?"

"Just do what I told you. You called for reinforcements. We're coming."

"Are you coming as the cavalry, blowing your bugles?"

"We're coming as the coalition that pays your second salary," Helene was frustrated.

EDGAR CHOSE THE Palmer House in the center of Chicago so he could soak up some civilization. He would go back to Washington to report to Helene and hopefully take her to the Kennedy Center. In his suite with Bill Haber he went over all of the fragments of data and information in the files which had been transmitted from Michelle. Edgar tried to visualize the traveling team and the relationships. Bill told him of the television coverage and the frequent tele-conferences which had been the source of some of the information Michelle had sent back.

From his portable Compaq plugged into the dataport on the phone he accessed the Internet and found out that Adrian was in Oklahoma at the University. He was the luncheon speaker before the faculty and there was to be a rally in the afternoon. He beeped Michelle using Bill's cell phone number. Three minutes later the phone rang.

"Hi, can you talk?" Bill asked.

"The luncheon is still going on," Michelle said.

"I'm with Edgar Slaughter at the Palmer House."

"Slaughter?"

"Yes, there is something he wants us to look for."

"I'm not supposed to do that."

"It's important. Here's Edgar."

"Hi, Michelle, how are you?"

"I'm good I guess, tired."

"I think that is the constant state of the traveling team. Don't they give you any relief?"

"Louise asked me to stay with her and I said 'yes,' otherwise I'd have some time off."

"That was the right thing to do. How is the mood?"

"They're elated by the debate."

"They should be. The latest report?"

"Daggett is almost up to 62%."

"Michelle, you have done a great job for us and your contribution has been significant as I think you know. We now have a special request."

"A special request?"

"Yes, we need to know the details of what Daggett was referring to in his response to the question about values in the debate. He said there would be something more about moral standards."

"How am I suppose to find out about that?" she said.

Edgar realized that this had to be done face-to-face. "You're going to Houston tonight and then to El Paso and Albuquerque. Where are you staying tonight?"

"At the Crowne Plaza in the Galleria."

"We'll try to get into that hotel so we can talk face-to-face."

"Are you bringing Bill?"

"Yes, I'll bring Bill."

"That will be nice."

"Call for us at the desk."

Edgar felt some unease at being at the same hotel as the Daggett campaign and all the reporters trailing it, but he could check into his suite before they arrived and stay there until they left. He got the last available bookings.

It was almost 11:00 p.m. before Michelle called. She asked for some time to freshen up and then appeared at their door in a beige and pink running suit. Her hair was combed and she smiled when she saw Bill.

"Kiss him," said Edgar. She stepped into a big hug and a long kiss.

Edgar was patient for a moment. "The sooner we get to business the sooner you'll be able to get down to the more serious stuff."

Michelle smiled and grabbed him around the neck and kissed his cheek. "I want to go home, Edgar. Even if home is Harbour Island." He could feel her voluptuous young body. She was tall, her cheekbone nearly opposite his jaw.

"I know you do," he said separating, "but there is an important assignment, shall we sit down?"

He got fruit juice from the refrigerator and some snacks from the serving bar and laid them out while he talked.

"Tell me about the state of the campaign," he said giving a general question to see how well she would focus.

"They're euphoric, everyone has stars in their eyes after the debate. Terry feels vindicated in his struggle against Mitchell Fiddler. They sense a victory."

"What do their polls show?"

"They have a good firm lead. They are showing development of a constituency. The management and employees of most manufacturing businesses are 80% for Daggett. In banking it's about the same. In financial services there is less of a majority. Executives and managers in large corporations favor him by 65%. There is a slim majority in small business where there is a tendency to vote against taxes. Among the races its 85% of the African-American, 70% of the Hispanic, and 96% of the Oriental which favor Daggett. Those in education are almost 70% for him. Among professionals of all types its 67%. Daggett will get more than half the union vote. A very large majority of the government employees are against Daggett. Retired military is 80% for Daggett. The main opposition comes from retirees as a whole, probably about 65% of them will vote against Daggett."

"What's happening with Mothers Against War?"

"There is evidence in the polls that they are having some effect."

"As I'm sure that you know, the debate was a disaster and I can tell you that Helene, Erla, and Marsha are all on their way to Washington with Yvonne and Ruth. They are setting up an office to have direct contact with the campaign on a daily basis. Helene blames Hatch for failing to prepare Hatford."

"It doesn't sound to me that there is much you could do debating Daggett."

"Well, they could have been very careful with what Hatford said instead of spouting off the usual nonsense. My gut feeling is that the Daggetts have an October surprise designed to put the election on ice. One step we have to take to mitigate the disaster is to find out what it is. As I told you, Daggett referred to some new proposal that would take a tangible step toward improving the country's overall morality. This could be it. He gave just a small hint.

"There hasn't been a lot of talk about that," said Michelle. "There is a program I've heard about, they call it 'the religion bomb,' but I don't know the details."

Edgar let that sink in for a moment. "How do we find out what it is, Michelle?"

"My orders are not to ask questions."

"We can change that," said Edgar. "Bill, do you have any thoughts about what this could be?"

"I read everything that Michelle sends me, I haven't seen anything yet."

"I think it is just talk, Edgar," said Michelle. "Why don't you make up your own program?"

That's difficult with the staff we have to work with. Who do you ask, Michelle, to find out what is happening, and how could you do it without arousing any suspicion?"

"I work for Louise. I guess I could ask her when I get the right opportunity."

"What do you consider to be the right opportunity?"

"When we're chatting about the future, making plans."

"How often do you do that?"

"Once or twice a week?"

"I think we have to do it faster than that," Edgar said.

"Okay, I'll try to initiate some conversation. I'm the person who handles the press and I need to know what's going on. I'm not involved in policy; people tell me what it is. But, I could ask what will be happening from now till the end of the campaign."

"Can you do that at lunch tomorrow?"

"Lunch tomorrow?" she paused. "No. I think we're with a gang of people. I'll look for the first opportunity."

"I would appreciate it very much, Michelle. Bill will go back to Chicago and I'll go to Washington. I'll stay there for a few days to support you."

"I'll still call Bill?"

"I'll give you a cell phone number."

He wrote the number down on the hotel pad and turned to them. "Now you better go to Bill's room or you will fall off your feet tomorrow, he can sleep late."

They both smiled at him. Michelle hugged him again. He felt the suppleness of her superb body. "Harbour Island. Soon," she said.

"Soon," Edgar replied.

He watched them go and he became very lonely for the woman he would like to hold close. He missed Helene. He wondered if going to Washington was a good idea.

Chapter 33

HELENE AND CAROLYN waited as long as they could after the debate before they stood Warren before the cameras at a press conference. They hoped the story would cool off to reduce the association with the obvious Daggett victory. They also wanted it to appear that there had been deliberation going on, even though the decision had been made within minutes after Senator Hatford left the stage.

Warren had to endure two afternoons of preparation for a 10 a.m. visit of the Washington press corps to the campaign briefing room. His statement alleged that the media bias and the failure of the moderator to control the audience was so profound that the campaign staff had urged the senator to withdraw from the scheduled second debate despite his desire to acquit himself before the public. This statement condemned the news media for pitching "softball" questions at Governor Daggett and hinted that they might have actually leaked the questions to him prior to the debate. Warren also alleged that the moderator had failed to gavel down the studio audience and had thus communicated a skewed perception to the television audience.

He took his first question from a young woman from one of the newsmagazines. "What perception are you trying to create here, Warren?"

He wasn't ready for that. "I'm telling you that the Senator wants to continue the debates, but we have determined that the evidence in the last debate is unacceptable media bias."

"What questions do you think showed media bias?"

"We will publish a detailed analysis of that," said Warren.

"I believe THE REALITY is," she said, "that your candidate was clawed bloody and you don't want it to happen again." Warren pointed to an older man, hoping his question would concern the future of the campaign instead of its past.

In the main conference room in Chicago, Terry Leelan watched his counterpart struggling and called his own press conference for the afternoon. He stated that the Daggett campaign and the Governor were deeply disappointed that the decision had been made not to continue the debates which had so clearly laid the distinctions before the American people. The media bias complaints of the opposition were another perception: the reality, he said, was that Senator Hatford had been mauled and didn't want to suffer again. Terry commented further on the broad constituency that was forming in the support of Adrian Daggett.

While the Vice Presidential candidates could not debate if the Presidential ones didn't, Helene and Carolyn had little doubt that Sandellot would chew up Thomas as badly as Daggett would chew up Hatford if they allowed another one. The withdrawal gave the Daggett campaign the opportunity to comment endlessly on the decision not to face Daggett again. Anne and Nancy made sure everyone in the country recalled the debate and Hatford's decision. While Adrian didn't mention it, the senior staff used every chance to bring up the subject and precipitated a series of editorials and press and TV commentary. They sought to keep the unwinding of the Hatford campaign going.

DAPHNE AND SHARON had two visitors whom they introduced at Valentine's and The Landing as former boyfriends from New York. The story was that the two knew each other and traveled together to see what the girls were doing on Harbour Island. Miles Ruskin was a wiry, gray haired, military-looking man. From a barstool at Valentine's, Cybill Chubb saw hard lines on his face. Sharon's date was introduced as Sam Black. He was a handsome African-American with large biceps and muscled legs which bulged against his slacks. He had been career military who jumped from enlisted to officer ranks. Cybill noticed he had a warmer, friendlier smile. POLACO security kept watch on the two from their arrival. The men shared the girl's bedrooms. Sharon thought the watchers should be convinced of romantic doings.

Daphne had told Cybill the men were coming and said she was surprised when they suddenly wanted to fly down to visit. Sharon found she liked Sam, and told him she wanted to see him when they got away from the island. He fell for this editor, a powerful woman of his race. He restrained himself sexually; he wanted a possible relationship.

The second night Daphne and Miles had "night caps" together. Daphne took off her clothes and found him to be a good lover; smooth and tender. She felt his military respect for women.

Edgar left word with his various agents to be notified as soon as the couples showed up inside any of the dinner or drinking places. Cybill reported she heard plans for their final night at Coral Sands. Edgar called Helene and asked her if she would like to go on a business date. He also invited Louis Fischer and Pat Stabler.

Pat didn't know they were going to meet Daphne and Sharon. On the spacious dining terrace they walked by several couples when she spotted Daphne and Sharon. She brought over Louis and was followed by Edgar and Helene. When Daphne introduced them the two men rose.

"Very nice to meet you, Daphne, I have been looking forward to it," said Helene. "I hope you're keeping her at work, Sharon. I'm anxious for your next book."

"Does he know anything about Harbour Island?" inquired Edgar gesturing at Miles.

"Not this one," Daphne smiled.

"We want the novel you write about the island," said Helene.

"I've already asked Daphne about that," Edgar said.

"Then another reader is interested."

"Have you ordered your dinner?" Edgar asked Miles.

"Yes, we have," Miles answered.

"Let me invite you to the bar after dinner to sample our local drink, Nassau Royale.

"Thank you, our pleasure," said Miles.

They gathered later for small talk.

On the way back to the POLACO compound Pat heard Edgar say to Louis, "They definitely are military and I don't think they knew those girls before they came here."

"How can you tell?" Louis asked surprised.

"They both stood up when they were introduced to us almost simultaneously. They both did it naturally. At the bar when we talked about our colleges, neither one of them knew where Daphne or Sharon went."

"How could you could tell that?" Louis asked.

"By the way that they answered the questions."

Louis was impressed.

At Valentine's another group sipped Nassau Royales that evening. Corrine Clayton, a striking looking blond, fended off the advances of one of the guests to talk with two friends at the bar. She had arrived on a motor yacht that morning and had stretched her shapely legs by walking several miles and then used a cart for further touring. In the afternoon she played tennis with another passenger on the yacht. She was the third officer of the PENMET rescue squad. Her tennis partner was her Sergeant, a former French paratrooper. The skipper of the chartered yacht was Captain Ansell Monroe.

PAT ASKED FOR a massage that evening. Louis happily obliged. He started by rubbing her neck and then she slipped off her clothes so he could rub the rest of her. Louis was ecstatically happy. While Pat had other motives, she found him an amiable lover who cared about her and not just the sex.

Laurie Pinta's parents gave her confidence, and she had had a relationship with her older brother much the same as Helene's. They had talked about it one time after playing tennis. She graduated from Mount Holyoke and stayed for her Master's. She enjoyed the Connecticut River Valley "Five College Faculty" as a serious student. She dated boys from the University of Massachusetts and fell in love with a Yale man, but she decided he was intellectually and socially immature. He made lame excuses when she beat him in tennis, and chess. He was, however, the boyfriend with whom she took her first steps to realizing her sexuality. Because she was a small person she exercised and ate carefully. She had strong legs and a flat hard stomach with strong shoulders. Her brother had promoted that. She could beat him in tennis.

She took the job at Harbour Island because of the money and the challenge. Preston was trying desperately to achieve a love life and she decided not unkindly to help him along. In her view it was a casual affair. He fell hard for her. He couldn't keep up with her athletically, but he could beat her in chess.

When she rejected him he was distraught and from that she got her hands on the disk that held the central secret to the founding of POLACO. He brought it to her. She duplicated it as a part of another project so as not to risk the original. Smuggling the duplicate disk out of the compound, she thought, would be easy enough.

The first indication of an irregularity came from the document control system. Edgar had perfected it over the months of having those who knew it existed try to spoof it. Half the time they were successful. Adjustments were made and lately the detection rate had improved. Laurie had to use her password to log into the computer duplicating the disks. Neither she nor Preston knew that the computer would detect the operation and isolate the disk which was not related to the others. The document control system worked, and Edgar and Cybill got their first clue about an issue which was more dangerous than losing the election to Daggett.

The document control system couldn't tell them exactly which document was copied, but it did tell them something was going on and who was involved. Neither Edgar nor Helene knew the contents of the founding contract. The original signers were still in office and they were the only ones who knew of the document. Its existence was a corporate secret so deep that copies were on disks encoded in a unique cipher. A special software was required to open them. The original was in a safe deposit box in Switzerland which could only be opened by Ward or Bernt. Murder had been used to assure that security.

Preston had warned Laurie about the difficulty of getting anything out of the POLACO compound. She intellectualized that she would be able to fool the security guards. She taped an envelope containing the disk to her stomach. She then put documents and disks and a note pad into a leather portfolio and started out on an electric cart to the gate. She told the guard she was going to get her hair cut and was taking some papers to work on while waiting. She hoped that this would give the impression of a diligent employee using her time efficiently. The guard, friendly as he had been trained to be, told her she couldn't take any disks out of the compound and he would have to inspect the papers. Laurie told him to keep the disks and she would pick them up on the way back. The guard continued to be friendly as he looked at memorandum which included her name on a list of people about whom Edgar wished to be notified should they leave the compound. He asked her to wait while he made a phone call. The desk sergeant informed him that he could let her pass. He smiled at her and she thanked him. Edgar and Cybill had already assigned operatives from Dunmore to follow Laurie. One of their own people kept her in sight as she headed into town. In a few minutes the second detective was ready and Cybill could conclude she was headed to the Coral Sands

Hotel. By the time she reached it the second operative was at the hotel climbing the stairs into the lobby. He went to the bar for a drink, then sat down in the lounge and watched.

Laurie came into the lobby and walked to the desk and spoke to a blond girl whom she apparently knew. After a few moments of conversation she went to the ladies' room which was adjacent to the bar and returned carrying something in her hand which she gave to the blonde girl. It was a gray shipping envelope for a 3 1/2 inch floppy disk. Two minutes after Laurie left he went out on the terrace facing the ocean, shiny blue on a calm day, he took out his phone.

"Chubb here," Cybill answered.

"The subject has given what looks like a gray floppy disk envelope to the clerk behind the front desk at the Coral Sands."

"My God, you got something."

"Apparently."

"Stay there, we must be sure no one gets that disk. Help will be on its way in minutes."

Cybill thought for a moment and then called Edgar. "Laurie has taken a disk out of the compound and given it to a friend at the Coral Sands."

"When?"

"A few moments ago."

"Good, she has led us to an accomplice and probably to a drop-off point. Make sure there is continued surveillance."

"Already on the way."

"I'll get the constables with a search warrant. You make sure that the package doesn't leave."

"We know it's a floppy disk, and the possible accomplice has put it into the hotel safe."

"Good for you. We'll replace it with a blank substitute and watch for a courier coming to retrieve it."

"After a search won't they stay away?"

"They might, or it may be important enough for them to take a risk, but we can't."

Two hours later after the local justice had been located, two constables in their smart uniforms of white sun helmets and jackets with black slacks arrived along with Edgar and Cybill. They approached the desk. Edgar spoke with the blonde. "Do I know you?"

"My name is Anneke, Mr. Slaughter."

"Anneke, we have reason to believe that some property that belongs to us has been stolen and was deposited here in your safe. We would like to view the contents of your safe to determine if that is true. We would like you to do it voluntarily, but I can tell you that we have a search warrant."

"I will have to talk to Mrs. Hinkens."

"Is she here?" Edgar asked.

"Upstairs in the office."

Word that the uniformed constables were in the hotel had reached the owner and she was on her way down. Edgar explained the problem and she went to the safe and opened it. Anneke almost hid behind her in fright. Edgar spotted the suspected package and looked through some other papers first. He deftly switched the envelope with an identical gray envelope which he had carried inside his shirt. After pondering the contents of the safe for another minute, he turned and said, "I guess we were mistaken. I don't see anything that could possibly be ours. Please forgive me."

"Not at all," the owner said. "Just remember that we appreciate your business."

Back in his office with the door closed Edgar put the disk in his private computer. He was unable to read the disk even using the standard decryption utilities.

He telephoned Ward and asked to see him. When he was ushered into the elegant office, Ward greeted him from behind his desk. "Good afternoon, Edgar, how are the moles?"

"Which, ours or theirs?"

"First ours."

"Liz Daley is basically inactive. She thinks Alvin Carter has spotted her. We see no danger in leaving her there, she can still observe. Michelle should be back to us shortly with the answer to the question about the October surprise. I think we have a leak point through Daphne Poltrac and Sharon Gillig. I suspect they're PENMET moles. We're leaving them alone. If they try to leave we'll have them arrested, but I would like some more proof."

"Do you think MacAulliffe sent them here because he found out we had our moles in his yard?

"Possibly. Possibly he only suspects their presence."

"What do you have?"

"This," said Edgar. "It's a disk Laurie Pinta smuggled out of the compound. There are no markings on it. I tried to bring it up on my computer that has all the standard text decoding software and I can't get anything." He handed the disk across the desk. Ward took it curiously slipped it into his disk drive and entered a few keystrokes.

"Where did you get this?"

"I took it from the safe at the Coral Sands where one of our operatives saw Laurie hand it over the desk to a friend of hers named Anneke. We got a search warrant. I substituted another disk for this one."

"Oh my God," said Ward. "Damn." He exited the Windows system he was using and typed in a code at the Dos-prompt. He didn't invite Edgar to look at the screen. After a few moments he saw words popping up and organizing into intelligible sentences. "I can't believe that she had this," Ward said, his face pale. He looked back at Edgar. "Laurie Pinta had this disk?"

"As best as we can determine."

"How the hell did she get it and how the hell did she get it out of here, Edgar?"

"I've interviewed the guard at the compound gate. He said Laurie came by in a cart with some disks and documents in a portfolio. Two days ago she copied a file she was not supposed to have, and we've been watching her. Last night she went to dinner at Romora Bay with Preston. We kept an eye on them, but nothing particular happened. They went back to his apartment."

"They have been a pair for a while, haven't they?"

"That's correct."

Ward thought for a moment. "Good job. The security worked. I appreciate your bringing this Edgar: I'll take care of the matter. It would be nice to know how she got it and who might try to pick it up at the Coral Sands."

"I doubt that anyone will come now that we have been there."

"You're the spy." Edgar didn't like being referred to as "the spy" and Ward knew it. He could tell that Ward was seriously disturbed by whatever was on that disk.

"I guess we could find out one way if we had to," said Edgar

"I'll let you know," said Ward. "Good work, thank you."

After Edgar left, Ward called Radion Gallosey in his office in Chicago.

"Radion, this is Ward."

"Good afternoon, Ward. I see our candidate is behind."

"Helene and Erla have gone up essentially to take over the campaign."

"His performance in the debate was miserable."

"He was up against a tough opponent, Radion."

"I know, but he was unprepared."

"That's why Helene is there."

"He'd better win."

"I called you about something else," Ward said. "I don't know how it happened, but Edgar Slaughter was able to recover a copy of the original contract on a disk at The Coral Sands."

"He what? God damn it, Ward! Say that again."

"Just what I said. Someone accessed a file with the original contract on it and tried to get out. They made the mistake of copying it which activated Edgar's document control system. Edgar couldn't identify the document, but he identified the unauthorized person who copied it."

There was a long pause. "Who did this?"

"Laurie Pinta. I don't know whether you have met her. A petite, good-looking girl who plays tennis with Helene. She must have somehow taped it to her body and gotten through the guards and the security."

"Who is this girl?"

"She is our software applications person. She writes our special applications and enhances our off-the-shelf software."

There was another pause. "How did she ever get hold of that file?"

"The only thing that I can think of, Radion, is that Mikla Alkasy realized that his two colleagues had been killed and expected that it would happen to him. So he left disks. Laurie found one."

"Or someone else found it and gave it to her."

"That's a possibility."

"You've got to get on this, Ward. You have the full ability to investigate things down there. Find out what you need to know. One question is how many other copies are loose."

"That's going to be difficult, because if I have my people work on this, they'll find out what we're after."

"Your right." There was another pause.

"I'll have to send Drago."

"Is that who did it last time?" Ward asked tentatively.

"Could be," Gallosey answered.

"What do you plan to do?"

"We'll find out how she got access to the file on the disk and who she was going to give it to."

"Edgar exchanged it for another identical disk. Someone may still try to fetch it."

"That was good thinking. How did he access it?"

"With a search warrant from the local constables."

"I'll call you back."

Drago himself came two days later with four men. They met with Edgar in the hotel conference room. When he entered the room the five were standing at the windows looking out over the beach of pink sand. Drago was dressed in a blazer and slacks with an open collar. The others wore shirts of tropical colors. Drago shook hands and smiled woodenly. He didn't introduce the others, but he gestured to them.

Edgar sat opposite Drago at the large conference table. The others sat beside Joe. As one descended into his chair he said, "What kinenna room is dis?"

Drago looked at him disapprovingly.

"We use this for small symposiums and other meetings, it is well equipped as you can see," Edgar said looking into the man's eyes. He could tell the man was unable to completely understand the sentence.

"Gallosey tells us you have a problem," said Drago looking in Edgar's eyes.

"I'm not sure I understand that fully."

"We do. We want the girl."

"What do you mean, 'you want the girl?'"

"We want to find out how she got the disk, who she was going to give it to and who else may be involved in this."

The difference between Paul Melius and Joe Drago was apparent to Edgar. Melius was a businessman who served his clients well. Joe was a sophisticated mercenary who sold his services to the highest bidder. The men he brought with him were killers. Edgar did not trust them to have charge of Laurie or any other suspects.

"If you wanted to ask questions we can do that," said Edgar.

"My orders are to ask the questions."

"From whom."

"You know whom."

"Mendos Sadovan?"

"Not him, he's a pansy, strictly a lawyers and money man. I mean Radion Gallosey. He uses whatever methods the situation requires."

Edgar wished he knew who really sent Drago.

"We have methods too," said Edgar. "Including the appropriate punishment and interrogation means."

Joe was prepared to be temporarily magnanimous; only part of his mission was the interrogation, not necessarily the most important part.

"Okay, you get the info. If you don't get the info, we get the girl."

"We'll get the information, Mr. Drago."

LAURIE FOUND IT hard to concentrate on her work. She and Pat Stabler, Daphne, and Sharon were now part of a dangerous conspiracy to expose POLACO. She worried about the reliability of Daphne and Sharon and about their prospects to escape. She was working on a problem trying to interface a data transfer between different applications residing on different computers when her phone rang.

"Hi Laurie," Carrie Watkins cheerily said. "Could you come down and visit for a minute."

"What about?"

"Just some issues in your file."

"When do you want me to come?"

"Anytime that is convenient for you."

"I'll come down in about a half-hour. I need to finish something."

When Laurie arrived at Carrie's office she found Edgar Slaughter, Cybill Chubb and one other detective around the conference table. Carrie got up and closed the door. "Sit down Laurie and make yourself comfortable." There was a tray with mineral water and glasses on the table. Laurie tried not to let her hand tremble as she reached for it and poured herself a glass. She sensed that they knew about the disk.

"Laurie, something irregular has happened. I couldn't tell you about it on the telephone. As you know security here is extremely important to us. We know that you copied a file that you weren't authorized to copy. You carried a disk containing the copied file to the Coral Sands Hotel and had someone put it in the safe there. I presume Anneke Krohmer is a friend of yours."

Laurie's heart began to pound and she swallowed before answering. "I don't know what you're talking about," she said.

"Laurie, after you copied the disk, Edgar Slaughter had you followed. You've been under surveillance for the last five days. We would like you to explain about some things that we observed including your overnight stay with Preston at Romora Bay."

"That's none of your business."

"It wouldn't be if you hadn't copied the file and taken it out of the compound."

"I don't know what you're talking about."

"We'll have Edgar tell you," said Carrie.

"Laurie," Edgar said as gently as he could, "we had a detective in the Coral Sands lobby who saw you enter the hotel and take a package that looked like a disk to the desk. You gave it to Anneke to put it in the hotel safe."

"You must be mistaken."

"There is no mistake."

"I haven't been to the Coral Sands Hotel."

"Laurie, there is no sense in trying to cover this, we followed you to the hotel. When we saw where you were going, we had another detective in front of you go to the hotel to be there when you arrived."

"There has to be a mistake."

"No mistake Laurie," said Cybill. "The best thing for you to do is to tell us all that you know about it and things will go back to normal. We want to know how you got the file and who you intended to give it to."

"I still don't know what you're talking about."

It was evident that she was frightened and had not prepared a cover story. She was not a mole, Edgar decided with some relief. She was, however, someone who had turned against POLACO. The bugging had picked out one suspicious conversation with Preston, which he now related to the file. Maybe Preston had found it. Preston would tell them, or would he? If he couldn't read it, would he inquire about it? He may have found decryption software left behind by Mikla Alkasy before he died. Edgar realized only Preston could answer these questions.

Edgar turned his head toward Carrie and motioned with his eyes.

"Laurie this is a security issue. It's important for you to get hold of yourself and answer our questions. We are confronting you with unquestionable evidence that you handed a disk that you took from our facility to your friend, Anneke, at the Coral Sands. You do remember? It was in a gray envelope."

"No, you're mistaken," said Laurie. She was terrified, and couldn't think. She was not going to admit anything if she could avoid it. Maybe they would just discharge her and she could leave. Her intellect told her that was unlikely. Taking the disk out of the compound was woefully wrong. She blundered into danger. She heard Carrie warn her about some serious consequences. A thick wall of panic was preventing her from fully comprehending Carrie's words.

"I'm going to order an interrogation Laurie because of where we are and the assets we have to protect. For interrogation we have to take you to our special facilities."

Laurie continued with barely coherent denials. Carrie motioned to Edgar and handed him an order. Edgar stood and left the room and came back with two of his detectives. One moved behind her chair and jerked her up by the arms and handcuffed her. The other slipped adhesive around her mouth and an elastic blindfold over her eyes. They guided her out of the room across the mezzanine.

When the blindfold came off and the handcuffs were released, she found herself in a small room with the hum of a ventilator. The door unlocked and a woman came with a tray of fruit juice, small sandwiches, and fruit. She recognized it as food prepared at the cafeteria. She drank some juice and ate one of the sandwiches and used the bathroom. She realized that she was in some kind of detention facility. She imagined scenes of interrogation and torture and knew she didn't have courage to resist. She walked around the room. There were chairs and a steel bed, she stretched out on it and closed her eyes. An hour later the door latch jiggled, and Carrie entered with two sinister figures shrouded in black masks and coveralls. Laurie sat up on the bed. The man rolled in a television set and a CD ROM player. "Our golden rule," Carrie said, "is that interrogation can only be ordered by people who have been through it. This is a tape of what they did to me." Laurie watched in horror as she saw Carrie naked and stretched on something and then touched with probes. Her fears were not wild fantasy; neither were the rumors she had heard.

"This is the final stop, Laurie, before I give you to these people. I would like to ask you a few questions and maybe you would like to answer them." She paused and waited for Laurie's reaction. "Do you know Anneke Krohmer who works at the Coral Sands?" She started with easy, neutral questions.

"Yes."

"How did you meet her?"

"At The Landing."

"What is her job?" Carrie tried to get Laurie answering.

"Anneke is a student from Holland who was here during the summer and decided to stay and help at the hotel because one of the desk managers resigned. She'll go back to school in January. She's studying hotel management."

"Did she agree to hold the package you gave her?'

"Yes."

"And that package was a 3 1/2 inch computer disk?"

"Yes."

"Did Preston give you that disk?"

"Yes."

"Do you know what is on the disk?"

"Yes."

"Does Preston?"

"Yes."

"Why did he give access to you?"

"I asked him for it."

"How much of the file did you read?"

"I couldn't get it to open."

"Preston, did he read all of it?"

"Yes."

"And, he told you what he read?"

"Yes."

Carrie was specifically instructed by Edgar, who got the word from Ward, not to ask what was on the disk.

"Is Ruth Farrencolt involved in this?"

"No."

"What about Julie and Jeff Spencer?"

"No."

"Is Pat Stabler involved?"

"Yes."

"Is Jimmy Connors involved?"

"No."

"How is Pat Stabler involved?"

"She and I wanted to get off the island. We thought that Daphne could help us."

"Why would you think that?"

"Pat suspected she was a mole for the Daggett campaign."

"Why would she think that?"

"Because we mistakenly gave her a lot of information about our campaign one night. The following day she left for New York and was gone two days.

"Has Pat Stabler seen this disk?"

"No."

"Does she know you had the disk?"

"No."

"Who was the disk for?"

"We weren't sure. Pat was going to offer it to Daphne," she lied.

"And Pat didn't know that you had the disk?"

"Not yet."

"That had better be the truth, Laurie."

"It is."

They talked a little further and then Cybill and her two associates left. Laurie was alone again. She wondered if this was some kind of psychological game and if there were subliminal messages being communicated to her.

Carrie returned and told her that the management was gratified that she had decided to cooperate. She should go back to work, but first she would have to retrieve the disk. Laurie wasn't sure she was getting off so easy, but she was taking no more chances. She lost no time in driving to the hotel and returning with the disk in hand.

TWO DAYS AFTER the debate Karen's 'political commando group' was scrambled to increase the liaison between the campaign and the individual congressional and senatorial campaigns. They would corral campaign managers and the candidates and offer them the soft ad, or appearances by the presidential or vice-presidential candidate in return for increased support of the national ticket. They predicted that Daggett would have very strong coattails, and urged the local candidates to take maximum advantage of these. Alan also wanted feedback to address any deficiencies or problems of the national campaign at the local level.

Just before leaving for the airport, they received the latest polls and analyses from Parker Lothan which showed that a cross constituency group was forming to support Adrian Daggett. He was winning the support of people who considered themselves informed, influential, patriotic, internationally aware, socially conscious, religious, professional, and hard working. The preference seemed to cross every possible traditional line. The groups included: businessmen, people in the top 20% of income, union members, other workers, professionals and managers, and executives in businesses or institutions of all sizes, military personnel, and retired military people. All the races and ethnic groups were scrambled into the mosaic behind Daggett. It was not exactly the way the campaign had planned to win the election, but this support was growing deeper and more reliable.

In the media struggle some single interest constituencies and advocate groups continued virulent attacks on Daggett. Daggett had flung down the gauntlet to them and they responded in a relentless and shrill chorus of disinformation. Karen's soft money ads countered by picking apart the claims made by these groups, through logical analysis and exposure of the underlying motivations.

Karen was assigned to Iowa, Nebraska, and South Dakota. She flew to Des Moines and in a rented car made a sweep to the west to Council Bluffs, over to Lincoln and Omaha, and then north and back through Sioux City. This was a different task. She was a diplomat for the campaign soliciting cooperation from potential allies. There were lunches and dinners and constant scrambling to catch up with candidates and their entourages. She presented the Daggett program and the polls, effectively injecting large doses of her own enthusiasm. Many of the local campaign staffs, responded that the debate had been decisive

Driving into Sioux City on a Friday evening she felt spasms of dizziness from fatigue. She knew the way to Earl's apartment, but had trouble finding it. She parked in the unloading zone and went to the door and buzzed him.

"Hi," he said.

"I'm so tired I can't carry my pocket book," she said.

"I'm on my way." In a few seconds he opened the door and looked at her. "Are you sure you can make it to the elevator?" He reached for her and pulled her to him and kissed her; then he swooped her up so he could carry her inside. She could feel his strong arms under her legs and around her shoulders. She held on to his neck. "I have to park my car."

"I can drive." He kept her in his arms in the elevator where they kissed again. On his floor he kicked open the door which he left ajar and carried her inside to the bedroom and laid her on the bed. "You snooze, I'll move your car." She handed him the keys and fell backwards.

When he came back she smiled blearily at him. "Thank you, I love you."

"I love you too, Karen, and you better stop whatever it is that's got you into this condition."

"Just hard work that never hurt anybody."

"You might try sleeping. I'd recommend about once a night."

"I'm too tired to sleep. When I lie down I think of all the things that I need to do."

"The ambition syndrome."

"I think of what it would be like if we lose."

"You're not going to lose," he said.

"But suppose we do."

"So, suppose you do. The sun will rise the next morning and I'll still love you."

"But it'll be awful to work so hard and then lose."

"It happens to a lot of people, Karen. People with persistence come back to win."

"But there is no chance to win again."

"Sure there is. Nixon lost the presidency and two years later lost the governor's race in California. Six years later he won the presidency."

"I want to win! I want to win this race, this time!"

"I know, Sweetie, winners hate losing. That is one of the reasons I love you so much."

"I'm hungry," she said.

"I'll make you some dinner."

"I thought about you all the way from Sioux Falls."

"I've been thinking about you for two weeks."

While she rested he cooked spaghetti with meatballs and a salad. He opened a bottle of Chianti. She came to dinner wearing one of his shirts.

"Do the absences really make us fonder?"

"It depends on how mature you are," he said.

"Are we mature enough?"

"It would seem so, but I don't want to be away from you anymore than necessary."

"If we win..."

"When you win," he interrupted.

"I'm going to be in Washington."

"I know, and I'm going to be there too. Everybody needs computer people."

"But you have such a great career at Gateway."

"There's more to do with other companies."

"But, you're designing computers."

"And software."

"You have started a career with this company."

"In the past you would have been expected to move wherever my career took me."

"But, I would have been only a housewife."

"I won't be a househusband, I'll pursue my career. Between us we might be able to afford to have somebody clean the flat."

"I want a house."

"So do I. You know where I grew up."

"How will we ever do that?"

Well, you're now 24 and doing extremely well. You're going to be in the National Government for 8 years, which will make you 33 or

34 when your finished. I'll be forty! Then we can start the family. I'll be the same age as Daggett was when his first child was born."

"Without five love affairs."

"How do you know?"

"If there were five, they would have been short ones. But you'll be giving up your seven years at Gateway. You're 32."

"I have technical skills and I keep improving and expanding them. I can work for a number of different companies. I could start my own company or work as a consultant. But, where could I ever find another girl like you? I know I won't. I'm not going to give you up for a career in Sioux Land. I'll go where you are. I want to wake up with you as many mornings as possible for the rest of my life."

She reached for him and they held each other. After a few moments, he could feel that her face was wet with tears.

MICHELLE FULFILLED HER duty to her employers by sending the Daggett October surprise in detail with scripts and press releases.

Helene reacted at once to the idea of teaching religion in schools. She saw that the Daggett campaign came up with an idea, which would last for years. It would be controversial and get continued media attention, but it would also be favored by a majority of Americans and particularly Republicans. Here was a chance to bring the religious right into the campaign from which they felt they had been excluded by the abortion issue. Daggett had marginalized the abortion issue and left it with the recommendation for an individual religious decision. Opposition to exclusion of religion in public schools was one leg of the stilts upon which the religious rights support of Republican candidates perched. Taking it away would cause much of this previously unshakable support to topple into the Democrats' camp.

She called in Erla and Marsha. Marsha disagreed. Her point was that it was bad politics to bring up a suggestion which was Constitutionally impossible. Helene wondered if it was, she called Louis Fischer to find out. In three hours she received a lengthy e-mail. The final decision involved the chief executives of the POLACO membership as well as the political staff. They looked at Hatford's schedule and noted that he was to appear at a religious conference in Atlanta two days later. It was enough time to put together a first class speech. Helene and Erla flew west to catch up with their candidate and Carolyn.

IT SEEMED LIKE things were normal to Laurie the next day. She pulled some analysis together and in the afternoon in the intelligence atrium, she spoke to Preston. He asked if he could come over to see her in the evening after dinner and she agreed. She worked late, ate dinner in the cafeteria, and then went back to straighten up her apartment. She put on a pair of her good shorts and a new paisley shirt that she ordered out of a catalog. Preston was late; she called him at 8:30, but there was no answer. A few minutes later there was a knock on the door. She opened it and saw Preston standing with three large and brutal-looking men. One grabbed her, clapped his hand around her mouth, and twisted her arm behind her back while the others pushed Preston through the door.

The man holding her whispered in her ear. "Make one sound and I bust your arm." The third man brandished a gun with a large silencer on it and whispered, "Say out loud, 'Hi, Preston' or I'll bruise your pretty little ass."

Laurie hesitated. The man's huge hand grabbed one of her cheeks and pinched. "Hi, Preston," she squeaked.

"It's nice out Laurie," he said with a quake in his voice, "let's take a walk on the beach." She felt the pressure on her buttock again. "Okay, Preston." They moved out and closed the door. Laurie felt her arms handcuffed and tape laid across her mouth. She watched the man do the same to Preston.

Outside a fourth man waited behind the wheel of a pick-up truck. The others lifted Preston into the back and pushed Laurie in beside him. One got into the cab, two jumped in back with Laurie and Preston and they headed down the beach road.

A half moon showed where the water met the sand. They stopped on the beach by a copse of trees. "Off, you two." She was raised up and made to jump over the side. With her hands behind her back she fell on the sand. Preston almost landed on top of her. One man grabbed her by the shoulder and stood her up. He pushed her forward to the edge of the water. Preston was behind her.

"Okay you two, strip," he then ordered. Laurie felt her hands released. She hesitated, after a few seconds she jumped as her other cheek was pinched.

"That means take off your clothes you prissy bitch." She turned and saw Preston shirtless and dropping his pants. She unbuttoned her shirt and slipped off her shorts. "Keep going."

She bent and pulled the knots off her tennis shoes and kicked them off. She unhooked her bra and dropped it and then pushed down her panties. She felt the gaze of the men on her body.

"Put these on." Two dark blue soft linen running suits were thrust at them. When she had zipped the jacket her arms were grabbed and cuffed again.

Laurie tried to be calm. She saw the pick-up go back up the road and shine a green light. On the water a green light flashed. In a few moments a large black rubber raft, which seemed to ride very close to the water, beached a few yards from them.

A push on her back made her understand that she was to wade out into the water and get into the raft. Its free board was low but the raft was deep in the water and she fell into it. The man at the tiller dragged her by the scruff of her neck back onto a thwart where she could sit. Preston fell and was dragged beside her. She saw his face was almost as white as the tape on his mouth. As the boat turned and thrust itself out into the Atlantic swells, one man turned to look forward while one sat and faced Preston and Laurie. She saw that the man at the tiller had a blackened face. The other two took cans from their pockets and spread black on their faces. The man facing them said "lean forward you," to Preston. Preston leaned forward and the man pushed the material onto his face and neck and into his light hair.

"Your hair is dark enough, dear." Laurie felt his massive mitt pull her head forward and he spread the black soot on her face and on her neck. He shifted and held her neck with his blackened hand and reached down inside the jacket with the other hand to her breasts. She squirmed and struggled.

"Don't do ya no good. You gonna be a peep show tonight." She shuddered as she looked at him. There was hardness in his face, unrelieved by smile lines. The dark hair and eyes made her feel she had seen him before. He was of that remorseless line of people from the city slums who grew up with neglect, poverty, violence, and early death. She felt she was looking into the face of a killer. But why? They couldn't want to kill Preston and her. It was something else. She and Preston were talented, worth too much, and would be very difficult to replace.

A long while later she saw lights ahead. White and green. It was a fishing yacht, a big cruiser with a flying bridge. There was a tall mast and from the base of the mast she saw a crane. She knew that would be used to hoist prizes up onto the deck or to hold them until the fisherman could be photographed with the catch before it was released. She remembered a sailfish her father had caught off of Florida. She started remembering other things about her father from her childhood; teaching her tennis, taking her to swimming lessons, and then to her tennis lessons. She remembered his hugging her when she was valedictorian of her high school class and again when she graduated cum laude from college and when she received her Master's Degree with distinction. She ruefully recalled starting her Ph.D. while working for an insurance company in Hartford only to be seduced by POLACO's salary offer and the prospect for adventure.

From a distance she saw a woman with white shorts and a blue sailing shirt. On the fore deck a man also dressed in white and blue motioned and waved to the woman to go below. When they approached the cockpit of the yacht, the man sitting forward jumped onto its deck with a line and secured it in a bit. The man with the motor moved the stern in so that the rubber raft was flush gunnel to gunnel. Laurie felt herself being lifted by the two men and pushed onto the yacht so that she fell on the deck. Preston was pushed and fell next to her.

She wiggled her way to a kneeling position and looked up to see an elegant gentleman sitting in a deck chair. He wore white linen slacks and white shoes. His shirt was musk colored with a perfectly selected tie to pick up the color with the blue of his blazer. His hair was carefully cropped. One leg was crossed. Beside his hand on a table was a glassful of ice with a lemon slice on top. Laurie realized how thirsty she was.

"Go below and clean off the black stuff."

"Yes, sir," one of them grunted. She felt herself being lifted up and pushed toward the companionway that went into a cabin. She saw the back of the woman who had been on the fore deck. She was pushed into a stateroom and over to a sink. Preston had been pushed into another on the opposite side of the companionway. She felt her arms loosened.

"Clean it off, honey." She reached for soap and a washcloth and looked into the mirror. The water was soothingly warm and she gratefully washed the greasy blackness away. Some of it ran on to the collar of her jacket. She was then pushed back up the companion way into the cockpit and against the aft rail where she and Preston were turned around. She saw the elegant gentleman. While he sipped his drink, he pointed at Laurie, "Let's see what we have here." One of the men came and started to unzip her jacket. She intervened and opened it herself and slipped it off her shoulders. The man gestured for her pants and she pushed them down and stood naked in front of them.

"A lovely body and probably a lovely personality," he gestured at the tape, it was pulled off her mouth.

"How do you keep so trim?" he asked.

She had to conquer the fear. "What are you doing to us?" she shouted.

"You'll find out all too soon, my dear," he said. "I promised my men they could have you for a while, if you were worth having. You are, indeed, lovely."

Preston suddenly made for one of the men who knocked him with the side of his hand. Preston fell back against the aft rail and dropped to the deck groaning. The third man who had been handling the boat came up from the companion way wearing bathing trunks. The other two went below, and they came back in shorts. With a sickening shock of recognition, she realized she was to be raped and murdered. The only hope was an intervention by a passing boat. Her captor was shrewd enough to have his men clean off the black they used to keep from being detected from the shore or from another boat and also let her and Preston wash it off. Little flicks of it remained around her neck. The night was warm but she quivered.

When the three men were back in the cockpit one of them unfastened the crane from its backstay and swung it toward the port side. He pulled down the hook and picked up some coils of line and began to drape them over the hook. Preston groaned. The man with the rope pulled him to his feet and told him to strip. He was still dizzy. "She's got a pretty good crotch there, let's see what he's got," said one of the men. They dragged off his clothes and laughed. "Kinda teensy-weensy." One of the other men held Preston upright while the man with the ropes looped one around his ankles and another around his wrists to tie his hands behind him. Then they lifted him up with the crane with a line under his shoulders. Laurie saw the ropes were tied with slipknots.

"Why are you doing this?"

"You really wish to know?" the elegant man asked.

"Yes, I do."

"Your death has been ordered by a Mr. Radion Gallosey and I do not know why."

Laurie knew who it was; Preston's suspicions were correct. He had ordered the murders of the other people who knew about the contract. She hoped for a passing boat and watched in horror as they swung Preston out over the rail. They pulled the tape off his mouth;

he was too frightened to scream. One man stood by with a large gleaming knife. Suddenly with one sweeping motion as Preston was hanging over the water, the man slit his throat. Then with expert strokes, he sawed open his belly from his crotch to the breastbone. Blood gushed. Laurie vomited violently. The man holding her pushed her head over the other rail. She heard a splash. One of the men reached down into the water with a small bucket and poured it over her face and neck. She thought about springing into the water to swim away. When she tried the man grabbed her hair and brought her back to the other rail to see Preston floating face down. The ropes had been pulled off his arms and ankles. Suddenly his body lurched to the right and back to the left. Fins appeared; then a large dark shape moving with sinister purpose. She saw the shark break into the feeding party of barracuda. There was thrashing in the water, the shark tearing into Preston's trunk and the barracuda snapping up bits of flesh. Soon the body disappeared. Laurie vomited again.

The elegant gentleman delicately took a sip of his drink. "Now you only have her to worry about."

"What about the other two?"

"My crew was told to lock themselves into the forward state room and make love until I personally came to them and knocked on the door."

"They ain't seen these people?"

"They haven't."

"You want her first boss?"

"I think not, I'll go to the flying bridge and keep watch. You take her below in the aft cabin. Make sure she doesn't scream."

Laurie remembered the two in the forward cabin. She opened her mouth to scream, but only got out a short cry before a clammy hand clamped across her mouth. She bit it and she felt him grab her throat and squeeze.

"Tape," said the elegant gentleman.

On the flying bridge he checked the radio frequency analyzer for any transmissions nearby and then the radar. This showed a blip a mile ahead crossing from the north. He guessed it was a fisherman headed for the ocean side of Eleuthera, always known for its harvest of grouper and lobster. In his night glasses he saw his guess was right. Over the starboard quarter toward Harbor Island, he could barely see the lights on the POLACO compound. On Edgar Slaughter's radar his boat would be mistaken for a night fisherman who had stopped to anchor. The yacht was large enough to look like a Spanish Wells boat or one from Nassau. He relaxed and enjoyed the soft sea air. He did-n't know that on the bridge of the boat to the east he was being watched by eyes enhanced by powerful, telescopic night vision lenses.

Laurie stumbled on the companion way as she came up to the cockpit. Behind her and holding a hand was one of the men whose firm grip kept her from leaving over the side. She was sitting on the deck when he came back down. She had not fought; there was no point in it. There might be some percentage to causing one of the thugs to want to keep her and she gave them each special attentions.

"A good woman boss, we ought to keep her."

"Sorry," he stood up and looked around the horizon and saw the boat ahead had apparently anchored.

"Let's get it done."

The crane was swung over her and she was quickly tied in the slip-knots and then hoisted up. She prayed the prayers of her childhood with a sudden fervent belief. When the knife severed her throat, it was both worse than and not as bad as she anticipated. When she died, she saw a beautiful light.

The elegant gentlemen looked down with dismay seeing that a tiny spot of blood had blemished the brilliant white of his trouser cuff.

When his two crewmembers heard the knock at their door, they saw nothing, but a clean deck. Later they noticed the kitchen garbage had been emptied. The three men who had come aboard were in their staterooms and the owner was at the wheel heading north at high speed toward Freeport. When they were clear of Eleuthera radar, he changed course toward the Berry Islands and Great Harbor where there would be no record that his craft ever left the port.

The fourth man drove the pick-up out of the POLACO compound and returned it to the rental agency. He carried his suitcase to a water taxi.

RUTH FARRENCOLT AND Jimmy Conlon came down to the water for their morning jog along the beach. They sometimes skinny-dipped. On the way back they saw the clothing that had been left on the sand near the bushes where there was some soft grass. They pre-sumed whoever had been swimming decided on a quickie. She thought she recognized the shorts as Laurie's. It was nice, she thought, that Preston had learned about quickies.

By 9:30 a.m., it was clear that Laurie and Preston were missing. Phone calls to their apartments were unanswered. A search of the compound, the swimming pool, the gym and the restaurant was unsuccessful. In town, Cybill Chubb made a quick check of the restaurants and hotels. A possibility that they fell asleep after making love in the bushes occurred to Edgar. He sent two of his people to look. They radioed back that he should come down to the beach. He told them to touch nothing. Next to the clothing he was shown deep tire tracks. He also saw vague footprints around the clothing. He had casts made of the tire tracks and the footprints. The tracks led only into water at high tide. He theorized that if both Laurie and Preston were victims of sharks, something would eventually wash up. Nothing did.

IN A TAXI headed for downtown Nassau after a helicopter ride from Norma, Ansell phoned Tony and left him a message to call him back at his lawyer's office on Bay Street. In the conference room, he had just started a cup of coffee when the secretary came to tell him that Tony was on the line.

"Good morning, Tony."

"Good morning, Captain."

"Tony, last night between about 22:30 and 23:00, I witnessed a dastardly crime. I had my infrared glasses on a fishing yacht anchored about four miles off Harbour Island. I was another mile to seaward beyond that anchored on a shoal where we fish. Four or five men were aboard when I saw a naked woman lifted over the water. Someone slit open her belly like they were gutting fish and dropped the body into the ocean. I saw a murder, Tony."

"Good God, Ansell." Murder was a new dimension. Tony had feared the possibility. "Can you describe the boat?"

"Sixty or seventy feet with a crane. That's how they lifted the girl."

"Any name?"

"Couldn't see the stern from my position. They took off north."

"We could get somebody down to Freeport to see if there had been any charters with boats matching that description."

"She would be hard to find. We don't know where she went."

"I'll have Alvin call you. We'll ask Daphne and Sharon if there is anyone missing at POLACO. You should have your attorneys prepare a sealed affidavit. We may need it."

Ansell's lawyer, whom he liked and respected, was a diminutive black man who was a member of the City Council. Ansell explained what he wanted and then dictated what he had seen giving the times and positions. After Ansell approved it and his lawyer friend had reviewed it, they signed three copies. Other members of the firm witnessed the signature and one of them notarized it.

Alvin Carter called Daphne. The following morning she told him that Laurie and Preston were missing and presumably had been attacked by sharks while skinny dipping two evenings before. Tony got back to Ansell to tell him he was not hallucinating.

Memorial services were held at the Anglican Church on Harbour Island.

☆ Chapter 34 ☆

WITH THE CLEAR victory in the debate, with Hatford shrinking from any further confrontation, and still with a major weapon poised and unused, the Chicago staff thought the election was in their grasp. They still had to deal with continuous hammering by the POLACO soft issue ads which refuted Adrian's proposals, and the campaign ads which speculated that Adrian was a dangerous man to elect. Regardless of this or because of their sincere replies, the constituency of thoughtful people in support of Daggett grew. Their main concern was a report from Daphne and Sharon that Helene, Erla, Harold Smalley, and Marsha with their supporting staffs were in Washington full time. They assumed POLACO senior people were totally in charge of the Hatford campaign. Instead of moving Warren out, with the media reaction that would precipitate, they quietly put Helene on top of him with her band of experts. With the obvious determination of their opponents, The reality was Daggett was still vulnerable.

Hatford was, however, wounded. They would launch the religion and morals teaching program which could be the decisive blow. All of the polls showed generally positive reaction to the idea of teaching religion in the public schools as long as the instruction centered on non-denominational, God-based morality. It would appeal to the 87% of Americans who believed in the Deity of the Old Testament and pry loose the religious right from the ranks of firm Hatford supporters. The schedule called for Adrian to broach the subject in a major speech on October 10th to the National Conference of Mayors in Atlanta.

On October 6th, there was a jarring surprise. At 10:00 a.m.

Central Time in Kansas City, Senator Hatford, before a meeting which included representatives of the religious groups of the Republican right, in specific detail, using language of the Daggett papers, described the Daggett program for teaching the history and philosophy of religion in the public schools as a major means to restore morality to American life. This was, however, portrayed as the new Hatford program. Roger Bennett hurriedly phoned Terry. The engineers in Chicago recorded a tape and prepared to play it on the TV in Terry's office. He called in Alan, Anne, Nancy, and Merrick to watch with him.

"Son-of-a-bitch, that's our program," Nancy yelled. "What in hell are they doing with our stuff?"

"I guess they don't have enough ideas of their own," said Terry. "I don't know of a precedent for this."

"It even sounds like our words," said Anne.

"Do they quote Wendy Heinz?" Alan asked.

"I haven't heard it," said Terry.

Merrick turned to Terry. "This was stolen from us and blatantly appropriated by the Hatford people."

"We suspected a mole," said Anne. "Have you sent this to Tony?"

"We should hear from him soon. He watched it with Stephie and Alvin."

"What do we do on the 10th?" Nancy wondered out loud.

"I guess we have to agree with our opponent. Something like this needs to be done."

"We can't let them get away with this, can we?" asked Nancy.

"We certainly can't take the opposite view point. We would destroy ourselves," said Merrick.

"The reason these people used our work verbatim," said Alan, "is they want us to agree with them, or they want us to take the opposite view point, or they want us to accuse them of plagiarism. They probably have a plan to exploit any of those options."

"Talk about unethical," Nancy said.

"These people have no concept of ethics. Maybe having ethics is a handicap in politics," said Anne.

The phone rang with word that Tony and the PENMET group was ready to tele-conference.

"It seems we do indeed have a mole," said Tony from Harrisburg. "What does this all mean? They're practically using our words."

"Not 'practically;' they are using our words," said Anne.

"What's the status of the investigation, Alvin?" Terry asked,

"If there is a mole in Cleveland, he's a former saint. Nobody there has a profile."

"Do we have to bite on one of these three hooks?" Stephanie asked.

"There might be a way out," said Anne. "When Adrian is asked, he has to agree with this program. We might be able to say that we were going to propose something similar or 'something surprisingly similar.' We could give it to an investigative reporter and see if a story can be put together. We could supply some very substantial evidence."

"I'm not sure about that, Anne," said Tony. "That could start a revelation cycle that could confuse the entire campaign."

"I wouldn't yield the issue," said Nancy. "We have to embrace the moral issue and prevent Hatford from monopolizing it."

Steven Hatford conducted a brilliant press conference on the subject of his new proposal. He was obviously well prepared for the questions and his statement was crisp and well organized. For the first time since the Republican Convention, Hatford appeared confident and in control.

At the mayors' convention Adrian bore down on the single-issue constituencies.

IN THEIR WASHINGTON office Helene, Erla, Harold, and Marsha met with Yvonne each morning at 7:30 to see the latest polls. At 7:45 a.m. Helene and Erla went to the campaign office for a meeting with Warren, Carolyn, and Ross Chamberlain. Warren hated these meetings because Helene was obviously in charge. Ross looked forward to them because they were focused and rational. He had huge respect for Helene and Erla. Carolyn was grateful for the meetings and Helene's presence because she needed help in the campaign.

"What is the next step?" Carolyn asked Helene the day after the October surprise was launched.

"Let's get some ads showing Steven Hatford doing tangible things to improve morality in America. We can use the Daggett theme that the changing social structure has caused a stress on family time."

"The role of the schools has to change," said Ross. "We'll do it."

"Can we make this television speech tomorrow night to the broadcasters?"

"What do you think?" Helene asked the group.

"It will show him telling off the broadcasters and getting tough directly with them," said Marsh. "I favor it. It'll play well in Peoria."

"I think she's right. Hatford vs. the evil purveyors of sex and violence."

And so Steven Hatford revealed himself to be a wolf among the sheep at the broadcasters convention. Many of them were cynical news people, or cynical moneymakers, who, like American politicians, slavishly followed polls and ratings to make their decisions. Steven Hatford told them that television had to vastly improve its programming even to regain its 60s status as "a vast waste land." He intended to do something about it by forcing changes in the program structure, which would eliminate the gratuitous sex, violence, and mindless sensationalism. The president of the association squealed like a cat that had been stepped on and ran behind his lawyers citing freedom of speech. Hatford pursued him at a press conference, saying that the Constitution didn't give them the right to fill the minds of American children with poisonous pap and casual cruelty.

Attacks on the media had been made before both by incumbents and by those running for office. The Hatford assault brought a new level of intensity and perceived commitment to control media excesses. The public took notice and Hatford's stature grew steadily as the perception of him as a moral champion was deftly nurtured by his political handlers.

NEW INSTRUCTIONS FROM Washington arrived at Harbour Island for a new TV ad almost daily. Pat Stabler was in the script conferences. Marsha had determined that a portion of the older female vote could be won by focusing continually on Adrian's five love affairs and a similar portion of the younger female vote by supporting Mother's Against War. The ads warned that Adrian would squander the lives of young Americans in foreign involvement and questioned Adrian's "family values."

That night Pat went to Valentine's, slipped into the office, and sat down at a desk. On Valentine's stationary, she wrote down from memory the dialogue and the visual treatments. At the bar she slipped it to Daphne who tucked it inside her shirt. Each day thereafter Pat did the same thing as the scripts were approved. In Chicago, Nancy and her writers prepared the responses. Ads battled ads.

At a press conference following Hatford's television speech, Daggett agreed again that television broadcasting should be reined in. He agreed that no first amendment rights were violated and he made a remark, "Since both Senator Hatford and I are committed to taking tangible steps to deal with America's moral advancement, I would like to suggest that you elect me President and leave Senator Hatford in the Senate where he would assure passage of the needed legislation."

Thereafter, Senator Hatford's recommendations became a promise.

ALVIN CARTER SERVED as the deputy commander of the operation to extricate Daphne and Sharon from the prospective clutches of a now murderous POLACO. From photographs, he made a detailed model of Harbour Island at the Scottish Village offices. The model showed the roadways and buildings between Valentine's and the girls' house and between the house, the government dock, and the secondary escape point north on Bay Street.

Alvin and Miles planned to bring in two large vessels. One carrying the soldiers in-bound would tie up at Valentine's. It would be the command center and would move to the government dock to serve as the primary escape route after the landing. The second would anchor off a shoal called "Girls Bank" and put two large rafts just off shore with light weapons mounted and manned. This was about 300 yards north of what was known as "the fisherman's dock." This would be the alternate evacuation route. Ansell Monroe would be in command to navigate the shallow water. He would lead the way out and then fall behind to cover the rear.

The expedition was a carefully planned, two-pronged maneuver. Four soldiers under Sam Black would head straight for Daphne's house. Eight others, under Corinne, would cover them blocking the roads from the POLACO gates. They also could come up on the rear of any POLACO forces guarding the house that resisted. Vehicles would be reserved in advance and picked up by soldiers in civilian clothes after the yacht's arrival. Miles and Alvin envisioned a rapid application of overwhelming force at the key point to get Daphne and Sharon, with a rapid retreat before POLACO could react with enough force to interfere. Sam Black would also use Daphne's jeep and cart in the escape.

On the model, they rehearsed the movements over and over again. Tony, who had authorized the operation, was frequently at the village and attended every meeting where decisions were made.

"I'm aghast that Daphne and Sharon are still talking with Pat Stabler and they are still sending information," he said one time.

"POLACO hasn't spotted the transfers in the bars of the scripts and treatments. When they do, that will stop," Alvin told him.

"Is that worth Pat risking her life?" Tony asked.

"I don't think Pat's risking her life."

"But what about the two that were murdered?"

"They apparently knew something they shouldn't have."

"It seems beyond belief that Ward would have someone killed."

"We don't know who did it yet, Tony," said Alvin.

"Are you going to be able to find out?"

"We think POLACO has used Joe Drago and Associates. Broderick tells us that they are a source of anything you want done."

"Including hits?"

"Apparently so."

Tony wondered if this was his baptism of fire in the high corporate responsibilities. It was going to cost nearly $300,000 to remove Daphne and Sharon from Harbour Island after he put them there. And, the fire could be live bullets from a POLACO speedboat or from the shore. Failure could mean injury or death to the rescuers and hostages. There could be civilian casualties. "Why can't we pull them out of Valentine's?"

"We have to expect POLACO security people to be there. It's too hard to control a situation there."

"So we are committed to this nighttime cutting-out action."

"Tony," Miles said, "we could send a few people to try to get Daphne and Sharon onto a yacht, but there is a marginal chance of it working. We've thought of trying to sneak them to a boat. Possible, but POLACO has fast craft. They could intercept. We would still need soldiers and automatic weapons."

"Why can't they intercept your yachts going out?"

"They will know we are armed."

"So?"

"They would have to risk an investigation of any serious shooting or use of missiles."

"You'll let the girls know when we're coming?"

"We'll send Corinne to find them."

"At one of the bars?"

"Or at the house."

Tony was concerned. It was a big commitment because to do anything less was to fumble his people into Edgar's hands. Once in the compound they would be rescued only on POLACO's terms. He would have to spend at least two days practicing handling the large yacht.

They had to set a date. They chose Halloween night.

THE MORAL CRUSADE of Steven Hatford gathered momentum. The polls showed increasing approval, the same support that the pollsters had expected for the Daggett campaign. Helene and her team had one main objective, to ride the issue into the final week with the lead and the momentum and to keep Adrian from riding the second hump of the camel.

Warren Hatch and his group, with the moral tide, wanted to keep pounding on the question of Adrian's values raising it by innuendo in the context of the Hatford theme. Ads from the Conservative Coalition were spread profusely in the states where they would do the most good. Helene's staff used them to enhance the moral crusade as a bulwark against the immoral taxes and immoral use of American forces proposed by Daggett.

The Daggett replys were precisely targeted counterattacks. To the statement about the immoral taxes and use of force, Anne and Nancy's response affirmed the wisdom of teaching moral standards in public schools, but attacked the allegations of the immorality of taxes and foreign engagements as calculated perception. Reality, they noted, was that fiscal stability was essential to democracy and the resolve of the United States in support of a reformed United Nations and was indispensable to long-term world peace which required America's full involvement.

While Steven Hatford concentrated on the morality crusade Adrian Daggett stayed on the issues and on his reality campaign. His advertising artillery pounded on the reality positions and the distinction between reality and perception. He continually questioned Hatford's ability and unwillingness to understand reality rather than foster unfounded perceptions. Strident Hatford advertisements accused Adrian of falsifying reality.

The Hatford campaign and coalition ads appeared almost twice as often as Daggett campaign and foundation ads. Surveys indicated that the Daggett ads were more effective but that they were being overwhelmed by the volume. When Karen was on the trip through Nebraska and Iowa, Lucile started a rewrite of some of the campaign and foundation ads to reflect the points made in the debate and new ads to reply to the POLACO barrage. More scripts and quick production at the Chicago headquarters and in the studios in New York and Los Angeles were the next assignment.

When Karen got back to her office, messages from the congressional campaign coordinators she had met requested foundation ads in their districts. She constructed a list on her computer with comments on the importance of each and carried them up to Anne's group. Anne's staff replied to the requests so Karen and Lucile could take a plane to New York. In two twelve-hour days at Evans & Copeland they wrote seven new foundation ads. Anne brought reinforcements from New York to Chicago to prepare campaign ads to respond to the script concepts transmitted up from Harbour Island by Daphne.

Anne looked at the edited scripts from New York and congratulated the two girls and their people there. A weekend of production followed in New York then a rush to Newark Airport. On a plane to Los Angeles where the ads would be produced, they fell asleep leaning on each other. A Continental flight attendant took away their dinner trays and covered them with blankets.

At headquarters the mood changed. Adrian led in the polls, but the lead was steadily diminishing. The new constituency promised to capture key states, but they were losing in others and fading from contention in the Bible belt. Daggett was also hopelessly behind in Maryland and Virginia because of the large number of government employees who feared his downsizing promise. He was behind in Florida and Arizona where retirees feared an increase in taxes. He was also behind in tax conscious states in the Midwest and New England. He was substantially ahead in the states with high tech economic bases except California where the retiree vote was canceling the aerospace industry vote. California also had favorite son support for Clayton Thomas as Vice President.

Terry reflected that the staff was drained as he lost concentration on the budgetary spreadsheet displayed on his terminal. They had all worked hard and they were brilliant at what they did. He was proud of the Cleveland achievements, the essence of the campaign. Anne and Nancy described substantive proposals to the electorate instead of slinging perceptions. The response from the public was, in a way, magnificent. Republicans, Independents, and Democrats all sent checks, first, to the campaign and then to the Liberty Foundation. Alan, Anne, and Nancy in a continuing campaign echoed the victory in the debate in every household that cared. What they had not calculated was the immensity of the opposition's ability to raise money. POLACO, under the guise of the Southern Conservative Coalition, was tapping into a deep financial well. Going over the latest statistics from Parker Lothan with Alan, Terry projected a win in a close election, but defeat was becoming ever more possible. He reached for the button on his phone for Tony Destito's private line.

"You only call when it's important," he heard Tony say.

"It is. I should fly to see you about this. You may realize that we are being smothered with POLACO's advertising."

"By how much?"

"About 1/3 of the soft ads on the air now are ours. They are out numbering us by 2-1. In the campaign ads it's about 3-2."

"I understood ours were considerably more effective."

"They are in the tests. Tony, we aren't talking about years of revenue over which you executives make your marketing adjustments. We are talking about one event, winner take all."

"I know what you mean," said Tony.

"We need another twenty million dollars for soft advertising."

"Wouldn't it be dangerous for us to put that in?"

"You could do it through the foundation."

"We don't want the scandals Bill Clinton suffered."

"If we don't win the election, we can't suffer the scandals. There is also something larger than the election at issue. You can see how determined they are."

"You have to hand it to Helene and Erla and their staff. They turned that campaign around even if they did steal our idea," Tony said.

"It would have been nice to win it in a walk."

"You want me to ask Ian for the money?"

"If you would. If he wants to talk I'll be there in the morning."

"I'll send a Lear up to Meigs."

"That would be appreciated."

"See if you can't get Mitchell to shake the fruit trees in his orchard."

"It's hard for me to ask, Tony. There also isn't enough time. He might bring in a million or two, but I want the insurance. This will also help us in our congressional elections. We do want a democratic congress beholden to Adrian."

"What about the campaign ads?"

"I think we'll be evenly matched in quantity and ours are better. I just don't want to take a chance losing the war of ideas."

"I'll get us some more ammunition," said Tony.

"Praise the Lord and pass it on down."

AMERICAN HALLOWEEN TRADITIONS had seeped over to the Bahamas and mingled with the Caribbean "Night of the Dead." There was no "Trick or Treat" in Dunmore. Neither children nor parents wished to encounter the dead on their night. For Americans, British and other Europeans, however, the resorts offered Halloween parties and encouraged costumes. The POLACO staff, as it expanded, added to the attendance. Carrie Watkins promoted the parties and even subsidized them to mitigate the lack of cultural activity and an urban variety of restaurant offerings.

The parties for the Americans ended at 11:00 p.m. to allow the Bahamian employees to be safely home before the witching hour. Normally at midnight Dunmore and Harbour Island would be quiet. Halloween minimized the civilian nighttime activity, providing the best environment for the operation.

Tony, wearing a uniform of khaki slacks and a light blue shirt with a white beaked cap, slowed the 70 foot cruising yacht "Winthrop" with the attack party and their gear packed into its state rooms, as he came south down the bay. Maneuvering the throttles and using bow thrusters he landed at the quay by Valentine's at 3:00 in the afternoon. Ansell would anchor another large fast cruiser "Ranger" opposite the beach of the alternate evacuation point. After waiting, the first mate went ashore with a crewman and a soldier in civilian clothes and picked up three vans, which they had reserved. They brought them back "for the use of their passengers."

Since it was such a large yacht, Miles suggested that more than one couple attend Valentine's party. They hoped to contact Daphne or Sharon without going near their house. They paired off Corinne and two other women in their force with three men. Costumed as pirates and sailors they joined the dancing. When Daphne arrived dressed in a peasant costume, Corinne told Bernard Napier, the Senior noncom, former paratrooper and her "date" for the evening, to ask Daphne to dance. At the next slow number, he approached her.

"If you are the well-known Daphne Poltrac, perhaps you would allow me the honor of dancing with you."

Daphne rose, smiled and complied. "How do you know my name?"

"From many pictures of you I have seen."

"On my books?"

"One time on a book, and a dozen of times in our briefings."

"Briefings?"

"Briefings. Military briefings. I and others are here to pick you up tonight."

"Tonight?"

"That is correct. We come at 2 a.m. You and Sharon should be dressed and ready. Make sure whoever is watching your house thinks you are in bed. Get out your weapons."

"What can we take?"

"Only your briefcases."

While they danced Daphne thought of what she would put in the briefcase: all of the disks of her work and her laptop computer. "How come we didn't know before?"

"Because it is too dangerous to make contact. I think we should stop worrying about it. Tell me about your life on Harbour Island."

"It's been spent in a good cause," said Daphne.

When the music stopped Bernard walked her to the table. He told her he was pleased to have been with such an attractive celebrity and went back to join Corinne. Daphne watched him with the others who were indistinguishable from the other tourists drinking the islands fruit drinks. She assumed there was no alcohol in them. Cybill Chubb, appropriately disguised in a sea creature costume, saw the contact. The suspicions were aroused by the big yacht, which had come to Harbour Island so early in the season. There were a dozen possible explanations.

Suddenly Daphne thought of Pat Stabler. Since there was a group coming to escort her and Sharon off the island, should she invite Pat to join them? The soldier she danced with told her to tell no one. But Pat was a special case. Someone who had provided information and assistance. She didn't want to leave Pat on the island if Pat wanted or needed to escape with them.

The POLACO detective assigned to watch Daphne was surprised to see her leave the party before 10:00 p.m. Rather than going to her car, she turned toward The Landing, 300 yards away. In the party there Daphne found Sharon. When she was sure that no one was watching she told her what was about to happen. Pat Stabler was not there, but came in with Louis Fischer. Daphne asked her to join her in the ladies' room where she told her of the opportunity. Louis was a complication. Pat would have to go back to his apartment with him and leave after he had fallen asleep, and then pack whatever she wanted to take. He was dressed as a bearded academic and Pat as his pupil in an academic gown. Pat said she would come down the beach. Daphne told her not to approach the house, but to wait and watch until the expedition took charge of the area. She suggested some places to hide.

Just before 9:00 p.m., Ansell glided "Ranger" down the channel using his searchlights on the markers and turned inshore to drop anchor opposite the embarkation point. On board were two extra mercenaries, a man and a woman who were ex-US Marines. They would handle the black rafts, which had been partially disassembled to be packed on the yacht to be reassembled in the water at Harbour Island. The rafts, each large enough to hold nine of the attacking party, were to be taken on shore with two electric motors, then swung with the bows facing the yacht. A line from each was attached to one of the yacht's winches. The rafts would be reeled in as occupants returned fire or just kept low profiles. On the stern of the rafts there was a plastic shield that would stop most bullets. A light machine gun was mounted to fire through it.

In the control room at POLACO security the Sergeant on duty noted activity on his radar. He called Cybill and told her. Normally there were two armed POLACO soldiers patrolling the town on a shift from 9:30 p.m. to 5:30 a.m. As much as possible they stayed out of sight and concentrated on Bay Street.

The operation was set to begin at 1:55 a.m. A countdown started at 11:00 p.m. with everyone in the main cabin for a final briefing with Miles Ruskin. He told them they should be confident because they were striking with surprise and also with what he believed was overwhelming force. If all went well, they calculated that they would be on shore no more than nine minutes. Alvin and Miles were uncertain of the POLACO patrol activity, but said that even if they were seen immediately they would still have time to deal with any opposition and escape. In the worst case, Corrinne's troops would stop any POLACO vehicles, buying time for the main contingent to complete their mission.

After the briefing, they began final preparations. Their equipment included a light body armor molded to each person. A light armor helmet covered the ears and contained a radio receiver, so communication would be instantaneous between the two leaders, Sam and Corinne, and their troops. There was to be complete radio silence until POLACO knew they were there. The coveralls were dark gray cotton linen with the name of the agent embroidered on the side. A logo of Special Forces, Inc. adorned the left arm and the officer's ranks were stitched on the collar. Corinne wore the three stripes of a captain. Sam wore a singlewide stripe with two narrow ones of a Major and Miles had three wide stripes of a Colonel. The noncoms wore stripes on their sleeves. At T minus 30 minutes there was an inspection in the main cabin by Corinne and Sam. They reported to Miles that all was ready.

With the two additional soldiers, the plan gave Corinne eight to block the approach of any POLACO force. Sam had four to make the rescue, but Corinne could move on any opposition from their rear. At T minus 15 there were two minutes of all the latest reports. The light condition was a three-quarter waning moon, which had risen at 8:00 p.m., partially obscured by clouds. At T minus 10 all was quiet. Alvin and Tony went out to the bridge of the yacht with infrared glasses to scan the town. They saw nothing. The only sound was the lapping of the water against the sides of the boats. At T minus 5 the two rafts began their way toward the evacuation beach from "Ranger." The soldiers filed over the gangway from "Winthrop" and down the pier. When they stepped ashore they heard the engine start. The lines were quickly cast off and fenders put over the starboard side so Tony could push into the government dock.

At the zero hour Edgar's patrol quietly navigated the shadows on Bay Street between Valentine's and The Landing. At the POLACO control room the radio jolted the desk sergeant to attention. "We have an attack by armed soldiers in uniforms coming in at the dock at Valentine's, large squad strength." The sergeant pushed a button that rang a speaker in Edgar's ear. He shook himself awake and heard this report. "TRIPLE ALARM...NOW, NOW, NOW!" He shouted and sprang out of bed toward his closet. Pulling on pants and grabbing everything else including his pistol belt and rifle he ran to the elevator to the security area leaving the lights on and the door open. His apartment was in the building immediately over the headquarters

After the third "NOW," the desk sergeant pushed another button which rang an alarm in 48 rooms around the compound. All the sleepy occupants picked up their phones and they heard the same message: ALARM, ALARM, ALARM, THIS IS NO DRILL-THIS IS NO DRILL!"

Ruth Farrencolt at first couldn't believe it. Then she rolled out of bed pushing Jimmy awake and turned on the lights. She rushed naked to one drawer and grabbed her undergarments. She put on her body armor and pulled on her coverall, socks, and boots. Carrying her Berretta 62 and her pistol belt with a helmet and ammunition case, she ran down the hall and out into the night. She was a thoroughly competent soldier in the second squad commanded by Cybill Chubb. The action station was behind the first squad headed by Mike

Anzarra who was in tactical command. The third squad would come behind them in a troop carrier and the fourth with trucks that would hold positions at the POLACO gates. The detective force would man an armed patrol boat, which would go off from the POLACO dock. All were under the overall command of Edgar Slaughter.

While Tony backed the yacht away from the quay a crewman in the electronics center told Alvin and Miles he thought he saw a brief radio transmission on his frequency scanner. Had Miles and Alvin been able to post observers without attracting suspicion, they would have seen lights go on in the POLACO compound and Edgar's soldiers running across the grounds to their armory.

Edgar ordered the patrol in the town to follow the penetrators and then to fall back to cover Bay Street as best they could. They could slow down the departure if need be. He looked at his model of the island and he wondered what exactly they were doing. He imagined the column was headed for Daphne's house with a covering force positioning between him and the house. The seconds ticked away. The radio crackled, "At Daphne's house. Others deployed south." He had guessed right, it was a rescue mission for Daphne and Sharon. What else could it be?

The crewman monitoring the frequency scanner reported more blips. Miles and Alvin weren't certain what it meant. They both went out onto the bridge with Tony. All was quiet as the bow swung around.

At Daphne's house on Colbrook Street, Sam knocked lightly on the door. Daphne and Sharon opened it. The two men and two women accompanying him spread out and took what cover they could. Their van was parked by Daphne's garage. Corinne's detachment drove their vans south of the house. She kept her group together by the vans ready to move.

"Pat Stabler is coming, Sam," Daphne said. "She should be watching and will come right down."

"We can't wait," said Sam.

"We have to, I told her we would take her out," said Daphne.

"That's a complication."

"She's been very helpful. She gave us the scripts."

"We can't wait."

"She should be right here."

"I'll give you two minutes. Get out the jeep and the cart."

All was silent around the house until the motors started. The "Winthrop" was under way now headed for the main dock with lights out.

"We'll assume that POLACO still doesn't know," Miles said.

"I hope not," said Alvin.

Edgar waited patiently for his troops to arrive. By phone, Anzarra reported they were ready and only one was absent. Edgar knew that was Helene. He looked at his watch. They had mobilized in seven minutes.

"GO, GO, GO," he said. "Mike, drop six at the main dock and get north on Bay and block Dunmore. Cybill, head for the house and flush them. Keep between them and the bay. Mike, Cybill we'll keep them from getting off wherever they intend to do it."

Corinne on the radio said, "I hear engines."

"Direction?" asked Miles.

"South-West." Miles looked at the area both on his map and the aerial photographs. "Lot's of radio traffic," the crewman said to Alvin and Miles.

"Use radio, Use radios," Miles said into the microphone. "Where are you? You're late."

"We're waiting for Pat Stabler."

"Return at once."

"We have to go," Sam said to Daphne. They ran to Daphne's jeep and the van.

"Proceeding to the main dock," said Sam.

"Fall back, Corinne," said Sam. "We'll leave by the main dock."

The radar showed that the large yacht was moving toward the main dock. Edgar broadcast. "The main dock may be the 'evac' route or it could be a decoy. The other 'evac' is a craft at anchor 700 yards to the north."

The POLACO troop carriers burst through a hidden gate and roared up Queen Street past the Romora Bay Club; turned west to Bay Street, and came wheeling toward the town. On the bridge Alvin could see the lights and hear the engines.

"We have only a minute until they're here," he said to Miles.

"RETREAT, RETREAT, RETREAT," said Miles. "Attackers coming from the south on the shore road."

"On which road?" he heard Corinne's voice.

"On the Shore Road."

"Damn," she said. "We expected they would come out the West gate."

"There apparently is a gate farther west."

Corinne yelled to her troops to follow her to cover Bay Street. They ran down York Street between Valentine's and the main dock. The POLACO carriers hurled themselves toward her. She yelled " FIRE!" Her troops found what cover they could and opened up at the carriers. The carriers kept coming and opened fire in return. Corinne saw the soldiers firing from above the cab. "Use your grenades, " Corinne shouted. The first carrier sped by as a grenade exploded against its side. The second carrier slowed and sprayed the intersection with bullets. For a moment she was in a crossfire with guns flashing at her from the rear of the carrier that passed. She waved her people back retreating under fire, but away from the dock. "I'm under fire by seven or eight of them at York Street," she whispered excitedly into her microphone.

"Acknowledge, affirmative, all proceed to alternate evac." Miles ordered.

"OFF, OFF, OFF!" Cybill shouted to her squad. The back of the carrier dropped down and they jumped. Ruth and four others ran forward across the lane behind the carrier. The rest deployed at the intersection. A grenade exploded.

"FLARE, FLARE!" Cybill yelled and within seconds the area illuminated nine crouching bodies scurrying to escape. They ran toward an alley behind the buildings heading north toward Church Street. Cybill yelled, "FIRE!" Seven Berrettas peppered the running figures with bullets and two fell. Cybill waved for Ruth and two others to run ahead and up the next lane to cut them off. The rest of her people gave chase. Cybill following Ruth, ordered, "Up Hill Street." Moving at full run they encircled Corinne's squad seeking cover behind trees. When Corinne and her six remaining soldiers came out, Cybill yelled, "drop your guns and put your arms in the air." Corinne saw her enemies were shielded and waved the squad to break for the alley. Cybill yelled, "FIRE." Ruth saw her bullets bring down another. Corinne's people fired at their pursuers and took two down. Ruth and two others crouching beside the entrance to the alley fired from their direction. Corinne, caught in yet another crossfire, saw their only hope was to try to sneak to the shore. She had lost three of nine and was opposed by twelve of this squad, and there was yet another squad ahead. Tony watched the skirmish as he steered the "Winthrop" into the dock. One crewman jumped overside with the lines. Another, a young woman brought an automatic rifle up to the bridge.

Sam saw the flare and heard the firing and sped toward the evacuation point. Corinne, he realized, had been flanked or overrun by the speeding vehicles. POLACO soldiers were now between her detachment and the dock. Sam headed toward King Street which would bring them to Bay Street opposite the rafts. The first POLACO squad followed on Bay Street. From his headquarters Edgar ordered the third squad to block Bay Street to the north at Duke Street. Estimating the size of the force that he was dealing with, Edgar ordered the fourth squad into town on Dunmore Street to block exits toward the beach. He saw no danger to the compound and didn't want to search for missing soldiers. He had his forces fully committed. The big yacht, he knew, was at the government dock, but he assumed the other vessel was the alternate escape plan.

Sam's small band was on the corner on King Street going onto Bay Street when he saw the POLACO carrier coming at him. It opened fire and he was left with no choice but to head back away from the rafts. Edgar brought the third squad down Dunmore Street far enough to block off Sam's escape and ordered Mike to bring four more soldiers from the government dock, leaving two with the patrol to hold it should the group Cybill was chasing get away.

Sam tried once more to get the group to the rafts through the back alley behind Crown Street. The first squad on the ground following between him and the shoreline fired, which made Sam retreat again. He ordered his cars into a driveway. The POLACO soldiers started running at him. He got everyone out of the driveway and tried to run down an alley to the shore by the rafts when they were spotted. A whole new squad fired at him. Everyone was thrown flat on the ground when the POLACO soldiers who had chased them came up behind them. He heard Mike say, "Stand up with your arms in the air where we can see them and throw your weapons to the ground." There was no choice. It was his five against twenty or more.

Corinne in the meantime was deciding whether to surrender or make one more attempt at the government dock. She saw a driveway which led to Bay Street, and with the remaining troops, began creeping down it hoping to evade notice. On Bay Street, however, she saw the four troops waiting behind one of her vans. A minute of silence passed when she realized soldiers were coming at her from all directions. Another flare went up and she heard Cybill's voice through the bullhorn, "Come out with your hands up; leave your weapons where they are." Three of her eight people were down and there was no place to go. She stood up and yelled, "Okay," and with the others raised her hands in the flare light. Into her microphone she said, "three down, surrounded by sixteen we're not coming out." The troops from the encirclement including Ruth pushed them into the road and faced them. A troop carrier and a jeep were brought up with spotlights.

"Strip," Cybill commanded. The two women and four men still standing began to take off their clothes. Corinne lifted off her helmet and shook out her yellow blonde-hair. She was helpless, but still in command of her own people. She unzipped the front of her uniform and bent down to undo her boots. She pulled them off and slipped off her coveralls with her rank on the collar. She unhooked the body armor and lifted it over her head.

One of the POLACO troops pulled plastic barrels off the truck and carried them to where their prisoners could put their clothes and boots into them. Cybill stepped up to Corinne where she stood in her bra and underpants. "How many were there?"

"Us and the three you hit."

Cybill smashed Corinne across the face. She fell backward and tried to return the swing but was stopped by two POLACO soldiers who grabbed her. One slipped on handcuffs. Cybill went back to her. "How many?"

"I told you." Cybill punched Corinne in the stomach and felt the strong muscles.

"Fourteen," called one of the other mercenaries who wished to cooperate with his captors. The prisoners were all handcuffed and then made to walk barefoot on the rough road down toward the dock.

At the bend at Bay Street, Ansell watched the same ceremony except in addition to the troops, Daphne and Sharon were made to undress to their underwear and were handcuffed. They were marched south on Bay Street toward the others. When the prisoners were together, a jeep came down Church Street toward the main dock. There was a large antenna on the rear and several other smaller ones. A large machine gun was mounted on it. Edgar climbed out of the seat and walked toward his squad commanders. They saluted and he returned it.

"Excellent job all of you. You trained your people well, and you led them well."

Mike said, "Thank you, sir."

Cybill smiled and Edgar stepped toward Sam Black.

"It would seem we have met before."

"Yes."

"Who is your second in command?"

"She is," Cybill said gesturing toward Corinne.

Edgar said, "Who sent you on this mission?"

"We only know the mission," said Sam.

"We'll see about that," Edgar said. In addition to the three mercenaries that were shot, he had three wounded as well. One might be crippled for life.

Tony saw it all as he backed the yacht away and headed north. As soon as Miles had the two manning the rafts aboard "Ranger" led Tony to the fairway. Watching the GPS when he was sure it was accurate Tony went to half speed and Ansell turned "Ranger" back to cover him. There was nothing more they could do.

Edgar looked out at the two ships in the harbor. He considered firing at them with his 40-caliber machine gun, but could see no purpose. His forces had proven themselves to be well trained and well motivated. He would design a combat ribbon.

"Okay Cybill, Mike, bring them back." The handcuffed mercenaries were blindfolded and pushed onto a truck. Corinne was jammed in skin to skin with her people.

When her blindfold was removed, she knew she had been in an elevator and was underground in a cell with the other women. There were four of them; the fifth was being worked on by the POLACO medical staff. She was told this was composed of an internist, a surgeon, an anesthetist, two surgical nurses, and two RN's all of whom were recruited in Eastern Europe enticed by dollars of Western dimension. Most of their time was spent treating inhabitants of the island, but they were there for routine preventive care of the staff and for emergencies.

One of the POLACO women in uniform came in and handed out orange shorts and tank tops except to Corinne. Behind her were two other women, one was armed with an Uzi. The other signaled for Corinne. Before she stepped out of the cell the guard turned her around and handcuffed her arms behind her and slipped on a blindfold. When she was backed out of the cell she was stopped and she felt hobbles being snapped on.

When the blindfold came off she was in an interrogation room. There was a table. Behind it she saw a gray-haired military man and the woman commander in the field who had slapped and slugged her when she lied about the number of penetrators. She knew as the second in command she would be the first to be questioned. Two soldiers stood behind her in dark coveralls.

Edgar scanned her body and saw everything he would expect with a military female. Looking into her eyes he could see she had brains.

"Please bring the lady a chair."

The woman who escorted her left and came back with a chair and Edgar gestured for her to sit down. They began to take off the hobbles and uncuffed her hands. She was able to sit down and cross her legs. Edgar still looked at her.

"How did someone like you get in this business?"

She didn't answer.

"There are no laws of war here, Corinne. We can talk. You are a perpetrator and you have trespassed. We can allege that you came here with the purpose of kidnapping. If that doesn't stick, we have enough other Bahamian laws related to bearing arms that should keep you and your friends in jail for at least five years. It is possible we won't file charges if you cooperate. If you're the observer I think you are, you'll recognize that we have other capabilities to make you talk. So, why don't we have a friendly conversation?

"Let me start by telling you that your three wounded all required surgery and we had to fly in some additional blood. They used up our supply. The doctors had to remove the spleen from the girl who was hit by a burst and bruised through her body armor. Her prognosis is good. The others should be all right."

"Thank you."

"So, where are you from, Corinne?"

"Flint, Michigan."

"Was your father in the automobile business?"

"He worked in the Chevy plant there."

"Where did you go to school?"

"I went to high school in Flint"

"You were in the top five percent of your class and lettered in every sport."

"That's right," she said with her chin up.

"You went to the Naval Academy."

"And became a Marine," Corinne replied.

"Infantry?"

"Special Forces."

"So when your five years was up, someone from a firm with broad interests contacted you?"

"That's right."

"They offered you four times your lieutenant's salary."

"I was a Captain."

"What assignments have you had?"

"I don't think that's relevant," Corrine said.

"Just interested in the nature of the business."

"We do security work in harbors on Africa and Asia. Once in a while in Eastern Europe. We work for shipping companies. We have stung a couple of pirate operations in Vietnam and hijackers in Poland and Russia."

"I've heard about that," Edgar said. "What happened in this operation? Why were you so slow?"

"I don't know. We were in position for a full three minutes longer than we were supposed to be."

"And you got flanked."

"I guess you call it that."

"You didn't know that we had armored personnel carriers."

"No, we didn't."

"I don't think you would have been able to stop us even if you were dug in. Who sent you?"

"I only follow orders."

"I think that you know more than that."

"Miles Ruskin gave us our orders and we were paid, that's all I know."

Edgar paused to think about that. Corinne was given orders not to reveal anything she knew about the client. Sam would be the same. He had met Miles Ruskin at the Coral Sands where he posed as Daphne's date. But he didn't have Miles, he had only Corinne and Sam.

"Corinne, in the course of planning this project you must have come in contact with someone representing the client."

"Actually, I didn't," Corinne said trying to persuade him of a lie.

"How did you conduct the briefings of Harbour Island?" he asked.

"We had them with Miles and Sam."

"You had been here?"

"Yes."

He thought that this was probably true. He only needed one or two names to connect. Like "Alvin" or "Broderick." It was unlikely that PENMET would use a buffer in this operation because of the need for secrecy. Corinne was not going to tell him until he forced it out of her if he could. But maybe he could get some cooperation with the two leaders together.

"Bring in Sam."

One of the POLACO guards left and returned with Sam. He was also handcuffed and hobbled and wore an orange shirt and shorts. His hard body made the clothes fit tight. The guard brought in another chair. Edgar paused letting the situation sink in. The two officers had lost their command and they were now helpless before the people they had attacked.

"As you might have guessed from what you have seen from this facility, we have the means to make both of you answer questions or find out you don't know the answers. If you make us do that, we're going to file charges against you and your troops. In the Bahamas, I can assure you we are powerful enough legally to see that everybody gets a prison sentence. That is the risk you took. Bahamian prisons are not luxurious, hard labor is required. That helps the government keep the streets reasonably safe. There is one alternative for you and your people. That is that you tell me who sent you here and what you know about it, and I mean all that you know about it. We will then drop you off on another island and let your clients know where you are.

"So, you have the lives of fourteen people in your hands. Remember that five of them are women who will be regularly raped in prison. Your choice is freedom or incarceration."

"You'll give us assurances?" Sam asked.

"You have my word, subject to the approval of the board."

Sam and Corinne thought along the same track. POLACO would not add fourteen murders to the others they had already committed. They could imprison fourteen people through the judicial process, which they probably controlled. Sam looked at Corinne. He knew she wouldn't give in unless he gave her the order.

"Our client is represented by a man named 'Alvin,'" said Sam. "We know this client is a foundation of some sort. Alvin is a former Chief of Detectives of the Cleveland Police." Edgar waited.

"We were told that we were rescuing Daphne Poltrac and Sharon Gilling who had been inserted on the island as moles for a political campaign and had been suspected. We verified that in our reconnaissance when we saw your people watching them." Edgar still waited.

"That's all we know."

"The only person that you have ever seen from this client is this man 'Alvin'?"

"One other was 'Tony.' He was in charge and sailed the big yacht."

Good, God! Tony Destito had been on the attack.

"Do you have anything to add, Corinne?"

"No."

"Were you at the briefings with this man Alvin?"

"Yes," she said. Edgar concluded she could lie effectively.

THE POLACO TROOPS patrolled the island for two hours looking for any other penetrators. At 5:00 a.m. Edgar assembled them in the armory to which their armored personal carriers had returned. Four squads lined up in ranks of two. When he, Mike and Cybill entered, someone called, "Attention," and he heard the clicking of heels and straightening of arms. While they were at attention he walked along the rows and looked at each one. He then stepped back in front of them. "At ease," he said. "You were highly successful tonight and demonstrated your training and hard work. No disciplined force could have done any better or have been any faster. You captured every perpetrator and you took them by surprise.

There are still goals that we should reach. There are personal goals of this military business that I want each of you to imagine and to work toward. Tonight could have been a fiasco of confusion and lateness. As it was, the enemy was late; and you were on time and decisive." He congratulated them again and relaxed the training and duty schedules except to deal with the prisoners.

Ruth Farrencolt carried her Berretta from the van, which delivered her to her apartment. She had started the military training with Helene's suggestion and had advanced beyond Helene. Her body had new strength and she had a new perspective on what she could do. She was also newly aware of what she would and wouldn't do. She would lead effectively. She would not panic under fire. She would shoot to kill.

Back at her apartment she took off the gear to store it where it would be quickly available. If there were a "next time" she would be faster to get to the assembly area.

Jimmy woke up, "What was it?"

"If you were in the military you'd know," she said with disdain, which accompanied her battle-born confidence.

"I heard explosions and firing. Are you all right?"

"There were explosions and a lot of shooting."

"Who was it?"

"They were trying to rescue Daphne and Sharon. We captured all of them."

"Daphne and Sharon? Where are they."

"Edgar has them all. Now sleep."

She was naked as she crawled into bed beside him. He reached for her but she pushed his hand away. It had been brief, but it was combat. It seemed ethereal yet more real than any other experience. She had abolished fear and had done what she was trained to do. Her relationship with Jimmy was already affected as she claimed membership in the elite club of combat-tested soldiers. Forever after she would be in that club.

WARD COWELL LOOKED up from Edgar's written report with reluctant appreciation.

Edgar saw to the confining of the prisoners and then slept for an hour on the couch in his office and then rose to dictate his report. When he finished and had edited it twice, he brought it up to Ward.

"Looks like your people did a great job. Was it PENMET?"

"No doubt," Edgar reported.

"What have you told the town?"

"The constables are putting out a press release that a group of apparent bandits attempted to seize control of the town and rob the bank and other establishments. The constables were aided in thwarting the attack by the security forces from the institute. The bandits, well armed, but unprofessionally led, were enveloped by the constables and the security force and surrendered when threatened with a gunfight. Approximately seventy shots were fired by the security forces and the constables. Three bandits were wounded before they gave up. Three members of the institute security organization were also injured. The bandits are in custody and being held in the institute. They will be transported to Nassau or deported to the United States for trial."

"Sounds good, you should probably have Madeline look at it."

"I will,"

"Let me read your report. I'll have to circulate it to the board."

"I understand. I'll be there when you talk with them if you like."

"I appreciate it, Edgar," Ward almost sighed. "This is something I'll have to handle myself."

"Keep in mind that three of our people have been spying on PEN-MET and the campaign."

"But they're in no physical danger," noted Ward.

"Not from PENMET," Edgar agreed.

ANSELL AT THE helm of "Ranger" led Tony in "Winthrop" into the harbor at Spanish Wells. After the yachts had fetched up to the quay Ansell climbed aboard the larger vessel. In the chart room they went over the situation with a sullen Miles Ruskin.

"Sam should not have waited. That was the big problem. But, we thought Corinne would have to deal with jeeps and trucks and not armored vehicles.

"They just overran her to seal off the escape route," said Alvin.

"We didn't know that they had those big armored carriers?" Tony asked.

"No one did. Even if Corinne was dug in, she couldn't have stopped them without armor piercing rockets."

"If we had known of the armored personal carriers we could have taken weapons to deal with them," said Miles.

"If we had known about them, we wouldn't have tried this," said Alvin.

"This tells us about the character and intentions of that organization which built the atriums and the caves," said Ansell.

"The problem was waiting for Pat Stabler. She didn't show."

They walked to Ansell's house to use the phone circuits to report to Ian.

Shuddering at the risks he had taken, Tony had to tell Ian twelve soldiers and two officers had been captured, three of them had been wounded, and that POLACO was holding Daphne and Sharon.

"Don't blame yourself, lad," said Ian. "We did what we thought was best. We couldn't leave the girls there."

"I didn't count on a military fiasco," said Tony.

"Military fiascoes happen," said Ian. "What is your next step, Tony?"

"We know that 'Cynthia Reese' is a mole. We need to find the other one and trade. I'll phone Gibson." He wasn't looking forward to that.

"Aye, get some legal advice."

AT THE LAST regular meeting of the Senior Staff Committee in Chicago each of them realized a stage of the adventure was coming to an end. Anne said, "We have convinced a lot of people to vote for Adrian because of his reality positions with the issues and Hatford is riding a morality crusade which was our idea. Hatford is closing the gap. We should be on the morality crusade and running away with the election."

"The attack on the television broadcasters is producing the same result in our polls," said Alan.

"Shit."

"We haven't lost yet," said Terry. "Our main constituency of support is still growing."

"We need to give Hatford one more good shot to the jaw," said Anne.

"Karen's celebrity ads are doing well, I think," said Nancy. "And we also have our special source of information about what our opponents are doing next. We are responding rapidly to cut off the perceptions and half truths."

"We also have two excellent candidates giving speeches," said Terry. "We give them material that probably no campaign has ever had."

"Somebody stole our idea," said Merrick. "Remember that."

"It doesn't do any good to say it."

"What could be their last minute surprise?"

"They will appoint an Ambassador to Africa."

Everyone laughed, but everyone felt the intense stress. They had poured themselves into the struggle. A political campaign has only one chance. It all happens in as little as twenty hours, from the time the voting starts in New England to the counting in California.

The Daggett staff was tired. Helene and her Washington strike force were comparatively fresh even though they worked seven-day weeks.

TONY AND ALVIN flew back to Harrisburg leaving Miles to unwind the logistics. Tony walked into his office the next morning feeling sullen when Joan handed him the best news he could get. One of Alvin Carter's investigators had identified the second mole at the campaign as Michelle Proust who was being run by Bill Haber from an apartment in Chicago where Michelle spent most of her time when she was in the city. The girl that Nancy and others had praised highly for her work and who was already being considered for a job in Washington, turned out to be the spy who handed POLACO the Daggett program on moral advancement or "The Religion Bomb." Tony read through the report after Alvin, also back in the office, handed it to him.

"Pretty, dark-haired, sexy Michelle, whom we all came to love," said Tony.

"She was a good plant," said Alvin. "Talented, good looking, devoted to her boyfriend who turns out to be running her."

"What proof do we have?"

"A lot of circumstantial evidence and phone taps. We've also connected 'Cynthia Reese' to Paul Melius and to one of his operatives.

Someday we'll find out how they got into the village offices."

"American politics at its best," Tony observed.

"We should pick these people up and make a trade," said Alvin.

"Isn't that kidnapping?"

"It's not as bad as what could happen to them if we brought criminal action."

"You mean we would forcibly hold Haber, Proust, and Cynthia; whoever she is, and release them in return for the release of our moles and our mercenaries."

"That's the gist," Alvin said.

"It doesn't sound like a very even trade," said Tony.

"You have to have a meeting with Helene and let her read Ansell's affidavit. Make it clear to her that we know about the murders."

"It should turn the trick as far as making the deal. What's the closing?"

"We invite Slaughter to deliver the mercenaries and the moles to Ansell Monroe in Spanish Wells."

"I don't want Ansell involved any further in this," Tony interrupted.

"He's already involved and Helene knows about him. It's a convenient way to deal with this large group and also to deliver those who are still in the hospital."

"And when we receive our people, what should we do?"

"Ansell will deliver their people to their dock. We'll fly them down. Edgar can send someone to Ansell's house to see that they're there."

"It seems simple enough." And so he gave the order for Alvin to commit a crime. Actually, three crimes. Other executives would wrangle with this decision looking for options. Tony saw the answer clearly. If he wanted to get his people off Harbour Island he had to act quickly and use all of the resources he could garner. He also wanted to act quickly before whoever ordered the other murders might take some action. He reached for the telephone while he punched up Helene's cell phone number on his computer.

The call was forwarded to her office in Washington, so he knew she was in. She called back 45 minutes later. His secretary announced her and, at the last moment, he didn't know what to say.

"Hi, Helene, how's the war?"

"We're going to win, Tony, what can I do for you?"

"We need to meet."

"On the matter of the mercenaries and the two moles?"

"That's right. We have your three."

"I don't think that bargaining position is very strong."

"I have something to show you."

"I'm very busy, Tony."

"I know, but perhaps you could use the night off," he visualized her body and the smile in her eyes and felt male longing.

"I wish I had the time."

"You need to see what I have."

"Have you something to trade for the people we're holding?"

"I think you'll be interested."

"Your word this is a vital matter that merits negotiation?"

"My word."

"Where should we meet?" she asked. She thought of the other places. Manchester, Quebec, and then St. Louis. A flash daydream of the great stonewalls at L'Noite on Ille d'Orleans materialized.

"We could meet in Baltimore or Pennsylvania. The city or the country."

"Baltimore, it's closer."

"I'll be checked in at the Hyatt Harborside this afternoon by 5:00 p.m."

"I'll get there as soon as I can."

She phoned him from the lobby. He had booked a suite. When he opened the double doors she saw a buffet table with hors d'oeuvres of smoked salmon and trout with a bottle of chilled Chardonnay. By reflex she stepped toward him and kissed his cheek and then turned so he could take her coat. He lifted it from her shoulders and she turned around to him. "Hello, Tony, " she said looking into his eyes. He saw lines of fatigue in her face and a few gray hairs in her coiffure, always perfect. He gestured toward the buffet. She declined the wine, but picked up a plate and selected some salmon and trout which she laid on pieces of toast and added the capers, chopped egg, and onion. She accepted a glass of mineral water and then sat down in an armchair facing Tony who sat on the couch. On the table between them he set several files for her to look at. They were thorough and well-written presentments against Elizabeth Daley, Michelle Proust, and Bill Haber. After a few minutes Helene looked up at him and said, "It took you a while."

"We've known about 'Cynthia Reese' for several months. We also knew that there was another mole and hoped she would lead us to it. We then found there were two."

"So."

"We have them."

"What do you mean 'you have them?'"

"We have them the same way you have Daphne and Sharon, Sam Black, Corinne, Napier, and the others."

"We are acting on behalf of the Royal Bahamas Police Force. What's your authority?"

"We're acting on behalf of the people of the United States who will indict these three for theft of intellectual property if we submit these."

"You've kidnapped them?" Helene asked evenly.

"You might say."

"You must be very certain that we will be able to come to an agreement."

"Isn't it reasonable for you to release our people in return for yours?"

"Why should we do that?"

"To end it, Helene."

"We are in the process of examining if Bahamian laws were broken by your moles and your mercenaries. We have every right to turn them over to the Bahamian police."

"Who will do whatever you ask them."

"We are a large investor in the Bahamas. It would seem that you have already broken a law and that you are holding people against their will."

"We have captured perpetrators in the act of committing a crime of theft of intellectual property and other information. I would say that we are investigating the circumstances before turning the perpetrators over to the authorities and to a federal grand jury."

"So, turn them over. You're not going to have a trial. Our lawyers have already prepared the defense motions. They only need to be dated. The judges will wonder how fast this work got done. We'll plea bargain to a fine. Nobody will go to jail, and virtually nobody will care about a routine intelligence operation conducted by one political party against another."

There were changes in Helene since he first met her so many months ago. "I think there is more to it. There are connections to an organization called Joe Drago & Associates. We know you have employed them."

"What does that have to do with the moles?"

"In reading British law did you come upon the rules of a sealed affidavit?"

"Yes."

"I have for you, Helene, a copy of a sealed affidavit by someone you know. I'm quite sure you'll keep it confidential."

He handed her a copy of Ansell's description of the murder of Preston and Laurie. She speed read it first, her face whitened, and she read it then word for word. She then looked slowly up at Tony.

"Are you sure this is the truth?"

"Why don't you start arguing?"

"It's supposed to have been a shark attack. It happens you know."

"According to Ansell Monroe, the sharks only finished the job, Helene."

There was silence.

"Go on."

"If we don't get a deal, the affidavit will be unsealed and handed to the American authorities. Federal authorities will begin a thorough investigation and examination of all charters on the southeast around the date and position. They will request the cooperation of the Bahamian authorities in reviewing charters in the Bahamas on or near the date of the murders. The checks, the credit cards will all be traced."

Helene saw the implications. She didn't believe Ward had ordered murders, but she knew who would. Exposure of this incident could destroy POLACO. PENMET would be damaged in the fallout, but would survive.

"I think that you want to be sure that the affidavit remains sealed."

"For the time being, Tony." She paused and he realized what she meant.

"We want our people delivered to Ansell Monroe at Spanish Wells. We'll send your people to Ansell. You can have someone verify they are there. Ansell will then take them to your dock at Harbour Island."

She thought about it for a moment. "Okay, Tony. When?"

"Tomorrow."

"Can I use your phone?"

"There's a private line in the bedroom."

He waited while she talked with Ward. She found out he was under an interdict from Radion Gallosey concerning the prisoners.

Ward called, and at first Gallosey claimed the affidavit was phony, but the date time and position were correct. Ward accused him of putting POLACO in jeopardy with his insistence on the murders. Gallosey argued the necessity of eliminating those that knew of and were prepared to disclose the POLACO charter. He wanted to up the intimidation quotient by punishing the captured mercenaries. The prisoners would be delivered to Spanish Wells according to the agreement, but not necessarily in perfect health. Ansell Monroe would already have the three from the mainland. He would complete the deal.

When she left to go back to work Helene kissed Tony's cheek again. She didn't tell him the details.

WARD ASKED EDGAR to join him in the morning. "What do you think of the value of putting these men and women through punishment, Edgar?"

"It's not exactly what one does with prisoners of war."

"Is there a value in your judgment of letting the word get around that people like them ought not to mess with us."

"My suspicion is that word would get around that assignments against us are very risky, but I don't like compromising secrecy of our methods or facilities."

Carrie and Madeline came in, Ward told them what Gallosey wanted. Ward wished Helene was there and able to focus on the problem, but she was in the final days of the campaign. It was obvious that the matter had to be settled quickly. The other side was ready to prosecute three of their people and apparently had a clear understanding that Laurie, at least, had not died of shark attack. A search for the remains could be renewed at the position of the boat. Something might be found far from any point to which they could swim. An international police search was hardly desirable. Tony Destito had in his hand the weapon that could make that happen.

Ward called Radion about Helene's policy. Neither Carrie nor Edgar would order the punishment. Ward made Radion poll the board and without Helene it was 3-2 with one abstention. Sadovan joined with Gallosey and Bernt. Madeline then ordered the punishment and the interrogation of Daphne and Sharon.

Edgar had Sam Black and Corinne brought to his office and told them what was going to happen. Regretful as he was, he still had his orders and he indicated that they would be carried out in the early afternoon, after which the group would be delivered to Spanish Wells. He turned it over to Carrie to see to the punishing and record it by videotape for Gallosey. The large military bodies were strapped to the straddle and received 18 shocks. Sam Black went first. He got up from the bonds and put on his orange outfit. Several of the others except Napier collapsed and had to be assisted in dressing. One screamed at the first touch. There were five women in the squad. One was still in the medical ward. Corinne stripped first. When the bonds were released she painfully stood up and put on her clothes.

Madeline had many questions for Daphne and Sharon.

When she was brought into the room, Madeline motioned to Daphne to strip. Her slender, exercised body was attractive in every way at age 45. Her breasts were firm, her stomach only slightly rounded. As she was stretched back and her legs were buckled she was asked to list the people who were cooperating with her and taking information out of POLACO. She revealed nothing during the ordeal when Edgar intervened. Released, she fell to the floor struggling with the agony and was vomiting when they bought Sharon in. Sharon fought Madeline as well. Both were able to protect Pat Stabler. Madeline showed her inexperience. She conducted the interrogation as if she were questioning a witness. Edgar didn't help her.

Several POLACO detectives and crewmen directed by Mike Anzarra walked or carried the group in orange clothing ashore at a dock near Ansell's house to which they were ferried in golf carts. Betsy saw the activity and came out to look. Corinne waved to Betsy and took her to Daphne and Sharon who were in coveralls. She pulled the zipper down Daphne's chest to show Betsy that she was covered with red welts. Betsy yelled, "Who did this to these girls?"

"It's been done to everybody, Lady," a POLACO soldier stated.

"But why?"

"A lesson and a warning to anyone foolish enough to try something similar," said Mike Anzarra.

"The captives were not supposed to be harmed."

"You got your merchandise. My superiors are expecting ours," he said.

Edgar sent along a note explaining that the effects of the welts would disappear in 48 hours. The message was delivered with two boxes. Betsy opened them and found four dozen morphine needles. She retrieved her nursing kit and immediately administered morphine to everyone.

When Ansell arrived he found Betsy had mobilized friends to help. They had put Daphne and Sharon in their bedroom with ice packs. The three wounded were in the local medical clinic. Betsy took Michelle, Bill Haber, and Liz Daley to see Daphne and Sharon. The POLACO moles were visibly shaken at the evidence of their employer's cruelty on the skin of their PENMET counterparts.

Late in the afternoon Ansell had the POLACO moles handcuffed and taken to the "Ranger" still under charter. He took three of his crew in addition to Broderick Rose's detectives who brought the three to North Eleuthera. He formed a plan as he piloted out of the narrow

Spanish Wells channel.

A half-hour later they made their wake down the fairway between Harbour Island and Eleuthera and steered toward the POLACO dock. He gave two long blasts on his siren and went into reverse. In his glasses he could see the port captain and others form on the deck above the landing. He bullhorned across the water. "We take full notice of the sorry condition of the people you returned to us." Then he brought up the three to the deck behind the bridge.

"Sorry Lad and Lassies, but your colleagues were treacherous, as you have seen. You are going to swim in naked. It's the least we can do since we don't use cattle prods or the like on people." He turned and told Haber to strip. Haber looked at him incredulously. "Take off your clothes boy."

Bill obeyed and stood naked. Two of the seamen stepped behind Haber and lifted him over the railing to drop to the water. Michelle didn't believe it.

Ansell turned to her "I'm sorry to do this to you, Lassie, but notice has to be given." Michelle lifted her blouse and then undid her tennis shoes. In a moment she showed her body, firm and buxom with a broad shoulders, a flat stomach and small hips. The grinning seamen lifted her so she could stand on the rail. She had never tried a dive that high, but she went off straight into the water. The splash was small enough.

Liz took off her jacket and blouse which she had already unbuttoned, she handed back her bra and pushed down her shorts and panties and pulled off her sneakers. There was interest on the part of Ansell's crew to see if she was a true blonde. They lifted her to the rail and she dove in.

Bill Haber had waited for Michelle and they hugged treading water while Liz joined them. Ansell followed the swimmers in with two of Broderick's men on the bow with rifles in case there was a cruising shark. A seaman collected the clothes, sealed them in a plastic bag and tossed it in the water. Bill climbed up a ladder to a low platform just above the tide and helped Michelle and Liz. Then they climbed the ladder to the dock. Someone came running with tablecloths. One of the men gave Liz his shirt.

Ansell backed out slowly and then he cut in the port engine full ahead and made a power turn to the right and steered north up the channel. The Bahamian flag flattened out over his stern as the stars and stripes ascended the signal mast. Three long blasts on the powerful boat horn sounded across the water and echoed from the shore.

PAT STABLER WATCHED the scene with others of the staff near the dock. She was not fully aware of the capability of Edgar's troops. Had she been captured with Daphne and Sharon she would have been in grave jeopardy. Had she been waiting near Daphne's house perhaps she would be on the way home.

Louis stayed up after they returned to his apartment and then wanted to make love. When he was finally asleep she calculated that there wasn't enough time to sneak out of the compound on the ocean beach and run to Daphne's house. She tried to telephone, but heard noises on the line and quickly hung up. Outside calls at this time she suspected were tapped. A few minutes later she heard the gunfire in the distance.

She was in bed with Louis in the morning when they heard the news of the attack. Louis kept her informed of developments with the prisoners. Her life might depend on whether Daphne or Sharon were forced to give her name. She followed the prisoner exchange, and planned the only possible escape of swimming across the bay. But, as the POLACO moles swam ashore, nothing had happened. Perhaps she would live to resume her role as a mole for the other side.

☆ Chapter 35 ☆

TWO WEEKS BEFORE the election, POLACO and the Hatford campaign launched inundating issue advertising to swamp the Daggett effort. The Southern Conservative Coalition seemed to buy every available space that would normally be filled with network or local TV advertising. Anne's buyers pursued openings with the assent of Mitchell Fiddler and a guarantee from Ian for another $10 million from the Liberty Foundation. Contributions still flowed in as more and more people resolved to support Adrian, but more was needed.

The last major accomplishment of the intelligence operation on Harbour Island was to report that the Hatford campaign ads were going negative with a vengeance.

Well-directed actors and actresses offered a new "Harry and Louise." They asked, "What gives Dr. Daggett the right to treat the United States with his bitter medicine?"

In other ads, body bags, military funerals and combat photographs appeared behind a discussion of yielding American foreign policy to the United Nations.

Another narration condemned Daggett for a policy of unfettered foreign involvement. Another cited alleged failures by the UN. And yet another complained of the breakup of the American health care system and the mitigation of freedom of choice. One character swore he would never allow the federal government to tell him what doctor to use for himself or his family.

Positive ads, carefully mixed in so the others would not appear to be so negative, trumpeted the moral crusade of Steven Hatford.

WITH THE WARNING of a final week of negatives, Nancy scrambled Karen and Lucile back from get-out-the-vote commando duties in North Carolina and Georgia.

An emergency meeting started on Saturday morning. By 8:00 in the evening they had a working script for four new ads to respond to the negatives with positives. In each of the ads, characters evaluated the Hatford campaign as a campaign of perceptions and the Daggett campaign as a campaign of real positions that invited reality-based debate. Production was completed by Tuesday afternoon. On Wednesday, when the responding ads were released, the effect on the polls was tangible. By early Friday, the impact of the POLACO ads appeared to be blunted, but the lead nationally and in many states was within the statistical margin of error.

Disappointment swept over the Daggett organization. They had anticipated marching toward the election in triumph. Their belief in their candidate and their ideals carried them to that assumption. Adrian stood for truth. How could he be opposed? Yet, the opposition was effective. Its interests provided almost unlimited financing.

Karen, Lucile, Louellen, and Jack were dispatched back to the Carolinas, Georgia, and Texas to help advance the final rallies.

As the final weekend approached, the whole staff went mobile with the candidate to speed decisions. Terry, Anne, Nancy, and Alan had their last minute meetings on the plane or at hotels. The schedule moved from east to west each day, following the clock. On Friday, Adrian barnstormed through Texas with rallies in San Antonio, Austin, Fort Worth, and Houston. He jumped to a big evening party in the French Quarter in New Orleans, but still got to an evening rally in San Diego where his defense and aerospace ideas were cheered.

Richard Sandellot appeared in Raleigh, Winston Salem, Knoxville, Nashville, and Memphis. On Saturday morning, with Karen in the advance party, Adrian relived the debate triumph in Charlotte. They filled the convention center. Richard Sandellot joined him. A big rally was staged in Philadelphia at lunchtime. In mid-afternoon, the two appeared in Harrisburg and Pittsburgh and then went west to Des Moines to relive that triumph, then up to Denver.

Sunday morning began with Daggett in Boston for a rally on the Common, after which they boarded a train that had stopped in Providence, New Haven, Stamford, New York, Newark, and Paterson, New Jersey by late afternoon. The planes were at Teterboro to zoom them to Buffalo and a football stadium filled with screaming supporters. A little rest was possible from there to Wichita. After a rally in that aerospace town, they lofted over the Rockies to San Francisco where Union Square was jammed with people shouting, "We want Daggett!" Sandellot covered any cities they missed from the Carolinas to Ohio.

The final day for Adrian began in Pittsburgh, and went to Cleveland, Minneapolis, Omaha, Tulsa, Lubbock, El Paso, and to a final tumultuous reception at the Los Angeles Coliseum. After the ceremonies and Adrian's speech, the party went on to 11:00 California time and ended after the first traditional votes were cast just after midnight in New Hampshire.

From Burbank Airport, the planes lifted off and steered toward Chicago. Adrian and Pamela slept in the private cabin. In her seat Anne dozed thinking she and Nancy now had two speeches to write: the victory speech and the concession. Both had to be ready.

From the plane at O'Hare, limousines scooted the Daggetts to the airport Hyatt where they showered and changed clothes for the traditional picture of their voting at their precinct in St. Charles. Following the voting photo-op, a helicopter took them to the Hyatt Lakefront, which would be the headquarters for the evening. The rest of the senior staff dispersed to their apartments or hotels.

AT THE SUITE she had kept at the Old Blackstone Hotel, Anne found the door ajar and opened it to see Bob waiting for her. She dropped her suitcase and her briefcase and fell into his arms. He could feel the exhaustion in her. They kissed for a long moment.

"Oh, what if we lose?" she asked.

"You won't lose."

"But all those ads, all the negatives. They ambushed us."

"You replied to them and you had some advance word."

"I don't want to lose. I'm afraid we're going to lose."

He pulled up her chin, "I think you need a massage."

"Oh, yes."

She relaxed under Bob's hands. He had gone down her back and flexed her buttocks and then her thighs and finally her calves. Bob touched her to roll over and he began to flex the front of her thighs and the muscles. She reached for him to hug him while she went to sleep.

TERRY KNOCKED ON his door, after she opened it, Annalee

kissed him. He dropped his bags by the living room sofa and headed for the bedroom where he kicked off his shoes and sat on the bed. Annalee sat down beside him rubbing his head and then his neck. She took his coat.

"It's over."

"What do you mean," she said.

"I'm not sure we're going to win."

"I am."

"They were too much. We were bushwhacked." Much the same, he thought, as Miles Ruskin's troops.

"You're going to win, dear. In an even race the best man wins."

"Not when his opponent has the momentum."

"You may be surprised."

Terry, who thought two glasses of Merlot was a lot to drink, asked for bourbon. He sat with her and sipped it while they talked. He had just enough strength to undress and crawl into bed. When he was asleep she closed the bedroom door and went to the kitchen to make his favorite lunch, vegetable beef stew which would be ready whenever he awoke.

Lying beside Pamela, who quickly fell asleep, Adrian tried to make his body relax as he looked at the ceiling of the Presidential suite. Would he be the President who would one day occupy this suite on a visit to Chicago? Or would it be Steven Hatford?

In political contests, the decision was sudden and complete. Several hundred million dollars on one day; one moment in the history of the United States – a moment that could change that history forever.

Behind it all loomed POLACO and their objectives. Adrian was supposed to be the winner and form a new government to sweep away the frustrations of so many Americans, on which the parasites in the American system were feeding. They had to win. And if not, they had to be the opposition that focused the issues. Either way, his life would be irretrievably changed unless Ian MacAuliffe gave up or sought a new spokesman. He would not give up.

Pamela turned in her sleep toward him. He put his arms around her.

Nancy unlocked the door to her apartment knowing no one was waiting. There was no man to hug her in her exhaustion or to make her a cup of tea or a little breakfast. She thought about getting a cat. After carrying her luggage to her bedroom she turned on her shower and pulled off her clothes and hung them in her closet. The shower was warm. She let it flow over her from head to foot for five minutes.

She turned it off and toweled herself dry and made it to the bed, pulled back the covers and scrunched in. She had done the best she could. She thought about her mistakes and how desperately she wanted to win. But in the last weeks she saw the seemingly perennial Daggett lead fade. She had visualized Adrian's running the moral crusade which would enrich the reality campaign. Instead, through a mole, the Hatford Group found the issue and exploited it. Had she and Anne handled it the right way? Was it possible they could have turned it into a scandal?

She wondered where Tony was. Terry had imposed a ban on PEN-MET people coming to the celebration if there was one. Two hours later she awoke restless, frightened of losing. She put on a running suit and jogged to the health club. She swam for a half-hour. At her apartment she ate a piece of skim milk cheese with low fat ham and a pear. She fell asleep again.

Alan Jacobs turned the key in his lock and found Lauren exercising in a full-length leotard. She ran to him, kissed him and held him. "You look like you've come from negotiating with the Russians."

"It's discouraging, honey, we put on such a good show for so long. We have every right to win, but they took one of our things."

"You're going to win," she said and kissed him. "You are on the side of righteousness."

"How were the last days? They looked good on TV. How did they feel?"

"Real good, Lover. Hatford got stale; Adrian still projected. Not good to be down on an Election Day. You're supposed to have hope regardless of the polls, and your polls aren't that bad."

"It's the trend."

"Damn the trend. Maybe you reversed it with this madcap last four days. I think it was very strong. Don't you?"

"I hope so."

AT THE CONGRESSIONAL Country Club in Washington, Helene concentrated on a passing shot and gave it all her strength to get by Ross Chamberlain before he could move sufficiently to his left after a long baseline rally. She was pleased with herself about her tennis. As for the election, she had brought the Hatford campaign back from the abyss. She had cut the lead of Adrian Daggett to be even with her candidate. There wasn't anything more she could have done. She was confident of victory, but, if they lost, she would live to fight another day. Carefully toeing the baseline and focusing inside the centerline of the ad court, she served an ace.

Helene had arranged for three television sets to be brought to her suite in the Canterbury. She would watch the election alone.

KAREN HAD THE "heart-in-mouth" feeling so much she thought her throat was swollen. Day-by-day she watched the percentage decline into what the staff called "the red zone." The morality crusade, germinated around a concept that the Daggett campaign delayed too long to launch, caught the fancy of many people. It seemed to merge with the "Assuring Freedom" theme. It frightened her.

On Tuesday, after saying goodbye to the state leaders with whom she had worked, she took a Continental luncheon flight to Chicago. She hoped, she prayed, and she wondered what she would do if they lost. Earl was on a plane to Chicago from Sioux City; at least she would see him. Her next job was to be with the staff greeting the invited guests at the Hyatt ballroom. She and Earl would stay at the hotel. Would it be the last time as a Daggett person? Or would it be as a new form of Daggett person? She had a sinking feeling.

Ian invited Tony, Stephie and her husband and Alvin and his wife to the mansion for dinner and later to watch the returns in the theater. Tony would have gone with Jean to the state party in Harrisburg, but he wanted to concentrate on the presidential race, and he would rather be with Ian. She said she understood and she would be home late.

At Harbour Island, Ward invited the senior staff to a buffet and to watch in the main conference room. Louis, Ed, and Julie prepared a program which would pick up local returns, process them and project them to the conference room screen.

THE DOORS TO the great chandeliered ballroom of the Lakefront Hyatt were opened at 5:30 Central Time. Tables of chaffing dishes and salads were being readied to roll in. The bars were stocked and the television sets were on. Hors d'oeuvres were on tables by the bars. Karen, holding on to Earl, with Jack, Louellen, George King and Bernadette, Lucile and John Nattaire, and Merrick and Marianne were down on the floor greeting people as they arrived. All of the state leaders were invited to Chicago for election night, a decision made weeks before when a Daggett victory seemed obvious. Now it was not obvious, and there was tension everywhere.

Anne and Nancy arrived from the command suite to mingle for a while with the press. CNN snapped up Anne, who appeared glamorous but subdued.

"Anne, you have been with the campaign all the way, what's your sense of these last weeks and of this night?"

"We have lost ground in the last few weeks," Anne admitted, "but we are still the best hope for the future. It's going to be a close election, and it may be decided in the final precincts in California sometime tomorrow morning. If anybody is out there who wants to vote for Adrian Daggett and who hasn't, I hope they go do it. We need every vote we can get."

"You're not confident."

"I'm confident in the judgment of the American people and that they will get out and vote for Adrian Daggett."

Nancy, in an interview with CBS, also plugged getting out to vote, particularly on the West Coast.

Merrick, Marianne, George King and Bernadette greeted the senior state people as they came in and ushered them to the suite where Adrian heard their reports. A special dinner for them was arranged which Adrian would attend.

The senior staff was particularly interested in record turnouts. They soon found out they had gotten them in Massachusetts, Connecticut, New York, New Jersey, Ohio, Wisconsin, Minnesota, North Carolina, Tennessee, Texas, and California – the states where they had worked very hard. They also saw records broken in Iowa, Nebraska, South Carolina, Louisiana, Washington, and Alaska. Everyone thought a heavy turnout in most states would favor Adrian.

The main floor guests multiplied with every passing minute: party officials of every rank, campaign workers, state and city officials, and old friends of the Daggetts. Around the ballroom were six large screens, three on either side, and at the head was a tally board for the 270 electoral votes that were required for election. There were screens for each of the four networks, for CNN and for CSPAN. At the entrance, each person was given a small receiver which could be switched to one of the six channels or to the totaling board. An eighth channel was available for special announcements that were flashed on the television screens. Around the side of the room were television sets tuned in to cameras in Adrian's suite.

Karen, Earl and the group by the front entrance had smiles pasted on their faces while their stomachs were knotted. Tom Haynes and

Harris Winthrop and their wives and some other staffers joined in the greeting and explaining of the sound system.

In the command suite there were televisions for the networks and the tally board. Alan and his wife Lauren sat in the corner sipping diet cokes. Anne talked to Bob Wentz and fielded phone calls. Nancy watched two televisions simultaneously and also did phone work. In the ballroom and in the command suite, many eyes watched the minute hand as it clicked toward the hour of 6 p.m. Central Time when the first polls would close. The staff in the command suite turned to watch CNN.

"Throughout this day, heavy voting, including record turnouts, has been reported in a number of states," the anchor said. "Both camps have indicated they consider the heavy vote to be an advantage. The hour is struck and the drama will begin. Polls will now close in New Hampshire, Maine, Maryland, and Virginia within the next few minutes. They will also close in West Virginia and Vermont. We'll be back to the results after these messages."

"At the first significant moment we have to be asked to buy somebody's new car," Anne commented.

"At least it won't be a Hatford commercial," said Nancy her dimples showing. She noticed that Bob Wentz was standing close to Anne this evening to give her the vibrations of support she might need. Annalee similarly brought Terry some soft drinks and refreshments as he chatted with the state leaders and others. She wished Tony were there to support her.

Adrian and Pamela went into the banquet room to eat with the state people and to circulate around the tables. In the dining room there was one large projecting television set tuned to CNN. The anchor came back. Stillness fell on the gathering.

"Ladies and gentlemen we now have additional returns from New Hampshire and exit surveys indicate that Steven Hatford has won that state and four electoral votes by 52% of the vote. This was the site of Daggett's first great primary victory."

"It was not," Anne said to the screen. "We swept them in Iowa."

"Returns are going to be in shortly from Maryland with 10 electoral votes and Virginia with 13, where Adrian Daggett is not expected to do well," the anchor said. "In fact, CNN now projects Hatford the victor in Virginia and Maryland by a margin of under 2%."

The anchor turned to the gathered experts in the broadcast booth. "We now have three states and Adrian Daggett has lost each one," he said.

"New Hampshire is a tax-conscious state," an expert offered. "Daggett ran there in the Democratic Primary and swept it, but it is Republican. It is disappointing that Virginia and Maryland have voted for Hatford on the issue of the reduction of government employment. They prefer the present system by which the administration mollycoddles them for their votes. Daggett could have tremendous authority to cut if he can amend the Civil Service Act, which is one of the first legislative initiatives that he pledges."

"Won't that influence other states?"

"It may," another expert said, "but the military will balance the civil service vote. The military wants Daggett's no-nonsense foreign policy and reality in general. The people also want a lower government payroll and to dismiss incompetents."

"What do you think the most significant states will be?" The anchor asked.

"New York, Texas, and California are obviously important," the first expert said, "but I think significant ones will be New Jersey, Pennsylvania, the Carolinas, and Tennessee. Tennessee and North and South Carolina are states in great transition from agricultural to technical and industrial, with surges of new entrepreneurism. Pennsylvania is a composite of the United States. New Jersey is a national microcosm."

"So," the anchor said. "We'll watch New Jersey, Pennsylvania, North Carolina, South Carolina and Tennessee. Are there any telltale states in the midwest or in the far west?"

"Iowa has always been a signal state because of education."

The anchor interrupted, "We now have returns coming in from Vermont and West Virginia. In West Virginia, with five electoral votes, CNN has declared Daggett the winner by 56%. Are we seeing some kind of early trend?"

"We expected that the states around Washington would go for Hatford and they did. I don't think this is a trend."

"Florida, with 25 electoral votes will be one of the next states with the polls closing at eight o'clock Eastern," said the anchor.

"Daggett was four points behind in Florida in the last poll," a third expert put in. "I don't think that he should expect to take it. The retirees will vote against taxation. You may well see him lose South Carolina for the same reason, despite his victory there in the Democratic primary."

"We shall see," said the anchor. "Now these messages."

Terry paced up to Nancy. "What intelligence do we have about Pennsylvania, North Carolina, and Tennessee?" he asked.

"There was heavy voting in North Carolina and Tennessee," Nancy said, " but it was lighter in Pennsylvania."

"What is the effect of the Hatford morality campaign on the Bible Belt?" he asked Alan.

"The polls indicate we are going to be disappointed," said Alan. "Parker's final rundown was not to expect to win in Georgia or Alabama. He said the black vote in Mississippi might move it to us."

"What about Louisiana?"

"That's where we have a combination of greater New Orleans, the growing industrialization and the black vote."

CNN came back on with the anchor. "Results are coming in from Florida with 25 electoral votes, you can see that Hatford is leading by about 5,000 to 4,000" he said. The computers are now verifying the exit polls. As soon as the results come in, CNN will declare a winner. We have results coming in from Vermont, where CNN has declared Daggett the winner by a substantial 54%."

"Well at least we have won two," said Terry. "Can you find out if it was the aerospace workers or the academics?"

Nancy turned to her phone and punched the code for Parker Lothan. He reported heavy voting in both Rutland and Burlington, Vermont.

"Does that indicate the heavy votes favor us?" Terry asked.

"Too early to tell," said Alan. "But, maybe."

Mitchell Fiddler had stayed on one side of the room with Dominick Kluczynski while Terry was on the other. Terry knew Fiddler was ready to blame him.

At the dinner, Adrian chatted away with the state leaders while everyone picked at their food waiting for the 8:00 closings. After four minutes of advertising, the anchor reappeared.

"We should in a moment have results from polls closing at 8:00 in Pennsylvania, Florida, New York, Massachusetts and Rhode Island," he said. "Also Ohio, Georgia, and the Carolinas. At the moment, Steven Hatford has 27 electoral votes to eight for Adrian Daggett. But, here is a big change: Hatford has been declared the winner in Florida with 25 electoral votes. His total has leapt forward to 52 electoral votes."

"Where is New York?" Alan asked sharply.

"That last report is long lines of voters in precincts in New York City and in Buffalo. No information until all the precincts are closed," said Nancy.

The analysis continued for a few moments, then the anchor

announced an interview with Warren Hatch.

The reporter said, "Warren, these early returns must be heartening to you."

"They certainly are, we are doing very well in key states," Hatch said. "We thought this would be a real race; now I think a very decisive showing by the Hatford campaign will win tonight."

"To what do you attribute such a win?"

"I think that we have an excellent candidate," Hatch said. "The people have realized what Steven Hatford intends to accomplish. There has been a great response to his initiatives concerning American morals. This has turned the tide in a number of states. We raised a lot of questions about the real meaning of the Daggett campaign."

"Do you think you will win in Texas and California?"

"We will not need to win in California," Hatch replied.

AT THE CANTERBURY, Helene's cell phone rang. She fumbled for it in her purse. It was Sadovan.

"I hope you are well," he said. "I had also hoped to spend this evening with you to watch the returns."

"I'm fine. That would have been nice."

"I'm glad that you said that because I'm on a plane in flight to National Airport. Can I see you?"

"I'm watching the returns at the Canterbury Hotel."

"Will I find you there?"

"I'm sure that I won't be going anywhere until the election is over."

"Is the dining room suitable?"

"More than suitable, you'll like it. Mediterranean."

"May I join you?"

"I would be delighted. I'll book you a suite."

"What's the score?"

"52 to 8."

"In favor of Daggett?"

"No, Hatford."

"You're amazing, Helene. I look forward to seeing you."

CNN SWITCHED TO the Hyatt in Chicago. The reporter in the ballroom proceeded to explain the nine-way audio portables and the televising of Adrian Daggett's suite. He was interrupted by the anchor.

"There is surprising news from one of the indicator states," he said. In Pennsylvania, where the polls closed 15 minutes ago, Senator Hatford has been declared the winner and gets 23 electoral votes. He is expected to poll less than 52%. Hatford now has 75 electoral votes to eight for Daggett."

AT THE MACAULLIFFE mansion the dinner party was separated from the gaggle of the television, but Susan's village manager had volunteered to serve as the statistician for the evening and maintain a summary of the returns. He had sent in several 4x6 cards with the score mounting on it. When Pennsylvania happened he entered the room and handed one to Ian.

"My God, they took Pennsylvania," Ian said, handing the card to Tony.

"There was a lot of pressure against adopting the Daggett line by Pennsylvania Democrats," said Tony.

"Then maybe this is good news," said Susan.

"It could be, let's pray it is."

The door opened and Lucinda entered with the entree, a succulent salmon grilled in thin slices prepared by the village chefs.

Adrian Daggett came out of the dinner with the state people, who remained to watch the returns. He and Pamela quickly made their way to the command suite. He came up to Terry holding Pamela's hand. "What's happening to us?" he asked

"I think it's not having New York and Ohio report yet," said Terry. There is heavy voting in Cleveland, Dayton and Cincinnati; there are still lines at polls in Manhattan, the Bronx, and Brooklyn. Same reported in New England."

"75 to 8?" asked Adrian of no one in particular.

"In just a few minutes we are going to be ahead I think, Adrian."

"Please, God," said Adrian. He turned to the CNN program.

"We have some better news for the Daggett supporters," the anchor said. "Massachusetts returns were delayed by heavy voting, but now CNN projects that state will go to Daggett with 12 electoral votes. Daggett is expected to score 62%. Connecticut with eight electoral votes has had similar heavy voting and will also go to Daggett by a big score of 59%. Rhode Island, with four electoral votes, has also been awarded to Adrian Daggett with 61% of the vote. Indications are that the Daggett total has affected the congressional races in those states. We'll have more details later."

"75 to 32 sounds better," Pamela observed. They now anticipated the 8 p.m. Central Time, when polls are closed in many of the Midwestern states and all of the east. Adrian had hoped to go into the Midwest with a big lead.

A bulletin flashed across the CNN screen that all of the polls had closed in New York State and Ohio and returns would be forthcoming in a few moments. Again the network went to its advertising, leaving everyone in suspense. They turned toward the other stations. NBC was reporting.

"You have just seen that the polls have now closed in New York 45 minutes late," the NBC anchor said. "Under the rules, anyone in line is allowed to vote. The polls are also closed in Cleveland, the final closing in the state of Ohio with 21 electoral votes, where NBC is now projecting Adrian Daggett the winner by at least 58%. This is Richard Sandellot's home state, which the Daggett campaign expected to handily win and they did. The score of electoral votes is 75 to 53."

When CNN came back from its advertising, it announced early results from New York and awarded the state to Daggett with 57% of the vote putting Daggett in the lead with 33 electoral votes. It was Daggett, 86 to 75. A wave of relief passed through the people in the Hyatt suite and the ballroom floor.

"I wonder what Warren Hatch would say in his interview now," said Anne.

Terry knew the 9 p.m. Central Time hour would be decisive. He and Alan knew the states they had to carry. Karen saw Iowa and Nebraska coming up where she had worked so hard.

With the score 86 to 75, the first state to come in was Indiana. Its 12 votes put Hatford back in the lead. A long evening of counting in the District of Columbia found it going Republican for the first time in history to give Hatford 90 electoral votes. Delaware fell to Hatford with three electoral votes to make it 93 to 86. Just as soon as the new total was announced, Missouri with its 11 electoral votes was awarded to Hatford to put him at 104 and Maine, after a to-close-to-call race fell to Hatford with four electoral votes putting him at 108.

The CNN anchor said to his panel of experts, "It would seem now that Steven Hatford is back in the lead, but we have not yet heard from Illinois. With 22 electoral votes certain to go to Daggett, his total would also be 108 votes. At this point they are exactly tied. Did any of you expect this?"

"I had certainly thought that Adrian Daggett would take Pennsylvania, which would have given him a delta of 46 votes. I also expected that he would have taken both Maine and New Hampshire," one of the experts ventured.

"Do you believe this is a trend toward Hatford?"

"I believe the people are speaking," another said. "They seem to be wondering about the reality campaign. There has been an immense amount of advertising pro and con on the issues Adrian Daggett has raised, and now people are struggling to make up their minds. Many are clearly more comfortable with Hatford."

"What's our latest news from Texas?" Terry asked Alan, who went to the telephone and pressed the number for the Texas headquarters. "Heavy voting continuing in Houston, Corpus Christi, Austin and San Antonio that will delay the count."

The CNN anchor came back on the air to announce the official score at 108 to 108, with Illinois awarded to Daggett. The tie was fleeting, however. Arkansas, Mississippi, Alabama and Georgia were all declared for Hatford which, brought his total to 143 electoral votes.

"We're in jeopardy," said Tony to Ian as they sat in the MacAuliffe mansion theater.

"It would seem that it depends on the results of the states which the experts consider critical," Ian said. "Which ones are those?"

"We expect to win in North Carolina, South Carolina and Tennessee which he mentioned as bellwether states. We also expect to win Iowa, Wisconsin and Minnesota."

"What about Texas?"

"We expect to take Texas and California, Ian."

"I pray you are right," he said. He looked at Susan. The two of them had invested 80 million dollars in defending the American Constitution by electing Adrian Daggett.

When the commercial break ended, the anchor came back and remarked to his panel, "You have named several states as bellwether to Adrian Daggett. One of those was Iowa, CNN has now awarded Iowa with seven electoral votes to Daggett by a thumping 58%."

Karen jumped in her excitement and kissed Earl.

"Does Warren Hatch with his prediction of victory before California include Tennessee, North and South Carolina as well as Texas in his forecast?" asked the anchor.

"The way it is adding up right now, if Senator Hatford, who has already won five southern states, can also win in the Carolinas, Tennessee and Texas, he will win the election because enough of the smaller states are going to vote for him if the trend is as we see it."

The anchor interrupted, "We now have an interview with Alan Jacobs, the political coordinator for Adrian Daggett who is on the ballroom floor at the Hyatt Lakefront in Chicago."

"This is our first interview with anyone of your campaign's senior people, Alan. What do you make of the vote so far?"

"We are obviously disappointed that we didn't get the win in Pennsylvania and in Georgia which is a metropolitan state," said Alan. "But, there are still many states to come. You have already indicated that Texas, Tennessee and the Carolinas would be critical states in the analysis of your panelists. I think that is true. We also expect to win in Texas and California which, along with the probable victories in the mid-west, would be enough."

"Warren Hatch expects to win in the Carolinas and he said he will declare victory before the votes are counted in California."

"Those are his perceptions," Alan smiled. "We'll see what the reality will be."

"Thank you, Mr. Jacobs."

When Alan got back to the suite, he found Adrian with Terry and Merrick going over the numbers again. Without Pennsylvania it was too close.

CNN announced that New Jersey, with its polls open long after the scheduled closing, had voted its 15 electoral votes for Daggett by 55%. Shortly afterward Nebraska and Minnesota also were awarded to Adrian giving him a total of 145 electoral votes to 143. The lead lasted only five minutes when CNN awarded Kentucky to Hatford to bring his total to 151.

Then a worse blow fell. The anchor said, "Our panel has not called it a bellwether state, but CNN has awarded Michigan with its 18 electoral votes to Senator Hatford."

Hatford has increased his lead to 169 to 145.

"Damn Porter and damn Zimmer," Merrick said aloud.

"Where are the Carolinas and Tennessee?" Terry asked. "They are now super critical, we win or lose with them."

HELENE OPENED THE door to her suite and found Sadovan. She hugged him, kissed his cheek and brought him in. "Its up to three states, the Carolinas and Tennessee," she said. "We have taken Michigan and Pennsylvania away from them."

"What about Texas and California?"

"If we get the Carolinas, Texas and Tennessee, we win."

"You didn't answer my question."

"Heavy voting in Houston, San Antonio, Fort Worth and Corpus Christi. Not good for Steven."

"Let's hope that Dallas and the west overcomes it."

She took his coat and offered him a drink from the service bar. He looked over the beers and selected a Heineken. She sat beside him on the couch.

"Further bad news from the west for the Daggett camp," said the CNN anchor. "Arizona and New Mexico with early poll closings were expected to fall to Steven Hatford and they did. Colorado is considered to be an important state. CNN has awarded Colorado to Hatford with 52% of the vote and CNN has also awarded Utah to Hatford with 52% of the vote. This brings the electoral total to 190. Hatford is winning, and is 80 electoral votes away from victory. We have still not heard from three of the critical states on which our panel had focused. Why are the Carolinas and Tennessee so important?"

"These are the newly industrialized states which like, New Jersey, are microcosms of the voting blocks in the United States," an expert said. " They have a large African-American vote. They have a large number of expatriates from other states who have come there in technical jobs. They have high tech industries. Memphis and Nashville are growing like the cities in Texas grew in the 70s and 80s."

"Do they also represent Texas?"

"Texas is like these states. I believe in this election whoever takes North Carolina and Tennessee will also win in Texas."

Sadovan said, "Let's hope it's our man." He put his beer on the table.

She turned to him. "I'm glad you came."

"I'm glad I was invited."

While CNN went to its advertising, he gently took her chin and they shared a kiss. She came back for a longer kiss.

"IT LOOKS LIKE we have to take Tennessee, the Carolinas, Texas and California or they've beaten us," Terry reflected.

"The mathematics are not that promising," said Merrick.

"What are our latest estimates?"

"According to the last polls we will win."

"What's holding up North Carolina?"

"There are long lines and some kind of difficulty with the voting machines in several precincts that need to be ironed out before they are able to report."

"And in Wisconsin?"

"We are going to win there."

"Like in Michigan?" said Nancy, suddenly feeling terror.

"Late voting in Milwaukee. They will be coming soon."

CNN came back on from its advertising and said," We have long-awaited developments in the upper mid-west. CNN declares Daggett the winner in Wisconsin. He has taken that state's 11 electoral votes with a relatively wide margin for this election of 56%. Daggett has also been declared the winner in Louisiana with nine electoral votes which will make his total 165, still 30 votes behind Senator Hatford who has 195. In the states he wins he is influencing the congressional results. In Louisiana the margin was 57%"

"If Senator Hatford were able to win in the Carolinas, Tennessee and Texas he would not need California because Hawaii is most certain to go to him on anti-tax," an expert said. " Alaska is a question mark and Hatford might need Alaska to reach 270, but some of the mountain states are still voting. Nevada is not in yet and there is a possibility that Hatford could win in Washington and Oregon, which would put him over the top."

"So, Daggett has to win Washington and Oregon as well."

AT THE MACAULLIFFE Mansion the dinner party moved into the theater where Max Bradford was doing the tabulations. He had programmed his computer to show what states needed to be won for both candidates and had some printouts waiting.

"Is it possible that we could lose, Tony?" asked Ian.

"Don't even mention it," said Susan.

"The polls look good in the states that we have to take, Ian."

"I'm still going to pray for the people in California," said Alvin holding his wife's hand.

Stephie Comstock was less optimistic. "We've lost Pennsylvania and Michigan, two states we should have taken with 41 votes, and we certainly should have done better in the South," she said. "At least in Georgia."

"We expected that we were going to win in those states," said Tony.

"You're right, then why are we so comfortable with the polls in the Carolinas, Tennessee, Texas and California?" asked Stephie.

"Wider margins," Tony said.

"Let's hope they hold."

"I'm beginning to think that I should bring out the scotch instead of the champagne," said Ian. They chuckled. There was a small bar in the theater where Francisco was laying out glasses.

"I think an after dinner drink might be more appropriate," said Francisco. "Who would like B&B, Grand Marnier or Remy Martin?"

During their first sips, they saw Hatford declared the winner in Oklahoma and North Dakota. The anchor announced "Steven Hatford, with 11 more electoral votes, has broken the 200 mark with 206 versus Daggett's 165."

IN THE BIG suite at the Hyatt Lakefront, Terry, Alan and Nancy stood together watching CNN. It was as though a hurricane were approaching.

"Now, what do we have to do to make it?" asked Terry.

"We obviously have to take both big ones," said Alan.

"We've got one big one so far."

"How did we ever lose in Michigan and Pennsylvania? Anne asked. "If we had them, we'd be across the line if we win Texas and the Carolinas."

"We know that the Southern Coalition spent huge amounts of money in the mountain states."

"So did the campaign," said Nancy. "They were looking for the leverage of the senatorial electors and for states where they could win with money."

CNN broke in on the regular broadcast. "Ladies and gentlemen, we've just received word from North Carolina that the irregularities in voting machines which had delayed the count have been cleared, and we are now have reports that Governor Daggett is leading Senator Hatford in a rapidly totaling vote. With 15% of the precincts reporting, Daggett has the lead with 54%. CNN now projects him to win the state's 14 electoral votes. The count is now 206 to 179.

"Daggett has won big in North Carolina," said a panelist. "Now we'll see what happens in Tennessee."

"The polls have now closed in the state of Texas and voting is complete," the anchor announced. "In early returns with 4% of the precincts reporting, Steven Hatford has the lead over Adrian Daggett."

Ten o'clock Central Time came. The staff group watching CNN saw Utah and Idaho fall to Hatford. The anchor remarked to the panel, "Senator Hatford's electoral total has now reached 213 as he edges closer to victory. He is within 57 votes of the magic number of 270. Did you look for this sweep of the mountain states?"

"There has been heavy advertising by the Southern Conservative Coalition and by the Hatford campaign in the mountain area."

"So, Hatford can now do what Warren Hatch said, win without California?"

"If they take the pivotal states and Kansas they can do it."

"We've come to the moment of truth," said Terry.

"Whether the polls are right and whether we win," said Alan. Anne was too emotional to talk. Nancy took her arm and they half-hugged and watched.

"Ladies and gentlemen," the anchor said, "we have been informed that the Governor of South Carolina has ordered the polls in his state to stay open until the last voters have voted. This has apparently brought out more voters to cast their ballots. In any event, the polls have now closed and the count has begun. With 7% of the precincts reporting, Daggett has a big lead. There will be a decision there in just a few minutes. We have the first reports from Tennessee, where the polls were scheduled to close at 8 p.m. Central Time, 9 p.m. Eastern Time. They have, in fact, just closed at 10:14 p.m.. Early reports show Adrian Daggett is leading with 8% of the vote reported."

To the relief of the four senior staffers, CNN awarded both Tennessee and South Carolina along with Kansas and South Dakota to Daggett, raising his total to 207 electoral votes. The anchor then reported that with 15% of the precincts in Texas reporting, Hatford was now ahead by 1%.

Karen saw that they had won in the three states where she had been most active in the campaign in a liaison role. Would they win in the state where she had been mostly active in a communication role?

NBC picked up with Warren Hatch.

"Warren we have just seen NBC and the other networks declare Daggett the winner in the Carolinas and Tennessee," the reporter said.

"We still expect to win," said Hatch. We have enough votes to win if we take Texas, which we expect that we will. If we need California, we will take that too. The polls showed that Daggett was favored in Pennsylvania and Michigan and you saw what actually happened."

"You're confident of victory," said the reporter.

"The Hatford campaign is going to win tonight."

THE STAFF STAYED off the ballroom floor and watched the crucial vote in Texas. While that was going on, the polls closed in Washington and Oregon. In ten minutes, Daggett was declared the winner not only in those two states, but also in Wyoming and Montana, which asserted their invulnerability to saturation advertising, giving Daggett the lead 228-213 for only the second time.

"It comes down to Texas and California," said Terry.

"I shouldn't have emphasized that," said Anne.

"You spoke the truth, the best thing to say."

Alan went to the telephone while all the others felt the tension come back. He reported, "Polls are still open in San Francisco, Los Angeles, San Jose, Bakersfield and in the San Jauquin. Agricultural workers go to work in the morning too."

"I THINK WE have just suffered a blow," said Sadovan to Helene.

"We needed those states to win without California, but we can still win with California and one other state."

"The aerospace industry in Texas and California is very powerful."

"California has a large number of retirees."

"We'll have to wait and see, shall we order dinner?" Helene realized she was hungry. Sadovan suggested lobsters and a salad.

THE STAFF THAT had been with Adrian and Richard since the beginning concentrated on CNN. When it went to advertising, they watched the other networks. The campaign crew televising the events in the suite picked up some of the action and passed it down to the TV sets on the ballroom floor. The polls in California were still open after the eleven o'clock Eastern hour. In Texas with 31% of the vote counted, Hatford edged toward a slim lead. The music in the ballroom played quietly. No one danced. All looked at the screens operating their receivers. Applause broke out when, with 44% of the vote counted in Texas, Daggett took the lead.

Alan went to the phone. He came back and told Terry the votes were coming in from Houston, San Antonio and Fort Worth. The Texas headquarters in Houston reported that Lubbock and Amarillo had gone for Daggett by 4-5% margins and the same had happened in El Paso. "Looks like the Lone Star State to the rescue," he said.

The Houston vote increased the Daggett percentage and the Texas coast added margin. When 63% of the vote was counted and Daggett was 2% ahead, CNN declared him the winner with an estimated margin of 54%. Cheers went up from the ballroom and the suite. The score was now Daggett 260 and Hatford 213.

"Next time we'll have to remind everyone how close it can be," said Anne. "If we had changed 5 electoral votes we wouldn't care about California."

"We can win with Nevada, Alaska and Hawaii," Alan said. "By one vote."

"Unfortunately that's not likely to happen," said Terry. " It will be done in California."

"Lots of aerospace," said Nancy.

"Lots of retirees and Dennis Thomas," said Mitchell Fiddler, who joined them. At 10:45 p.m. Central Time, the bulletin finally came. The polls were closed in California.

"The early count will be from the places where the polls had already closed," Alan said. The count quickly rose to 14% of the precincts with Hatford in a 2% lead."

"If that's San Diego and Riverside county, it's good news."

CNN shot its broadcast to Hatford headquarters, where Warren Hatch was waiting.

"Warren, you have seen the race come down to the final big state as many have predicted, what's your thinking?" asked the anchor.

"We're ahead."

"Does your information indicate the senator is going to prevail in California and be elected? This is the closest presidential race since Wilson's re-election."

"We're going to take Hawaii and we expect to win in California. Senator Hatford will be the President-elect within the next hour. He has prepared his victory speech and will be giving it by midnight Central Time."

"Thank you, Warren."

The anchor posed the question to his panel, "To what do you attribute the victory in Texas, and what do you think will happen in California?"

"The Daggett campaign did a great job in Texas," a panelist said. "They had soft ads going of Texans talking to Texans about issues. There was a huge amount of advertising by Hatford in the last six weeks that sought to counter that by overwhelming the issues with contrary material of questionable logic. The majority of Texans in Houston and Fort Worth, San Antonio and down the coast to Corpus Christi didn't buy it."

"California? Anyone venture a prediction?"

"The aerospace vote in Los Angeles, the San Juaquin agricultural vote, the Silicon Valley techies and San Francisco and Oakland ought to do it for Daggett."

"Despite Dennis Thomas?"

"I disagree," said another panelist. "California is Hatford's."

"On that we will let the audience listen to these messages," said the anchor.

As the advertising came on CNN, the group in the suite turned to the networks. Merrick rejoined them. Terry asked Alan to phone California for the latest report. While Alan was on the phone, they were joined by Adrian, Mitchell and Dominick.

"The vote was heavy in San Francisco and Oakland and down The Peninsula," Alan said. "It was heavy in Los Angeles and Orange counties and very heavy in the San Juaquin. A challenge has stopped everything; there was apparently something wrong with the voting machines that led to the delay."

"What's the forecast?" asked Adrian.

"By the latest poll, we have a good chance."

"But, Hatford's still ahead," Mitchell observed. He wanted to win, but if they lost his views would be vindicated.

"Should we send Merrick down to meet the flesh eaters? They have been feeding on our younger people. Karen, Louellen and Jack need some relief."

"It might be a good idea to let them know that we are still here," said Anne.

"Wear your flak jacket," Nancy joked. They laughed nervously.

Merrick appeared on the floor and strode to the stage. He was immediately engulfed in television reporters, one of whom seemed about to jam a microphone down his throat. Several of the security people pushed them away. Merrick climbed onto the stage and stepped up to the microphones.

"On my own behalf, I want to thank all of the state leaders who are here with us tonight for their momentous effort in what we hope will be a victorious campaign," he said. A cheer went up from the audience anxious to cheer something.

"Governor Daggett and Pamela; Richard and Martha Sandellot; the senior staff and the other guests are in the suite, as you can see by the television originating from there. Because of the great effort everyone has put forth, we believe that victory is forthcoming. We will win in California."

A loud cheer rang out in the ballroom.

"But," said one reporter, "Senator Hatford is ahead in California."

"We know that."

"But how could you claim the state if Senator Hatford is ahead?"

"He was also ahead in Texas in the early count."

"Have you seen our interviews with Warren Hatch? He also claims that his polls show they will win in California."

"I'm sure that they have very competent polls, but we may have a different technique in polling or we may read the numbers differently."

The broadcast of Merrick's statement gave way to the CNN anchor on the screen.

"The race is coming to the finish line with both sides claiming victory," he said. The Republicans are slightly ahead. With 27% of the vote counted in California, Senator Hatford has a 51% lead. Governor Daggett has something less than 49%. This vote is too close for CNN computers to call. Now these messages from our good advertisers."

"Just the right touch," said Nancy.

"What would you expect from Merrick?" asked Anne. They went back to watching the California total which was now in the center of every screen. The count slowed because of the voting machine difficulties in the area of Bakersfield. Nancy occasionally had a nervous twitch in her left eye. She felt it start.

The CNN anchor returned. "This is a remarkable election for its closeness and it has been a remarkable election for its dichotomy," he said. "There has been a real difference between the proposals of Adrian Daggett and those of Steven Hatford, who represents a more status quo approach to things. It now appears that Adrian Daggett will win the popular vote, regardless of who wins in California, by at least 52%. Senator Hatford, if he wins would be only the second president to take office without a majority or plurality of the popular vote. Further, in the states where he has been victorious, Adrian Daggett's coattails have been very strong. Senator Hatford, if he wins, will face a Democratic congress with a majority of about eight or nine votes. While that majority is not necessarily alarming, the Democratic majority means that all the committee chairs will pass back to the Democrats. The power of a committee chairperson to influence legislation and the direction of events is substantial."

KAREN AND EARL were talking to the NBC people off camera when a cheer went up in the ballroom. Adrian Daggett had suddenly taken the lead with 43% of the precincts reporting. Ten minutes later it changed back for Hatford with 47% of the precincts reporting. No one could do anything but watch. There was no music; there was no dancing; there was just the count. Each tenth of a percent change in the vote total brought applause or groans.

CBS brought on Warren Hatch. "Are you still confident that you're going to win in California?"

"We have virtual proof that we are going to win from our polls," said Hatch. "We're doing well in Orange and Riverside counties and we expect to do well on The Peninsula and in San Francisco. We see a pattern coming together."

"Judging by comments from the Daggett suite, they think you're not going to take enough votes in Riverside County or Orange County to overcome the aerospace and related votes."

"We'll stick by our polls and the Daggetts can stick by theirs."

"Thank you, Warren. Back to you."

Only the murmurs of quiet voices could be heard in the ballroom; there was silence in the suite. The thoughts everyone had of victory or defeat ran through their minds. They watched Hatford's lead click down two tenths, then up one, then down again and then down to even. It went back up; then Adrian took a lead of a tenth. A cheer went up and then silence again.

Adrian held the small one-tenth of a percent lead for several minutes, then suddenly he went to three-tenths, then back to two and down to one and Hatford took the lead of a tenth with 54% of the precincts reporting.

"That's ominous," said Terry.

"Let's hope the late polls are coming in last, they will be our best," said Alan.

"Pray for the people who do the stoop labor in the San Juaquin Valley," Nancy recited.

"Pray for those who bend over their computers in aerospace and silicon electronics," said Anne.

All was quiet. Hatford held his lead and then expanded it by a tenth. He then fell back and Adrian jumped ahead. There was a loud cheer in the suite and on the floor because it was a full three- tenths jump. He quickly added another tenth of a percent and the lead grew. Each advance was cheered and the floor began to buzz. In the suite, Alan gave the thumbs up sign to the camera. The count advanced past 70% of the precincts with Adrian up to a 1% lead. At 85% the lead was more than 2%. CNN flashed that there would be a decision, but ABC was first. Their anchor said, "The ABC election center computers having now evaluated the data from California, where Adrian Daggett leads by 2.2%t with 86% of the vote counted, now project that Adrian Daggett will win the state of California and with it, Ladies and Gentlemen, the election."

The multitude in the Hyatt ballroom went wild. Some jumped up in the air while others fell on their knees. The band started to play "God Bless America" and everyone sang it and felt it. Adrian was overcome by feeling. Anne came up and hugged him. Everyone was hugging. Than everyone came to embrace Adrian and Pamela.

In the ballroom Earl hugged Karen and they also shared a long kiss. Tears streamed down her face. They embraced Louellen and Jack. Lucile wept openly, holding on to John.

As the cheering continued on the floor of the ballroom, Adrian spoke to the gathering in the suite. "I think at this moment all of us may have something to say to our God," he said, "and perhaps we should hold hands and say it silently, although I may add a few words."

In silence they formed a circle around chairs, couches and tables; everyone held hands.

With his voice nearly breaking, Adrian said, "It has pleased Almighty God to sustain our spirits, to enrich our intellects, to inspire us to high goals and to warm the hearts of the people who have elected us. Let us ask that He give us the energy and the strength to achieve as we go forward, and that He nurture and sustain our high goals."

When they broke up, there was still more hugging and crying. Louise Sczyniac was sent to the floor. When she arrived at the podium, applause and cheering broke out anew. After an appropriate time the music was waved silent as she leaned toward the phalanx of microphones. She looked fresh, her dark hair shining, her eyes glistening.

"Ladies and gentlemen, as you have all received the word of the networks' decision concerning this election, we send our good wishes to Senator and Barbara Hatford and the others who have worked so hard. We have been the fortunate victor and we would like to give Senator Hatford the opportunity to speak first as soon as he is ready, but by 12:30 a.m. Central Time. We offer him the opportunity to receive the acclaim of his people first. Thank you." There was applause all around the room. The media was stymied. Louise smiled and left.

AT THE CANTERBURY Hotel, Helene was snuggled beside Sadovan with her head against his shoulder. She felt his warmth and he felt hers. "I should call Warren and tell him to take advantage," she said. "That was a nice gesture."

"They should consider any possible challenge," said Sadovan.

"That never works," said Helene. "It's a waste of time and money. Maybe you would like to have some kissing time while we wait for the speeches. She twisted herself so she was on his lap facing him and they began to kiss. After a minute he ignored the television.

IN ST. LOUIS there was a council. Warren wanted to challenge the registrations in the San Juaquin Valley. Would they find irregularities? Carolyn wondered if they should let Adrian claim it. Someone called the Hirsch Organization and the projection was confirmed.

Hatford wanted to wait as long as they could. He knew, when the agricultural union began to quietly register their people in Southern California and in the San Juaquin Valley. Louis Fisher tracked the effort. Helene, Steven and Carolyn knew considerably more about it than the Daggett campaign whose California leaders were never officially informed. Carlos Himenez wanted to make sure of California. He did his work well and made no mistakes.

Carolyn, with tears in her eyes, handed Hatford the concession speech.

With 91% of California reporting and Adrian leading by 2%, Hatford made the traditional phone call to offer Adrian his congratulations. "I want you to know that we sincerely believed that we would win this," he said. "Warren Hatch wasn't bullshitting; that's what we thought."

"You had good grounds to think that," said Adrian.

"I don't think you realize what you have done," said Hatford. "You have turned politics upside down. You have defied what had been accepted practice over the past 30 years. I just can't believe it."

"I hope you'll help us make the key reforms," said Adrian.

"I'm going to have to think about it," said Hatford.

At 20 minutes after midnight Central Time, Steven Hatford entered the ballroom of the Adams Mark Hotel to a loud standing ovation. He smiled all around the room and Barbara was behind him. A chant started: "RECOUNT, RECOUNT, RECOUNT!"

Steven Hatford, smiling, shook his head. In gracious remarks, he profusely thanked his supporters and workers and conceded the election. There was no word of future cooperation in the nation's interest.

Inside a gaggle of Secret Service men and women, he went into the crowd with Barbara, Carolyn and Warren to greet everyone. The cries for a recount subsided.

WHEN THE TV networks switched back to the Hyatt ballroom, it was vibrating with anticipation. The TV camera in the suite showed Adrian and Pamela leaving amid a small crowd. The Secret Service appeared in the ballroom for the final check, then Adrian and Pamela, followed by the staff with their spouses, came out on the platform. Pandemonium erupted. They stood at the podium and waved at the cheering, happy crowd. As they recognized people in the crowd, they pointed and waved. Adrian turned and gestured to the staff to come forward.

In every state, in every city and town, in their homes or clubs or in hotel rooms tens of millions of people joined in the moment. In millions of living rooms, families clapped along with the applause on the Hyatt ballroom floor. The reality campaign had won. On their televisions they heard the anchors commenting on who was there and saw close-ups of the staff people, some of whom they would soon know well.

Then the crowd realized it wanted to hear what Adrian wanted to say. They responded to his raised arms. He thanked them for their hard work, and for their support. He introduced Terry, Alan, Anne, Tom Haynes, George, Merrick and Nancy. He embraced each of them and their partners. Richard did the same again to rousing cheers and a chant of DAGGETT, DAGGETT, DAGGETT.

Adrian then offered his good wishes to Senator Hatford and his staff and said that he looked forward to working with him on the issues on which they agreed, particularly on the moral crusade. He said it was time to savor the victory, but not to savor it too long because of the huge tasks ahead. Their reality government was chosen by the American people and now they had to deliver.

He also said that they should continue the party, but the budget had run out and they could only afford potato chips, pretzels and beer. Mitchell Fiddler waved and said they could do better than that.

Adrian asked the band to start playing. It was a lively tune and he turned to Pamela to dance. For an hour the staff and the candidates were part of the crowd. They danced with wives and husbands as they met. They toasted victory with the champagne Mitchell had personally ordered for everyone. With some idea of the huge audience they had, the networks and cable channels stayed on it.

AT THE MACAULLIFFE mansion champagne was passed out while they watched the celebration. Ian offered overnight accommodations for everyone, but they declined. Alvin lived close by. The Comstocks and Tony headed for Harrisburg, Susan and Ian went to their bedroom suite.

" I wish we could be in Chicago," Ian said, as he slumped onto a sofa. "I would like to feel what's happening and see the people."

"So do I, but Terry and Anne are right," said Susan. "We can't give the demons any hints. Any attack on you automatically becomes an attack on Adrian. Lets have our own toast." She went to the refrigerator in the pantry. The confidential phone line in the bedroom rang. Ian picked it up, and a security officer informed him he had a call from the president-elect.

Ian chuckled and told him to put the call through.

"I didn't think you would be sleeping," Adrian said. "And I wasn't going to end the night without calling you."

"Well, I'm very glad you did," said Ian, "so I can offer my congratulations."

"I should be offering the congratulations," said Adrian. "I couldn't have done this without your help."

"I was the one who asked for your help," said Ian.

"Well then, thank you for asking me," Adrian said. "I'm going to fight to save this country, and I consider this the highest honor a man can have."

"We've only fought round one," said Ian. "But I have confidence in you. I remember a saying from the Book of Tao, which I read in my student days: "When the country is confused and in chaos, loyal ministers appear.'"

"Thank you very much for the opportunity," said Adrian. "I hope you don't want Nancy back."

Ian chuckled.

"Just stay away from Stephie Comstock," he said. "Get Mitch Fiddler for your Office of Management of Budget. And don't bother Tony Destito for a while. He's going to have his hands full with this company."

"Thank you," said Adrian.

As the party wound down at the Hyatt, the word was passed to all of the permanent staff members to gather in the suite. Adrian thanked them all and invited them to lunch that day at 1:00 p.m. in a private dining room at the Hyatt. Then he, Pamela, Richard and Martha hugged them all again and sent them to bed. At the end it was Terry and Annalee with Adrian and Pamela.

"It came out the way you predicted," said Adrian.

"Our enemies were vicious," said Terry.

"I hope we discouraged them."

"I expect not," said Adrian. "You and I have discussed the transition. Tomorrow I would like to give everyone their prospective assignments. Shall we meet at ten? Anne wants to have a press conference at 4:00 p.m.."

"To show that we are going right at it, I agree," said Terry.

WHEN THEY GOT inside their hotel room door Earl spun Karen to him and held her tightly and kissed her. He felt her lean body against him. "I told you we would win."

"I'm drained."

"I know you are."

"Let's take a shower, I've been in a cold sweat all night."

When they had toweled dry they snuggled under the covers.

AT HIS HOUSE, Tony found Jean sitting in the library. He put down his coat and asked her if she would like a refill. She held up her glass and he poured some more port and filled a glass for himself. Her dress was several shades of blue and white and off-the-shoulder, showing off her hair and her tanned skin.

She looked up at him, "Go ahead and say it."

"Say what?"

"That we almost lost it for you."

"I never thought that."

"Two big states didn't follow the Daggett line, Michigan and Pennsylvania, and we lost in both."

"How many seats did you gain?"

"Only one. The Senate was very close."

"Well you won."

She didn't respond.

"Why don't we carry these up to bed?" said Tony.

"I think you should sleep in the guest room tonight," Jean said.

"What's this about?"

"I don't feel like sleeping with you. In fact, maybe you should plan on sleeping in the other room, at least when the children aren't here."

"Jean..."

"No, Tony, not tonight. I've been unhappy for a long time. I think there is only one way out."

"Jean, I don't want that way out."

"You're never here for me or for the children. You're cheating, I think."

"I think you're cheating," he said.

"Maybe I am," she said. She grimaced then looked him crudely in the eye. "Maybe that is what needs to come out. I like being with another man, Tony."

"It's too late to talk about this."

"Just sleep in the other room."

He went into their bedroom and gathered up the clothes he would wear tomorrow and took them to the guestroom. He found his suitcase which always had a toilet kit ready to go and he used that for brushing his teeth and taking some Pepcid. He took a tranquilizer. There was no sense in thinking about it now. He needed rest and tomorrow he would contemplate the cost of the Adrian Daggett victory in his personal terms.

Lying down on the bed, Tony thought briefly about Helene and their pledge in Quebec to be there for each other when it was all over. That pledge was a long time ago. They were on opposite sides, and it was far from over.

On impulse he took out his cell phone and called Nancy's apartment. He got the answering machine.

"Hi, this is Tony," he said. "Congratulations."

AT THE CANTERBURY, after the victory statement, Helene snapped off the television set and turned to Sadovan, " I don't like to lose," she said.

"Neither do I," he said, "but sometimes we must accept it."

She looked into his eyes and reached to pick up her drink and sipped it. "It's not over yet," she said.

Why don't we just go to bed and sleep as long as we like and we'll talk to Ward after breakfast."

"I think you need a day's rest or more."

Helene thought she would want to sleep, but after she undressed and he came into the bedroom she beckoned to him. He was such a good lover, why waste the opportunity?

PAMELA AND ADRIAN were finally alone in their suite as the secret service man bid them good night and closed the door. She turned to him and put her arms around his neck and kissed him. "I'm so proud of you. I love you, Adrian. I know you are going to ask a lot, but I will do it. I will do what you ask."

"For so long it didn't seem like a struggle and then all of a sudden it was."

"I know. The struggles to come will be worse."

"We are going to prepare the staff for that tomorrow." She saw someone had placed a bottle of champagne in ice with fruit, cheese and crackers on the coffee table.

"Let's get our clothes off and have a quiet toast."

She wore her favorite Japanese robe and he the one supplied by the hotel. They sat together on the couch and kissed again. In a while she twisted the cork off the champagne and blinked when it popped. She reached, handing Adrian a glass and poured his champagne and then her own. They clinked glasses and she looked into his eyes. "Victory."

"There are going to be many fights. I appreciate what you said. Our lives haven't been our own since Ian came out to see us. Now they really won't be ours."

"We will have to try for little bits of time."

She scooched over to him and hugged him. "You're too tired to think, or even to talk."

"Some sleep." He went to the bed and took his robe off and climbed in between the sheets. He watched, admiring her, as she removed her robe and lay it on the sofa. She turned out the light. He fell asleep feeling her warmth.

THE "MORNING AFTER media ritual" was interviews with the winning staff. The Today show tracked down Anne for half an hour of the 7-8 a.m. segment. She was cheerful and bright at 6 a.m. Central Time with barely three hours sleep. Alan was on *Good Morning America*, Nancy on CNBC. Terry, exhausted, appeared with Merrick from the hotel on the early segment of the CNN morning show and then on BBC and CBC. They saw each other in the lobby, as those going to studios were collected by limousines. Anne and Nancy appeared on the PBS *News Hour*. Terry went on *60 Minutes*. Nancy agreed to a long interview with CSPAN. All were signed up for the Sunday shows. Pamela agreed to *Larry King Live* and *Oprah* so she could get some sleep and wake up with Adrian. Even Karen got a call from CNN to join with Jack Wood and Louellen for a special sequel on the campaign from their perspective.

At 10 a.m. with juices flowing, Adrian came into Terry's office. He closed the door and Terry rose from behind his desk. They shook hands, "A superb job, Terry, worthy of all the compliments you have received."

"Yours is the victory, Adrian. A lesser man would have failed."

"I've come to ask you to be my White House Chief of Staff, and if you accept we will proceed to discuss the forming of an administration."

"You still want to see me everyday?"

"I don't want anyone else in that job, Terry."

"I would like to be able to say 'no'."

"Why's that?"

"I would rather have an agency."

"The power is in the White House until we change it."

"I know that. I accept." They shook hands again.

"I want to show that an administration is being formed and the transition is developing quickly. Would you also head the transition team?"

"If you'll give me a week off."

"If you must," Adrian joked. They laughed.

"The first thing I want to do is reorganize the White House staff. There are too many positions, too many senior people, too many overlaps and too much intramural politics."

"We can pare down to all the positions that are legislatively required."

"Probably, then we'll let people build their own organizations as their missions require."

"Just keep in mind there is a fearsome amount of traffic from Capitol Hill, from the agencies, from business and the special interests, and from the public. It all has to be handled."

"I would like to give everyone who has been with us their prospective roles. Something to think about while I order them to take some time off. I have a list."

"Then shall we look at it?"

"Richard will be here in a few minutes. We can write each one a note."

"Reality One" was dispatched to Cleveland to pick up the issues staff. Adrian, Pamela, Richard and Martha were at the door of the small ballroom where the luncheon was to be held. They greeted everyone individually and thanked them for the great effort.

It was a happy if still tired group, particularly the ones who had obliged the media. When dessert was served Adrian went to a single podium. Richard stood and went to one of the secret service agents for a portfolio which he had been told was highly confidential and to be given only to one of the two candidates. In it were the notes they had written.

"I told you once before that at the lowest moments of moods, I would think of this staff and be quickly rejuvenated. You are publicized to be the best that ever ran a national campaign. There is no doubt that you are." They cheered. "Now, however, you face an even greater challenge. That is to govern. The majority of the American people voted for a great change in Washington. They want the government to tell the truth and to face it. They have voted away government by public relations so long practiced. We must deliver on all of our promises to accomplish that." There was more applause and cheers.

"We're up to another vacation time again," Adrian said. "I want everyone to get a good rest. A week from Monday we'll be in Washington at Blair House and I want each of you to visit." Terry, after being persuaded that he didn't want to be a cabinet officer, accepted the job of Chief of Staff at the White House. Tom Haynes with a promise of a lot of action will be Richard's Chief of Staff. The White House Staff will be much reduced. Everyone will be too busy with the business of the reality government to have any time for infighting which has engulfed and deteriorated many recent administrations.

"We want to make a few announcements today. Richard has an envelope for each of you suggesting what job we'd like you to consider. You have ten days to think it over and tell us what you'd like. For now; Mitchell Fiddler will be the Director of the Office of Management and Budget; Nancy will be Director of Communication; Merrick will be Director of Congressional Affairs; Alan will be the Director of Political Affairs and Anne will be Domestic Policy Advisor. Now we can bring this to a close. Thank you all for your hard work and great enthusiasm. God bless you all and keep you safe in your travels. Thank you." They applauded some more and then a line formed at the door.

When Earl looked up the salary of Karen's job as Special Assistant for Legislative Affairs, he was astounded. It paid $72,000 plus the use of a White House car with full expenses. "I'll have to spend some on clothes," she told him after they watched the afternoon press conference.

"We also will need an apartment in Washington. There will be a lot for sale. You need to be close to the White House or the Capitol."

"I'd rather be away from it on weekends. Washington is also expensive. We need to save."

"We'll live on your salary and save mine. How's that?" She turned to him when she realized what he meant. He embraced her and kissed her and told her he would start looking for a job in Washington when they returned from Montecello, Davenport and five days at the Tanque Verde Ranch in Tucson. In Montecello, he told her, he would ask her father for her hand. She was sure, she said, that he would agree.

MENDOS SADOVAN AND Helene sat together in the rear of his airplane after it took off heading due south from Bridgeport after they had brought Helene's children home. He had picked them up there and was host for Quebec City and skiing at Mont. Saint Anne. They stayed at the Chateau Frontenac in separate rooms except that Helene's adjoined Sadovan's suite. She woke up the next morning and felt especially happy that her children would be with her that day. She sensed they were happy that she was with them. She hoped it wasn't the luxurious lifestyle that Sadovan could afford. The price she had to pay was missing them. There had been many weekends during the campaign and now she would be back at Harbour Island. She would see what would happen next, although she could probably write the script.

Sadovan had the plane land at Fort Lauderdale in time for Helene to catch the afternoon Continental flight to North Eleuthera. He arrived first and waited for her with Ward Cowell. The occasion was a meeting of the Executive Committee. Radion Gallosey, Ryan Keeley and Alex Peterson were playing golf. Bernt Umrich, sailing from Great Harbor, had radioed that they had passed Spanish Wells and would be at Harbour Island for dinner.

They ate on the terrace with the ocean breeze smelling sweet and the splashing of the waves in the background. A full moon rose red over the water. It was idyllic, except the meeting was scheduled to start. In an hour it was clear that the mandate to POLACO was to resist Daggett in every possible way and to switch the Congress against him at the mid-term election. At the end Helene thought of the things she would do in Washington. Certain special interest and single-issue constituencies could be aroused against Daggett picking the right policy points. The irresponsible or unknowing Republicans would be fertile ground. She would form alliances and would leverage the skills of the staff and the resources of Louis Fischer to stop the Daggett initiatives. The war plan crystallized in her mind. It included Rollin Tinton at the job of unseating Daggett supporters in Congress. Erla would complete her ideologue philosophy. Perceptions would rule again. Perceptions that confused reality and prevented understanding by the electorate. That was her job. She bid them all "good evening" knowing Sadovan would join her in her apartment. He found her on her balcony. The moonlight made diamonds glisten on the waves. It was so bright she thought she could feel the pink of the sand.

THREE HUNDRED MILES to the west, trailed by Secret Service agents, Adrian and Pamela walked on the beach at Fort Myers under the same moon. One stress was over; a new one was about to begin. Tomorrow they would fly to Washington. Adrian, rested, looked forward to seeing his people again. They had won the opportunity to serve. They would make momentous changes. The fate of America and the world could depend on their success. Every time he thought of that he prayed briefly.

Pamela was awed at what they faced. As a student she was determined to be successful and to make her mark on the world. Fate or a divine plan had joined her to Adrian. They shared a great love and were a great team. She would continue to be his best friend and counselor. She prayed that God would protect them from the evils they would seek to dispel from American government. She was aware of their power.

"Those who are wise will shine like
the brightness of the heavens,
and those who lead many to
righteousness, like the stars forever..."

The New International Bible
Daniel, chapter 12, verse 3

Author's Acknowledgements

A first-time large novel with a large concept is more work than ever anticipated. It also requires more thanks than ever anticipated. Jeffrey Keller and Dennis Gawera performed the editing. Betty Barnard, jumped into the final readings. Jennifer Washburn contributed many excellent comments and the line editing. Caldie Barnard and Leslie Washburn helped in the final preparation. Jolisa Magara coordinated it all with unfailing focus and good humor and added many ideas for improvement. Margaret, my wife, put up with the task and read it in several iterations giving corrections and suggestions. The Reverend Wendy Heinz reviewed the concept. Marilyn Martin designed the cover and the set-ups for the excellent photography of Richard Smith. She also did the layout and with Cherish Coddington the formatting and managed production.

Kristin Delcamp, Jodi Guido, and Sharley Cole typed from dictation and did never ending redrafts. Dena Jo Delcamp worked to meet goals of transcriptions and redrafts with useful comment. Duane Palmer assisted, encouraged, commented, and drafted several segments. Sally Hertz inspired the early work and provided continued guidance, advice, and fundamental ideas. Norman Coddington initiated the map.

Appearing in the photography were Dennis Gawera, Marshall Hall, Wendy Johnson, Greg Mayer, Christine Kinn, Caldie Barnard, Walter Duprey, and Jim Frasier.

To all my deep appreciation for their interest and commitment.

Gerry Balcar